JOYCE CAROL OATES is a recipient of the National Book Award and the PEN/Malamud Award for Excellence in Short Fiction. She has written some of the most enduring fiction of our time, including *We Were the Mulvaneys*, which was an Oprah Book Club Choice, and *Blonde*, which was nominated for the National Book Award. She is the Roger S. Berlind Distinguished Professor of Humanities at Princeton University.

From the reviews of *The Gravedigger's Daughter*:

'When Joyce Carol Oates is at her best, as she so often is in this bleak, gothic powerhouse of a book, she truly deserves the title of The Great American Novelist . . . This is masterful storytelling from Oates . . . her writing is electrifying and what makes it so powerful – and painful – is that there is nothing she will not say'   *Scotland on Sunday*

'A moving and surprisingly gruesome tale of one family's experience of immigration to America . . . Joyce Carol Oates is a storyteller of astounding grace and in *The Gravedigger's Daughter* she has produced an intricate and provocative novel . . . a captivating exploration of identity, isolation and freedom'   *Literary Review*

'A richly nuanced portrait of a woman who survives more than her share of abuse and loss. Few writers write more convincingly about male violence than Oates, and her depiction of its effects on her heroine is memorable'   *Sunday Times*

'The excellent Joyce Carol Oates conjures an America that few of us could know . . . There is a Dickensian sweep to her great adventure'   *Irish Independent*

'*The Gravedigger's Daughter* is a rather nightmarish celebration of the American dream, of the transformative powers of ambition, talent and love. Its style is a fitting combination of the harsh and lyrical, and has a powerful, seemingly unconscious fluency'   *Daily Telegraph*

'Joyce Carol Oates, that prolific, intense observer of American life . . . succeeds in evoking the perilous complexity of complete cultural integration, the faulty foundations of American life'   *TLS*

By the same author

JOYCE CAROL OATES

The Gravedigger's Daughter

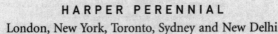

HARPER PERENNIAL
London, New York, Toronto, Sydney and New Delhi

Harper Perennial
An imprint of HarperCollins*Publishers*
77–85 Fulham Palace Road
Hammersmith
London W6 8JB

www.harperperennial.co.uk
Visit our authors' blog at www.fifthestate.co.uk

This Harper Perennial edition published 2008

4

First published in Great Britain by Fourth Estate in 2007

Copyright © The Ontario Review 2007

PS Section: Portrait of Joyce Carol Oates copyright © Eithne Farry 2004

PS™ is a trademark of HarperCollins*Publishers* Ltd

Joyce Carol Oates asserts the moral right
to be identified as the author of this work

A catalogue record for this book is available from the British Library

ISBN 978-0-00-725846-8

Set in Garamond

Printed and bound in Great Britain by Clays Ltd, St Ives plc

FSC is a non-profit international organisation established to promote the
responsible management of the world's forests. Products carrying the FSC
label are independently certified to assure consumers that they come
from forests that are managed to meet the social, economic and
ecological needs of present and future generations.

Find out more about HarperCollins and the environment at
www.harpercollins.co.uk/green

Mixed Sources
Product group from well-managed
forests and other controlled sources
www.fsc.org Cert no. SW-COC-1806
© 1996 Forest Stewardship Council

acknowledgments

Sections from Part I were originally published, in slightly different forms, in *Witness*, Summer/Fall 2003.

Chapters 6 and 7 were originally published in *Conjunctions*, Fall/Winter 2003.

Chapters 16 and 17 were originally published, in different forms, in *Childhood*, editor Marian Wright Edelman, Houghton Mifflin, 2003.

I

IN THE CHAUTAUQUA VALLEY

prologue

"In animal life the weak are quickly disposed of."

He'd been dead for ten years. Buried in his mangled parts for ten years. Unmourned for ten years. You would think that she, his adult daughter, a man's wife now and the mother of her own child, would be rid of him by now. God damn she had tried! She hated him. His kerosene eyes, his boiled-tomato face. She gnawed her lips raw hating him. Where she was most vulnerable, at work. On the assembly line at Niagara Fiber Tubing where the noise lulled her into a trance she heard him. Where her teeth rattled from the conveyor belt vibrations she heard him. Where her mouth tasted like dried cow shit she heard him. Hated him! Turning in a crouch thinking it might be a joke, a crude trick, one of her asshole co-workers shouting into her ear. Like some guy's fingers poking her breasts through the cover-alls or digging into her crotch and she's paralyzed unable to turn her attention away from the strips of tubing on the rubber belt moving jerkily along and always faster than you wanted. Damned steamed-up goggles hurting her face. Shutting her eyes breathing the foul dusty air through her mouth which she knew better than to do. An instant of shame, soul-withering, live-or-die-what-the-hell that came over her sometimes in moments of exhaustion or sorrow and she groped for the object on the belt that in that instant had no name, no identity, and no purpose, risking her hand being hooked by the stamping machine and half the fingers smashed before she could shake her head free and clear of him who spoke calmly knowing he would be heard above the machine clatter. "So you must hide your weakness, Rebecca." His face close to hers as if they were conspirators. They were not, they had nothing in common. They looked in no way alike. She hated the sour smell of his mouth. That face that was a boiled, burst tomato. She'd seen that face exploding in blood, gristle, brains. She'd wiped that face off her bare forearms. She'd wiped that face off her own damn face! She'd picked that face out of her hair. Ten years ago. Ten years and almost four months to the day. For never would she forget that day. She was not his. She had never been his. Nor had she belonged to her mother. You could discern no resemblance among them. She was an adult woman now twenty-three years old which astonished her, she had lived so long. She had survived them. She was not a terrified child now. She was the wife of a man who was a true man and not a sniveling coward and a murderer, and this man had given her a baby, a son, whom he, her dead father, would never see. What pleasure that gave her, he would never see his grandson. Never utter his poison-words into the child's ears. Yet still he approached her. He knew her weakness. When she was exhausted, when her soul shrank to the size of a wizened grape. In this clamorous place where his words had acquired a powerful machine rhythm and authority that beat beat beat her into stunned submission.

"In animal life the weak are quickly disposed of. So you must hide your weakness, Rebecca. We must."

chautauqua falls, new york

I

❋ ❋ ❋

One afternoon in September 1959 a young woman factory worker was walking home on the towpath of the Erie Barge Canal, east of the small city of Chautauqua Falls, when she began to notice that she was being followed, at a distance of about thirty feet, by a man in a panama hat.

A panama hat! And strange light-colored clothes, of a kind not commonly seen in Chautauqua Falls.

The young woman's name was Rebecca Tignor. She was married, her husband's name Tignor was one of which she was terribly vain.

"Tignor."

So in love, and so childish in her vanity, though not a girl any longer, a married woman a mother. Still she uttered "Tignor" a dozen times a day.

Thinking now as she began to walk faster *He better not be following me, Tignor won't like it.*

To discourage the man in the panama hat from wishing to catch up with her and talk to her as men sometimes, not often but sometimes, did, Rebecca dug the heels of her work shoes into the towpath, gracelessly. She was nerved-up anyway, irritable as a horse tormented by flies.

She'd almost smashed her hand in a press, that day. God damn she'd been distracted!

And now this. This guy! Sent him a mean look over her shoulder, not to be encouraged.

No one she knew?

Didn't look like he belonged here.

In Chautauqua Falls, men followed her sometimes. At least, with their eyes. Most times Rebecca tried not to notice. She'd lived with brothers, she knew "men." She wasn't the shy fearful little-girl type. She was strong, fleshy. Wanting to think she could take care of herself.

But this afternoon felt different, somehow. One of those wan warm sepia-tinted days. A day to make you feel like crying, Christ knew why.

Not that Rebecca Tignor cried. Never.

And: the towpath was deserted. If she shouted for help . . .

This stretch of towpath she knew like the back of her hand. A forty-minute walk home, little under two miles. Five days a week Rebecca hiked the towpath to Chautauqua Falls, and five days a week she hiked back home. Quick as she could manage in her damn clumsy work shoes.

Sometimes a barge passed her on the canal. Livening things up a little. Exchanging greetings, wisecracks with guys on the barges. Got to know a few of them.

But the canal was empty now, both directions.

God damn she was nervous! Nape of her neck sweating. And inside her clothes, armpits leaking. And her heart beating in that way that hurt like something sharp was caught between her ribs.

"Tignor. Where the hell are *you*."

She didn't blame him, really. Oh but hell she blamed him.

Tignor had brought her here to live. In late summer 1956. First thing Rebecca read in the Chautauqua Falls newspaper was so nasty she could not believe it: a local man who'd murdered his wife, beat her and threw her into the canal somewhere along this very-same deserted stretch, and threw rocks at her until she drowned. Rocks! It had taken maybe ten minutes, the man told police. He had not boasted but he had not been ashamed, either.

Bitch was tryin to leave me, he said.

Wantin to take my son.

Such a nasty story, Rebecca wished she'd never read it. The worst thing was, every guy who read it, including Niles Tignor, shook his head, made a sniggering noise with his mouth.

Rebecca asked Tignor what the hell that meant: laughing?

"You make your bed, now lay in it."

That's what Tignor said.

Rebecca had a theory, every female in the Chautauqua Valley knew that story, or one like it. What to do if a man throws you into the canal. (Could be the river, too. Same difference.) So when she'd started working in town, hiking the towpath, Rebecca dreamt up a way of saving herself if/when the time came.

Her thoughts were so bright and vivid she'd soon come to imagine it had already happened to her, or almost. Somebody (no face, no name, a guy bigger than she was) shoved her into the muddy-looking water, and she had to struggle to save her life. *Right away pry off your left shoe with the toe of your right shoe then the other quick! And then—* She'd have only a few seconds, the heavy work shoes would sink her like anvils. Once the shoes were off she'd have a chance at least, tearing at her jacket, getting it off before it was soaked through. Damn work pants would be hard to get off, with a fly front, and buttons, and the legs kind of tight at the thighs, Oh shit she'd have to be swimming, too, in the direction the opposite of her murderer . . .

Christ! Rebecca was beginning to scare herself. This guy behind her, guy in a panama hat, probably it was just coincidence. He wasn't *following her* only just *behind her*.

Not deliberate only *just accident*.

Yet: the bastard had to know she was conscious of him, he was scaring her. A man following a woman, a lonely place like this.

God damn she hated to be followed! Hated any man following her with his eyes, even.

Ma had put the fear of the Lord in her, years ago. *You would not want anything to happen to you, Rebecca! A girl by herself, men will follow. Even boys you know, you can't trust.*

Even Rebecca's big brother Herschel, Ma had worried he might do something to her. Poor Ma!

Nothing had happened to Rebecca, for all Ma's worrying.

At least, nothing she could remember.

Ma had been wrong about so many damn things . . .

Rebecca smiled to think of that old life of hers when she'd been a girl in Milburn. Not yet a married woman. A "vir-gin." She never thought of it now, all that was past. Niles Tignor had rescued her. Niles Tignor was her hero. He'd taken her from Milburn in his car, they'd eloped to Niagara

Falls. Her girlfriends had been envious. Every girl in Milburn adored Niles Tignor from afar. He'd brought his bride Rebecca then to live in the country east and a little north of Chautauqua Falls. Four Corners, it was called.

Their son Niles Tignor, Jr. had been born here. Niley would be three years old, end of November.

She was vain of being Mrs. Tignor, and she was vain of being a mother. Wanting to shout at the man in the panama hat *You have no right to follow me! I can protect myself.*

It was so. Rebecca had a sharp piece of scrap metal in her jacket pocket. In secret, nervously she was fingering it.

If it's the last thing I do mister I WILL MARK YOU.

In school in Milburn, Rebecca had had to fight sometimes. She was the town gravedigger's daughter, other kids taunted her. She had tried to ignore them, best as she could. Her mother had so advised her. *But you must not stoop to their level Rebecca.* She had, though. Frantic flailing and kicking fights, she'd had to defend herself. Damn bastard principal had expelled her, one day.

Of course she had never attacked another. She had never hurt any of her classmates not really, even the ones who'd deserved to be hurt. But she didn't doubt that if she was desperate enough fighting for her life she could hurt another person, bad.

Ah! the point of the steel was sharp as an ice pick. She would have to stab it deep into the man's chest, or throat . . .

"Think I can't do it, asshole? I can."

Rebecca wondered if the man in the panama hat, a stranger to her, was someone Tignor knew. Someone who knew Tignor.

Her husband was in the brewery business. He was often on the road for days, even weeks. Usually he appeared to be prospering but sometimes he complained of being short of cash. He spoke of the business of brewing, marketing, and delivering beer and ale to retailers through New York State as *cutthroat competitive*. The way Tignor spoke, with such zest, you were made to think of slashed and bleeding throats. You were made to think that *cutthroat competitive* was a good thing.

There were rivalries in the brewery business. There were unions, there were strikes and layoffs and labor disputes and picketing. The business employed men like Niles Tignor, who could handle themselves in difficult situations. Tignor had told Rebecca that there were enemies of his who would never dare approach him—"But a wife, she'd be different."

Tignor had told Rebecca that he would murder with his bare hands anyone who approached her.

The man in the panama hat, Rebecca wanted to think, did not really look like a man in the brewery business. His sporty straw hat, tinted glasses, and cream-colored trousers were more appropriate for the lakeshore in summer than the industrial edge of Chautauqua Falls in autumn. A long-sleeved white shirt, probably high-quality cotton or even linen. And a bow tie. A bow tie! No one in Chautauqua Falls wore bow ties, and certainly no one of Tignor's acquaintance.

It was like seeing Bing Crosby on the street, or that astonishing agile dancer: Fred Astaire. The man in the panama hat was of that type. A man who didn't look as if he would sweat, a man who might smile if he saw something beautiful, a man not altogether real.

Not a man to track a woman into a desolate place and accost her.

(Was he?)

Rebecca was wishing it wasn't so late in the afternoon. In full daylight, she would not feel so uneasy.

Each day now in September, dusk was coming earlier. You took notice of the days shortening, once Labor Day was past. Time seemed to speed up. Shadows rose more visibly from the underbrush beside the canal and the snaky-glittery dark water like certain thoughts you try to push away except in a weak time you can't. The sky was massed with clouds like a fibrous substance that has been squeezed, and then released. There was a strange quivering malevolent *livingness* to it. Through the cloud-mass, the sun appeared like a fierce crazed eye, that glared, and made each grass blade beside the towpath distinct. You saw too vividly, your eyes dazzled. And then, the sun disappeared. What had been distinct became blurred, smudged.

Heavy thunderheads blowing down from Lake Ontario. Such humidity, flies were biting.

Buzzing close to Rebecca's head, so she gave little cries of disgust and alarm, and tried to brush them away.

At Niagara Tubing, the air had been sultry hot as in midsummer. Stifling at 110° F. Windows opaque with grime were shoved at a slant and half the fans broken or so slow-moving they were useless.

It was only temporary work, at Niagara Tubing. Rebecca could bear it for another few months . . .

Punching in at 8:58 A.M. Punching out at 5:02 P.M. Eight hours. Five days a week. You had to wear safety goggles, gloves. Sometimes a safety apron: so heavy! hot! And work shoes with reinforced toes. The foreman inspected them, sometimes. The women.

Before the factory, Rebecca had worked in a hotel: maid, she was called. She'd had to wear a uniform, she had hated it.

For eight hours, Rebecca earned $16.80. Before taxes.

"It's for Niley. I'm doing it for Niley."

She wasn't wearing a watch, never wore a watch at Niagara Tubing. The fine dust got into a watch's mechanism and ruined it. But she knew it was getting on toward 6 P.M. She would pick up Niley at her neighbor's house just after 6 P.M. No son of a bitch trailing her on the towpath was going to prevent her.

Preparing herself to run. If, suddenly. If he, behind her. She knew of a hiding place somewhere ahead, on the other side of the canal embankment, not visible from the towpath, a foul-smelling culvert: made of corrugated sheet metal, a tunnel about twelve feet in depth, five feet in diameter, she could duck and run through it and into a field, unless it was a marsh, the man in the panama hat would not immediately see where she'd gone and if he did, he might not want to follow her . . .

Even as Rebecca thought of this escape route, she dismissed it: the culvert opened into a fetid marsh, an open drainage field, if she ran into it she would stumble, fall . . .

The towpath was an ideal place to track a victim, Rebecca supposed. You could not see beyond the embankments. The horizon was unnaturally close. If you wished to see the sky from the towpath you had to look up. Had to lift your head, crane your neck. On their own, your eyes did not naturally discover the sky.

Rebecca felt the injustice, *he* had followed her here! Where always she was relieved, grateful to be out of the factory. Always she admired the landscape, though it was slovenly, a wilderness. Always she thought of her son, eagerly awaiting her.

She knew: she must not weaken. She must not show her fear.

She would turn and confront him, the man in the panama hat. She would turn, hands on her hips, Tignor-style she would stare him down.

She mouthed the words she would say to him: "You! Are you following me?"

Or, "Hey mister: not following me, are you?"

Or, her heart quickened in hatred, "God damn you, who are you to follow *me*?"

She was not a shy young woman, and she was not weak. Not in her body, or in her instincts. She was not a very feminine woman. There was nothing soft, pliant, melting about her; rather she believed herself hard, sinewy. She had a striking face, large deep-set very dark eyes, with dark brows heavy as a man's, and something of a man's stance, in confronting others. In essence, she despised the feminine. Except, there was her attachment to Tignor. She did not wish to be Tignor, but only to be loved by Tignor. Yet Tignor was not an ordinary man, in Rebecca's judgment. Otherwise, she despised the weakness of women, deep in her soul. She was ashamed, infuriated. For this was the ancient weakness of women, her mother Anna Schwart's weakness. The weakness of a defeated race.

At the factory, men let her alone, usually. Knowing she was married. Seeing she gave no signals to welcome their interest. She never met their eyes. What thoughts they might have of her, she did not consider.

Yet: the week before she had had to confront a smirking asshole who was always passing close behind her as she stood at the assembly line, a man who eyed her up-and-down to embarrass her, she'd told him to leave her alone God damn she would complain to the foreman but in the midst of the rush of words she had suddenly swallowed and her voice choked and the smirking asshole just grinned at her. *Mmmm baby! I like you.*

Yet she would not quit the factory. Damned if she would quit.

Since March she'd been working at Niagara Tubing. Assembly line, unskilled labor. Still the factories paid better than most other jobs for women—waitress, cleaning woman, salesclerk. You had no need to smile at customers, to be "nice." The work was only just temporary she'd told her friend Rita, who also worked on the line at Niagara Tubing, and Rita had laughed saying sure, Niagara Tubing was just temporary for her, too. "Going on seven years."

This foreshortened horizon, it made you anxious because you couldn't plot an escape route. Into underbrush? There were briars, wild rose, tangles of poison ivy. Into the trees? And out of sight of the towpath, where anything might happen?

The bridge at the Poor Farm Road was at least a mile away. How many minutes, she couldn't estimate: twenty? And she could not run. She wondered what would happen during those twenty minutes.

The canal surface rippled like the hide of a great slumbering beast whose head you could not see. Only its length, stretching to the horizon.

Except there was no horizon ahead, really. The canal faded into a shadowy haze in the distance. Like train tracks where your eyes trick you into thinking that the tracks narrow, shrink in upon themselves and disappear as if running out of the present time and into a future you can't see.

Hide your weakness. Can't remain a child forever.

She was hardly a child. She was a married woman, a mother. She had a job at Niagara Fiber Tubing in Chautauqua Falls, New York.

She was not a minor dependent upon the charity of adults. She was not a ward of the county living in Milburn. The gravedigger's daughter to be pitied.

These were boom times in American industry, post-war. So you were told. So it seemed. Factories working to capacity in Chautauqua Falls as in other cities and towns in upstate New York where the largest and most prosperous city was Buffalo. All day long the sky of the Chautauqua Valley was streaked with two kinds of cloud: the natural, horizontal clouds and the vertical columnar clouds of factory smoke. Distinctive hues they were, rising from identical smokestacks. Always you could recognize the steely-powder rubbery-smelling smoke erupting upward from Niagara Fiber Tubing.

At work she wore her long thick hair coiled in loose braids around her head, covered with a head scarf. Yet when she brushed it out it smelled of the factory anyway. Her hair that had been beautiful glossy black, gypsy-hair Tignor called it, was becoming dry and brittle and corroded like iron.

She was only twenty-three and already she was discovering gray hairs! And her fingers were calloused, her nails discolored, though she wore work gloves on the job. The heavy safety goggles left a pale imprint on her face and dents on the sides of her nose.

She was a married woman, why was this happening to her!

Tignor had been crazy for her once. She didn't want to think that time had passed.

He had not liked her pregnant. Belly swollen big and tight as a drum. Pale blue veins visible in her flesh looking as if they might burst. Her ankles, feet swollen. Her breath short. The heat of her skin that was a strange sexual heat, a fever that repelled a man.

She was tall, five feet eight. She weighed about 115 pounds. Pregnant with Niley, she'd weighed 140. Strong as a horse Tignor had said of her.

The man behind her would be led to think Rebecca was a tough woman, she thought. The kind of woman to fight back.

She wondered if he knew her, in some way. And so maybe he knew she was living alone with her son. Living in an old remote farmhouse in the country. But if he knew these facts, he might also know that Rebecca's son was watched during weekdays by a neighbor; and if Rebecca was late picking him up, if Rebecca failed to appear, Mrs. Meltzer would guess that something had happened to her.

But how long a time would pass, before Mrs. Meltzer called the police?

The Meltzers were not likely to call the police if they could avoid it. Any more than Tignor would call the police. What they would do is go out looking for you. And not finding you, they'd decide what to do next.

How long this would require: maybe hours.

If she'd brought the bread knife from home. That morning. The towpath was a desolate place. If Tignor knew, his wife walking along the canal like a tramp. Sometimes there were derelicts hanging out in the railroad yard. Solitary fishermen at the bridge over the canal. Solitary men.

If the canal wasn't so beautiful, she wouldn't be drawn to it. In the morning the sky was likely to be clear and so the surface of the canal appeared clear. When the sky was heavy and leaden with clouds, the surface of the canal appeared opaque. Like you could walk on it.

How deep the canal was exactly, Rebecca didn't know. But it was deep.

Over a man's head. Twenty feet? Couldn't hope to save yourself by wading out. The banks were steep, you'd have to lift yourself soaking wet out of the water by the sheer strength of your arms and if somebody was kicking at you, you were doomed.

She was a strong swimmer! Though since Niles, Jr. she had not swum. She feared discovering that her body had lost its girlish buoyancy, its youth. Ignominiously she would sink like a rock. She feared that truth-telling you confront in water over your head exerting your arms and legs to keep afloat.

She turned abruptly and saw: the man in the panama hat, at about the same distance behind her. He wasn't trying to catch up with her, at least. But he did seem to be following her. And watching her.

"You! Better leave me alone."

Rebecca's voice was sharp, high-pitched. It didn't sound like her own voice at all.

She turned back, and walked faster. Had he actually *smiled*? Was he *smiling at her*?

A smile can be taunting. A smile like her own, deceased father's smile. Mock-eager. Mock-tender.

"Bastard. You have no right . . ."

Rebecca remembered now, she'd seen this man the previous day.

At the time she'd taken little notice. She'd been leaving the factory at the end of her shift, 5 P.M., with a crowd of other workers. If she'd noticed the man in the panama hat, she'd have had no reason to suppose he was interested in her.

Today, his following her, might be random. He couldn't know her name—could he?

Her mind worked swiftly, desperately. It was possible that the stranger had simply chosen a woman to follow at random. He'd been in the vicinity of the factory as a hunter awaits prey, alert to any possibility. Or, what was equally plausible: he had been waiting for someone else but she had not turned up or, if she had, it wasn't practical for him to follow her at that time.

Her heart beat in fury. Yet she was frightened.

"My husband will kill you . . ."

She didn't want to think that this man might know Tignor. That he had a score to settle with Tignor. *One of those guys that think they know me.*

You never knew, with Tignor, what such a remark meant. That he had true enemies, or that there were men, unidentified, unreasonable, who believed they were his enemies.

One of those guys, they'd like to cut off my balls.

Tignor laughed, saying such things. He was a man who thought well of himself and his laughter was quick and assured.

Futile for Rebecca to ask what he meant. Tignor never answered a question directly, and especially not from a woman.

"No right! No right to follow me! Fucker."

In her right-hand pocket Rebecca stroked the piece of steel.

She'd had the impression that the man, the stranger, had made a gesture to take off his hat.

Had he smiled?

She was weak with doubt, suddenly. For he'd made no threatening gesture toward her. He hadn't called to her as a man might do, to unnerve her. He had made no move to catch up with her. She might be imagining danger. She was thinking of her little boy waiting for her and of how she wanted desperately to be with him to console both him and herself. At the treeline a crazed-eye sun appeared briefly between massed clouds and she thought, with the eagerness with which a drowning woman might reach for something to haul her up *His clothes.*

Trousers of some unlikely cream-colored fabric. A white, long-sleeved shirt and a bow tie.

It seemed to her, the man in the panama hat possessed a light floating quality, a hopefulness, not like the mean concentrated look of a man who wants to sexually humiliate or hurt a woman.

"Maybe he lives out here. He's just walking home, like me."

The towpath was a public place. It was possible he was taking the identical shortcut Rebecca was taking. She'd just never seen him before. Parallel with the canal was the asphalt Stuyvesant Road and a half-mile ahead was the gravel Poor Farm Road that crossed the canal on a single-lane wooden bridge. At the juncture of the roads was a small settlement, Four Corners.

A storefront post office, a general store with a large Sealtest sign in the window, Meltzer's Gas & Auto Repair. An operating granary, an old stone church, a cemetery. Rebecca's husband had rented a ramshackle farmhouse here, for her second pregnancy.

They'd lost the first baby. Miscarriage.

Nature's way of correcting a mistake the doctor had told her, to suggest maybe it had not been a bad thing . . .

"Fuck it."

Rebecca was thinking she should have taken off her jacket, soon as she'd left work. Now, it was too late. Couldn't make any move like that, taking off an item of clothing with that bastard behind her watching. A signal, he'd interpret it. Sure. She could feel him watching her ass, her hips, legs as she walked fast guessing she wanted badly to start running but didn't dare.

It was like a dog: turn your back, start running, he's on you.

Fear has a smell. A predator can smell it.

When she'd seen this man the previous day, he hadn't been wearing a hat. He'd been standing across the street from the factory gate, leaning back against a wall beneath an awning. In that short block were a café, a shoe repair, a butcher shop, a small grocery. The man had been lounging between the café and the shoe repair. There were many people around, this was a busy time of day. Rebecca wouldn't have taken the slightest notice of him except now, she was forced to.

Remembering backward is the easy thing. If you could remember forward, you could save yourself . . .

Traffic was always congested at 5 P.M. when the factories let out. Niagara Tubing, Empire Paper Products, Arcadia Canning Goods, Chautauqua Sheet Metal. A block away, Union Carbide Steel, the city's largest employer. Hundreds of men and women working the day shift erupted out onto the streets, as if released from hell.

Bats out of hell, it was an apt expression.

Whenever Rebecca left Niagara Tubing, she looked for Tignor out on the street. When he'd been gone for a while she lived in a state that might be defined as waiting-for-Tignor and involuntarily, without knowing what she did, she sought his tall broad figure in any public place. She was hopeful of seeing him yet dreaded seeing him for she never knew what emotions she might feel nor could she guess what Tignor might be feeling. Twice since March he had re-entered her life in this way: casual-seeming, parked in his car, a 1959 silver-green Pontiac, at the curb waiting for her as if his absence from her and their son—days, weeks, most recently five weeks in succession—was no more than something Rebecca had imagined. He would call out, "Hey babe: here."

He would signal her to come to him. And she would.

Twice, she had. It was shameful but it was so. Seeing Tignor smiling at her, signaling her, she'd hurried to him. You would think if you'd seen them that a husband was picking up his wife after work, as so many wives picked up their husbands.

"Hey kid, calm down. People are watching."

Or he'd say, "Gimme a kiss, babe. I miss you."

But Tignor had not been there. Not the day before, and not today.

Vaguely Rebecca was expecting a call from him on Sunday. Or so she told herself. Last thing she knew of Tignor he'd been up in Port au Roche at the Canadian border on Lake Champlain where he owned or co-owned property: a hotel, a tavern, maybe a marina. Rebecca had never seen Port au Roche but she understood that it was a resort town, far more beautiful than Chautauqua Falls at this time of year, and always ten degrees cooler. It was not reasonable to blame a man for preferring Lake Champlain to Chautauqua Falls.

Not Tignor but someone else, Rita had nudged Rebecca to notice.

"Lookit the hotshot. Who's he?"

A stranger, maybe mid-thirties, lounging beneath the awning across the street. He hadn't been wearing cream-colored trousers but he'd been quirkily well dressed. A striped sport coat, beige trousers. Gray-blond hair that was crimped-looking and tinted glasses that gave him a movie-actor flair.

Eight hours on the line yet Rita still felt, or wished to give the impression that she felt, an avid if derisive sexual interest in an attractive stranger.

"Ever seen him before?"

"No."

Rebecca had no more than glanced at the man. She had no interest in whoever it was.

If not Tignor, no one.

This afternoon she'd left the factory alone. She had not wanted to look for Tignor on the street knowing he wouldn't be there, yet she had looked, her eyes glancing swiftly about, snatching at male phantom-figures. Almost it was relief she felt, not seeing him.

For she'd come to hate him, he had so lacerated her heart.

Her pride, too. Knowing she should leave Tignor, take the child and simply leave him. Yet lacking the strength.

Love! It was the supreme weakness. And now the child who was the bond between them, forever.

She'd yanked off the damn sweaty kerchief and stuffed it into her pocket. A rivulet of sweat at the nape of her neck like an insect crawling. Quickly she walked away. The factory fumes made her sick.

A block away was the Buffalo & Chautauqua railroad yard, through which she cut to get to the canal. She knew the way so well by now, she scarcely had to look up. Hadn't noticed a man behind her until she was partway through the yard and then it was purely chance.

Out of place, in his city clothes. In the panama hat. Making his way so deliberately through the railroad yard between boxcars smelling of cattle and chemical fertilizers.

Who is he! And why, here!

It was rare, but sometimes you'd see a man or men in suits, in the railroad yard. In the streets near the factories. Never knew who they were except they were in charge, they'd come to the site in new-model cars and they were usually inspecting something or engaged in earnest conversations with one another and they wouldn't be out-of-doors long.

This one, in the panama hat, appeared different, though. He didn't seem to know where he was going, exactly. Crossing the weedy terrain as if his shoes hurt him.

Rebecca walked ahead, knowing where she was going. Through oil-splotched weeds, concrete broken like jagged ice chunks. Sure-footed as a mountain goat.

Each day at Niagara Tubing was like the first: raw, clamorous, suffocating. Airless air stinking of burnt fibres. You got used to the noise by deadening yourself against it, like a paralyzed limb. No solitude. No privacy except in the lavatory and there you could not stay long, the smells were even worse. How many days she'd clocked since March first and each week managed to save as much as she could, a few dollars, a handful of change, in a secret cache in the house for her and the child if ever there was an emergency.

Worse-come-to-worst was the expression. A married woman saves in secret, not in a bank but somewhere in her house, for that day of reckoning *worse-come-to-worst.*

Rebecca leapt over a drainage ditch. Pushed through a torn chain-link fence. Always at this point as she neared the canal, and the outskirts of town, she began to feel better. The towpath was usually deserted, the air would be cooler. A smell of the canal, and that earthy-rotted smell of leaves. She was a country girl, she'd grown up tramping the fields, woods, country roads of Milburn ninety miles to the east, always she felt exhilarated at such times. She would arrive at Mrs. Meltzer's and there Niley would be waiting for her crying *Mom-ma!* running at her with a look of such pained love, she could scarcely bear it.

It was at this moment, by chance, she happened to see: the odd-looking man in the panama hat, a stranger to her, appeared to be headed in the same direction in which she was headed. She had no reason to think that he might be following her, or that he was even aware of her. But she saw him, at this moment.

She saw, and chose to ignore the fact.

She crossed another ditch, that emitted a foul odor like sulphur. Nearby in the railroad yard, boxcars were being uncoupled: the noise came in sharp scimitar blows. She was thinking, in that way that isn't precisely thinking, not deliberate and not purposeful, that the man in the panama hat, dressed as he was, would turn back soon. He wasn't the type to walk here, on these paths used mostly by boys and derelicts.

Tignor wouldn't like her tramping about like this, either. Like her mother years ago. But Tignor didn't know, as Anna Schwart had not known all that Rebecca did, in secret.

Later Rebecca would recall how she'd halfway known, at this point, that it was risky to continue walking here, but she'd continued anyway. Once she descended the embankment and began walking along the towpath, she would probably be alone; and if the man in the panama hat really was following her, she wouldn't want to be alone. And so she had a choice: she could turn back abruptly, and run toward a side street nearby where children were playing; or she could continue to the towpath.

She didn't turn back. She continued on.

Not even thinking *I have no need to be afraid of such a man, he isn't a man to frighten me.*

Except: in resourcefulness and cunning, for she was the gravedigger's daughter after all, she took from a barrel of scrap metal a strip of steel about seven inches long, and an inch wide, and this she slipped into the right pocket of her khaki jacket. So quickly, she could not think that the man in the panama hat had seen her.

The piece of steel was sharp, all right. Except it lacked a handle, it resembled an ice pick.

If she had to use it, her hand would be cut. Yet she smiled thinking *At least I will hurt him. If he touches me he will regret it.*

Now the sky had darkened, it was nearly dusk. A sombre, sulky evening. There was no beauty in the canal now. Only at the horizon was the sun dimly visible like flame amid smoldering ashes.

The Poor Farm Road was a quarter-mile ahead: she could see the plank bridge. Her heart thudded heavily in her chest. She was desperate to get to the bridge, to climb up the embankment to the road, and to safety. She would run in the middle of the road to the Meltzers' house a half-mile away . . .

Then, the man in the panama hat made his move.

She heard a sound like breaking glass unexpected close behind her: footsteps in dried leaves. At once she panicked. She did not look back but ran blindly up the embankment. She clutched at briars, thistles, tall grasses to help pull herself up. She was desperate, terrified. In a flash came memories of trying to pull herself up onto fences, or roofs, as her brothers did so easily, and she could not. She heard the man behind her speak, he was calling after her, she began to fall, the incline was too steep. Her ankle twisted, she fell heavily. The pain was shocking, sickening. She had partly broken her fall with the fleshy edge of her right hand.

But she was fallen now, helpless. In that instant her vision darkened, like an eclipse of the sun. Of course she was a woman, this man sought her as a woman. He would be on her, now.

"Miss, wait! Excuse me! Please! I won't hurt you."

Rebecca was on her haunches, panting. The man in the panama hat approached her, with a pained expression. Cautiously, as one might approach a snarling dog.

"Don't! Don't come any nearer! Get away."

Rebecca fumbled for the piece of steel in her pocket. Her hand was bleeding, numbed. She could not force it into her pocket.

The man in the panama hat, seeing the expression in Rebecca's face, had stopped dead in his tracks. Concerned, he removed his tinted glasses to peer at her. There was the strange thing about him Rebecca would long remember: his curious, staring, naked eyes. They were eyes of wonderment, calculation, yearning. They appeared to have no lashes. Something about the right eye looked damaged, like a burnt-out filament in a lightbulb. The whites of both eyes were discolored as old ivory. He was a young-old man, a boyish demeanor in a creased face, weakly handsome, yet something fading about him, insubstantial. Rebecca saw, such a man could be no danger to her unless he had a weapon. And if he had a weapon, by now he would have shown it.

She was flooded with relief, what a fool she'd been to so misjudge this stranger!

He was saying, awkwardly, "Please forgive me! I didn't mean to frighten you. That was the last thing I mean, truly. Are you hurt, dear?"

Dear! Rebecca felt a tinge of contempt.

"No. I'm not hurt."

"But—may I help? You've twisted your ankle, I think."

He offered to help Rebecca to her feet, but Rebecca gestured for him to keep his distance. "Mister, I don't need your help. Get away."

Rebecca was on her feet, shakily. Her heart was still pounding. Her blood was up, she was furious with this man for having frightened her, humiliated her. She was furious with herself, even more. If anyone who knew her saw her cowering like this . . . She hated it, the way the stranger stared at her with his queer lashless eyes.

He said, suddenly, yet almost wistfully, "It's Hazel—yes? Hazel Jones?"

Rebecca stared at the man, not knowing what she'd heard.

"You are Hazel, aren't you? Yes?"

"Hazel? Who?"

" 'Hazel Jones.' "

"No."

"But you look so like her. Surely you are Hazel . . ."

"I said no. Whoever it is, I am not."

The man in the panama hat smiled, tentatively. He was at least as agitated as Rebecca, and perspiring. His checked bow tie was crooked, and his long-sleeved shirt was damp, showing the unflattering imprint of his undershirt beneath. Such perfect teeth, they had to be dentures.

"My dear, you look so much like her—'Hazel Jones.' I simply can't believe that there could be two young women, very attractive young women, looking so much alike, and living in the same region . . ."

Rebecca had limped back to the towpath. She tested her weight on the ankle, gauging if she could walk on it, or run. Her face was flushed with embarrassment. She brushed at her clothes, that had picked up crumbly loose dirt and burrs. How annoyed she was! And the man in the panama hat still staring at her, convinced she was someone she was not.

She saw that he'd removed the panama hat, and was turning it nervously in his hands. He had crimped-looking gray-blond hair that looked like a mannequin's hair, molded, hardly disturbed by the hat.

"I got to go now, mister. Don't follow me."

"Oh, but—wait! Hazel—"

Now the stranger was sounding just subtly reproachful. As if he knew, and she knew, that she was deceiving him; and he could not comprehend why. He was so clearly a well-intentioned man, and a gentleman, unaccustomed to being treated rudely, he could not comprehend why. Saying, courteously, with his air of maddening persistence: "Your eyes are so like Hazel's, and your hair has grown a little darker, I think. And your way of carrying yourself is a little harsher for which," he said hurriedly, "I am to blame, frightening you. It's just that I had no idea how to approach you, dear. I saw you on the street yesterday, I mean I believed it was you I had seen, Hazel Jones after so many years, and now today . . . I had to follow you."

Rebecca stared at him, deliberating. It did seem to her that this earnest man was telling the truth: the truth as he saw it. He was deceived, but didn't appear to be deranged. He spoke with relative calmness and his reasoning, granted the circumstances, was logical.

He thinks I am her, and I am lying.

Rebecca laughed, this was so unexpected! So strange.

She wished she could tell Tignor about it, when Tignor called. They might have laughed together. Except Tignor was inclined to be jealous, and you don't tell a man with such inclinations that you have been followed by another man wanting to think that you are another woman beloved by him.

"Mister, I'm sorry. I'm just not her."

"But . . ."

He was approaching her, slowly. Though she'd told him, warned him, to stay away. He seemed not to know what he did, and Rebecca wasn't fully aware, either. He did seem harmless. Hardly taller than Rebecca, and wearing brown oxford shoes covered in dust. The cuffs of his cream-colored trousers were soiled, too. Rebecca smelled a sweet cologne or aftershave. As he was a young-old man, so he was a weak-strong man, too. A man you misjudge as weak, but in fact he's strong. His will was that of a young coiled-up copperhead snake. You might think the snake was paralyzed with fear, in terror of being killed, but it was not; it was simply biding its time, preparing to strike. Long ago Rebecca's father Jacob Schwart the gravedigger of Milburn had been a weak-strong man, only his family had known of his terrible strength, his reptile will, beneath the meek-seeming exterior. Rebecca sensed a similar doubleness here, in this man. He was apologetic, yet not humble. Not a strain of humility in his soul. He thought well of himself, obviously. He knew Hazel Jones, he'd followed Hazel Jones, he would not give up on Hazel Jones, not easily.

Tignor would misjudge a man like this, for Tignor was affably blunt in his opinions, and never revised them. But this man was a man with money, and an education. Very likely, family money. He had a bachelor look, yet a cared-for look. His clothes were of good quality if now slightly rumpled, disheveled.

On his right hand he wore a gold signet ring with a black stone.

"I don't know why you deny me, Hazel. What I've done to so alienate you. I am Dr. Hendricks's son—you must recognize me."

He spoke half-wistfully, insinuatingly.

Rebecca laughed, she knew no one named Hendricks. Yet she said, as if to bait him, "Dr. Hendricks's *son*?"

"Father passed away last November. He was eighty-four."

"I'm sorry to hear that. But—"

"I'm Byron. You must remember Byron?"

"I'm afraid, no I don't. I told you."

"You were no more than twelve or thirteen! Such a young girl. I was just graduated from medical school. You perceived me as an adult. An abyss of a generation separated us. Now, the abyss is not so profound, is it? You must have wondered about us, Hazel. I am a doctor now, following my father's example. But in Port Oriskany, not in the Valley. Twice a year I return to Chautauqua Falls to see relatives, to look after family property. And to tend my father's grave."

Rebecca stood silent. Damn if she was going to respond to this!

Quickly Byron Hendricks continued, "If you feel that you were mistreated, Hazel . . . You, and your mother . . ."

"I told you no! I'm not even from Chautauqua Falls. My husband brought me here to live. I'm married."

Rebecca spoke hotly, impatiently. Wished she'd worn her ring to shove into this man's face. But she never wore her pretty ring at Niagara Tubing.

Byron Hendricks sighed. "Married!" He had not considered this, it seemed.

He said, "There is something for you, Hazel. Through his long and sometimes troubled life my father never forgot you. I realize it's too late for your poor mother, but . . . Will you take my card, at least, dear? If you should ever wish to contact me."

He handed her a small white business card. The neatly printed black letters seemed to Rebecca a rebuke of some kind.

Byron Hendricks, M. D.
General & Family Medicine
Wigner Building, Suite 414
1630 Owego Avenue
Port Oriskany, New York
tel. 693–4661

Rebecca said, furious, "Why the hell should I contact you?"

Rebecca laughed, and tore the card into small pieces, and tossed them down onto the towpath. Hendricks stared at her in dismay. His lashless myopic eyes quivered.

Rebecca turned, and walked away. Maybe it was a mistake: turning her back on this guy. He was calling after her, "I am so very sorry if I offended you! You must have a very good reason, dear, for such rudeness. I don't judge others, Hazel. I am a man of science and reason. I don't judge *you*. This newly harsh way of yours, this . . . hardness. But I don't judge."

Rebecca said nothing. She wasn't going to look back.

God damn, he'd scared her! She was shaking, still.

He was following her again, at a short distance. Persisting, "Hazel! I think I understand. You were hurt, or were told you were. And so you wish to hurt, in turn. As I said, dear—there is something for you. My father did not forget you in his will."

Rebecca wanted to press her hands over her ears. No, no!

"Will you call me someday, dear? In Port Oriskany? Or—come to see me? Tell me we are forgiven. And accept from me what Dr. Hendricks has left you, that is your legacy."

But Rebecca was now climbing the embankment to the road. A narrow, steep dirt path she knew well. Though she favored her ankle, she wasn't going to fall. Behind her Byron Hendricks remained, looking after her. He would be gripping his ridiculous panama hat in both hands, in a suppliant pose. Yet Rebecca had sensed the man's will, she shuddered to think of it. She'd had to pass so close to him, he might have reached out and grabbed her. The way he'd crept up behind her, only the dried leaves had warned her, she would remember for a long time.

In his will.

Legacy.

It was a lie, had to be. A trick. She did not believe a word of it. Almost, Rebecca wished that Hendricks had tried to touch her. She would have liked to stab him with the piece of steel, or to try.

2

✸ ✸ ✸

"Mom-*my*!"

The child rushed at her as soon as she entered the Meltzers' kitchen, hugging her legs. His small careening body was electric with energy, excitement. His eyes were a feral animal's eyes, gleaming and fiery. Rebecca stooped to hug him, laughing. Yet she was trembling, too. His cry tore at her heart, she felt such guilt at being away from him. "Niley, you didn't think Mommy wasn't coming back, did you? I always do."

His relief at her arrival was absurd, hurtful. He wanted to punish her, she thought. And for Tignor's absence, he wanted to punish her. It was often like this. Damn she felt the injustice, she should be doubly punished by both the child and his father!

"Niley? You do know Mommy has to work, don't you?"

Niley shook his head stubbornly, no.

Rebecca kissed him. His fevered face.

Now she must endure being told by Edna Meltzer that Niley had been fretting through the day, demanding to listen to the radio and moving restlessly from window to window as soon as the sun passed behind the treeline, waiting for Mommy.

"He don't like the daylight shortening, he can tell it's getting on night faster. This winter, I don't know how he'll be." Mrs. Meltzer was frowning, fussing. Between her and Rebecca there was an air of muted tension, like a telephone dial humming. "Oh, that child would hang out on the road if I didn't watch him every minute," she laughed. "He'd trot along the canal to meet you like a lovesick little puppy if I let him."

Lovesick little puppy! Rebecca hated such flowery speech.

She hid her face against the child's warm neck and held him tight. Her heart beat in the aftermath of relief, that nothing had happened to her on the towpath, and no one would ever know.

She asked if Niley had been a good boy, or a naughty boy. She told him that if he'd been naughty the Great Spider would get him. He shrieked with laughter as she tickled his sides to weaken his grip on her legs.

Edna Meltzer observed, "You're in a good mood tonight, Rebecca."

Mrs. Meltzer was a stout, solid woman with billowing breasts and a sugary pudding face. Her manner was benign, maternal; yet always subtly accusing.

Shouldn't I be in a good mood? I'm alive.

"I'm out of that hellhole till tomorrow. That's why."

Rebecca smelled frankly of female sweat, her skin felt clammy-pale, feverish. Her eyes were bloodshot. She shied from Mrs. Meltzer observing her so closely. The older woman was wondering maybe if Rebecca had been drinking. A quick drink with co-workers in town instead of coming directly home? For she seemed excited, distracted. Her laughter was rather wild.

"Huh! What happened, hon, did you fall?"

Before Rebecca could draw away, Edna Meltzer took her right hand, and lifted it to the light. The fleshy edge of her hand had been chafed raw in the dirt, blood oozed out now in slow drops glistening like gems. There were thinner cuts on her fingers, that had barely bled, caused by the sharp piece of steel she'd been gripping in her pocket.

Rebecca drew her hand from the older woman's grasp. She murmured it was nothing, she didn't know what it was, no she had not fallen. She would have wiped her hand on her coverall except Edna Meltzer stopped her. "Better wash this, hon. You don't want to catch what's it—*tet'nis.*"

Niley clamored to know what *tet'nis* was. Edna Meltzer told him it was something very bad that happened to you if you cut yourself out in the wild and didn't wash it very clean with good strong soap.

Rebecca washed her hands at the kitchen sink as Mrs. Meltzer insisted. She was flushed with annoyance for she hated to be told what to do. And in Niley's presence! Washing her damn hands like a child with a bar of grainy gray soap, 20 Mule Team was the brand name, a laborer's soap useful for removing dirt embedded in the skin, the nastiest dirt and grime. Edna Meltzer was married to Howie Meltzer, who owned the Esso station.

Rebecca's father had used such harsh soap to clean himself of grave-dirt. Except of course you can never clean yourself entirely of grave-dirt.

Excitedly Niley was crying, "Tet'nis! Tet'nis!" and crowded beside Rebecca, wanting to wash his hands, too. He was of an age when new words thrilled him as if they were gaily feathered birds flying about his head.

The windowpane above the sink had darkened. In it Rebecca could see Mrs. Meltzer observing her. Tignor disliked the Meltzers for no reason except they were friendly with his wife, in his absence. Rebecca was herself undecided whether she was very fond of Edna Meltzer, a woman of the age Rebecca's mother would have been if she hadn't died young, or whether in fact she resented her. Always so righteous, so maternal! Always telling Rebecca the young, inexperienced mother what to do.

Mrs. Meltzer had had five children. Out of that compact fleshy body, five babies. The thought made Rebecca feel faint. All the Meltzers' children were now grown and gone. Rebecca wondered how Edna Meltzer could bear it: having babies, loving them with such tenderness and ferocity, enduring so much on their behalf, and then losing them to time. It was like gazing into the sun, your eyes are blinded, so Rebecca could not comprehend a time when Niley would be grown and gone from her. Her little boy who so adored her and clung to her.

"Mom-*my*! Love *you*!"

"Mommy loves you too, honey. Not so loud, now!"

"He's been like that all day, Rebecca. Wouldn't settle down for a nap. Wouldn't hardly eat. We were outside in the garden, and what'd he want but the radio on the porch railing, turned up high so he could hear it." Mrs. Meltzer shook her head, laughing.

The child believed that certain radio broadcasters might be his father, their voices sounded like Tignor's voice. Rebecca had tried to explain to him that this was not so, but Niley had his own ideas.

"I'm sorry," Rebecca said, embarrassed. She was confused, and could not think what to say.

"Oh, it's nothing," Mrs. Meltzer said quickly. "You know what children are like, these things they 'believe in,' they don't really. Just like us."

Preparing to take Niley home, Rebecca heard herself ask casually if Mrs. Meltzer had ever heard of a person named Hazel Jones.

"Somebody lives around here? That's who she is?"

"She lives in Chautauqua Falls, I think."

But was that right? The man in the panama hat had possibly said that Hazel Jones had once lived in Chautauqua Falls, as a girl.

"Why're you asking? Who is she?"

"Oh, someone asked if that was my name."

But this, too, was inaccurate. The man who was Dr. Hendricks's son had asked if Rebecca was Hazel Jones. There was a significant difference.

"Asked if that was your name? Why'd anybody ask such a question?"

Edna Meltzer screwed up her broad fattish face, and laughed.

It was the response to anything out-of-the-ordinary by local standards: a derisive laugh.

Niley ran outside, letting the screen door slam. Rebecca would have followed him except Mrs. Meltzer touched her arm, to speak with her in a lowered voice. The younger woman felt a pang of revulsion for that touch, and for the forced intimacy between them. "Is Tignor expected home sometime soon, Rebecca? It's been a while."

Rebecca felt her face throb with heat.

"Has it!"

But Mrs. Meltzer persisted. "I think it has, yes. Weeks. And the child—"

Rebecca said, in her bright, blithe way, to forestall such intimacy, "My husband is a businessman, Edna. He travels, he's on the road. He owns *property*."

Rebecca pushed out the screen door blindly, and let it fall back. There was Niley running in the grass, flailing his hands and screeching in childish excitement. How healthy the little boy was, how like a self-possessed little animal! Rebecca resented this woman speaking to her, the child's mother, in such a tone. Inside the kitchen Mrs. Meltzer was saying, in her patient, prodding, maddening voice, "Niley keeps asking about 'Daddy,' and I don't know what to tell him."

"That's right, Edna," Rebecca said coldly. "You don't know. Good night."

Back in their place, a small two-storey farmhouse Tignor rented for them at the end of a dirt lane off the Poor Farm Road, Rebecca printed out the new word for Niley: *TETANUS*.

Even before she removed her sweaty clothes and washed the grime of Niagara Tubing off her body, and out of her matted hair, she looked up the word in her dictionary. A battered old *Webster's* it was, from the time when she'd lived in Milburn and gone to the grammar school there; she'd won it in a spelling bee, sponsored by a local newspaper. Niley was fascinated by the bookplate inside:

SPELLING CHAMPION MILBURN DISRICT #3

*** 1946 ***

REBECCA ESHTER SCHWART

For in that place and in that time she'd been her parents' daughter, bearing the name her father had taken in the New World: Schwart.

(Rebecca had not wanted to correct the misspelling of "Esther." She had not wanted to defile the handsome printed bookplate.)

From the time Niley was two, Rebecca began to look up words in the dictionary to spell out for him. She herself had not been encouraged to spell, to read, even to think until she'd been much older, but she did not intend to emulate her parents in the raising of her child. First, Rebecca carefully printed the word onto a sheet of stiff paper. Then Niley tried to imitate her. Gripping a crayon in his stubby child-fingers, and moving it with a fierce and unswerving concentration across the paper. Rebecca was struck by the child's deep mortification when his laboriously printed word failed to resemble Mommy's; as Niley was deeply mortified by other mishaps of his—spilling food, wetting his bed. Sometimes he burst into tears, and sometimes he was furious, kicking and whining. With his baby fists he struck out at Mommy. He struck his own face.

Rebecca quickly embraced him at such times. Held him tight!

She loved him passionately, as she loved his father. Yet she feared for him, he was developing something of his father's temper. But he was avid to learn, and in that way different from Tignor. In the past several months he'd astonished her, he'd become so captivated by alphabet letters and the way they connected into "words" and were meant to represent "things."

She'd been poorly educated herself. She'd never graduated from high school, her life had been interrupted. Sometimes she felt faint with shame, to think of all that she did not know and could not know and could not even fathom not-knowing for the very scope of her ignorance was beyond her ability to imagine. She saw herself stuck in a bog, quicksand to the ankles, to the knees.

This earth is a shit hole. Ignorance!—stupidity!—cruelty!—confusion! And madness over all, be sure.

Rebecca shuddered, remembering. His voice. The levity of his bitterness.

"Mom-*my*? Look."

Niley had printed, with excruciating slowness, $TETANUS$ on a sheet of paper. He squinted up at her, anxious. He looked nothing like his father, certainly nothing like Rebecca's father. He had fine, fair-brown hair; his skin was fair as well, susceptible to rashes; his features were rather small, pinched. His eyes were like Rebecca's, deep-set and intense.

As usual Niley had slanted his letters oddly downward so that he ran out of space, the final letters had had to be crowded together—*NUS*. Rebecca smiled, Niley was so funny. As an infant he'd reminded her of a little monkey, wizen-faced, intense.

Running out of space on the sheet of paper might set off a temper tantrum, though. Rebecca quickly took away the paper, and provided another.

"O.K., sweetie! Let's both do 'tetanus' again."

Eagerly Niley took up the red crayon. This time, he would do better.

Rebecca vowed: she would not make mistakes with her son at this time in his life. So young, before he began school. When a child is at the mercy of his parents almost exclusively. That was why Rebecca looked up words in the dictionary. And she had high school textbooks, too. To get things right. To get those things right that you could, amid so much that you could not.

3

❀ ❀ ❀

A voice in Rebecca's ear harsh and urgent: "Jesus, watch out!"

She woke from her trance. She laughed nervously. Her right hand, bulky in the safety glove, had been trailing dangerously near the stamping machine.

She thanked whoever it was. Her face flushed with embarrassment, indignation. God damn it had been like this most of the morning: her mind trailing off, losing her concentration. Taking risks, like she'd just begun the job and didn't know by now how dangerous it could be.

Clamoring machines. Airless air. Heat tasting of singed rubber. Sweat inside her work clothes. And mixed with the noise was a new urgent sound she could not decode, was it hopeful, was it seductive, was it mocking. HAZEL JONES HAZEL JONES HAZEL JONES.

The foreman came by. Not to speak with Rebecca but to let her see him: his presence. Son of a bitch, she saw.

No one at Niagara Tubing knew much about her. Even Rita, who was her friend. They might have known that she was married, and some of them might have known to whom she was married, the name Niles Tignor was known in some quarters in Chautauqua Falls. All they knew of Rebecca was that she kept to herself. She had a stubborn manner, a certain stiff-backed dignity. She wouldn't take bullshit from anybody.

Even when she was tired to the point of dazedness. Unsteady on her feet and needing to use the lavatory, to splash tepid water on her face. It wasn't just the few women workers who became light-headed at Niagara Tubing but men, too. Veterans of many years on the line.

The first week she'd begun in the assembly room, Rebecca had been nauseated by the smell, the rapid pace, the noise. Noise-noise-noise. At such a decibel, noise isn't just sound but something physical, visceral, like electric current pumping through your body. It frightens you, it winds you tight, and tighter. Your heart is racing to keep pace. Your brain is racing but going nowhere. You can't keep a coherent thought. Thoughts spill like beads from a broken string . . .

She'd been terrified, she might go crazy. Her brain would break into pieces. You had to shout to be heard, shout in somebody's ear and people shouted in your ear, in your face. It was the raw, pulsing, primal life. There were no personalities here, no subtleties of the soul. The delicate soul of the child, like Niley, would be destroyed here. In the machines, in the hell-hole of the factory, there was a strange primal life that mimicked the pulse-beat of natural life. And the living heart, the living brain, were overcome by this mock-life. The machines had their rhythm, their beat-beat-beat. Their noises overlapped with the noises of other machines and obliterated all natural sound. The machines had no words, only just noise. And this noise overwhelmed. There was a chaos inside it, though there was the mechanical repetition, a mock-orderliness, rhythm. There was the mimicry of a natural pulse-beat. And some of the machines, the more complicated, mimicked a crude sort of human thought.

Rebecca had told herself she could not bear it!

More calmly telling herself she had no choice.

Tignor had promised Rebecca she would not have to work, as his wife. He was a man of pride, easily offended. He did not approve of his wife working in a factory and yet: he no longer provided her with enough money, she had no choice.

Since summer, Rebecca was better adjusted. But, Christ she would never be adjusted.

It was only temporary work of course. Until . . .

He had looked at her with such certainty! HAZEL JONES.

Seeming to know her. Not Rebecca in her filth-stiffened work clothes but another individual, beneath.

He'd known her heart. HAZEL JONES HAZEL ARE YOU HAZEL JONES YOU ARE HAZEL JONES ARE YOU. In the long morning hours HAZEL JONES HAZEL JONES lulling, seductive as a murmurous voice in Rebecca's ear and in the afternoon HAZEL JONES HAZEL JONES had become a jeering din.

"No. I am not. God damn you leave me alone."

Him removing his glasses. Prissy tinted glasses. So she could see his eyes. How sincere he was, and pleading. The injured iris of one eye, like something burnt-out. Possibly he was blind in that eye. Smiling at her, hopeful.

"Like I was somebody special. 'Hazel Jones.' "

She had no wish to think about Hazel Jones. Still less did she want to think about the man in the panama hat. She'd have liked to scream into his face. Seeing again his shock, when she'd torn up his card. That gesture, she'd done right.

But why: why did she detest him?

She had to concede, he was a civilized man. A gentleman. A man who'd been educated, who had money. Like no one else she knew, or had ever known. And he'd made such an appeal to her.

He was kind-hearted, he meant to do right.

"Was it just I'm 'Hazel Jones' or—maybe, it was *me*."

Remembered you. In his will.

Legacy.

"See, I am not her. The one you think I am."

Must remember me, Dr. Hendricks's son.

"I told you, I don't."

God damn she'd told him *no*, she'd been truthful from the start. But he'd kept on and on like a three-year-old insisting what could not be, was. He'd continued to speak to her as if he had heard *yes* where she'd been saying *no*. Like he was seeing into her soul, he knew her in some way she didn't know herself.

"Mister, I told you. I'm not *her*."

So tired. Late afternoon is when you're susceptible to accidents. Even the old-timers. You get slack, fatigued. SAFETY FIRST!—posters nobody glanced at anymore, so familiar. 10 SAFETY REMINDERS. One of them was KEEP YOUR EYES ON YOUR WORK AT ALL TIMES.

When Rebecca's vision began to waver inside the goggles, and she saw things as if underwater, that was the warning sign: falling asleep on her feet. But it was so . . . It was so lulling. Like Niley falling asleep, his eyelids closing. A wonderment in it, how human beings fall asleep same as animals. What is the *person* in *personality* and where does it go when you fall asleep. Niley's father Tignor sleeping so deeply, and sometimes his breath came in strange erratic surges she worried he might cease breathing, his big heart would cease pumping and then: what? He had married her in a "civil cere-mony" in Niagara Falls. She'd been seventeen at the time. Somewhere, lost amid his things, was the Certificate of Marriage.

"I am. I am Mrs. Niles Tignor. The wedding was real."

Rebecca jerked her head up, quickly. Where'd she been . . . ?

She poked her fingers inside the goggles, wiping her eyes. But had to take off her safety gloves first. So awkward! She wanted to cry in frustra-tion. . . . *hurt. Or were told you were. I don't judge.* He was watching her from the doorway, he was speaking about her with one of the bosses. She saw him, in the corner of her eye; she would not stare, and allow them to know that she was aware of them. He wore cream-colored clothes, and the pan-ama hat. Others would glance at him, quizzically. Obviously, he was one of the owners. Investors. Not a manager, not dressed for an office. Yet he was a doctor, too . . .

Why'd Rebecca rip up his card! The meanness in her, taking after her gravedigger father. She was ashamed of herself, thinking of how he'd been shocked by her, and hurt.

Yet: he did not judge.

"Wake *up*. Girl, you better *wake up*."

Again Rebecca had almost fallen asleep. Almost got her hand mangled, left hand this time.

Smiled thinking crazily: the fingers on the left hand you would not miss so much. She was right-handed.

She knew: the man in the panama hat wasn't in the factory. She must have seen, in the blurry corner of her eye, the plant manager. A man of about that height and age who wore a short-sleeved white shirt, most days. No bow tie, and for sure no panama hat.

After work she would almost-see him again. Across the street, beneath the shoe repair awning. Quickly she turned away, walked away not looking back.

"He isn't there. Not Tignor, and now not him."

No one saw: she made sure.

Looking for pieces of Hendricks's card she'd ripped up. On the towpath she found a few very small scraps. Not certain what they were. Whatever was printed on them was blurred, lost.

"Just as well. I don't want to know."

This time, disgusted with herself, she squeezed the pieces into a pellet and tossed it out onto the canal where it bobbed and floated on the dark water like a water bug.

Sunday passed, and Tignor did not call.

To distract the restless child she began telling him the story of the man-on-the-canal-towpath. The man-with-the-panama-hat.

"Niley, this man, this strange man, followed me along the towpath, and guess what he said to me?"

The Mommy-voice was bright, vibrant. If you were to color it in crayons it was a bold sunny yellow tinged with red.

Niley listened eagerly, uncertain if he should smile: if this was a happy story, or a story to make him worry.

"Mommy, what man?"

"Just a man, Niley. Nobody we know: a stranger. But—"

" 'Stang-er'—"

" 'Strang-er.' Meaning somebody we don't know, see? A man we don't know."

Niley glanced anxiously about the room. (His cubbyhole of a bedroom with a slanted ceiling, that opened onto her bedroom.) He was blinking rapidly peering at the window. It was night, the single window reflected only the blurred undersea interior of the room.

"He isn't here now, Niley. Don't be afraid. He's gone. I'm telling you about a nice kind man, I think. A friendly man. My friend, he wants to be. Our friend. He had a special message for me."

But Niley was still anxious, glancing about. To capture his attention Mommy had to grip his little shoulders and hold him still.

A squirmy little eel, he was. She wanted to shake him. She wanted to hug him tight, and protect him.

"Mommy? *Where?*"

"On the canal towpath, honey. When I was coming home from work, coming to get you at Mrs. Meltzer's."

"Today, Mommy?"

"Not today, Niley. The other day."

It was later than usual, the child hadn't yet gone to bed. Ten o'clock and she'd only just managed to get him into his pajamas by making a game of it. Tugging off his clothes, his shoes, as he lay passive and not-quite-resisting. It had been a difficult day, Edna Meltzer had complained to Rebecca. At the delicate juncture of bones at the child's forehead Rebecca saw a nerve pulsing.

She kissed the nerve. She resumed her story. She was very tired.

The three-year-old had been too cranky to be bathed in the big tub, Mommy had had to struggle to wash him with a washcloth, and then not very well. He was too cranky to be read to. Only the radio would comfort him, that damned radio Rebecca would have liked to toss out the window.

"A man, a very nice man. A man in a panama hat—"

"Mommy, what? A banana hat?"

Niley laughed in disbelief. Rebecca laughed, too.

Why the hell had she begun telling this story, she couldn't imagine. To impress a three-year-old? Out of the crayon box she selected a black crayon to draw a stick-man and on the stick-man's silly round head with the yellow crayon she drew a banana hat. The banana was disproportionately large for the stick-man's head, and upright. Niley giggled and kicked and squirmed with pleasure. He grabbed at the crayons to draw his own stick-man with a tilted-over banana hat.

"For Dad-*dy*. Banana hat."

"Daddy doesn't wear a hat, sweetie."

"Why not? Why doesn't Dad-dy wear a hat?"

"Well, we can get Daddy a hat. A banana hat. We can make a banana hat for Daddy . . ."

They laughed together, planning Daddy's banana hat. Rebecca gave in to childish nonsense, she supposed it must be harmless. The things that child imagines!—Mrs. Meltzer shook her head, you could not determine if she was amused, or alarmed. Rebecca smiled, Rebecca shook her head, too. She worried that Niley wasn't developing as other children developed. His brain seemed to function like the jerky conveyor belt. His attention span was fierce but brief. You could not hope to follow through a line of thinking or of speaking, Niley had no patience for tales that went on for more than a few seconds. Unless you imposed your will upon the child, as Rebecca sometimes did, in exasperation. Otherwise the child led you wandering, stumbling. A blizzard of broken-off thoughts, snatches of misheard words. She felt at such times that she would drown in the child's small fevered brain, she was a tiny adult figure trapped in a child's brain.

She had wanted desperately to be a mother. And so she was a mother.

She had wanted desperately to be Niles Tignor's wife. And so she was Niles Tignor's wife.

These irrefutable facts she was trying to explain to the man in the panama hat who stood gazing at her with his small, hurt smile. His eyes were myopic, almost you could see the fine scrim of myopia over them, like scum on water. His gray-blond hair so curiously molded. Smile lines deep-etched in his face that was an old-young face, faded and yet strangely boyish, hopeful. He was a courteous man you could see, a gentleman. Convinced that the slatternly young woman in the factory clothes was lying to him yet appealing to her anyway.

A man of science and reason.

At least take my card.

If you should ever wish to . . .

———

In the telephone directory for the Greater Chautauqua Valley she looked up *Jones*. There were eleven *Joneses* all of them male, or initials which might mean male or female. Not a single woman, so designated. Not a single listing *H. Jones*.

This didn't surprise her. For obviously, Byron Hendricks must have consulted the directory, many times. He must have called some of these Joneses, in his search for Hazel Jones.

"Asshole! What a stupid thing to do."

One night Rebecca woke from sleep to the realization, that struck her like a punch to the gut, that she was a careless mother, a bad mother: she'd stuck away the makeshift weapon, the seven-inch piece of steel, in a bureau drawer, where Niley who was always rummaging through her things might find it.

She took it out, and examined it. The steel was nasty-looking but not so sharp, overall. She'd have had to stab desperately with it to defend herself.

Anyway, she'd been wrong about the man in the panama hat. He had not meant to hurt her, he'd only just confused her with someone else. Why she'd become so upset, she didn't know. She, Rebecca, was low, primitive in her suspicions.

Yet she didn't throw the piece of steel away, but wrapped it in a tattered old sweater of hers kept high on a closet shelf where Niley, and Tignor, would never find it.

Two nights later, Tignor called.

"Yes? Who is it?"

"Who'd you think, girl?"

He had that power: to render her helpless.

She sank onto a kitchen chair, suddenly weak. Somehow, Niley knew. Running from the other room crying, "Dad-*dy*? Dad-*dy*?"

Niley plunged into his mother's lap, hot, eel-like, quivering with excitement. His devotion for his father was ardent and unquestioning as a young puppy's for its master. Still, he knew not to snatch at the phone, as he wanted to; he knew he would speak with Daddy when Daddy was ready to speak with him, and not before.

Rebecca would recall afterward that she'd had no premonition that Tignor would call that night. Since falling in love with the man she had become superstitious, it was a weakness of love she supposed, even a skeptical mind is prey to omens, portents. But she had not expected to hear Tignor's voice on the other end of the line, she'd had no preparation.

Tignor was telling Rebecca he would be back, back with her and the boy, by the end of the week.

Tignor never said he'd be back *home*. Only just *back with you and the boy*.

Rebecca asked where Tignor was, was he still in Port au Roche?—but Tignor ignored the question. He never answered questions put bluntly to him. And his telephone voice was one of forced heartiness, jovial and impersonal as a radio announcer's voice.

Only in close quarters, was Tignor capable of intimacy. Only where he could touch, stroke, squeeze. Only when he made love to her, was Rebecca really certain that he was with her.

Physically, at least.

Telling her now there'd been a little trouble. But it was *blown over* now.

"Trouble? What kind of . . . ?"

But Tignor wouldn't answer, Rebecca knew. It was some kind of business trouble, rivalry with another brewery maybe. She had not heard of any trouble, and so it was best to fall in with Tignor's tone. *Blown over*.

When Tignor was away, Rebecca kept a road map of New York state spread out onto the floor, to show Niley where Daddy was, or where Mommy believed Daddy was. She dreaded the child guessing that Mommy didn't always know. That Mommy might be misinformed. For Daddy's territory was vast, from Chautauqua Falls where they lived at the western edge of the state across the breadth of the state to the Hudson Valley, and north to the Adirondack Mountains and east to Lake Champlain where a town the size of Port au Roche was no more than a poppy-seed-sized dot on the map, even smaller than Chautauqua Falls.

Now, what was Tignor telling her? Something to make her laugh?

She understood: *I must laugh*.

This was important. Early on, in her relationship with Niles Tignor, she knew to laugh at his jokes, and to make jokes, herself. Nobody wants a heavy-hearted girl for Christ sake.

And: in the places Tignor frequented there were numerous girls and women vying with one another to laugh at his jokes. There always had been, before Rebecca had known Tignor, and there always would be, though he was her husband. She understood *I am one of these. I owe it to him, to be happy.*

"Niley, behave! Be good."

She whispered in the boy's ear, he was becoming impatient.

But Tignor was speaking to someone at the other end of the line. His hand over the receiver, she couldn't make out his words. Was he arguing? Or just explaining something?

How uncomfortable she was: in this chair, Niley squirming on her lap, her heart beating so hard it ached, snarly hair, damp from being washed, trailing down her back wetting her clothes.

She wondered what the man in the panama hat would think, seeing her. At least, he would recognize that she was a mother, and a wife. He would not confuse her with . . .

Tignor asked to speak with Niley. Rebecca handed over the phone.

"Dad-*dy*! H'lo Dad-*dy*!"

Niley's crunched-up little face came alive with pleasure. A child so suddenly happy, you understood there was anguish beforehand, pain. Rebecca staggered away, leaving him with the phone. She was dazed, exhausted. She stumbled into the next room, sank onto the sofa. A sofa with broken springs, covered with a not-clean blanket. A roaring in her ears like Niagara Tubing. Like the falls below the locks in Milburn, she'd stared into for long sickly fascinated minutes as a young girl.

Why could she not accuse Tignor of neglecting her. Why could she not tell Tignor she loved him even so, she forgave him.

He wasn't required to ask her forgiveness. She knew he never would. Only, if he would accept her forgiveness!

"You called me only three times. Sent me God damn sixty-five dollars and no message, no return address on the envelope. Fuck you."

And she had to accept it, the way Niley was chattering away to Daddy. *Loves Daddy more than he loves Mommy. Always has.*

Rebecca returned to the kitchen. She would take the receiver back from Niley. "Niley! Tell Daddy I need to talk to him, before he—"

But when Niley handed the receiver to his mother, Tignor must have already hung up for the line had gone dead.

It wasn't the music. Not the music that grated against her nerves. It was the announcers' voices. Radio voices. Advertisements. Those bright-brassy jolly-rollicking rapidly recited advertisements! And Niley crouched near, listening with frowning concentration. His small head bowed, attentive, in a pose that was not at all child-like. Listening for Daddy's voice in the radio! Rebecca felt a pang of hurt, and of fury, that her child should be so willfully deluded, and so oblivious of her.

"Niley, turn that off."

But Niley did not hear. Niley would not hear Mommy.

"Niley, I said turn that God-damned thing *off.*"

And so Niley might turn the radio volume down, reluctantly. Yet not off. So that Rebecca could still hear the voices like her rapid-chattering thoughts.

She told him no no no. That was not Daddy.

Not Daddy in the radio. No!

None of them. None of the radio voices.

(Did he believe Mommy? Was he even listening to Mommy?)

(And why should he believe Mommy? She was helpless as he was, to know whether Daddy would really return to them this time.)

Yet she too took comfort in it, often. Radio music.

Half-hearing in her sleep. Smiling as a dream of surpassing beauty enveloped her. There was Niley, not a spindly-limbed little boy you worried wasn't growing right, wasn't developing right, but a boy of perhaps fifteen, sixteen; a boy who was no longer a vulnerable child, yet not a hurtful man; a boy whose blurred face was handsome, and whose posture was excellent;

as he sat at a piano playing for an audience so large, Rebecca could not see to the edges of it.

"He will. He will do this. Here is the promise."

Her mother had made the promise, Rebecca seemed to think. They had listened to radio music together, in secret. How angry Pa would have been, if he'd known! But Pa had not known.

Pa had suspected, of course. But Pa had not known.

Anna Schwart had played piano, as a girl. A very long time ago in the *old world*. Before the *crossing*.

In the dream, Rebecca was suffused with happiness. And made to know how simple happiness is. Like smoothing a wrinkled cloth, dampening the cloth and ironing it, with care. That simple.

"You are a mother, Rebecca. You know what must be done."

Niley's favorite music wasn't piano music, though. Melancholy-whiny country-and-western. Bright pop tunes that made you want to dance. No matter how heavy-hearted she was feeling, Rebecca had to laugh seeing the three-year-old rocking from side to side on short, stubby legs, baby-legs that looked as if they were only just flesh and no bones inside. Inspired, Niley flailed his arms about. He screeched, he trilled. Rebecca pushed aside whatever the hell she was doing, danced with him, his pudgy little hands snatched up in hers. A wildness overcame her, she loved him so. Tignor had not liked her during her pregnancy, and so fuck Tignor: here was the result of the pregnancy, and he was hers.

Careening and banging around the house, reckless colliding with furniture, knocking over a chair, banging/bruising their legs, like a drunk couple overcome by fits of mirth.

"You love Mommy best, don't you! You *do*."

The music stopped, though. Abruptly, music stops.

Announcers' voices, so grating. God! You came to hate some of these voices like you came to hate people you saw too often, like at school, or at work. Always the same (male) voices. And Niley's expression changed, for now he was listening to hear: Daddy's voice?

Rebecca had tried to explain. Sometimes she didn't trust herself, just walked away.

See the humor in it, girl. Walk away.

Don't touch the child. The terrible rage in you, let it stay in you.

What most scared her, she might hurt Niley. Shake shake shake the obstinate little brat until his teeth rattled, eyes rolled back in his head. For so she'd been disciplined, as a child. She wanted to recall that it had been her father who'd disciplined her but in fact it had been both her mother and her father. She wanted to recall that the discipline had been deserved, necessary, and just but she wasn't so certain that this was so.

Tignor would return perhaps on Sunday.

Why Rebecca thought this, she didn't know. Just a premonition.

Except: it was possible that Tignor would show up outside the factory gate on Friday afternoon, or Monday afternoon. His silver-green 1959 Pontiac idling at the curb.

Hey kid: here.

Almost, Rebecca could hear his voice. She smiled, as she would smile when she heard it.

Hey you night owl folks out there this is Buffalo Radio Wonderful WBEN Zack Zacharias broadcasting the best in jazz through the wee hours.

Niley fell asleep most nights listening to this program. Yet she couldn't enter his room to switch off the radio because he woke so easily; she couldn't enter his room even to switch off the light. If Niley was wakened at such times he was likely to be frightened, and Rebecca would end up having to stay with him.

At least in the night Niley allowed the radio volume to be kept low. He could lie very quietly in his bed a few inches from the radio and take consolation from it.

At least with the door shut between their rooms Rebecca wasn't kept awake by the light.

"When Daddy returns, all this will stop."

Beside Niley's bed was a lamp in the shape of a milk glass bunny from a Chautauqua Falls furniture store. The bunny had upright ears and a pink nose, a small peach-colored shade in some fuzzy fabric. Rebecca admired the lamp, the wan warm glow on the child's sleeping face was comforting to her. The bulb was only sixty watts. You would not want a harsher light in a child's room.

She wondered: had her mother stood over her, gazed upon her as she'd slept? So long ago. She smiled to think yes, maybe.

The danger in motherhood. You relive your early self, through the eyes of your own mother.

In the doorway watching Niley sleep. Long entranced minutes that might have been hours. Her heart pounded with happiness, certainty. A mother knows only that the child *is*. A mother knows only that the child *is* because she, the mother, has made it so.

Of course there is the father. But not always.

Niles, Jr. She hoped he would take on some of his father's strength. He seemed to her a child of yearning, impulse. A spring was wound tight in him, like the spring of a toy that clatters about, deranged. Except when he slept, then Niley was fine. His tight-wound soul was quiet.

A glisten of saliva on his mouth like a stray thought. She wanted to kiss it away. But better not.

Strand of damp hair stuck to his forehead. She wanted to brush it away but no, better not.

Hazel Jones's secret son.

The radio on the windowsill was turned low. The music was jazz. The radio, like the lamp, emitted a comforting glow. Rebecca was becoming adjusted to it, no longer so annoyed. The announcer's voice was nothing like the daytime radio voices. Was Zack Zacharias a Negro? His voice was softly modulated, a singing sort of voice, rather playful, teasing. An intimate voice in your ear.

And the music. Rebecca was coming to like the music.

Cool, moody jazz. Seductive. Rebecca recognized piano music of course but knew few other instruments. Clarinet, saxophone? She hated it, that she knew so little.

An ignorant woman, a factory worker. Wife, mother. Had not graduated from high school, even. So ashamed!

Only once had she heard classical music on her father's radio. Only once, in her mother's company. Her father had not known and would have forbidden it. *This radio is mine. This news is mine. I am the father, all facts are mine. All knowledge of the world outside this house of sorrow is mine to keep from you, my children.*

Tignor had not asked much about Rebecca's parents. He knew a little, and might not have wanted to know more.

Rebecca's brother Herschel used to say, Christ that ain't even his name. "Schwart" ain't even our fuckin' name.

It was all a joke to Herschel. Baring his big wet braying-donkey teeth.

Rebecca asked what was their name, then? If it wasn't "Schwart" what had it been?

Herschel shrugged. Who the hell knew, who the hell cared?

Old-world bullshit, Herschel said. Nobody gives a damn about it in the U.S. of A., I sure don't.

Rebecca begged to know their name if it wasn't Schwart but Herschel walked away with a rude gesture.

If Jacob Schwart had lived, he would now be sixty-three.

Sixty-three! Old, but not really old.

Yet in his soul the man had been elderly even then. Rebecca could remember her father only as old, worn-out.

Upsetting to think such thoughts. It was rare for her, in her new life, to think such thoughts.

Hazel Jones did not think such thoughts.

"Mamama . . ."

Niley moaned in his sleep, suddenly. As if he'd become aware of Rebecca standing over him.

His smooth child-face was wizened, ugly. Oh, he looked like an elderly man! His skin was waxy-pale. His eyelids fluttered, and that nerve in his forehead. As if a wrong-sized dream, all sharp corners, had poked itself into his brain.

"Niley."

Rebecca's heart was torn, seeing her son trapped in a dream. Her instinct was to save him from such dreams, immediately. But no, better not. Mommy could not always be saving him. He must learn to save himself.

The dream was passing, and would pass. Niley would relax in another minute. He was a child of the new era: born in 1956. You would not call

Niles Tignor, Jr. "post-war" (for everything was "post-war") but "post-post-war." Nothing of the past could matter much to him. As World War I was to Rebecca's generation, so World War II would be to Niley's. Old-world bullshit as Herschel said.

Nothing of the Schwarts would prevail in him who had never known them.

That line was extinct, the old, rotted European lineage was broken.

Niley's dream seemed to have vanished. He was sleeping as before, breathing wetly through his mouth. The bunny lamp glowed on his bedside table. The radio on the windowsill emitted a steady, soothing sound of piano-jazz. Rebecca smiled, and backed away. She too would sleep, now. Niley would be all right, she had no need to wake him. Wouldn't kiss him, as she wanted to do. Still he would know (she was sure) that his mother loved him, always his mother was close by, watching, protecting him. Through his life, he would know.

"I have no God to witness. But I vow."

Sunday, in three days. Rebecca counted on her fingers. She smiled to think that Niley's daddy would return to them then. She had a premonition!

4

❀ ❀ ❀

Gypsy girl. Jewess . . .

Tignor's voice was a low helpless moan, a sliding-down moan, delicious to hear. His thick-muscled body quivered with desire as if electric currents ran through it.

Rebecca smiled, recalling. But the blood beat hard and hot in her face. She was no gypsy-girl, and she was no Jewess!

And the blood beat hard and hot between her legs, where she was so lonely.

"God damn." She was having trouble sleeping. In her and Tignor's bed. All this day, these days since the canal towpath, oh Christ her nerves were strung tight like wire.

The weather was turning at last. Wind from the great roiling-dark lake forty miles to the north seemed to push against the windowpanes of the old farmhouse. By morning the dreamy Indian-summer weather would have been blown away, the air would be sharper, colder, damp. That taste of winter to come. Winter in the Chautauqua Valley, in the foothills of the mountains . . .

But no. She would not think about it. Not *the future* beyond the next few days.

As her parents had gradually ceased thinking about *the future*.

Like animals they'd become, at the end. With no future, that was what happened to you.

Desperate to sleep! Within a few hours she'd have to get up, return to

Niagara Fiber Tubing. Not the thin pale froth-sleep that washed over her aching brain and brought little nourishment but the deeper more profound sleep she required, the sleep that slowed your heartbeat toward death, the sleep that stripped from you all awareness of time, place, who you are or have ever been.

"Tignor. I want you! I want you inside me. I want you . . ."

He'd urged her to say his special words to him: *fuck, fuck me. Hurt me some.*

The more hesitant she'd been, the more embarrassed, shame-faced, the more Tignor had loved it. You could see that the man's pleasure was increased immeasurably, a tall stein into which ale was being poured, poured-poured-poured until, foaming, it overflowed.

He'd been her only lover. Niles Tignor. What he did to her, what he taught her to do to him. How painful it was to lie here in this bed and not think of him, not think of those things, her heartbeat quickened in desire.

Futile, this desire. For even if she touched herself it was not Tignor.

Before Tignor she had never slept in so large a bed. She didn't feel that she deserved so large a bed. (Yet it was just an ordinary bed, she supposed. Secondhand, bought here in Chautauqua Falls. It had a slightly tarnished brass frame and a new, hard, unyielding mattress that had quickly become stained with Tignor's salty sweat.)

She turned, to lie on her back. In the adjacent room, turned low, the damn radio was playing. She couldn't hear the music but she felt the beat. She spread out her arms, her armpits were wet. Her thick hair dense as a horse's mane had dried at last and was fanned out around her head on the pillow in that way that Tignor, face taut with a hard, sensual pleasure, sometimes arranged it with his clumsy hands.

This is what you want, Gypsy-girl, eh? Is it?

He had other women, she knew. She'd known before she married him what he was. In the hotel in which she'd worked there were tales of Niles Tignor. Through the Chautauqua Valley, and beyond. She understood it wasn't reasonable for any woman of Tignor's to expect a man like him to be faithful in the way that ordinary men are faithful to women. Hadn't Tignor said to Rebecca, shortly after they were married, not cruelly but with an air of genuine surprise that she should be jealous: "Jesus, kid—they like me, too."

Rebecca laughed, remembering. Knuckles jammed against her mouth.

But it was funny. You had to have a sense of humor to appreciate Niles Tignor. He expected you to make him laugh.

She lay on her back now. Sometimes that worked. Her muscles began to twitch. There was her damn hand drifting near the God damn stamping machine . . . She drew it back just in time.

In some other universe it might've happened. Her hand mangled like meat. Severed from her arm. What she deserved, stupid cunt not watching what she was doing.

How Tignor would stare! Rebecca had to laugh, imagining.

He'd hated her big-whale belly. Staring in fascination, and couldn't keep his hands off.

The way the wind blew in the yew trees. A sound like voices jeering. This was the old Wertenbacher farm, so-called still in the neighborhood. By now, three years later, Rebecca would have thought they would have their own house.

He did love them. Her and Niley. In his heart he was not unfaithful.

In his heart, her father Jacob Schwart had loved her. He had loved them all. He had not meant to hurt them, he had only meant to erase history.

You are one of them. Born here.

Was this so? She hugged herself, smiling. Drifting at last into sleep as into a stone well so deep it had no bottom.

milburn, new york

I

❀ ❀ ❀

November 1936. By bus the Schwart family arrived in this small town in upstate New York. Out of nowhere they seemed to have come, with bulging suitcases, valises, bags. Their eyes were haggard in their faces. Their clothes were disheveled, their hair uncombed. Obviously, they were foreigners. "Immigrants." It would be said of the Schwarts that they looked like they'd been on the run from the Führer (in 1936, in such places as Milburn, New York, it was possible to think of Adolf Hitler with his mustache and military posture and stark staring eyes as comical, not unlike Charlie Chaplin) without stopping to eat, breathe, wash.

The smell that came off 'em!—the bus driver would so comment, rolling his eyes.

It seemed appropriate that Jacob Schwart, the head of the family, would find work as caretaker of the Milburn Township Cemetery, a non-denominational cemetery at the ragged edge of town. He and his family—wife, two sons, infant daughter—would live in the weathered stone cottage just inside the cemetery gates. This "cottage" was rent-free, which made the job attractive to a man desperate for a place to live.

Mr. Schwart was profusely grateful to the township officials who hired him though he'd had no experience as a cemetery caretaker, nor even as a gravedigger.

He was a good worker, he insisted. With his hands, and with his head.

"You will not regret, sirs. I will assure you."

At the time they'd moved into the cobwebby stone cottage in the cemetery, that had been only casually cleared after the departure of the previous tenants, and smelled strongly of something like liquid lye, the Schwarts' youngest child Rebecca was a sickly five-month-old infant tightly wrapped in her mother's filthy shawl. For much of the bus ride from downstate New York, this shawl had functioned as a sort of secondary diaper for the fretting infant.

So little she was, her brother Herschel would afterward recall, she looked like some hairless thing like a baby pig, and smelled like one, too. "Pa wouldna look at you hardly, he was thinkin you would die I guess."

Had she been Rebecca Esther Schwart then? She'd had no name and no identity, so young. Of those early days and weeks, months, and finally years in Milburn she would recall so little. For there was little memory in the Schwart family.

There was Ma, who nursed her. Ma who sometimes pushed her away with a grunt, as if her touch was painful.

There was Pa. "Jacob Schwart" he was. You could not predict Pa. Like the sky Pa was always changing. Like the ugly coal-burning stove in the kitchen Pa was smoldering sometimes, flaring-up sometimes. You would not wish to press your fingers experimentally against the stove when the fire was up inside.

Other times, the stove was empty of fire. Cold, dead.

Jacob Schwart was profusely grateful to be hired by strangers in this small country town. Yet Pa, brooding in the stone cottage, expressed a different sentiment.

"Like a dog they wish to treat me, eh! 'Jay-cob' I am, eh! Because I am foreign, I am not-rich, I am not one of them! One day they will see, who is a dog and who is a man."

Already as an infant she would begin to acquire an instinctive sense that her father, this powerful presence that leaned over her crib, sometimes poked her with wondering fingers, and even lifted her in his arms, had been grievously wounded in his soul; and would bear the disfigurement of this wound, like a twisted spine, through his life. She seemed to know, even as she shrank from such terrible knowledge, that she, the last-born of the family, the *little one*, had not been wanted by Jacob Schwart and was an outward sign of his wound.

She would not know why, a child does not ask why.

She would remember her panicked mother stumbling to her crib, clamping a moist hand over her mouth to muffle her crying. That Pa not be wakened from his exhausted sleep in the next room.

"No! Please no! He will murder us both."

2

❀ ❀ ❀

And so Jacob Schwart slept. Twitching and moaning in his sleep like an injured animal. After ten, twelve hours working in the cemetery in those early days he fell onto the bed in his work clothes, stinking of sweat, heavy mud-splattered boots still laced to his feet.

These boots he'd found in the shed. They had belonged to the previous Milburn cemetery caretaker, he supposed.

Too big for his feet. He'd stuffed the toes with rags.

Like hooves they seemed to him, his feet in these boots. Heavy, bestial. He dreamt of plunging into water, into the ocean, wearing such boots and being unable to unlace them, to swim and save himself.

3

⊛ ⊛ ⊛

History has no existence. All that exists are individuals, and of these, only individual moments as broken off from one another as shattered vertebrae. These words he hand-printed, gripping a pencil clumsily in his stiffening fingers. He had so many thoughts! In the cemetery his head was invaded by hornet-thoughts he could not control.

Clumsily he wrote down these thoughts. He wondered if they were his. He stared at them, and pondered them, then crumpled the paper in his hand and tossed it into the stove.

4

❋ ❋ ❋

You saw him at a distance: the gravedigger Schwart.

Like a troll he appeared. Somewhat hunched, head lowered.

In the cemetery amid the gravestones. Grimacing to himself as he wielded a scythe, a sickle, a rake; as he pushed the rusted hand-mower in fierce and unvarying swaths through the dense crabgrass; as he dug out a grave, and carted away excess soil in a tipsy wheelbarrow; as he paused to wipe his forehead, and to drink from a jar he carried in his coverall pocket. Tipping back his head, eyes shut and gulping like a thirsty dog.

Schoolboys sometimes squatted behind the cemetery wall that was about three feet in height, made of crude rocks and chunks of mortar, in poor repair. Briars, poison ivy and sumac grew wild along the wall. At the front entrance of the cemetery there was a wrought iron gate that could be dragged shut only with difficulty, and an eroded gravel drive, and the caretaker's stone cottage; beyond these, there were several sheds and outbuildings. The oldest gravestones ran up practically to the rear of the cottage. To the grassy area where the caretaker's wife hung laundry on clotheslines stretching between two weathered posts. If the schoolboys couldn't get close enough to Mr. Schwart to taunt him, or to toss chestnuts or stones at him, they sometimes settled for Mrs. Schwart, who would give a sharp little cry of alarm, hurt, pain, terror, drop what she was doing in the grass, and run panicked into the rear of hovel-house in a way that was very funny.

It would be pointed out that harassment of the cemetery caretaker predated Jacob Schwart's arrival. His predecessor had been similarly taunted, and his predecessor's predecessor. In Milburn, as in other country towns in that era, harassment of gravediggers and acts of vandalism in cemeteries were not uncommon.

Some of the schoolboys who harassed Jacob Schwart were as young as ten, eleven years old. In time, others would be older. And some weren't schoolboys any longer, but young men in their twenties. Not immediately, in the 1930s, but in later years. Their shouts wayward and capricious and seemingly brainless as the raucous cries of crows in the tall oaks at the rear of the cemetery.

Gravedigger! Kraut! Nazi! Jew!

5

❋ ❋ ❋

"Anna?"

He'd had a premonition. This was in the early winter of 1936, they'd been living here for only a few weeks. Clearing away storm debris from the cemetery he'd paused as if to hear . . .

Not jeering schoolboys. Not that day. He was alone that day, the cemetery was empty of visitors.

Run, run! His heart plunged in his chest.

He was confused. Somehow thinking that Anna was having the baby now, the baby was stuck inside her distended body now, Anna was screaming, writhing on the filthy blood-soaked mattress . . .

Even as he knew he was elsewhere. In a snow-encrusted cemetery amid crosses.

In a place he could not have named except it was rural, and had a fierce desolate beauty now that most of the leaves had been blown from the trees. And the sky overhead massed with clouds heavy with rain.

"Anna!"

She wasn't in the kitchen, she wasn't in the bedroom. Not in any of the four cramped rooms of the stone cottage. In the woodshed he found her, that opened off the kitchen; in a shadowy corner of the cluttered shed, crouched on the earthen floor—could that be Anna?

In the shed was a strong smell of kerosene. Enough to make you gag but there was Anna huddled with a blanket around her shoulders, matted hair and her breasts loose and flaccid inside what looked to be a dingy nightgown. And there was the baby on her lap, partly hidden in the filthy blanket, mouth agape, eyes watery crescents in the doll-face, unmoving as if in a coma. And he, the husband and the father, he, Jacob Schwart, trembling above them not daring to ask what was wrong, why in hell was she here, what was she hiding from now, had something happened, had someone knocked at the door of the cottage, what had she done to their daughter, *had she smothered her?*

For he was frightened, yet also he was furious. He could not believe that the woman was collapsing like this, after all they had endured.

"Anna! Explain yourself."

By degrees Anna became aware of him. She had been asleep, or in one of her trances. You could snap your fingers in Anna's face at such times and out of stubbornness she would scarcely hear you.

Her eyes shifted in their sockets. In this place called Milburn amid the crosses and stone angels and *those others* staring after her in the street she'd become furtive as a feral cat.

"Anna. I said . . ."

She licked her lips but did not speak. Hunched beneath the filthy blanket as if she could hide from him.

He would yank the blanket from her, to expose her.

Ridiculous woman!

"Give me the little one, then. Would you like me to strangle her?"

This was a jest of course. An angry jest, of the kind Anna could drive a man to.

It was not Jacob Schwart speaking but—who? The cemetery man. Gravedigger. A troll in work clothes and boots stuffed with rags grinning at her, clenching his fists. Not the man who'd adored her and begged her to marry him and promised to protect her forever.

It was not the baby's father, obviously. Hunched above them panting like a winded bull.

Yet, without a word, Anna lifted the baby to him.

6

❋ ❋ ❋

In America. Surrounded by crosses.

He'd brought his family across the Atlantic Ocean to this: a graveyard of stone crosses.

"What a joke! Joke-on-Jay-cob."

He laughed, there was genuine merriment in his laughter. His fingers scratching his underarms, his belly, his crotch for God is a joker. Weak with laughter sometimes, snorting with merriment leaning on his shovel until tears streamed down his whiskery cheeks and dribbled the shovel with rust.

"Jay-cob rubs his eyes, this is a dream! I have shat in my pants, this is my dream! *Am-er-i-ka*. Every morning the identical dream, eh? Jay-cob a ghost wandering this place tending the Christian dead."

Talk to yourself, there's no one else. Could not talk to Anna. Could not talk to his children. Saw in their eyes how they feared him. Saw in the eyes of *those others* how they pitied him.

But there was the *little one*. He had not wanted to love her for he had expected her to die. Yet she had not died of the bronchial infection, she had not died of the measles.

"Rebecca."

He was coming to speak that name, slowly. For a long time he had not dared.

One day, Rebecca was old enough to walk unassisted! Old enough to play Not-See with her father. First inside the house, and then outside in the cemetery.

Oh! oh! where is the little one hiding!

Behind that grave marker, is she? He would Not-See her.

She would giggle, and squeal in excitement, peeking out. And still Pa would Not-See.

Eyes squinted and pinched for he'd lost his damn glasses somewhere. Taken from him and snapped in two.

The owl of Minerva soars only at dusk.

That was Hegel: the very priest of philosophy admitting the failure of human reason.

Oh! Pa's eyes scraped over the *little one* without seeing her!

It was a wild tickle of a game. So funny!

Not a large man but in his cunning he'd become strong. He was a short stocky man with the hands and feet, shameful to him, of a woman. Yet he wore the previous caretaker's boots, cleverly fitted out with rags.

To the Milburn officials he had presented himself with such courtesy, for a common laborer, they had had to be impressed, yes?

"Gentlemen, I am suited. For such labor. I am not a large man but I am strong, I promise. And I am"—(what were the words? he knew the words!)—"a faithful one. I do not *cease*."

In the game of Not-See the *little one* would slip from the house and follow him into the cemetery. This was so delicious! Hiding from him she was invisible, peeking out to see him she was invisible, ducking back behind a grave marker quivering like a little animal, and his eyes scraping over her as if she was no more than one of those tiny white butterflies hovering in the grass . . .

"Nobody. There is nobody there. Is there? A little ghostie, I see? No!—nobody."

At this early hour, Pa would not be drinking. He would not be impatient with her. He would wink at her, and make the smack-smack noise with his lips, even as (oh, she could see this, it was like light fading) he was forgetting her.

His work trousers were tucked into his rubber boots, his flannel shirt loosely tucked into the beltless waist of his trousers. Shirt sleeves rolled up, the wiry hairs on his forearms glinting like metal. He wore the gray cloth cap. His shirt was open at the collar. His jaws moved, he smiled and grimaced as he swung the scythe, turning from her.

"Little ghostie, go back to the house, eh? Go, now."

The wonderful game of Not-See was over—was it? How could you tell when the game was over? For suddenly Pa would not-see her, as if his eyes had gone blind. Like the bulb-eyes of the stone angels in the cemetery, that made her feel so strange when she approached them. For if Pa didn't see her, she was not his *little one*; she was not *Rebecca*; she had no name.

Like the tiny grave markers, some of them laid down flat in the grass like tablets, so weathered and worn you could not see the names any longer. Graves of babies and small children, these were.

"Pa . . . !"

She didn't want to be invisible anymore. Behind a squat little grave marker tilting above a hillock of grass she stood, trembling.

Could she ride in the wheelbarrow? Would he push her? She would not kick or squeal or act silly she promised! If there was mown grass in the wheelbarrow not briars or grave-dirt, he would push her. The funny old wheelbarrow lurching and bumping like a drunken horse.

Her plaintive voice lifted thinly. "Pa . . . ?"

He seemed not to hear her. He was absorbed in his work. He was lost to her now. Her child-heart contracted in hurt, and in shame.

She was jealous of her brothers. Herschel and August helped Pa in the cemetery because they were boys. Herschel was growing tall like his father but Gus was still a little boy, spindly-limbed, his hair shaved close to his bumpy skull so that his head was small and silly as a doll's bald head.

Gus had been sent home from school with lice. Crying 'cause he'd been called Cootie! Cootie! and some of the kids had thrown stones at him. It was Ma who shaved his head, for Pa would not come near.

Who was she: Rebecca? "Reb-ek-ah." Ma said it was a beautiful name for it was the name of her great-grandmother who had lived a long time ago across the ocean. But Rebecca wasn't so sure she liked her name. Nor did she like who-she-was: *girl.*

There were the two: *boy*, *girl*.

Her brothers were *boys*. So it was left to her to be *girl*.

There was a logic to this, she could understand. Yet she felt the injustice.

For her brothers could play in the marsh, in the tall snakeroot if they wanted. But she could not. (Had she been stung by a bee, had she cried hard? Or had Ma scared her, pinching her arm to show what a bee sting is?)

Each morning Ma brushed her hair that was girl-hair, plaiting the hair to make her scalp hurt. And scolding if she squirmed. And if she tore her clothes, or got dirty. Or made loud noises.

Rebecca! You are a *girl* not a *boy* like your brothers.

Almost she could hear Ma's voice. Except she was in the cemetery trailing after Pa asking could she help? Could she help him?

"Pa?"

Oh yes she could help Pa! Rebecca could yank out small weeds, drag broken tree limbs and storm debris to the wheelbarrow. She would not scratch herself on the damn briars as Pa called them or stumble and hurt herself. (Her legs were covered in bruises. Her elbows were scabbed.) She was desperate to help Pa, to make him see her again and make that luscious smack-smack noise that was a noise only for *her*.

That light in Pa's eyes, she yearned to see. That flash of love for her even if it quickly faded.

She ran, and she stumbled.

Pa's voice came quick: "Damn you! Didn't I say *no*."

He was not smiling. His face was shut up tight as a fist.

He was pushing the wheelbarrow through the dense grass as if he hoped to break it. His back was to her, his flannel shirt sweated through. In a sudden terror of childish helplessness she watched him move away from her as if oblivious of her. This was Not-Seeing, now. This was death.

Pa shouted to her brothers who were working some distance away. His words were scarcely more than grunts with an edge of annoyance, no affection in them and yet: she yearned for him to speak to her in that way, as his helper, not a mere girl to be sent back to the house.

Back to Ma, in the house that smelled of kerosene and cooking odors.

———

Deeply wounded she was. So many times. Till at last she would tell herself that she hated him. Long before his death and the terrible circumstances of his death she would come to hate him. Long she would have forgotten how once she'd adored him, when she was a little girl and he had seemed to love her, sometimes.

The game of Not-See.

7

❀ ❀ ❀

Herschel growled, Promise you won't tell 'em?

Oh, she promised!

'Cause if she did, Herschel warned, what he'd do is shove the poker up her little be-hind—"Red hot, too."

Rebecca giggled, and shivered. Her big brother Herschel was always scaring her like this. Oh no oh *no*. She would *never tell*.

It was Herschel who told her how she'd been born.

Been born like this was something Rebecca had done for herself but could not remember, it was so long ago.

Never would Rebecca's parents have told her. Never-never!

No more speaking of such a secret thing than they would have disrobed and displayed their naked bodies before their staring children.

So it was Herschel. Saying how she, just a tiny wriggly thing, had gotten born on the boat from Europe, she'd been born in *New York harbor*.

On the boat, see? On the water.

The only one of the damn family, Herschel said, born this side of the 'Lantic Ozean that never needed any damn vissas or papers.

Rebecca was astonished, and listened eagerly. No one would tell her such things as her big brother Herschel would tell her, in all the world.

But it was scary, what Herschel might say. Words flew out of Herschel's mouth like bats. For in the Milburn cemetery amid the crosses, funerals, mourners and graves festooned with flowerpots, in the village of Milburn where boys called after him *Gravedigger! Kraut!* Herschel was growing into a rough mean-mouth boy himself. He hadn't been a child for very long. His eyes were small and lashless and gave an unnerving impression of being on opposing sides of his face like a fish's eyes. And his face was angular, with a bony forehead and a predator's wide jaws. His skin was coarse, mottled, with a scattering of moles and pimples that flared into rashes when he was upset or angry, which was often. Like their father he had fleshy, wormy lips whose natural expression was disdainful. His teeth were big and chunky and discolored. By the age of twelve, Herschel stood as tall as Jacob Schwart who was a man of moderate height, five feet eight or nine, though with rounded shoulders and a stooped head that made him appear shorter. From working with his father in the cemetery, Herschel was acquiring a bull-neck and a back and shoulders dense with muscle; by degrees he was coming more and more to resemble Jacob Schwart, but a Jacob Schwart smudged, distorted, coarsened: a dwarf grown man-sized. Herschel had bitterly disappointed his father by doing poorly in school, "kept behind" not once but twice.

As soon as they'd arrived in Milburn, Jacob Schwart had forbidden the speaking of German by his family, for this was an era of German-hatred in America and a suspicion of German spies everywhere. Also, his native language had become loathsome to Jacob Schwart—"a language of beasts." And so Herschel, who'd learned German as a child, was forbidden to speak it now; yet scarcely knew the "new" language, either. Often he spoke with an explosive stammer. Often it sounded as if he was trying not to laugh. Talkin, it was some kind of joke? Was it? You had to know the right sounds to talk, how to move your mouth, God damn they had to be the sounds other people knew, but how'd these people *know*? The connection between a sound coming out of a mouth (where your damn tongue got in the way) and what it was supposed to mean drove him wild. And printed words! Books! Fuckin school! That some stranger, an adult, would talk to *him*, he was expected to sit his ass in a desk where his damn legs didn't fit, because it was New York state fuckin law, an look in their damn face? With them little kids, half his size? That stared at him scared like he was some kind of freak? And some old bitch titless female teacher? Why the hell? At the Milburn school where Herschel Schwart was ostensibly in seventh grade, by far the biggest boy in his class, he took "special education" courses and under state law would be allowed to quit at age sixteen. What a relief, to his teachers and classmates! As he could not speak any language coherently he could not read at all. His father's effort to teach him simple arithmetic came to nothing. Printed materials aroused him to scorn and, beyond scorn, if they weren't quickly removed from his glaring eyes, fury. His brother Gus's textbooks and even his sister's primers had been discovered torn and mutilated, tossed on the floor. In the Port Oriskany newspaper which Jacob Schwart occasionally brought home, only the comic strips engaged Herschel's interest and some of these—"Terry and the Pirates," "Dick Tracy"—gave him difficulty. Herschel had always been fond of his baby sister the *little one* as she was called in the household and yet he often teased her, a wicked light came into his yellowish eyes and she could not trust him not to make her cry. Herschel would tug at her braids that had been so neatly plaited by their mother, he would grin and tickle her roughly beneath the arms, on her belly, between her legs to make her squeal and kick. Here he comes! Herschel would warn her. The *boa 'stricter*! This was a giant snake that wrapped itself around you but also had the power to tickle.

Even with Ma in the room staring at Herschel he would so behave. Even with Ma rushing at him crying *Schwein! Flegel!* slapping and punching him about the head, he would so behave. Physical blows from their mother made him laugh, even blows from their father. Rebecca feared her hulking big brother yet was fascinated by him, those lips expelling the most astonishing words like spittle.

That day, when Herschel told Rebecca the story of how she'd been born.

Been born! She was such a little girl, her brain had yet to comprehend that she hadn't always *been*.

Yah she was a squirmy red-face monkey-thing, Herschel said fondly. Ugliest little thing you ever saw like somethin' skinned. No hair, neither.

'Cause why it took so long, eleven damn hours, and everybody else dis-em-barkin' the fuckin' ship except them, her baby-head come out backwards and her arm got twisted up. So it took time. Why there was so much blood.

So she *got born*. All slimy and red, out of their Ma. What's it called—

'gina. Ma's hole, like. A hairy hole it is, Herschel had never seen anything like it. Nasty! Like a big open bloody mouth. Later he'd seen it, the hairs, between Ma's legs and up on Ma's belly like a man's whiskers, in the bedroom by accident pushing open the damn door and there's Ma tryin to hide, changin' her nightgown or tryin' to wash. You ever seen it? Thick hairs like a squirrel.

Hey, Herschel said, snapping his fingers in Rebecca's blank face.

Hey you think I'm fuckin' lyin' or somethin'? Lookin' at me like that?

Rebecca tried to smile. There was a roaring like thousands of mosquitoes in her ears.

You askin for the *boa 'stricter*, honey, are you?

Not the *boa 'stricter*, oh! Please not him.

Herschel liked to see his sister scared, it calmed him some. Saying she maybe thought he was makin all this up, but he wa'nt. How'd you think you got born, eh? *You* somebody special? How'd you think anybody gets born? Out of their Ma's hole. Not her asshole, nah not like a shit, that's somethin else, there's this other hole it starts out small then gets bigger, girls and wimmen got 'em, you got one too, want me ta show ya?

Rebecca shook her head no. No no!

You're just a li'l gal so you got one but it'd be real small like pea-size but for sure it's there inside your legs where you go pee-pee and where you're gonna get pinched, see? You don't b'lieve your brother Hershl.

Quickly Rebecca said, yes she believed him! She did.

Herschel scratched his chest, frowning. Trying to recall. The shit-hole cabin they was stayin' in, on the ship. Size of a dog house. No windows. "Bunk beds." Damn mess of rags, squashed roaches an' stale puke from Gus being sick, and everywhere stinkin' of shit. Then, Ma's blood. Stuff comin out of her layin' in the bunk bed. At last they was in New York harbor and everybody crazy to leave the stinkin' boat except them, they had to stay behind, 'cause of *her* wantin' to be born. Pa said you wa'nt spost to be born for another month, like he could argue with it. We was all starvin', Christ sake. Ma got so 'lirious, it was like she wudna h'self but some wild animal-like. Screamin, some muscle or somethin in her throat broke, why she don't talk right now. An you know she ain't right in the head neither.

Some old lady was gonna help Ma get you born, but there we wuz "em-

barkin" so she had to leave the boat, see. So it was just Pa. Poor Pa out of
his head. All along, Pa was goin' nuts with worry he said. Sayin' what if they
wudna let us land? in the Yoo Ess? what if they send us back to fuckin'
Nazizz they're gonna kill us like hogs. See, these Nazizz was comin' after
Pa at where he worked, he hadta leave. We hadta leave, where we was livin'.
We didn't always live like animals, see, we wa'nt like this ... Shit, I don't
remember too well, I was just a little kid scared all the time. They was tellin
us there's Nazizz submarines—"torpedoes"—tryin to sink us, why we was
zigzaggin an took so long to cross. Poor Pa, all the time he's lookin through
this "money-belt" thing he got around his middle checkin the papers, the
vissas. God damn you got to have them vissas with all kinds-a stamps an
things, you ain't a Yoo Ess cit'zen, see the fuckers won't let you in if they
can. Fuckers sure didn't want us lookin at us like we stunk! Like we was
worse'n hogs 'cause we cudna speak right. All Pa could worry about on the
boat was this papers gonna be stolen. Everybody stealin what they could,
see. That's where I learned, snatchin things. You run, old people ain't gonna
run after you. You're little enough, you can hide like a rat. A rat is littler
than I am, I learned from em. Pa goes around sayin his guts was eat out by
rats on that crossin. It's some joke of Pa's you got to 'preciate the old man's
sense-humor. My guts was eat out by rats on the 'Lantic Ozean I heard him
sayin to some old lady in the cemetery here she's puttin flowers on some
grave an Pa gets to talkin to her, like he says for us never to do, talkin to
those others you can't trust, but he's talkin an laughin that dog-bark laugh of
his so she's lookin at him like she's scared of him. So I was thinkin Pa is
drunk, he ain't got his right judgment.

On the boat, we had to eat what they give us. Spoiled food with weevils
in it, roaches. You pick em out, squash em under your foot and keep on
eatin, you're hungry enough. It's that or starve. All our guts was eat out by
the time we landed and everybody shittin bloody stuff like pus but Pa was
the worst 'cause of ulcers he said the fuckin Nazizz give Pa ulcers way back
years before. Pa's guts ain't normal, see. Look at Pa, he wa'nt always like he
is now.

Rebecca wanted to know how Pa used to be.

A vague look came over Herschel like a thought the wrong size for his
skull. He scratched at his crotch.

Oh shit, I dunno. He wa'nt so excitable I guess. He was more happy I guess. Before the trouble started. Before I got too big, he'd carry me around, see? Like he does with you. Used to call me *Leeeb*—somethin like that. Used to kiss me! Yeah, he did. And this music him an Ma liked, loud singin on the radio—"oper-a." In the house they'd be singin. Pa would sing some, and Ma she'd be in some other room and she'd sing back, an they'd laugh, like.

Rebecca tried, but could not imagine her parents singing.

She could not imagine her father kissing Herschel!

They was diffr'nt then, see. They was younger. Leavin where we lived wore em out, see. They was scared, like somebody was followin em. Like the police maybe. "Nazizz." There was trains we rode on, real noisy. Real crowded. And the damn boat, you'd think the 'Lantic Ozean would be nice to look at, but it ain't, all-the-time the wind's blowin and it's damn cold an people pushin you an coughin in your damn face. I was little then, not like now, see nobody gave a damn about a kid if they stepped on me the bastids! The crossing, that wore em out. Havin' you 'bout killed Ma, an him, too. Nah it wa'nt your fault, honey, don't feel bad. It's the Nazizz. "Storm trooperz." Ma had nice soft hair and was pretty. Talkin diffr'nt langidge, see. Christ I was talkin this diffr'nt langidge "Ger-man" it was, bettern I can talk what-the-fuck's-this-now—"Eng-lish." God damn why they got to be so diffr'nt I don't know! Makin more trouble. I mostly forget that other now but I don't know fuckin Eng-lish worth shit, either. Pa was like that, too. He knew to talk real well. He was a schoolteacher they said. Now, Christ they'd laugh! 'Magine Pa teachin in school!

Herschel guffawed. Rebecca giggled. It was funny: seeing Pa in front of a classroom, in his old work clothes and cloth cap, a stick of chalk in his hands, blinking and squinting.

No. You could not. You could not 'magine.

Herschel had been nine years old at the time of the 'Lantic crossing and would not forget through his fuckin life except he could not remember, either. Not clearly. Some kind of mist came down over his brain that ain't lifted since. For when Rebecca asked how long did it take to cross the ocean, how many days, Herschel began to count on his fingers slowly then gave up saying it was a long fuckin time an there was lots of people died an' dumped over the side of the boat like garbage for the sharks to eat, you was always scared you would die, this "dyzen-tery" sickness in the guts— that's all he knew. A long time.

Ten days? Rebecca asked. Twenty?

Nah it wa'nt days it was fuckin weeks, Herschel snorted.

Rebecca was just a little girl but already she needed to know: numbers, facts. What was *real* and what was only *made-up*.

Ask Pa, Herschel said, flaring up suddenly. Herschel would get mad if you asked him any question he couldn't answer like he'd gotten mad at his teacher at school once, she'd run out of the classroom for help. That cobweb look in Herschel's eyes and baring his yellow teeth like a dog. Saying, Ask Pa you're so hot to know all this old crap.

Looming over her, and his hand shot out, the edge of his hand, *whack*! on the side of her face so, next thing Rebecca knew, she was fallen over sideways like a rag doll, too surprised to cry, and Herschel was stomping out of the room.

Ask Pa. But Rebecca knew not to ask their father anything, none of them dared approach Pa in any way likely to *set him off*.

8

❀ ❀ ❀

Schwart! That's a Jew-name, yes? Or do I mean——He-brew?

No. A German name. He and his family were German Protestants. Their Christian faith derived from a Protestant sect founded by a contemporary of Martin Luther in the sixteenth century.

A very small sect with very few followers in America.

9

❁ ❁ ❁

Swallow your pride like phlegm Jay-cob.

In this American place mysterious and ever-shifting to him as a dream not his own: Milburn, New York.

On the banks of that so strangely named canal: Erie.

It was musical in its way—"Ear-ee"—both syllables equally stressed.

And there was the Chautauqua River a quarter-mile north of the cemetery, beyond the town limits: an Indian name, "Cha-taa-kwa." No matter how many times he pronounced this word he could not master it, his tongue was thick and clumsy in his mouth.

This region in which he and his family dwelt, this place in which they had taken temporary refuge, was the Chautauqua Valley. In the foothills of the Chautauqua Mountains.

A beautiful landscape, farmland, forests, open fields. If with a broken back and eyes smudged with dirt and your meanly beating troll-heart you wished to perceive it that way.

And there was the U.S.: the "Yoo Ess." You did not mumble or swallow such words but spoke them outright with an air of pride. You would not say "America"—"Ameri-ka"—for that was a word only immigrants used. Yoo Ess was the word.

As he would one day learn to say "Ale-lied": Allied. The Allied Forces. The Allied Forces that would one day "liberate" Europe from the Axis Powers.

"Fascists." That ugly word, Jacob Schwart had no difficulty saying though in public he would never say it.

Nor "Nazi"—"Nazis." These words too he knew well though he would not utter them.

Swallow pride. Grateful is happy. You are a happy man.

He was. For here in Milburn he was known: the caretaker of the cemetery, the gravedigger. The cemetery was several acres of hilly, rocky soil. By the standards of North America it was an old cemetery, the earliest markers dating from 1791.

These were the most peaceful dead. Almost, you could envy them.

A prudent man, Jacob Schwart did not inquire into the fate of his predecessor nor did anyone volunteer information about "Liam McEnnis." (An Irish name? Miscellaneous pieces of mail had continued to arrive for McEnnis months after the Schwarts had moved in. Worthless items like advertising flyers but Jacob took care to print NOT HERE on each and place them in the mailbox by the road for the mailman to take away again.) He was not an inquisitive man, not one to pry into another's business. He would do his work, he would earn the respect and the wages paid to him by the Milburn officials who'd hired him and persisted in calling him, in their awkward, genial, American way, "*Jay*-cob."

Like a dog they'd hired. Or one of their Negro ex-slaves.

In turn, Jacob Schwart was careful to address them with the utmost respect. He'd been a schoolteacher and knew how important it was to assuage the pettiness of such officials. "Sirs"—"gentlemen"—he called them always. Speaking his slow, awkward English, very polite, at that time clean-shaven, in reasonably clean clothes. He had gripped his cloth cap in both hands and took care in lifting his eyes, that were not timid but fierce, brimming with resentment, hesitantly to theirs.

Thanking them for their kindness. Hiring him, and providing him with a "cottage" in which to live on the cemetery grounds.

So grateful. Thank you sirs!

(Cottage! A strange word for that dank stone hovel. Four cramped rooms with plank floorboards, crude stone walls and a single coal-burning stove whose fumes pervaded the space drying their nostrils so they bled.

There was his baby girl, his daughter Rebecca, it tore at his heart to see her coughing and spitting up her food, wiping blood from her nose.)

This time of madness in Europe. I thank you in the name of my wife and my children also.

He was a broken man. He was a man whose guts had been eaten out by rats. Yet he was a stubborn man, too. Devious.

Seeing how *these others* smiled at him in pity, some slight revulsion. They would not wish to shake his hand of course. Yet he believed they were sympathetic with him. He would insist to Anna, these people are sympathetic with us, they are not scornful. They can see that we are good decent hardworking people not what is called "traz"—"trass"—in this country.

For once they determined you were *trass*, they would not hesitate to fire you.

Out on your ass—a colorful American expression.

His papers were in order. The visa issued to him, after much delay, anguish, and the payment of bribes to key individuals, by the American consul in Marseilles. The documents stamped by U.S. Immigration at Ellis Island.

What he would not tell *those others*: how in Munich he'd been a math instructor in a boys' school as well as a popular soccer coach and when he'd been dismissed from the faculty he had been an assistant pressman for a printer specializing in scientific texts. His proofreading skills were extolled. His patience, his exactitude. He had not been paid so much as he might have been paid in other circumstances but it had been a decent wage and he and his family had owned their house, with their own furniture, including a piano for his wife, at a good address close by her parents and relatives. He did not tell *those others* whom he perceived to be his adversaries as early as 1936 that he was an educated man, for he understood that none of them was educated beyond what was called high school; he understood that his university degree, like his intelligence, would make of him even more of a freak in their eyes, and in addition make them suspicious.

In any case Jacob Schwart wasn't so educated as he wished and it became his plan that his sons would be better educated than he had been. It was not his plan for them to remain the sons of the Milburn gravedigger for long, his sojourn here would be temporary.

A year, possibly two. He would humble himself, he would save money. His boys would learn English and speak it like true Americans—quickly, even carelessly, not needing to be precise. There was public education in this country, they would study to be—engineers? doctors? businessmen? Maybe, one day Schwart & Sons Printers. Very fine printers. The most difficult scientific and mathematical texts. Not in Milburn of course but in a large, prosperous American city: Chicago? San Francisco?

He smiled, it was rare that Jacob Schwart allowed himself the luxury of a smile, thinking such thoughts. Of Rebecca Esther, the little one, he wished to think less clearly. She would grow up, she would marry one of *those others*. In time, he would lose her. But not Herschel and August, his sons.

In the night, in their lumpy bed. Amid the smells. Saying to Anna, "It is a matter of one day to follow another, yes? Do your duty. Never weaken. Never before the children, weaken. We must all. I will save pennies, dollars. I will move us from this terrible place within the year, I vow."

Beside him, turned toward the wall in whose stony crevices spiders nested, the woman who was Jacob Schwart's wife made no reply.

10

❊ ❊ ❊

Not Ma either. You lived in dread of *setting Ma off*.

As Herschel said it was worsen Pa, somehow. With Pa, he'd haul off and hit you if you said the wrong damn thing but poor Ma, she'd quiver and quake like she was wettin her pants, and start to cry. So you felt like shit. So you wanted to run out of there, and keep on runnin.

"Why'd you want to know that? Who is asking you such things? Somebody been askin you? Like at that school? Somebody spyin' on us?"

Like a match tossed into kerosene it was, how Ma would flare up excited and stammering if you asked the most innocent question. If you said some words Ma could not comprehend or had not even heard clearly (Ma was always humming and talking and laughing to herself in the kitchen, she'd pretend not to notice you when you came inside, not even glancing around, like a deaf woman) or asked some question she could not answer. Her mouth went ugly. Her soft sliding-down body began to tremble. Her eyes, that seemed to Rebecca beautiful eyes, immediately flooded with tears. Her voice was hoarse and cracked-sounding like dried cornstalks when the wind blows through them. Through her life she would speak her new language with the confidence of a crippled woman making her way across a patch of treacherous, cracking ice. She could not seem to mimic the sounds her children learned so readily, and even her husband could mimic in his own brusque way: "Anna, you must try. Not 'da'—'the.' Not 'ta'—'to.' Say it!"

Poor Anna Schwart spoke in a whisper, cringing in shame.

(And Rebecca was ashamed, too. In secret. She would never laugh openly at Ma like her brothers.)

There were stores in Milburn, the grocer's for instance, and the pharmacy, even Woolworth's, where Anna Schwart dared not speak but mutely handed over lists hand-printed by Jacob Schwart (initially, though in time Rebecca would make up these lists) so there could be no misunderstandings. (Still, there were misunderstandings.) Everybody laughed at her, she said. Not even waiting till her back was turned or she was out of earshot. Calling her "Mrs. Schwarz"—"Mrs. Schwartz"—"Mrs. Schwazz"—"Mrs. Warts." She heard them!

The boys, Herschel in particular, were embarrassed of their mother. Bad enough they were the gravedigger's sons, they were the sons of the gravedigger's wife. God damn!

(Ma can't help it, her nerves, Gus told Herschel, and Herschel said he knew it, fuck he knew it but that didn't make it easier did it? Two of em not right in the fuckin head, but at least Pa could take care of himself, Pa could speak English so you could make sense of him at least and also Pa had, what's it called, had to hand it to the old man, Pa had *dignity*.)

Once, when Rebecca was a little girl too young yet for school, she was in the kitchen with Ma when a visitor knocked at the front door of the caretaker's cottage.

A visitor! She was a middle-aged woman with fattish hips and thighs, a wide, ruddy face like something rubbed with a rag, and a cotton scarf tied around her head.

She was a farmer's wife who lived about six miles away. She had heard of the Schwarts, that they were from Munich? She, too, was from Munich: she'd been born there, in 1902! Today she was visiting the cemetery to tend to her father's grave, and she was bringing Anna Schwart an apple kuchen she'd baked that morning . . .

And there was Ma trembling in the doorway like a woman woken from a nightmare sleep. Her face was going sick, sallow as if blood were draining out of it. Her eyes were blinking rapidly, flooded with tears. Stammering she was busy, she was so busy. Rebecca heard the visitor address Ma in a strange harsh speech, yet warmly, as if they were sisters, uttering words too quickly for Rebecca to grasp—*Sie?* she heard—*haben?*—*Nachbarschaft?* But Ma shut the door in the woman's face. Ma stumbled away into the back bedroom and shut that door, too.

The rest of that afternoon, Ma hid in the bedroom. Rebecca, frightened, shut outside, heard the bedsprings creak. She heard her mother talking, quarreling with someone in that forbidden language.

"Ma?"—Rebecca jammed her fingers into her mouth, to keep from being heard.

She was desperate to be with her mother, wanted to cuddle with Ma, for sometimes Ma did allow that, sometimes Ma hummed and sang by the side of Rebecca's little bed, sometimes plaiting Rebecca's hair Ma blew into her ears, blew the tiny hair-wisps at the back of Rebecca's neck to tickle her just a little; not like Herschel who tickled so rough. Even Ma's sweat-smell that was mixed with cooking fats and the stink of kerosene, she was desperate to breathe.

Only toward dusk did Ma reappear, her face washed and her hair tightly plaited and coiled around her head in that way that made Rebecca think of baby snakes, you saw coiled together sometimes, in the grass in cold weather stunned and slow-moving. Ma had fastened the neck to her dress, that had been unbuttoned. Her vague reddened eyes blinked at Rebecca. In her hoarse whispery voice she told Rebecca not to tell Pa. Not to tell Pa that anybody had come to their door that day.

"He would murder me if he knew. But I didn't let her in. I would not let her in. Did I say a word to her?—I did not. Oh, I did not. I would not. Never!"

Through a window they could see movement in a far corner of the cemetery. A funeral, a large funeral with many mourners, and Pa would be busy well after the last mourner departed.

"Hey! Somebody left us some cake, looks like."

It was Herschel, home from school. Lurching into the kitchen carrying a baking tin, covered in wax paper. It was the apple kuchen, that had been left by the farmer's wife on the front step of the house.

Ma, guilt-stricken, folded her arms over her breasts and could not speak. A fierce blush like a hemorrhage rose into her face.

Rebecca jammed her fingers into her mouth and said nothing.

"Pa's gonna say it's some bastids wantin to pizzin us," Herschel laughed, breaking off a large piece of the coffee cake and chewing it, noisily. "But the old man ain't here yet, huh?"

❋ ❋ ❋

11

"We will have to live with it, for now."

So he'd said. Many times. Months and now years had passed.

Yet: they were so often sick. August, who was small for his age, edgy, rat-like, blinking as if his eyes were weak. (And were the boy's eyes weak? It was too far to drive him to an eye doctor, in the nearest city which was Chautauqua Falls.) And Rebecca was so often sick with respiratory ailments. And Anna.

The Schwart family, in the gravedigger's hovel.

More and more he was noticing the steeply slanting earth of the cemetery. Of course he'd noticed from the start, but had not wished to see.

The cemetery slanted upward, gradually. For the river was at their back, and this was a valley. At the road, at the front entrance where the house was built, the earth was more level. *Death leaks downward.*

When he'd applied for the job he had asked about the well water hesitantly, for he had not wanted to offend the township officials. It was clear that they were doing him a favor, yes? Just to speak with him, to suffer through his slow excruciating broken English, yes?

With their genial smiles they'd assured him that the well was a "pure" underground spring in no way affected by leakage from the graves.

Yes, certainly. The water had been tested by the county.

"At regular intervals" all the wells in Chautauqua County were tested. Certainly!

Jacob Schwart had listened, and had nodded.

Yes sirs. Thank you. I am only concerned . . .

He hadn't pursued the issue. He'd been dazed with exhaustion at the time. And so much to think about: housing his family, feeding his family. Oh, he'd been desperate! That ravaging will of which Schopenhauer wrote so eloquently, to exist, to survive, to persevere. The baby daughter who lacerated his heart with her astonishing miniature beauty yet maddened him, fretting through the night, crying loud as a bellows, vomiting her mother's milk as if it were poison. Crying until in a dream dense as glue he saw himself clamping his hand over her tiny wet mouth.

Anna spoke worriedly of the "grave water"—she was sure there was danger. Jacob tried to convince her there was no danger, she must not be ridiculous. He told her what the township officials had told him: the water in their well had been tested recently, it was pure spring water.

"And we won't be living here long."

Though later, he would tell her bluntly, "We will have to live with it, for now."

Was there an odor in the cemetery? A smell after rain of something sickly-sweet, moldering? A rancid-meat smell, a maggoty-meat smell, a putrescence-smell?

Not when the wind blew from the north. And the wind was always blowing from the north, it seemed. In these foothills of the Chautauqua Mountains south of Lake Ontario.

What you smelled in the Milburn cemetery was earth, grass. Mown grass rotting in compost piles. In summer, a pungent odor of sunshine, heat. Decomposing organic matter that was half-pleasurable to the nostrils, Jacob Schwart thought.

It would come to be Jacob Schwart's unmistakable smell. Permeating his weathered skin and what remained of his straggly hair. All his clothing, that, within a short period of time, not even 20 Mule Team Borax could fully clean.

Of course he knew: his children had to endure ignorant taunts at school. Herschel was big enough now to fend for himself but August was a timorous child, another disappointment to his father, tongue-tied and vulnerable. And there was little Rebecca, so vulnerable.

It sickened him to think of his daughter whom he could not protect laughed at by her classmates, even by ignorant teachers at her school.

Gravedigger's daughter!

He told her, solemnly as if she were of an age to understand such words, "Humankind is fearful of death, you see. So they make jokes about it. In me, they see a servant of death. In you, the daughter of such a one. But they do not know us, Rebecca. Not you, and not me. Hide your weakness from them and one day we will repay them! Our enemies who mock us."

All human actions aim at the good.

So Hegel, following Aristotle, had argued. In Hegel's time (he died in 1831) it had been possible to believe that there is "progress" in the history of humankind; history itself progresses from the abstract to the concrete, in this way realized in time. Hegel had believed, too, that nature is of necessity, and determined; while humankind knows freedom.

Jacob had read Schopenhauer, too. Of course. They had all read Schopenhauer, in Jacob's circle. But he hadn't succumbed to the philosopher's pessimism. *The world is my idea. The individual is confusion. Life is ceaseless struggle, strife. All is will: the blind frenzy of insects to copulate before the first frost kills them.* He'd read Ludwig Feuerbach for whom he had a special predilection: it thrilled him to discover the philosopher's savage critique of religion, which Feuerbach exposed as no more than a creation of the human mind, the projection of mankind's highest values in the form of God. Of course! It had to be so! The pagan gods of antiquity, thunderous Yehovah of the Jews, Jesus Christ on His cross so mournful and martyred—and triumphant, in resurrection. "It was all a ruse. A dream." So Jacob told himself, at the age of twenty. Such blindness, superstition, the old rites of sacrifice given a "civilized" cast: all were the way of the past, dying or extinct in the twentieth century.

He read Karl Marx, and became an ardent socialist.

To his friends he defined himself as an agnostic, a freethinker, and a German.

. . . a *German!* What a bitter joke, in retrospect.

Hegel, that fantasist, had been right about one thing: the owl of Minerva flying only at dusk. For philosophy comes too late, invariably. Understanding comes too late. By the time human intelligence grasps what is happening, it is in the hands of the brutes, and becomes history.

Broken-off pieces, like vertebrae.

Oh! I could listen to you talk forever, you have such wisdom.

Early in their love the young Anna had told Jacob this. Her eyes brimming with adoration of him. He'd spoken passionately to her of his socialist beliefs and she'd been dazzled, if slightly scandalized, by his certainty. No religion? No God? None? Anna's religious background had been similar to his, her people were very like his, proud of their "assimilation" into German middle-class culture. In his presence she believed as he believed, she learned to mimic certain of his words. *The future. Mankind. Shapers of our own destiny.*

Now they rarely spoke. Between them was a heavy, palpable silence. Clumsy rocks and boulders of silence. Like eyeless undersea creatures they moved in intimate proximity to each other and were keenly aware of each other and sometimes they spoke, and sometimes they touched, but there was only deadness between them now. Anna knew him as no one living knew him: he was a broken man, a coward. He had been unmanned. The rats had devoured his conscience, too. He'd had to fight to save himself and his young family, he'd betrayed a number of his relatives who had trusted him, and Anna's as well; he might have done worse if he'd had the opportunity. Anna would not accuse him for she had been his accomplice, as she'd been the mother of his sons. How he had acquired the exorbitant sums of money needed for their escape from Munich, their flight through France and their booking on the ship in Marseilles, Anna had not asked. She'd been pregnant with their third child then. She had their sons Herschel and August. She had come to see that nothing mattered to her except her children, that they not die.

"We will live for them, yes? We will not look back."

He made such vows, as a man might make, though he'd been unmanned, he had no sex. The rats had devoured his sex, too. Where his genitals had been was something useless now, soft-rotted fruit. Pathetic, comical. Through such a flesh-knob he managed to urinate, sometimes with difficulty. Oh, that was enough!

"I *said*. We will have to live with it, *for now*."

As she would not speak of her fear of contaminated water, even after heavy rains when the well water was so cloudy, and the children gagged and spat it out, so Anna would not speak of their future. She would not ask him any questions. How much money he'd saved, for instance. When they might be leaving Milburn.

And what was his salary, as caretaker of the cemetery?

If Anna had dared to ask, Jacob would have told her it was no business of hers. She was wife, mother. She was a woman. He would give her money each week: one-, five-, ten-dollar bills with which to shop. Counting out coins on the kitchen table, frowning and sweating in the halo of the bare-bulb light overhead.

Yes: Jacob Schwart had a savings account. Behind the stately neo-Grecian facade of the First Bank of Chautauqua on Main Street. It would not be an exaggeration to say that Jacob thought of this bank account, its exact sum, almost constantly; even when he was not consciously thinking of it, it hovered at the back of his mind.

My money. Mine.

The small black bankbook in the name of *Jacob Schwart* was so cleverly hidden away, wrapped in waterproof canvas on a shelf in the lawnmower shed, no one but *Jacob Schwart* could ever hope to find it.

Each week since his first salary check he had tried—oh, he had tried!—to save something, if only pennies. For a man must save something. Yet by October 1940 he had saved only just two hundred sixteen dollars and seventy-five cents. After four years! Still, the sum drew interest at 3 percent, a few pennies, dollars.

You didn't need to be a mathematical genius to know: *pennies add up*!

Soon, he would ask the Milburn township officials for a raise.

Very courteously in his second year as caretaker of the cemetery he'd asked. Very humbly he'd asked. Their replies had been stiff, guarded.

Well, Jay-cob! Maybe next year.

Depends upon the budget. County taxes, see?

Politely he pointed out to them that they had the unpaid labor of his elder son who helped him many hours a week now. Also his younger son, sometimes.

They pointed out to him, he lived in the caretaker's cottage for no rent. And paid no property taxes, either.

Not like the rest of us citizens, Jay-cob. *We* pay taxes.

They laughed. They were genial jovial men. *Those others* who regarded him like a dog teetering on its hind legs.

Was he doing a satisfactory job as caretaker, well yes—he was doing a satisfactory job. Unskilled labor it was, maintaining the cemetery, except you had to have some skills, in fact. Except you could not belong to any union. Except you would receive no pension, no insurance, like other township employees.

Except you were fearful in the end of seeming to complain. You were fearful of becoming known in Milburn, New York, as *Schwart-who-complains*.

Schwart-the-Kraut they called him behind his back. He knew.

Schwart-the-Jew.

(For hadn't Schwart a Jew nose? No one in Milburn had ever seen an actual Jew except now, *Life* magazine for instance, *Collier's*, were reproducing Nazi anti-Semitic cartoons and caricatures side by side with amusing photographs of inept British civilians training for the defense of their homeland.)

Damn he vowed he would show them! *Those others* who insulted him and his family. *Those others* whose secret allegiance was with Hitler. He had secrets of his own, saving money for his escape. He had escaped Hitler and he would escape Milburn, New York. So carefully saving his pennies for though Jacob Schwart was not a Jew (he was not a Jew) he possessed the ancient Jewish cunning, to slip through the clutches of the adversary, to prosper, and to take revenge. In time.

12

❊ ❊ ❊

The day Gus came running home from school snot-nosed and sniveling asking Ma what's a Jew, what's a damn Jew, those bastards on the Post Road were teasing him and Hank Diggles threw corncobs at him and everybody was laughing like they hated him, some of them he thought were his friends. And Ma was near to fainting, looking like a drowning woman, tied a scarf over her hair and ran to find Pa in the cemetery, stammering and panting for breath and it was the first time in memory he'd seen her, his wife, this far from the house, outside in the cemetery where he was using a scythe on tall grasses and wild rose infesting a hillside, he was shocked how frightened she appeared, how disheveled, in her shapeless housedress and in fact her stockings were rolled down to her ankles, her legs were glaring-white and covered in fair brown hairs, fattish legs, and her face now was puffy, bloated, where once she'd been a slender pretty girl smiling shyly in adoration of her schoolteacher husband and she'd played Chopin, Beethoven, Mendelssohn, God how he had loved her!— and now this clumsy woman stammering broken English so that he had trouble figuring out what the hell she was saying, he'd thought it might be those damn kids hiding behind the wall and tossing corncobs at the laundry on the line or at her and then he heard, he heard *Jew Jew Jew* he heard, and took hold of her shoulders and shook her telling her to shut her mouth and get back inside the house; and that evening when he saw Gus,

who was ten years old at this time, fifth grade at the Milburn grammar
school, Jacob Schwart slapped the boy open-handed across the face saying
these words Gus would long recall as would his sister Rebecca standing
close by:

"Never say it."

13

⁂ ⁂ ⁂

It was one of the astonishing acts of his life in America.

From a tradesman in Milburn, in the cold wet spring of 1940, he bought the radio. He, Jacob Schwart! His impulsiveness frightened him. His absurd trust in a stranger's integrity. For the radio was secondhand, and came with no guarantee. In this reckless gesture he was violating his principles of healthy distrust of *those others* he meant to inculcate in his children to protect them from disaster.

"What have I done! What . . ."

Like a random act of adultery, it had been. Or violence.

He, *he!*—who was assuredly not a man of violence but a civilized man, in exile now from his true life.

Yet the purchase had been premeditated for weeks. The quickening news in Europe was such, he could not bear to remain in ignorance. Local newspapers were inadequate. Nothing would satisfy him except a radio with which to hear daily, nightly news from as many sources as possible.

In a state of barely controlled agitation he had presented himself to the teller at the First Bank of Chautauqua. Shyly yet decisively he'd pushed his bankbook beneath the wicket. The teller, an individual of no earthly significance except he held Jacob Schwart's bankbook in his hand, frowned at the inked figures as if poised to glance up sternly at him—this cringing troll-figure in the soiled work clothes and cloth cap, "Jacob Schwart"—and inform him that no such savings account existed, he was totally mistaken. Instead, as if this were an everyday transaction, the teller mechanically counted out bills, not once but twice; and stiff freshly minted bills they were, which pleased Jacob Schwart absurdly. As the teller pushed both money and bankbook back beneath the wicket he seemed almost to wink at his customer. *I know what you're going to do with this money, Jacob Schwart!*

For days afterward Jacob would suffer stomach cramps and diarrhea, so stricken with guilt. Or so elated, and so stricken with guilt. A radio! In the caretaker's hovel! A Motorola, *the very best manufacturer of radios in the world.* The cabinet was made of wood, the dial warmly glowed as soon as the radio was turned on. It was a miracle how, switching the knob to *on*, you felt immediately the vibrating life of the marvelous instrument inside the cabinet like a thrumming soul.

Of course, Jacob had bought the radio without telling Anna. He no longer troubled to tell his wife much of what he did. Obscurely, they had become resentful of each other. Their stony silences lasted for hours. A day, a night. Who had wounded whom? When had it begun? Like dumb blind undersea creatures they lived together in their shadowy cave with only a minimal awareness of each other. Jacob learned to make his wishes known by grunting, pointing, grimacing, shrugging, shifting his body abruptly in his chair, glancing toward Anna. She was his wife, his servant. She must obey. He controlled all their finances, all transactions with the outside world were his. Since he'd forbidden the intimidated woman to speak their native language even when they were alone together in their bedroom, even in their bed in the dark, Anna was at a disadvantage, and came to resent having to speak English at any time.

Anna, too, was profoundly shocked by her husband's impulsive purchase of the radio, which she interpreted as an act not only of uncharacteristic profligacy but also of marital infidelity. *He is mad. This is the beginning.* When they had so little money, and the children needed clothes, and visits to the dentist. And the price of coal, and the prices of food . . . Anna was shocked, and frightened, and could not speak of it without stammering.

Jacob interrupted, "The radio is secondhand, Anna. A bargain. And a *Motorola.*"

He was jeering at her, she knew. For Anna Schwart had no idea what *Motorola* was, or meant; no more than she could have recited the names of the moons of Jupiter.

That first evening, Jacob was giddy, magnanimous: he invited his family into the parlor to listen to the big box-like object installed beside his chair. Anna stayed away, but the boys and Rebecca were enthralled. But it was an error in judgment, Jacob came to realize, for the news that evening was of an attack in the North Sea, the British destroyer *Glowworm* sunk by German warships, but survivors of the attack had been rescued from drowning by the crew of one of the German ships . . . Immediately Jacob changed his mind about his children listening to the radio, and ordered them out of the parlor.

German warships! Rescuing British sailors! What did it mean . . .

"No. It is not predictable. There is ugliness in it. It is not for young ears."

It was the news, he meant. Unpredictable, and therefore ugly.

Nineteen years later, hearing the radio in Niley's room murmuring and humming through the night, Rebecca would recall her father's radio that came to be such a fixture in the household. Like a malevolent god it was, demanding attention, exerting an irresistible influence, yet unapproachable, unknowable. For as no one but Pa ever dared to sit in Pa's chair (a finely cracked old leather chair with a hassock and a solid, almost straight back, because of Pa's aching spine) so no one but Pa was to switch on, or even to touch, the radio.

"You hear? No one."

He was serious. His voice quavered.

Mostly it was Herschel and August he warned. Anna, he understood would scorn to touch the radio. Rebecca he knew would never disobey.

Pa was jealous of the damn thing like it was (this was Herschel's sniggering observation) some lady friend of his. You had to wonder what the old man was doin with it, some nights, huh?

During the day, when Pa was working in the cemetery, the radio was unprotected in the parlor. More than once Pa suddenly appeared in the house, stalking into the parlor to check the tubes at the rear of the radio: if they were hot, or even lukewarm, there would be hell to pay for somebody, usually Herschel.

The reason for such frugality was *electricity doesn't grow on trees.*

And as Pa said repeatedly, grimly *war news isn't for the ears of the young.*

Behind the old man's back Herschel sputtered indignantly, "Fuck 'war newzz.' Fuck like there ain't other things on a radyo, like muzik an' jokin, it wouldna kill the old bastid to let us lissen." Herschel was old enough to know what a radio was, he had friends in town whose families owned radios, and everybody listened to them all the time, and not just fuckin' war newzz!

Yet, night after night, Pa shut the parlor door against them.

The more Pa drank at supper, the more firmly he shut the door against them.

Some nights, the yearning to hear the radio was so powerful, both Rebecca's brothers whined through the door.

"C'n we lissen too, Pa?"

"We won't talk or nothin . . ."

"Yeah! We won't."

Herschel was daring enough to rap his scraped knuckles against the door, though not too loudly. He was growing so fast his wrists protruded from his shirtsleeves, and his collar was too tight to button over his Adam's apple. Soon, the lower half of his face would sprout wire-like hairs he would be obliged to shave off before coming to school, or be sent back home by his teacher.

Through the door they (Herschel, August, Rebecca) could hear a radio voice that rose and fell like waves, but they could not distinguish any words, for Pa kept the volume turned low. What was the voice saying? Why was "news" so important? Rebecca was too young to know what war was ("Fightin' like with guns, bombs, an there's airplanes, too," Herschel said) but Ma told her it was all happening far away in Europe: thousands of miles away. Herschel and August spoke knowingly of "Nazizz"—"Hittler"—but said they were far away, too. No one wanted the war to come to the Yoo Ess. Anyway there was the 'Lantic Ozean in-between. The war would never come to a place like Milburn with a single lock on the barge canal. "This place," Herschel said scornfully, "the fuckin Nazizz wouldna bother with."

Rebecca's mother scorned the radio as what she called a *toy-thing* of her father's they could not afford, yet he had bought it. He had bought it! She would never forgive him.

Month followed month in that year 1940. And in 1941. What was happening in the *war-news*? Pa said it was ugly, and getting uglier all the time. But the Yoo Ess was staying out of it like damn cowwards not wanting to get hurt. You'd think, if they didn't give a damn about Poland, France, Belgium, Russia, they'd give a damn about Britain . . .

Ma was nervous, and began to hum loudly. Sometimes she would hiss in her hoarse, cracked voice, " 'War news isn't for the ears of the young.' "

Rebecca was confused: Pa wanted the war to come here? Was that what Pa wanted?

There were nights when, in the midst of eating supper, Pa became distracted so you knew he was thinking of the *war-news* in the next room. That sick-eager look in his eyes. Gradually he would cease eating and push his plate away and take swallows of his drink instead, like medicine. Sometimes his drink was beer, sometimes hard cider (purchased from the Milburn cider mill a mile away on the river, that smelled so strong when the wind blew from that direction), and sometimes whiskey. Pa's stomach was eat out by rats he liked to say. On that damn boat from Mar-say. Lost his guts and lost his youth Pa said. This was meant to be a joke, Rebecca knew. But it seemed so sad to her! Unconsciously Pa would drift his eyes on her, not seeing her exactly but the *little one*, the unwanted one; the baby born after eleven hours of her mother's labor in a filthy cabin in a filthy, docked boat in New York harbor from which the other passengers had fled. She was too young to know such a thing, yet she knew. When Pa uttered one of his jokes he laughed his snigger-laugh. Herschel would echo this laugh and, less certainly, August. But never Ma. Rebecca would not recall her mother laughing at any joke or witticism of her father's, ever.

The worst was when Pa came into the house in a bad mood, limping and cursing, too tired to wash up after working ten, twelve hours in the cemetery and not even the promise of the *war-news* could liven him. At supper he chewed his food as if it pained him, or was making him ill. More and more he would drink the liquid in his glass. With a fork he pushed fatty chunks of meat off his plate onto the oilcloth covering and finally he would shove away his plate with a sigh of disgust. "Huh! Somebody must think this is a family of hogs, feeding us such swill."

At the supper table, Rebecca's mother stiffened. Her flushed, soft-sliding girl's face that was pinched inside her other, older and tireder face showed no sign of hurt, nor even of hearing what Pa had said. The boys would laugh, but not Rebecca who felt the stab of pain in her mother's heart as if it was her own.

Pa grunted he'd had enough. Shoved his chair back from the table, grabbed his bottle to take into the parlor with him, shut the door hard against his family. In his wake, there was an awkward embarrassed silence. Even Herschel, his ears reddening, stared down at his plate and gnawed his lower lip. In the parlor, you could hear a stranger's voice: muffled, teasing-taunting. Ma rose quickly from the table and began to hum and would continue to hum, fierce as a swarm of bees, crashing pans and cutlery in the sink as she washed the dishes in water heated from the stove. Every night, now that she was a big girl and no longer a toddler, Rebecca helped Ma by drying. These were happy times for Rebecca. Without Ma giving a sign of noticing, still less of being annoyed, Rebecca could draw close against Ma's legs, that exuded such warmth. Through her almost-shut eyes she might glance up, to see Ma peeking down at her. Was it a game? The game of Not-See, but with her mother?

Supper was over abruptly. The boys had gone out. Pa was gone into the parlor. Only Rebecca and Ma remained in the kitchen, doing dishes. From time to time Ma muttered under her breath words in that strange sibilant language the farmer's wife had spoken at their front door, passing too swiftly for Rebecca to grasp, that she knew she was not meant to hear.

When the last dish was dried and put away, Ma said, not smiling at Rebecca, speaking in a sudden sharp voice like a woman waking from sleep, "You were wanted, Rebecca. God wanted you. And I wanted you. Never believe what that man says."

14

❀ ❀ ❀

Never say it.

And there would be other things *never-to-be-said*. That, in time, vanished into oblivion.

Marea was one of these.

Marea—a sound like music, mysterious.

When Rebecca was five years old, in the summer of 1941.

Later, the memory of *Marea* would be obliterated by her father's emotion at the time of "Pearl Harbor."

Marea—"Pearl Harbor"—"World War Too" (for so it sounded to Rebecca's ears). In that time when Rebecca was still a little girl too young to go to school.

One evening after supper instead of going into the parlor, Pa remained in the kitchen. He and Ma had a surprise for them.

Of Herschel and August it was asked, Would you like a brother?

Of Rebecca it was asked, Would you like two sisters?

Pa was the one to speak so, mysteriously. But there was Ma beside him, very nervous. Giddy and girlish and her eyes shining.

As the children stared, Pa removed from an envelope photographs to be spread carefully on the oilcloth cover of the kitchen table. It was a warm

June evening, the cemetery was alive with the sounds of nocturnal insects and there were two or three small moths inside the kitchen, throwing themselves against the bare lightbulb overhead. In his excitement Pa nudged the dangling lightbulb with his head so that the halo of light swung, veered drunkenly across the table; it was Ma who reached out to steady the bulb.

Their cousins. From the town of Kaufbeuren in Germany across the ocean.

And these: their uncle Leon, and their aunt Dora who was their mother's younger sister.

The boys stared. Rebecca stared. *Your cousins. Your uncle, aunt.* Never had they heard such words before from their father's mouth.

"Herschel will remember them, yes? Uncle Leon, Aunt Dora. El-zbieta, your little cousin, maybe you do not. She was just a baby then."

Herschel crouched over the table to frown at the strangers in the photographs, who squinted up at him in miniature beside Pa's splayed thumb. He was breathing hoarsely through his nose. "Why'd I remember 'em?"

"Because you saw them, Herschel. As a child in Munich."

" 'Mew-nik' "?—what the hell's that?"

Pa spoke hurriedly, as if the words pained him. "Where we lived. Where you were born. In that other place before this one."

"Nah," Herschel said, shaking his head now so vehemently the flesh of his mouth quivered, "I wadna. Not me."

Their mother touched Pa's arm. Saying quietly, "Maybe Herschel does not remember, he was so young. And so much since . . ."

Pa said bluntly, "He remembers."

"Fuck I don't! I was born in the fuckin Yoo Ess."

Ma said, "Herschel."

Now was a dangerous time. Pa's hands were shaking. He pushed one of the photographs toward Herschel, to look at. Rebecca saw that the photographs were bent and wrinkled as if they were old, or had come a long distance. When Herschel picked up the photograph to hold to the light, squinting as he peered at the couple, Rebecca worried that he might tear the photograph in two; it was like her older brother to do sudden wild things.

Instead, Herschel grunted and shrugged. Maybe yes, maybe no.

This placated Pa who snatched the photograph back from Herschel and smoothed it out on the table as if it were something precious.

There were five photographs, and each was wrinkled, and somewhat faded. Ma was saying to Rebecca, "Your new sisters, Rebecca? See?"

Rebecca asked what were their names.

Ma spoke the names of the children in the photograph as if they were very special names: "Elzbieta, Freyda, Joel."

Rebecca repeated in her earnest child-voice: "Elz-bee-ta. Frey-da. Jo-el."

Elzbieta was the oldest, Ma said. Twelve or thirteen. Freyda, she was the youngest, Rebecca's age. And Joel was somewhere between.

Rebecca had seen pictures of people in newspapers and magazines but she had never seen photographs, that you could hold in your hand. The Schwarts did not own a camera, for such was a luxury and they could not afford luxuries as Pa said. Strange it seemed to Rebecca, and wonderful, that a picture could be of someone you knew, whose name was known to you. And of children! A little girl Rebecca's age!

Ma said these were her little nieces and nephew. Her sister Dora's children.

So strange to hear Anna Schwart speak of *nieces, nephews. Sister!*

These attractive strangers were not Schwarts but Morgensterns. The name "Morgenstern" was utterly new, and melodic.

In the photographs the Morgenstern children were smiling uncertainly. Almost you might think they were looking at you, because you could look so closely at them. Elzbieta was frowning as she smiled. Or maybe she was not smiling at all. Nor Joel, who squinted as if a light was shining in his eyes. The smallest, Freyda, was the most beautiful child, though you could not see her face clearly for she stood with her head bowed. Shyly she smiled as if to beg *Don't look at me please!*

In that instant Rebecca saw that Freyda was her sister.

In that instant Rebecca saw that Freyda had the same dark, shadowed eyes that she had. And except that Freyda had fluffy bangs brushed down on her forehead, and Rebecca's forehead was bare, their braided hair was the same. In one picture, Rebecca's favorite for you could see Freyda the clearest, the little girl appeared to be tugging at her braid over her left shoulder in the way that Rebecca sometimes did with hers when she was nervous.

" 'Frey-da.' She can sleep in my bed."

"That's right, Rebecca," Ma said, squeezing her arm in approval, "she can sleep in your bed."

Pa was saying that the Morgensterns would be "making the crossing" along with nine hundred other passengers on a ship called the *Marea*, in mid-July, sailing from Lisbon, Portugal, to New York City. They would be journeying then upstate to Milburn, to stay with the Schwarts until they were "settled" in this country.

Rebecca was excited to hear this: her cousins would be crossing the ocean, that Rebecca's family had crossed before she was born? A strange little story came to her the way such stories often did, like dreams, swift as an eyeblink and vanished before she knew it: that another baby girl would be born, then. The way Rebecca had been born. And so when the Morgensterns came to live with them—would there be a new baby?

It would seem to Rebecca that, yes there would be a new baby in the house. But she knew not to mention this to anyone, not even Ma, for she was beginning to understand that some things she believed to be true were only dreams inside her head.

Herschel said sullenly there wouldn't be enough room for them all if these new people came, Chrissake would there? "Bad enough livin like hogs."

Quickly Gus said his cousin Joel could sleep with him in his bed.

And quickly Ma said yes there would be room!

Pa seemed not so certain as Ma, more worried, stoop-shouldered and rubbing his knuckles against his eyes in that way he had, that made him look so tired, and old-seeming, saying yes the house was small, but he and his brother-in-law could enlarge it, maybe. Convert the woodshed into an extra room. Leon was a carpenter, they could work together. Before the Morgensterns arrived, he and the boys could start. Clear out the trash and level the dirt floor and lay down planks for floorboards. Get some tar paper sheets, for insulation.

"Tar paper!" Herschel snorted. "Like from the dump, huh?"

A mile away on the Quarry Road was the Milburn township dump.

Herschel and Gus often explored there, as did other neighborhood children. Sometimes they dragged things home, useful items like castoff rugs, chairs, lamp shades. It was believed that Jacob Schwart, too, explored the dump, though never at any hour when he might be observed.

The dump was one of the places Rebecca was forbidden to go, ever. Not with her brothers and especially not alone.

Ma was saying in her quick warm voice she could fix all the rooms nicer. She had never gotten around to doing all she'd meant to do, she'd been so tired when they first moved in. Now she could put up curtains. She would sew curtains herself. Ma was speaking in a way that made her children uneasy for they had not heard her speak like this before. Ma was smiling a bright nervous smile showing the crack between her teeth, and Ma was brushing at her hair with both hands as if the moths had gotten into it.

Ma said, "Yes you will see. There is room."

Herschel shifted his shoulders inside his shirt that was missing half its buttons, and said the house was too small for how-many people to live in: ten? "Ten fuckin people like in a animal pen, that's bad enough now for Chrissake. The fuckin stove ain't any good except for this room, an the God-damn well water tastes like skunk, an me an Gus is always bumpin into each other in our damn room, how're you gonna fit a new 'brother' in it? Shit."

Without warning, swift as a copperhead snake striking, Pa's hand flew out to whack Herschel on the side of the head. Herschel recoiled howling his damn eardrum was burst.

"That won't be all that's going to be burst, you don't shut your mouth and keep it shut."

Ma said, pleading, "Oh please."

Gus who was still hunched over the table, unmoving, afraid to look up at his father, said another time that Joel could sleep with him, it was O.K. with him.

Herschel said loudly, "Who in hell is gonna sleep with *him*, pissin the bed every night! It's bad enough sleepin in the same damn room like hogs."

But Herschel was laughing now. Rubbing his left ear that Pa had hit, in a way to show it didn't hurt much.

Saying, "Fuck I don't care, I ain't gonna stay in this shit-hole. If there's a war, see, I'm gonna en-list. Guys I know, they're gonna en-list an so am I, I'm gonna fly a plane an drop bombs like what's-it—the Blitz. Yeah, I'm gonna."

Rebecca tried not to hear the loud voices. She was peering at Freyda, her sister Freyda who (you could almost believe this!) was peering up at her. Now they knew each other. Now they would have secrets between them. Rebecca dared to lift the photograph to the light to look inside it somehow. Oh, she wanted to see Freyda's feet, what kind of shoes Freyda was wearing! She seemed to know that Freyda was wearing nicer shoes than she, Rebecca, had. Because Freyda's little jumper-dress was nicer than anything Rebecca had. *Kaufbeuren* Rebecca was thinking *in Germany across the sea*.

It seemed to Rebecca, yes she could see into the photograph just a little. Her cousins were standing outside, behind a house somewhere. There were trees in the background. In the grass, what looked like a dog with white markings on his face, a pointy-nosed little dog, his tail outstretched.

Rebecca whispered: "Frey-da."

It was so, Freyda's hair had been parted in the center of her head neatly, and plaited like Rebecca's. In two thick pigtails the way Ma plaited Rebecca's hair that was inclined to snarl, Ma said, like tiny spider nests. Ma plaited Rebecca's hair tight so that it made her temples ache, Ma said it was the only way to tame flyaway hair.

The only way to tame flyaway little girls.

"Frey-da." They would brush and plait each other's hair, they promised!

It was time for the younger children to go to bed. Herschel stomped out of the house without another word but Gus and Rebecca wanted to linger, to ask more questions about their cousins from *Kaufbeuren, Germany*.

Pa said no. He was returning the photographs to an envelope Rebecca had not seen before, of tissue-thin blue paper.

Still the moths fluttered around the bare lightbulb. There were more now, tiny white animated wings. Gus was saying he never knew there was cousins in the family before. Damn he never knew there was anybody in the family!

15

❀ ❀ ❀

Those summer weeks when she was never alone. Always Rebecca would remember. Playing by herself it wasn't by herself but with her new sister Freyda. Always the girls were chattering and whispering together. Oh, Rebecca was never lonely now!—no need to hang around her mother so much, nudging Ma's knees till Ma pushed her away complaining it was too hot for fooling around.

Herschel was always giving his little sister presents, things he found in the dump he'd bring home for her, there were two dolls he'd brought for her called Maggie and Minnie, and now Maggie was Freyda's doll, and Minnie was Rebecca's doll, and the four of them played together around the side of the house in the hollyhocks. Maggie was the prettier of the dolls, so Rebecca gave Maggie to Freyda because Freyda was the prettier of the sisters, and more special because she was from *Kaufbeuren in Germany across the ocean*. Maggie was a girl-doll with plastic rippled brown hair and wide-open blue eyes but Minnie was just a naked rubber doll-baby with a bald head and a corroded pug face, very dirty. The way Herschel had given Minnie to Rebecca, he'd tossed the rubber doll high into the air making a wailing-baby noise with his mouth and it landed with a thud at Rebecca's feet scaring her so she'd almost wetted herself. So when Minnie was bad you could discipline her by throwing her onto the ground and it would hardly hurt her but you would not wish to throw Maggie down, ever, for Maggie might break and so Maggie was the better-behaved of the dolls, and obviously smarter because she was older. And Maggie could read words, a little. Pa's old newspapers and magazines Maggie could read while Minnie was just a baby and could not even speak. Of such matters Rebecca and Freyda whispered endlessly in the wild-growing hollyhocks in the very heat of midday so Ma was drawn to come outside to peer at them in wonderment, hands on her hips.

Asking Rebecca what on earth was she doing in that hot dusty place, who was she talking to?—and her voice was throaty and cracked and alarmed, and Rebecca turned away blushing and sullen refusing to look up from the dolls as if no one had spoken at all.

Go away! Go away Freyda and I don't need you.

But Monday was laundry day, and both girls were eager to help.

For Anna Schwart did not leave the stone cottage often, and this was a special time. She would tie a scarf hurriedly around her head to partially hide her face. On even very hot days she would wear one of Herschel's jackets over her shapeless housedress. So that if someone was spying on her (from the cemetery, from behind the crumbling stone wall) they could not see her clearly. Jacob Schwart had tried to shame his wife out of such eccentric behavior, for cemetery visitors certainly noticed her, shook their heads and laughed at the gravedigger's crazy wife, but Anna Schwart ignored him for what did Jacob Schwart know for all his radio-listening and newspaper-reading he knew nothing about their Milburn neighbors. *She* knew.

Yet the laundry had to be washed in the old washing machine in the shed, and the soaking-wet clothes pressed through the hand-wringer, and placed in the wicker basket, and the basket had to be hauled out into the backyard, into the bright sunshine and gusty air. And Rebecca helped carry the basket. And Rebecca and Freyda handed Ma things from the basket to be pinned on the old rope clothesline tied between two posts to flap and slap and clapclapclap on windy days. Rebecca made Freyda laugh by pulling an undershirt over her head when Ma's back was turned, or letting a pair of shorts fall into the grass accidentally-on-purpose like they'd squirmed out of Rebecca's hands, but Freyda took away the undershirt and the shorts to hand to Ma for Freyda was a good girl, Freyda was a serious girl, often Freyda put her forefinger to her lips *Shhhh!* when Rebecca was being loud or silly.

In Rebecca's bed, they snuggled and cuddled and hugged and sometimes tickled. Rebecca slid Freyda's warm bare arm across her side, over
her ribs to snuggle closer so Rebecca could sleep not hearing Pa's radio
voices in the night.

Oh, that delicious swoon of a dream: Rebecca and her new sister Freyda
walking to school together in matching jumpers and shiny patent leather
shoes along the Quarry Road, and along the Milburn Post Road, a mile-
and-a-half walk it was to the Milburn Grammar School, and they would be
hand in hand like sisters. And they would not be afraid because there were
two of them. Except Ma had been saying this year was too soon, she would
not let Rebecca go yet. *I want my little girl safe with me long as I can*. Pa said that
Rebecca would have to go to school, she would have to start first grade,
why not this year since she knew her ABC's and numerals and could almost
read, but Ma insisted *No. Not yet. Not for another year. If they come to ask us we
will say that she is too young, she is not well, she coughs and cries all the time.*

But Rebecca thought: Freyda will be with me now. And Elzbieta.

The sisters would all walk to school together.

Rebecca felt a thrill of triumph, her mother would not be able to prevent her now.

How strange it was that in those weeks of July 1941 there was such
excitement in the stone cottage like the humming of bees in the powdery
snakeroot flowers you were not supposed to play near for you would be
stung, and a sickish sensation beneath like running faster and faster down
a hill until you are in danger of falling yet the name *Morgenstern* was rarely
spoken and then only in whispers. By *Morgenstern* was meant adults as well
as children yet Rebecca gave not the slightest thought to her cousins' parents. *Freyda!* was the only name she cared for. It was as if the others even
Elzbieta and Joel did not exist. Especially the adults did not exist.

Or, if these Morgensterns existed, they were but strangers in photographs, a man and a woman in a setting drained of all color, beginning to
fade like ghosts.

16

❀ ❀ ❀

And so they waited, in the caretaker's stone cottage just inside the front gates of the Milburn cemetery.

And so they waited patiently at first and then with increasing restlessness and anxiety through the second half of July, and into the terrible damp heat of early August in the Chautauqua Valley.

And the Morgensterns who were Anna Schwart's relatives did not come. The uncle, the aunt, the cousins did not come. Though the cottage had been prepared for them, the woodshed cleared out, curtains hung at windows, they did not come. And there was a day, an hour, when at last it was clear that they would not be coming, and Jacob Schwart drove into Milburn to make telephone calls to ascertain that this was true.

"Ask God why: why such things happen. Not me."

There was the voice of her father, that pierced her heart in its fury, and shame.

It made her feel faint, dazed as if the very floorboards tilted beneath her bare feet, to hear his voice in this way. Yet there was a curious exhilaration in his voice, too. A kind of relief that the worst had happened, he'd anticipated from the start. He had been right, and Anna had been wrong, to have hoped.

"Turned back! Nine hundred refugees turned back, to die."

Above the roaring in her ears and the panicked beat of her heart

Rebecca heard her parents in the kitchen. Her father's words that were sharp and distinct and her mother's that were not words but sounds, moans of grief.

The shock of hearing her mother crying! Choked ugly sounds like an animal in pain.

Rebecca dared to push open the door a crack. She saw only her father's back, a few feet away. He wore a shirt soaked through with sweat. His hair was graying and straggled past his collar, so thin at the top of his head that his scalp showed through like a pale glimmering sickle-moon. He was speaking now in an almost calm voice yet still there was the exhilaration beneath, the obscene gloating. For now he had no hope, he would have no hope. The hope of the past weeks had been lacerating to Jacob Schwart, who wished for the worst, that the worst might be over with, and his life over. Rebecca was a child of only five, and yet she knew.

"Why not kill them on the ship, set the ship on fire? In New York harbor, for all the world to see? 'This is the fate of the Jews.' It would be mercy for these Christians, eh? Hypocrite bastard Roosevelt may his soul rot in hell, better to kill them here than send them back to die like cattle."

Desperately she wanted to run past her father to her mother yet she could not, Jacob Schwart blocked her way.

Unconsciously Rebecca reached for Freyda's fingers. Since the evening the photographs had been spread across the kitchen table she had not been apart from Freyda. You would not see one of the sisters without the other! Rebecca and Freyda were of a height, their hair plaited in the same way and their eyes identical dark-shadowed eyes set deep in their sockets, watchful and alert. Yet now, Rebecca reached for Freyda's fingers, and felt only air.

She could not now turn to see Freyda pressing a forefinger against her lips *Shhhh Rebecca!* because Freyda herself was air.

Rebecca pushed the door open, and entered the kitchen. She was barefoot, and trembling. She saw how her father turned to her with a look of annoyance, his face flushed, livid eyes that held no love for her in that instant, nor even recognition. She stammered asking what was wrong? where was Freyda? wasn't Freyda coming?

Her father told her to go away, out of here.

Rebecca whimpered Ma? Ma? but her mother paid no heed to her, turned away at the sink, sobbing. Her mother's chafed hands hid her face and she wept without sound, her soft slipping-down body shaking as if with merriment. Rebecca ran to her mother to tug at her arm but Pa intervened, grabbing her hard. "I said *no*."

Rebecca stared up at him, and saw how he hated her.

She would wonder what Jacob Schwart saw, in her: what there was in her, a child of five, he so despised.

She would be too young for years to consider *He hates himself, in me*. Still less *It is life he hates, in all his children*.

She ran outside. Stumbling, barefoot. The cemetery was a forbidden place, she was not to wander in the cemetery amid the rows of gravestones that signaled the resting places of the dead in the earth and were the possessions of others, *those others* who helped to pay Jacob Schwart's wages; she knew, she had been told numberless times that *those others* did not want to see a child prowling aimless in the cemetery that belonged to them. Her brothers too were forbidden to enter the cemetery except as their father's helpers.

Rebecca ran, blinded by tears. Where her father had grabbed her shoulder, she felt a throbbing pain. She whispered, "Freyda—" but it was useless, she knew it was useless, she was alone now and would be alone, she had no sister.

The cemetery was deserted, there were no visitors. The air was gusty and wet-tasting, the white-striated bark of birch trees shone with an unnatural glisten. In the taller trees, crows called raucously to one another. Where you could not hear Jacob Schwart's voice, and could not see Anna Schwart turned away sobbing and broken in defeat, it was as if nothing had happened.

The cries of the burning passengers of the *Marea*—she could hear them. In her memory it would seem, yes the *Marea* had been set afire, she had seen the fire herself, she had seen her sister Freyda burned alive.

Why?—"Ask God why: why such things happen. Not me."

She would hide in the cemetery, frightened for hours.

No one would call her name. No one would miss her.

The previous day there had been a funeral, a procession of cars and pallbearers carrying a coffin to an open grave site scrupulously prepared by Jacob Schwart, Rebecca had watched from a distance the mourners, she had counted twenty-nine of *those others*, some had lingered at the grave as if reluctant to leave and when at last they departed there came Jacob Schwart dark-clad and silent as a scavenger bird to fill in the grave, to cover the coffin with moist crumbly dirt, until there was only earth, the curve of earth, and a smooth granite headstone engraved with letters, numerals. And flowers in pots, set with care at intervals about the rectangular grave.

Rebecca approached this grave, that was some distance from the stone cottage. She was barefoot, limping. She had cut her left foot on a stone. In the summers she was a dark-tanned Indian-looking child furtive in appearance and often dirty, her tight-plaited hair beginning to pull loose in wisps. No wonder such a child was forbidden to wander in the cemetery where visitors might be startled and annoyed to see her.

Only when she saw her father's pickup truck being driven away would she emerge from hiding to return to the house, and to her mother. She would take to Ma a handful of beautiful pale-blue cluster-flowers broken off from one of the potted plants.

17

❀ ❀ ❀

Not-to-be-said from that time onward in the stone cottage in the Milburn cemetery were such words as "cousins"—"Morgenstern"—"boat"— *Marea.* Certainly you would not say "Kaufbeuren"—"Aunt Dora"— "Freyda"—"Germany." Not that Ma might hear, or in her nervous confusion imagine she heard. Not that Pa might hear for he would fly into one of his spittle-rages.

Rebecca asked her brothers what had happened? what had happened to their cousins? was it so, the *Marea* had been set on fire? but Herschel shrugged and grimaced saying how in fuck would he know, he never thought anybody was comin' to Milburn anyway, not so far across the ozean with submarines now, and bombs. Also there was sure to be trouble about those damn vissas, like Pa had worried about for them.

"See, there ain't room for everybody over here. There's these miz'rable people worsen us, a million maybe. Like this damn house, you can figure it ain't big enough for anybody else! You can figure it. The Yoo Ess Immigradion can figure it."

Rebecca asked what that was: the Yoo Ess Immigradion.

"The police, like. Soldiers. They got to guard the Yoo Ess so it don't get crowded with refugees, like. People tryin to get away from Hitler, you can't blame em. But over here, you can't blame em either, tryin to keep people out. Why they let us in," Herschel said, grinning, scratching at the crotch of his overalls, *"I* sure as hell don't know. See I'm gonna en-list in the navy pilots, soon as I can. I'm hopin we go to war real soon."

In that late summer of 1941 and well into the fall, Ma was in bed. Ma was sleeping, or Ma was lying awake-not-sleeping with her eyes closed, or Ma was lying awake-not-sleeping with her eyes open but unfocused, covered in a thin film like mucus that, drying, stuck to her eyelashes. If Rebecca whispered, Ma?—there would be no response usually. Maybe a flicker of Ma's eyelids, as if a fly had buzzed too near.

Mostly the bedroom door was shut against the family except of course Pa could enter at any time (for there could be no room in the stone cottage from which Jacob Schwart might be barred) and at certain times Rebecca hesitantly entered bringing her mother food, and taking away dirtied plates and glasses to be washed, by Rebecca who had to stand on a chair for the task, at the kitchen sink. The bedroom was a small room only just large enough to hold a double bed and a chest of drawers. It was airless, smelly, dank as a cave. Ma refused to allow the window to be opened even a crack. As she tasted death in the well water so now she smelled death in the humid greeny-tinged air of the cemetery. A cracked and discolored blind was drawn on the window at all times of the day and night so that no one could peer inside.

For *those others* were keenly aware of the Schwarts in their stone cottage in the cemetery. All of Milburn, New York, was keenly aware. Since the *Marea* had been turned back in New York harbor surely everyone knew, and laughed their cruel, crude laughter like hyenas. You had to imagine how they laughed speaking of "Mrs. Schwarz"—"Mrs. Warts"—"the gravedigger's wife"—who had ceased to appear in town and was believed now to be sick with some wasting disease like T.B., brain tumor, cancer of the uterus.

When Jacob Schwart was stone cold sober he entered his wife's sickroom in finicky silence, and in silence undressed; he must have slept beside the woman's inert fleshy perspiring body in silence; in the early morning, before dawn, he arose, and dressed, and departed. No doctor would be summoned, for Anna Schwart would have screamed and fought like a panicked wildcat if any stranger attempted to enter her place of refuge, nor did Jacob Schwart seem to consider that she was ill enough to require a doctor. Frugality had become so instinctive in him, he had no need even to consider those platitudes he had learned to mimic out of an infinity of word-formulae available to him in this new, still awkward and improvised language *Dollar bills do not grow on trees. Want not waste not.*

When Pa was drinking he became noisy and belligerent and stumbling-into-things, Rebecca could hear from her bed where she lay open-eyed in the dark waiting for something to happen that would in fact not happen for eight years. Sometimes when Pa was drunk he became jovial, garrulous talking to himself. He would curse, and he would laugh. Never would there be any audible response from Anna Schwart. When he settled heavily on the bed, you would hear the bedsprings creak as if the bed was about to break, and then often you would hear a spasm of coughing, phlegmy staccato coughing. Probably Pa would not trouble to undress, even to pull off his mud-splattered work shoes for the damn laces were hopelessly knotted.

After his death those misshapen work shoes would have to be cut off his feet, as if like hooves they were merged with the man's very flesh.

There were no longer meals in the stone cottage, only just isolated and often ravenous episodes of eating. Often the food was devoured out of the heavy iron frying pan that remained more or less continuously on the stove, so coated and encrusted with grease it did not need ever to be cleaned. There was also oatmeal, in a pot on the stove that was never cleaned. There was always bread, hunks and crusts of bread, and there were Ritz crackers, eaten in handfuls; there were canned goods—peas, corn, beets, sauerkraut, kidney beans and baked beans hungrily spooned out of the cans. From a neighboring farm dairy there were fresh eggs, which were prepared swimming with grease in the frying pan; and there was fresh milk, in bottles, kept in the icebox close beside the slow-melting block of ice, for Jacob Schwart did believe in milk for children ("So that your bones will not bend and break, like mine"). When he was sober, he had a taste for milk himself, which he drank directly from the bottle as he might drink ale, gulping thirstily, without seeming to savor or even to taste what he drank, head thrown back and feet apart in a classic drinking stance. He had begun to chew tobacco and so the milk often tasted of tobacco-tinged saliva, after he'd been drinking it.

Rebecca drank this milk, gagging. Most days she was so hungry, she had no choice.

In time, Anna Schwart would emerge from her sickbed and resume, to a limited degree, her duties as housewife and mother. In time, with the catastrophe of Pearl Harbor on December 7, 1941, and the long-awaited United States declaration of war against the Axis powers, Jacob Schwart would resume some of his old embittered energy.

"In animal life the weak are quickly disposed of. So you must hide your weakness, Rebecca."

Yes, Pa.

"When *those others* ask where you are from, whose people are your people, you must tell them 'The Yoo Ess. I was born here.' "

Yes, Pa.

"Why this world is a shit-hole, eh! Ask Him who casts the dice! Not one who is no more than dice. No more than a shadow passing over the face of the deep." His scarred-scabby hand cupped to his ear in an exaggerated gesture, he laughed. "Hear? Eh? A whirring of wings? 'The owl of Minerva soaring at dusk.' "

Bleakly she smiled, yes Pa. Yes.

She would wonder: was there an owl? In the tall trees, yes there were screech owls sometimes, in the night: that high-pitched eerie cry of rapidly descending notes, that meant a screech owl. What "Minerva" was, she had no idea.

Pa's breath, too, that stank of alcohol and something dank and sweetly rotted made her gag. His dirt-stiffened clothing, his unwashed body. His oily hair, unkempt whiskers. Yet she could not run from him. She dared not run from him. For of his children she, the *little one*, the unwanted one, was coming to be Jacob Schwart's favorite. His sons had disappointed him, often he could not bear to look at them. Herschel was sullen and slovenly and resentful of working with his father in the cemetery, for no pay; Gus was growing into a skinny boy with spider-arms and -legs and a perpetual squint, as if fearing a blow out of nowhere. (When his mother disappeared into the bedroom Gus ceased speaking of her and, weeks later, when she reappeared, he averted his eyes from her as if the very sight of Anna Schwart's raddled girl's face was distressing to him, shameful.)

And so, those evenings Pa turned to her, the *little one*, taking her hands and pulling her to him, laughing, teasing, whispering to her of such strange fanciful things she could not comprehend, how should she resist, how should she run from him, oh she could not!

And there was Ma, who would seem never to change. For the remainder of Rebecca's childhood she would seem never to change.

Though since her mysterious protracted illness she was ever more withdrawn from her family. Her sons, gangling clumsy boys, she scarcely seemed to see, and they, in turn, were acutely conscious of her, and embarrassed by her in that way of adolescent boys for whom the physical, sexual being is predominant. For Anna Schwart's body was so fleshy, straining against the fabric of her housedresses; her breasts were so lavish, big-nippled, and fallen; her stomach bloated, her varicose-veined legs and ankles swollen—how could her sons tear their eyes from her? Perversely, her face remained relatively youthful, her skin flushed and rosy as if with fever. Though Ma was morbidly self-conscious and fearful of being spied upon yet, to her sons' dismay, she seemed oblivious of how she looked hanging laundry on the clothesline in wind that outlined her back, buttocks, thighs through her carelessly fastened clothes. In an agony of shame they saw their mother, invariably outside when funeral processions passed by the stone cottage, so very slowly. Herschel complained that Ma's tits were like damn cow udders hangin' down, why didn't she get a braz-zir like women do, fix herself up right? and Gus protested Ma couldn't help it, her nerves, Herschel should know that. And Herschel said shit I know it! I know it but that don't help none.

Rebecca was less keenly aware of her mother's appearance. For Anna Schwart so fascinated her, alarmed and worried her, Rebecca scarcely knew what she looked like in others' eyes. Rebecca felt the distance between them, even in the cramped rooms of the stone cottage. How even at mealtimes, even as she served them food, Ma's damp heated face was vacant, preoccupied; her eyes were vague and dreamy as if, inside her head, she heard voices no one else could hear, of infinitely more interest than the crude, quarrelsome voices of her family. At such times Rebecca felt a pang of loss, and of jealousy. Almost, she hated her mother for abandoning her to the others. Her father, her brothers! When it was her mother she wanted.

For Rebecca no longer had a sister. Even in dreams she had lost Freyda. With childish logic she blamed Anna Schwart for this loss. What right had the woman to speak of *my little nieces, nephew, your little cousins*! What right to show them those photographs, and now to turn away aloof and oblivious!

Especially Rebecca resented her mother talking to herself. Why could Ma not talk to *her*, instead of these others? Ghost-figures they were, making Anna Schwart smile in a way her living family could no longer make her smile. In the back rooms Rebecca heard her mother murmuring, laughing sadly, sighing. Dropping an armload of wood into the stove, noisily pumping water out of the hand pump at the sink, running the carpet sweeper repeatedly over the frayed carpets, Anna Schwart talked to herself in a bright murmurous voice like water rippling over rock. *She is speaking with the dead* Rebecca came to realize. *She is speaking with her family left behind in Germany.*

One winter day when the men returned home, it was to discover that Ma had removed the curtains from all the windows. The very curtains she'd sewed with such excitement, back in July. In the kitchen there had been daffodil-colored ruffled curtains, in the parlor pale rose gauzy panels, floral print curtains elsewhere.

Why?—because it was time, Ma said.

Asked what the hell that meant, Ma said imperturbably that it was time to take the curtains down because she would be using them for rags and a rag should not be dusty because a rag would be used for dusting.

Into the rag-bag in the closet, that bulged with Anna Schwart's spoils! Jacob Schwart joked to his children that one day he would wind up in their mother's rag-bag, bones picked clean.

Herschel and Gus laughed, uneasily. Rebecca bit her thumbnail until it bled seeing how her mother stared smiling at the floor, silent.

Except then rousing herself to say, with a disdainful laugh, Why'd anybody want old picked bones in a rag-bag? Not her.

Calmly Pa said, You despise me, don't you.

Calmly Pa said, Tell you what, Ma. I'll buy a gun. Shotgun. You can blow Jacob Schwart's head off, Ma. Spray his brains all over your precious wall.

But Rebecca's mother had drifted away, indifferent.

Those lonely hours even after she'd started first grade. Following Ma around like a puppy. Hoping that Ma might say, Help me with this, Rebecca. Or, Rebecca, come here! And Rebecca would come eagerly running.

Those years. Rebecca would remember how they'd worked together, often in silence. From the time Rebecca was a little girl until the age of thirteen, when Anna Schwart died.

Died Rebecca would say. Not wishing to say *Was killed*.

Not wishing to say *Was murdered*.

And yet during all these years (preparing meals, cleaning up after meals, doing laundry, dusting and scrubbing and shaking out rugs) they never spoke of serious things. Never of essential things.

Rebecca's mother became enlivened, a catch in her voice, only when she warned Rebecca of danger.

Don't wander along the road! Stay away from people you don't know! And even if you know them don't climb into any car or truck! And stay away from that canal! There's fishermen that come there to fish, and there's men on the canal, in boats.

See, you don't want anything to happen to you, Rebecca. You will be blamed if something happens to you.

You're a *girl*, see.

At that school you be careful, things happen to girls at school. Plenty of things. Nasty things. Boys calling to you like from a cellar, or inside something, or hiding in a ditch you run away from them hard as you can, see you're a *girl*.

Ma worked herself up into a passion, speaking at such length. Never, at other times, did Ma speak at such length. Warning too that Rebecca should not make the mistake of following her brothers, they were boys and they'd run off and leave her, you're a *girl*.

Rebecca came to see that it was like a wound. Being a *girl*.

School! It was the great event of Rebecca's young life.

Her mother had bitterly opposed her going. Her mother had tried to keep her home until the very last day. For Rebecca had to walk by herself a half-mile along the Quarry Road before being joined by other children; and, in any case, Ma did not trust these other children for they lived in a run-down shack close by the town dump.

Yet Ma showed no interest in Rebecca's school, apart from these theoretical dangers. It was as if, when the dangers failed to materialize, she was scornful of school as she was of Milburn and their neighbors. Of course, she would not visit the school as other parents did. (Nor would Jacob Schwart visit the school.) Neither of Rebecca's parents would do more than glance at Rebecca's report cards. It would be years before Rebecca realized that her mother could not read English, and so she disdained all printed materials: she was capable of tossing out Rebecca's schoolbooks with her husband's old newspapers and magazines they meant so little to her. She paused only to look at photographs, occasionally. Once, Rebecca saw her in the kitchen staring at a photography feature in *Life* of fallen, bloodied, part-naked men, women, and children, sprawled amid rubble in some far-off city. When Rebecca came closer to peer at the caption, her mother jerked the magazine away and slapped Rebecca's face with it.

"No. It is not for a girl's eyes. *Bad*."

And once I saw her, who had expressed such a terror of snakes, kill a snake with a hoe. We were hanging clothes on the line and a copperhead came out from under the house, in the grass about twelve inches from my feet and Ma said nothing but went for the hoe that was leaning against the side of the house and chopped at the snake chopped and chopped wildly at it until the snake was dead, bleeding and mangled.

At the Milburn Elementary School, Rebecca's first grade teacher was Miss Lutter who identified herself on the first day of school as a Christian. Miss Lutter was a thin woman with dust-colored hair and teeth that poked through her tight-pursed lips when she smiled. She told Rebecca and the others that they had souls that were "little flames" inside their bodies, in the area of their hearts; these little flames would never go out, unlike ordinary fire.

Rebecca, who had never heard such a thing before, knew at once that this must be so.

For: the coal-burning stove and the wood-burning stove in the Schwarts' house were all that kept the house from freezing in the bitter cold of winter, so it was that the flames inside a person kept him or her from freezing, too. Almost, Rebecca could see the flames inside her father and mother, behind their eyes; yet she knew she must not speak of this to them. For any authority outside the family would enrage them.

Any belief of *those others* told to their children would enrage them.

And there is a fire in me, too.

This revelation made Rebecca so happy, she wished there was her sister Freyda to share it with.

18

❀ ❀ ❀

" 'Rebecca Esther Schwart.' "

He was making fun of her, was he? Her name? Or—who she was?

For she felt its impact, here amid strangers. How harsh the final blunt syllable *Schwart* struck the ear like the flat of a shovel wielded as a weapon.

" 'Rebecca'—are you here?"

Miss Lutter nudged her. She woke from her trance, rose and tremulously made her way into the aisle, and up to the lighted stage. A roaring of blood in her ears mingled with the applause of the audience—so loud! Like flames crackling. Rows of strangers, *those others* Pa would disdain them, yet smiling at her as vigorously they clapped their hands as if for these fleeting seconds in their lives the dark-haired gypsy-looking Schwart girl, the gravedigger's daughter, wasn't a figure to be pitied.

" 'Rebecca'?—congratulations."

She was too frightened to murmur Thank you. She could not clearly see the face of the man who was addressing her, glittery glasses, a striped necktie, she'd been told his name and who he was and of course she'd forgotten. Desperately she reached for whatever-it-was the man was handing her—a hefty book, a dictionary—there was a tittering of amusement in the audience when, not expecting the book to be so heavy, Rebecca nearly dropped it. The glittery-glasses man laughed and caught the book— "Whoops, Little Miss!"—to hand to her more securely and in that instant she saw him staring at her curiously, as if memorizing her *the Schwart girl the gravedigger's daughter poor child sent to school looking like a savage.*

In a haze of embarrassment and confusion Rebecca stumbled back off stage and returned to her row, and to her seat, where Miss Lutter was smiling at her, as the next name was being called.

It was April 1946. She was ten years old, and a winner of the Milburn School Township Spelling Bee. She had represented her grammar school, that was District #3. For weeks she had memorized lists of words. Such words as *profligate, precipitant, precipitate, epithet, dysphoria, expurgate, quotidian, lapidarian, lacrymose, stationary, stationery, unparalleled, inchoate, heinous, dais, dour, err, harass, impious, forte, slough, prophecy, prophesy, forgo, forego, resuscitate, genealogy, sacrilegious, braggadocio, gnomic, tortuous, fortuitous, contingency, autarky, temerarious, encomium*. Like other students who'd memorized these word-spellings Rebecca had only the dimmest idea of what they meant. They were mysterious sounds, syllables that might as readily have been in a foreign language as in the language known as English. A game it was, learning-to-spell. Yet it was a game that made you nervous, twitchy and sweaty through the night. Miss Lutter had insisted that Rebecca could compete with older students in the junior high school and so out of a terror of failing and disappointing her teacher Rebecca had memorized the words and Rebecca had won over the other children and now Miss Lutter was proud of her, and squeezing her icy hand; and the roaring in her ears began to subside.

Except she would remember *looking for them in the audience at the rear of the high school auditorium though knowing they would not come of course. Not her mother Anna Schwart, not her father Jacob Schwart. Never would they have come to this public place to see their daughter honored.* After the ceremony making her way like a furtive animal through the foyer of the high school, where a "reception" was being held for the spelling bee winners, their relatives and teachers and other adults. She was awkward and self-conscious among them, a solitary child without a family. Her face smarted with hurt, shame. Yet she knew how her parents would disdain this place and these people.

Those others you must never trust, our enemies.

"Rebecca?"—her name was being called but amid the confusion of voices and laughter Rebecca could not be expected to hear. She was headed for a side door marked EXIT.

"Rebecca Schwart? Please come over here."

Someone clutched at her. She was surrounded by adults. A woman with a bronze helmet-head and staring eyes. And there was the man with the glittery glasses and striped necktie, principal of Milburn High School, who gripped Rebecca firmly by the elbow and led her to a group of students and adults being photographed for the *Milburn Weekly Journal* and the *Chautauqua Valley Gazette*. Rebecca, the youngest and smallest of the spelling bee winners, was made to stand in front, center. She was told to smile, and so she smiled. Cameras flashed. Her startled squinting smile she held, the cameras flashed again. Hearing and not-hearing a murmured conversation not quite out of earshot.

"That Schwart girl—where are her parents?"

"Not here."

"For God's sake why not?"

"They just aren't."

And then Rebecca was released, and headed for the exit. From somewhere behind her she heard Miss Lutter calling—"Rebecca, don't you need a ride home?"—but this time she didn't turn back.

She had not planned to show the dictionary to them. Not to anyone in the family. She'd told her father about the spelling bee and the awards ceremony and he'd scarcely listened, nor had her mother listened. And now, she would hide the dictionary beneath her bed knowing how they would scorn it.

And there was the danger that one of them might toss it into the stove.

A long time ago Jacob Schwart had hoped that his sons would do well in school but neither Herschel nor Gus had done well and so he had become indifferent to the schooling of his children, he was contemptuous of Rebecca's primer school books leafing through them sometimes saying they were fairy tales, trash. Newspapers and magazines he brought home he was likely to read thoroughly, with a perverse ardor, yet these too he dismissed as trash. Since the war had ended he no longer listened to the radio after supper yet he did not wish others in the family to listen to it. "Words are lies." This pronouncement he made often, with a jocular screwing-up of his face. If he was chewing tobacco, he spat.

For so much since the war was a joke to him. But you could not always know what would be a joke, and what would not. What would make him laugh so hard his laughter shaded into wheezing coughing spasms, or what would *set Pa off*.

Something in the newspapers, maybe.

Shaking the front page of the paper, face contorted in derision and outrage. Slamming his fist against the paper flattening it onto the oilcloth cover of the kitchen table. Jacob Schwart had a particular loathing for the sleek-black-haired black-mustached little-man governor of New York State, his mouth worked in speechless fury seeing the governor's photograph. Why exactly, no one in the family knew. Jacob Schwart detested Republicans, yes but Jacob Schwart detested F.D.R. and F.D.R. was a Democrat, wasn't he. Rebecca tried to keep these names straight. What meant so much to Pa should mean something to her, too.

Those others. Our enemies. We are dirt to them, to scrape off their shoes.

"What the hell's this? *You?*"

It was a shock, Pa tossing the *Milburn Weekly* onto the table, flattening it with his fist and confronting his daughter.

He was incensed, insulted. Rebecca had rarely seen him so upset. For there was *Rebecca Esther Schwart of Milburn District #3*, in a group photograph on the front page of the paper. *Spelling Bee Winners. Awards Ceremony at Milburn High.* Pa yanked Rebecca to the table, to stare at herself, a diminutive and startled image of herself, amid the gathering of smiling strangers. She had forgotten the occasion, she could not have anticipated that anything real would come of the flashbulbs and the jocular, jokey *Smile, please!* And now her father was demanding to know what was this! what this meant! Saying, wiping at his mouth, "*I* never knew anything about this, did I? God damn to hell, I don't like any child of mine acting behind my back."

Rebecca stammered saying she had told him, she had tried to tell him, but Pa continued to rage. He was one whose rage fed on itself, ecstatic. He wrenched the newspaper toward the light, at differing angles, to see the incriminating front page more clearly. Finally turning to Rebecca, disbelieving, "It's you, huh! God damn to hell. Behind my back, my daughter."

"I t-told you about it, Pa. The spelling bee."

" 'Spelling'—what?"

" 'Spelling bee.' Words you spell. In school."

" 'Words' I tell you words: bullshit. Every word that has ever been uttered by mankind is bullshit."

Herschel and Gus, drawn by the commotion, examined the scandalous front-page photograph and article, amazed. Gus said it was good news wasn't it?

Pa said, sputtering, "Bring the damn 'prize' out, I want to see this damn 'prize' for myself. Fast!"

Rebecca ran to get the dictionary where she'd hidden it. Beneath her bed. Shame-shame, she'd known it would get her into trouble, why she'd hidden the dictionary *beneath her bed*.

As if anything could be hidden from Jacob Schwart. As if any secret would not be exposed, like soiled underwear or bedclothes, in time.

Rebecca's face was very warm, her eyes stung with tears. (Where was Ma? Why wasn't Ma here, to intercede? Was Ma hiding away in the bedroom from Pa's raised voice?)

Rebecca brought the *Webster's Dictionary* to her father, she would obey him even as she feared and hated him. Seeming to know beforehand, with a child's resignation to fate, as a doomed animal bares its throat to a predator, that he would toss the dictionary into the stove with a curse.

Almost, Rebecca would remember he'd done this. Tossed her dictionary into the stove, and laughed.

In fact, Pa did not. He took the heavy book from her, and laid it on the table, suddenly quieter, as if intimidated. Such a heavy book, and so obviously expensive!

His mind would calculate rapidly what a book this size might cost: five dollars? Six?

Gilt letters on the spine and cover. Marbleized endpapers. Almost two thousand pages.

With a flourish Pa opened the front cover, and saw the bookplate:

SPELLING CHAMPION MILBURN DISTRICT #3

*** 1946 ***

REBECCA ESHTER SCHWART

Immediately Pa saw the misspelling, he laughed harshly, and was triumphant. "Eh, you see? They are insulting you—'Eshter.' They are insulting us. This is no accident, this is calculated. Spelling the child's name wrong to insult who named her." Pa showed the bookplate to Herschel, who peered at it, unable to read. In frustration he poked the dictionary as you'd poke a snake with a stick, saying, "Jezuz. Keep the fuckin thing from me, I'm *lergic*." This provoked Pa to laugh heartily, he had a weakness for his older son's crude humor.

Gus objected. "God damn, Hersch'l, somebody in this family got something for once, I think it's damn *nice*." Gus would have liked to say more, but Pa and Herschel ridiculed him.

Pa shut the dictionary. Now was the moment, Rebecca knew, when he would lean over with a grunt, and open the stove door, and toss the dictionary inside . . .

Instead, Pa said, brooding, "God damn I don't like for any child of Jacob Schwart sneaking behind my back like a weasel. In this hellhole where everybody's watching us, you can be sure. Damn picture in the paper for everybody to see. Next time . . ."

Desperately Rebecca said, "I won't, Pa! I won't do it again."

Seeing with relief that her father seemed to be losing interest in the subject, as he often did when no one opposed him. Suddenly he was bored, and shoved the dictionary aside.

"Take the damn thing, just don't let me see it again."

Rebecca snatched up the heavy book. Pa and her brothers had to laugh at her, she was so desperate, and so clumsy nearly dropping the book on herself.

She hurried back to her bed. She would hide it again, beneath her bed.

Hearing behind her Jacob Schwart haranguing his sons: "What are words, words are bullshit and lies, lies! You'll learn."

There came Herschel's insolent laugh.

"So tell us somethin that ain't bullshit, Pa, you're the fuckin *jeen-yus*, eh?"

19

✵ ✵ ✵

A bright summer day. The blinds in the parlor were drawn. Rebecca would recall this day trying to calculate how old she'd been, how old her mother had been, how many months before Anna Schwart's death. Yet she could not, the brightness of the air so dazzled her even in memory.

It was summer, she knew: a time of no school. She had been tramping through a sprawling wooded area behind the cemetery, she'd been tramping along the canal towpath watching the barges, waving at the pilots who waved at her, as she'd been forbidden. She'd been at the township dump, too. Alone, and not with her friends.

For Rebecca had friends now. Mostly they were girls like herself, living at the edge of Milburn. Quarry Road, Milburn Post Road, Canal Road. These girls lived in run-down old farmhouses, tar paper shanties, trailers propped up on concrete blocks amid weedy trash-strewn yards. To such girls Rebecca Schwart was not scorned as the gravedigger's daughter. For the fathers of such girls, if they had fathers, were not so very different from Jacob Schwart.

Their brothers, if they had brothers, were not so very different from Herschel and Gus.

And their mothers . . .

"What's your ma like?"—so Rebecca's friends asked her. "Is she sick? Something wrong with her? Don't she like us?"

Rebecca shrugged. Her shut-up sullen expression meant *None of your damn business.*

None of Rebecca's friends had ever had a glimpse of Anna Schwart, though their mothers might recall having seen her, years ago, in downtown Milburn. But now Anna Schwart no longer ventured into town, nor even left the vicinity of the stone cottage. And of course Rebecca could not bring any friends home.

That day there was a funeral in the cemetery, Rebecca saw. She paused to watch the slow procession of vehicles from behind one of the sheds, not wanting to be seen. Her coarse dark hair straggled down her back like a mane, her skin was rough and tanned. She wore khaki shorts and a soiled sleeveless shirt covered in burrs. Except for her hair she might have been mistaken for a lanky, long-legged boy.

The hearse! Stately, darkly gleaming, with tinted windows. Rebecca stared feeling her heart begin to beat strangely. *There is death, death is inside.* Seven cars followed the hearse, their tires crackling in the gravel drive. Rebecca glimpsed faces inside these cars, women with veiled hats, men staring straight before them. Now and then a younger face. Especially, Rebecca shrank from being seen by anyone her age, who might know her.

A funeral in the Milburn cemetery meant that, the previous day, Jacob Schwart had prepared a grave site. Most of the newer graves were in hilly terrain at the rear of the cemetery where tall oaks and elms grew and their roots were tangled in the rocky soil. Gravedigging was an arduous task. For Jacob Schwart had to dig the graves with a shovel, it was back-breaking labor and he hadn't mechanical tools to aid him.

Rebecca shaded her eyes sighting her father at the rear of the cemetery. A troll-man, Jacob Schwart was. Like a creature who has emerged from the earth, slightly bent, broken-backed and with his head carried at an awkward angle so that he seemed always to be peering at the world suspiciously, from the side. He'd torn a ligament in his knee and now walked with a limp, one of his shoulders was carried higher than the other. Always he wore work clothes, always a cloth cap on his head. He was one to know his place among funeral directors and mourners whom he called *sir, ma'am* and with whom he was unfailingly deferential. Herschel spoke of seeing their father downtown on Main Street headed for the First Bank of Chautauqua, what a sight the old guy was in his gravedigger clothes and boots, walking with his head down not seeing how he was being stared at, and not giving a damn if he walked into somebody who didn't get out of his way fast enough.

Herschel warned Rebecca, if she was in town and saw Pa, not to let Pa see her—"That'd make the old bastid mad as hell. Like us kids is spyin' on him, see, goin' into the bank? Like anybody give a shit what the old bastid is up to, he thinks nobody knows."

So many millions dead and shoved into pits, just meat.

Ask why: ask God why such things are allowed.

Gazing upon her father when he wasn't aware of her, Rebecca sometimes shuddered as if seeing him through another's eyes.

"Ma . . . ?"

The interior of the stone cottage was dim, humid, cobwebby on this sun-bright day. In the kitchen dishes were soaking in the sink, the frying pan remained on the stove from breakfast. A smell of grease prevailed. Since her illness Rebecca's mother had become careless about housekeeping, or indifferent. Since the *Marea*, Rebecca thought.

Blinds were drawn on all the windows, at midday.

From the parlor came a strange sound: rapid and fiery like breaking glass. The door was shut.

Now that Pa no longer listened to the news every night after supper, the radio was rarely played. Pa would not allow it when he was in the house grumbling *Electricity doesn't grow on trees, want not waste not*. But Rebecca heard the radio now.

"Ma? Can I—come in?"

There was no answer. Cautiously Rebecca pushed the door open.

Her mother was inside, seated close beside the floor-model Motorola as if for warmth. She'd pulled a stool close beside it, she was not sitting in Pa's chair. Rebecca saw how the radio dial glowed a rich thrumming orange like something living. Out of the dust-latticed speaker emerged sounds so beautiful, rapid yet precisely rendered, Rebecca listened in amazement. A piano, was it? Piano music?

Rebecca's mother glanced toward her as if to ascertain this wasn't Jacob Schwart, there was no danger. Her eyelids fluttered. She was lost in concentration, and did not want to be distracted. A forefinger to her lips signaling *Don't speak! Be quiet!* So Rebecca kept very still, sitting at her mother's feet and listening.

Beyond the Motorola, beyond the dim-lighted mildew-smelling parlor of the old stone cottage in the cemetery, there was nothing.

Beyond Ma leaning to the radio, nodding and smiling with the piano music, beyond this moment, beyond the happiness of this moment, there was nothing.

When there came a break in the music, the briefest of breaks between movements of the sonata, Rebecca's mother whispered to her, "It is Artur Schnabel. It is Beethoven that is played. 'Appassionata' it is called." Rebecca listened eagerly, with no idea what most of her mother's words meant. She had heard of Beethoven, that was all. She saw that her mother's soft-raddled girl's face shone with tears that were not tears of hurt or grief or humiliation. And her mother's eyes were beautiful eyes, dark, lustrous, with a startling intensity, that made you uneasy, to see close up. "When I was a girl in the old country, I played this 'Apassionata.' Not like Schnabel I played, but I attempted." Ma fumbled for Rebecca's hand, squeezing her fingers as she had not done in years.

The piano music resumed. Mother and daughter listened together. Rebecca held on to her mother's hand as if she were in danger of falling from a great height.

Such beauty, and the intimacy of such beauty, Rebecca would cherish through her life.

❀ ❀ ❀

20

"Pa! Get the hell out here."

There came Herschel careening and panting in the kitchen door. He was a tall lumbering horsey boy with unshaven jaws and a raw braying voice. He was breathing on his knuckles, it was a cold autumn morning.

It was the morning of Hallowe'en, 1948. Rebecca was twelve years old and in seventh grade.

It was shortly past dawn. In the night there had been a frost and a light dusting of snow. Now the sky was gray and twilit and in the east beyond the Chautauqua mountains the sun was a faintly glowing hooded eye.

Rebecca was helping Ma prepare breakfast. Gus hadn't yet emerged from his bedroom. Pa in coveralls stood at the sink pumping water, coughing and noisily spitting in that way of his that made Rebecca feel sickish. Pa looked up at Herschel sharply, asking, "What? What's it?"

"You best come outside by y'self, Pa."

Herschel spoke with uncharacteristic grimness. You looked to see if he'd wink, screw up his eyes, wriggle his mouth in that comical way of his, give some sign he was fooling, but he was serious, he did not even glance at Rebecca.

Jacob Schwart stared at his elder son, saw something in the boy's face—fury, hurt, bafflement, and quivering animal excitement—he had not seen before. He cursed, and reached for the poker beside the cast-iron stove. Herschel laughed harshly saying, "It's too late for any fuckin poker, Pa."

Pa followed Herschel outside, limping. Rebecca would have followed but Pa turned as if by instinct to warn her, "Stay inside, girl." By this time Gus had stumbled out of the bedroom, spiky-haired and disheveled; at nineteen he was nearly Herschel's height, six feet two, but thirty pounds lighter, rail-thin and skittish.

Anna Schwart, at the stove, looking at no one, removed the heavy iron frying pan from the burner and set it to the side.

"Fuck! Fuckers."

Herschel led the way, Pa followed close behind him swaying like a drunken man, staring. The night before Hallowe'en was known as Devil's Night. In the Chautauqua Valley it seemed to be an old, in some way revered tradition. "Pranks" were committed by unknown parties who came in stealth, in the dark. "Mischief." You were meant to take it as a joke.

The Milburn cemetery had long been a target for Devil's Night pranks, before Jacob Schwart became caretaker. So they would tell him, they would insist.

"Think I don't know who done this, Chrissake I *do*. I got a good idea, see!"

Herschel spoke in disgust, his voice trembling. Jacob Schwart was barely listening to his son. The night before, he'd dragged the iron gates to the front entrance shut and fastened them with a chain, of course he knew what Devil's Night was, there'd been damage to the cemetery in past years, he'd tried to stay awake to protect the property but (he'd been exhausted, and he'd been drinking) he'd fallen asleep by midnight and in any case he had no weapon, no gun. Men and boys as young as twelve owned rifles, shotguns, but Jacob Schwart had not yet armed himself. He had a horror of firearms, he was not a hunter. A part of him had long cautioned against the irrevocable step. *Arm yourself! One day it will be too late.* A part of him wanted neither to kill nor to be killed but in the end his enemies were giving him no choice.

Vandals hadn't been deterred by the shut gates, they'd only just climbed over the cemetery wall. You could see where they'd knocked part of the wall down, a hundred or so yards back from the road.

There was no keeping them out. Marauding young men and boys. Their faces would be known to him, maybe. Their names. They were Milburn residents. Some were likely to be neighbors on the Quarry Road. *Those others* who despised the Schwarts. Looked down upon the Schwarts. Herschel seemed to know who they were, or to suspect. Jacob Schwart stumbled behind his son, wiping at his eyes. A twitch of a smile, dazed, ghastly, played about his lips.

No keeping your enemies out, if you are unarmed. He would not make that mistake again.

Crockery and flowerpots had been broken amid the graves. Pumpkins had been smashed with a look of frenzied revelry, their spilled seeds and juicy flesh looking like spilled brains. Already, crows had been feasting on these spilled brains.

"Get away, fuckers! Sonsabitches."

Herschel clapped his hands to scatter the crows. His father seemed scarcely to notice them.

Crows! What did he care for crows! Brute, innocent creatures.

A number of the younger birch trees had been cruelly bent to the ground, and were now broken-backed, and would not recover. Several of the oldest and most frail of the gravestones, dating back to 1791, had been kicked over, and were cracked. All four tires on the caretaker's 1939 Ford pickup had been slashed so that the truck sagged on its wheel rims like a beaten, toothless creature. And on the truck's sides were marks in tar, ugly marks with the authority of jeering shouts.

And on the caretaker's sheds, and on the front door of the caretaker's stone cottage, so that the ugly marks were fully visible from the gravel drive, and would be seen by all visitors to the cemetery.

Gus had run outside, and Rebecca followed, hugging herself in the cold. She was too confused to be frightened, at first. Yet how strange it was: her father was silent, while Herschel cursed *Fuck! fuckers!* Her father Jacob Schwart so strangely silent, only just blinking and staring at the glistening tar marks.

"Pa? What's it mean?"

Pa ignored her. Rebecca put out her hand to touch the tar where it had been scrawled on the side of a shed, the tar was cold, hardened. She couldn't remember what the marks were called, something ugly—sounding beginning with *s*, but she knew what they meant—Germany? Nazis? The Axis Powers, that had been defeated in the war?

But the war had been over for a long time now, hadn't it?

Rebecca calculated: she'd been in fourth grade when the Milburn fire siren had gone off, and all classes at the grammar school were canceled for the day. Now she was in seventh grade. Three years: the Germans had surrendered to the Allies in May of 1945. This seemed to her a very long time ago, when she'd been a little girl.

She wasn't a little girl now. Her heart pounded in anger and indignation.

Herschel and Gus were talking excitedly. Still, Pa stood staring and squinting. It was not like Jacob Schwart to be so quiet, his children were aware of him, uneasy. He had hurried outside without a jacket or his cloth cap. He seemed confused, older than Rebecca had ever seen him. Like one of those homeless men, derelicts they were called, who gathered at the bus station in Milburn, and in good weather hung about the canal bridge. In the stark morning light Pa's face looked battered, misshapen. His eyes were ringed in fatigue and his nose was swollen with broken capillaries like tiny spiderwebs. His mouth worked helplessly as if he couldn't chew what had been thrust into it, couldn't swallow or spit it out. Herschel was saying again how he had a damn good idea who the fuckers were who'd done this and Gus, aroused and indignant, was agreeing.

Rebecca wiped at her eyes, that were watering in the cold. The eastern sky was lightening now, there were breaks and fissures in the clouds overhead. She was seeing the ugly marks—"swastikas," she remembered they were called—through her father's eyes. How could you remove them, black tar that had hardened worse than any paint? How could you clean them off, scrub them off, *tar*? And how upset Ma would be! Oh, if they could hide the marks from Ma, somehow . . .

But Rebecca's mother would know. Of course, she already knew. Anna Schwart's instinct was to fear, to suspect the worst; by now she would be cowering behind the window, peering out. Not just the swastikas but the birch trees, that tore at your heart to see. And the broken flowerpots, and smashed pumpkins, cracked gravestones that could not be replaced.

"Why do they hate us?"

Rebecca spoke aloud, but too softly for her brothers or father to hear.

Yet her father heard her, it seemed. He turned toward her, and came limping toward her. "You! God damn what'd I tell you, girl! Get inside with your God damn *ma*."

Jacob Schwart had become furious suddenly. He lunged at her, even with his bad knee he moved swiftly. Grabbing Rebecca by her upper arm and dragging her back to the house. Cursing her, hurting her so that Rebecca cried out in protest, and both her brothers protested, "Pa, hey—" though keeping their distance and not daring to touch him. "In-side, I *said*. And if you tell your God damn *ma* about this I will break your ass."

His fingers would leave bruises in Rebecca's flesh, she would contemplate for days. Like swastika marks they were, these ugly purplish-orange bruises.

And the fury with which he'd uttered *ma*. That short blunt syllable in Jacob Schwart's mouth sounding like a curse.

He is the one who hates us.
But why?

That day. Hallowe'en, 1948. Her mother had wanted her to stay home from school but no, she'd insisted upon going to school as usual.

She was twelve, in seventh grade. She knew, at the school, that some of her classmates would know about the desecration to the cemetery, they would know about the swastikas. She didn't want to think that some of her classmates, in the company of their older brothers, might have been involved in the vandalism.

Names came to mind: Diggles, LaMont, Meunzer, Kreznick. Loud jeering boys at the high school, or dropouts like Rebecca's own brothers.

In town, among children at Rebecca's school, there was always excitement about Hallowe'en. Wearing masks and costumes (purchased at Woolworth's Five-and-Dime, where there was a front-window display of witches, devils, skeletons amid grinning plastic jack-o'-lanterns), going door to door in the darkness calling out *Trick or treat!* There was something thrilling about it, Rebecca thought. Hiding behind a mask, wearing a costume. Beginning in first grade she'd begged to be allowed to go out on Hallowe'en night, but Jacob Schwart would not allow it, of course. Not his sons, and certainly not his daughter. Hallowe'en was a pagan custom, Pa said, demeaning and dangerous. Next thing to begging! And what if, Pa said with a sly smile, some individual fed up with kids coming to his door and annoying him decided to put rat poison in the candy treats?

Rebecca had laughed. "Oh, Pa! Why'd anybody do such a mean thing?" and Pa said, cocking his head at her as if he meant to impart a bit of wisdom to a naive little girl, "Because there is meanness in the world. And we are in the world."

There had been Devil's Night mischief in Milburn, Rebecca saw as she walked to school. Toilet paper tossed up into tree limbs, pumpkins smashed on the front steps of houses, battered mailboxes, soaped and waxed windows. (Soaped windows were easy to clean off but waxed windows required finicky labor with razor blades. Kids at school spoke of waxing the windows of neighbors they didn't like, or anybody who didn't give them very good treats. Sometimes, out of sheer meanness, they waxed store windows on Main Street because the big plate glass windows were such targets.) It made Rebecca nervous to see the Devil's Night mischief in the unsparing light of morning. At the junior high school, kids stood about pointing and laughing: many ground-floor windows had been waxed, tomatoes and eggs had been thrown against the concrete walls, yet more pumpkins smashed on the steps. Like broken bodies they seemed, destroyed in a gleeful rage. You were made to realize, Rebecca thought, how mischief could be committed all the time, each night, if there was nobody to stop it.

"Look! Lookit here!"—someone was pointing at more damage to the school, a jagged crack in the plate glass window of one of the front doors, that had been crudely mended with masking tape by the school janitor.

Yet there were no tar marks in town, anywhere Rebecca had seen. No "swastikas."

Why, Rebecca wondered. Why were the swastikas only at the cemetery, only at her family's house?

She would not ask anyone. Not even her close girlfriends. Nor would anyone speak to her about the swastikas, if they knew.

In English class, God damn! Mrs. Krause who was always trying to make her seventh grade students like her had this idea, they would read aloud a short story about Hallowe'en and ghosts: a shortened version of "The Legend of Sleepy Hollow" by some old dead author named Washington Irving. It was like Mrs. Krause, whose gums sparkled when she smiled, to make them read some old-fashioned prose nobody could follow; damn big words nobody could pronounce let alone comprehend. (Rebecca wondered if Mrs. Krause comprehended them.) Row after row, student after student stumbled through a few paragraphs of dense, slow-moving "The Legend of Sleepy Hollow"; they were faltering and sullen, especially the boys who read so poorly that the exasperated teacher finally interrupted to ask Rebecca to read. "And the rest of the class, sit quietly and listen."

Rebecca's face burned. She squirmed in her seat, in misery.

Wanting to tell Mrs. Krause she had a sore throat, she couldn't read. Oh, she couldn't!

Everybody staring at her. Even her friends, the girls she believed to be her friends, staring in resentment.

"Rebecca? You will begin."

What a nightmare! For Rebecca, who was one of the better students, was always self-conscious when any teacher singled her out. And the story was so slow, so tortuous, its sentences lengthy, words like snarls—*apparition—cognomen—enraptured—superstitious—supernumerary*. When Rebecca mispronounced a word, and Mrs. Krause prissily corrected her, the other students laughed. When Rebecca pronounced such silly names as "Ichabod Crane"—"Brom Bones"—"Baltus Van Tassel"—"Hans Van Ripper"—they laughed. Of the thirty students in the classroom perhaps five or six were trying to make sense of the story, listening quietly; the others were restless, mirthful. The boy who sat behind Rebecca jiggled her desk, that was attached to his. A wad of something struck her between the shoulder blades. *Gravedigger! Jew-gravedigger!*

"Rebecca? Please continue."

She'd stopped, and lost her place. Mrs. Krause was annoyed, and beginning to be disappointed.

What was a Jew, Rebecca knew not to ask. Her father had forbidden them to ask.

She couldn't remember why. It had something to do with Gus.

I am not Rebecca thought. *I am not that.*

In a haze of embarrassment and misery she stumbled through the story. Seeing again the vandalized cemetery of that morning, the smashed pumpkins and the noisy wide-winged crows flapping up in alarm as Herschel clapped his hands and shouted at them. She saw the ugly marks that had so frightened her father.

Felt his fingers closing on her upper arm. She knew the bruises had formed, she hadn't yet wanted to see.

It had been nice of her brothers to protest, when Pa grabbed her like that. Indoors, when their father was mean to her, or made a threatening gesture, it was likely to be Ma who would mutter or make a little warning cry, not words exactly, for Anna Schwart and her husband rarely spoke to each other in the presence of their children, but a sound, an uplifted hand, a gesture to dissuade him.

A gesture to signify *I see you, I am watching.*

A gesture to signify *I will protect her, my daughter.*

How she hated stupid old ugly old Ichabod Crane who reminded her of Jacob Schwart! She liked it that handsome dashing Brom Bones threw the pumpkin-head at Ichabod, and scared him out of Sleepy Hollow forever. Maybe Ichabod even drowned in the brook . . . That would serve him right, Rebecca thought, for being so pompous and freaky.

By the time she finished reading "The Legend of Sleepy Hollow," Rebecca was dazed and exhausted as if she'd been crawling on her hands and knees for hours. She hated Mrs. Krause, never would she smile at Mrs. Krause again. Never would she look forward to coming to school again. Her voice was hoarse and fading as the very voice of Ichabod Crane's ghost—" 'at a distance, chanting a melancholy psalm tune among the tranquil solitudes of Sleepy Hollow.' "

"We are not Nazis! Do you think that we are Nazis? *We are not.* We came to this country twelve years ago. The war is over. The Germans are defeated. We have nothing to do with Nazis. *We are Americans like you.*"

It would be told and retold and laughed over in Milburn how frenzied Jacob Schwart was on that Hallowe'en morning. How, limping badly, he'd hiked up the road to the Esso station where he made telephone calls to the Chautauqua County sheriff's office and to the Milburn Township Office reporting the Devil's Night damage at the cemetery, and insisting that "authorities" come to investigate.

Jacob Schwart then hiked back home where he ignored his wife's pleas to come inside the house, instead he waited at the entrance gates, pacing in the road in a lightly falling freezing rain, until at last, around noon, two Chautauqua County deputies arrived in a police cruiser. These were men who knew Jacob Schwart, or knew of him; their manner with him was familiar, bemused. "Mr. Schwarzz, what seems to be your trouble?"

"You can see! If you are not blind, you can see!"

Not only had Jacob Schwart's truck tires been slashed, damage had been done to the truck's motor. He was desperate, he would need a replacement immediately! The truck was owned by the Township, not by him, the Township must replace it immediately! He had not the money to buy a vehicle himself.

The truck was the Township's responsibility, the deputies told him. The sheriff's office had nothing to do with the Township.

Jacob Schwart told them that he and his sons could clean up most of the damage in the cemetery, but how to remove tar! How to remove tar! "The criminals who have done this, they are the ones to remove it. They must be arrested, and made to remove it. You will find them, eh? You will arrest them? 'Destruction of property'—eh? It is a serious crime, yes?"

The deputies listened to Jacob Schwart with neutral expressions. They were polite, but clearly not very interested in his complaints. They made a show of examining the damage, including the swastika marks, saying only that it was just Hallowe'en, just kids acting up, nothing personal.

"See, Mr. Schwarzz, cem'teries are always targets on Devil's Night. Everywhere in the Valley. Damn kids. Getting worse. Lucky they don't set fires like some places. Nothing personal, Mr. Schwarzz. Nothing against you and your family."

The elder deputy spoke in a flat, nasal drawl, taking desultory notes with a pencil stub. His partner, prodding at one of the broken gravestones with his boot, smirked and suppressed a yawn.

Through the blood in his eyes Jacob Schwart saw suddenly how they mocked him.

He saw, like the sun breaking through clouds, and his battered hands shook with the yearning to grip a poker, a shovel, a hoe.

He had no weapon. The deputies carried pistols, holstered, on their hips. They were cunning coarse-faced peasants. They were storm trooper Nazi brutes. They were of the very stock that had saluted Hitler, had marched and wished to die for Hitler. He would buy a twelve-gauge double-barreled shotgun to protect himself against them. But he had not the shotgun yet. Only his bare, battered hands, which were useless against brutes with guns.

It would be reported everywhere in Milburn how Jacob Schwart began to rave, excitedly. His ridiculous accent so strong, he was practically indecipherable.

"You are related to these 'kids,' eh? You are knowing them, eh?"

For suddenly it was clear, why the deputies had driven out here. Not to help him but to laugh at a man's misery. To mock a man before his family.

"Yes. You are all related here. This hellhole, you protect one another. You will give one like me no help. You will make no arrest of the criminals. In other years, you have not arrested them. This is the worst of it, and you will not arrest them. I am an American citizen yet you scorn my family and me like animals. 'Life unworthy life'—eh? You are thinking, seeing Jacob Schwart? Goebbels you admired, eh? Yet Goebbels was a cripple too. Goebbels killed his family and himself, yes? So why you do admire the Nazi? Go away then, get out of here and to hell, damn your Nazi souls to hell, I am in not need of you."

In his vehemence Jacob Schwart misspoke. His sons, listening unseen to his ravings from one of the sheds, winced in shame.

What an outburst! Like some kind of hopped-up dwarf, gesturing and spitting and you couldn't understand half of what he said. The deputies would joke afterward it was damned lucky they were armed, that poor bastard Schwarzz looking like he was some kind of smashed Hallowe'en pumpkin himself.

One-quarter Seneca blood.

Somehow he'd acquired that reputation. In the Chautauqua Valley among those who knew Herschel Schwart without knowing his family.

He'd quit school at sixteen. He'd been suspended from Milburn High for fighting and during the two-week suspension he had turned sixteen and so he'd quit. God damn he'd been relieved! Kept behind in ninth grade, biggest kid in his class and made to feel shamed and murderous. Immediately he got a job at the Milburn lumber mill. Friends of his worked there, none of them had graduated from high school and they made good wages.

He still lived at home. He still helped the old man in the cemetery, sometimes. He felt sorry for Jacob Schwart. Each time he quarreled with the old man he made plans to move out, but by the age of twenty-one in October 1948 he had not yet moved out. It was inertia binding him to the stone cottage. It was his mother binding him. Her meals he devoured always hungrily, her tending to him in silence and without reproach. He would not have said *I love her, I could not leave her with him*.

He would not have said *My sister, too. I could not leave her with the two of them*.

His brother Gus, he knew could take care of himself. Gus was all right. Gus, too, had quit school on his sixteenth birthday, at their father's urging, to help in the damn cemetery like a common laborer, full-time. But Herschel was too smart for that.

How, the eldest son of German-born immigrants, he had acquired a local reputation as part-Seneca, Herschel himself could not have said. Certainly he had not made such a claim. Neither did he deny it. His straggly dark hair that was lank and without lustre, his eyes too that were glassy-dark and without lustre, his quick temper and eccentric manner of speech suggested an exotic background of some kind, perhaps unknowable. A shrewder young man would have smiled to think *Better Seneca than Kraut*.

By the age of eighteen he bore an angular horsey face scarred like filigree about the mouth, eyes, and ears from bare-knuckled fights. At the age of twenty he'd been wounded by another young man wielding a broken beer bottle, twelve clumsily executed stitches across Herschel's forehead. (Reticent, stubborn, Herschel had not told the sheriff's deputies who had wounded him. He had revenged himself upon the young man, in time.) His teeth had been rotting in his head all his life. He was missing several teeth back and front. When he grinned, his mouth seemed to be winking. His nose had been broken and flattened at the bridge. Though he frightened most Milburn girls he was an attractive figure to certain older divorced or separated women who appreciated what was special about Herschel Schwart. They liked his face. They liked his good-natured if explosive and unpredictable manner. His loud braying laugh, his nerved-up sinewy body that gave off heat like a horse. His ropey penis that remained a marvel even when its bearer was staggering drunk, or comatose. These were women who drew their fingertips in fascination over his skin—chest, back, sides, belly, thighs, legs—that was coarse as leather, covered in bristling hairs and dimpled with moles and pimples like shot.

These were women of coarse affable appetites who teased their young lover inquiring *which part of him was Seneca?*

It was no secret, Herschel Schwart had a police record in Chautauqua County. More than once he'd been taken into custody by law enforcement officers. Always he'd been in the company of other young men at the time of the arrests, and always he'd been drinking. He was not perceived by county officers as dangerous in himself and he had never been kept in jail more than three nights in succession. He was a brawler, his crimes were public and boisterous, he lacked the subtlety of slyness or premeditation. Not cruel, not malicious or woman-hating; not one to break into houses, to steal or rob. In fact Herschel was careless with money, likely to be generous when he drank. In this he was admired, and perceived to be utterly different from his old man Jacob Schwart the gravedigger who it was said would *jew you out of your last penny if he could.*

And yet the tale would be told through Milburn for years how, on that Hallowe'en night, the night following the vandalism in the Milburn cemetery, several young men were surprised and attacked by Herschel Schwart who acted alone. The first of these, Hank Diggles, dragged out of his pickup truck in the dimly lighted parking lot of the Mott Street Tavern, could not claim to have seen Herschel Schwart but only to have felt him and smelled him, before he was beaten by his assailant's fists into unconsciousness. There were no witnesses to the Diggles beating, nor to the even bloodier beating of Ernie LaMont in the vestibule of his apartment building just off Main Street, about twenty minutes after the Diggles beating. But there were eyewitnesses to the attack on Jeb Meunzer outside the Meunzers' house on the Post Road: at about midnight Herschel showed up on the front porch, long after the last of the trick-or-treaters in their Hallowe'en costumes had gone home, he'd pounded on the door and demanded to see Jeb, and when Jeb appeared Herschel immediately grabbed him and dragged him outside, threw him onto the ground and began beating and kicking him, with no more explanation than *Who's a Nazi? Fucker who's a fuckin Nazi?* Jeb's mother and a twelve-year-old sister saw the beating from the porch, and cried out for Herschel to stop. They knew Herschel of course, he'd gone to school with Jeb and intermittently the two boys had been friends, though they were not friends at this time. Mrs. Meunzer and Jeb's sister would describe how "crazed" Herschel was, terrifying them by stabbing at Jeb with what appeared to be a fishing knife and all the while cursing *Who's a Nazi now? Fucker who's a fuckin Nazi now?* Though Jeb was Herschel's size and had a reputation for brawling, he appeared to be overcome by Herschel, unable to defend himself. He, too, was terrified and begged his assailant not to kill him as with both knees Herschel pinned him to the ground and, with the knife, crudely carved into his forehead this mark—

that would scar Jeb Meunzer for the remainder of his life.

It would be told how Herschel Schwart then wiped the bloody knife calmly on his victim's trousers, rose from him and waved insolently at the stunned, staring Mrs. Meunzer and her daughter, and turned to run into the darkness. It would be said that, at a bend in the Post Road, a car or pickup truck was idling, with its headlights off; and that Herschel climbed into this vehicle and drove away, or was driven away by an accomplice, to vanish from the Chautauqua Valley forever.

21

❀ ❀ ❀

Earnestly he insisted, "My son, he is a good boy! Like all your boys. Your Milburn boys. *He* would not harm another. Never!"

And, "My son Herschel, where he is gone I do not know. He is a good boy always, working hard to give his wages to his mother and father. He will return to explain himself, I know."

So Jacob Schwart claimed when Chautauqua County deputies came to question him about Herschel. How adamant the poor man was, in not-knowing! In a craven posture clutching his cloth cap in both hands and speaking rapidly, in heavily accented English. It would have required men of more subtlety than the literal-minded deputies to decipher the gravedig-ger's sly mockery and so the men would say afterward of Jacob Schwart *Poor bastard ain't right in the head is he?*

Among your enemies, Rebecca's father advised, it is wise to hide your intelligence as to hide your weakness.

A police warrant had been drawn charging Herschel with three counts of "aggravated assault with intent to commit murder." Of his three vic-tims, two had been hospitalized. The swastika-mutilation to Jeb Meunzer's face was severe. No one in the Milburn area had ever been so attacked. Bulletins had been issued through New York state and at the Canadian border describing the "dangerous fugitive" Herschel Schwart, twenty-one.

The deputies did not question Anna Schwart at length. The agitated woman shrank from them trembling and squinting like a nocturnal crea-ture terrified of daylight. In her confusion she seemed to think Herschel had himself been injured and hospitalized. Her voice was quavering and near-inaudible and her English so heavily accented, the deputies could barely understand her.

No! She did not know . . .

. . . knew nothing of where Herschel had gone.

(Was he hurt? Her son? What had they done to him? Where had they taken him? She wanted to see him!)

The deputies exchanged glances of pity, impatience. It was useless to question this simple-minded foreign-born woman who seemed not only to know nothing about her murderous son but also to be frightened of her gravedigger husband.

The deputies questioned August, or "Gus," Herschel's younger brother, but he too claimed to know nothing. "Maybe you helped your brother, eh?" But Gus shook his head quizzically. "Helped him how?"

And there was Rebecca, the twelve-year-old sister.

She, too, claimed to know nothing about what her older brother might have done, and where he'd fled. She shook her head wordlessly as the deputies questioned her.

At twelve, Rebecca still wore her hair in thick, shoulder-length braids, as her mother insisted. Her dark-brown hair was parted, not very evenly, in the center of her head and gave off a rich rank odor for her hair was not often washed. None of the Schwarts bathed frequently for hot water in large pails had to be heated on the stove, a tedious and time-consuming task.

In the face of adult authority Rebecca's expression was inclined to be sullen.

" 'Rebecca,' that's your name? Is there anyone in your family in contact with your brother, Rebecca?"

The deputy spoke sternly. Rebecca, not raising her eyes, shook her head *no*.

"*You* haven't been in contact with your brother?"

Rebecca shook her head *no*.

"If your brother comes back, miss, or you learn where he's hiding, or that someone is in contact with him, for instance providing him with money, you're obliged to inform us immediately, or you'll be charged as an accessory after the fact to the crimes he's been charged with—d'you understand, miss?"

Stubbornly, Rebecca stared at the floor. The worn linoleum floor of the kitchen.

It was true, she knew nothing of Herschel. She supposed that, yes he was the man the deputies wanted. Almost, she was proud of what Herschel had done: punishing their enemies. Carving a swastika on Jeb Meunzer's mean face!

But she was frightened, too. For Herschel might now be hunted down, and himself injured. It was known that fugitives *resisting arrest* were vulnerable to severe beatings at the hands of their pursuers, sometimes death. And if Herschel was sent to state prison . . .

Jacob Schwart intervened: "Officers, my daughter knows nothing! She is a quiet girl, not so bright. You see. You must not frighten her, officers. I plead you."

Rebecca felt a pang of resentment, that her father should misspeak. And malign her.

Not so bright. Was it true?

The deputies prepared to leave. They were dissatisfied with the Schwarts, and promised to return. With his sly mock-servile smile Jacob Schwart saw them to the door. Again telling them that his elder son was a boy who prayed often to God, who would not raise a fist even to a brute deserving of harm. Nor would Herschel abandon his family for he was a very loyal son.

" 'Innocent until guilty'—yes? That is your law?"

Watching the deputies drive away in their green-and-white police cruiser, Rebecca's father laughed with rare gusto.

"Gestapo. They are brutes, but they are fools, to be led by the nose like bulls. We will see!"

Gus laughed. Rebecca forced herself to smile. Ma had crept away into a back room, to weep. Almost you would think, seeing Jacob Schwart strut in his kitchen, thrusting a wad of Mail Pouch chewing tobacco into his mouth, that something exhilarating had happened, that *these others* had brought good news of Herschel and not a warrant for his arrest.

In the days following, it was clear that Jacob Schwart took pride in what Herschel had done, or was generally believed to have done. He overcame his customary frugality by buying several newspapers carrying articles on the assaults. His favorite was a front-page feature in the *Milburn Weekly* with a prominent headline:

THREE BRUTAL HALLOWE´EN ASSAULTS
LINKED TO 21-YEAR-OLD SUSPECT
Area Youth a Fugitive Considered Dangerous

In each of us there is a flame that will never die, Rebecca!
That flame is lighted by Jesus Christ and nourished by His love.
How badly Rebecca wanted to believe in these words of her former teacher Miss Lutter! But it was so hard. Like trying to lift herself onto the tar paper roof of the toolshed using just her arms, when she'd been a little girl imitating her brothers. They'd laughed at their little sister struggling behind them, too weak-armed at the time, her legs too thin, lacking muscle. Where they scrambled up onto the roof deft as cats, she'd fallen back helplessly to the ground.

Sometimes one of her brothers would lean over to give her a hand and hoist her up onto the roof. But sometimes not.

In each of us a flame. Rebecca, believe!

Jacob Schwart mocked *those others* for being Christian. In his mouth the word "Chriss-tyian" was a comical hissing noise.

Rebecca's father said how Jesus Christ had been a deranged Messiah-Jew who could save neither himself nor anybody else from the grave and what the fuss was about him, almost two thousand years after his death, God knows!

This, too, was a joke. Jacob Schwart was always grinning when the word "God" popped out of his mouth like a playful tongue. Pa would say, for instance, "God chases us into a corner. God is stamping his big boot-foot, to obliterate us. And yet there is a way out. Remember, children: always there is a way out. If you can make yourself small enough, like a worm."

He laughed, almost in mirth. His rotted teeth shone.

And so it became Rebecca's secret from her family: her wish to believe in Miss Lutter's friend Jesus Christ who was Jacob Schwart's enemy.

Miss Lutter had given Rebecca Bible cards, to be hidden in Rebecca's school books and smuggled home. "Our secret, Rebecca!"

The cards were slightly larger than playing cards. They were full-color depictions of Bible scenes so precisely rendered, Rebecca thought, you might think they were photographs. There was the Wise Men from the East (Matthew 2:1) in their flowing robes. There was Jesus Christ seen in profile, in a yet more flowing, surprisingly colorful robe (Matthew 6:28). There was the Crucifixion (John 19:26), and there was the Ascension (Acts 1:10): Jesus Christ, His bearded face barely visible, in a now snow-white robe floating above the head of his prayerful disciples. (Rebecca wondered: where did Jesus's robes come from? Were there stores in that far-off land, as in Milburn? You could not buy such a garment in any store in Milburn but you could purchase the material, and sew it. But who had sewed Jesus's robes, and how had they been laundered? And were they ironed? It was one of Rebecca's household tasks, to iron flat things for her mother, that didn't wrinkle easily.) Rebecca's favorite Bible card was the Raising of Jairus's Daughter (Mark 5:41) for Jairus's daughter had been twelve years old, she'd been given up for dead except Jesus Christ had come to her father and said *Why make ye this ado, and weep? The damsel is not dead, but sleepest.* And so it was, Jesus took the girl by the hand, wakened her, and she rose, and was well again.

Miss Lutter had not understood that the Schwarts did not own a Bible, and Rebecca had never wished her to know this. There were many things of which the gravedigger's daughter felt shame. Yet she did not wish to betray her parents, either. Now in seventh grade she was not Miss Lutter's pupil any longer, and saw her infrequently. She remembered Miss Lutter's words, however. *You have only to believe in Jesus Christ the Son of God and He will enter your heart, He will love you and protect you forever.*

So she tried, tried to believe!—and could not, not quite. Yet almost she did believe! Each day, since Herschel's disappearance, and the upset in her family's life, and the widespread dislike with which all the Schwarts were now regarded, Rebecca especially wanted to believe.

When she was alone, and no one observing her. No one sneering at her, cursing her. Bumping against her in the seventh grade corridor, or on the school stairs. Walking quickly home from school cutting through alleys, vacant lots, fields. She was becoming a feral cat, furtive and wary. Her legs were strong now, she could run, run, run if pursued. A not-bright girl, you might think. A girl from a poor family, in mismatched clothes, ugly braids swinging beside her head. There was a certain hill above the railroad embankment, just before Quarry Road, where, as she descended it, skidding and slipping in the loose gravel, Rebecca felt her heart knock against her ribs for she was allowed to know *If you deserve to fall and injure yourself, it will happen now*.

Rebecca had recently learned to bargain in this way. To offer herself as a victim. It was in place of others in her family being punished. She wanted to believe that God would act justly.

Sometimes she did fall, and cut her knees. But most often she did not. Even when she became aware of the wraith-like figure in a flowing white robe and white headdress approaching her she did not lose her balance, her body had become agile and cunning.

Columns of mist, fog, lifted out of the deep drainage ditches on either side of Quarry Road, that was an unpaved country road on the outskirts of Milburn. Here there was a stark cold odor of mud, stone.

Rebecca was allowed to speak if she did not move her lips, and did not utter any sound.

Would Herschel be returned to them?

Jesus said in a low, kindly voice, "In time your brother will return to you."

Would the police arrest him? hurt him? Would he go to prison?

Jesus said, "Nothing will happen that is not meant to be, Rebecca."

Rebecca! Jesus knew her name.

She was so afraid, Rebecca told Jesus. Her lips quivered, she was in danger of speaking out loud.

Jesus said, just slightly reproachfully, "*Why* make ye this ado, Rebecca? I am beside you."

But Rebecca must know: would something happen to them? Would something terrible happen to—her mother?

It was the first time Rebecca had mentioned her mother to Jesus.

It was the first time (her mind rapidly calculated, she knew that Jesus too must be thinking this) she had alluded to her father, indirectly.

Jesus said, an edge of irritation to His voice, "Nothing will happen that is not meant to be, my child."

But this was no consolation! Rebecca turned in confusion, and saw Jesus staring at her. The man looked nothing like Jesus on the Bible cards. He wasn't wearing a flowing white robe after all, nor a headdress. He was bareheaded and his hair was straggling and greasy, tinged with gray. His jaws were stubbled, his face was creased with deep wrinkles. In fact Jesus resembled the scummy-eyed men, derelicts they were called, bums, who hung about the railroad yard and the worst of the taverns on South Main Street. Those shabbily dressed men of whom Rebecca's mother warned her repeatedly to keep clear, to avoid.

This Jesus resembled Jacob Schwart, too. Smiling at her in angry mockery *If you believe me you are indeed a fool.*

And then a car came rattling along the Quarry Road, and He vanished.

22

❀ ❀ ❀

Nothing will happen that is not meant to be.

These were the words of the mocking derelict Jesus. Rebecca heard them taunting her through that long winter and into the freezing spring of 1949 which would be her final year in the old stone house in the cemetery.

It would be said in Milburn that the end came for the Schwarts soon after Herschel's criminal behavior, and his flight as a fugitive, but in fact eight months intervened. This was a time of stasis and confusion: when one is locked in the paralysis of sleep, even as the dream is broken, disintegrating. Rebecca knew only that her father's episodes of fury and despair, anxiety and sodden alcoholic depression, alternated more frequently, and were not to be predicted.

More and more, Jacob Schwart found fault with his remaining son. The boy's very name filled him with contempt: " 'Gus.' What is this 'gus'—'gas'? Who is named 'gas'?" Jacob laughed, this was very amusing. Even when he hadn't been drinking he tormented the boy:

"If our Nazi enemies took one of my sons, why not *you*? Eh?"

And, "God is a joker, we know: taking my firstborn son and leaving behind *you*."

Strange, Jacob Schwart's English speech was becoming ever more heavily accented, as if he'd been living in the Chautauqua Valley only a few weeks and not more than a decade.

Gus mumbled, to Rebecca, "Why's he hate *me*? I never made Herschel go nuts like that."

Unlike Herschel, Gus could not seem to stand up to their father. And Jacob Schwart was a man who, when unopposed, grew yet more contemptuous, cruel. Rebecca had seen how at school if she tried to ignore the other children's taunts, the taunts were only intensified. You could not placate a bully. You could not wait for a bully to tire of his cruelty, and find another target. Only if Rebecca fought back immediately did her tormentors let her alone.

Temporarily, at least.

Poor Gus, who had no work outside the cemetery. No life outside the stone cottage. Their father refused to let him get a job, as Herschel had done, and earn his own wages. Nor did Gus have the strength to break away from home, for their mother was dependent upon him. By the age of nineteen he'd become Jacob Schwart's (unpaid) assistant. "Get out here! Get your ass here! I am *waiting*." In the smallest matters, Gus must obey his father; Rebecca thought he was craven as a boy-soldier, terrified of disobeying his superior officer. She'd loved Gus when they were younger, now she shrank from him in disgust. By degrees Gus had become a captive animal, his spirit was squelched. His hair that was thin, fawn-colored, was seriously thinning, he scratched his scalp so. His forehead was becoming furrowed as an old man's. He suffered from mysterious skin rashes, always he was scratching with his nails. Rebecca cringed seeing Gus poke his forefinger deep, deep into his ear canal to scratch wildly as if hoping to claw out his brains.

Since Herschel had left home, the persecution was worsening. But it had begun years before when Jacob Schwart insisted that Gus quit school on his sixteenth birthday.

Jacob had said, matter-of-factly, "Son, you are not bright. School does nothing for one like you. On the terrible sea voyage, you were afflicted with dysentery and fever. Once the brain starts to melt like wax there is no recovery of intelligence. At that school you are surrounded by our enemies. Crude, coarse peasants who laugh at you, and through you laugh at your family. At your mother! It is not to be tolerated, son!" When Pa worked himself up into righteous anger, there was no reasoning with him.

It was true, Gus had to concede. His grades were poor, he had few friends, the majority of his classmates avoided him. Yet he'd never caused trouble, he'd never hurt anyone! It was his inflamed skin that exuded a look of fury. It was his small close-set eyes that regarded the world with such distrust.

So Gus obeyed his father, and quit school. Now he had no life outside the cemetery, beyond Jacob Schwart's domain. Rebecca worried that one day her father would insist that she, too, quit school. He had so bitterly repudiated the world of learning, of books, *words*. And Rebecca's mother would wish it, too. *You are a girl, you don't want something to happen to you.*

(Rebecca was puzzled: would she be punished because she was a girl, or because she was the gravedigger's daughter?)

One day in late March, when Gus was helping their father clear away storm debris from the cemetery, Jacob Schwart became impatient with his son, who worked clumsily and distractedly; Jacob cursed him, and feinted with his shovel as if to strike him. Of course, Jacob was only joking. But Gus's cringing response, the look of abject fear in his face, infuriated the older man who lost his temper and struck Gus on the back with the flat of the shovel—"Fool! Donkey!" The blow wasn't a hard one, Jacob Schwart would insist, yet out of perversity Gus fell, striking his head against a gravestone and cutting himself. A short distance away, several visitors to one of the grave sites were watching. A man called over asking what was wrong, what was going on, but Jacob Schwart ignored him, cursing his fallen son and commanding him to get up—"You are shameful, to behave so. Pretending to be hurt like a baby." When Gus struggled to his feet, wiping at his bleeding face, Jacob raged at him. "Look at you! God-damn baby! Go, go to your mama, suckle Mama's teats. Go!"

Gus turned to his father, staring. There was no look of abject fear in his face now. Bleeding from a cut in his forehead, Gus regarded the older man with an expression of hatred. His fingers twitched, gripping a wide-pronged metal rake.

"Do you dare! Do you! *You! You* do not dare, go suckle Mama's teats!"— so Jacob Schwart raged, as his son advanced upon him with the uplifted rake. At the same time, the man who'd called to them was now approaching them, cautiously, speaking calmly, trying to dissuade them from more violence. At the grave site, two women clutched at each other, whimpering in alarm.

"Try! Try to strike your father! You cripple-baby, you can*not*."

Gus held the rake in his trembling hands and then, abruptly, let it fall. He had not spoken, and would not speak. As Jacob Schwart continued to rage at him, he turned and walked away, unsteady on his feet, dripping blood on the snow, determined not to fall like a man making his way across the deck of a pitching ship.

When Gus entered the house, there was Anna Schwart awaiting him, quivering with emotion.

"*He? He* did this to you?"

"Ma, no. I fell. I did it to myself."

Anna tried awkwardly to embrace her son, who would not be embraced or impeded at this time.

She was begging, pleading. "He loves you, August! It is just his way, to hurt. To harm where he loves. The Nazis—"

"Fuck the Nazis. He's a Nazi. Fuck *him*."

Anna soaked a towel in cold water, to press against Gus's bleeding forehead. But he had no patience with her nursing, he seemed hardly to feel pain, the bleeding was only annoying to him. "Shit, Ma, let me go. I'm O.K." With surprising roughness he shoved Anna aside. In his bedroom he emptied bureau drawers onto his bed, yanked his few items of clothing out of his closet, threw everything into a pile. He would fashion a crude bundle out of a flannel blanket, and tie up his meager possessions inside. His distraught mother could not believe what she was seeing: her wounded son, her only remaining son, so elated? Smiling, laughing to himself? August, who'd rarely smiled since the terrible morning of the swastikas.

On the kitchen floor, in the hallway and in the bedroom, bloodstains would gleam in August Schwart's wake like exotic coins Rebecca would discover when she returned home from school to the silent, devastated stone house.

Like the other he never said goodbye. Left without seeing me never said goodbye.

23

❈ ❈ ❈

Both his sons were gone. In his fury he would come to think they had abandoned him—"My plans for them. Betrayers!"

With time, with brooding, drinking late into the night staring toward his blurred reflection in a window, that looked like a drowning man, he would come to see that his sons had been taken from him.

It was a conspiracy. A plan. For they hated Jacob Schwart. His enemies.

Wandering in the cemetery, amid the thawing dripping trees.

He read aloud: " 'I am the Resurrection and the Life.' " It was a blunt statement, wasn't it?—a remarkable claim of power, and consolation. Words carved into a weatherworn gravestone from the year 1928.

Jacob's voice was playful but hoarse. Nicotine had scorched the interior of his mouth. He was thinking how, when Herschel had been still in school, years ago, he'd been working with his son here and he'd read these very words aloud to Herschel and Herschel had scratched his head asking what the hell was that—" 'Rez-rectshun' "—and Jacob said it meant that a Messiah had come to save the Christians, only the Christians; also it meant that the Christians expected to be resurrected in their own bodies, when Jesus Christ returned to earth.

Herschel made a sniggering noise, perplexed.

"What th' fuck *bodiez*, Pa? Like, dead bodiez inna *grave*?"

Yes, that was it. Dead bodies in graves.

Herschel laughed his breathy heehaw laugh. As if this was a joke. Jacob Schwart had to smile: his elder, illiterate son had an eye for the tragic farce of human delusion as perceptive as that of the great German pessimist Arthur Schopenhauer. He did!

"Jeezus, Pa, they'd be nasty-lookin, eh? An how in fuckin hell they gonna get *out*?"

Herschel struck the rounded curve of a grave with the flat of his shovel as if to waken, and to mock, whatever lay inside, beneath the grass.

God damn: he missed Herschel. Now his son (whom he'd been barely able to stomach, in fact) had been missing for months, now Jacob missed Herschel like something eaten out of his gut. To Anna he might grunt, "All of that, that we had then. Gone with him."

Anna did not reply. Yet Anna knew what Jacob meant.

All that we had then, when we were young. In the old country. When Herschel was born. Before the Nazis. Gone.

Here was a theory: Herschel had been hunted down like a dog, shot in a ditch by Chautauqua County sheriff's deputies. Gestapo. They would claim self-defense. "Resisting arrest." In the mountains, it might've been. Often you heard gunfire from the mountains—"hunters."

Herschel hadn't been armed, so far as Jacob knew. Maybe a knife. Nothing more. He'd been shot, left to bleed to death in a ditch. Residents of Milburn would never forgive Herschel for beating and scarring their Nazi-sons.

"*I* will exact justice. I will not be unarmed."

It was a freezing spring! A hell of a spring. Too many funerals, the gravedigger was kept busy. This accursed year 1949. He missed his younger son, too. The puny whining one with the skin rashes—"August."

"August"—named for a favorite, older uncle of Anna's who had died at about the time Anna and Jacob were married.

For a while he was furious with August for behaving so insolently and stupidly and running off where Jacob Schwart could not find him to talk sense into him but then it seemed to him only logical, August too had been taken from him, to render Jacob Schwart helpless. For hadn't the boy been beaten, streaming blood from a nasty gash in his face . . .

A slow-witted boy but a good worker. A good son. And August could read, at least. August could do grade-school arithmetic.

"I will not be unarmed . . . I will not be 'meek.' "

Strange, and terrible: the paralysis that had overcome those declared enemies of the German Reich. Like hypnotized creatures, as the predator approaches. Hitler had not obfuscated. Hitler had been forthright, unambiguous. Jacob Schwart had forced himself to read *Mein Kampf.* At least, he had read into *Mein Kampf.* The lunatic certainty! The passion! *My battle, my campaign. My struggle. My war.*

Set beside Hitler's rantings, and Hitler's demon logic, how flimsy, how vulnerable, how merely *words* were the great works of philosophy! How merely *words* the dream of mankind for a god!

Among his enemies here in the Chautauqua Valley, Jacob Schwart would not be hypnotized. He would not be surprised, and he would not be unarmed. History would not repeat itself.

He blamed his enemies for this, too: that he, Jacob Schwart, a refined and educated individual, formerly a citizen of Germany, should be forced to behave in such a barbaric manner.

He, a former math teacher at a prestigious boys' school. A former respected employee of a most distinguished Munich printing firm specializing in scientific publications.

Now, a gravedigger. A caretaker of *these others*, his enemies.

Their Christian cemetery he must maintain. Their grave sites he must keep trimmed. Crosses!—crucifixions!—ridiculous stone angels!

He maintained the graves, oh yes. When no one observed there was Jacob Schwart "watering" the graves with his hot-acid piss.

He and Herschel, years ago. Laughing wild as braying donkeys.

Gus had never. You couldn't joke with Gus, like that. Pissing with his father, unzipping his trousers and taking out his penis, the boy would be mortified, embarrassed. More like a girl, Jacob thought.

That was his shame, he had lost his sons.

For this, he would come to blame the Township board. For it was too confusing otherwise.

"You will see. Soon, your blind eyes will be blasted open."

He'd memorized their names. They were *Madrick, Drury, Simcoe, Harwell, McCarren, Boyd* . . . He wasn't sure of their faces but he knew names and he could learn where they lived, if necessary.

So grateful, sirs. Thank you sirs!

Rural idiots. Wrinkling their noses at his smell. Seeing that he was unshaven, a troll-man with a broken back, twisting his cloth cap in his hands . . . In pity of him, in contempt of him, explaining to him shameless in their duplicity that the budget, the budget was, budget cuts were, maybe next year Jacob, possibly next year we will see Jacob. Thank you for coming in, Jacob!

Some kind of a long gun he would purchase. A deer rifle, or a shotgun. He had money saved. In the First Bank of Chautauqua, he had nearly two hundred dollars saved.

" 'Genocide' it is called. You are young now, you are ignorant and are being falsely educated in that school but one day you must know. In animal life the weak are quickly disposed of. You must hide your weakness, Rebecca!"

He spoke with alarming vehemence. As if she had dared to doubt him. Though in fact she was nodding, yes Pa.

No idea what he was saying. Uneasy that in his excitement he might spit at her. For he chewed an enormous wad of tobacco, acid juices leaked down his chin. The more vehemently he spoke the more spittle flew from his lips. And if he should lapse into one of his coughing spasms . . .

"You are listening, Rebecca? You are hearing me?"

His sorrow was, he had no sons remaining. He had been castrated, unmanned. His shame.

Only the girl. He must love the wretched girl, he had no one else.

And so he told her, he lapsed into telling her, in the evenings sometimes, couldn't recall what he'd said or when he'd begun instructing her, how in

Europe their enemies had wished not only to kill him and his kind "as in an action of war" but to exterminate them utterly. For they were believed to be "pollutants"—"toxins." And so it was not merely war, which is a political action, but genocide, which is a moral, you might say a metaphysical action. For genocide, if carried out, is an action that time cannot undo.

"Here is a puzzle worthy of Zeno: that, in history, there can be actions that history—all of 'time'—cannot undo."

A profound statement. Yet the girl merely stared at him.

Damn, she annoyed him! Awkward child with skin olive-dark as his own. A Gypsy look. Beautiful dark-luminous eyes. Not-young eyes. Anna was to blame, obscurely he blamed Anna for the girl. Not that he did not love the girl of course. But, who knows why, in a family a mother is blamed sometimes, simply for giving birth.

Another child? I cannot bear it. No.

In the blood-soaked bunk bed, in that windowless "cabin" of unspeakable filth. How easily the infant girl might have been smothered. And what a mercy to smother her. An adult hand pressed over the small wizened face red as a boiled tomato. Before she could draw breath and begin to howl. Before the boys saw, and understood that they had a sister. And in the days of Anna's dazed slovenly nursing she might have been suffocated as well. Might have been dropped onto the floor. Might have been lifted carelessly out of her crib, her disproportionately heavy head not supported on its fragile neck by an adult's protective hand. (His!) The infant might have been taken sick, mucus might have clotted her tiny lungs. Pneumonia. Diphtheria. Nature has provided a wondrous assortment of exits from life. Yet somehow little Rebecca had not perished but survived.

To bring a child into the hellhole of the twentieth century, how could it be borne!

And now she was twelve years old. In her presence, Jacob felt his gnarled heart contract with an emotion he could not define.

It wasn't love, perhaps it was pity. For Rebecca was Jacob's daughter, unmistakably. She more resembled him than either of his sons resembled him. She had his sharp cheekbones, and a widow's peak he'd had (when he'd had more hair). She had his restless hungry eyes. She was intelligent, as he was; and distrustful. So very different from her mother who'd been sweet-faced and pretty as a girl, fair-skinned, with fine, fair-brown hair and a way of laughing that was so delightful, you were drawn to laugh with her at the most trivial things. Long ago when Anna had laughed . . . But Rebecca, their daughter, was not one to laugh. Maybe as a child she'd sensed how close she had come to not-existing. She had a melancholy spirit, and she was stubborn. Like her father. Heavy of heart. Her eyebrows were growing in thick and straight as a man's and never would any man condescend to her by calling her "pretty."

Jacob did not trust females. Schopenhauer knew well: the female is mere flesh, fecundity. The female tempts the (weak, amorous) male into mating, and, against the inclination of his desire, into monogamy. At least, in theory. Always the result is the same: the species is continued. Always the desire, the mating, always the next generation, always the species! Blind brainless insatiable will. Out of their innocent joyous love of a long-ago time had come their firstborn, Herschel: born 1927. And then came August, and at last the little one Rebecca. Each was an individual and yet: the individual scarcely matters, only the species. In the service of that blind will, the secret female softness, moist smells; the folded-in, roseate, *insides* of the female, that a man might penetrate numberless times yet could not perceive or comprehend. Out of the female body had sprung the labyrinth, the maze. The honeycomb with but one way in and no way out.

Well! That his daughter so closely resembled him and yet was a small female seemed to Jacob all the more repellent, for it was as if Jacob Schwart did not fully know himself; and could not trust himself.

Saying, chiding, "Yes. You are ignorant now. You know nothing of this hellhole the world."

He tugged at her arm, he had something to show her, outside.

Telling her how, in the twentieth century, with the actions of Germany and the so-called Axis Powers, all of the effort of civilization from the Greeks onward had been swept aside, with a demonic joy; abandoned and obliterated, in the interests of the beast. The Germans made no secret of it—"The worship of the beast." Not a one of them now living regretted the war, only that they lost the war and were humbled, humiliated; and thwarted in their wish to exterminate their enemies. "Many in this country were of their beliefs, Rebecca. Many here in Milburn. And many Nazis have been protected, and will be protected. None of this you will learn in your schoolbooks. Your ridiculous 'history' books, I have examined. Outwardly now the war is over, since 1945. But only see how this country rewards the warrior Germans. So many millions of dollars given to Germany, lair of the beast! And why, if not to reward them? Inwardly, the war wages. Never will the war end until the last of us has died."

He was excited, his spittle flew. Fortunately, in the open air, Rebecca could avoid being struck by any of it.

"You see, eh? Here."

He'd brought her to the graveled lane that led past the house, into the interior of the cemetery. It was the caretaker's responsibility to maintain this lane, to spread gravel evenly on it; yet, in the night, his enemies had come with a rake or a hoe, to taunt him.

Rebecca was staring at the lane. What was she supposed to see?

"Are you blind, girl? Do you not *see*? How our enemies persecute us?"

For there, unmistakably, were swastikas raked into the gravel, not blatant like the tar-swastikas of Hallowe'en but more devious.

"You *see*?"

Ah, the stubborn child! She stared, and could not reply.

Angrily Jacob dragged his heel through the gravel, destroying the most obvious of the mocking lines.

Months ago, at the time of the initial desecration, he'd exhausted himself removing the tar-markings. He'd scraped tar off the front door of the stone house in a frenzy of loathing and yet!—he had failed to remove it entirely. All he could do was repaint the damned door a somber dark green, except: a large shadowy  was visible beneath the paint, if you looked closely enough. He and Gus had repainted parts of the sheds, and tried to scour the defaced gravestones clean. Still the swastikas remained, if you knew where to look.

"Eh! You are one of *them*."

A senseless remark, he knew even as he uttered it. But he was the father of this child, he might say anything that flew into his head and she must honor it.

His stupid, stubborn daughter unable to see what was before her eyes, at her very feet! He lost patience with her, grabbed her shoulder and shook, shook, shook her until she whimpered with pain. "One of *them*! One of *them*! Now go bawling to your ma!" He flung her from him, onto the lane, the sharp pebbly gravel, and left her there panting and swiping at her nose, staring at him with widened eyes, dilated in terror. He stalked off cursing to get a rake to erase the taunting swastikas, another time.

Dybbuks! He had not thought of it.

He was a man of reason, of course he had not thought of such a thing. And yet.

A *dybbuk*, cunning and agile as a snake, could take over a weak-minded female. In the Munich zoo he'd seen an extraordinary eight-foot snake, a cobra, so amazingly supple, moving in what appeared to be a continuous stream, like water; the snake "running" on its numerous ribs, inside its scaly, glittering, rather beautiful skin. His eyes rolled in his head, almost he felt faint, imagining how the snake-dybbuk would enter the female.

Up between the legs, and inside.

For he could not trust either of them: wife, daughter.

As a man of reason he did not want to believe in dybbuks and yet perhaps that was the explanation. Dybbuks had come alive, out of the primeval mud of Europe. And here in Milburn. Prowling the cemetery, and the countryside beyond. Dybbuks rising like mist out of the tall damp grasses that shivered in the wind. Snakeroot, cattails. Dybbuks blown by the wind against the loose-fitting windows of the old stone house, scratching their claws against the glass, desperate to gain entry. And dybbuks seeking entry into human bodies in which the souls are loose-fitting, primitive.

Anna. His wife of twenty-three years. Could he trust Anna, in her femaleness?

Like her body, Anna's mind had softened with time. She had never fully recovered from the third pregnancy, the anguish of that third birth. In fact she had never fully recovered from their panicked flight from Germany.

She blamed him, he felt. That he was her husband and a man, and yet not a man to protect her and their children.

Yet in the night, another Anna came alive. In her sleep, in her lustful dreams. Ah, he knew! He heard her groaning, breathing rapidly. He felt her flesh-tremors. Their bed reeked with her sweat, her female secretions. By day she turned from him, averting her eyes. As he averted his eyes from her nakedness. She had never loved him, he supposed. For hers had been a girl's soul, shallow and easily swayed by emotion. In their circle of young people in Munich, Anna had laughed and flirted with many young men; you could see how they were attracted to her, and she had basked in their attention. Now he could acknowledge, Jacob Schwart had been but one of these. Perhaps she had loved another, who had not loved her. And there came Jacob Schwart, blinded by love. Begging her to marry him. On their wedding night he had not known to ask himself *Is my bride a virgin? Is hers a virgin-love?* The act of love had been overwhelming to Jacob, explosive, annihilating. He'd had so little experience. He had had no judgment, and would have none for years.

It was on the ocean crossing that the dybbuk-Anna had first emerged. She'd been delirious, muttering and raving and striking at him with her fists. Her eyes held no love for him, nor even recognition. Demon eyes, tawny-glowing eyes! The coarsest German profanities and obscenities had leapt from Anna's lips, not those of an innocent young wife and mother but the words of a demon, a dybbuk.

That day he'd found Anna in the shed. Hiding there, with the little one wrapped in a dirty shawl. *Would you like me to strangle her?* Had she been serious, or taunting him?—he had not known.

Now, he could not trust Anna to prepare their meals correctly. It was her practice to boil their well water, for very likely the well water was contaminated, and yet he knew, she was careless and indifferent. And so they were being poisoned, by degrees. And he could not trust her with other men. Any man who saw Anna saw at once her femaleness, as evident as nakedness. For there was something slatternly and erotic in Anna's soft, raddled body and slack girl's face; her moist, brainless gaze that excited masculine desire, even as it revulsed.

The sheriff's deputies, for instance. Since Herschel's disappearance they came by the house from time to time, to make inquiries. Jacob wasn't always home when they came, Anna had to answer the door and speak to them. Jacob was coming to suspect, these inquiries might be mere pretense.

Often there were men wandering in the cemetery, amid the graves. Seemingly visiting the graves. Mourners. Or assuming that role.

Anna Schwart had become devious, defiant. He knew she'd disobeyed him by daring to turn on his radio, more than once. He had never caught her, for she was too clever; yet he knew. Now the radio tubes were burnt out and would not be replaced, so no one could listen to the damned radio. There was that satisfaction, at least.

(Jacob had loosened the radio tubes himself. To thwart Anna. Then he'd forgotten he had loosened them. When he switched on the radio now, there was silence.)

And there was Rebecca, his daughter.

Her lanky body was filling out, taking on the contours of the female. Through a part-closed door he'd glimpsed her, washing her upper body with an expression of frowning concentration. The shock of the girl's small, startlingly white breasts, the nipples small as grape seeds. Her underarms that were sprouting fine dark hairs, and her legs . . . He had known that he could no longer trust her, when she'd refused to acknowledge the swastika marks raked in the lane. And years before, when he'd discovered her picture in the Milburn newspaper. Spelling champion! *Rebecca Esther Schwart!* The first he'd heard of such a thing. She had kept it secret from him, and from Anna.

The girl would grow up swiftly, he knew. Once she'd begun school she had begun to turn into one of *those others*. He had seen her with the slatternly Greb girl. She would grow up, she would leave him. A man must surrender his daughter to another man unless he claims her for his own, which is forbidden.

"And so I must harden my heart against them both."

From the proprietor of the Milburn Feed Store he would acquire secondhand a Remington twelve-gauge double-barrel shotgun, a bargain at seventy-five dollars.

Five dollars more for a near-full box of fifty shells.

For hunting, Mr. Schwart?

For protection of my property.

Pheasant season isn't till fall. Second week of October.

Protection of my home. My family.

It's got a kick, a twelve-gauge.

My wife, my daughter. We are alone out there. The sheriff will not protect us. We are alone in the country. We are U.S. citizens.

A good gun for protection if you know how to use it. Remember it has a kick, Mr. Schwart.

A kick?

In the shoulder. If you grip the stock too loosely when you pull the trigger. If you are not practiced. A kick like a mule.

Jacob Schwart laughed heartily, baring nicotine-stained teeth in a happy smile. *Kick like a mule, eh? Well! I am a mule.*

"Fools! There was no one."

Sometime in the slow dripping spring of 1949 the realization came to him. His deepest contempt wasn't for the ignorant peasants who surrounded him but for the elderly Jews of his long-ago youth in skullcaps and prayer shawls muttering to their ridiculous god.

An extinct volcano god Yehovah.

In the night such truths came to him. He sat in the kitchen or in the doorway of the house, drinking. Exclusively now he drank hard cider from the mill down the road, that was cheap, and potent. The shotgun close by. In case of prowlers, vandals. He had no fear of the dead. A dybbuk is not dead. A dybbuk is fierce with life, insatiable. In this place where the tide of history had washed him ashore and abandoned him like trash. Yet his deepest contempt was for the bearded black-clad troll-elders of his long-ago boyhood in Munich. Cruelly he laughed seeing the sick terror in their eyes as at last they understood.

"No one, you see? God is no one, and nowhere."

And Jacob Schwart was not a son of that tribe.

24

❁ ❁ ❁

As if she'd only just thought of it, Katy Greb said, "You could stay with me, Rebecca. Sleep in my bed, there's room."

Always Katy spoke with the impulsiveness of one for whom there is no hesitation between a wish and its immediate expression.

Rebecca stammered she didn't know.

"Sure! Momma won't mind, Momma likes you real well."

Momma likes you real well.

So touched, Rebecca couldn't speak at first. Wasn't watching where she was walking, stubbed her toe on a rock at the side of the Quarry Road.

Katy Greb was the only girl to whom Rebecca had said certain private things.

Katy was the only girl who knew how frightened Rebecca was of her father.

"Not what he'd do to me. But to Ma. Some night when he's drunk."

Katy grunted as if such a revelation, daring for Rebecca to make, was no surprise to *her*.

"My pa, he's the same way. Except he ain't around right now, so Ma misses him."

The girls laughed together. You had to laugh at older people, they were so ridiculous.

Of course there was no room for Rebecca in the Grebs' ramshackle wood-frame house. No room for a twelve-year-old girl, almost thirteen, tall for her age, awkward and brooding.

Somehow it had happened, in seventh grade, that Katy Greb was Rebecca's closest (secret) friend. Katy was a big-boned girl with straw-hair and teeth that smelled like brackish ditch water and a face big and florid as a sunflower. Her laughter was high-pitched and contagious. Her breasts were jiggly nubs in her chest like fists bunched up inside her hand-me-down sweaters.

Katy was a year older than Rebecca, but in Rebecca's seventh grade homeroom at the Milburn junior high. She was Rebecca's (secret) friend because neither Rebecca's father nor Rebecca's mother approved of her having friends. *Those others* who could not be trusted.

Rebecca wished that Katy was her sister. Or she was Katy's sister. Living then with the Grebs, and only just neighbors of the Schwarts who lived a half-mile away.

Katy was always saying how her momma believed that Rebecca was a "good influence" on her because Rebecca took her school studies seriously and didn't "horse around" like the other kids.

Rebecca laughed as if she'd been tickled. It wasn't true but she loved to hear that Mrs. Greb spoke of her in such a flattering way. It was like Leora Greb to say extravagant things based on not much evidence. "Horse around" was a common expression of hers, almost you could see young horses galloping and frolicking in a field.

The Grebs were the Schwarts' closest neighbors on the Quarry Road. Leora Greb had five children of whom the two youngest appeared to be retarded. A seven-year-old boy still in diapers, not yet potty-trained. A six-year-old girl whimpering and jabbering in frustration at being unable to speak as others did. The Grebs' house was partly covered in asphalt siding, close by the dump. Worse than where the Schwarts live, Rebecca thought. When the wind blew from the direction of the dump there was a sickish stink of garbage and smoldering tires in the Grebs' house.

Katy's father Bud Greb, whom Rebecca had never seen, was said to be away at Plattsburgh, at the Canadian border. *Incarcerated* at the men's maximum security prison there.

In-car-cer-ated. An unexpected dignity accrued to these syllables, when Bud Greb was spoken of.

What a surprise for Rebecca, to learn that Leora Greb wasn't any younger than Anna Schwart! Rebecca did the calculations, both women were in their early forties. And yet, how different they were: Leora's hair was an eye-catching blond, she wore makeup that gave her a youthful, glamorous look, her eyes were alert, laughing. Even with Mr. Greb away at Plattsburgh (his sentence was seven-to-ten, for armed robbery) Leora was likely to be in a good mood most days.

Leora was a part-time chambermaid at the General Washington Hotel in Milburn, which called itself the "premiere" hotel in this part of the Chautauqua Valley. The General Washington was a large boxy building with a granite facade, white-shuttered windows, and a painted sign at the front meant to depict General Washington's head, his tight-curled hair like a sheep's and his big-jawed face, in some long-ago improbable year 1776. Leora was always bringing back from the General Washington cellophane packages of peanuts, pretzels, potato chips that had been opened by patrons in the tavern but not depleted.

Leora was one to utter wise sayings. A favorite was a variant of Jacob Schwart's: "Waste not, want not."

Another, spoken with a downturn smirk of her mouth: "You made your bed, now lie in it."

Leora drove a 1945 Dodge sedan left in her care by the incarcerated Bud Greb and sometimes, in one of her good moods, she could be prevailed upon to drive Katy and Rebecca into town, or along the Chautauqua River to Drottstown and back.

What was puzzling about Leora Greb, that Rebecca had yet to fully comprehend, was: she seemed to like her family, crowded together in that house. Leora seemed to like her life!

Katy acknowledged they did miss their pa, sometimes. But it was a whole lot easier without him. Not so much fighting, and friends of his hanging out at the house, and the cops showing up in the middle of the damn night shining their lights through the windows scaring the shit out of everybody.

"What they do, they yell through a bullhorn. Y'ever heard one of them?"

Rebecca shook her head, no. She wasn't planning on hearing one if she could help it.

Katy told Rebecca, with the air of one confiding a secret, that Leora had boyfriends, guys she met at the hotel. "We ain't supposed to know but hell, we do."

These men gave Leora things, or left things in their hotel rooms for her, Leora passed on to her daughters. Or they'd give her actual money which was, in Leora's voice, that was lyric and teasing as a radio voice, "Al-ways wel-come."

It was true, Leora drank sometimes and could be a real bitch picking and nagging her kids. But mostly she was so nice.

Asking Rebecca one day, out of the blue it seemed, "There ain't any-thing wrong over at your place, hon, is there?"

Five of them were playing cards at the Grebs' kitchen table covered in sticky oilcloth. At first, just Katy and Rebecca were playing double solitaire which was a fad at school. Then Leora came home, and got the younger kids, for a game of gin rummy. Rebecca was new to the game but picked it up quickly.

Basking in Leora's casual praise she had a *natural ap'tude* for cards.

Rebecca had to adjust, what to expect of a family. What to expect of a mother. At first it shocked her how the Grebs crowded together at the table, jostling one another and laughing over the silliest things. Leora could get in a mood, she wasn't much different from Katy and Rebecca. Except she smoked, one cigarette after the other; and drank Black Horse ale straight from the bottle. (Yet her mannerisms were fussy, ladylike. Stick-ing out her little finger as she lifted the bottle to her mouth.) Rebecca squirmed to think what Anna Schwart would say of such a woman.

And the way Leora snorted with laughter when the cards turned against her, as if bad luck was some kind of joke.

Leora dealt first. Next, Katy. Then Conroy, Katy's eleven-year-old brother. Then Molly who was only ten. Then Rebecca who was self-conscious at first, fumbling the cards in her excitement at being included in the game.

She was surprised by Leora's casual question. She mumbled something vague meant to convey *no*.

Leora said, briskly dealing out cards, "Well, O.K. I'm real glad to hear that, Rebecca."

It was an awkward time. Rebecca was close to crying. But Rebecca would not cry. Katy said, that whiny edge to her voice, "I told Rebecca, Momma, she could stay with us. If she didn't, y'know, want to go home. Some night."

There was a buzzing in Rebecca's head. Must've told Katy some things she had not meant to tell. How she was afraid of her father, sometimes. How she missed her brothers and wished they'd taken her with them.

Rebecca's exact words had been reckless, extravagant. Like somebody in a comic strip she'd said *Wished they'd taken me with them to Hell if that's where they went*.

Leora said, exhaling smoke through her nostrils, "That Herschel! He was a real character, I always favored Herschel. *Is* a real character, I mean. He's alive, ain't he?"

Rebecca was stunned by the question. For a moment she could not respond.

"I mean to ask, did you people hear from him? That you know?"

Rebecca mumbled *no*. Not that she knew.

" 'Course if your pa heard from Herschel, he might not tell you. Might not want word to get out. Account of, y'know, Herschel's *fugitive status*."

This was a term, both alarming and thrilling, Rebecca had never heard before: *fugitive status*.

Leora went on in her rambling way, to speak of Herschel. Katy said of her mother if you listened to her she'd tell you plenty, a lot of it maybe not intended. It was a revelation to Rebecca, Leora seemed to know Herschel so well. Even Bud Greb had known Herschel, before being sent away to prison. And Herschel had even played gin rummy and poker, right here at this table!

Rebecca was moved, to see how her brother was known to people in ways not-known to his family. It was a strange thing, you could live close to somebody and not know as much about him as others did. It made Rebecca miss him all the more, though his way of teasing had not been nice. Leora was saying, with girlish vehemence, "What Herschel did, hon, those bastards deserved. Taking the damn law in your own hands sometimes you got to do."

Katy agreed. So did Conroy.

Rebecca wiped at her eyes. It made her want to cry, Leora saying such things about her brother.

Like shifting a mirror, just a little. You see an edge to something, an angle of vision you had not known. Such a surprise!

At school, nobody ever said a nice thing about Herschel. Only he was a *fugitive from justice, wanted by the police* and he'd be sent to Attica for sure where Ne-gro prisoners from Buffalo would cut him up good, himself. Get what he deserved.

The game continued. Slap-slap-slap of sticky cards. Leora offered Rebecca a sip of her ale and Rebecca declined at first then said O.K. and choked a little swallowing the strong liquid and the others laughed, but not meanly. Then Rebecca heard herself say, as if to surprise, "My pa's some damn old drunk, I hate him."

Rebecca expected Katy to burst into giggles as Katy always did when a girlfriend complained in harsh comic tones of her family. It was what you did! But here in the Grebs' kitchen something was wrong, Leora stared hard at her holding an uplifted card and Rebecca knew to her shame that she'd misspoken.

Leora shifted her Chesterfield from one hand to the other, scattering ashes. Must've been the Black Horse ale that had provoked Rebecca to utter such words, making her want to choke and laugh at the same time.

"Your pa," Leora said thoughtfully, "is a man hard to fathom. People say. I would not claim to fathom Joseph Schwart."

Joseph! Leora didn't even know Rebecca's father's name.

Rebecca shrank, in shame. The harsh monosyllable *Schwart* was stinging to hear. To know that others might utter it, might speak of her father in a way both impersonal and familiar, was shocking to her.

Yet Rebecca heard herself say, half in defiance, "You don't have to 'fathom' him, I'm the one. And Ma."

Carefully Leora said, not looking at Rebecca now, "What about your ma, Rebecca? She keeps to herself, eh?"

Rebecca laughed, a harsh mirthless sound.

Katy said, to Leora, in a whiny triumphant voice as if the two had been arguing, and this was the crushing point, "Momma, see? I told R'becca she can stay with us. If she needs to."

Too slowly, Leora sucked on what remained of her cigarette.

"Well . . ."

Rebecca had been smiling. All this while, smiling. The hot sour liquid she'd swallowed was a gaseous bubble in her gut, she could feel it and worried she might vomit it back up. Her cheeks were burning as if they'd been slapped.

All this while, Conroy and Molly were fiddling with their cards, oblivious of this exchange. They had not the slightest awareness that Rebecca Schwart had betrayed her parents, nor that Katy had put it to Leora, with Rebecca as a witness, that Rebecca might come live with them, and Leora was hesitant, unwilling to agree. Not the slightest awareness! Conroy was a large-boned child with sniffles and a nasty habit of wiping his nose every few minutes on the back of his hand and the mean thought came to Rebecca *If he was mine, I'd strangle him* and the wish to tell this to Leora was so strong, Rebecca had to grip her cards tight.

Hearts, diamonds, clubs . . . Trying to make sense of what she'd been dealt.

Can a king of hearts save you? Ten of clubs? Queen-and-jack pair? Wished she had seven cards in the same suit, she'd lay them down on the table with a flourish. The Grebs would be goggle-eyed!

Wanting nothing more than to keep playing rummy forever with Katy's family. Laughing, making wisecracks, sipping ale and when Leora invited her to stay for supper Rebecca would say with true regret *Thanks but I can't, I guess, they want me back home* but instead there was Rebecca tossing down her cards suddenly, some of them falling onto the floor, Rebecca pushed her chair away from the table skidding and noisy, God damn if she was going to cry! Fuck the Grebs if they expected that.

"I hate you, too! You can all go to hell!"

Before anyone could say a word, Rebecca slammed out the screen door. Running, stumbling out to the road. Inside, the Grebs must have stared after her, astonished.

There came Katy's voice, almost too faint to be heard, "Rebecca? Hey c'mon back, what's wrong?"

Never. She would not.

In April, this was. The week after Gus left.

My pa's some damn old drunk, I hate him.

She could not believe she had uttered those words. For all the Grebs to hear!

Of course they would tell everyone. Even Katy who liked Rebecca would tell everyone with ears.

At school, forever afterward Rebecca ignored Katy Greb. Would not look at Katy Greb. In the morning, her strategy was to wait until Katy and the others were out of sight walking along the road, before she followed behind them; or, she took one of her secret routes through fields and pine woods and, her favorite, along the railroad embankment that was elevated by five feet. So happy! She was a young horse galloping, her legs so springy and strong, she laughed aloud out of very happiness, she could run-run-run forever arriving reluctantly at school, nerved-up, sweaty, itching for a fight, bad as Herschel wanting somebody to look at her cross-eyed or mouth *Gravedigger!* or some bullshit like that, Christ she was too restless to calm down to fit into a desk! Herschel had said he'd have liked to break the damn desk, squeezing his knees under and lifting, exerting his muscles, and Rebecca felt the same way, exactly.

"Hey, R'becca—"

Go to hell. Leave me alone.

Hatred for Katy Greb and for Leora Greb and all of the Grebs and many others became a strange, potent consolation, like sucking something bitter.

Hardening her heart against dopey Katy Greb. Friendly good-natured not-too-bright girl who'd been Rebecca Schwart's closest friend from third grade on, till Katy stared at Rebecca in hurt, in bewilderment, and finally in resentment and dislike. "Fuck you too, Schwart. Fuck *you*."

A group of girls, Katy at the center. Smiling in scorn speaking of Rebecca Schwart.

Well, Rebecca had wanted this, didn't she? Wanted them to hate her and leave her alone.

All that spring, their enmity wafted after her like the stink of smoldering rubber *Gravedigger's daughter she can go fuck herself.*

25

❀ ❀ ❀

"Ma? Ma—"

In the end she would not need to run away from home. It was her home
that would expel her. Always she would recall that irony: her punishment
at last.

May 11, 1949. A weekday. She'd stayed away after school for as long as
she'd dared. In dread of returning home as if sensing beforehand what
awaited.

She called for her mother. Her voice rose in childish terror. She was
panicked stumbling to the front door that was partly open . . . The crude
wooden door he'd painted over after the Hallowe'en vandalism in thick
furious swaths of dark green paint to obscure the markings beneath that
could not be obscured. "Ma . . . ? It's me." Beyond a corner of the house as
if in mockery of her alarm was a vision of laundry on the clothesline,
frayed towels and a sheet stirring in the wind and so it was logical for Rebecca who believed in magical thinking to tell herself *If Ma has hung out
wash today . . .*

. . . if today, laundry on the line, Ma's washday . . .

Still she was short of breath. She'd been running. From the Quarry
Road, she'd been running. It was hours after school had ended for the
day. It was near six o'clock, and still the sun was prominent in the sky.
Her heart was pounding in her chest like a deranged bell. As an animal
smells fear, injured flesh, spilled blood she knew instinctively that something had happened.

At the edge of her blurred vision, in the interior of the cemetery, some distance away a car or cars were parked on the graveled lane and so she'd thought possibly there had been a funeral, and something had gone wrong, and Jacob Schwart had been blamed through no fault of his. Even as she was plunging toward the front door of the house. Even as she was hearing raised voices. With childish obstinacy not wishing to hear a woman crying, "Don't go in there!—stop her!"

She was thinking of her mother Anna. Her mother trapped in that house.

For how could Rebecca not enter, knowing that her mother was inside, trapped.

Ask God why: why such things are allowed. Not me.

In that spring, that season of desultory and defiant wandering. Like a stray dog she wandered. Reluctant to return to the stone house in the cemetery which she would one day recall having been built into the side of a massive hill like a cellar or a sepulchre though in fact it was neither, only just a weatherworn stone-and-stucco dwelling with few windows, and those windows small, and square, and coated on the outside with a near-opaque winter grime.

Hating to return to the house though she knew her mother was waiting for her. Hating to return since Herschel had left, since Gus had left hitching a ride with a trucker bound for somewhere west. Both her brothers had left without a word, not a word of affection or regret or explanation or even farewell for their sister who'd loved them. Now in fury thinking *I hate them, both of them. Fuckers!*

This angry language she was beginning to savor. At first under her breath, and then aloud. A pulse beat hard and hot in her throat in the angry joy of hating her brothers who'd abandoned her and their mother to the madman Jacob Schwart.

She knew: her father was mad. Yet not raving-mad, not helpless-mad, so that someone in authority might come to help them.

Yet: *they know, but they don't care. Even that he has bought a shotgun, they don't care. For why should they think of us, who are but jokes to them.*

One day soon, Rebecca would run away, too. She didn't require Katy

Greb to take her in. Didn't require anyone to take her in or feel sorry for her. *Fuckers* they were all of them, she turned from them in scorn.

After the spring thaw it became increasingly difficult for Rebecca to stay in school for a full day. More and more she found herself abruptly walking out. Scarcely knowing what she did only that she could not bear the stifling classrooms, the cafeteria that smelled of milk and scorched and greasy food, the corridors in which her classmates passed jostling one another like brainless, blind animals rushing through a chute. She walked out a rear exit not caring who might be watching and would report her. If an adult voice called after her stern and admonishing—*Rebecca! Rebecca Schwart where are you going!*—she didn't trouble even to glance back but broke into a run.

Her grades were mostly C's and D's now. Even in English, that had been her best subject. Her teachers had grown wary of her as you'd be wary of a cornered rat.

Like her brothers, Rebecca Schwart was becoming. This girl who'd once been so promising . . .

Run, run! Through the weedy vacant lot adjacent to the school, along a street of brownstone row houses and small shops, into an alley, and so to an open field and the Buffalo & Chautauqua railroad embankment which she would follow downtown to Canal Street. The Canal Street bridge, off South Main, was so wide that parking was allowed on it. Where the taverns were. A block away on its peak of a hill was the General Washington Hotel. Several streets including South Main converged here at the bridge. In Milburn, all hills sloped down to the Erie Barge Canal and the canal itself had been out through bedrock, into the interior of the earth. At the bridge idle men leaned on the railings thirty feet above the rushing water, smoking, sometimes sipping from bottles hidden inside paper bags. This was a slipping-down place, a place inclined to muteness, like a cemetery where things came to rest.

Why Rebecca was drawn here, she could not have said. She kept her distance from strangers.

Some of the men were war veterans. There was a man of about Jacob Schwart's age on crutches, with a melted-away face. Another wore thick glasses with one of the lenses blacked out, so you knew he was missing an eye. Others had faces that were not-old and yet deeply lined, ravaged. There were tremulous hands, stiffened necks and legs. An obese man with a stump-knee sometimes sprawled on a concrete ledge in good weather, sunning himself like a reptile, repulsive and yet fascinating to observe. His hair was gray-grizzled and thin as Jacob Schwart's hair and if Rebecca dared to draw close she could hear the man's hoarse, moist breathing that was like her father's breathing when he was agitated. Once, she saw that the reptile-man had wakened from his slumber and was observing her, with a sly little smile, through quivering eyelids. She wanted to turn quickly away, but could not. She believed that, if she ran, the reptile-man would become angry and call after her and everyone would see.

There were no more than twelve feet separating them. Rebecca could not comprehend how she'd dared to come so close.

"No school today, girlie? Eh? 'Sa holiday, eh?"

He was teasing, though with an air of threat. As if he might report her for truancy.

Rebecca said nothing. She was leaning against the bridge railing, staring down at the water far below. In the countryside, the canal was flat and placid-seeming; here at the forty-foot lock, the current was swift and perilous, rushing over the lock in ceaseless agitation, churning, frothy, making a noise like wildfire. Almost, you could not hear the sound of traffic on the bridge. You could not hear the metallic chiming of the hour from the bell tower at the First Bank of Chautauqua. You could not hear another's voice unless he spoke loudly, provocatively.

"I'm talkin to you, girlie. 'Sa holiday is it?"

Still Rebecca did not reply. Nor did she turn away. In the corner of her eye she saw him, sprawled in the sun, panting. He chuckled and rubbed his hands over his groin that looked fattish, like a goiter.

"I see you, girlie! And you see me."

Run, run! That spring of 1949.

Always Milburn had been an old country town, you could see where post-war newness was taking hold. The gaunt red-brick facades of Main Street were being replaced by sleek modern buildings with plate glass windows. In some of the newer buildings were revolving doors, elevators. The old Milburn post office, cabin-sized, would be replaced by a beige-brick post office that shared its quarters with the YM-YWCA. Grovers Feed Mill, Midtown Lumber, Jos. Miller Dry Goods were being crowded out by Montgomery Ward, Woolworth's, Norban's, a new A & P with its own as-phalt parking lot. (Jos. Miller Dry Goods had been the store to which Re-becca had come with her mother, to select material for the curtains Anna Schwart sewed in preparation for the Morgensterns' visit nearly eight years before. Rebecca's father had driven them into town in the caretaker's pickup truck. It had been a rare outing for Anna Schwart, and her last. It had been the only time that Rebecca had been brought into town with her mother and she would afterward recall that trip and the excitement of that trip with faint disbelief even as, staring at the site of the old store, replaced now by another, she was having difficulty recalling it.)

Only just recently, Adams Bros. Haberdashery had been replaced by Thom McAn Shoes. An impressive new bank had been built kitty-corner from the First Bank of Chautauqua, calling itself New Milburn Savings & Loan. The General Washington Hotel had begun expansion and renova-tion. There was a newly refurbished Capitol Theater with its splendid mar-quee that gleamed and glittered by night. A five-storey office building (doctors, dentists, lawyers) was erected at Main and Seneca streets, the first of its kind in Milburn.

(To this building Jacob Schwart had allegedly come, in the spring of 1949. It would be told of how he'd entered a lawyer's office on the ground floor without an appointment and insisted upon "presenting his case" to the astonished young lawyer; Mr. Schwart had been rambling, incoherent, alternately incensed and resigned, claiming that he had been cheated for twelve years of his "due merit" by the Milburn Township which refused to pay him decent wages and had rejected others of his requests.)

On South Main Street, the taverns were little changed. Like the pool hall, the bowling alleys, Reddings Smoke Shop. At the Army-Navy Discount on Erie Street, a tunnel-like store with oppressively bright lighting and crowded shelves and counters, you could buy camouflage jackets and trousers, long woollen underwear, soldiers' infantry boots and sailors' caps, cowhide ammunition pouches marketed as purses for high school girls.

When she'd been friends with Katy Greb, Rebecca had often come into the Army-Navy store with Katy, for things were always "on sale" here. The girls drifted also into Woolworth's, Norban's, Montgomery Ward. Rarely to buy, mostly to look. Without Katy, Rebecca no longer dared to enter these stores. She knew how the salesclerks' eyes would shift upon her, in suspicion and dislike. For she had an Indian look to her. (There was a Seneca reservation north of Chautauqua Falls.) Yet she was drawn to gaze into the display windows. So much! So many things! And a girl's wan, ghostly reflection super-imposed upon them, magically.

The loneliness of the solitary life. Consoling herself she was invisible, no one cared enough to see her.

Only once, Rebecca happened to see her father in Milburn. Downtown, as he was crossing a side street en route to the First Bank of Chautauqua.

Out of nowhere Jacob Schwart had seemed to emerge, exuding a strange dark radiance. A troll-man, broken-backed and limping, in soiled work clothes and a cloth cap that looked as if they'd been hacked out of a substance harsher than mere cloth; making his way along the sidewalk with no apparent awareness of how others, glancing at him in curiosity and alarm, stepped out of his way.

Rebecca shrank back, stepping into an alley. Oh, she knew! She must not let Pa see her.

Herschel had warned *Don't let the old bastid see you, anywhere outside the house. 'Cause if he does he flies off the handle like some nut. Says you're followin him, spyin on him to tell Ma what he's doin, crazy shit like that.*

This was in April 1949. At the time Jacob Schwart closed out his savings account and bought the twelve-gauge double-barreled shotgun and the box of shells.

That day, May 11. Could not bear going to school and instead she wandered along the railway embankment, and so to the canal towpath. An acrid odor blew from the direction of the dump, she avoided it by crossing the canal at the Drumm Road bridge. There, beneath the bridge, was one of Rebecca's hiding places.

Hate hate hate them both of them. Wish they were dead.

Both of them. And then I would . . .

But what would she do? Run away as her brothers had done? Where?

Such thoughts came to her, mutinous and exciting, beneath the Drumm Road bridge where she crouched amid boulders and rocks, old rusted pipes, broken concrete, metal rods protruding from the shallow water near shore. This was debris from the bridge's construction twenty years before.

She was thirteen now. Her birthday had gone unremarked in the stone house in the cemetery, as so much else there went unremarked.

She liked being thirteen. She wanted to be older, as her brothers were older. She was impatient with remaining a child, trapped in that house. She hadn't yet begun to bleed, to have "periods"—"cramps"—as Katy and other girls did each month. She knew it must happen to her soon and what she dreaded most about it was having to tell Ma. For Ma would have to know, and Ma would be deeply embarrassed and even resentful, having to know.

Rebecca had grown apart from Anna Schwart, since Herschel's disappearance. She believed that her mother no longer listened to music on the radio, for Pa claimed that the radio was broken. Rebecca had not listened with her mother in so long, she would come to wonder if she'd ever listened.

Piano music. Beethoven. But what had been the name of the sonata— a name like "Passionata"?

She must go home, soon. It was beginning to be late afternoon, Ma was awaiting her. Always there were household tasks but predominantly Anna Schwart wanted her daughter home. Not to speak with her and certainly not to touch her, scarcely even to look at her. But to know that Rebecca was home, and safe.

On the underside of the plank bridge were ravishing faces! Ghost-faces reflected upward from the rippling water below. Rebecca stared at these faces that were often those of her lost cousins Freyda, Elzbieta, Joel. And more recently the faces of Herschel and Gus. Dreamily she observed them, and wondered if they could see her.

She'd known why her brothers had disappeared, but she had not known why her cousins and their parents had been sent back to the old world. To die there, Pa had said. Like animals.

Why? Ask God why.

Ask that hypocrite F.D.R. why!

Rebecca recalled her dolls Maggie and Minnie. One of the dolls had been Freyda's doll. The memory was so vivid, Maggie cuddled in Freyda's arms, almost Rebecca believed it must have been so.

Both Maggie and Minnie had disappeared a long time ago. Very likely, Ma had disposed of them. Ma had a way of disposing of things when *it was time*. She had no other need to explain herself, nor would Rebecca have wished to ask.

Minnie, the sad ugly bald rubber doll, had been Rebecca's doll. Minnie was so debased, you could not injure her further. There was a comfort in that! Hairless as a wizened baby. A corpse-baby. (In the cemetery, there were corpse-babies buried. Of course Rebecca had not seen any of these but she knew there were baby-sized coffins, in baby-sized plots. Often these dead had no names except Baby.) Rebecca winced to think she'd ever been so childish, to play with dolls. Katy's retarded sister, a child with fat cheeks and glassy staring eyes, was always hugging an old bald doll in a way pathetic and repulsive to see. Katy said with a shrug, she thinks it's real.

Except for the ghost-faces, the underside of the Drumm Road bridge was ugly. There were rusted girders and big screws and massive spider-webs. That look of the underside of things, like skeletons you are not meant to see.

On days of bright sunshine, like this day, the shadows beneath the bridge were sharp and cutting.

Often it was said of the Erie Barge Canal it's deeper than it appears. Sometimes, in the heat of summer, the canal looks as if you could walk on its surface opaque as lead.

My good girl who is all I have, I must trust you.

And so, how could Rebecca run away from home? She could not.

Now that Herschel and Gus were gone, she was Anna Schwart's only child remaining.

A girl, you must not wander alone. You don't want something to happen to you.

"God damn I do. I do want something to happen to me. I *do*."

How Anna would stare at her, astonished and hurt.

A farmer's flatbed truck was approaching the bridge. Rebecca clamped her arms over her head, stiffening. There came a clattering noise, the bridge shuddered and vibrated not ten feet above Rebecca's head. Bits of grit and dust sifted downward.

On her way home, on Quarry Road, she heard gunfire.

Hunters. Often there were hunters, in the scrubby pine woods along Quarry Road.

Never would Rebecca know. But Rebecca would imagine.

How to the Milburn Township Cemetery in the late afternoon of May 11, 1949 there had come two brothers, Elroy and Willis Simcoe, with their sixty-six-year-old aunt. They had come to visit their parents' grave site, that was marked with a heavy, handsome granite stone engraved with the words THY KINGDOM COME THY WILL BE DONE. Elroy Simcoe who was an insurance agent in Milburn and a longtime member of the Township board had lived in Milburn all his life, Willis had moved to the small city of Strykersville forty miles to the west. The Simcoe brothers were well known in the area. They were middle-aged, paunchy, and nattily dressed. They wore sport coats and white cotton shirts open at the throat. Elroy had driven his brother and aunt to the cemetery in a new-model gray Oldsmobile shaped like a box car. As soon as they passed through the cemetery gate they began to notice that the grounds were not so fastidiously kept as one might wish. A profusion of dandelions was in bloom, tall thistles had sprung up around the gravestones. An erratic swath had been mowed through grass with a look of drunken abandon or contempt and, most jarring to the eye, there were piles of soil heaped beside the newer graves like refuse that should have been carted away.

A fallen tree limb lay slantwise across the graveled drive. In a very bad mood, Willis Simcoe climbed out of the Oldsmobile to drag the limb aside.

As Elroy drove on, he and his brother noticed the cemetery caretaker working with a small scythe, not very energetically, about fifty feet from the graveled drive. Elroy did not slow the Oldsmobile, there was no exchange of words at this point. The workman, whose name was known to Elroy Simcoe as "Schwart," did not so much as glance up as the Simcoes passed by, his back to them.

Of course he was aware. Jacob Schwart was aware. Of all visitors to the cemetery, Jacob Schwart was keenly aware.

At the elder Simcoe's grave, the brothers and their elderly aunt were shocked to see untrimmed grasses and dandelions. Pots of hyacinth and geraniums that had been lovingly placed about the grave on Easter Sunday, not long before, now lay on their sides, broken and dessicated.

Elroy Simcoe, a short-tempered man, cupped his hands to his mouth to call over to the caretaker, "You, Schwart!" Elroy meant to *chew him out* as Elroy would later testify. But the caretaker, his back still turned, refused to so much as glance around. Elroy called, in a louder voice, "Mr. Schwart! I'm talking to you, sir!" His sarcasm seemed to be lost on the caretaker, who continued to ignore him.

Though laying down the scythe in the grass, for the last time. Retreating without haste, or a backward glance. And limping Schwart went to a storage shed adjacent to the caretaker's stone house and disappeared inside it and shortly afterward reappeared now limping purposefully in the direction of the Simcoes in the interior of the cemetery and now—so unexpectedly!—pushing a wheelbarrow with a strip of canvas tossed over its contents, bump-bump-bump through the grass! And no turning back now! *Knowing what must be done. Now his enemies had begun their attack, no longer surreptitiously but openly*. As Jacob Schwart approached the Simcoe brothers who stood watching him pushing the wheelbarrow apparently in their direction, watching the peculiar little troll-man with expressions of bemusement and irritation, there may have been harsh words exchanged. Elroy Simcoe, the surviving brother, and his elderly aunt would later testify that Jacob Schwart was the one to speak first, his face contorted with rage: "Nazi murderers! No more!" At this point both Simcoe brothers shouted at him, seeing the man was mad; and suddenly, with no warning, when Schwart had pushed the wheelbarrow to within twelve feet of Willis Simcoe, he pulled the canvas away and lifted a shotgun that looked massive in his diminutive hands, aimed it at Willis and in virtually the same moment pulled the trigger.

The stricken man would die of a gaping wound in the chest. His right forearm, lifted in a futile attempt to protect his torso, would be blasted away, white bones protruding through mangled flesh.

Now you see, eh! Now! The pogrom is done.

She was calling, "Ma? Ma—" childish and pleading.

Somehow she'd entered the stone house. Knowing perhaps she should not, there was danger here. A woman, a stranger, had called at her, to warn her. Rebecca had not listened, and Rebecca had not clearly seen the wounded man lying on the ground, in the cemetery.

She had not! She would claim she had not, afterward.

What she did remember was: laundry flapping on the clothesline.

Her belated realization, Ma would be mad as hell at her. For Rebecca should have helped with the laundry as always.

Yet: *It can't happen, today is washday.*

In the kitchen something blocked her way, and this was a wrong thing: a chair, sprawled on its back. Rebecca collided with the chair like a blind girl, wincing with pain.

"Ma?"

Calling for her mother but her voice came so faint, Anna Schwart could not have heard had Anna Schwart been capable of hearing.

Then she called for her father—"Pa? Pa?"—reasoning even in this moment of terror *He would want me to acknowledge him, to respect him.*

She was in the kitchen of the old stone house, and hearing the sound of struggle in one of the back rooms. Her parents' bedroom?

She was panting, covered in a film of cold sweat. Her heart was beating erratically as a wounded bird beating its wings. All that she knew, she was forgetting. Laundry? Washday? She was forgetting. Already she'd forgotten the unknown woman crying *Don't go in there!—stop her!* She'd forgotten having heard gunshots; she could not have said how many shots she'd heard. And so she would not have thought *He has reloaded. He is prepared.*

For it is an important distinction in such matters: if a man acts impulsively, or with premeditation.

She heard them. The floorboards vibrated with their struggle. Her father's excited, eager voice and her mother's short breathless cries, that sound that Rebecca would later realize was Anna Schwart pleading for her life, as Anna Schwart had never pleaded before in Rebecca's hearing. Her mother's fleshy indifference, her stubborn composure were gone, vanished as if they had never been; her air of stoic calm, that had seemed to welcome humiliation, hurt, even grief, had vanished. A woman pleading for her life and there was Jacob Schwart interrupting to say, as if gloating, "Anna! No! They are coming now, Anna. It is time."

Since Rebecca had started to run for home, out on the Quarry Road, there'd been a faint roaring in her ears. A sound as of water rushing over the forty-foot lock in the canal at Milburn. And now there came a deafening noise, an explosion so close by, Rebecca would think, panicked, that she'd been hit herself.

She was in the hall outside the bedroom. The door was ajar. She might have turned and run. She might have escaped. She was not behaving with the panicked instinct of an animal bent upon survival. Instead she cried, "Ma! Oh, Ma!" another time and pushed into the bedroom, that cramped dim-lit room at the rear of the house in which Anna and Jacob Schwart had slept in the same bed for more than a decade and into which the Schwart children had rarely ventured. She nearly collided with her father who was panting and moaning, and who may have been muttering to himself, her father gripping the unwieldy shotgun in both his hands, the barrels pointing upward. In this room there was a powerful stink of gunsmoke. In the pallid light from a grimy window Jacob Schwart's face was a hot boiled-tomato hue and his eyes glittered like kerosene. And he was smiling.

"To spare her, eh? They leave no choice . . ."

On the floor by the bed was a shape, a sprawled motionless shape that might have been a body but Rebecca could not see the head, where the head had been, or possibly there was a head, or part of a head, yes but it lay in darkness beyond the foot of the bed; though the darkness was glistening, the darkness was wet, and spreading like spilled paint. Rebecca was not capable of thinking and yet the thought came to her lightly and whimsically blown as milkweed seed *It is almost over, it will stop then. I can take down the laundry myself.*

Her father Jacob Schwart was speaking to her. His face and the front of his work clothes were splattered with the dark liquid. He may have been trying to block her vision of what lay on the floor even as, smiling harder, as a father smiles at a recalcitrant child to distract her attention from something that must be done for the child's own good, he was trying, in that tight space, to maneuver the gun barrels around, to take aim at her. Yet Pa seemed not to wish to touch her, to jostle her bodily. Not for a long time had Pa touched his daughter. Instead he backed away. But the edge of the bed prevented him from moving far. He was saying, "*You*—you are born here. They will not hurt you." He had changed his mind about her, then. He was aiming the barrels at his own head, clumsily at his jaws outthrust like a turtle's. For there was a second shell remaining to be discharged. He was sweating and panting as if he'd been running uphill. He set his jaws tight, he clenched his stained teeth. The last look Jacob Schwart would give his daughter was one of indignation, reproach, as he fumbled to pull the trigger.

"Pa, no—"

Again the blast was deafening. The windowpanes behind Jacob Schwart would be shattered. In that instant father and daughter were one, obliterated.

26

❀ ❀ ❀

Each of us is a living flame, and Jesus Christ has lighted that flame. Rebecca, remember!

These words of Rose Lutter's echoed in her ears. Still she was trying to believe.

She was thirteen years old, a minor. She would be a ward of Chautauqua County until the age of eighteen. Though it was expected that, at sixteen, she would quit public school and take full-time employment to support herself, as other indigent orphans had done in the past.

For she had no parents. She had no relatives to take her in. (One of her brothers was twenty-one. But Herschel Schwart was a notorious fugitive from justice.) Apart from a few shabby items removed in haste from the old stone house in the cemetery, she had no inheritance, not a penny. Jacob Schwart had closed out his savings account at the First Bank of Chautauqua and what he'd done with his money, apart from purchasing a shotgun and shells, was not known. The words *pauper, destitute* were uttered on Rebecca's behalf, in her hearing in the family court of the Chautauqua County courthouse.

What to do with the gravedigger's daughter!

There was a proposal to send Rebecca to a home for "indigent orphans" in Port Oriskany, that was associated with the United Methodist Church. There was a proposal to board her with a local family named Cadwaller, where two other child-wards of the county were currently living amid a slatternly mix of five Cadwaller children: the Cadwallers owned a ten-acre pig farm, and all the children worked. There was a proposal to board her with a childless couple in their sixties who owned several Doberman pinschers. There was a proposal to board her with a Mrs. Heinrich Schmidt who in fact operated a boardinghouse on South Main Street, Milburn, where mostly solitary men lived, ranging in age from twenty to seventy-seven; some of these boarders were World War II veterans, and most were on county welfare subsidies.

The obese reptile-man! In her dreamy state Rebecca seemed to know that he boarded at Mrs. Schmidt's. He awaited her there, smiling his sly wet smile.

"Girlie! Welcome."

27

And yet: "Jesus has arranged this, Rebecca. We must think so. 'I am a light come into the world that whosoever believeth on me should not abide in darkness.' You are welcome to live with me, Rebecca. I have made the arrangements with the county. Together we will pray to discover what this terrible thing means, that has touched your young life."

For it wasn't Mrs. Schmidt but Miss Rose Lutter, Rebecca's former schoolteacher, with whom she could live as a ward of Chautauqua County for two and a half years.

Out of nowhere it would seem to Rebecca, her former schoolteacher had come. Yet there was the sense, that would grow upon Rebecca over time, that Miss Lutter had been waiting for Rebecca, for years.

Rose Lutter was the sole party in Milburn to offer to pay not only for much of Rebecca Schwart's upkeep (the term "upkeep" was frequently noted) but also for a burial plot in the very Milburn cemetery for which he'd been a caretaker, for the deceased, disgraced Jacob Schwart and his wife Anna. Except for Rose Lutter's generosity, the Schwarts' remains would have been buried at county expense, in an unmarked and untended section of the cemetery reserved for indigents.

Paupers' graves these were called. No headstones, no markers.

But Miss Lutter would not hear of this. Miss Lutter was a Christian, a bearer of mercy. Though she had retired early from public school teaching for reasons of health and lived now on a modest pension supplemented by a family annuity, she arranged for Jacob and Anna Schwart to be properly buried and for a small aluminum marker to be set into the earth at the head of the grave site. Since Rebecca had not been capable of providing information about her parents, their birth dates for instance, and since no one in Milburn much wished to rummage through the morass of old, yellowed, moldering documents that Jacob Schwart had left behind in boxes in the stone house, all that was indicated on the marker was:

SCHWARD Anna & Jacob d. 4-11-49

Rebecca perceived the errors here. The misspelled name, the inaccurate death-date. Of course she said nothing. For who could care that an immigrant gravedigger had killed his sickly wife with a single shotgun blast, and himself with a second shotgun blast, on a weekday in April, or in May?

Who could care that someone named Schwart, or Schward, had lived or died, let alone when?

And so in the Chautauqua County Courthouse when Miss Rose Lutter appeared amid a gathering of strangers, and all of these strangers men, and clutched at Rebecca's hands in triumph, and uttered such extravagant words as *special destiny, singled out by God* Rebecca did not protest.

"Jesus, I will believe. Jesus, help me to believe in You."

He was observing her, she knew. In the corner of her eye sometimes she saw Him. But when she turned her head, however slowly, He retreated. Vaguely she recalled that He had taunted her, once—hadn't He? She would pretend not to remember.

She would come to know, in time: the man whom her father had shot in the cemetery was named Simcoe, fifty-one years old and a former Milburn resident and unknown to Jacob Schwart and his death by Jacob Schwart "unprovoked." He had died en route to the Chautauqua Falls hospital in an ambulance, of massive gunshot wounds to the chest. His left forearm, uplifted in a futile gesture to protect himself against an explosion of buckshot at close range, had been shredded, a splintered white bone protruding.

This death was the outrage, the injustice. This death was the crime.

The Schwart deaths were lesser, of course. You could see the logic. The shotgun death of Anna Schwart, also at close range. Massive injuries to the head. The self-death of Jacob Schwart, at close range. Strangers would ask the daughter what she knew, what she could tell them. So slowly she spoke and with such confusion and often her voice trailed off into baffled silence so there were observers who believed that she must be mentally retarded or in some way "damaged" like others in the family perhaps, the wife Anna for instance, and at least one of the sons, or both.

And there was the father, the madman.

How Rebecca had left the stone house on that day, where she'd been taken and by whom, she would not recall clearly. What had been sticky and coagulating in her hair, that had to be cut out by a frowning nurse in whose fingers the scissors trembled.

"Girl! Try to stay *still.*"

In a strange bed nonetheless she slept for twelve, sometimes fourteen hours even with morning sun shining on her mask-face. Slept with her limbs entwined like snakes in winter, in a burrow. Her mouth was open, agape. Her bare feet, icy at the toes, twitched and paddled to keep her from falling. Inside her empty head water rushed rushed rushed over the gigantic ten-foot lock in a ceaseless stream. *Damned lucky to be alive! don't you ever forget damned lucky I didn't blow your head off you are one of them aren't you! born here why I couldn't trust you going behind my back and wasn't I right?*

No memory of how she'd left the stone house. Maybe she'd run outside desperate and screaming. Maybe she'd run panicked as a wounded animal trailing blood, something soft and liquidy in her hair, on her face and arms. Maybe she'd fainted, and someone had lifted her. Onto a stretcher?

Thinking that she, too, had been shot, wounded? A dying girl, looks like about thirteen.

In the startling intimacy of Miss Lutter's kitchen. Where on a shelf with several pots of beautifully blooming African violets, in a tasteful oval mirror-frame, the handsome olive-skinned and dark-bearded likeness of Jesus Christ lifted His hand in a casual blessing as, at the Capitol Theater, in a movie poster Cary Grant, Henry Fonda, James Stewart might lift his hand in a casual smiling greeting to warm the heart.

There were two pieces of raisin bread toast, smeared with honey. Set before her.

"Rebecca, eat. You *must*."

"Jesus, I will believe. Jesus, help me to believe in You."

Personal possessions they were called. Brought to her from the old stone house in the cemetery.

Rebecca's clothes, her shoes and boots. Such shabby items, Rebecca was shamed to see turn up in Miss Lutter's tidy house, dumped out of cardboard boxes. Even her schoolbooks looked shabby! And there was the dictionary she'd won as a champion speller of 1946, now warped from the damp in the old stone house and smelling of mildew. Some of Anna's clothing had been mixed with Rebecca's, a wrinkled white cotton eyelet blouse far too large for Rebecca, box-shaped housedresses, cotton stockings twisted together like snakes, black suede gloves Rebecca hadn't known her mother had owned, a much-laundered flannel nightgown big and shapeless as a tent . . . Seeing the frightened look in Rebecca's face, Miss Lutter quickly folded up Anna Schwart's things, and placed them back inside the box.

Here was a surprise: the Motorola console radio that had been shut away in the parlor for years, Jacob Schwart's most prized possession. In the frayed cardboard box in which it was carried into Miss Lutter's house it, too, appeared shabby, diminished like something hauled from the dump. Rebecca stared at the radio, unable to speak. Numbly she drew her fingers over the wooden cabinet: she fumbled to turn the dial *on*, though of course the radio wasn't plugged in and hadn't Pa told them with bitter satisfaction that the tubes were burnt out . . .

Politely Miss Lutter told the delivery men to please take it away. "I have my own radio, thank you."

Most of the *personal possessions* were given to the Milburn Good Will shop, by Miss Lutter. So ever afterward so long as Rebecca lived in Milburn, and even after she moved away with Niles Tignor to live elsewhere, she instinctively shrank from glancing into the windows of such secondhand stores as Good Will or Salvation Army out of a dread of seeing her family's despoiled things on display: old, ugly clothes, battered furniture, the pathetic Motorola console radio in its scuffed imitation-wood cabinet.

In the fall of 1949, the old stone house in the cemetery was razed.

No one had lived in it since the murder-suicide. No one had attempted to even clean it. The Township voted to replace it with another dwelling in which the new cemetery caretaker and his family could live.

By this time Rebecca had been living for nearly five months in Rose Lutter's tidy beige-brick house at 114 Rush Street, in a residential neighborhood of similar small brick and shingle-board homes. A block away was the First Presbyterian Church, to which Miss Lutter avidly belonged. Her house had a small front stoop upon which, in appropriate seasons, Miss Lutter placed pots of geraniums, mums, and hydrangea. Inside, Miss Lutter's house wasn't really much larger than the stone house had been, and yet: how different!

The most startling difference was that Miss Lutter's house contained no strong *smells*. Not a smell of kerosene, not woodsmoke, not old, rancid food, or rotting wood, or damp earth close beneath the floorboards. Not that smell of human bodies in cramped quarters.

Only just, in Rose Lutter's house, most noticeable on Fridays, a smell of furniture polish. And, beneath, a faint sweet prevailing fragrance of what Miss Lutter called her *potpourri*.

Potpourri was a mix of wildflowers, herbs, and spices prepared by Miss

Lutter herself and allowed to dry. Potpourri was placed in bowls through the house including the bathroom where its position was on the back of the gleaming-white porcelain toilet.

Miss Lutter's mother, now deceased, had always had potpourri in her house. And Miss Lutter's grandmother, long deceased.

Rebecca had never heard of *potpourri* and she had never smelled anything like it before. It made her feel almost dizzy sometimes. When she stepped into the house, and the fragrance struck her. Or when she wakened in the morning, and it awaited her.

Blinking her eyes uncertain of where she was, what this meant.

Another startling thing was, the walls of Miss Lutter's house were so *clean*. Some of the walls were covered in floral-print wallpaper, and some had been painted white. And all of the ceilings were white. In all the rooms there were windows!—even the bathroom. And at each of these windows, even the tiny window on the back door, there were curtains.

Mornings when Rebecca opened her eyes in the room designated as hers, in the rear, left corner of Miss Lutter's house, what she saw first was pale pink organdy curtains facing her bed.

Wished she was friends still with Katy Greb! God damn she'd have liked to show Katy this room. The curtains, and the pink-rosebud wallpaper, and the fluffy "throw" rug, and the step-in closet . . . Not boast but just to show her. For Katy would be impressed. And she would be sure to tell Leora.

Is Rebecca lucky now, Momma! You should see her room . . .

Another remarkable thing was, how few cobwebs you saw in Miss Lutter's house. Even in the summer, not many flies. None of those crazed stinging flies that hung out in kitchens and privies and made your life miserable. Rebecca helped Miss Lutter with keeping the house clean, and it was rare for her to discover dust-balls beneath furniture, or a patina of grime on any surface. So this was how people lived, in real houses in Milburn! The world of *those others* that had eluded the Schwarts.

There was a procedure to life, Rebecca saw. It wasn't meant to be haphazard and made up as you went along.

As Miss Lutter had been a scrupulous teacher at the Milburn grammar school, so she was a scrupulous housekeeper. She owned not only a carpet sweeper but a General Electric vacuum cleaner. A heavy upright mechanism with a roaring motor and a bag that swelled up like a balloon with dust and grit and roller-wheels to be pushed along the floor. Of all of the household tasks, Rebecca liked vacuuming most. The roaring motor filled her head and drove out all thoughts. The very weight of the vacuum cleaner, tugging at her arms, making her short of breath, was like wrestling with someone who was strong and stubborn but finally tractable, and became an ally. Soon Rebecca was entrusted with vacuuming all of the rooms of the beige-brick house at 114 Rush Street.

Always there is a way out. If you can make yourself small enough, like a worm.

For two and a half years Rebecca would live with Rose Lutter, and for two and a half years she would await Jesus.

She'd given up expecting her brothers to come for her. Not Herschel, not Gus. Herschel was still a *fugitive from justice* and Gus had simply disappeared. It seemed to Rebecca that they must know what had happened for in her dazed state she believed that all the world must know. When she left Miss Lutter's house to walk to school, when she appeared with Miss Lutter at church services in the First Presbyterian Church, everyone who saw her knew, as if a glimmering halo of light surrounded her, like those halos of light surrounding figures in Bible pictures: Jesus stilling the storm, Jesus healing the leper, Jesus presiding over the miraculous draught of fishes, but also Daniel in the lions' den, Solomon dedicating the temple, Moses and the brazen serpent, Mary visited by the angel. Some were singled out for attention, and could not hope to hide.

In Sunday school, in the basement of the First Presbyterian Church, Rebecca learned to clap hands as she sang with other, mostly younger children:

> *This little light of mine!*
> *I'm going to let it shine!*
> *Let it shine all over God's mountain!*
> *I'm going to LET IT SHINE!*

For the news of the Gospels was good news, Rebecca was told. It was all about Christ and the coming-again of Christ and Christ entering your heart.

Sometimes, Rebecca saw the minister's wife Mrs. Deegan watching her above the heads of the younger children. At such times Rebecca smiled, and sang louder. The palms of her hands stung pleasantly with clapping.

"Very good, Rebecca! What a nice voice you have, Rebecca. Do you know what it is? A *contralto.*"

Rebecca ducked her head, too shy to thank Mrs. Deegan. Her voice was scratchy as sandpaper and it hurt her throat when she sang, especially it hurt her to sing loudly. Still, she would sing.

She would sing children's songs to please the minister's wife, who wore her hair in twisty little bangs on her forehead, and who would tell Reverend Deegan what a good girl Rebecca Schwart was. Miss Lutter would be informed, too. Make no mistake about that. They were keeping close watch on the gravedigger's daughter, she knew.

She knew, and she accepted. She was a ward of Chautauqua County, a charity case.

"Rebecca! Put on your gloves, dear. And hurry."

Sunday school began promptly at 9 A.M. and promptly at 9:50 A.M. Miss Lutter appeared in the schoolroom doorway, to take Rebecca to church services upstairs. If Rebecca had left her white cotton gloves back at the house, Miss Lutter would have discovered them, and brought them to give to Rebecca.

You could see that churchgoing was the very center of Miss Lutter's quiet week. Always she wore dazzling white gloves, and one of her pert little hats with a veil; she wore "pumps" that gave her an unexpected, giddy height, of about five foot one. (Already by the age of thirteen Rebecca was taller than Miss Lutter, and heavier.) In warm weather Miss Lutter wore floral-print dresses with flared skirts and crinolines beneath, that made a frothy sound when she moved. Her thin cheeks glowed with pleasure, or with rouge. Her thin lips had been reddened. Her sparrow-colored hair was curled tightly as a child's.

"We mustn't be late, dear. Come!"

Sometimes in her enthusiasm Miss Lutter took Rebecca's hand, to pull the shy gawky girl along.

It was like the Red Sea parting in the Bible picture, Rebecca thought. When Miss Lutter made her way importantly along the center aisle of the church to her pew near the front, with Rebecca in tow. "Hello!"— "Hello!"—"Good morning!"—"Hello!" So many friendly curious faces, for Miss Lutter to address, somewhat breathlessly. So many eyes sliding past her, and onto Rebecca.

Miss Lutter had bought Rebecca several girlish dresses with flared skirts, that were already too tight for her, in the bodice and armpits. She'd bought silk ribbons for Rebecca's hair. At Thom McAn's Shoes for the Family she bought Rebecca a pair of beautiful black patent leather shoes to be worn with white anklet socks. And white gloves to match Miss Lutter's, a size larger than hers.

In all, Miss Lutter would be obliged to buy several more dresses for Rebecca, pairs of shoes, gloves. For goodness how the girl *grew*!

And her hair that was thick, coarsely wavy, inclined to snarls—Miss Lutter insisted that Rebecca brush, brush, brush it with a wire handbrush until it shone, and her wrist ached with weariness. Like a horse's mane, Miss Lutter sighed. Yet she touched Rebecca's hair, with a fascinated repugnance.

"Sometimes I think you're part-horsy, Rebecca. A wild roan pony."

Rebecca laughed, uneasily. She was never certain whether Miss Lutter was joking, or meant such extravagant remarks.

When manly Reverend Deegan strode to the pulpit to preach his sermon, Miss Lutter sat upright in the pew before him, rapt with attention as if she were the sole person in the room. The minister had been a U.S. Army chaplain, he'd served in the war, in the Pacific. So it was frequently noted, in Reverend Deegan's sermons. He spoke in a gliding-and-dipping voice, a voice trained as a singer's; he frowned, he smiled. Almost inaudibly Miss Lutter murmured *Yes yes yes. Amen, yes.* Her lips parted moist as a child's, her eyelids fluttered. Rebecca tried very hard to hear what Miss Lutter was hearing for she wanted very badly to believe for if she failed to believe, Jesus would not enter her heart and her soul would be as nettles cast upon the earth, and not seeds. And the stones that the Jews took up to throw at Jesus for His blasphemy would be her lot.

How hard Rebecca tried, week following week! Still it was like trying to haul herself up by her arms onto the shed roof, when she'd been a little girl and her brothers had scrambled ahead of her laughing at her.

It was strange: how when Rebecca was alone, it was not so difficult to believe in Jesus Christ. Almost she could sense that Jesus was watching her, smiling His enigmatic smile. For Jesus, too, had laughed at Rebecca, on the Quarry Road. Yet Jesus had forgiven her. Yet Jesus had saved her life and for what reason?

Miss Lutter had promised that they would discover, one day.

Miss Lutter had taken her to her parents' grave site, that was so plain, and covered in weeds. Miss Lutter had taken no notice (out of tact, or because her eyes were weak) of the factual errors in the marker. *They had no religion, I was told. But we will pray for them.*

But here in church all that was difficult to believe. Though Rebecca tried to concentrate. The more earnestly Reverend Deegan spoke of Jesus, the less real Jesus seemed. Amid this congregation of good decent people. Amid the polished hardwood pews, robust voices uplifted in song. Women's talcum powder, men's hair oil and shaving lotion.

Time to take up the hymnal. Reverend Deegan's smile flashed wetly white. "My brothers and sisters in Christ, make a joyful noise unto the Lord."

They stood. Miss Lutter sang as earnestly as the others. Her weak soprano voice. Her head uplifted in hope, her mouth like a hungry little beak, working. *A mighty fortress, a mighty fortress is our Lord.* The lady organist with the snow-white floating hair struck her shrill chords. The crinoline beneath Miss Lutter's rayon dress quivered. Rebecca sang, shutting her eyes. She loved the swell of the music, that mixed with the roar of the water over the gigantic lock. Her heart beat strangely, she became excited. Oh, suddenly there was hope. Shut her eyes tight in hope of catching a glimpse of the remote Jesus, in his filmy white robe, floating. She did not like to think of the crucifixion, she wanted Jesus to be remote, like an angel; like a beautiful high-scudding cloud, borne by the wind overhead; for the most beautiful clouds were shaped above the lake, and scattered by the wind in all directions; and no one except Rebecca Schwart saw. She would explain to Miss

Lutter: for she loved Miss Lutter, and was so grateful for Miss Lutter having saved her life, having taken her in, a ward of Chautauqua County, a charity case, almost she could not look Miss Lutter in the face, almost she could not speak without stammering. She loved Jesus that he was remote and ascended to the Father but like a willful child she hated it more and more that Jesus was a dead body on a cross like any other dead body dripping blood and shortly it would begin to decompose, and smell. Jesus need not be resurrected if He had not died and He need not have died if He had not submitted to His enemies, and escaped. Or better yet why had He not struck His enemies dead? For was not Jesus the Son of God, possessed of the power of life and death?

Words are bullshit, lies. Every word that has ever been uttered, has ever been used is a lie.

The singing was over. The congregation was seated. Rebecca opened her eyes, and Jesus had vanished. Ridiculous to think that Jesus would ever be here, summoned by Reverend Deegan of the First Presbyterian Church of Milburn, New York.

Rebecca tried to forestall a yawn. One of those powerful jaw-breaking yawns that spilled tears down her cheeks. Miss Lutter would notice and be hurt (for Miss Lutter was easily hurt) and would afterward scold in her elliptical-nasal manner.

Now Rebecca was restless, itchy. Each Sunday it was worse.

She tried to sit still. Tried to be good. Oh but it was so stupid! Bullshit it was, all of it. Yet telling herself how grateful she was. To Miss Lutter, grateful. Grateful to be alive. Damn lucky. She knew! She might be mistaken for retarded but she was an intelligent girl with eyes in the back of her head and so she knew exactly how Milburn viewed her, and spoke of her. She knew how Rose Lutter was admired, and in some quarters resented. The retired schoolteacher who'd taken in the gravedigger's daughter, the orphan. Her underarms were itching, and her ankles in the little white anklet socks she hated. She rubbed one ankle against the other, beneath the pew. Hard. Except for where she was and who might be watching she would've dug at the patch of wiry hair between her legs, hard enough to draw blood.

28

❀ ❀ ❀

She would not wait until her sixteenth birthday to quit school.

She would be expelled in November 1951, and she would not return.

She would break Rose Lutter's heart, for it could not be helped.

For that day she'd had enough. Fuck it she'd had enough. Long they had harassed her at the high school. Her teachers knew, and the principal knew, and did nothing to intervene. In the tenth grade corridor at the stairs the older Meunzer girl shoved Rebecca from behind and instead of behaving as if she hadn't noticed, turning the other cheek as Miss Lutter advised, walking quickly away without a backward glance, Rebecca turned and threw her books at her assailant and began to hit her, striking with her fists as a boy might strike, not overhand but from the shoulder, and beneath. And a second assailant flew at her, a boy. And others joined in against Rebecca. Cursing, scratching, punching. A thrill as of wildfire spread through the corridor, once Rebecca was wrestled down to the floor and kicked, and kicked, and kicked.

They hated her that she was Herschel Schwart's sister, and Herschel had left Jeb Meunzer's face disfigured by scars. They hated her that she was the daughter of the gravedigger Jacob Schwart who'd killed a man named Simcoe, a name well known in Milburn, and had escaped by killing himself and would not die in the electric chair. Long they'd resented Rebecca, that she persisted among them. That she would not humble herself. That her manner was often arrogant, aloof. Both with her classmates, and with her teachers who were uneasy in her presence, and seated her with other misfits and troublemakers at the back of their classrooms.

All who'd been involved in the fight were expelled from Milburn High and ordered by the principal to leave the school premises at once. It made no difference that Rebecca had been first attacked, he would allow no fighting at his school. There was a possibility of appealing the principal's decision, in the new year. But Rebecca refused.

She was out, she would not return.

Miss Lutter was stunned by the news, devastated. Rebecca had never seen the older woman so distraught.

"Rebecca, you can't mean this! You're upset. I will talk with the principal, you must graduate from high school. You were the one who was attacked, you were only defending yourself. This is a dreadful injustice that must be rectified . . ." Miss Lutter pressed a tremulous hand against her chest, as if her heart were beating erratically. Almost in that moment Rebecca weakened, and gave in.

But no: she'd had enough of Milburn High. She'd had enough of the same faces year following year, the same staring impudent eyes. Imagining that they knew *her*, when they only knew *of her*. Imagining that they were superior to her, because of her family.

Her grades were only average, or poor. Often she cut classes out of boredom. The course she disliked most was algebra. For what did equations have to do with actual *things*? In English class they were forced to memorize poems by Longfellow, Whittier, Poe, ridiculous singsong rhymes, what did rhymes in poems have to do with *things*? She'd had enough of school, she would get a job in Milburn and support herself.

For days Miss Lutter pleaded with Rebecca. You would have thought that Rose Lutter's future itself was endangered. She told Rebecca that she should not let those ignorant barbarians ruin her life. She had to persevere, to graduate. Only if she had a high school degree could Rebecca hope to find a decent job and lead a decent life.

Rebecca laughed, this was ridiculous. Decent life! She had no hope of a decent life.

As if what Jacob Schwart had done surrounded her like a halo.

Everywhere Rebecca went, this halo followed. It was invisible to her but very visible to others. It gave off an odor as of smoldering rubber at the town dump.

One day Rose Lutter confessed to Rebecca, she had retired early from teaching because she could not bear the ignorant, increasingly insolent children. She'd begun to be allergic to chalk dust, her sinus passages were chronically inflamed. She'd been threatened by white-trash parents. The principal of her school had been too cowardly to defend her. Then a ten-year-old boy bit her hand when she'd tried to break up a fight between him and a smaller boy and her doctor had had to give her a prescription for nerves and heart palpitations and the school district granted her a medical leave and at the end of three months when she'd re-entered the school building she had had a tachycardia attack and had nearly collapsed and her doctor advised the school district to retire her with a medical disability and so she had conceded, it was probably for the best; and yet she wanted so very badly for Rebecca not to give up, for Rebecca was young and had all her life before her.

"You must not replicate the past, Rebecca. You must rise above the past. In your soul you are so superior to . . ."

Rebecca felt the insult, as if Rose Lutter had slapped her.

"Superior to who?"

Miss Lutter's voice quavered. She tried to take Rebecca's stiff cold hands, but Rebecca would not allow it.

Touch me not! Of the myriad remarks of Jesus Christ she had come to learn, since moving into Rose Lutter's house, *touch me not!* had most impressed her.

". . . your background, dear. And those who are your enemies at the school. Throughout the world, barbarians who wish to pull the civilized down. They are enemies of Jesus Christ, too. Rebecca, you must know."

Rebecca ran abruptly from the room, to prevent herself from screaming at the nagging old woman *Go to hell! You and Jesus Christ go to hell!*

———

"But she has been so good to me. She loves me . . ."

Yet the end would come soon now, Rebecca knew. The break between them Rebecca halfway wished for, and dreaded.

For she would not return to that school, no matter how Miss Lutter pleaded. No matter how Miss Lutter scolded, threatened. Never!

More and more she began to stay away from the tidy beige-brick house on Rush Street, as once she'd stayed away from the old stone house in the cemetery. The potpourri fragrance seemed to her sickening. She stayed away from church services, too. After dark, sometimes as late as midnight, when every other house on Rush Street was darkened and utterly still, she returned guilty and defiant. "Why do you wait up for me, Miss Lutter? I wish you wouldn't. I hate it, seeing all these lights on."

I hate you, I hate you waiting. Leave me alone!

The tension between them grew tighter, ever tighter. For Rebecca refused to tell Miss Lutter where she went. With whom she spent her time. (Now that she was out of school, she was making new acquaintances. Katy Greb had quit school the previous year, she and Katy were again close friends.) Since she'd been attacked at school, so viciously, so publicly, ugly welts and bruises lasting for weeks on her back, thighs, buttocks, even her breasts and belly, she had come to see herself differently, and she liked what she saw. Her skin shone with a strange olive pallor. Her eyebrows were so fierce and dark, like a man's nearly touching above the bridge of her nose. A rich rank animal-smell accrued to her skin, when she sweated. With what sudden inspired strength she'd struck Gloria Meunzer and other of her assailants with her fists, she'd made them wince with surprise and pain, she'd drawn blood.

Smiling to think how like the outlaw Herschel she was, in her heart.

And there was Miss Lutter, persisting. "I am your court-appointed guardian, Rebecca. I have an official responsibility. Of course I want only what is best for you. I have been praying, I have been trying to think how I've failed you . . ."

Rebecca bit her lip to keep from screaming.

"You haven't. You haven't failed me, Miss Lutter."

The very name *Miss Lutter* made her smile, in derision. *Rose Lutter, Miss Rose Lutter.* She could not bear it.

"I haven't?" Miss Lutter spoke with mock wistfulness. Her thin faded hair had been crimped and wadded up somehow, flattened against her skull beneath a hairnet. Her soft skin that was lined terribly about her near-sighted eyes, and sagged at her chin, glistened with a medicinal-smelling night cream. She was in her nightgown, a royal blue rayon robe over it, tightly tied about her very narrow waist. Rebecca could not keep from staring at Miss Lutter's chest that was so flat, bony. "Of course I have, dear. Your life . . ."

Rebecca protested, "My life is my life! My own life! I haven't done anything wrong."

"But you must return to school, dear. I will see the principal, he's a man of integrity whom I know. I will make an appeal in writing. I'm sure that he's waiting for us to appeal. I can't allow you to be treated unjustly."

Rebecca would have pushed past Miss Lutter in the narrow hall, but the older woman blocked her way with surprising firmness. Though Rebecca was taller than Rose Lutter and heavier by perhaps fifteen pounds, she could not confront her.

"Your destiny, dear. It is bound up with my own. 'Sow not your seed in a stony place.' "

"Jesus didn't say that! Not those words, you made it up."

"Jesus did say that. Perhaps not those exact words, but yes He did."

"You can't make up what Jesus says, Miss Lutter! You can't!"

"It is the essence of what Jesus said. If He were here, you can be sure He would speak to you as I am. Jesus would try to talk some sense into you, my child."

In scrubby areas of Milburn you saw scrawled on walls and sidewalks and the sides of freight cars the words FUCK FUCK YOU FUK YOU which were not for girls to utter aloud. Boys uttered such words constantly, boys shouted them gleefully, but "good" girls were meant to look away, deeply embarrassed. Now Rebecca bit her lower lip, to keep such words back. FUCK FUCK YOU ROSE LUTTER. FUK FUK FUK ROSE LUTTER. A spasm of hilarity overtook her, like a sneeze. Miss Lutter stared at her, wounded.

"Ah, what is so funny, now? At such a time, Rebecca, what is so very funny? I wish that I could share your mirth."

Now Rebecca did push past Miss Lutter, into her room slamming the door.

Damned lucky and you know it. You! It was so, she knew. He was reproaching her. For a father had the right.

Always in that dim-lighted room where time passed so swiftly she was missing something. Always she strained to see, and to hear. It was a strain that made her spine ache. Her eyes ached. Living again those confused fleeting seconds in the stone house that would mark the abrupt and irrevocable termination of her life in the stone house as a daughter of that house. The termination of what she would not have known to call her childhood let alone her girlhood.

The smell of potpourri confused her, mixed with the smells of that other bedroom. She struggled to wake breathing rapidly and sweating and her eyeballs rolled in her head in the agitation of trying finally to *see* . . . what lay on the floor, obscured in shadow.

A wet glistening shadow beyond the bed. The soft fallen body that might have been (in the semi-darkness, in the confusion of the moment) simply discarded clothes, or bedclothes.

Ma? Ma—

No. She could not see. He was blocking her view. He would not allow it. When she was neither fully awake nor fully asleep she had the power to summon again the vision of her father Jacob Schwart smiling tightly at her and his eyes wet and fierce as he tried to maneuver the awkward weapon, trying to shift the barrels unobtrusively in that tight space, for he wanted to aim the gun at her and yet he did not want to touch her. For with his fatherly puritanical tact he would not wish to touch his daughter's breasts even by way of an intervening object. Rebecca had seen her father staring at her chest, frequently in the past year, not knowing how he stared and that Rebecca saw, instinctively she turned aside, and thought no more of it. Nor would he wish to touch her throat with the gun barrels, where an artery was beating wildly. Still she tried to see past him, to where her mother lay unmoving. Where the upper body of what had been her mother dis-

solved into a shapeless darkness. She would see, she must see!—except not
clearly. So long as her eyes did not open and she hovered in that twilight
state between sleep and wakefulness she could see into that room and by
an act of will she could see *backward*.

Again approaching the stone house from the gravel drive. And there
was the crudely painted front door. And there, in the backyard of the house,
the clothesline, and on the clothesline laundry stirring in the wind for it was
a windy May afternoon, the sky overhead was splotched with swollen rain
clouds. Towels, a sheet, his shirts. His underwear. So long as the laundry
flapped on the line it was an ordinary washday, always there is something
comical and reassuring about laundry, there could be no danger waiting
inside the house. Even as a stranger's voice came urgent and jarring *Don't go
in there!—stop her!* A woman's voice, distracting. And yet already it was too
late. For in history there are actions that no act of history can undo.

She was missing something! Always she was missing something, she'd
failed to see sufficiently, or to hear. She must begin again.

Running along the Quarry Road, panting. And into the cemetery on the
gravel lane that had become shabby in recent months, pebbles scattered in
the grass at the sides of the lane, and weeds emerging. Dandelions everywhere! For the caretaker of the Milburn cemetery was not so fastidious as
he'd once been. For the caretaker of the Milburn cemetery was not so
courteous and deferential as he'd once been. There was a vehicle or vehicles in the interior of the cemetery. And something was wrong, there was
some upset there. And a woman calling to Rebecca, who gave no sign of
hearing. Calling *Ma?* in a voice so absurdly weak, how could Anna Schwart
have heard it! Rebecca was inside the house when the explosion erupted.
The very air shook, vibrated. She would believe that she had witnessed the
shooting, the impact of the buckshot at a distance of approximately six
inches from its soft, defenseless target, yet she had not witnessed it, she
had only heard it. In fact the explosion was so deafening she had not heard
it. Her ears had not the capacity to hear it. Her brain had not the capacity
to absorb it. She might have fled in panic as an animal would have fled but
she did not. A recklessness born of the stubborn inviolable vanity of the
young, that cannot believe that they might die, might have carried her inside the bedroom where virtually in the doorway, for the room was so

small, Jacob Schwart was standing blocking Rebecca's way. She was pleading with him. He was smiling his familiar smile. It was a mocking smile of stained and rotted teeth like a crudely carved jack-o'-lantern smile yet it was (she would see it so, she who was his only daughter and the only child remaining to him now) a mordantly tender smile. A reproachful smile and yet a forgiving smile. *You! Born here. They will not hurt you.* His words were senseless like so much of what he said and yet she, his daughter, understood. Always she would understand him though she could not have articulated what it was she understood in his despairing and jocular face as, grunting, he managed to turn the shotgun against himself and there came a second explosion far louder than the first, far more massive, obliterating; and something wet, fleshy and sticky flew at her, onto her face, into her hair where it would coagulate and have to be carefully scissored out by a stranger.

Yet: Rebecca had missed something, again. God damn it all passed so fast, she could not *see.*

The crucifixion of Christ, that was a mystery.

The crucifixion of Christ, she came to detest.

Listening stony-hearted and unmoved as Reverend Deegan preached his Good Friday sermon. That Rebecca had heard before, and more than once. The man's bulldog face and whiny, blustering voice. Betrayal of Judas, hypocrisy of the Jews. Pontius Pilate washing his hands of guilt with the excuse *What is truth?* And afterward at the house she'd wanted to escape yet could not for Miss Lutter must read aloud from the Book of St. John as if Rebecca were not capable of reading for herself. And Miss Lutter shook her head, sighing. Cruelly Rebecca thought *It's for yourself you feel sorry, not for Him.* And Rebecca heard herself ask, with childlike logic, "*Why* did Jesus let them crucify Him, Miss Lutter? He didn't have to, did He? If He was the Son of God?"

Warily Rose Lutter glanced up from her Bible, frowning at Rebecca through silver-rimmed bifocals as if, one more time, to Rose Lutter's disgust, Rebecca had muttered a profanity under her breath.

"Well, why? I'm just asking, Miss Lutter."

Hating the way the older woman was always looking so hurt, lately. When it wasn't true hurt but anger she felt. A schoolteacher's anger at her authority being challenged.

Rebecca persisted, "If Jesus really was God, He could do whatever He wanted. So if He didn't, how could He be God?"

It was supreme adolescent logic. It was an unassailable logic, Rebecca thought.

Rose Lutter gave a moist, pained cry. With dignity the older woman rose, shut up her precious soft-leather Bible, and walked out of the room murmuring, for Rebecca to overhear, "Forgive her, Father. She knows not what she says."

I do, though. I know exactly what I say.

That night Rebecca slept poorly, waking often. Smelling the damned pot-pourri on her bureau. At last, barefoot and stealthy, she carried it out of her room to hide in a hall closet, beneath the lowest shelf where, to her chagrin, Rose Lutter would discover it only after Rebecca was gone.

29

❀ ❀ ❀

She was free! She would support herself, she would live in downtown Milburn after all. Not at Mrs. Schmidt's disreputable rooming house but just around the corner on Ferry Street, in a ramshackle brownstone partitioned into a warren of rooms and small apartments. Here, Katy Greb and Katy's older cousin LaVerne were living, and invited Rebecca to move in with them. Her share of the rent was only a few dollars a week—"Whatever you can afford, Rebecca." For the first several weeks Rebecca slept on a pile of blankets on the floor, such exhausted sleep it scarcely mattered where she slept! She worked as a waitress, she worked as a merchandise clerk, finally she became a chambermaid at the General Washington Hotel.

It was Leora Greb, now Rebecca's friend again, who helped to get her the job at the hotel. "Say you're eighteen," Leora advised. "Nobody will know."

Rebecca was paid in cash, counted out into the palm of her hand. The hotel would not report her earnings to Internal Revenue, and so she would not be taxed. Nor would the hotel pay into her Social Security fund. "Off the books, eh? Makes things easier." Amos Hrube, in charge of the cleaning and kitchen staff, winked at Rebecca as if there was a fond joke between them. Before Rebecca could draw back, Hrube pinched her cheek between the second and third fingers of his right hand.

"Don't! That hurts."

Hrube's expression was pouting, playful. As an adult might pretend to sympathize with a child who has hurt herself in some silly inconsequential way.

"Well! Sor-*ry*."

Hrube had an ugly flat face, a mashed-looking mouth. He might have been any age between thirty-five and fifty-five. On a wall behind his desk was a framed photo of a young man in a U.S. Army dress uniform, dark-haired, lean, yet bearing the unmistakable features of the elder Hrube. His office was a windowless cubbyhole at the rear of the hotel. Leora said not to mind Hrube for he tried such behavior with all the female help and some of them liked fooling around, and some did not. "He's basically good-hearted. He's done me some favors. He'll respect you if that's what you want and if you work hard. See," Leora said, as if this was good news, "they can't fire us all."

Rebecca laughed. In fact this was good news. Her previous jobs had brought her into an unwanted proximity with men-who-hired. Always they'd been aware of her, eyeing and judging her. They had known who she was, too: the daughter of Jacob Schwart. At the General Washington there were many employees. Chambermaids were mostly invisible. And Leora had promised not to tell Hrube, or anyone, who she was, whose daughter. "Anyway that's old news in Milburn. Like the war, people start to forget. Most people, anyway."

Was this true? Rebecca wanted to think so.

Always she'd been aware of the General Washington Hotel on a hilly block of Main Street, but until Leora took her there to apply for a job, Rebecca had never entered it. The busy front lobby with its gleaming black tile floor, its leather furnishings and brass fixtures, potted ferns, ornamental chandeliers and mirrors, had to be one of the largest interior spaces Rebecca had ever been in, and certainly the most impressive. She asked Leora what the price of a room for one night was and when Leora told her, Rebecca said, shocked, "So much money just to *sleep*? And you have nothing to show for it, afterward?"

Leora laughed at this. She was steering Rebecca through the lobby, toward a door marked EMPLOYEES ONLY at the rear. She said, "Rebecca, people who stay in a hotel like this have money, and people who have money leave tips. And you meet a better class of men—sometimes."

She was hired *off the books*, and in her naiveté she thought this was a very good thing. No taxes!

She liked it that there were so many employees at the General Washington. Most of these wore uniforms that indicated their work, and their rank. The most striking uniforms were men's: head doorman, doorman's assistants, bellboys. (Not all the bellboys were "boys": some were quite mature men.) Managerial staff wore business suits and ties. There were only waiters in the better of the hotel's two restaurants, and these were elegantly attired. Female staff were switchboard operators, secretaries, waitresses in the lesser of the restaurants and in the boisterous Tap Room; kitchen workers, chambermaids. A small army of chambermaids. The oldest of these was a stout, white-haired woman in her sixties who proudly claimed to have worked at the General Washington since the hotel had opened its doors in 1922. Rebecca was the youngest.

Chambermaids wore white rayon uniforms with skirts that fell to mid-calf, and short boxy sleeves. The uniform issued to Rebecca was too large in the bust and too tight in the shoulders and beneath the arms and Rebecca hated the slithery sensation of the fabric against her skin; especially she hated the requirement that, as an employee of the General Washington, she must wear stockings at all times.

God damn she could not, would not. In the humid Chautauqua Valley summer, dragging a vacuum cleaner, mopping floors. It was too much to ask!

Leora said, "There's where you want Amos Hrube on your side, hon. He likes you, it makes a difference. He don't like you, he can be a stickler for the rules. A real sonuvabitch."

Just surfaces. I can do this.

She liked it, pushing her maid's cart along the corridor. Her cart was stocked with bed linens, towels, cleaning supplies, small fragrant bars of soap. In her dowdy white-rayon costume she was invisible to most hotel guests and she never met their eyes even when some of them (male, invariably) spoke to her.

"Good morning!"

"Nice day, eh?"

"If you want to make up my room now, miss, I can wait."

But she never cleaned any room with a guest inside, watching.

Never remained in any room with a guest, and the door closed.

It was the solitude of such work she loved. Stripping beds, removing soiled towels from bathrooms, vacuuming carpets she could lapse into a shallow hypnotic dream. An empty hotel room, and no one to observe her. She liked best the moment of unlocking the door and stepping inside. For as a maid she had a passkey to all the guest rooms. *She*, Rebecca Schwart who was no one. Yet she could pass through the rooms of the General Washington Hotel, invisible.

One-of-many. "Chambermaids!"

It was a word she'd never known before. She saw his mouth twisting in derision as he pronounced it.

Chamber-maid! Cleaning up after swine.

My daughter.

But even Jacob Schwart would have been impressed by the guest rooms at the General Washington Hotel. Such tall windows, reaching nearly to the ten-foot ceilings! Brocade draw-drapes, and filmy white curtain panels inside. It was true that, in some of the smaller rooms, the wine-dark carpet was worn in places; yet clearly it was of high quality, made of wool. Gleaming mirrors flashed Rebecca's lithe white-rayon figure, her face olive-pale, blurred. Very rarely did Rebecca glance at herself in these mirrors for the point of the hotel was anonymity.

In Miss Lutter's tidy little house everything had been too personal. Everything had meant too much. In the General Washington, nothing was personal and nothing meant anything except what you saw. Except for the top, seventh-floor suites (which Rebecca had never seen) rooms were identically furnished. There were identical bedspreads, lampshades, sheets of stationery and memo pads gilt-embossed with the hotel's name on identical desks. Even, on the walls, identical reproductions of nineteenth-century paintings depicting scenes on the Erie Barge Canal in the late 1800s.

Maybe, in the identical beds, there were identical dreams?

No one would know. For no one would wish to acknowledge, his dreams were identical with the dreams of others.

Here was the solace of the impersonal! Guests checked into the hotel, and guests checked out. Rooms were occupied, then abruptly vacated. Very often Rebecca didn't even glimpse these strangers. Passing them in the corridor, she lowered her eyes. She knew never to unlock any door without rapping sharply on it and identifying herself, even when she was certain the room was empty. Most of the guests at the General Washington were men, businessmen traveling by car or train; weekends there were likely to be more women, and couples. It was the custom for these strangers to leave tips for the chambermaid, on a bureau, but Rebecca soon learned not to expect anything. She might discover as much as two dollars, she might discover a few nickels and dimes. And sometimes nothing. Men were likely to tip, Leora said, except if there was a wife along, sometimes the wife pocketed the tip without the man knowing.

(And how did Leora know this? Rebecca wondered.)

Older men tended to tip more generously than younger. And if you'd exchanged a few words with a guest, if you'd smiled at him, almost certainly he would leave a tip.

Katy and LaVerne teased Leora about certain "hotel friends" of hers who traveled frequently through Milburn.

Leora said, with an angry laugh, "They're gentlemen, at least. Not like some bastards."

It was no secret that the Tap Room bartender was a friend of Leora's who'd introduced her to some of these "hotel friends" over the years.

He had approached Rebecca, too. But Rebecca had told him *no*.

Not even for a fifty-dollar tip, honey?

No, *no*!

(In fact, Rebecca didn't allow herself to think whether a fifty-dollar tip was a possibility, or one of Mulingar's jokes. For her six-day, eight-hour workweek she was paid precisely forty-eight dollars, counted out into her hand by a smirking Amos Hrube.)

Rebecca felt revulsion, at the thought of being touched by a stranger. The prospect of sex-for-money was not one she wanted to think about since she knew (but had to pretend not to know) that both Katy and LaVerne sometimes took money from their "dates," as well as Leora. As Katy said with a shrug *It's just something that happens it ain't like it's planned.*

It was so, such encounters seemed to be unplanned. If you were a girl, young and seemingly alone and unprotected. A man would return to his hotel room claiming to have forgotten something, while Rebecca was making up the room. A man would glance up smiling at her in the corridor as if he hadn't seen her until that moment and begin speaking with her with an air of nerved-up intimacy and Rebecca would smile politely and continue pushing her maid's cart along the corridor shaking her head as if uncomprehending and except if a man was very drunk or very aggressive he would not follow.

"All right, honey. Have it your way."

Or, weirdly echoing Amos Hrube: "Eh! Sor-*ree*."

No predicting how Rebecca might be tipped after such an encounter. She might be left a few pennies scattered among soiled bedsheets, or a five-dollar bill folded on the dresser. She might be left a ravaged room. A filthy bathroom, an unflushed toilet.

Even so, Rebecca understood that it was nothing personal. It did not mean anything.

Even when there'd been no encounter, when she had not glimpsed a hotel guest, nor he her, Rebecca was sometimes wakened from her chambermaid trance by a room left in a disgusting state. As soon as you entered, you knew: a smell. Spilled whiskey, beer. Spilled food. Sex-smells, toilet smells. Unmistakable.

There were bedclothes dragged onto the floor as if in a drunken frolic. There were stained sheets, cigarette-scorched blankets, pillowcases soaked through with hair oil. Stained carpets, brocade drapes ripped from their fastenings and lying in heaps on the floor. Bathtubs ringed in filth, pubic hair in drains. (Each drain in each guest bathroom had to be clean. Not just clean but what Amos Hrube called sparkly-clean. Hrube was known to spot-check the rooms.) The worst was a filthy toilet, urine and even excrement splattered onto the floor.

Yet in this too there was the perverse satisfaction. *I can do this, I'm strong enough.* All chambermaids had such experiences, eventually. To be a housewife and a mother would not be so very different.

As the hotel room was cleaned, as Rebecca mopped, scrubbed, scoured, vacuumed, re-made the bed, restored order to what had been so ugly, she began to feel elated. As the harsh odor of cleanser replaced other odors in the bathroom and the mirror and white porcelain sink brightened, so her spirits revived.

How easy this is! Surfaces.

She would live like this, unthinking. From day to day she would drift. Her mother's mistake had been to marry, to have babies. From that mistake all the rest had followed.

Wanting to exhaust herself so that, at night, she could sink into sleep without dreaming. Or, if she dreamt, without memory. *Damned lucky and you know it! You, born here!* Some days making her way like a sleepwalker scarcely aware of her surroundings in the high-ceilinged corridors of the General Washington Hotel into which, in life, Jacob Schwart had never once stepped.

"A chambermaid, Pa. That's what I am."

It was her revenge upon him, was it? Or her revenge upon her mother?

She'd left Rose Lutter abruptly, she felt guilt for her behavior. One night when the house was darkened she slipped away, furtive and cowardly. It was a few days after Easter. Never would she have to hear one of Reverend Deegan's sermons again. Never again, see Miss Lutter's look of hurt and reproach cast sidelong at her like a fishhook. She had made secret plans with Katy and LaVerne, who'd invited her to stay with them and so while Miss Lutter slept Rebecca made up her bed neatly for the final time and left, on her pillow, a brief note.

This damned note had been so hard to write! Rebecca tried, and tried, and could come up with only:

Dear Miss Lutter,

Thank you for all that you have given me.

~~I wish that~~

This was stiffly written in the schoolgirl "Parker Penmanship" that Miss Lutter had instilled in her pupils in grade school. Rebecca tried to think of something further to say and felt sweat break out in all her pores, damn she was ashamed of herself and she resented this, wasting time on Rose Lutter while her friends were eagerly awaiting her in their place on Ferry Street and she was impatient to join them for already it was past midnight. She was taking with her only her special possessions: the prize dictionary she'd won, and a very few items of clothing Miss Lutter had purchased for her that still fit her, and weren't too young-looking, and silly on her tall rangy frame.

At last she ripped up the note she'd written, and tried again.

Miss Lutter,

Thank you for all that you have given me.

Jesus will be nicer to you than I can be. I am sorry!

Rebecca Esther Schwart

❋ ❋ ❋

30

"First time I saw you, girl. I knew."

These would be Niles Tignor's words. Delivered in Tignor's blunt dead-pan manner. So that you gazed up at the man knowing yourself off-balance as if he'd reached out to poke you, not hard, but hard enough, his big fore-finger into your breastbone.

It was August 1953. A sultry afternoon and no air-conditioning in most parts of the General Washington Hotel and the interior corridors airless, stifling. Rebecca was pushing her maid's cart heaped with soiled linens and towels on the fifth floor when she saw, to her annoyance, a door at the far end of the corridor being pushed open with teasing slowness. This was room 557, she knew: the man in that room, registered as H. Baumgarten, was one who'd been giving her trouble. Baumgarten had paid for several nights at the hotel in advance, which wasn't typical of most guests, but then Baumgarten wasn't typical. He seemed to have little to do apart from lingering in his room, and drinking in the cocktail lounge and Tap Room on the first floor. Always he was lurking in the corridor hoping to speak with Rebecca who tried to be courteous with him though she hated such men, she hated such games! If she complained of Baumgarten to the hotel manager, he would want to blame her, she knew. From prior experience, she knew.

"Bastard. You have no right."

Rebecca was seventeen years old, three months. Not so young any longer. Not the youngest of the female workers at the General Washington any longer.

She liked her work less. Brainless labor it was, mechanical and repetitive and yet the solitude was still a kind of drug to her, she could move through her days in a waking sleep like an animal that has no need to glance up from the ground before it. Except when she was wakened rudely by the unwanted interference of another, like the man in room 557.

She saw that the door had ceased opening, at a space of about two inches. Baumgarten must have been watching her from inside. And he would want Rebecca to know, to be uneasily aware of him watching her and her not able to see him not knowing if he was fully clothed or in his underwear, or worse yet naked. Baumgarten would be enjoying the chambermaid's embarrassment, her very dislike of him.

It was early afternoon and Rebecca had been working for hours. She was bare-legged, stockingless. Damned if she would wear ridiculous stockings because the hotel management wanted her to. In this heat! She would not, and did not. If Amos Hrube had noticed, he hadn't yet reprimanded her.

The Schwart girl Hrube spoke of her. Not to her face but within her hearing. He didn't like her but he had come to respect her, as Leora had predicted.

She was a good worker. Her arm- and shoulder-muscles were small, hard, and compact. She could lift her own weight. She rarely complained. In her sobriety and concentration on her work she appeared older than her age. In hot weather she partially plaited her thick hair and wrapped it around her head to keep it out of her face and off her neck, that was strangely sensitive in the heat as if the skin had been burnt. Now her white-rayon uniform was sticky with sweat and a film of sweat shone on her upper lip. She was very tired and there was a sharp ache between her shoulder blades and a sharper ache beginning between her eyes.

The man in room 557 had introduced himself to Rebecca as a frequent guest at the General Washington who was on "friendly terms" with the management and staff including several of the chambermaids for whom he left generous tips—"When merited, of course."

Rebecca had noted the sweet sickish odor of whiskey on his breath. And a quivering of his hands, making exaggerated nervous motions as he spoke. Another time he'd tried to waylay her when Rebecca was cleaning the room next to his, eager to inform her that he had crucial business in the Chautauqua Valley—"Some of it family, some of it purely financial, and none of it of the slightest *value*."

Pronouncing the word *value* he'd fixed Rebecca with a yellow-tinged stare. As if this should mean something to her, suggest some link between them.

Baumgarten had been barefoot, which looked very wrong, very offensive to Rebecca's eye, in this setting. He'd worn a festive Hawaiian-print shirt partly unbuttoned to show grizzled-gray chest hairs. His soft, flaccid jaws had been clumsily shaved, with a myriad of tiny cuts. A man in his forties, a drinker, unsteady on his feet and his yellowish eyes snatching at her in shameless yearning. "My name is Bumstead, dear. You have seen me in the comic pages. I am not an actual man which is why I am smiling. Would you believe, dear, I was once your age?" He chuckled, and swiped at his flushed pug nose.

It was then that Rebecca saw, Baumgarten's rumpled trousers were only partway zipped. He must have been naked beneath for boiled-looking flesh and pubic hairs were visible. Disgusted, Rebecca ducked past him pushing her maid's cart into the room and quickly shut the door behind her so that Baumgarten couldn't follow. Yet he dared to rap on the door for some minutes, speaking to her in a plaintive, pleading voice, words she couldn't hear as she began work in the bathroom.

She hadn't yet cleaned Baumgarten's room. His PRIVACY PLEASE card was always looped over his doorknob. Rebecca dreaded the pigsty that would await her. But so long as the sign was up, she could not enter the room even if she knew that Baumgarten was out; and she would not enter it, so long as Baumgarten was in the vicinity, even when he invited her. She had hoped that Baumgarten would be checking out that morning, but he'd hinted he might be staying longer.

Now, the following day, Baumgarten was playing another of his games. No escaping him!

As Rebecca approached room 557 she saw that the door was still ajar.

But Baumgarten had stepped back from it. (Unless he was hiding behind it, to leap out at her.) A fattish hulking figure she dreaded glimpsing naked. Yet she had no choice but to glance inside the room.

"Mister? Is anyone . . . ?"

The room was a pigsty, as she'd expected. God damn there were clothes and towels scattered everywhere, a single man's dress shoe overturned on the carpet just inside the door. Though it was midday the heavy brocaded drapes were drawn tightly shut. A lamp with a crooked shade was lighted. A smell of whiskey and hair pomade prevailed. The man himself lay on the bed, on his back. He was breathing with difficulty, eyes shut and arms flung out at his sides; he was wearing trousers, haphazardly zipped up, and belt-less, and a thin cotton undershirt; again, he was barefoot; his head was turned at an awkward angle and his mouth gaped open, damp with spittle. On the bedside table was an empty glass and a near-empty bottle of whis-key. Rebecca stared, seeing what looked like blood dribbled across Baumgarten's throat and torso.

"Mister! Is something . . ."

On the floor near the bed several objects had been arranged as in a store window display: a man's wallet, a man's gold stretch-band wristwatch, a woman's ring with a large pale-purple stone, a leather change purse and a matching leather toiletry kit. Several bills had been pulled partway out of the wallet so that their denominations were visible: twenties, a single fifty.

For me Rebecca thought calmly.

Yet she could not touch these items. She would not.

She had come to stand close beside the bed, uncertain what to do. If Baumgarten had seriously injured himself with a razor or a knife, there would have been more blood, she knew. Yet: maybe he'd cut himself in the bathroom, and staggered back into the bedroom. Maybe there were wounds she couldn't see. And maybe he'd drunk so much, he had lapsed into a coma and might be dying, she must call the front desk . . .

Rebecca made a move toward the phone, to lift the receiver. But she would have to come very close to the man, if she did. And maybe this was a game of his. Baumgarten would open his yellowish eyes, he would wink at her . . .

"Mister, wake up! You need to wake up."

Rebecca's voice rose sharply. She saw veins on the man's ruined face, like incandescent wires. The greasy pug nose, damp gaping mouth like a fish's. Thin gray hair lay in disheveled strands across the bumpy crown of his head. Only his teeth were perfect, and must have been dentures. His eyelids fluttered, he moaned and breathed noisily, erratically. In that instant, Rebecca felt pity for him.

If he is dying I am his final witness.

If he is dying there is no one except me.

She was about to lift the phone receiver and dial the front desk when the stricken man slyly opened one eye, and grinned at her. The porcelain-white dentures gleamed. Before Rebecca could draw away, Baumgarten grabbed hold of her wrist with surprisingly strong fingers.

"Eh! My dear! What a pleasant surprise."

Rebecca screamed and pushed at him, struggling to get free. But Baumgarten gripped her tight.

"Let me alone! God damn you—"

She clawed at Baumgarten's hands. He cursed her, sitting up now, having swung his legs around; using his legs, as a wrestler would do, to grip Rebecca around the hips. In their struggle Baumgarten managed to pull Rebecca onto the bed beside him, wheezing, laughing. She would afterward recall the harsh whiskey smell of his breath and a fouler, darker smell beneath of something fetid, rotting. She would recall how close she'd come to fainting.

"Hey: what the hell's going on here?"

A tall man with stiff, nickel-colored hair had entered the room. Like a bear on its hind legs he moved with startling swiftness. Baumgarten protested—"Get out! This is a private room, this is a private matter"—but the man paid no heed, seized him by a flabby shoulder and began to shake him, hard. "Let the girl go, fucker. I'll break your ass." Rebecca slipped from Baumgarten's grasp. The men struggled, and the stranger struck Baumgarten with his fists even as Baumgarten tried feebly to defend himself. With one blow of the stranger's fist, Baumgarten's nose was broken. With another blow, the gleaming-white dentures were broken. Whatever Baumgarten had dribbled on himself must not have been blood because there was now a sudden spray of fresh blood, very red blood, on his grimacing face and torso.

Rebecca backed away. The last she saw of Baumgarten/Bumstead he was begging for his life as the man with the nickel-colored hair gripped his head and slammed it—once, twice, a third time—against the rattling mahogany headboard of the bed.

Rebecca fled. She left her maid's cart in the fifth-floor corridor, she would retrieve it another time.

The man, the stranger: who was he?

Discreetly, for days after the "savage beating" in room 557, Rebecca would make inquiries about the tall solidly-built man with the nickel-colored hair: who was he, what was his name? She would not involve him with the beating of H. Baumgarten in room 557, which police were investigating. Never would she have involved him, who had intervened on her behalf.

Let the girl go. Let the girl go . . .

So strange, to think of herself as a *girl!* A *girl* requiring intervention, protection, in another's eyes.

In fact, Rebecca had glimpsed the man with the nickel-colored hair in the General Washington Hotel, from time to time. He must have been a frequent patron of the hotel or the tavern. She'd seen him in the company of the Tap Room bartender Mulingar: he was in his mid-thirties, well over six feet tall, distinctive with his steely hair and deep-chested laughter.

A man admired by others. And knowing he was admired by others.

If he'd killed Baumgarten . . .

Rebecca would have kept his secret. Wouldn't have told the hotel management, or the police. Wouldn't have come forward as a witness to the "savage" beating.

Baumgarten had lied to police, saying two (male) intruders had broken into his hotel room, beaten and robbed him. Two! He claimed to have been lying on his bed, asleep. Hadn't seen their faces except to know that they were white men and they were "unknown to him." Baumgarten's nose, lower jaw and several ribs were broken. Both his eyes blackened. Bleeding from head wounds, he'd lain helpless for more than an hour before he revived and had the strength to reach for the telephone.

Baumgarten would claim that "thieves" had taken his wallet, his wristwatch, and other personal items worth approximately six hundred dollars.

Baumgarten would say nothing about Rebecca. Not a word about the chambermaid he had lured into his room. For a week, Rebecca worried that police would come to question her. But no one did. She smiled thinking *He's ashamed, he wants to forget.*

Rebecca resented it, that Baumgarten told lies about having been robbed. The man who'd beaten him certainly wasn't the type to have robbed him! Baumgarten must have hidden away his things, to make a false claim. He could sue the hotel management, perhaps. He could file an insurance claim.

Too injured to walk, Baumgarten had been carried on a stretcher to an ambulance waiting outside the hotel entrance, and by ambulance he had been taken to the Chautauqua Falls General Hospital. He would not return to the General Washington Hotel, Rebecca would not see him again.

"Niles Tignor."

As Leora Greb said, no mistaking Tignor for anyone else.

He was a brewery representative, or agent. He traveled through the state negotiating with hotel, restaurant, and tavern owners on behalf of the Black Horse Brewery of Port Oriskany. His salary depended upon commissions. He was said to be the most aggressive and overall the more successful of the brewery agents. He passed through Milburn from time to time and always stayed at the General Washington Hotel. He left generous tips.

It was said of Tignor that he was a man with "secrets."

It was said of Tignor that he was a man you never got to know—but what you did know, you were impressed by.

It was said of Tignor that he liked women but that he was "dangerous" to women. No: he was "gallant" to women. He had women who adored him scattered through the state from the eastern edge of Lake Erie to the northwestern edge of Lake Champlain at the Canadian border. (Did Tignor have women in Canada, too? No doubt!) Yet it was said of Tignor that he was "protective" of women. He'd been married years ago and his young wife had died in a "tragic accident" . . .

It was said of Tignor that he trusted no one.

It was said of Tignor that he'd once killed a man. Maybe it was self-defence. With his bare hands, his fists. A tavern fight, in the Adirondacks. Or had it been Port Oriskany, in the winter of 1938 to 1939 during the infamous brewery wars.

"If you're a man, you don't want to mess with Tignor. If you're a woman . . ."

Rebecca smiled thinking *But he wouldn't hurt me. There is a special feeling between him and me.*

It was said that Tignor wasn't a native of the region. He had been born over in Crown Point, north of Ticonderoga on Lake Champlain, his ancestor was General Adams Tignor who had fought to a draw the British general John Burgoyne, in 1777, when Fort Ticonderoga was burnt to the ground by the departing British army.

No: Tignor was a native of the region. He'd been born in Port Oriskany, one of a number of illegitimate sons of Esdras Tignor who was a Democratic party official in the 1920s involved in smuggling whiskey from Ontario, Canada, into the United States during Prohibition, gunned down in a Port Oriskany street by competitors in 1927 . . .

It was said of Tignor that you must not approach the man, you must wait for him to approach you.

31

❀ ❀ ❀

"Somebody wants to meet you, Rebecca. If you're the 'black-haired Gypsy-looking chambermaid' who works on the fifth floor."

This was the first Rebecca heard, that Niles Tignor was interested in her. Amos Hrube with his smirky, insinuating smile.

Later that day, Mulingar, beefy and mustached, bartender in the Tap Room. "R'becca! Got a friend who'd like to meet you, next time he's in town."

It was Colleen Donner, a switchboard operator at the hotel, a new friend of Rebecca's, who made the arrangements. Tignor would be in town the last week of October. He would be staying at the hotel for just two nights.

At first Rebecca could not speak. Then she said yes, yes I will.

She was sick with apprehension. But she would go through with it. For she loved Niles Tignor, at a distance. There was no man Rebecca had loved in all her life, and she loved Niles Tignor.

"Only I know. I know *him*."

So she consoled herself. In her loneliness, she was fervent to believe. For Jesus Christ had long since ceased to appear to her, wraith-like and seductive in the corner of her eye.

Since leaving Miss Lutter, Rebecca had ceased to think of Jesus Christ, altogether.

Let the girl go, fucker.
I'll break your ass.

This loud furious voice she heard almost continuously. In her thoughts it was always present. Cleaning rooms, pushing her maid's cart, smiling to herself, avoiding the eyes of strangers. Miss? Miss? Excuse me, miss? But Rebecca was courteous and evasive. All men she kept at a distance as she kept her distance from all hotel guests, including women, whom she could not trust, in their authority over her. For it was the prerogative of any hotel guest to accuse any member of the staff of rudeness, poor performance, theft.

Let the girl go . . .

She was dreamy, and she was agitated. She was unaccountably excited, and she was stricken with an almost erotic lassitude. She had never been involved with any boy or man, until now. At the high school, there had been boys who were attracted to her, but only crudely, sexually. For she'd been the gravedigger's daughter, from outside Milburn. She'd been a Quarry Road girl, like Katy Greb.

When she thought of Niles Tignor, she felt a cruel, voluptuous sensation pass over her. Of course, she hadn't known his name at the time he had entered Baumgarten's room and yet somehow she had known him. She wanted to think that they had exchanged a glance at the time. *I know you, girl. I have come here for you.*

That day, a Friday in October 1953, Rebecca worked her eight-hour shift at the hotel. Not tired! Not tired at all. Returned to Ferry Street, bathed, shampooed her hair, brushed and brushed her long wavy hair that fell past her shoulders, halfway down her back. Katy gave her a tube of lipstick, to smear on her mouth: bright peony-red. "Christ, you look good. Like Ruth Roman." Rebecca laughed, she had only a vague idea who the film actress Ruth Roman was. She said, " 'Ruth'—'Rebecca.' Maybe we're sisters." She wore a lime-green sweater that fit her bust tightly, and a gray flannel skirt that fell to mid-calf, a "tailored" skirt as a salesgirl at Norban's described it. LaVerne gave her a little silk scarf to tie around her neck, such "neckerchiefs" were in vogue.

Stockings! Rebecca had a pair without a run. And high-heeled black leather shoes, she'd bought for $7.98, for the occasion.

She met Colleen outside the rear entrance of the hotel. As employees, they would not have dared to enter through the lobby.

Colleen scolded, "Rebecca! Don't look like you're going to some damn funeral, try to *smile*. Nothing's gonna happen to you, you don't want to happen."

It was early evening, and the Tap Room was beginning to fill. At once Rebecca saw Niles Tignor at the bar: a tall broad-backed man with peculiar, nickel-colored hair that seemed to lift from his head. He surprised her, for he stood at the bar with other, ordinary men.

She stared, suddenly frightened. It was a mistake, meeting him. Here was not the man she remembered, exactly. Here was a man whose booming laughter she could hear across the room, above the din of men's voices.

He was talking with the men at the bar, he'd taken not the slightest interest in Colleen and Rebecca who were approaching slowly. The symmetry of his face seemed wrong, as if the bones beneath the skin had been broken, and one side had set higher than the other. His skin looked heated, the hue of red clay. He was larger than Rebecca remembered: his face, his head, his shoulders, his torso that resembled a barrel in which the staves were horizontal and not vertical, a rib cage dense with muscle. Yet he wore a sport coat, dull gray with darker stripes, that fitted him tightly in the shoulders. He wore dark trousers, and a white shirt open at the throat.

Rebecca was pulling at Colleen's arm, weakly. But Colleen, trying to get the attention of her friend Mulingar, behind the bar, pushed her off.

It was a mistake, yet it would happen. Rebecca felt the crust of lipstick on her mouth, bright and smiling as a clown's mouth.

Tignor was a man to hold the attention of other men, you could see. He was telling a story, just concluding a story, the others listened intently, already beginning to laugh. At the ending, which might have been unexpected, there was explosive laughter. Six, seven men including the bartender were gathered around Tignor. At this moment, Mulingar glanced around to see Colleen and Rebecca, girls alone in the Tap Room, amid so many men, and beginning to draw attention. Mulingar winked at Colleen, and signaled her to come closer. He leaned over to speak into Tignor's ear, smiling his sly, lewd smile.

Tignor, however, broke off his conversation with the other men, and turned to see them. Immediately, smiling, his hand extended, he approached them.

"Girls! H'lo."

He was squinting at them. At Rebecca. The way a hunter squints along a rifle barrel. Rebecca who was smiling felt a rush of blood into her face, a hemorrhage of blood. Only dimly could she see, her vision was blurred.

Colleen and Niles Tignor spoke, animatedly. Through the roaring in her ears Rebecca heard her name, and felt the man's grasp, tight, very warm, gripping her hand and releasing it.

" 'R'becca.' H'*lo*."

Tignor escorted the girls to a booth in another part of the tavern, where it was quieter. Close by was a large fieldstone fireplace in which birch logs were burning.

How nice it was here! The oldest, "historic" part of the General Washington Hotel, that Rebecca had never before seen.

Colleen was twenty-one, and so could drink: Tignor ordered a draft beer for her. Rebecca was under-age and so could only have a soft drink. Tignor gave their orders and spoke with them politely, rather formally, at first. His manner with the girls was very different from his manner with the men.

Clearly, Tignor was taken with Rebecca, though his initial conversation was with Colleen, a flirty sort of banter. How big the man's teeth were, a horse's teeth! Somewhat crooked, and of the hue of rotted corncobs. And his odd broke-looking face. And his eyes that were pale, metallic gray, lighter than his skin; their glisten, fixed upon Rebecca, made her uneasy, yet exhilarated. Her heart was beating as it had beat in the high school that morning when Gloria Meunzer pushed into her from behind and Rebecca had known that she wasn't going to run this time, she would turn, confront her enemies, she would fight.

Tignor smiled, asking Rebecca about her work at the hotel.

"Must be, a chambermaid sees lots of things, eh? Bet you could tell some stories."

Rebecca laughed. She was very shy, with Tignor focusing upon her so. She said, "No. I don't tell stories."

Tignor laughed, approving. "Good girl! That's a good girl."

He would know, she had not spoken of him to the police. There was the secret between them, that Colleen could not guess.

On the sly, Rebecca drank from Colleen's glass. For there was the pretense that the hotel management must not see, here was an underaged customer. Tignor ordered two more draft beers, Black Horse of course, for the table.

Damn Rebecca had no intention of remaining sober that night. She was sick of always-so-serious, God-damned *heavy heart* as her friends chided her. Looking like a funeral God damn. No guy wants to go out with a girl with a *heavy heart*. Rebecca heard herself laughing, and she felt her face flush, and she knew she looked damned good, that was why Niles Tignor was attracted to her. She would drink as much as Colleen drank, and she would not get drunk, or sick to her stomach. And when Tignor made a show of offering them Chesterfield cigarettes from his fancy silver cigarette case, engraved with the initials *NT*, Rebecca saw her fingers extract a cigarette just as readily as Colleen did, and this too made her laugh.

It was then that Tignor said, unexpectedly, frowning, in his awkward, head-on way, " 'R'becca Schwart.' I have heard of you, and I am sorry for your loss."

It was a painful moment. Rebecca wasn't sure at first what she had heard.

Bit her lip to keep from laughing. But she could not keep from laughing.

Why do you think I have a loss! I don't. I don't care. I wanted them dead, I hated them both.

It was a purely nervous reflex, Rebecca's laugh. Both Tignor and Colleen stared at her. Rebecca wanted to hide her face in her hands. She wanted to leave the booth, and escape from this place. She managed to say, to Tignor, "I . . . don't think about it, now."

Tignor cupped a hand to his ear, he hadn't heard.

Rebecca repeated her faltering words. By now her face was throbbing again with blood. Tignor nodded. "That's right, girl. Good." There were things of which Niles Tignor did not wish to think, either.

He squeezed her hand. She felt that she would faint, at the touch.

Rebecca's hand was hardly a small, delicate female hand and yet, in Tignor's grip, it became so; his fingers, squeezing, with unconscious strength, made her wince.

Girl he'd called her.

They'd known each other a long time.

"Like this, Rebecca. *Don't* breathe in right away, wait till you get more used to it."

Colleen was showing Rebecca how to smoke. As Tignor looked on, amused. A Technicolor movie it was, music billowing beneath. Not Ruth Roman but Debbie Reynolds, June Allyson. Rebecca was behaving like these pretty, pert film actresses. She was a good-girl-learning-to-smoke, she coughed, tears spilled from her eyes. She was a girl learning-to-drink. She was a girl to please a man, not just any man but a man like Niles Tignor, and though she looked like a slut, in her tight sweater and tight skirt and her mouth a lurid lipstick red, and her hair wavy and tangled down her back, yet she wanted you to think she was a good girl, and naive.

A girl a man wanted to protect, and to love.

Why this happened, Rebecca didn't know: Colleen leaned over and kissed her on the lips!

A joke, it must have been. Tignor laughed.

Oh, but tobacco had such an ugly taste. Mixed in her mind with milk . . .

Damn Rebecca was not going to puke. Not here! Not her.

Luckily, the subject shifted. Rebecca let her cigarette go out. Washed away the taste with a swallow of her lukewarm cola. Colleen, a shrewd girl who'd "dated" many men, and some of these men old as Niles Tignor, knew the questions to ask of their escort: where did he travel, where did he like best, did he have girlfriends all over the state like people said, where was he headed after Milburn, did he have an actual home, anywhere?

Tignor answered most of these questions with a pose of seriousness. He liked everywhere he went but favored Lake Champlain and the Adirondacks. He liked all the people he met! For sure, he liked the General Washington: the hotel was a damn good Black Horse customer.

He had no "home"—maybe. He wasn't one to especially want a "home" like other people. Near as he could figure, "home" was a weight dragging at your ankle. Unless "home" could be something he could take with him anywhere he went, like his car.

Rebecca was struck by Tignor's words. She knew no one who had ever articulated such thoughts. There was a precision here of thinking, though Tignor's actual words were commonplace, that thrilled her. Like Herschel, he was. A crude expression yet something subtle beneath, and unexpected. For wasn't "home" a trap, really? Confinement, a prison. A dank airless cave. You crawled into your cave, to die. What would a man like Niles Tignor want with a mere *home*?

Rebecca said eagerly, "I don't have one, either. A 'home.' Just someplace I keep things. I live on Ferry Street with my friends but it isn't my home. I could sleep out anywhere—by the canal, or in a car."

Tignor laughed, and stared at her, and drank. Rebecca was drinking beer now, from a glass someone had set before her.

It was past nine o'clock: Tignor ordered food for them.

Roast beef on kimmelwick bread, a specialty of the Tap Room. French fries, dill pickles. Foaming glasses of Black Horse draft ale. Rebecca would not have thought she could eat, in Niles Tignor's presence, yet she was surprisingly hungry. Tignor devoured not one but two of the enormous roast beef sandwiches, washed down with ale. His big teeth flashed, he was utterly happy.

"Gin rummy, girls. Know it?"

Rebecca opened her heavy-lidded eyes. Suddenly there was Tignor shuffling cards.

Out of nowhere, a shiny, new-looking deck of playing cards! With remarkable skill Tignor shuffled, caused cards to flash in the air in a kind of waterfall, fascinating to observe. Rebecca had never seen anything like Tignor's skill with cards. And such big, ungainly hands! "Cut, babe." He'd slapped down the deck, Rebecca cut it, and Tignor snatched up the deck again and continued to shuffle, grinning at his audience. Like glittering blades he dealt cards to Colleen, to Rebecca, to himself, to Colleen, to Rebecca, to himself . . . When had it been decided that they would play cards? Rebecca recalled the gin rummy games she'd played at the Greb house, and wondered if Leora had taught them correctly.

Tignor announced this game would be Gypsy-gin-rummy, a variation of the other.

Gypsy-gin-rummy? Neither Colleen nor Rebecca had heard of it.

Tignor removed his jacket and flung it across the back of the booth. His white cotton shirt was of good quality but had become damp and rumpled. His face too was damp, a rivulet of sweat at his temple. The strange steely hair looked like a cap of wires. His eyes were pale, as if luminescent against his ruddy face. A deep-sea predator's eyes, Rebecca thought. For a man of his type Tignor had surprisingly clean fingernails, close cut, though thick and somewhat discolored. He wore a wristwatch with a black leather band, not Baumgarten's watch. And a ring on his right hand, a strange figure like a lion, with a human face, in bas-relief, in gold. "Pick up your cards, Rebecca. See what you have."

She picked up her cards, eager but fumbling. Tried to recall what the point of the game was. You counted cards in a sequence, of the same suit; or in a group, of identical value. There were two piles of cards on the table, the discard and the stock and you were expected to do something with these. The object was to accumulate points and *go gin*.

Colleen was disappointed with her cards. She laughed but bit her lower lip, pouting.

Rebecca stared at the shining cards in her hand. The queen of spades? Ten of spades? Jack, ace . . . ?

Her fingers trembled slightly. The smoldering smoke of the birch logs distracted her. She had a vision of birch trees, beautifully white birches marked with striations in black, bent to the ground, broken-backed to the ground . . . She had no need to draw, or to discard. She played out the hand. She was too naive a cardplayer to question the odds of such a hand.

Tignor laughed, and congratulated her. He was keeping score with a stub of a pencil, on a cocktail napkin.

The game continued. Tignor dealt. The girls insisted, he must be the dealer for they loved to watch him shuffle the cards. Though Colleen complained, "Rebecca has all the luck. Shit!" A pretty frowning girl with a fleshy deep-pink mouth, large breasts firmly erect in a black knit jersey top, glittery hoop earrings. Rebecca sensed how desperate Colleen was to snag Tignor's eye, to engage his interest that kept drifting onto Rebecca. "D'you need extra cards, girls? It's Gypsy-rummy. Ask me, I'll hit you."

They laughed. They had no idea what Tignor was talking about.

Rebecca had been noticing how amid the busyness and frantic hilarity of the Tap Room, Tignor seemed to hold himself apart. If he was aware of others glancing in their direction from time to time, men who might have imagined themselves friends of his, or friendly acquaintances, hoping to be invited to join Tignor in his booth, he gave no sign. For he was not like the other men: he was so supremely self-possessed. He was not quite laughing at Colleen and Rebecca, these credulous girls who picked up the cards he dealt them, like children.

"Oh, look at my hand . . ."

"Oh, look . . . !"

Rebecca laughed, she had such beautiful shining cards king queen jack of clubs . . . She'd given up counting their value, she would trust to Tignor to keep score.

Tignor hunched over his own cards, and sucked at his mouth in dissatisfaction, or a pretense of dissatisfaction, saying, suddenly, "Your race, Rebecca. You are wanderers."

"Race? What race?"

"The race to which you were born."

This was so abrupt, Rebecca had no idea what they were talking about. Her eyelids, that were heavy, and stinging from the smoke, now lifted in antagonism. "I'm the same race as you. The same damn race as anybody."

She was furious with Niles Tignor, suddenly. She felt a savage dislike of him in her soul, in that instant. He had tricked her into trusting him. All that evening he'd been leaning forward on his elbows watching her, bemused. She would have liked to claw his big-boned face that was so smug.

Yet Tignor frowned, his question seemed sincere: "What race is that, Rebecca?"

"The human race."

These words were so fiercely uttered, both Tignor and Colleen burst into laughter. And Rebecca laughed, seeing this was meant to be playful—was it? She liked it that she could make Niles Tignor laugh. She had a gift for beguiling men, if she wished to. Catching their eyes, making them want her. The outside of her, that they could see. Since Tignor had greeted her she'd been intensely aware of him, the sexual heat that exuded from him. For of course Tignor wanted sex with her: he wanted sex from her. God damn if she would go upstairs with him to his hotel room, or out into his car for a nightime drive along the river . . . She felt the thrill of her will in opposition to his. She felt almost faint, exulting in her opposition.

Tignor was dealing. More flashing cards. Tignor's fingers, the sphinx-ring on his right hand, snaky rivulet of sweat running down his forehead, and those big horsey teeth grinning at her. "Don't need to be hit, eh? So show us your cards, girl."

Rebecca spread her cards on the sticky tabletop: king, queen, jack, ten, seven, ace . . . all diamonds.

Unexpectedly then Rebecca began to cry. Tears spilled down her warm cheeks, stinging as acid.

32

⊛ ⊛ ⊛

They would become lovers, in time. For Tignor must have her. He would
marry her if there was no other way.

He went away from Milburn, and he returned. In the winter of 1953 to
1954 he was sometimes gone for a month, sometimes two. Yet in January,
he unexpectedly returned after only two weeks. There was no pattern in his
schedule that Rebecca could discern. He never told her when he might be
back or even whether he would be back and out of pride she refused to ask
him. For Rebecca, too, was stubborn telling the man only goodbye calmly
and maddeningly as if each time she accepted it, this might be the last time
she saw him.

She kissed his cheek. He seized her head, and kissed her mouth hurting her.

Teasing, "Don't you love me, girl?"

And, "Ain't you curious what it might be, to love me?"

And, "You ain't gonna make me marry you, girl? That's it?"

She kept Tignor at a little distance from her, she would not sleep with
him. It was painful to her, yet she would not.

For Rebecca knew: Tignor would use her and discard her like Kleenex.
He would not love her in return—would he?

It was a risk. Like slapping down a playing card, irrevocably.

"You don't want to fall in love with that man, Rebecca. That would be a damn sorry mistake for a girl like you."

This was Leora Greb. But others were jealous of her, too. It riled them that Niles Tignor should seek out Rebecca Schwart who was so young, scarcely half his age. Rebecca Schwart who was graceless in their eyes, not-pretty and headstrong.

Rebecca asked Leora, "What's that, Leora—'a girl like you'?"

Leora said, "A young girl. A girl who doesn't know shit about men. A girl who . . ." Leora paused, frowning. About to say *A girl with no mother, no father* but thinking better of it.

Rebecca said hotly, "Why would I fall in love with Tignor, or with any man! I don't trust any damn man."

She knew: when Tignor was away from Milburn, he forgot her, she simply ceased to exist for him. And yet she could not forget him.

When he was in Milburn, at the General Washington, always he wanted to see her. Somehow, at some time. He had "business appointments" through much of the day and often for dinner and so he must fit Rebecca in, late in the evening. Was she available? Did she want to see him? She'd given him her telephone number, at the Ferry Street apartment. Out of nowhere he would call her. His voice was always a shock to her, so intimate in her ear.

Rebecca tried to manage a light, bantering tone when he called. Often Katy and LaVerne were close by, listening. She would ask Tignor where he was, and Tignor would say, "A block up, on Ferry Street at a pay phone. Fact is, I can see your windows. Where'd you think I was, girl?"

Girl he called her, teasing. Sometimes *Gypsy-girl.*

Rebecca told him she was not a Gypsy! Told him she had been born in the United States just like him.

I won't sleep with him. But I will marry him.

It was ridiculous, truly she didn't believe. Any more than years before she had believed truly that Jesus Christ was her savior: that Jesus Christ had any awareness of Rebecca Schwart at all.

She hadn't wanted to fall in love with Niles Tignor or any man. Love was the poisoned bait, she knew! Sexual love, the love of the senses. Though she could not recall her parents ever having touched each other with affection, yet she had to suppose that they had been *in love*, once. They had been young, they had loved each other and they had married. Long ago, in what Anna Schwart had called the old country. For hadn't Herschel astonished Rebecca by telling her *Pa would sing some, and Ma would sing back, an they'd laugh, like*. And Herschel had told her that Pa had kissed *him*! Love was the trap, that drew you into the cave. And once in that cave, you could not escape.

Sexual love. That meant wanting. Wanting bad, so it ached between the legs. Rebecca knew what this was (she guessed) and knew it was stronger in men, not to be trifled with. Recalling her brother Herschel looming over her grunting and whimpering wanting to rub himself against her behind when she'd been a little girl: the raw wet need in the boy's eyes, an anguish in his face you might mistake (if you saw just the face, the uprolled glistening eyes) for a spiritual longing. Herschel, whom Ma had had to drag away from his little sister slapping the big gangling boy about the head.

Yet Rebecca thought constantly of Tignor. When he was away from Milburn which was most of the time. She recalled with excruciating embarrassment how she had fled the Tap Room that night, desperate to escape. Why she'd burst into tears she didn't know. A hand of shining cards, all diamonds . . . Colleen had tried to follow Rebecca but Rebecca had hidden from her in a back stairway of the hotel.

She'd had too much to drink, that must have been it. Unaccustomed to alcohol. Unaccustomed to such close physical proximity with a man, and knowing he wants you. And such shining cards . . .

Rebecca had supposed in her shame that Niles Tignor would never have wanted to see her again. But he had.

Her trance-like hours of work at the hotel were invaded by Tignor. Especially when she pushed her cart along the fifth-floor corridor. Unlocking the door to room 557, stepping inside. As in a waking dream she saw

Tignor another time striding to the bed, a tall man with nickel-colored hair and a face flushed with anger; she heard Tignor's furious words *Let the girl go* as he grabbed hold of Baumgarten and began to beat him.

For Rebecca's sake, Tignor had risked arrest. He had not known her at the time: he'd heard only her cries for help.

They drove along the Chautauqua River. Westward out of Milburn, toward Beardstown. Where fine, powdery, new-fallen snow had not drifted on the ice, the frozen river was scintillant, blue-tinged in the sun. It was February 1954. Rebecca had not seen Tignor for several weeks. He'd arrived in Milburn driving a new-model Studebaker, robin's-egg-blue, a sedan with the widest windows, front and rear, Rebecca had ever seen on any vehicle. "D'you like it? Want to come for a ride?"

She did. Of course, she did.

Tignor had an opened bottle of Black Horse ale snug between his knees as he drove. From time to time he lifted it to his mouth and drank, and passed it to Rebecca who drank sparingly though she'd grown not to dislike the strong acrid taste of ale. Only in Tignor's company did Rebecca drink and so she associated drinking, the smell of beer or ale, the warm buzzing at the base of her skull, with the anxious happiness she felt with Tignor.

Tignor nudged her with his elbow. "C'mon, babe: drink up. It's no good me drinking alone."

They were not yet lovers. There was that tension between them, an edginess and a reproach on Tignor's part. Rebecca understood that they would become lovers soon.

This afternoon, a Sunday, they would stop at several taverns and hotels along the river. Their destination was the Beardstown Inn. In all these places the Black Horse Brewery had business accounts, and Niles Tignor was known and well liked. It was a pleasure to see strangers' faces lighten when Tignor stepped into a bar, and men glanced up. The camaraderie of men drinking together, even at midday. As a woman Rebecca would never know it and would not have wished to know it and yet: in Tignor's company, in the green plaid woollen coat he'd given her at Christmas, to replace her shabby old brown wool coat he'd said looked like a horse blanket, Rebecca too was made to feel special.

That your new girl, Tignor? Kind of young ain't she?

Maybe for you, pal. Not for me.

As in the corner of her eye Rebecca was aware of Tignor tall and looming like a bear on its hind legs so often she overheard such exchanges between Tignor and other men, strangers to her.

Jesus, Tignor! This one looks hot.

Rebecca overheard, and gave no sign of hearing. Moving off to the women's room so that the men could talk together as crudely and as jocularly as they wished, without her.

Men liked to be seen with good-looking girls. The younger, the better. Could you blame them? You could not! It was jealousy on Leora Greb's part, Leora was past forty and no man would ever look at her again the way Tignor looked at Rebecca.

Younger women in Milburn were jealous of Rebecca, too. Some of them had gone out with Tignor. He'd driven them in one or another of his cars, no doubt he'd given them presents. But their time was past, now was Rebecca's time.

"Could be, honey, I got a surprise for you today."

"Tignor, what? Don't tease!"

He would, though. Tignor was a terrible tease.

Rebecca loved riding with Tignor in the robin's-egg blue Studebaker that was unlike any other vehicle you'd be likely to see in the hilly countryside between Milburn and Beardstown, thirty miles away. Farmers' cars, pickups and jalopies driven by young men passed them from time to time but mostly the road was deserted. Rebecca wanted to think that they were the only two people remaining in the world: no destination ahead, and no General Washington Hotel of Milburn behind where Niles Tignor was a prize guest and Rebecca Schwart was a chambermaid whose wages were paid in cash, off the books.

The Chautauqua River was frozen, ice-locked. Rebecca had never been so far upriver. All of the landscape was new to her, and made beautiful and mysterious by snow. In the distance were the Chautauqua Mountains, pale and fading in winter mist. Nearer were farms, farm land, stretches of un-cultivated land. Rebecca was struck by cornfields in whose ragged and stubbled interiors she sometimes glimpsed the ghost-shapes of white-tailed deer. Mostly the herds were does and nearly grown eight-month fawns in their dull thick winter coats but occasionally she saw a buck: big-chested, massive, with elaborate antlers. When she saw a buck, Rebecca whispered, "Oh, Tignor! Look." Tignor slowed the car to squint out into rows of broken cornstalks.

No creature so beautiful as a fully grown white-tailed buck with a full head of antlers. Tignor whistled through his teeth in admiration for one of his own kind.

"Jesus, girl! Wish I had my rifle."

"You wouldn't shoot him, would you, Tignor? Then he'd just be dead."

Tignor laughed. It was impossible to know what he meant.

Rebecca thought calmly *He has killed. Somebody, or something.*

In her pride and vanity thinking *But he won't kill me!*

Liking her to snuggle against him as he drove. Liking her to rest her head against his shoulder. He stroked her knee, her thigh through layers of winter clothing. He stroked her hand and her forearm up inside the coat sleeve where her skin shivered. As if his hand were moving of its own ac-cord or in accordance with Rebecca's desire. She began to feel excited, anxious. For Rebecca, sexual excitement was indistinguishable from anxi-ety. Wanting to push away from the man, and yet wanting him not to stop.

Her body was alight, glowing. In her breasts, and in the pit of her belly. Suffused through her very soul like a liquidy sunlight.

He has killed, I'm afraid of him.

I shouldn't be here. I've come too far. This is wrong.

He will marry me. Someday!

Tignor had told her he was crazy for her. Told her he wanted to be with her. *Be with.* Rebecca knew what that meant.

Sex. This desire. Only through the sex was there the possibility of love. She had to be cautious of the man, she dreaded becoming pregnant like other girls she knew in Milburn, high school dropouts, some of them younger than Rebecca and already mothers. Tignor had warned her he wasn't a man to marry.

Yet if he loved me. Then!

She knew that ugly things were said of Tignor. Even Mulingar who counted himself a friend of Tignor's repeated rumors. He'd been married, more than once. No doubt he was married now. He had a family at Lake Champlain who knew little of his life elsewhere. He had a family in Buffalo. The remnants of families scattered through the state: his former wives mourning him and his children fatherless.

But not me. He would not leave me. I will be different.

"What is this surprise, Tignor?"

"Wouldn't be any surprise, honey, would it? If I told you too soon."

"Is it something to make me happy or . . ."

Rebecca's voice trailed off. What was she thinking of, to hint such things to any man. That a surprise, to her, might make her unhappy.

Tignor grunted yes. He thought so.

She was wearing a peach-colored angora sweater she'd found in a wastebasket in one of the rooms at the General Washington whose stretched neck she hid with a knotted scarf, and a black wool skirt that fitted her hips snugly, and shiny black boots to mid-calf. So happy!

At the Beardstown Inn, Tignor had the use of a room.

A private room, a room-with-a-double-bed, and a bathroom.

A second-floor room available at the historic old inn for the Black Horse Brewery agent whenever he came there on business. Rebecca wondered uneasily was she meant to stay with Tignor, to sleep with him in that bed?

Tignor gave no sign. He was brusque, matter-of-fact. He left her in the room and went downstairs and would be gone more than an hour having drinks and "talking business" with the hotel manager. Rebecca used the bathroom cautiously and dried her hands not on a fresh-laundered white towel virtually identical with the towels at the General Washington but with toilet paper. She sat in a hard-cushioned chair by a drafty window, she would not stretch out on the bed, on an earthen-colored brocade bedspread that exuded a wintry chill.

My surprise, what is my surprise . . .
Tignor, don't tease!

The Beardstown Inn was smaller than the General Washington, but of a comparable age. Like that hotel, it had originally been a stagecoach stop a very long time ago. The oldest parts of both hotels were their taverns, "tap rooms." It was known that brothels—"whore houses"—were often part of these services for men.

Rebecca was made to think, shivering in a room at the Beardstown Inn: so long ago, girls and women designated as "whores," how frightened and desperate they must have been, in the wilderness of the Chautauqua Valley. They would have been homeless, penniless. No families. No husbands to protect them. Some must have been mentally retarded. In time, they would become pregnant, they would become diseased. And yet there was something comical about the very words *whore—whore house*. You could not utter such vulgar words without smirking.

This room, Rebecca saw, with a critical eye, had been flawlessly made up. The bed, that was just slightly higher than beds at the General Washington, with a plainer headboard and old-fashioned bedposts, was perfectly made. The ugly velvet drapes were arranged just so. A faint smell of cleanser prevailed. And a deeper smell of age, moldering plaster. The carpet was nearly threadbare in places and the walls were papered in a floral print with an off-white background that looked discolored. The ceiling was water-stained in a way to make you think of long-legged spiders scuttling overhead. The tall, gaunt window beside her, framed by heavy velvet drapes, overlooked a snowy waste of a side yard crisscrossed with numberless dog tracks, and now the sun was setting, these tracks were darkening like mysterious markings in code.

Tignor returned, in a heightened mood. His pale eyes lit upon Rebecca, seeing she had not removed her coat, nor even unbuttoned it, and he laughed, telling her to take it off: "You look like somebody waiting for a bus, girl. We're not leaving yet. We're having supper here, for sure. Relax." When Rebecca stood, and fumbled with the cloth-covered buttons, Tignor tugged at them, and a button flew off, rolling across the carpet in a way that would have made Rebecca laugh at another time.

Tignor pulled off her coat, and tossed it carelessly onto a chair atop his own coat he'd tossed there earlier. He smiled at her with his big glistening teeth, stroked her shoulders and hair and kissed her wetly on the mouth. His mouth seemed to be swallowing hers the way a snake would swallow its small paralyzed prey. His tongue tasted of whiskey, and cigarette smoke, yet was oddly cool. Rebecca pushed from him and began to shiver uncontrollably.

"Tignor, I can't. I can't stay here. Do you expect me to stay here tonight? Is this the surprise? I can't, see I don't have my things. I don't have a, a change of clothes. I have to work tomorrow, Tignor. By seven A.M. I have to be at the hotel. They will fire me if . . ."

Tignor let her chatter nervously. He smiled at her, bemused.

"No fuckers are gonna fire *you*, sweetheart. Take my word."

What did this mean? Rebecca was feeling faint.

"I can't stay the night. I . . ."

"I didn't say we were staying the night. I just said I have this room. It's here."

He spoke like a father reproving a small willful child. Rebecca felt the sting, she could not bear to be rebuked.

Tignor went to use the bathroom not shutting the door. Rebecca pressed her hands over her ears not wanting to hear the zestful splash of his urine that went on, and on. She hoped he had not splashed up onto the toilet seat or onto the tile wall. Not that!

She would clean it away, if he had. She would not leave such evidence behind for the chambermaid to clean.

Just as Tignor returned to the room, zipping up his trousers, whistling, there was a cautious knock at the door: he'd ordered a bottle of bourbon, two glasses, a bowl of mixed nuts. The bourbon Tignor ceremoniously poured into glasses for Rebecca and himself insisting: "It's no good a man drinking alone, Rebecca. That's my girl!"

Tignor clicked his glass against Rebecca's, and they drank. The bourbon was liquid flame going down Rebecca's throat.

"First time I saw you, girl. I knew."

He had never before alluded to their first encounter. Even now, it wasn't clear what Tignor meant, and Rebecca knew she must not question him. A man who chose his words carefully, and yet awkwardly, Tignor would not wish to be interrupted.

"See, you're a beautiful girl. I saw that right away. In your maid-uniform, and ugly flat shoes, I saw. Only you need to smile more, honey. You go around looking like you're thinking your own thoughts, and they sure ain't making you happy." Tignor leaned foward and kissed Rebecca on the mouth, lightly. He was smiling at her, his eyes were of the same pale metallic hue as his hair, and he was breathing quickly.

Rebecca tried to smile. Rebecca smiled.

"That's better, honey. That's a whole lot better."

Rebecca was seated on the old-fashioned, hard-cushioned chair, that Tignor had dragged close to the bed, and Tignor was seated on the edge of the bed, pleasantly heated, giving off an aroma of male sweat, male desire, bourbon-and-cigarette-smoke, looming over Rebecca. She was thinking that she was drawn to Niles Tignor because of his size, he was a man to make a not-small girl like herself feel precious as a doll.

Out of his trouser pocket Tignor pulled a handful of loose dollar bills. He tossed them onto the bed beside him, watching Rebecca closely. Like a card trick, this was. "For you, Gypsy-girl."

Shocked, Rebecca stared at the fluttering bills. She could not believe what she was seeing.

". . . for me? But why . . ."

Several of the bills were ten-dollar bills. One was a twenty. Others were five-dollar bills, one-dollar bills. And there came another twenty. In all, there might have been twenty bills.

Tignor laughed at the expression in Rebecca's face.

"Told you there was a surprise waiting in Beardstown, didn't I?"

"But . . . why?"

Rebecca was trying again to smile. She would recall how important it had seemed to her, at this moment, as at the crucial moment when her father Jacob Schwart was trying to maneuver the shotgun around to fire at her, to smile.

Tignor said, expansively, " 'Cause somebody is thinking of you, I guess. Feels guilty about you maybe."

"Tignor, I don't understand."

"Baby, I was up in Quebec last week. In Montreal on business. Saw your brother there."

"My brother? Which brother?"

Tignor paused as if he hadn't known that Rebecca had two brothers.

"Herschel."

"Herschel!"

Rebecca was stunned. She had not heard her brother's name spoken in a very long time and had come half-consciously to think that Herschel might be dead.

"Herschel sent this money for you, see. 'Cause he ain't coming back to the States, ever. They'd arrest him at the border. It ain't a helluva lot of money but he wants you to have it, Rebecca. So I told him I'd give it to you."

It did not occur to Rebecca to doubt any of this. Tignor spoke so persuasively, it was always easier to give in than to doubt him.

"But—how is Herschel? Is he all right?"

"Looked all right to me. But like I said, he ain't gonna come back to the States. One day, maybe you can see him in Canada. Might be we could go together."

Anxiously Rebecca asked what was Herschel doing? how was he getting along? was he working? and Tignor shrugged affably, his pale eyes becoming evasive. "Must be working, he's sending you this money."

Rebecca persisted, "Why doesn't Herschel call me, if he's thinking of me? You told him I work at the General Washington, did you? And you have my telephone number, did you give it to him? He could call me, then."

"Sure."

Rebecca stared at the bills scattered on the bed. She was reluctant to touch them for what would that mean? What did any of this mean? She could not bear to take up the bills, to count them.

"Herschel went away and left me, I hated him for a long time."

Her words sounded so harsh. Tignor frowned, uncertain.

"I'm not so sure I will see Herschel again. He might be moving on," he said.

"Moving on—where?"

"Somewhere out west. What they call 'prairie provinces.' There's jobs opening up in Canada."

Rebecca was trying to think. The bourbon had gone swiftly to her head, her thoughts came to her in slow floating amber-tinted shapes like clouds. Yet she was anxious, for something was wrong here. And she should not be here, in the Beardstown Inn with Niles Tignor.

She wondered why Tignor had surprised her in this way? Scattering dollar bills on a hotel bed. Her chest ached, as if a nerve were pinching her heart.

With renewed energy, Tignor said, "But this ain't my surprise for you, Rebecca. That's Herschel, now there's *me*."

Tignor stood, went to rummage through the pockets of his tossed-down coat, and returned with a small package wrapped in glittery paper: not a box, only just wrapping paper clumsily taped to enclose a very small item.

At once Rebecca thought *A ring. He is giving me a ring.*

It was absurd to think so. Greedily, Rebecca's eyes fastened on the small glittery package that Tignor was presenting to her with a flourish, in the way he shuffled and dealt out cards.

"Oh, Tignor. What is it . . ."

Her hands shook, she could barely open the wrapping paper. Inside was a ring: a milky-pale stone, not transparent but opaque, oval-shaped, of about the size of a pumpkin seed. The setting was silver, and appeared just slightly tarnished.

Still, the ring was beautiful. Rebecca had never been given a ring.

"Oh, Tignor."

Rebecca felt weak. This was what she had wished for, and now she was frightened of it. Fumbling with the beautiful little ring, fearful of dropping it.

"Go on, girl. Try it. See if it fits."

Seeing that Rebecca was blinded by tears, Tignor, with his clumsy fingers, took the ring from her and tried to push it onto the third finger of her right hand. Almost, the ring fit. If he had wanted to push harder, it would fit.

Faintly Rebecca said, "It's so beautiful. Tignor, thank you . . ."

She was nearly overcome with emotion. Yet a part of her mind remained detached, mocking. *It's that ring. He stole it from that room. That man he almost killed. He's waiting for you to recognize it, to accuse him.*

Rebecca took the ring from Tignor and slipped it onto a smaller finger, where it fit loosely.

She kissed Tignor. She heard herself laughing gaily.

"Tignor, does this mean we're engaged?"

Tignor snorted in derision. "Hell it does, girl. What it means is I gave you a damn pretty ring, that's what it means." He was very pleased with himself.

Beyond the tall gaunt window framed by heavy velvet drapes the winter sun had nearly disappeared below the treeline. The snow was glowering a somber shadowy white, the myriad dog tracks that had troubled Rebecca's eye had vanished. Rebecca laughed again, the rich flamey bourbon was making her laugh. So many surprises in this room, that had gone to her head. She was short of breath as if she'd been running.

She was in Tignor's arms, and kissing him recklessly. Like one throwing herself from a height, falling, diving into water below, blindly trusting that the water would receive her and not crush her.

"Tignor! I love you. Don't leave me, Tignor . . . "

She spoke fiercely, she was half-sobbing. Clutching at him, the fatty-muscled flesh of his shoulders. Tignor kissed her, his mouth was unexpectedly soft. Now Rebecca had come to him, now he was startled by her passion, almost hesitant himself, holding back. Always in their lovemaking it was Rebecca who stiffened, who held back. Now she was kissing him hard, in a kind of frenzy, her eyes shut hard seeing the brilliant glittering ice on the river, blue-tinted in the sun, that hardness she wished for herself. She tightened her arms around his neck in triumph. If she was afraid of him now, his maleness, she would give no sign. If he had stolen the ring he had stolen it for her, it would be hers now. She opened her mouth to his. She would have him now, she would give herself over to him. She hated it, her soul so exposed. The man's eyes seeing her, that had seen so many other women naked. She could not bear it, such exposure, yet she would have him now. Her body, that was a woman's body now, the heavy breasts, the belly, the patch of wiry black pubic hair that trailed upward to her navel, like seaweed, that filled her with angry shame.

Like tossing a lighted match onto dried kindling, Rebecca kissing Niles Tignor in this way.

Hurriedly he pulled off their clothing. He took no care that the neck of the angora sweater was stretched and soiled, he had no more awareness of Rebecca's clothing than he had of the floral-print wallpaper surrounding them. Where he could not unbutton or unfasten, he yanked. And his own clothes, too, he would open partway, fumbling in haste. He dragged back the heavy bedspread, throwing it onto the floor, scattering the dollar bills another time, onto the carpet. Some of these bills would be lost, hidden inside the folds of the brocade bedspread, for a chambermaid to discover. He was impatient to make love to Rebecca yet Tignor was an experienced lover of inexperienced girls, he had presence of mind enough to bring out from the bathroom not one but three towels, the very towels Rebecca had been too shy to soil with her wetted hands, and these towels he folded deftly, and lay on the opened bed, beneath Rebecca's hips.

Rebecca wondered why, why such precaution. Then she knew.

33

⁂ ⁂ ⁂

And then he was gone again. On the road, and gone again. A day and a night after they returned from Beardstown and he was gone with just *Goodbye*! And she had no word from him, or of him. Until one day at the end of February she forced herself to speak with Mulingar, there was Mulingar lazily swabbing the Tap Room bar with a rag and Rebecca Schwart in her white maid's uniform and her hair plaited and coiled around her head quietly asking when he thought Tignor would be back in Milburn; and Mulingar smiled insolently at Rebecca and said, "Who wants to know, baby? *You?*"

Even then, quickly walking away, not glancing back at the man leaning over the bar observing her retreating body, her hips and muscled legs, not thinking *I knew this, I deserve this humiliation* but no less adamant than before *He will marry me, he loves me! Here is proof* running her finger over the smooth pale-purple stone in the setting that was just slightly tarnished, she believed to be genuine silver.

34

❀ ❀ ❀

First time I saw you, girl. I knew.

He was gone, and he would return. Rebecca knew: for he had promised.

At work, Rebecca removed the ring for safekeeping. She wrapped it in tissue and carried it close to her heart, in a pocket of her white rayon uniform. When she removed the uniform at the end of her shift, she replaced the silver ring on the smallest finger of her left hand.

Now, it fit perfectly. Katy had showed her how to tighten the ring with a narrow strip of transparent tape.

It was generally known, in Rebecca's small circle of acquaintances, that Niles Tignor had given her this ring. *Are you engaged? You spent the night with him—didn't you?* But Rebecca would not speak of Tignor. She was not one to speak casually of her personal life. She was not one to laugh and joke about men, as other women did. Her feeling for Tignor went too deep.

She hated it, the levity with which women spoke of men, when no men were near. Vulgar remarks, mocking, meant to be funny: as if women were not in awe of male power, the authority of a man like Tignor. The very carelessness of the male who might spread his seed with the abandon of milkweed or maple seeds swirling madly in gusty spring winds. Female mockery was merely defensive, desperate.

So Rebecca would not speak of Tignor, though her friends persisted in asking her. *Was* she engaged? And when would he be back in Milburn? She protested, "He isn't the man you think you know. He is . . ." Behind her back she knew they laughed at her, and pitied her.

In the old stone cottage in the cemetery there had been many words but these had been the words of Death. Now, Rebecca did not trust words. Certainly there were no adequate words to speak of what had passed between her and Tignor, in Beardstown.

We are lovers now. We have made love together. We love each other . . .

Ugly words scrawled by boys on walls and pavement in Milburn. On Hallowe'en morning, invariably FUCK FUK YOU waxed in foot-high letters on store windows, school windows.

It was so, Rebecca thought. Words lie.

She felt confident that Tignor would return to her, for he had promised. There was the ring. There was their lovemaking, the way Tignor had loved her with his body, that could not have been false.

No erotic event exists in isolation, to be experienced merely once, and forgotten. The erotic exists solely in memory: recalled, re-imagined, re-lived, and re-lived in a ceaseless present. So Rebecca understood, now. She was haunted by the memory of those hours in Beardstown that seemed to be taking place in a ceaseless present to which she alone had access. No matter if she was working, in the General Washington Hotel, or in the company of others, talking with them and seemingly alert, engaged: yet she was with Tignor, in the Beardstown Inn. In their bed, in that room.

Their bed it had come to seem, in her memory. Not merely *the bed*.

"Tignor! Pour me some bourbon."

This Tignor would do, happily. For Tignor too needed a drink.

Lifting the glass to Rebecca's chafed lips as she lay in the churned soiled sheets. Her hair was sticking to her sweaty face and neck, her breasts and belly were slick with sweat, her own and Tignor's. He had made her bleed, the folded towels had only just been adequate to absorb the bleeding.

Making love to her, Tignor had been heedless of her muffled cries. Moving upon her massive and obliterating as a landslide. The weight of him! The bulk, and the heat! Rebecca had never experienced anything like it. So shocked, her eyes flew open. The man pumping himself into her, as if this action were his very life, he could not control its urgency that ran through him flame-like, catastrophic. He had scarcely known her, he could not have been aware of her attempts to caress him, to kiss him, to speak his name.

Afterward, she'd tried to hide the bleeding. But Tignor saw, and whistled through his teeth. "God *damn.*"

Rebecca was all right, though. If there was pain, throbbing pain, not only between her legs where she was raw, lacerated, as if he'd shoved his fist up inside her, but her backbone, and the reddened chafed skin of her breasts, and the marks of his teeth on her neck, yet she would not cry, God damn she refused to cry. She understood that Tignor was feeling some repentance. Now the flame-like urgency had passed, now he'd pumped his life into her, he was feeling a male shame, and a dread of her breaking into helpless sobs for then he must console her, and his sexual nature was not one comfortable with consolation. Guilt would madden Niles Tignor, like a horse beset by horseflies.

He hadn't *taken caution* as he called it, either. This he had certainly meant to do.

Rebecca knew, by instinct, that she must not make Tignor feel guilty, or remorseful. He would dislike her, then. He would not want to make love to her again. He would not love her, and he would not marry her.

Ah, how good the bourbon tasted, going down! They drank from the same glass. Rebecca closed her fingers around Tignor's big fingers, on the glass. She loved it, that his hand was so much larger than her own. The knuckles were pronounced, nickel-colored hairs grew lavish as pelt on the backs of his hands.

She was naked, and the man was naked. In this room in their bed at the Beardstown Inn, where they were spending the night together.

Abruptly now, they were intimate. The shock of nakedness had passed over into something so very strange: this intimacy, and the sweaty closeness of their flesh. If they kissed now, the kiss was one of this new intimacy. They were lovers and this fact could not be altered.

Rebecca smiled, greedy in this knowledge. What Tignor had done to her, to her body, was like a shotgun blast, irrevocable.

"You love me, Tignor, don't you? Say you do."

" 'You do.' "

She laughed, and swatted him. In play, in this new dazzling intimacy where she, Rebecca Schwart, had the right now to lightly chastise her lover.

"Tignor! Say you *do*."

"Sure, baby."

In the sticky smelly sheets they lay dazed, exhausted. Like swimmers who have exerted themselves and lay now panting on the sand. What they had done would seem to matter less than that they'd done it, and had survived.

Tignor drifted by quick degrees into sleep. His body twitched, and quivered, with its powerful inner life. Rebecca marveled at him, the fact of him. Awkwardly in her arms, the weight of his left shoulder crushing her right arm. *What does this mean, that we have done together?* She felt the angry hurt throbbing between her legs and yet: the pain was distant, it could be endured. The flamey bourbon coursed through her veins, she too would sleep.

Waking later, in the night. And the bedside lamp was still on.

Her throat burned from the bourbon, she was very thirsty. And the seeping of blood in her loins, that had not ceased. Almost, she felt panic. Almost, she could not think of the man's name.

She peered at him, from a distance of mere inches. So close, it's difficult to see. His skin was ruddy and coarse and still very warm. He was a man who normally sweated when he slept, for his sleep was twitchy, restless. He grunted in his sleep, moaned and whimpered in surprise like a child. His metallic hair that lifted from his forehead, in damp spikes . . . His eyebrows were of that same glinting hue, and the beard pushing through the skin of his jaws. He had turned onto his back, sprawled luxuriantly across the bed, his left arm flung over Rebecca. She lay in its shelter, beneath its numbing weight.

How hard the man breathed, in his sleep! He half-snored, a wet clicking sound rhythmic in his throat like the cries of a nocturnal insect.

Rebecca slipped from the bed, that was unusually high from the floor. She winced, the pain in her groin was knife-like. And still she was bleeding, and had better take a towel with her, to prevent bloodstains on the carpet.

"So ashamed. Oh, Christ."

Yet it was only natural wasn't it: she knew.

Katy and the others would be eager to know, what had happened in Beardstown. They knew, or thought they knew, that Rebecca had never *been with* a man before. Now they would be ravenous to know, and would interrogate her. Though she would tell them nothing yet they would talk of her behind her back, they would wonder.

Niles Tignor! That was the man's name.

Rebecca made her way stiffly into the bathroom, and shut the door. What relief, to be alone!

With shaky fingers Rebecca washed between the legs, using wetted toilet paper. She would not flush it down the toilet until she was certain the bleeding had stopped, for she dreaded waking Tignor. It was 3:20 A.M. The hotel was silent. The plumbing was antique, and noisy. She was dismayed to see that, yes there was fresh blood seeping from her, though more slowly than before.

"You will be all right. You will not bleed to death."

In the mirror above the sink she was surprised to see: her flushed face, her wild disheveled hair. No lipstick remained on her mouth that looked raw, swollen. Her eyes appeared cracked, with tiny red threads. Her nose shone, oily. How ugly she was, how could any man love her!

Still, she smiled. She was Niles Tignor's girl, this blood was proof.

The bleeding would cease by morning. This wasn't menstrual blood that would continue for days. It wasn't dark as that blood, and not clotted. Its odor was different. She would wash, wash, wash herself clean and the man would think no more of it.

Her *hymen* he'd torn, Rebecca knew the word from her dictionary. She'd smiled, years ago seeing how close *hymen* was to *hymn, hymnal.*

Suddenly she recalled how, in the Presbyterian church, beside Rose Lutter who had been so kind to her, Rebecca had not really listened to the minister's sermons. Her mind had drifted off onto men, and maleness, and sex. But with unease, disdain, for she had not yet met Niles Tignor.

In the morning though groggy and hungover, Tignor would need to make love. His breath foul as ditch water yet he would need to make love. For he was fully aroused, and mad with love for her. Couldn't keep his hands off her, he said. Crazy about her she was so beautiful, he said. *My Gypsy-girl. My Jewess. Oh, Jesus . . .*

Later Rebecca would say, in Tignor's car driving back to Milburn, her head resting against his shoulder, "You know, I'm not a Gypsy, Tignor. I'm not a 'Jewess.' "

Tignor, bleary-eyed in the raw morning air, jaws glinting with stubble where he'd shaved in haste, seemed not to hear. Like a fisherman casting his line out, out into a fast-moving stream, he was thinking ahead to Milburn, and what awaited him. And beyond.

"Sure, kid. Me neither."

The ring: it wasn't the ring Baumgarten/Bumstead had placed at the foot of his bed to beguile Rebecca. She was certain, now she had time to examine it. The stone in the other ring had been a darker purple than this stone, square- or rectangular-cut, and clear as glass. (Very likely, it had been glass.) This small oval stone was purple, and opaque.

She was not pregnant. Yet she was pregnant with her feeling for the man, that accompanied her everywhere and at all times.

It was mid-March yet still winter, very cold at night. Only the days were lengthening, there were ever-longer periods of sunshine, thawing and dripping ice. Rebecca was stubborn in her belief that Tignor would return, check into the General Washington Hotel as usual, and call her. She knew, she had not doubted him. Yet when the phone rang in the early evening, and LaVerne Tracy answered, Rebecca came to the doorway to listen, her heart beating in dread. LaVerne was a blowsy blond woman of twenty-three whose attitude toward men was both flirtatious and mocking; always you could tell if LaVerne was speaking with a man on the phone, by her malicious smile.

"Rebecca? I don't know if she's home, I'll see."

Rebecca asked who the caller was.

LaVerne covered the receiver with the flat of her hand, indifferently. "Him."

Rebecca laughed, and took the call.

Tignor wanted to see her, that night. After 10 P.M. if she was free. His voice was a shock in her ear, so close. He sounded edgy, not so bluff and assured as Rebecca recalled. His laughter sounded forced, unconvincing.

Rebecca said yes, she would see him. But only for a while, she had to work the next morning.

Tignor said stiffly so did he have to work the next morning—"I'm in Milburn on business, honey."

In February, Rebecca had had no excuse to give Amos Hrube for being late for work, when Tignor brought her back at midday from Beardstown. She'd stood mute and sullen as Hrube scolded her, saying another chambermaid had had to take over her rooms. Tignor had wanted to speak to Hrube on Rebecca's behalf, but Rebecca wouldn't let him. The last thing she wanted was talk of her and Tignor among the hotel staff, beyond what the staff was already saying.

It was 10:20 P.M. when Tignor's Studebaker pulled up outside the brownstone on Ferry Street. Tignor wasn't one to come upstairs to knock on the apartment door, instead he entered only the vestibule and called Rebecca's name up the stairs, with an air of impatience.

LaVerne said, "Tell that fucker to go to hell. Fuck he thinks he's hot shit, yelling for you like that."

LaVerne had known Niles Tignor before Rebecca had met him. Their relationship was vague to Rebecca, enigmatic.

Rebecca laughed, and told LaVerne she didn't mind.

"Well, I mind," LaVerne said hotly. "That fucker."

Rebecca left the flat. She knew how LaVerne would complain of her to Katy, and how Katy would laugh, and shrug.

Shit it's a man's world, what can you do . . .

If Niles Tignor snapped his fingers for her, Rebecca would come to him. She would come initially, but on her own terms. For she must see the man again, and be with him, to re-establish the intimate connection between them.

She was wearing the green plaid coat Tignor had given her, of which she was so vain. Rarely did Rebecca wear this coat for it was too good for Milburn, and for the hotel chambermaid. She'd smeared lipstick on her mouth: a lurid moist peony-red. On her finger was the silver ring with the small oval milky-purple stone, Rebecca had learned by this time was an opal.

"Tignor! Hello . . ."

When Tignor saw her on the stairs, his smile faded. Something seemed to break in his face. He began to speak, he meant to be jocular in his easy, bantering way, but his voice failed. Quickly he came to Rebecca, and took her hand, hard, clumsy in possession. "Rebecca. Jesus . . ." Through her lowered eyelashes Rebecca assessed the man who was her lover and would be her husband: ruddy-faced, sensual, this man who'd seduced her and whose wish it was to break her, to use and discard her as if she were of no more consequence than a tissue: she saw him, in that instant exposed, naked. Beneath Tignor's good-natured gregariousness was a ghastly nullity, chaos. His soul was a deep stone well nearly emptied of water, its rock sides steep, treacherous.

Rebecca shuddered, knowing.

Yet she lifted her face to his, to be kissed. For these are the rituals that must be performed. She would be without subterfuge, lifting her young, eager face to his, the moist red mouth that so aroused him. For she wished him to think she trusted him utterly, not to hurt her.

Tignor hesitated, and kissed her. Rebecca understood that, at the last moment, he had not wanted to kiss her. The light in the vestibule was glaring, overhead. The vestibule was shabby, unswept. Tenants on the first floor had a young child whose tricycle Tignor stumbled against, greeting Rebecca. He meant to kiss her lightly, a kiss of mere greeting, yet even this kiss Tignor mismanaged. He was stammering, as no one in Milburn had heard Niles Tignor stammer, "I—I guess I been—missing you. Jesus, Rebecca . . ." Tignor's voice trailed off, he stood abashed.

Outside on Ferry Street was the robin's-egg blue Studebaker, idling at the curb and expelling clouds of exhaust.

In the car, Tignor fumbled to turn the key in the ignition, but the key had already been turned, the motor was on. He cursed, and laughed. The interior of the car no longer smelled of smart new upholstery but of bourbon, cigar smoke. In the backseat Rebecca saw amid scattered newspapers, a valise and a pair of man's shoes, the glint of a bottle. She wondered if the bottle was empty or yet contained bourbon and, if so, if she would be expected to drink from it.

Tignor said, "Honey, we can go to the hotel. Where I'm staying."

He did not look at Rebecca. He was driving slowly along Ferry Street as if not altogether certain where he was.

Quietly Rebecca said no. "Not the hotel."

Tignor said, "Why not? I have a room."

When Rebecca did not reply, Tignor said, "It's my private business at the hotel, who I bring. Nobody is going to interfere. They know me there and they respect my privacy. I have a suite on the seventh floor you will like."

Again, quietly Rebecca said no. Not the hotel.

"There's windows looking out toward the canal, over some roofs. I'll order some supper, room service. Drinks."

No, no! Rebecca would not. She was smiling, biting her lower lip.

Tignor was driving now more swiftly along Ferry, turning off onto Main. At the top of the steep hill the General Washington Hotel glittered with lights, amid blocks of mostly darkened buildings.

Rebecca said, "Not that hotel, Tignor. You know why."

"Shit, then. We'll go somewhere else."

"Not any hotel, Tignor."

In the fleeting light from the street, Rebecca saw him staring at her. She might have reached over to slap him. She might have laughed at him, mocked him. She saw his surprise, his hurt, slow-dawning as physical pain. And his resentment of her, the obdurate resisting female. His jaws tightened, yet he forced himself to smile.

"You're the boss, then. Sure."

He drove then to Sandusky's, a tavern on the river. It was two miles away and during the drive he said nothing to Rebecca, nor did she speak to him.

Rebecca thought calmly *He would not touch me. He would not want to hurt me.*

As soon as they entered the smoky interior of the tavern, men called out to Tignor: "Hey, Tignor! H'lo, man"—"Tignor! How the hell are you?"

Rebecca sensed how it gratified Tignor, to be so recognized, and well liked. Tignor swaggered, and called back greetings. Of course he knew Sandusky, the tavern owner; he knew the bartenders. He shook hands, he thumped shoulders. He declined invitations to join men at the bar, where they were eager to have him. He did not trouble to introduce Rebecca, who hung back, at a little distance. She saw the men assessing her, and liking what they saw.

Tignor's girl.

A new, young one.

Some of these Milburn men must have known her, or of her. The Schwart girl. The gravedigger's daughter. Yet she was older now, not a child. In Niles Tignor's flashy company, they would not recognize her.

"C'mere, honey. Where it's quiet."

Tignor brought Rebecca to sit in a booth, away from the bar. A string of festive green and red lights, left over from Christmas, sparkled overhead. Tignor ordered Black Horse draft ale for himself, two glasses. And a Coke for Rebecca. She would drink ale if she wished, from Tignor's glass. He hoped so.

"Hungry? Christ, I could eat a horse."

Tignor ordered two platters of roast beef sandwiches, fried onions, french fries and ketchup. He wanted potato chips, too. And salty peanuts. Dill pickles, a plate of dill pickles. He spoke to Rebecca now in his easy, bantering way. In this place, where others might be observing them, he did not wish to be perceived as a man ill at ease with his girl. He talked of his recent travels through the state, in the Hudson Valley, south into the Catskill region, but very generally. He would tell her nothing crucial of himself, Rebecca knew. In Beardstown, when there had been the opportunity, he had not. He had gorged himself on food, drink, and Rebecca's body, he had wanted nothing more.

"Last two nights, I was in Rochester. At the big hotel there, the Statler. I heard a jazz quartet in a nightclub. D'ya like jazz? Don't know jazz? Well, someday. I'll take you there, maybe. To Rochester."

Rebecca smiled. "I hope so, yes."

In the flickering lights Rebecca was a beautiful girl, perhaps. Since Tignor had made love to her, she had become more beautiful. He was powerfully drawn to her, remembering. He resented it, this power the girl had over him, to distract him. For he did not want to think of the past. He did not want the past, of even a few weeks ago, to exert any influence upon him, in the present. He would have said that to be so influenced, as a man, was to be weak, unmanly. He wanted to live in the present, solely. Yet he could not comprehend it, how Rebecca held herself apart from him, now. She was smiling, but wary. Her olive-dark skin had a fervid glow, her eyes were remarkably clear, the lashes dark, thick, with a curious oblique slyness.

"So! You don't love me, eh? Not like last time."

Tignor, leaning on his elbows, was wistful, half-joking, but his eyes were anxious. Not that Tignor wanted to love any woman but he wanted to be loved, very badly.

Rebecca said, "I do, Tignor. I do love you."

She spoke in a strange, exultant, unsettling voice. The noise in the tavern was such, Tignor could pretend not to have heard. His pale flat eyes went opaque. A dull flush rose into his face. If he'd heard Rebecca, he had no idea what to make of her remark.

The roast beef platters arrived. Tignor ate his food, and much of Rebecca's. He finished both glasses of ale, and ordered a third. He lurched from the booth to use the men's room—"Gotta take a leak, honey. Be right back."

Crude! He was crude, maddening. He went away from the booth, but was not right back.

Rebecca, idly chewing stumps of greasy french fries, saw Tignor dropping by other booths, and at the bar. A half-dozen men at the bar seemed to know him. There was a woman with puffed-up blond hair in a turquoise sweater, who persisted in slipping an arm around Tignor's neck as she spoke earnestly with him. And there was the tavern owner Sandusky with whom Tignor had a lengthy conversation punctuated by explosions of laughter. *He wants to hide among them* Rebecca thought. *As if he is one of them*.

She felt the triumph of possession, that she knew the man intimately. None of these others knew Tignor, as she knew him.

Yet he stayed away from her, purposefully. She knew, she knew what he was doing; he had not telephoned her in weeks, he had forgotten about her.

She knew, and would accept it. She would come like a dog when he snapped his fingers, but only initially: he could not make her do anything more.

When Tignor returned to Rebecca, carrying a draft ale, his face was damply flushed and he walked with the mincing precision of a man on a tilting deck. His eyes snatched at hers, in that curious admixture of anxiety and resentment. "Sorry, baby. Got involved over there." Tignor did not sound very apologetic but he leaned over to kiss Rebecca's cheek. He touched her hair, stroked her hair. His hand lingered on her shoulder. He said, "Know what, I'm gonna get you some earrings, R'becca. Gold hoop earrings. That Gypsy-look, that's so sexy."

Rebecca touched her earlobes. Katy had pierced Rebecca's ears with a hat pin "sanitized" by holding it in a candle flame, so that she would wear pierced earrings, but the tiny slit-wounds had not healed well.

Rebecca said, unexpectedly, "I don't need earrings, Tignor. But thank you."

"A girl who 'don't need' earrings, Jesus . . ." Tignor sat across from Rebecca, heavily. In a gesture of drunken well-being he ran his hands robustly through his hair, and rubbed at his reddened eyelids. He said, genially, as if he had only now thought of it, "Somebody was telling me, R'becca, you're a, what?—'ward of the state.' "

Rebecca frowned, not liking this. God damn, people talking of her, to Niles Tignor!

"I am a ward of Chautauqua County. Because my parents are dead, and I'm under eighteen."

Never had Rebecca uttered those words before.

My parents are dead.

For she had not been thinking of Jacob and Anna Schwart as dead, exactly. They awaited her in the old stone cottage in the cemetery.

Tignor, drinking, was waiting for Rebecca to say more, so she told him, with schoolgirl brightness, "A woman, a former schoolteacher, was appointed my guardian by the county court. I lived with her for a while. But now I'm out of school, and working, I don't need a guardian. I am 'self-supporting.' And when I'm eighteen, I won't be a ward any longer."

"When's that?"

"In May."

Tignor smiled, but he was troubled, uneasy. Seventeen: so young!

Tignor was twice that age, at least.

"This guardian, who's she?"

"A woman. A Christian woman. She was"—Rebecca hesitated, not wanting to say Rose Lutter's name—"very nice to me."

Rebecca felt a stab of guilt. She'd behaved badly to Miss Lutter, she was so ashamed. Not just leaving Miss Lutter without saying goodbye but three times Miss Lutter had tried to contact Rebecca at the General Washington Hotel, and Rebecca had ripped up her messages.

Tignor persisted, "Why'd the court appoint *her*?"

"Because she was my grade school teacher. Because there was no one else."

Rebecca spoke with an air of impatience, she wished Tignor would drop the subject!

"Hell, *I* could be your guardian, girl. You don't need no stranger."

Rebecca smiled, uncertain. She'd become warm, discomfited, being interrogated by Tignor. What he meant by this remark she wasn't sure. Probably just teasing.

Tignor said, "You don't like talking about this 'ward' stuff, I guess?"

Rebecca shook her head. No, no! Why the hell didn't he leave her alone.

She liked Tignor to tease her, yes. In that impersonal way of his that allowed her to laugh, and to feel sexy. But this, it was like him jamming his fist up inside her, making her squirm and squeal, for fun.

Rebecca hid her face, that thought was so ugly.

Where had such a thought come from, so ugly!

"Baby, what the hell? Are you crying?"

Tignor pulled Rebecca's hands away from her face. She was not crying, but would not meet his eye.

"Wish you liked me better tonight, baby. There's something gone wrong between us, I guess."

Tignor spoke mock-wistfully. He was stymied by her, balked by her will in opposition to his own. He was not accustomed to women in opposition to him for very long.

Rebecca said, "I like you, Tignor. You know that."

"Except you won't come back with me. To the hotel."

"Because I'm not your whore, Tignor. I am not a whore."

Tignor winced as if she'd slapped him. This kind of talk, from a woman, was deeply shocking to him. He began to stammer:

"Why'd you think—that? Nobody ever said—that! Jesus, Rebecca— what kind of talk is that? I'm not a man who goes to—whores. God damn I am *not*."

It was the man's pride she'd insulted. As if she'd leaned over the table and slapped him hard in the face for all in Sandusky's to see.

Rebecca had spoken hotly, impulsively. Now she'd begun she could not stop. She had not tasted Tignor's ale that evening yet she felt the reckless exhilaration of drunkenness. "You gave me money, Tignor. You gave me eighty-four dollars. I picked up those bills from the floor, the ones I could find. You didn't help me. You watched me. You said the money was from my brother Herschel in Montreal, but I don't believe you."

Until this moment Rebecca hadn't known what she believed. She hadn't wanted to be suspicious of Tignor, she hadn't wanted to think about it. Eighty-four dollars! And this money, too, *off the books*. Now it seemed probable, Tignor had played a trick on her. She was so stupidly naive. He had paid Rebecca Schwart for being a whore and he'd done it so deftly, in his way of shuffling and dealing cards, you could argue that Rebecca Schwart had not been a whore.

Tignor was protesting, "What the hell are you saying, you? I made it up? He—what's-his-name—'Herschel'—did give me that money, for you. Your own brother, that loves you, for Christ's sake you should be grateful."

Rebecca pressed her hands over her ears. Now it seemed so clear to her, and everyone must have known.

"Look, you took the money, didn't you? I didn't see you leaving it be- hind on the floor, baby."

Baby Tignor uttered in a voice heavy with sarcasm.

"Yes, I took it. I did."

She had not wanted to question the money, at the time. Within a few days she'd spent it. She'd bought food for lavish meals, for her roommates and herself. She'd bought nice things for the living room. She had never been able to contribute as much to the apartment as Katy and LaVerne, always she'd felt guilty.

Now she saw, the others must have guessed who the money was really from. She had told them *Herschel* but surely they were thinking *Tignor*. Katy had told her, taking money for sex was only just something that happened, sometimes.

Tignor's eyes glistened meanly. "And you took the ring, R'becca. You're wearing the ring, aren't you?"

"I'll give it back! I don't want it."

Rebecca tried to remove the ring from her finger but Tignor was too quick for her. He clamped his hand over her hand, hard against the table-top. He was furious, that she should draw attention to them, he was exposed, humiliated. Rebecca whimpered with pain, she worried he would crush the bones of her hand, that were so much smaller than his own. She saw by the flushed glistening look in the man's face that he would have liked to murder her.

"We're leaving. Take your coat. Fuck, you won't take it, I will." Tignor grabbed Rebecca's coat, and his jacket, without releasing her hand. He dragged her from the booth. She stumbled, she nearly fell. People were watching them, but no one would intervene. In Sandusky's, no one would wish to challenge Niles Tignor.

Yet in the Studebaker, in the tavern parking lot, the struggle continued. As soon as Tignor released Rebecca's hand, a flame of madness came over her, she tugged at the ring. She would not wear it a moment longer! And so Tignor slapped her, with the back of his hand, and threatened to do worse. "I hate you. I don't love you. I never did. I think you are an animal, disgusting." Rebecca spoke quietly, almost calmly. She cringed against the passenger's door, her eyes glaring out of the darkness reflecting neon lights like the eyes of a feral cat. Clumsily she was kicking at him. She drew back both her knees to her chest, and kicked him. Tignor was so taken by surprise, he could not protect himself. He cursed her, and punched her. His aim was off, the steering wheel was in his way. Rebecca clawed at his face and would have raked his cheeks if she had been able to reach him. She was so reckless, fighting a man with the strength to break her face in a single blow, Tignor marveled at her. Almost, he had to laugh at her—"Jesus, girl!" She caught him with a flailing blow, bloodying his lip. Tignor wiped his mouth discovering blood. Now he did laugh, the girl was so brazen not seeming to know what he might do to her, in her need to hurt him.

She had not forgiven him, for not calling her. Those weeks. That was the crux of it, Tignor understood.

Somehow, Tignor managed to start the car motor. He kept Rebecca at arm's length. Blood ran down his chin in tusk-like rivulets, his suede sheepskin jacket would be ruined. He backed the Studebaker around, and managed to drive nearly to the road, before Rebecca attacked again. This time, he grabbed her by her thick long hair, shut his fist in her hair and slammed her against the passenger's door so hard, her head against the window, she must have lost consciousness for a moment. He hoped to hell he had not cracked the window. By this time, men had followed them out into the parking lot, to see what was happening. Yet even now, no one would intervene. Sandusky himself who was Tignor's friend had hurried outside, bareheaded in the freezing air, but damn if Sandusky would intervene. This was between Tignor and the girl. You had to suppose there was a purpose to whatever Tignor had to do in such circumstances, and justice.

Rebecca was weakened now, sobbing quietly. That last blow had calmed her, Tignor was able to drive back into Milburn, and to Ferry Street. He would have helped Rebecca out of his car except as he braked at the curb she had the door open, she shrank from him to run away, stumbling up the brownstone steps and into the house. Tignor, panting, gunned the motor, and drove away. He was bleeding not only from the mouth but from a single vertical cut on his right cheek, where Rebecca's nails had caught him. "Bitch. Fucking bitch." Yet he was so flooded with adrenaline, he felt little pain. He guessed that the girl was looking pretty beat-up, too. He hoped he had not broken any of her bones. Probably he'd blackened an eye, maybe both eyes. He hoped to hell nobody called the police. In the parking lot behind the hotel he switched on the overhead light in the Studebaker and saw, as he knew he would see, on the front seat, tossed down in contempt of him, the little opal ring.

The girl's coat lay trampled on the floor.

"It's over, then. Good!"

35

❀ ❀ ❀

Next morning, Rebecca's face was so bruised and swollen, and she walked so stiffly, Katy insisted on calling Amos Hrube to tell him she was sick and couldn't work that day.

LaVerne said hotly, "We should call the police! That fucker."

Katy said, less certainly, "Should we take you to a doctor, Rebecca? You look like hell."

Rebecca was sitting at the kitchen table pressing ice chunks, wrapped in a washcloth, against her face. Her left eye had shut, enlarged and discolored as a goiter. Her mouth was swollen to twice its size. A hand mirror lay on the table, facedown.

Rebecca thanked Katy and LaVerne and told them she was all right: it would be all right.

LaVerne said, "What if he comes back to hurt you worse? That's what guys do, they don't kill you the first time."

Rebecca said no, Tignor would not be back.

LaVerne lifted the telephone from the kitchen counter, and set it onto the table beside Rebecca. "In case you need to call the police."

Katy and LaVerne left for their jobs. Rebecca was alone in the apartment when Tignor arrived later that morning. She had heard a vehicle brake to a stop at the curb outside, and she'd heard a car door slammed shut with jarring loudness. She was feeling too light-headed to go to the window to look out.

The girls' second-floor apartment was only three rooms. There was but a single door, opening out onto the stairway landing. Rebecca heard Tignor's heavy footsteps ascending, and then he was rapping his knuckles on the door. "Rebecca?"

Rebecca sat very still, listening. She'd locked the door after Katy and LaVerne had left but the lock was flimsy, Tignor could kick open the door if he wished.

"Rebecca? Are you in there? Open up, it's Tignor."

As if the bastard needed to identify himself! Rebecca would have laughed except for the pain in her mouth.

Tignor's voice sounded sober, raw and aggrieved. She had never heard her name uttered with such yearning. She saw the doorknob being turned, frantically.

"Go to hell, you! I don't want you."

"Rebecca? Let me in. I won't hurt you, I promise. I have something to tell you."

"No. Go away."

But Tignor would not go away. Rebecca knew he would not.

And yet: she could not bring herself to call the police. She knew she must, but she could not. For if the police tried to arrest Tignor, he would fight them, and they would hurt him, badly. As in a dream she had already seen her lover shot in the chest, on his knees bleeding from a chest wound onto the linoleum floor of the kitchen . . .

Rebecca shook her vision clear. It had not happened, it had been only a dream. A dream of Jacob Schwart's, when the Gestapo had hunted him down in the stone house in the cemetery.

To protect Tignor, Rebecca had no choice but to unlock the door.

"Hey, girl: you're my girl, eh?"

Tignor came inside at once, elated. Rebecca smiled to see that his face, too, had been marked: his upper lip swollen, with an ugly moist scab. In his right cheek was a jagged vertical scratch from her raking nails.

Tignor stared at her: the evidence of his hands on her.

A slow pained smile, almost a look of shyness, that Rebecca bore such visible signs of what he'd done to her. "Pack your things, we're going on a trip."

Taken by surprise, Rebecca laughed. " 'Trip'? Where?"

"You'll see."

Tignor reached for her, Rebecca eluded him. She wanted to strike at him again, to slap his hands away. "You're crazy, I'm not going anywhere with you. I have a job, damn you you know I have to work, this afternoon—"

"That's over. You're not going back to the hotel."

"What? Why?" Rebecca heard herself laugh, now frightened.

"Just get your things, Rebecca. We're leaving Milburn."

"Why the hell d'you think I'd go anywhere with you?—damn bastard like you, a man hitting a girl, treating me with such disrespect—"

Calmly Tignor said, "That won't happen again, Rebecca."

There was a roaring in her ears. Her brain had gone blank, like overexposed film. Tignor was stroking her hair, that was coarse, matted. "C'mon, honey. We got to hurry, we got a little drive ahead—to Niagara Falls."

On the kitchen table beside the squat black rotary telephone Rebecca left the hastily printed note for Katy Greb and LaVerne Tracy to discover that evening:

Dear Katy, and dear LaVerne—Goodbye I am gone to get married.
Rebecca

36

❀ ❀ ❀

Mrs. Niles Tignor.

Each time she signed her new name, it seemed to her that her handwriting was altered.

"There's enemies of mine out there, honey, they'd never approach me. But a wife, she'd be different."

Tignor, frowning, made this pronouncement on the night of March 19, 1954, as they drank champagne in the honeymoon suite of the luxurious Hotel Niagara Falls that overlooked, through scrims of drifting mist, the fabled Horseshoe Falls. The suite was on the eighth floor of the hotel, Tignor had booked it for three nights. Rebecca shivered, but made herself laugh knowing that Tignor needed her to laugh, he'd been brooding much of the day. She came to sit on his lap, and kissed him. She was shivering, he would comfort her. In her new lace-trimmed silk dressing gown that was unlike any item of clothing Rebecca had ever seen let alone worn. Tignor grunted with satisfaction, and began to stroke her hips and thighs with hard, caressing motions of his strong hands. He liked her naked inside the dressing gown, her breasts loose, heavy as if milk-filled against his mouth. He liked to prod, to poke, to tease. He liked her to squeal when he tickled her. He liked to jam his tongue into her mouth, into her ear, into her tight little belly button, into her hot damp armpit that had never been shaved.

Rebecca did not ask what Tignor meant by his enigmatic words, for she supposed he would explain, if he meant to explain; if not, not. She had been Niles Tignor's wife for less than twelve hours, but already she understood.

Clamped between his knees as he drove, a pint bottle of bourbon. The drive from Milburn north and east to Niagara Falls was approximately ninety miles. This landscape, layered with snow like rock strata, passed by Rebecca in a blur. When Tignor lifted the bottle to Rebecca, to drink from it, as you'd prod a child to drink from a bottle by nudging her mouth, he did not like her to hesitate, and so she swallowed the smallest sips she dared. Thinking *Never say no to this man.* The thought was comforting, as if a mystery had been explained.

"Tignor, my man! She's of age, eh?"

"She is."

"Birth certificate?"

"Lost in a fire."

"She's sixteen, at least?"

"Eighteen in May. She says."

"And ain't been c'erced, has she? Looks like both of you been in a car crash'r somethin."

C'erced Rebecca heard as *cursed.* No idea what this squat bald man with tufted eyebrows, said by Tignor to be a trusted acquaintance, and a justice of the peace who could marry them, was speaking of.

Tignor responded with dignity: nobody was being *c'erced.* Not the girl, and not him.

"Well! See what we can do, man."

Strange that the office of a justice of the peace was in a private house, small brick bungalow on a residential street, Niagara Falls nowhere near the Falls. And that his wife—"Mrs. Mack"—would be the sole witness to the wedding.

Tignor steadied her, she'd had to be helped into the house for bourbon on an empty stomach had made her legs weak as melted licorice. The vision in her left eye, that was what's known as a *shiner*, was gauzy. Her swollen mouth throbbed not with ordinary pain but with a wild hunger to be kissed.

It was a "civil" ceremony she was told. It was very brief, requiring less than five minutes. It passed in a blur like turning the dial on a radio, the stations fade in and out.

"Do you, Rebecca . . ."

(As Rebecca began to cough, then to hiccup. So ashamed!)

" . . . your awfully, I mean lawfully wedding husband . . . "

(As Rebecca lapsed into a fit of giggles, in panic.)

"Say 'I do,' my dear. *Do* you?"

"Y-Yes. I do."

"And do you, Niles Tignor—"

"Hell yes."

In a mock-severe voice intoning: "By the authority vested in me by the State of New York and the County of Niagara on this nineteenth teenth day of March 1954 I hereby pronounce you . . . "

Somewhere outside, at a distance a siren passed. An emergency vehicle. Rebecca smiled, danger was far away.

"Bridegroom, you may kiss the bride. Take care!"

But Tignor only closed his arms around Rebecca, as if to shield her with his body. She felt his fist-sized heart beating against her warm, bruised face. She would have closed her arms around him, but he held her fixed, fast. His arms were heavy with fleshy muscle, his sport coat was scratchy against her skin. Her thoughts came to her in slow floating balloons *Now I am married, I will be a wife.*

There was someone she wanted to tell: she had not seen in a long time.

"Mrs. Mack" had documents to be signed, and a two-pound box of Fanny Farmer chocolates. This woman, squat like her husband, with thin-penciled eyebrows and a fluttery manner, had forms for Tignor and Rebecca to sign, and a Certificate of Marriage to take away with them. Tignor was impatient, signing his name in a scrawl that might have been *N. Tignor* if you peered closely. Rebecca had trouble holding the pen in her fingers, hadn't realized that all the fingers of both her hands were slightly swollen, and her concentration faded in and out of focus, so Tignor had to guide her hand: *Rebecca Schard*.

"Mrs. Mack" thanked them. She wrested the box of chocolates out of her husband's hands (the box had been opened, Mr. Mack was helping himself and chewing vigorously), and handed it over to Tignor like a prize.

"These're included in the price, see? You get to take 'em with you on your honeymoon."

"My mother was always warning me, something bad would happen to me. But nothing ever did happen. And now I'm *married*."

Rebecca smiled so happily with her banged-up mouth, Tignor laughed, and gave her a big wet smacking kiss in full view of whoever, in the lobby of the Hotel Niagara Falls, might be watching.

"Me too, R'becca."

Never at the General Washington Hotel had Rebecca seen any room like the honeymoon suite at the Hotel Niagara Falls. Two good-sized rooms: bedroom with canopied bed, sitting room with velvet sofa, chairs, a Motorola floor-model television set, silver ice bucket and tray, crystal glasses. Here too Tignor playfully carried his bride over the threshold, fell with her onto the bed tugging at her clothes, gripping her squirmy body in his arms like a wrestler, and Rebecca shut her eyes to stop the ceiling from spinning, the bed-canopy overhead, Oh! oh! oh! gripping Tignor's shoulders with the desperation of one gripping the edge of a parapet, as Tignor fumbled to open his trousers, fumbled to push himself into her more tentatively at first than he'd done in Beardstown, in a muffled choked voice murmuring what might have been Rebecca's name; and Rebecca shut her eyes tighter for her thoughts were scattering like panicked birds before the wrath of hunters as their explosive shots filled the air and the birds fled skyward for their lives and she was seeing again her father's face realizing for the first time it was a skin-mask, a mask-of-skin and not a face, she saw his mad eyes that were her own, saw his tremulous hands and for the first time too it came to her *I must take it from him, that's what he wants of me, he has called me to him for this, to take his death from him.* Yet she did not. She was paralyzed, she could not move. She watched as he managed to maneuver the bulky shotgun around in that tight space, to aim at himself, and pull the trigger.

Tignor groaned, as if struck by a mallet.

"Oh, baby . . ."

It was her privilege to kiss him, as his wife.

The heavily sleeping man as oblivious of Rebecca kissing his sweaty face at his hairline as he was of the single forlorn fly buzzing trapped in the silken canopy of the bed, overhead.

In the night she found it, that she had not known she'd been looking for: in a "secret" compartment of Tignor's suitcase, in the bathroom that was also a dressing room.

During the day, when they left the hotel, Tignor kept his suitcase locked. But not at night.

It was 3 A.M., Tignor was sleeping. He would sleep deeply and profoundly until at least 10 A.M.

In the bathroom that gleamed and glittered with pearly tiles, brass fixtures, mirrors in gold-gilt scalloped frames like no bathroom she had ever seen at the General Washington, Rebecca stood barefoot, naked and shivering. Tignor had pulled off her lacy new nightgown and tossed it beneath the bed. He wanted her naked beside him, he liked to wake to female nakedness.

"He wouldn't mind. Why would he mind. Now we are husband-and-wife . . ."

Certainly Tignor would mind. He had a short temper, if anyone so much as questioned him in ways he didn't like. A girl did not pry into Niles Tignor's personal life. A girl did not tease the man by slipping her hand into his pocket (for his cigarette case, or lighter), for instance.

Leora Greb had warned Rebecca: never go through a guest's suitcase, they can set traps for you and you'll get hell.

Possibly Rebecca was looking for the Certificate of Marriage. Tignor had folded it carelessly, hidden it away among his things.

Not looking for money! (She seemed to know, Tignor would give her as much money as she wanted, so long as he loved her.) Not looking for brewery-business documents and papers. (Tignor kept these in a valise locked in the trunk of the car.) Yet in one of several zippered compartments in the suitcase she found it: a gun.

It appeared to be a revolver, with a dull blue-black barrel of about five inches. Its handle was wood. It did not appear to be newly purchased. Rebecca had no idea what caliber it was, if the safety lock was on, if it was loaded. (Of course, it must be loaded. What would Tignor want with an unloaded gun?)

It was as she'd known in the car speeding to Niagara Falls to be married: *Never say no to this man.*

Rebecca had no wish to remove the gun from the compartment. Quietly she zipped the compartment back up, and quietly she closed the suitcase. It was a man's suitcase, impracticably heavy, made of good leather but now rather scuffed. A brass monogram gleamed *NT.*

37

She was waiting to become pregnant. Now she was a man's wife, next she would be a baby's mother.

Always *on the move*! Tignor boasted it was the only life.

In those years they lived nowhere. Through 1954 and into the spring of 1955 (when Rebecca became pregnant for the first time) they lived nowhere but in Tignor's car and in a succession of hotels, furnished rooms and, less frequently, apartments rented by the week. Most of their stops were overnight. You could say they lived nowhere but only just stopped for varying lengths of time. They stopped in Buffalo, Port Oriskany, and Rochester. They stopped in Syracuse, Albany, Schenectady, Rome. They stopped in Binghamton and Lockport and Chautauqua Falls and in the small country towns Hammond, Elmira, Chateaugay, Lake Shaheen. They stopped in Potsdam, and in Salamanca. They stopped in Lake George, Lake Canandaigua, Schroon Lake. They stopped in Lodi, Owego, Schoharie, Port au Roche on the northern shore of Lake Champlain. In some of these places, Rebecca understood that Tignor was negotiating to buy property, or had already bought property. In all of these places, Tignor had friends and what he called *contacts*.

Tignor returned regularly to Milburn, of course. He continued to stay at the General Washington Hotel. But at these times he left Rebecca in another town, for she could not bear returning to Milburn.

To the hotel, she'd told Tignor. Not that!

In fact it was Milburn itself. Where she was the gravedigger's daughter and where, if she cared to seek it out, she could visit her parents' weedy grave sites in a shabby corner of the Milburn Township Cemetery.

She had never returned to Ferry Street to pick up the remainder of her things. In such haste she'd left, on that first, astonishing morning of her new life.

But, months later, she'd written to Katy and LaVerne. Her mood was repentant, nostalgia. She worried that her friends had come to dislike her out of jealousy. *I miss you! I am very happy as a married woman, Tignor & I travel all the time on business staying in the best hotels but I miss you both, & Leora. I am hoping to have a baby* . . . What was this: this girlish-gushing tone? Was this the voice of Mrs. Niles Tignor? Rebecca felt a thrill of sheer revulsion, for the voice emerging from her, writing rapidly as she could propel a pen across a sheet of Schroon Lake Inn stationery, in the eerie stillness of the hotel room. *I am sending some money here, please buy something nice for the apartment, new curtains? a lamp? Oh I miss us together staying up late, laughing; I miss Leora dropping by; I would call you but Tignor would not like it, I am afraid. Husbands are jealous of their wives! I should not be surprised, I suppose. Especially, Tignor is jealous of other men of course. He says he knows what men are "in their hearts" & does not trust his wife with any of them.* Rebecca paused, for a moment unable to continue. She could not allow herself to read what she'd written. She could not allow herself to imagine what Tignor would say, should he read what she'd written. *May I ask a favor? If you would please send me some of the things I left behind there, my dictionary especially? I know this is a big favor, for you to wrap & mail something so heavy, I guess that I could buy a new dictionary, for Tignor is very generous giving me money to spend as his wife. But that dictionary is special to me.* Rebecca paused, blinking away tears. Her battered old dictionary: and her name misspelled inside. But it was her dictionary, Pa had not tossed it into the stove but had relented, as if, in that instant, that flooded back upon her now with the power of hallucination, Pa had loved her after all. *Please send to Mrs. Niles Tignor c/o P.O. Box 91, Hammondsville, NY (which is where Tignor receives mail, as it is central to his travels in NY State). Here is $3. Thank you! Give Leora a hug & kiss for me will you? I miss our old days playing rummy after school Katy don't you? Your friend Rebecca.* How tired she was, suddenly. How stricken with unease. For this voice was not hers; no word was hers; as Rebecca, she had no words; as Mrs. Niles Tignor, each word that escaped from her was somehow false. Hurriedly she reread the letter, and wondered if she should rip it up; yet, the point of the letter was to ask for her dictionary to be sent to her. How tired she was feeling, her head ached with anxiety: Tignor would be returning to the room, she dared not allow him to see her writing a letter.

Hastily she added a P.S., that made her smile:

Tell Leora to pass on to that asshole Amos Hrube I DO NOT MISS HIS UGLY FACE.

Each month she was ever closer to becoming pregnant, Rebecca believed. For less frequently now did Tignor *take caution*. Especially if he'd been drinking, and there just wasn't time. Even as they made love Rebecca rehearsed telling him *Tignor? I have news*. Or, *Tignor! Guess what you're going to be, darling. And me, too*. Brushing aside as you'd brush aside an annoying fly any memory of those rumors of Niles Tignor she'd heard back in Milburn that the man had children of all ages scattered across the state, that his young wives came to harm, that even now he had at least one wife and young children, he'd only recently abandoned.

Some months, she would swear she *was*. Just *had to be*.

Her breasts felt heavy, the nipples so sensitive she winced when Tignor sucked them. And her belly hard and round and tight as a drum. Tignor was crazy for her, said it was like a drug to him, her and him together he couldn't get enough of. And not *taking caution* signaled to Rebecca he wanted a baby just as she did.

Rebecca had not wished to ask Tignor straight out if he wanted children, nor would Tignor have asked Rebecca for there was a curious reticence between them in such matters. Tignor spoke crudely and casually using such words as *fuck, screw, suck, shit* but he would have been deeply embarrassed to utter such an expression as *having sexual intercourse*. No more could Tignor have spoken of *making love* to Rebecca than he could have spoken in a foreign language.

It was all right for Rebecca to become emotional, such behavior was expected of a woman. "You love me, Tignor, don't you? A little?" Rebecca would ask, plaintive as a kitten, and Tignor would mutter, "Sure." Laughing, on the edge of being annoyed, "Why'd I marry you, sweetheart, if I didn't?"

Her reward was, and would be: the man's weight upon her.

How big Tignor was, and how heavy! It was like the sky falling on you. Panting and spent and his skin that was coarse and mismatched-looking glowed with an uncanny sort of beauty.

Rebecca believed that her love for Niles Tignor would endure for a lifetime, always she would be grateful to him. He had not needed to marry her, she knew. He might have tossed her away like a used tissue, for perhaps that was what she deserved.

Somewhere amid his things it existed: the Certificate of Marriage. Rebecca had seen it, her hand had even signed it.

Without Tignor's weight holding her fixed, fast, she would be broken and scattered like dried leaves blown by the wind. And of no more account than dried leaves blown by the wind.

She was coming to love him, sexually. She would take from him a fleeting sexual pleasure. It was not the powerful sensation Tignor seemed to feel, that so annihilated him. Rebecca did not want to feel any sensation so extreme. She did not want to shatter in his arms, she did not want to scream like a wounded creature. It was the weight of the man she wanted, that was all. And Tignor's sudden tenderness in the drift to sleep in her arms.

The first baby would be a boy, Rebecca hoped. Niles, Jr. they would call him.

If a girl . . . Rebecca had no idea.

On the move! For the brewery business was *cutthroat competitive*. As an agent Tignor earned a base salary but his real money came from commissions.

What Tignor's yearly income was, Rebecca had no idea. She would no more have asked him than she would have asked her father what his income was. Certainly if she'd asked, Tignor would not have told her. He would have laughed in her face.

Possibly, if she'd misjudged his mood, he'd slap her in the face.

For *getting out of line* he might slap her. For *smart-mouthing* him.

Tignor never hit her hard, and not with a closed fist. Tignor spoke with contempt of men who hit women in such a way.

Once, Rebecca naively asked when would she meet his family?—and Tignor, lighting a cigar, laughed at her, genially, and said, "Tignors don't have no family, honey." He fell silent then, and a few minutes later, abruptly he turned on her and slapped her with the back of his hand demanding to know who she'd been talking to?

Rebecca stammered, no one!

"Anybody talks to you about me, or asks questions about me, you come to me, honey. And I'll deal with it."

It was so, as Rebecca had boasted to Katy and LaVerne, Tignor was a generous husband. In the first year of their marriage. Long as he was crazy for her. He bought her presents, costume jewelry, perfume, sexy clothing and underwear, silky things, that aroused him sexually just to see, as Rebecca pulled them from their tissue wrappings to hold up against herself.

"Oh, Tignor! This is beautiful. Thank you."

"Put it on, baby. Let's see how it fits."

And what a tease Tignor was: it helped if Rebecca had had a drink or two, to fall in with his mood.

Scattering money for her onto the bed of their hotel room, as he'd done in Beardstown so he did in Binghamton, Lake George, Schoharie. Pulling bills out of his wallet, tossing ten- and twenty-dollar bills and sometimes fifty-dollar bills into the air to flutter and sink like wounded butterflies.

"For you, Gypsy-girl. Now you're my wife, not my whore."

She knew: he had married her but had not forgiven her. For the insult that he, Niles Tignor, might be perceived as a man who needs to pay women for sex. One day, he would make her regret this insult.

———

How restless Tignor was! It was an almost physical reaction, like an itchy rash.

A few days in one place. Sometimes only just overnight. The worst time was the end of the year, the so-called holiday season. Mid-December through New Year's Day Tignor's business came to a virtual halt. There was plenty of drinking, and Tignor had arranged to stay at the Buffalo Statler Hotel, he had friends in the Buffalo-Niagara Falls area with whom he could drink and play cards and still: he was *fucking bored*. Rebecca knew not to irritate him by saying the wrong thing or by getting in his way.

She drank with him, in the early hours of the morning when he couldn't sleep. Sometimes she touched him, gently. With the caution of a woman touching a wounded dog that might turn on her, snarling. Stroking his warm forehead, his stiff metallic hair, in a gentle teasing way that Tignor liked, making of Niles Tignor a riddle to himself.

"Tignor, are you a man who travels all the time because he's restless, or have you become a man who becomes restless because he travels all the time?"

Tignor frowned, wondering at this.

"Jesus, I don't know. Both, maybe."

Saying, after a pause, "But your race is a wandering one, too. Ain't it, R'becca?"

Sometimes after they'd just checked into a hotel, Tignor would make a telephone call, or receive one, and announce to Rebecca that something had "come up"—he had "business-on-top-of-business"—and would have to leave, immediately. His mood at such times was excited, aroused. That air of urgency about him that signaled to Rebecca to stand back, not to expect him to return for a while. And not to ask questions.

Business-on-top-of-business meant business unrelated to the Black Horse Brewery, Rebecca gathered. For more than once when Tignor disappeared like this, a call came to him at the hotel from brewery headquarters in Port Oriskany, and Rebecca had to make the excuse that Tignor was visiting local friends, they'd taken him on an overnight hunting trip . . . When Tignor returned, and Rebecca passed on the message to him, Tignor shrugged. "So? Fuck 'em."

Rebecca was lonely, at such times. But she never doubted that Tignor would return to her. On these impromptu trips he left most of his things behind, including the big scuffed-leather suitcase.

Tignor didn't leave the revolver behind, though. He took it with him.

Mrs. Niles Tignor. She loved signing this name, beneath *Niles Tignor* in the hotel registers. Always there was her anticipation that a desk clerk or a manager would question was Rebecca really Tignor's wife but none ever did.

Mrs. Niles Tignor. She'd come to think she was so smart. But like any young wife she made mistakes.

It was as she'd told Katy and LaVerne, Tignor had a jealous streak. She supposed it meant he loved her, no one had ever loved her like this, there was a danger in it, like bringing a match too close to flammable material. For Tignor was a man not accustomed to sharing a woman's attention with other men, though he liked men to look at Rebecca, he often brought her with him to restaurants, bars, taverns to keep him company. Yet he did not like Rebecca to look at other men, even friends of his. Especially he did not like Rebecca talking and laughing more than briefly with these men. "A man has got one idea, looking at you. And you're my wife, that idea is mine." Rebecca was meant to smile at this but to take the warning seriously. Yet more upsetting to Tignor was the prospect of Rebecca becoming friendly with strangers, behind his back. These might be other male guests in the hotel, hotel employees, even Negro bellboys whose faces brightened at the sight of "Mis-tah Tig-ger" who never failed to tip so generously.

"Anybody gets out of line with you, girl, you come to me. I'll deal with it."

And what would you do? Rebecca thought of Tignor's fists striking the helpless Baumgarten, breaking his face like melon. She thought of the revolver with the wooden handle.

"You don't look like you live around here."

A man in a navy jacket, a navy cap pulled low on his forehead. He'd come to sit beside Rebecca at the counter, at a diner in Hammond, or maybe it was Potsdam. One of the small upstate cities of that winter

1955. Rebecca smiled at the stranger sidelong, not meaning to smile exactly. She said, "That's right. I don't live here." His elbow on the counter beside her arm, and he was leaning onto the palm of his hand, bringing his face uncomfortably close to hers, and about to ask her something further when Rebecca turned abruptly from him, left a dollar on the counter to pay for her coffee, and walked quickly out of the diner.

It was February. Sky like a blackboard carelessly erased of chalk markings. A lightly falling snow on a river whose name Rebecca could not recall no more than, in her nerved-up state, she could have recalled the name of the city they'd stopped in for several days.

Until that morning she'd believed she might be pregnant. But her period had come at last, unmistakable, cramps and bleeding and a mild fever, and so she knew *Not this time. I am spared telling Tignor.* In the hotel room she'd become restless, Tignor would be away until that evening. Trying to read one of her paperback books. She had her dictionary, too. Looked up her old spelling-bee words *precipitant, prophecy, contingency, inchoate.* So long ago! She'd been a little girl, she had known nothing. Yet it was a comfort to Rebecca, that the words, useless to her, were still in the dictionary and would outlive her. In the wintry light that fell through the hotel windows she was lonely, and restless. The maid hadn't yet come to make up the room, she'd pulled the heavy bedspread over the tumbled sheets that smelled of sweat, semen, Tignor's yeasty body.

Had to get out! She put on her coat, boots. Walking in the lightly falling snow in the downtown area near the hotel until she was shivering with cold, stopped in a diner to have a cup of coffee, and would have remained at the counter basking in warmth except the man in the navy jacket approached her. *A man has got one idea.* And on the street she happened to glance back over her shoulder and saw the man behind her, and wondered if he was following her. And it seemed to her then that she'd seen this man, or someone who closely resembled him, in the lobby of the hotel, as she'd crossed from the elevators to the front entrance. He had followed her from the hotel—had he? She'd had only a vague impression of him. He was in his thirties perhaps. He quickened his pace when she quickened hers, abruptly turning a corner, crossing a street just far enough behind Rebecca so that she might not have seen him unless she'd known to look for him.

One idea. One idea. A man has got one idea. She was alarmed but not really frightened. She walked faster, she began to run. Pedestrians glanced at her, curious. Yet how good to run in the lightly falling snow, drawing sharp, cold air deep into her lungs! As she'd run in Milburn as a girl so she was running now in Potsdam, or in Hammond.

Blindly she entered a woman's clothing store. She was a surprise to the salesclerks, exiting at the rear. She doubled back to the hotel, she'd eluded the man in the navy jacket. She thought no more of him. Except that evening entering the tap room of the hotel to meet Tignor, she saw the man who'd followed her with Tignor, at the bar. They were talking, laughing. The man wasn't wearing the navy jacket but Rebecca was sure it was him.

A test! Tignor was testing me.

Rebecca would never know. When she joined Tignor, Tignor was alone at the bar. The other man had slipped away. Tignor was in one of his warm, expansive moods, he must have had a good day.

"How's my girl? Did you miss your old husband?"

This time, it was a fact. Not speculation.

Waking one morning and her breasts were heavy-feeling, and abnormally sensitive. Her belly felt bloated. There was a tingling through her body like a mild electric current. In bed in Tignor's arms she dared to wake him, to whisper to him her apprehension. For suddenly, Rebecca was frightened. She felt as if she'd been pushed to the edge of something like a parapet, she was risking too much. Tignor's response was surprising to her. She had expected him to react with a grunt of disapproval, but he did not. He was waking fully, he was thinking. She could feel his brain churning with thought. And then he said nothing, he only just kissed her, a hard wet aggressive kiss. He kneaded her breasts, he sucked at the nipples that were so sensitive, Rebecca winced. He whispered, "How's that feel? You want more?"

Rebecca held the man tight, tight for dear life.

Dear Katy, and dear LaVerne lying on a hotel bed writing on hotel stationery, one of Tignor's almost-emptied glasses of bourbon on the bedside table from the previous night. *I have such exciting news, I AM PREGNANT. Tignor took me to a doctor in Port Oriskany. The baby is due in December he says. I AM SO EXCITED.*

Rebecca reread what she'd written to her friends who were faraway and becoming increasingly vague to her, and added *Tignor wants the baby, too, he says if it will make me happy that is what he wants, too.* And again reread the letter, and ripped it up in disgust.

It was so, as Jacob Schwart had said. Words are lies.

Now she was pregnant, and so cozy-feeling. Even what's called morning sickness came to be familiar, reassuring. The doctor had been so nice. He'd told her what to expect, stage by stage. His nurse had given her a pamphlet. Not for a moment had they appeared to doubt that she was Niles Tignor's wife, in fact they were both acquainted with Tignor and pleased to see him. Rebecca lay cuddled against Tignor in bed saying, "We will need a place to stay, Tignor. For the baby. Won't we, Tignor?" and Tignor said, in his sleepy-affable voice, "Sure, honey," and Rebecca said, "Because just stopping in hotels like we do . . . That would be hard, with a tiny baby."

It was a pregnancy-sign, that Rebecca would say *tiny baby*. She was beginning to speak, and to think, in baby-talk. *Tiny!* She jammed her fist against her mouth to keep from laughing. A tiny baby would be the size of a mouse.

In these drowsy-loving talks with Tignor she did not say *home*. She knew how Tignor would screw up his face at *home*.

And yet, Tignor was not to be predicted. He surprised Rebecca by saying he'd been thinking of renting a furnished apartment for her anyway. In Chautauqua Falls, out along the canal in the country where it was quiet, he knew of a place. "You and the baby would live there. Daddy would be there when he could." So tenderly Tignor spoke, Rebecca could have no reason to think this was the end of anything.

———

Lying on a hotel bed writing a letter on hotel stationery, a glass of bourbon on the bedside table. So delicious, by lamplight! She wasn't so lonely
with Tignor away, now she had the baby snug inside her. This letter
she would work damn hard at, she would make a first draft and copy
it over.

April 19, 1955

Dear Miss Lutter,

I am sending you this little Easter gift, I thought of you when I saw it in
a store here in Schenectady. I hope you can wear it on your Easter coat
or dress. "Mother-of-pearl" is so beautiful, I think.

I guess I never told you, I am married and moved away from Milburn.
My husband and I will have a residence in Chautauqua Falls. My husband is Niles Tignor, he is a businessman with the Black Horse Brewery you have heard of. He is often traveling on business. He is a handsome "older man."

We will have our first baby in December!

I will be 18 in three weeks. I am quite "grown up" now! I was very
ignorant when I came to live with you and could not appreciate your
goodness kindness.

At 18 I would no longer be a ward of the county, if I was not married.
So it will be all legal that

Miss Lutter there is something for me to tell you I don't know how to
find the words

I am so ashamed of

I am so sorry for

I hope that you will remember me in your prayers. I wish

"Bullshit."

It had taken Rebecca almost an hour to stammer out these halting lines. And when she reread them she was overcome with disgust. How stupid she sounded! How childish. She'd had to look up the simplest words in the dictionary yet she'd managed to misspell *residence* anyway. She tore the letter into pieces.

Later, she sent Miss Lutter the mother-of-pearl brooch with just an Easter card. *Your friend Rebecca.*

The brooch was in the shape of a small white camellia that seemed to Rebecca very beautiful. It had cost twenty dollars.

"Twenty dollars! If Ma could know."

She included no return address on the little package. So that Miss Lutter could not write back to thank her. And so that Rebecca could never know if her former teacher would have written to thank her.

"Mrs. Tignor. Good to meet you."

They were burly good-natured men like Tignor whom you would not wish to cross. In taverns and hotel tap rooms they drank with Tignor and they looked and behaved like Tignor's other drinking companions but they were police officers: not the kind to wear uniforms, as Tignor explained. (Rebecca hadn't known there were police officers who didn't wear uniforms. They had higher ranks: detective, lieutenant.)

These men mingled easily with the others. They were hearty eaters and drinkers. They picked their teeth thoughtfully with wooden toothpicks placed in whiskey shot glasses on bars beside pickled pigs' feet and fried onion rings. They favored cigars over cigarettes. They favored Black Horse ale which was on the house wherever Niles Tignor drank. They were respectful of Rebecca whom they never failed to call "Mrs. Tignor"—with sometimes a hint of a wink over her head, to Tignor.

They've met other women of his. But never a wife.

She smiled to think this. She was so young, damned good-looking she knew they were saying, nudging one another. In envy of Niles Tignor who was their friend.

If they carried guns inside their bulky clothes, Rebecca never saw the guns. If Tignor sometimes carried his gun, Rebecca never saw it.

38

❀ ❀ ❀

She was Niles Tignor's wife, and she was having Niles Tignor's baby. These were days, weeks, months of surpassing happiness. And yet, like any young wife, Rebecca made a mistake.

She knew: Tignor did not like her behaving in any over-friendly way with men. He had made it clear to her. He had warned her, more than once. Now she was pregnant, her skin glowed darkish-pale as if lit from within by a candle flame. There was often a flush in her cheeks, often she was breathless, moist-eyed. Her breasts and hips were more ample, womanly. Tignor teased her, she was eating more than he was. Almost hourly, the baby in her womb seemed to be growing.

Of course Rebecca knew (from the illustrated pamphlet *Your Body, Your Baby & You*), that in fact the "fetus" more resembled a frog than a human being, yet by the twelfth week, in May, she fantasized that Baby Niles had already acquired a face, and a soul.

"There are men crazy for pregnant women. A woman blown up like a goddam whale, still there's men who . . ." Tignor's voice, bemused and disdainful, trailed off. You could see that he, Tignor, was not inclined to such perversity.

And so Rebecca knew, to shun the attentions of men. Even elderly men. She was aloof and indifferent to the most innocuous of greetings — "Good morning!" — "Fine morning isn't it?" —cast in her direction by men in hotel corridors, elevators, restaurants. Yet she had a weakness for women. Now in her pregnancy, she was avid for the company of women. Tignor was annoyed by her *gabbing with* waitresses, salesclerks, chambermaids for more than a minute or two. He liked his exotically good-looking young wife to be admired, to be vivacious, and to display "personality": but he did not like too much of this, behind his back. In the hotels in which Niles Tignor was known as a frequent guest he knew he was talked-of by the staff, he knew and accepted this but he did not want Rebecca to tell tales of him, that might become exaggerated in the re-telling, and make him into a figure of fun. And now that his wife was pregnant, and would soon begin to show her pregnancy, he was particularly sensitive.

It was in May 1955, that Tignor returned unexpectedly to their room in the Hotel Henry Hudson in Troy, to discover Rebecca not only *gabbing with* the chambermaid who was making up the room, but helping the woman change the bed. In the corridor just outside the door Tignor froze, observing.

For there was his wife deftly tucking in bedsheets, tugging at a sheet as the other woman tugged at the other end. With girlish eagerness Rebecca was saying, ". . . this baby, he's always *hungry*! He takes after his daddy for sure. His daddy wants him bad as I do. I was so surprised! I thought my heart would burst, I was . . . well, I was so surprised. You don't expect men to have those kinds of feelings, do you? My birthday was last week, I'm nineteen and that's plenty old enough to have a baby, my doctor says. I guess I'm a little scared. But I'm very healthy. My husband is always traveling, we stay in the best hotels like this one. He has an important position with the Black Horse Brewery, maybe you know. You know him, I guess?— Niles Tignor?"

When Rebecca glanced around, to see why the maid was staring so fixedly past her shoulder, she saw Tignor in the doorway.

Quietly Tignor told the maid, "Out. I need to speak with my wife."

She would not try to elude him. Vividly she recalled her father needing to discipline her. Not once but many times. And Tignor had been sparing with her, until now. Pa's way had not been to slap but to grab her by the upper arm and shake-shake-shake until her teeth rattled. *You are one of them. One of them!* Rebecca no longer knew if she had ever known what Pa had meant by these words and what she had done to provoke him but she knew she'd deserved it, her punishment. You always know.

The bleeding began a half-hour later. Cramps in the pit of her belly, and a sudden hot surging of blood. Tignor had not struck her there, Tignor was not to blame. Niles Tignor was not a man to strike a woman with his fists, and not a pregnant woman in the belly. Yet the bleeding began, a *miscarriage* it would be called. Tignor poured bourbon into glasses for them both.

"The next one, you can keep."

39

❀ ❀ ❀

It was so. He kept his promise. She had not doubted him.

"You'll be safe here. It's quiet here. Not like in town. Not like on the road, that ain't good for a woman trying to have a baby. See, there's a food store here. Five-minute walk. Anytime you want, if I'm not here you can walk to town, along the canal. You like to walk, eh? Most walking-girl I ever known! Or you could get a ride, there's plenty of neighbors here. Meltzer's wife, she'll take you when she goes in. I'll pay for a telephone, and for sure I'll call you when I'm on the road. I'll make sure you have everything you need. This time, you got to take better care of yourself. Maybe cut back on the drinking. That's my fault, I kind of encouraged you, I guess. That's my weakness, too. And I'll be here as much as I can. I'm getting tired of the road, frankly. I'm looking into some property in town, maybe buying into a tavern. Well!"

Kissing her, baring his big horsey teeth in a grin.

"Y'know I'm crazy about you, girl, eh?"

She knew. She was four weeks' pregnant again, and this time she would have the baby.

"Why's it called 'Poor Farm Road'?"

She was frightened, naturally she asked jokey questions.

Yet Tignor surprised her, he knew the answer: a long time ago, could have been a hundred years ago, there'd been an actual "poor farm"—"a farm for poor people"—about a mile down the road where the school-house was, now. Vaguely Tignor thought it might've had something to do with the canal being dug.

Edna Meltzer said it was so, there had been an actual poor farm just up the road: "I remember it real well from when I was little. Mostly old people. That got sick or too old and couldn't work their farms, and had to sell them cheap. There wasn't this 'welfare' we have now to take care of people—there wasn't 'income tax'—'Social Security'—any kind of thing like that." Mrs. Meltzer made a snorting sound that might have meant she was disgusted that life had ever been so cruel, or might have meant she was disgusted how people were coddled now in modern times. She was a stout pudding-faced woman with sharp little eyes and a motherly air that seemed to suck oxygen out of the room.

The Meltzers, who lived approximately a quarter-mile away, were Rebecca's nearest neighbors on the Poor Farm Road. Mr. Meltzer owned Meltzer's Gas & Auto Repair with a big round red-letter ESSO sign out front of his garage. There was some kind of connection between Meltzer and Niles Tignor, Rebecca hadn't figured out. The men were known to each other yet not exactly friends.

Tignor warned, "Take care you don't go gabbing with the old woman, eh? An old bag like that, her kids're grown up, she'll be wanting to ask you all kinds of things ain't her business, see? But you know better, I guess." Tignor stroked Rebecca's head, her hair. Since the *miscarriage*, he'd been gentle with her, and patient. But Rebecca knew not to talk carelessly with anyone. Whether Tignor was around, or whether Tignor was away.

It was a ramshackle old farmhouse at the end of a dirt lane—not where you'd expect Niles Tignor to live! Rebecca had expected a rented house or an apartment in one of Tignor's favored cities, at least a residence in Chautauqua Falls instead of in the deep countryside. Tignor kept saying, "Nice, ain't it? Real private." No other house was visible from the upstairs windows of this house. Nor could you see the road, that was a narrow gravel road. Except for the slow-rising smoke-haze to the east, you could not have guessed in which direction Chautauqua Falls was. All that remained of the farm's original ninety acres were a few overgrown fields and pastures, a faded-red falling-down hay barn and several outbuildings, and a thirty-foot-deep stone well that yielded water so cold it made your mouth ache, and tasted faintly of metal.

"It's beautiful, Tignor. It will be special to us."

From the driveway, the farmhouse looked impressive, bordered by fierce craggy yew trees, but up close it was clearly shabby, in need of repair. Yet when Tignor was home, though he did not call it *home*, he appeared to be in a heightened mood.

He ate the meals Rebecca nervously prepared for him, from cookbook recipes. Tignor was easy to please: meat, meat, meat! And always potatoes: mashed, oven-roasted, boiled. In his spending moods he took her to Chautauqua Falls to buy supplies. "It's our honeymoon, kid. A little delayed." The old house was partly furnished but a new gas stove was badly needed, a refrigerator to replace the smelly old icebox, a new mattress for their bed, curtains and carpets. And baby things: bassinet, stroller, baby-bath. "One of those rubber-things where you pour the water in, you heat the water and pour it in, and there's a little hose, like, and it drains out the bottom. And it's on wheels."

Rebecca laughed and nudged Tignor's ribs. "You've been a daddy before, haven't you? How many times?" She spoke so playfully, not at all accusingly, Tignor could hardly take offense.

Ruefully Tignor said, "Honey, it's always for the first time. Everything that matters is."

This remark so struck Rebecca, she wanted to cry. It was love's perfect answer.

He won't leave me, then. He will stay.

For some time Tignor behaved as if the run-down farmhouse was *home* to him, maybe it was true as he'd said he had grown tired of traveling. Maybe he'd grown tired of cutthroat competition. Though even when Tignor was officially home he was often away on what he called day trips. Driving out in the morning, returning after dark. Rebecca came to wonder if her husband was still an agent for the Black Horse Brewery? He was a man of secrets, like one of those fires that smolder underground for weeks, months, years. She wanted to think that one day he would surprise her with a house he'd bought for them, their own house in town. Tignor was a big battered-face moon in the night sky, you saw only the brightly lighted part, glaring like a coin, but you knew that there was another, dark and secret side. The two sides of the pockmarked moon were simultaneous yet you wanted to think, like a child, that there was only the light.

He means to leave me.

No: he loves me. He has promised.

Since Rebecca's miscarriage, and the fever she'd had for days afterward, the feeling between her and Tignor had changed, subtly. Tignor was not so jovial any longer, so loud-laughing. Not so likely to shove her, shake her. Rarely did he touch her except when they were in bed. She saw him regarding her with narrowed eyes. As if she was a riddle to him, and he didn't like riddles. He was repentant, and yet still he was angry. For Tignor was not a man to forget anger.

For Rebecca had caused the miscarriage, with her reckless behavior. Talking about Tignor to a chambermaid! Helping a chambermaid make up the room! When she was Mrs. Niles Tignor, and should have had dignity.

In her loneliness on the Poor Farm Road she would come to think that there must have been a logic to it, her behavior. In the way that, as a girl, she'd stayed away from the old stone house in the cemetery and so had saved herself from what might have been done to her on that last day. Couldn't have known what she was doing and yet—a part of her, with the cunning of a trapped creature gnawing at its own leg to save itself, had known.

For Niles, Jr. would be born. The other (a girl? in her dreams, a girl) had been sacrificed, that their son would be born.

Dr. Rice explained: a miscarriage is often "nature's way of correcting a mistake." For instance, a "malforming" fetus.

A blessing in disguise, sometimes.

Dr. Rice explained: "Of course, the pregnant woman can experience grief almost as if she has lost an actual baby. And grief can linger, into the start of a new pregnancy."

Grief! Rebecca wanted to laugh at the know-it-all doctor, an obstetrician, in angry dislike.

Dr. Rice of Chautauqua Falls. Examining Rebecca like a slab of meat on his examination table, prissy yet crude, fussy yet hurting her with his damn rubber-gloved hands and cold metal instruments like ice picks, she'd had to bite her lip to keep from screaming and kicking him in the belly. Yet afterward in his office, when Rebecca was dressed again, and trying to regain her composure, he offended her worse by telling her this crap.

"Doctor, I'm not 'grieving'! I sure am not. I'm not the kind of woman to grieve over the past. See, I look forward to the future like my husband Tignor does. If this new baby is healthy and gets born—that's all we care about, doctor."

Dr. Rice blinked at Rebecca. Had he underestimated Mrs. Niles Tignor, mistaking her for some wishy-washy weepy girl? Quickly saying, "That's a very wise philosophy, Mrs. Tignor. I wish that more of my patients were so wise."

Home! By the time Niles, Jr. was born, in late November 1956, Rebecca would come to love it.

"It's beautiful, Tignor. It will be special to us."

She'd uttered these words more than once. Like words of a love song, to make Tignor smile and maybe hug her.

The old Wertenbacher place the farmhouse was called, locally. About two miles north of Chautauqua Falls in a hilly area of small farms, grazing land, open fields and marshes. It was at the western edge of the Chautauqua Mountains, in the foothills. By chance (Rebecca did not believe in coincidences, she believed in pure chance) Chautauqua Falls was an old canal town like Milburn, eighty miles west of Milburn. Unlike Milburn, it had become a small city: its population was 16,800. It was an industrial city with factories, clothing and canning mills on the Chautauqua River. There was canal traffic. The largest employer was Union Carbide, that had expanded its facilities in the boom years 1955 and 1956. One day, Rebecca would work the assembly line at Niagara Tubing. But it was the countryside outside Chautauqua Falls to which Tignor brought her, a crossroads settlement called Four Corners. Here at the juncture of the Poor Farm Road and the Stuyvesant Road were a small post office, a coal depot, a granary, Ike's Food Store with a large Sealtest sign in its window, Meltzer's Gas & Auto Repair. There was a two-room schoolhouse on the grounds of the former poor farm. There was a volunteer firemen's station. There was a clapboard Methodist church and a cemetery behind the church. Walking sometimes past this church Rebecca heard singing inside, and felt a pang of loss.

Edna Meltzer attended this church and several times invited Rebecca to come with her. "There's a joyful feeling in that church, Rebecca! You smile just stepping inside."

Rebecca murmured vaguely she would like that, maybe. Someday.

"When your baby is born? You'll want it baptized."

Rebecca murmured vaguely that would depend upon what the baby's father wanted.

"Tignor, he's religious, is he? Nah!"

Mrs. Meltzer surprised Rebecca, the familiar way she laughed. As if Tignor was well known to her. Rebecca frowned, uneasy.

"Your own people, Rebecca: what kind of religion were they?"

Mrs. Meltzer put this question to Rebecca in a pleasant, casual manner as if she'd only just thought of it. She seemed wholly unconscious of *were*.

Why *were* and not *are*? Rebecca wondered.

For a long moment she could not think how to answer this question. And there was the woman waiting for her, Tignor had warned her against.

They were in Ike's. Rebecca was just leaving, Mrs. Meltzer was just entering. It was mid-September, dry and very warm. Tignor was away in Lake Shaheen looking at "waterfront property." Rebecca was seven months' pregnant and did not want to estimate how many pounds she'd gained beyond twenty. She was all belly, that hummed and quivered with life. Her brain had ceased to function significantly, like a broken radio. Her head was empty as an icebox tossed away in a dump.

Without saying another word to Edna Meltzer, Rebecca walked out of the store. The bell above the door rang sharply in her wake. She was oblivious of Mrs. Meltzer staring after her and took no heed for how her neighbor would speak of her to Ike's wife Elsie behind the counter. *That girl! She's a strange one ain't she! Almost you could feel sorry for her, what's in store.*

Through the autumn, as the days began to shorten, the air sharpened, it seemed to Rebecca that the farm was more beautiful than previously. Everywhere she walked, everywhere she explored was slovenly and beautiful. The canal: she was drawn to the canal, to the towpath. She liked to watch for the slow-moving barges. Men waving to her. As she stood flat-footed, balancing her weight on her heels, big-bellied and smiling, laughing at how ridiculous she must seem to them, how unalluring. Anna Schwart would not warn her now *Something will happen to you* for no man would want a woman so visibly pregnant.

And the sky, that autumn. Marbled clouds, thunderhead clouds, high pale cirrus clouds that dissolved even as you watched. Rebecca stood staring at these for long dreamy minutes, hands clasped over her belly.

The next one, you can keep.

. . . in their bed, in the old Wertenbacher house on the Poor Farm Road. Tignor pressed his face against her hard, hot belly. He kneaded her thighs, her buttocks. He kneaded her breasts. He was jealous of the infant who would suckle those breasts. When he returned to the house he did not wish to speak of where he'd been, he told her he hadn't married her to be questioned by her. She had asked him only how long he'd been driving, and was he hungry? She felt his dislike of her, the big belly that interfered with lovemaking. Yet he wanted to touch her. He could not keep his hands from her. Kneading her pelvis, the bristling public hair that radiated upward to her navel. Pressing his ear against her belly so hard it hurt, claiming he could hear the baby's heartbeat. He'd been drinking but he did not appear to be drunk. He said, aggrieved, "They cast me out when I was a baby. I had these thoughts, I would find them someday. I would make them pay."

In Troy, in the hotel room where she'd bled into a thick wad of towels, toilet paper, and tissues, Rebecca had been the one to comfort Tignor. *It isn't your fault. It isn't your fault.* She'd peered into his soul, she'd seen what lay broken and shattered there like glittering glass. She believed that she was strong enough to save him, as she had not been strong enough to save Jacob Schwart.

40

❀ ❀ ❀

A woman was shouting at her as if Rebecca was slow-witted.

"It will come when it's damn good and ready, hon. And once it's out, you won't give a damn what led to it."

In the bumpy rear of the Meltzers' low-slung Chevy sedan Rebecca lay spread-eagled, whimpering with pain. Lightning-flashes of pain. These were contractions, she was supposed to be counting between them yet the surprise of the pain—! She was not so self-assured now. She was not so pleased with herself now. She had intended not even to show Edna Meltzer the baby for she feared and disliked the woman and yet here she was in the Meltzers' car being driven to the hospital in Chautauqua Falls. She'd had to call the Meltzers when the pains began. Tignor had promised her, he would not be away at this time. He had promised her, she would not be alone. She had no number for Tignor and so she'd called the Meltzers. Somehow she was upside-down in the backseat of their car. Seeing the rushing landscape outside the car windows, a strip of white sky, from the bottom up. She would have little memory of this drive except Howie Meltzer in his greasy Esso cap behind the wheel chewing a toothpick and Edna Meltzer grunting as she leaned over the back of the passenger's seat to grip one of Rebecca's flailing hands, smiling sternly to show there was no cause for panic.

"Hon, I told you: it will come when it's damn good and ready. You just get a hold of yourself, *I got you*."

That hand of Edna Meltzer's Rebecca squeezed, and squeezed.

———

... a druggy delirium in which waves of excruciating pain were confused with a sound as of high-pitched frantic singing. She called for the baby's father but the man was nowhere near. Called and called until her throat was scraped raw but the man was nowhere near. Oh but he had promised, he would be with her! He had promised, she would not be alone when the baby was born. When the first of the contractions began and she'd sunk to her knees in shock, though she'd prepared beforehand like a diligent schoolgirl reading and underlining and memorizing passages from *Your Body, Your Baby & You*. She gripped her enormous belly with both hands. She cried for help but there was no one. And no number to call, to reach Niles Tignor. No idea where he was. In her desperation she did what he had not even needed to forbid her ever to do, called Port Oriskany information, the Black Horse Brewery, a disdainful female voice informed her no one by the name of Niles Tignor was employed by the Brewery at the present time.

But he was! Rebecca protested he'd been working as an agent for the Brewery for years!

A disdainful female voice informed her no one by the name of Niles Tignor was employed by the Brewery at the present time.

She would stumble to the Meltzers' house a quarter-mile away.

She would plead for help, she was alone and had no one.

Her nightgown, toiletries were already packed. And a paperback book for reading in the hospital for in her naiveté she had thought there might be leisure time for reading ... She would waste precious minutes in a futile search for the Certificate of Marriage in case she had to prove to the Chautauqua Falls Hospital authorities that she was a legally married woman, this birth was legitimate.

... a druggy delirium afterward to be described as eleven hours' labor which she, at its center, would recall vaguely as one might recall a film seen long ago in childhood and even at that time not comprehended. As the baby would afterward be described as *boy, eight pounds three ounces. Niles Tignor, Jr.* who had not yet a name, as he had not yet drawn breath to cry. A fierce thing shoving its head hard and lethal as a bowling ball bizarrely crammed up inside her. And this bowling ball a phenomenon of solid heat inside which, you would wish to believe, a tiny soul translucent as a creek slug dwelled. *Something will happen to you, a girl. You would not want.* Now that it was too late, she knew what her mother had warned her against.

... druggy delirium out of which nonetheless she emerged to her astonishment hearing what sounded like a cat's wail, so strangely in this brightly lighted room. Someone was saying *Mrs. Tignor?* She blinked to clear her occluded vision. She saw hands placing a naked flailing and kicking infant at first against her flattened, flaccid belly, then up between her breasts. *Your baby Mrs. Tignor. Baby boy Mrs. Tignor.* Such voices came to her from far away. She scarcely heard. For how hard the infant was crying, that deafening cat-wail! She laughed to see how angry it was, and so small; like its father furious, and dangerous; eyes shut and tiny fists flailing. Puckered monkey-face, soft coconut head covered in coarse black hairs. She laughed, she saw the tiny penis and had to laugh. Oh she'd never seen anything like this baby they were saying was hers! Wanting to joke *This one's daddy must've been a monkey!* but knowing that such a joke at such a time and place might be misinterpreted.

And already her breasts were leaking milk, one of the nurses was helping the sucking little mouth find its way.

" 'Give birth.' That's how a man would talk, I guess! Like 'birth' was something it was up to you, to 'give.' My God."

So dazed and happy now that she was home from the hospital and had her baby it was like the buzz you got drinking draft beer mixed with bourbon. Loving to nurse the hot-skinned little monkey that was hungry every few hours and as he sucked-sucked-sucked greedily at one fat breast and then the other, she, the new Momma, just wanted to talk-talk-talk. Oh, she had so much to say! Oh, she loved this little monkey! All this was so—wild-and-strange!

Edna brought the girl a copy of the *Chautauqua Falls Weekly*. Turned to the back pages, obituaries, weddings, and birth announcements. There were photos of the newly deceased and the newly wed but none of the new mothers who were identified as their husband's wives. Rebecca read aloud, " 'Mrs. Niles Tignor of Poor Farm Road, Four Corners, gave birth to an eight-pound three-ounce boy, Niles Tignor, Jr. at the Chautauqua Falls General Hospital, November 29.' " She laughed, her bright harsh laugh that grated against the ear, and tears leaked from her eyes. Going on and on about *giving birth* as Edna would report like she was drunk, or worse.

To her credit, this girl Rebecca had not been badly prepared for a new baby, Edna had to concede. She had a good supply of diapers, a few baby clothes. A crib and a baby-bath. She'd been studying some baby pamphlet a doctor had given her. There was food, mostly canned things, in the kitchen. And for sure Edna had castoff baby things at their house, to donate. And Elsie Drott had, too. And other women neighbors, if it came to that. Within a circumference of as many as four miles, women knew of Rebecca Tignor, some of them without knowing her actual name. *A new mother, just a girl. No family, it looks like. The father of the baby just ain't around. Seems like he's abandoned her, out in the country. That old Wertenbacher house that's practically falling down.*

If the girl was worried about the future, she wasn't showing it, yet. This, Edna Meltzer found annoying.

"He left you some money, I guess?"

"Oh, yes! Sure he did."

Edna frowned, as if needing to be convinced.

Oh, Rebecca had had enough of Mrs. Meltzer for right now! Baby had ceased nursing and was drowsing slack-mouthed in her arms, here was a rare opportunity for Momma to nap, too.

Sweet delicious sleep like a stone well you could fall into, and fall and fall.

On an evening in early December, twelve days after their baby was born, there stood Tignor in the doorway of their bedroom, staring. Rebecca heard a faint breathy whistle—"Jesus!" Tignor's face was in shadow, she could not see his expression. He stood very still, wary. For a tense moment Rebecca halfway expected him to turn away. "Tignor. Here." Rebecca lifted the baby to Tignor, smiling. Here was a perfect baby, Tignor would see. It had only just awakened from its nap, staring and blinking at the stranger in the doorway. It began to make its comical blowing noises, bubbles of spittle on its lips. It kicked, flailed its tiny fists. Slowly Tignor came to the bedside, to take the baby from Rebecca. In infant astonishment the baby gaped at Tignor's face, that must have seemed gigantic and luminous as a moon. Gingerly, Tignor held the baby. Rebecca saw that he knew to cup the small head on its delicate neck. Before entering the house he'd tossed away his cigar yet still he smelled of smoke, the baby began to fret. With his nicotine-stained thumb he stroked the baby's forehead. "It's mine, is it?"

41

❀ ❀ ❀

Hey you night-owl folks this is Buffalo Radio Wonderful WBEN broadcasting the best in jazz through the wee hours. You are listening to Zack Zacharias your all-night host bringing you up-next vintage Thelonious Monk... She was lying awake in the dark, hands clasped behind her head. Thinking of her life strung out behind her like beads of myriad shapes, in memory crowded, confusing as in life each had been singular, and had defined itself with the slowness of the sun's trajectory across the sky. You knew the sun was moving yet you never saw it move.

In the room adjoining Rebecca's bedroom, Niley was sleeping. At least she hoped he was sleeping. In his sleep listening to the radio desperate to be not-alone even in his sleep and desperate to hear his father's voice amid the voices of strangers. Rebecca was thinking how she'd given birth to Niley without knowing who Niley would be, she'd opened her body to pain so excruciating it could not be recalled in consciousness and so it was exactly as Edna Meltzer had predicted *Once it's out you won't give a damn what led up to it.*

She smiled, yes this was so. That was the one true fact of her life.

She'd opened her body, too, to Niles Tignor. Without knowing in the slightest who Niles Tignor was. Except for Niley, this had perhaps been a mistake. And yet, Niley was no mistake.

What she knew of Tignor now, she would never have dared approach the man. Yet she could not leave him, he would never allow it. She could not leave him, her heart clenched in anticipation simply of seeing him again.

Hey girl: love me?

Christ you know I'm crazy about you.

At the end of the lane, out on the Poor Farm Road, there was a tin mailbox on a rotted wooden post with the faded black letters WERTEN-BACHER still visible. No mail ever came for Niles Tignor or his wife except advertisements, flyers stuffed into the mailbox. But one day back in March, soon after Rebecca had started working at Niagara Tubing (was there some connection? had to be!), she went to empty the mailbox, and discovered amid the trash mail a neatly folded front page from the *Port Oriskany Journal*. Fascinated, Rebecca read an article with the headline TWO MEN SLAIN, ONE WOUNDED IN LAKESIDE "AMBUSH": two men had died of gunshot wounds and a third wounded, in the parking lot of a popular Port Oriskany tavern and marina, police had made no arrests yet but had taken into custody one Niles Tignor, forty-two, a resident of Buffalo, as a material witness. The attack was believed by police to be related to extortion and racketeering in the Niagara lakeside area.

Rebecca read and reread the article. Her heart beat hard, she worried she might faint. Niley, who'd come with her to empty the mailbox, fretted and nudged against her legs.

Taken into custody! Forty-two years old! Resident of Buffalo!

"Material witness": what did that mean?

At this time Tignor had been away for a week, in the Catskill area. At least, Rebecca believed that Tignor was in that part of the state: he'd called her, once. The ambush had taken place in late February, three weeks before. So whatever had happened, Tignor had been released.

He had told her nothing about this, of course. Nor could Rebecca remember anything unusual in his manner, his mood.

Maybe in fact Tignor had been in an unusually good mood recently.

He'd driven home in a new car: silver-green Pontiac sedan with gleaming chrome fixtures. Taken his little family, as he called them, for a Sunday outing up at Lake Shaheen . . .

Rebecca would make inquiries, and learned what "material witness" meant: an individual who police had reason to believe might be helpful in an investigation. In the Chautauqua Falls library she searched through back issues of the Port Oriskany newspaper but could find no further information about the shootings. She called the Port Oriskany police to inquire, and was told that the investigation was still under way, and was confidential—"And who are you, ma'am? And why do you want to know?"

Rebecca said, "No one. I'm no one. Thank you."

She hung up, and resolved not to think about it. For what good would come of thinking about it . . .

(Tignor, forty-two years old: she would have thought him years younger. And a resident of Buffalo: how was that possible! He was a resident of Chautauqua Falls.)

(What mattered was: he was Niley's father, and he was her husband. Whoever Niles Tignor was, they loved him. Rebecca had no right to pry into his life apart from her, that had so preceded her.)

It was not quite three years since Tignor had come to this house, and into this bedroom, and held his son in his hands for the first time. A lifetime ago it seemed to Rebecca, yet perhaps it was only a beginning.

It's mine, is it?

Whose else?—Rebecca had needed to make a joke of it, to make them both laugh.

But Tignor hadn't laughed. Rebecca belatedly guessed you didn't joke with a man about such things. Tignor frowned, looking as he had when Rebecca had uttered the word *whore*. Holding the squirming infant in the palm of one hand, staring at its flushed, squeezed-in little face. A long moment passed before Tignor smiled, and then laughed.

He's got my temper, eh? Little pisspot.

Tignor had told Rebecca he was sorry he'd been away, he had not wanted her to be alone at such a time. He had tried to call her several times but always the line was busy. Sure he'd worried about her, alone in the farmhouse. But he'd known that nothing bad would happen, because they had luck on their side.

Luck! Rebecca smiled.

Tignor had brought back things for the house: a brass floor lamp with a three-way bulb, a jade ashtray on a carved-elephant pedestal. These were showy items fit for a hotel lobby. For Rebecca, a new lacy champagne-colored negligee to replace the old, that was becoming frayed; a black satin dress with a sequined bodice ("for New Year's Eve"); a pair of high-heeled kidskin shoes (size six, and Rebecca's feet were size seven and a half). Rebecca shook her head, seeing it was like Tignor had forgotten she'd been pregnant when he'd driven off. It was like Tignor had forgotten there was a baby coming, entirely.

At first, Tignor was enthralled with his son. He seemed always to be bearing him aloft like a prize. He loved to carry the baby on his shoulders, making Niley kick and squeal with excitement. A warm ruddy glow suffused Tignor's broad face at such times and Rebecca felt a small pang of jealousy even as she thought *I can forgive him anything, for this*. They laughed that Niley's first coherent word wasn't "Ma-ma" but "Da-*da*" uttered in a cry of infant astonishment. Though Tignor did not wish to get his hands wet bathing Niley, he loved to towel him dry, vigorously. And he was drawn to watch Rebecca nurse the baby, kneeling beside Rebecca's chair, bringing his face close to the baby's eagerly sucking little mouth until at last Tignor could not bear it, he had to kiss and suck at Rebecca's other breast, so aroused he needed to make love to her . . . Rebecca was still sore from childbirth but knew she must not say no to this man.

But at such times Tignor often wanted her only to stroke him, swiftly and expediently to orgasm. His face contorted and shut against her, his teeth bared. He was ashamed afterward, he would dislike his wife for being a witness to such raw animal need. He went away from her, drove away in the car and Rebecca was left wondering when he would be back.

The novelty of the new baby began to fade for Tignor after a few months. Even Niley's delight in Da-*da* was not enough. For Niley was a fretful baby, refusing food, rarely sleeping for more than three hours at a time. He was lively, alert, curious, yet easily frightened and made anxious. He had his father's short temper, but not his father's assurance. His cries were shrill, deafening. You could not believe that such infant-lungs were capable of such a volume of sound. Rebecca became so deprived of sleep she staggered about dazed and hallucinating. No sooner did Tignor return home than he threatened to leave again. "Nurse him, get him to sleep. You're his mother for Christ sake."

You're his mother came to be a familiar utterance. Rebecca did not want to think it was an accusation.

"Mom-my? C'n I sleep with you, Mom-my?"—there came Niley wanting to crawl into bed with her.

Rebecca protested, "Oh, sweetie! You have your own bed like a big boy, don't you?"

But Niley wanted to sleep with Mom-my, he was lonely he said.

There were things in that room with him, that scared him. He wanted to sleep with Mom-my.

Rebecca scolded, "All right for now, but when Daddy is back you won't be able to sleep here. Daddy won't spoil you like I do."

She hauled the child up inside the covers. They would snuggle together and drift off to sleep listening to WBEN Radio Wonderful in the next room.

❀ ❀ ❀

42

It was the first week of October 1959. Twelve days after the man in the panama hat. Now came less seductively HAZEL JONES HAZEL JONES ARE YOU HAZEL JONES in the clamor and burnt-rubber stink of the assembly line at Niagara Tubing, Rebecca was beginning to forget.

She was a practical-minded young woman. She was the mother of a small child, she would learn for his sake to forget.

And then, Tignor returned.

She came to the Meltzers' to pick up Niley, and was told by Mrs. Meltzer that Tignor had already been there, he'd taken the boy home.

Rebecca stammered, "Here? Tignor is—here? He's *back*?"

Edna Meltzer said yes, Tignor was back. Hadn't Rebecca known her husband was coming home that day?

It was shameful to Rebecca, to be so exposed. Having to say she had not known. She hated it, that Edna Meltzer should see her confusion, and would speak of her pityingly, to others.

She left the Meltzers' house, she ran the rest of the way home. Her heart knocked in her chest. She had expected Tignor the previous Sunday, and he had not come, and he had not called. She had wished to think that he would come to Niagara Tubing to pick her up and drive her home . . . Niles Tignor in his shining car, at the curb waiting for her. In the new-model silver-green Pontiac at which others would glance in admiration. There was something wrong here, Rebecca could not think what it was. *He has taken Niley away. I will never see Niley again.*

But there was the Pontiac parked at the end of the weedy driveway. Inside, there was Tignor's tall broad-backed figure in the kitchen, with Niley; firing questions at Niley in his ebullient radio-announcer voice—"And then? Then what? What'd you do? You and 'Mom-my'? Eh?"—that meant he was talking but not listening, in an elevated mood. The kitchen smelled of cigar smoke and a fresh-opened ale. Rebecca stepped inside, and was stunned to see that something had happened to Tignor . . . His head was partially shaved. His beautiful thick metallic hair had been shorn, he looked older, uncertain. His eyes swung onto her, he bared his teeth in a grimace of a smile. "You're back then, girl, are you? From the factory."

It was one of Tignor's senseless remarks. Like a boxer's jab. To throw you off balance, to confuse. There was no way to reply that would not sound guilty or defensive. Rebecca murmured, yes she was back. Every night at this time. She came to Tignor, who had not moved toward her, and slid her arms around him. For days she had had such mutinous thoughts of this man, now she was stricken with emotion, she wanted only to hide her face against him, to burrow into his arms. Niley was jumping about them chattering of Dad-*dy*, Dad-*dy*. Dad-*dy* had bought him presents, did Mommy want to see?

Tignor did not kiss Rebecca, but allowed her to kiss him. His jaws were stubbled. His breath was not fresh. He appeared slightly disoriented, as if he'd come to the wrong house. And possibly he was looking over her head, squinting toward the door as if half-expecting someone else to appear. He was stroking her back and shoulders, rather hard, distracted. "Baby. My girl. You missed your old husband, eh? Did you?" Roughly he pulled off the scarf she'd tied around her hair, shook out her hair that was tangled, not very clean, to fall halfway down her back. "Uh. You smell like burnt rubber." But he laughed, he kissed her after all.

Rebecca hesitated to touch Tignor's head, stroke his hair, that was so changed. "See you looking at me, eh? Shit, I had a little accident, over in Albany. Had to have a few stitches."

Tignor showed her, at the back of his head, where his hair had been shaved to the scalp, an ugly raw-looking scab of about five inches in length.

Rebecca asked what kind of accident and Tignor said, with a shrug, "The kind that won't be repeated."

"But, Tignor—what happened?"

"I said, it won't be repeated."

Tignor had tossed his valise, suitcase, jacket onto chairs in the kitchen. Rebecca helped him carry these into the bedroom at the rear of the house. This room, to Rebecca the special room of their house, she kept in readiness for her husband's unpredictable return: the bed was made, and covered with a quilted spread; all her clothes were neatly hung away in a closet; all surfaces were free of dust; there was even a vase of straw flowers on the bureau. Tignor stared at the interior of the room as if he'd never seen it before.

Tignor grunted what sounded like *Mmmm!*

Tignor pushed Niley outside the bedroom, to whimper at the shut door. Suddenly he was aroused, excited. He half-carried Rebecca to the bed, she was kissing him as he pulled at her clothes and his own, and within minutes he'd discharged his pent-up tension into her eager body. Rebecca clutched at his back that was ridged with fleshy muscle. She bit her lower lip to keep from crying. Her voice was low, near-inaudible, pleading. ". . . love you so, Tignor. Please don't leave us again. We love you, don't hurt us . . ."

Tignor sighed with massive pleasure. His face with its curious broken symmetry glowed warm, ruddy. He rolled over onto his back, wiping his forehead with a brawny forearm. Suddenly he was exhausted, Rebecca felt the heaviness in all his limbs. At the latched door Niley was scratching and calling Dad-*dy*? Mom-*my*? plaintive as a starving cat. Tignor muttered irritably, "Quiet the kid, will you? I need to sleep."

That first night. Tignor's return, she had so long awaited.

Not wanting to think what it meant. How long he would be with her this time.

Rebecca left the bedroom silently, carrying her clothes. She would bathe before making supper. She would bathe, and wash her lank greasy hair, to please him. She walked unsteadily as if she'd been mysteriously wounded. Tignor's lovemaking had been hard, harsh, expedient. He had not made love to her for nearly six weeks. Almost she felt as if this had been the first time, since Niley's birth.

That massive wound of childbirth. Rebecca wondered if you could grow in again, heal completely. Had Hazel Jones ever married? Had Hazel Jones had a baby?

Niley needed to be assured, Daddy was really home, and would be staying home for a while; Daddy was sleeping now, and did not want to be disturbed. Still, Niley begged to peek through the crack of the doorway.

Whispering, "Is that him? Is that Dad-dy? That man?"

Later, after supper, Tignor was drinking, and repentant. He had missed them, he said. His little family in Chautauqua Falls.

Rebecca said lightly, "Just one 'little family'? Where are the others?"

Tignor laughed. He was watching Niley struggle with the shiny red wagon he'd brought for him, too large and unwieldy for a three-year-old.

"There needs to be some changes in my life, Jesus I know. It's time."

He'd bought lakeshore property up at Shaheen, he told her. And he was negotiating a deal, a restaurant and tavern in Chautauqua Falls. And there were other properties . . . Ruefully Tignor stroked the back of his head, where his scalp was scarred. "This accident was some bastard tried to kill me. Skimmed my head with a bullet."

"Who? Who tried to kill you?"

"But he didn't. And like I said, it won't happen again."

Rebecca sat silent, thinking of the gun she'd found in Tignor's suitcase. She supposed it was in his suitcase even now. She supposed he'd had reason to use it.

Hazel Jones might have a son like Niley. Hazel Jones would not have a husband like Niles Tignor.

"I know about what happened in Port Oriskany. Where you were taken into custody as a 'material witness.'"

The words came out suddenly, impulsively.

Tignor said, "And how d'you know, baby? Somebody told you?"

"I read about it in the Port Oriskany newspaper. The 'ambush.' The shootings. And your name . . ."

"And how did you happen to see that newspaper? Somebody showed you, who lives around here?"

Still Tignor's tone was affable, mildly curious.

"It was left in the mailbox. Just the front page."

"This was a while back, Rebecca. Last winter."

"And is it over now? Whatever it was, is it—over?"

"Yes. It's over."

Undressing for bed, Tignor watched Rebecca brushing out her hair. Her hand wielding the brush moved deftly, with deliberation. Now her hair had been newly washed it was very dark, lustrous; it smelled of a fragrant shampoo, and not of the factory; it seemed to throw off sparks. Through the mirror, Rebecca saw Tignor approach her. She began to shiver in anticipation, but her hand did not slow its movement. Tignor was naked, massive; torso and belly covered in coarse glinting hairs. Between his thick legs, out of a dense swirl of pubic hair, his penis lifted, semi-erect. Tignor touched her hair, he stroked the nape of her neck that was so sensitive. Pressed himself against her, moaning softly. Rebecca heard his breath quicken.

She was frightened, her mind had gone empty.

She could not think how to behave. What she might have done, in the past.

Quietly Tignor said, as if it were a secret between them, "You've been with a man, have you?"

Rebecca stared at him through the mirror. "A man? What man?"

"How the hell would I know, what man?"

Tignor laughed. He'd pulled Rebecca to her feet, he was pulling her toward the bed, that had been neatly opened, top sheet pulled back over the blanket precisely three inches. They swayed together like clumsy dancers. Tignor had been drinking for hours and was in a jovial mood. Caught his toe on the shag rug beside the bed, cursed then laughed again for something was very funny. "The one who gave you the newspaper, maybe. Or his friend. Or all their friends. You tell me what man, baby." Rebecca panicked and tried to push from Tignor but Tignor was too quick, grabbed her hair, shut his fist in her hair and shook her, not so hard as he might have but gently, reprovingly, as you might shake a recalcitrant child.

"You tell me, Gypsy-girl. We got all night."

43

❀ ❀ ❀

. . . an hour and twenty minutes late for work next morning. His car in the driveway but she did not have the keys and did not dare to ask him, the man so deeply sunk in sleep. She moved stiffly. Her hair was hidden in a head scarf. On the assembly line it was observed that her face was swollen, sullen. When she removed her plastic-rimmed sunglasses of the cheap cheery kind sold in drugstores and replaced them with her safety goggles it was observed that her left eye was swollen and discolored. When Rita nudged her, spoke in her ear—"Oh honey, he's back? Is that it?"—she had nothing to say.

44

❀ ❀ ❀

And so she knew: she would leave him.

Knew before she fully realized. Before the knowledge came to her calm and irrevocable and irrefutable. Before the terrible words sounded in her brain relentless as the machines at Niagara Tubing *What choice, you have no choice, he will kill you both.* Before she began to make her desperate calculations: where she might go, what she could take with her, how she could take the child. Before counting the small sum of money—forty-three dollars!— she had imagined there would be more—she'd managed to save from her paycheck, and had hidden in a closet in the house. Before in his playful mock-teasing way he began to be more abusive to both her and the child. Before he began to blame her, that the child shrank from him. Before the terror of her situation came to her in the night in her bed in the remote farmhouse on the Poor Farm Road where she lay sleepless beside the man in heavy sodden sleep. That smell of damp grass, damp earth rising through the floorboards. That sweet-rotten smell. When she was an infant wrapped in a soiled shawl to be carried in haste into the shed and held against her mother's heavy breasts as her mother hid panting, crouched in the darkness for much of an afternoon until a figure threw the door open, indignant, outraged *Would you like me to strangle her?*

And so she knew. Before even that morning in October when the sun had only just appeared behind a bank of clouds at the tree line and Niley was still sleeping in the next room and she dared to follow him outside, and to the road, and across the road to the canal; before she hid watching him from a distance of about thirty feet, how he walked slowly along the tow-path and then paused, and lit a cigarette and smoked, and brooded; a solitary masculine figure of some mysterious distinction of whom it is reasonable to ask *Who is he?* Rebecca watched from behind a thicket of brambles, saw Tignor at last glance casually over his shoulder, and in both directions along the flat dark glittering waterway (it was deserted, no barges in sight, no human activity on the towpath), then remove from his coat pocket an awkward-sized object she knew at once to be, though it was wrapped in canvas, the revolver. He weighed the object in his hand. He hesitated, with an air of regret. Then, as Tignor did most things, he tossed it indifferently into the canal where it sank at once.

Rebecca thought *He has used that gun, he has killed someone. But he won't kill me.*

When they'd first been married Tignor had taught Rebecca to drive. Often he'd promised to buy her a car—"Nice little coupe for my girl. Convertible, maybe." Tignor had seemed sincere and yet he'd never gotten around to buying the car.

There was Tignor's Pontiac in the driveway, she dared not ask to drive. Even to shop in Chautauqua Falls, or to drive to work. Some mornings, if he was awake that early, or if he'd only just come home from the previous night, Tignor drove Rebecca to Niagara Tubing; some afternoons, if he was in the vicinity, he picked her up at the end of her shift. But Rebecca could not rely upon him. Most of the time she continued to walk the mile and a half along the towpath as she always had.

It wasn't so clear what to do with Niley. Tignor objected to Edna Melt-zer looking after his son—the old bag sticking her nose in Tignor's business!—and yet, Tignor could hardly be expected to stay in the house and look after a three-year-old himself. If Rebecca left Niley with Tignor, she might return to discover the Pontiac gone and the child wandering outside in disheveled soiled clothes, if not part-naked. She might discover Niley barefoot in pajamas trying to pull his shiny red wagon along the rutted driveway, or playing at the thirty-foot well where the plank coverings were rotted, or prowling in the dilapidated hay barn amid the filthy encrustations of decades of bird droppings. Once, he'd made his way to Ike's Food Store.

Edna Meltzer said, "But I don't mind! Niley is like my own grandson. And any time Tignor wants him back, he comes over and takes him."

At first, Tignor had been interested in Niley's childish drawings and scribblings. His attempts at spelling, under Rebecca's guidance. Tignor hadn't the patience to read to Niley, the very act of reading aloud bored him, but he would lie sprawled on the sofa smoking and sipping ale and listening to Rebecca read to Niley, who insisted that Rebecca move her finger along beneath the words she was reading, that he could repeat them after her. Tignor said, amused, "This kid! He's smart, I guess. For his age." Rebecca smiled, wondering if Tignor knew his son's age. Or what the average three-year-old was like. She said, yes she thought Niley was very smart for his age. And he had musical talent, too.

" 'Musical talent'? Since when?"

Anytime there was music on the radio, Rebecca said, he stopped whatever he was doing to listen. He seemed excited by music. He tried to sing, dance. Tignor said, "No kid of mine is going to be a dancer, for sure. Some tap-dancing darkie." Tignor spoke with the teasing exaggeration of one who means to be funny, but Rebecca saw his face tighten.

"Not a dancer but a pianist, maybe."

" 'Pianist'—what's that? Piano player?"

Tignor sneered, he was coming to dislike his wife's big words and pretensions. Yet he was sometimes touched by these, too, as he was touched by his son's clumsy crayon drawings and attempts at walking-fast-like-Daddy.

Tignor came upon the sheet of paper with Niley's crayon-printed *TE TANUS*. And others: *AIRPLANE, PURPLE, SKUNK*. Tignor laughed, shaking his head. "Jesus. You could teach the kid every word in the damn dictionary, like this."

"Niley loves words. He loves the feeling of 'spelling' even if he doesn't know the alphabet yet."

"Why doesn't he know the alphabet?"

"He knows some of it. But it's a little long for him, twenty-six letters."

Tignor frowned, considering. Rebecca hoped he wouldn't ask Niley to recite the alphabet, this would end in a paroxysm of tears. Though she suspected that Tignor didn't know the alphabet, either. Not all twenty-six letters!

"This is more like you'd expect, from a kid." Tignor was looking at Niley's banana hat drawing. A figure meant to be Daddy (but Tignor didn't know this clumsily drawn fattish cartoon figure was meant to be Daddy) with a yellow banana sticking from its head, half the figure's size.

Later, restless and prowling the old house, upstairs where Rebecca kept her private things, Tignor found her word sheets and scribbled doodlings. She was stricken with embarrassment.

Mostly these were lists comprised from her dictionary. And from discarded public school textbooks in biology, math, history. Tignor read aloud, amused: "*gymnosperms—angiosperms.* What the hell's this—*sperms?*" He glared at her in mock disdain. "*Chlorophyll—chloroplast—photosynthesis.*" He was having difficulty pronouncing the words, his face reddened. "*Cranium—vertebra—pelvis—femur—*"

Femur he uttered in a growl of disgust as *feeeemur.*

Rebecca took the pages from him, her face smarting.

Tignor laughed. "Like some high school kid, eh? How the hell old are you, anyway?"

Rebecca said nothing. She was confused, thinking he'd taken the dictionary from her too, and thrown it into the stove.

Her dictionary! It was her most secret possession.

Grunting, Tignor stooped to pick something fallen onto the floor. This was a sheet of paper upon which Rebecca had written, in a lazy sloping script floating down the page—

Hazel Jones

Hazel

Hendricks Byron
"Hazel"

"Who're these? Friends of yours?"

Now Rebecca was stricken with fear. The way Tignor was glaring at her.

"No. They're no one, Tignor. Just . . . names."

Tignor snorted in derision, crumpled the page and tossed it at Rebecca, striking her chest. It was a harmless blow with no weight behind it yet it left her breathless as if he'd punched her.

Yet he wasn't in a really mean mood. Rebecca heard him laughing to himself, whistling on the stairs.

"Mommy, what's wrong?"

Niley saw her pressing both her fists against her forehead. Her eyes reddened, shut tight.

"Mommy is ashamed."

" 'Shamed' . . . ?"

Niley came to stroke Mommy's heated forehead. Niley was frowning, that old-young look to his face.

God damn why hadn't she hidden her papers from Tignor! Better yet, thrown them away.

Now that Tignor was home, she needed to keep the run-down old house clean and neat and "sparkly" as possible. As much like the rooms of a good hotel as she could manage.

No mess. No clothes tossed about. (Tignor's clothes and things, Rebecca put away without a word.)

The irony was, she'd stopped thinking about Hazel Jones. The man in the panama hat. The look of urgency in his face. All that seemed long ago now, remote and improbable as something in one of Niley's picture books.

Why'd anybody give a shit about you, girl!

A man's scornful voice. She wasn't sure whose.

Niley was sick. A bad cold, and now flu.

Rebecca tried to take his temperature: 101° F?

Her hand trembled, holding the thermometer to the light.

"Tignor? Niley needs to see a doctor."

"A doctor where?"

It was a question that made no sense. Tignor seemed confused, shaken.

Yet he carried Niley, wrapped in a blanket, out to his car. He drove Niley and Rebecca into Chautauqua Falls and waited in the car in the parking lot outside the doctor's office, smoking. He'd given Rebecca a fifty-dollar bill for the doctor but had not offered to come inside. Rebecca thought *He's afraid. Of sickness, of any kind of weakness.*

She was angry with him, in that instant. Shoving a fifty-dollar bill at her, the mother of the sick child. She would not give him change from the fifty dollars, she would hide it away in her closet.

Tignor was away from home often. But never more than two or three days at a stretch. Rebecca was coming to see he'd lost his job with the brewery. Yet she could not ask him, he'd have been furious with her. She could not plead with him *What has happened to you? Why can't you talk to me?*

When Rebecca returned to the car with Niley, an hour later, she saw Tignor on his feet, leaning against a front fender, smoking. In the instant before he glanced up at her she thought *That man! He is no one I know.*

Quickly she said, "Niley just has a touch of the flu, Tignor. The doctor says not to worry. He says—"

"Did he give you a prescription?"

"He says just to give Niley some children's aspirin. I have some at home, I've been giving him."

Tignor frowned. "Nothing stronger?"

"It's just flu, Tignor. This aspirin is supposed to be strong enough."

"It better be, honey. If it ain't, this 'peedy-trician' is gonna get his head broke."

Tignor spoke with defiance, bravado. Rebecca stooped to kiss Niley's warm forehead in consolation.

They drove back to Four Corners. Rebecca held Niley on her lap in the passenger's seat, beside Tignor who was silent and brooding as if he'd been obscurely insulted. "I'd think you would be relieved, Tignor, like me. The doctor was very nice."

Rebecca leaned against Tignor, just slightly. The contact with the man's warm, somehow aggrieved skin gave her pleasure. A small jolt of pleasure she hadn't felt in some time.

"The doctor says that Niley is very healthy, overall. His growth. His 'reflexes.' Listening through a stethoscope to his heart and lungs." She paused, knowing that Tignor was listening, and that this was good news.

Tignor drove for another few minutes in silence but he was softening, melting. Glancing down at Rebecca, his girl. His Gypsy-girl. At last he squeezed Rebecca's thigh, hard enough to hurt. He reached over to tousle Niley's damp hair.

"Hey you two: love ya."

Love ya. It was the first time Tignor had ever said such a thing to them.

And so she thought *I will never leave him.*

"He loves us. He loves his son. He would never hurt us. He is only just . . . Sometimes . . ."

Waiting? Was Tignor waiting?

But for what was Tignor waiting?

He'd ceased to shave every day. His clothes were not so stylish as they'd been. He no longer had his hair trimmed regularly by a hotel barber. He no longer had his clothes laundered and dry cleaned in hotels. He'd spent money to look good though he'd never been overly fastidious, fussy. Now he wore the same shirt for several days in a row. He slept in his underwear. Kicked dirty socks into a corner of the bedroom for his wife to discover.

Of course, Rebecca was expected to launder and iron most of Tignor's clothes now. What required dry cleaning, he didn't trouble to have cleaned.

The damned old washing machine Rebecca was expected to use—! Almost as bad as her mother's had been. It broke down often, spilling soapy water onto the linoleum floor of the washroom. And then Rebecca had to iron, or try to iron, Tignor's white cotton shirts.

The iron was heavy, her wrist ached. Bad as Niagara Tubing except the smells weren't so sickening. Ma had taught her to iron but only just flat things, sheets, towels. Pa's few shirts she'd ironed herself taking care frowning over the ironing board as if all of her life, her female yearning, had been bound up in a man's shirt spread out before her.

"Jesus. A blind cripple could do better than this."

It was Tignor, examining one of his shirts. The iron had made creases at the collar. Ma had told her *The collar is the hardest part, next are the shoulders. Front, back, and sleeves are easy.*

"Oh, Tignor. I'm sorry."

"I can't wear this shit! You'll have to wash it again, and iron it again."

Rebecca took the shirt from him. It was a white cotton dress shirt with long sleeves. Still warm from the iron. She would not re-wash it, only just soak it and hang it to dry and try ironing it again in the morning.

In fact she stood mute, sullen. After Tignor went away. God damn she worked eight hours five days a week at fucking Niagara Tubing, did all the housework, took care of Niley and him and why wasn't that enough?

"This factory job. What's it pay?"

Out of nowhere came Tignor's question. But Rebecca had the idea Tignor had wanted to ask for a long time.

She hesitated. Then told him.

(If she lied, and he found out. He would know then that she was trying to save money out of the salary.)

"*That* little? For a forty-hour week? Christ."

Tignor was personally hurt, insulted.

"Tignor, it's just the machine shop. I didn't have any experience. They don't want women."

It was nearing the end of October. The sky was a hard steely knife-blade-blue. By midday the air was still cold, begrudging. Rebecca had not wished to think *How will we endure the winter together in this old house!*

She'd missed Tignor, in his absences. Now that Tignor was living with them, she missed her old loneliness.

And she was frightened of him: his physical presence, the swerve of his emotions, his eyes like the eyes of a blind man who has suddenly been gifted with sight, and doesn't like what he sees.

Tignor's new habit was running both his hands through his ravaged hair in a gesture of impatience. His hair had grown back slowly, was no longer thick. It was the hair of an ordinary man now: thin, lank, faded brown. Beneath, his skull was bony to the touch.

Tignor was ashamed for Rebecca and of her and of himself as her husband, for a long trembling moment he could not speak. Then he said, spitting the words, "I told you, Rebecca. You wouldn't have to work anymore, that day we drove to Niagara Falls I told you. Didn't I?"

He was almost pleading. Rebecca felt a stab of love for him, she knew she must console him. Yet she said:

"You said I didn't have to work at the hotel. That's all you said."

"God damn, I meant any kind of job. That's what I meant and you fucking know it."

He was becoming angry. She knew, she knew!—she must not provoke him. Yet she said:

"I only took the job at Niagara Tubing because I needed money for Niley and me. A young child needs clothes, Tignor. And food. And you were away, Tignor, I hadn't heard from you . . ."

"Bullshit. I sent you money. In the U.S. mail, I sent it."

No. You did not.

You are remembering wrongly. You are lying.

Rebecca knew the warning signals, she must say nothing more.

Tignor went away, furious. She heard his footsteps. Vibrations of footsteps pulsing in her head. So Jacob Schwart in his righteous anger had walked heavily, on the heels of his boots. That after his shotgun-death had had to be cut from his feet like hooves grown into the flesh.

Jacob Schwart: a man, in his home. A man, head of his family. Heavily on his heels he walks signaling displeasure.

"At the factory, is he? This guy?"

Rebecca opened her eyes, confused. Tignor was standing before her, hadn't he walked away?

"Foreman, is he? Some local big shot? *Boss?*"

Rebecca tried to smile. She believed that Tignor was only taunting, he wasn't serious. Yet he could be dangerous.

Saying, "Hell no, not a boss. One of those assholes drives a Caddie.

Not you. Look at you. Used to be damned good-looking. Used to have a real happy smile like a girl. Where's it now? Anybody fucking you now, he's got to be on the floor. I smell him on you: that burnt-rubbery stink and sweat like a nigger."

Rebecca backed away.

"Tignor, please. Don't say such ugly things, Niley might hear."

"Let the kid hear! He's got to know, his hot-shit mommy is a *w-h-o-r-e*."

"Tignor, you don't mean that."

"Don't, eh? Don't 'mean' what, baby?"

"What you're saying."

"Exactly what'm I saying? You tell me."

Rebecca said, trying not to stammer, "I love you, Tignor. I don't know any man except you. There has never been any other man except you. You must know that! I have never—"

There was Niley crouched beside the sofa, listening. Niley who should have been in bed by now.

The previous night Tignor had been playing poker with friends in Chautauqua Falls. Exactly where, Rebecca didn't know. He'd hinted it had been a "damn worthwhile" night and he was in a generous mood, in his soul.

He was! Fuck it, his mood wasn't going to be ruined.

Tignor sank onto the sofa, heavily. Pulled Niley onto his lap. He seemed not to notice, unless it amused him, how the boy winced at his rough strong fingers.

Tignor hadn't shaved today. His stubbled jaws glinted gray. He looked like a giant predator fish in an illustrated book: Niley stared. Daddy's eyes were bloodshot, he'd rolled his shirtsleeves up tight over his biceps. Droplets of perspiration gleamed on his skin that looked like myriad skins, stitched together, just perceptibly mismatched.

"Niley, my boy! Tell Daddy does a man come to the house here to see Mommy?"

Niley stared as if not hearing. Tignor gave him a shake.

"A man? Some man? Maybe at night? When you're supposed to be asleep but you ain't? Tell Daddy."

Niley shook his head faintly.

"What's that? No?"

"No, Daddy."

"Swear? Cross your heart and hope-to-die?"

Niley nodded, smiling uncertainly at Tignor.

"Not once? Never a man in this house? Eh?"

Niley was becoming confused, frightened. Rebecca ached to pull him from Tignor's arms.

Tignor was demanding, "*Never* a man? Not *ever*? Not one man, *never-ever*? You haven't waked up, and heard someone here? A man's voice, eh?

Niley tried to hold himself very still. He would not look at Rebecca, if he did he would burst into tears and cry for her. He was facing Tignor, eyelids partly closed, quivering.

Rebecca knew he was thinking: radio voices? Was that what Daddy meant?

Niley whispered what sounded like *yes*. It was almost inaudible, pleading.

Tignor said sharply, "A man? Eh? Here?"

Rebecca touched Tignor's hand, that was gripping Niley's thin shoulder. "Tignor, you're scaring him. It's the radio he's thinking of."

"Radio? What radio?"

"The radio. Radio voices."

"Hell, he's told me, baby. He's spilled the beans."

"Tignor, you don't mean any of this. You—"

"Niley admitted there's been a man here. He has heard the voice. Mommy's man."

Rebecca tried to laugh, this could only be a joke.

She had a sense of things-falling-away. Walking on thin rubbery ice as it starts to sink, crack.

"It's the radio, Tignor! I told you. Niley has to have the radio on all day and all night, he has some notion in his head the men's voices are *you*."

"Bullshit."

Tignor was enjoying this, Rebecca saw. The color was up in his face. This was as good as drinking. As good as winning at poker with his friends. Not for a moment did he believe any of it. Yet he seemed unable to stop.

Rebecca could have walked from the room. Waving her hand in disgust. Walked away, and began to run. Where?

Impossible, she could not leave Niley. Tignor was on his feet suddenly, dumping Niley to the floor. He caught hold of her elbow.

"Admit it, Jew-girl."

"Why do you hate me, Tignor? When I love you . . ."

Tignor's face flushed with blood. His mean wet eyes shrank from hers, he was ashamed. In that instant she saw his shame. Yet he was furious with her for defying him before the child.

"You are a Jew, aren't you? Gypsy-Jew! Hell, I was warned."

"What do you mean, 'warned'? By who?"

"Everybody. Everybody who knew you and your crazy old man."

"We weren't Jewish! I am not—"

"You aren't? Sure you are. 'Schwart.' "

"What if I was? What's wrong with Jews?"

Tignor made a disdainful face. He shrugged, as if he knew himself above such prejudice.

"*I* don't say it, baby, it's other people. 'Dirty Jews'—you hear that all the time. What's it mean, people say that? It's in the papers. It's in books."

"People are ignorant. They say all sorts of ignorant things."

"Jews, niggers. A nigger is next thing to an ape but the Jew is too smart for his own damn good. 'Jew' you down—pick your pocket, stab you in the back, and sue you! There's got to be some damn good reason, the Germans wanted to get rid of you. The Germans are a damn smart race."

Tignor laughed crudely. He didn't mean any of this, Rebecca thought. Yet he could not stop himself as, during lovemaking, he could not stop himself from thrashing and moaning helplessly in her arms.

Rebecca said, pleading, "Why did you marry me, then? If you don't love me."

A shrewd, sly look came over Tignor's face. Rebecca thought *He never did marry me. We aren't married.*

"Sure I love you. Why the hell'd I be here, in this dump, with this antsy kid, half-Jew kid, if I didn't? Bullshit."

Niley had begun to whimper, Tignor stalked out of the room in disgust. Rebecca hoped she would hear him slam out of the house, she and Niley would cower together hearing the car start, and back out of the driveway . . .

But Tignor didn't appear to be leaving. He'd only gone to the refrigerator for another ale.

That sensation of things-falling-away. Once the ice begins to crack, it will happen swiftly.

She would put the child to bed, quickly. Desperate to get him in bed, and the door to his room shut. She wanted to think that once the door was shut, Niley quieted and in bed, Tignor would forget him.

She was dazed, disoriented. It had happened so quickly.

Isn't my husband, never was my husband. I never had a husband.

The revelation was a blinding light in her face. She was sickened, humiliated. And yet, she'd known.

At the time, in the shabby brick house in Niagara Falls. Hastily married by an acquaintance of Niles Tignor's said to be a justice of the peace. She'd known.

She was tucking Niley into bed, the child pulled and clutched at her. "Don't cry! Try not to cry. If you have to cry, hide your face in your pillow. It makes Daddy upset to hear you cry, Daddy loves you so. And stay in this bed. Don't get out of this bed. No matter what you hear, Niley. Stay in this bed, don't come out. Promise?"

Niley was too agitated to promise. Rebecca switched off the bedside lamp, and left him.

Since Tignor had returned, Niley's rabbit-lamp did not burn through the night. The radio was no longer on his windowsill but back in the kitchen where, when Tignor was home, it was turned on only once a day, for the evening news.

It was Rebecca's intention to head off Tignor, to get into the front of the house and so prevent him from entering the bedroom. But there in the bedroom was Tignor, disheveled, glaring, a bottle of foaming ale in his fist.

"Hiding him away, eh? Making him afraid of his father."

Rebecca tried to explain it was Niley's bedtime. Far past his bedtime.

"You been poisoning him against me, haven't you? All this time."

Rebecca shook her head, no!

"Turning him against me. Why he's so afraid of me. Nervous like a kicked dog. *I* never raised a hand to him."

Rebecca was standing very still, staring at a spot on the floor.

Neither agreeing nor disagreeing. No resistance, and no defiance.

"Like I don't love him, and you. Like I ain't doing a damn good job. All the thanks I get." Tignor spoke in an aggrieved voice, searching in his pocket for something. He was clumsy, urgent. He took out his wallet, fumbled to pull out bills. "Gypsy-girl! Always wanting money, eh? Like I don't provide enough. Like for five fucking years you haven't been bleeding me dry." He began to toss bills at her, in that way that Rebecca loathed. She was certain now that he'd lied about Herschel, he'd never met Herschel in his life, that episode had been deceptive, demeaning. She hated dollar bills being tossed at her yet she tried to smile. Even now, she tried to smile. She knew it was necessary for Tignor to see himself as amusing and not threatening. If he sensed how frightened she was of him, he would be even angrier.

"Take 'em! Pick 'em up! This is what you want from me, isn't it?"

The bills fluttered to the floor at Rebecca's feet. She smiled harder, as Niley smiled in terror of his teasing Daddy. She knew she must perform, somehow. Must abase herself another time, to protect the child. She no longer cared about herself, she was so tired. She would not be one of those mothers (in Milburn you heard of them, sometimes) who failed to protect their children from harm. Always it seems so simple, self-evident *For God's sake why didn't she take the children, why didn't she run for help, why wait until it was too late* yet now that it was happening to her she understood the strange inertia, the wish that the storm might blow over, the male fury would spend itself and cease. For Tignor was very drunk, unsteady on his feet. His bloodshot eyes caught at hers in hurt, shame. Yet the fury had hold of him, and would not yet release him.

In a mock-amorous voice saying, "Jew-girl. Whore."

Crumpling bills into balls and throwing them at Rebecca, at her face. Her eyes filled with moisture, she was blinded.

"What's wrong? Too proud? You make your own money now, do you? On your back? Opening your legs? That's it?"

Tignor had set the bottle of ale on the floor. Not noticing that he'd knocked it over. He grabbed Rebecca, laughing as he tried to stuff a wad of bills down the front of her shirt. He tore at her slacks, that were made of black corduroy, worn at the knees and seat. These were factory clothes, she hadn't had time to change. He was stuffing bills inside the slacks, inside her underwear and between her legs as she struggled to get away. He was hurting her, his big fingers clawed at her vagina. But he was laughing, and Rebecca wanted to think *He isn't angry then, if he is laughing. He won't hurt me, if he is laughing.*

She was desperate hoping that Tignor wouldn't hear Niley pleading *Mom-my*!

Tignor had stopped hurting her, Rebecca thought it might be over, except there came a sudden explosion of light at the side of her head. Suddenly she was on the floor, dazed. Something had struck the side of her head. She had no clear idea that it had been a man's fist or that the man who'd struck her was Tignor.

He stood over her, prodding with his foot. The toe of his shoe between her legs, making her writhe in pain. "Eh, baby? What you like, is it?" Rebecca was too slow and dazed to react as Tignor wished, he lost patience and straddled her. Now he was truly angry, cursing her. So very angry now, and she had no idea why. For she had not fought him, she had tried not to provoke him. Yet he was shutting his hands around her neck, just to frighten her. Teach her a lesson. Shaming him in front of their son! Thump-thump-thumping the back of her head against the floorboards. Rebecca was choking, losing consciousness. Yet even in her distress she could feel cold air rising through the cracks of the floorboards, from the cellar below. The child in the next room was screaming now, she knew the man would blame her. *He will kill you now, can't help himself.* Like one who has ventured out on thin ice in full confidence that he can turn back at any time, he is safe so long as he can turn back even as in her terror she was thinking he must stop soon, of course he would stop soon, he had never gone on so long, never seriously hurt her in the past. There was the understanding between them—wasn't there?—he would never seriously hurt her. He would threaten, but he would not. Yet he was choking her, and stuffing bills into her mouth, trying to shove bills down her throat. Never had he done anything like this before, this was entirely new. Rebecca could not breathe, she was choking. She struggled to save herself, panic flooded her veins. The man was jeering, "Jew! Bitch! Whore!" He was furious, exuding a terrible righteous heat.

In all, the beating would last forty minutes.

She would believe afterward that she had not lost consciousness.

Yet there was Tignor shaking her: "Hey. There's nothing wrong with you, cunt. Wake up."

He pulled her to her feet, trying to make her stand. Though Tignor himself was swaying, like a man on a tilting deck.

"Come on! Stop faking."

Rebecca's knees had no strength. The hope came to her, quick as a lightning flash, that, if she sank to her knees, Tignor would take pity on her at last and allow her to crawl away like a kicked dog. And somehow, in that instant, it seemed to her that this had already happened. She would hide beneath the stairs, she would hide in the cellar. She would crawl into the cistern (the cistern was dry, the gutters and drainpipes of the old house were badly rusted and rainwater could not accumulate) and hug her knees to her chest, she would never testify against him even if he killed her. She would never!

But she hadn't crawled away. She was still in that room. A lighted room, and not the cellar. Through the webby fabric she saw it: the neatly made bed with the quilt spread, Rebecca hadn't yet turned back with her chambermaid's exactitude, for nighttime; dark-gold circular shag rugs bought for $2.98 in Chautauqua Falls, in the post-Christmas sales; the straw flowers on the bureau that Miss Lutter would have admired. Tignor was grunting, "Wake up! Open your eyes! I'll break your ass if—" He was shaking her, slamming her against a wall. The windowpanes vibrated.

Something had fallen and was rolling across the floor, emitting foam. Rebecca would have slipped down like a rag doll except the man held her, striking her face.

"Talk back to me, will you! Shame a man in his own son's eyes."

Tignor dragged Rebecca to the bed. Her clothes were torn, and strangely wet. Her shirt had been ripped open. It would infuriate him to see her breasts, she must hide her breasts. Her naked female flesh would madden him. Tignor threw her onto the bed, he fumbled at his trousers. He blamed her, stupid cunt. His trousers were no longer sharply pressed. In the farmhouse on the Poor Farm Road, Niles Tignor had lost himself. He had lost his manhood, his dignity. His shirts were clumsily ironed, creases at the collar. A blind cripple could do better!

There was Niley, pulling at Daddy's legs, screaming for him to stop.

"Little fucker."

Rebecca knew now: she had made a terrible mistake. The worst mistake a mother can make. She had endangered her child out of stupidity and carelessness.

A bright blood-blossom on the child's mouth, nose.

Rebecca pleaded with the man straddling her: not to hit Niley, to hit her.

Not him: her.

"Baby! Damn cry-baby!" Tignor lifted the screaming child by an arm, and threw him at the wall.

Niley ceased crying. He lay quietly on the floor, where he'd fallen. And Rebecca, on the bed, lay quietly now.

The fabric over her face had tightened. She was blind, her brain was close to extinction. She could not breathe through her nose, something was broken, blocked. Like a gasping fish she sucked for air through her mouth, all her strength went into this effort. Yet she could hear, her hearing was sharpened.

A man's heavy panting, beside her. Wet snorting noise in his throat. Tignor had lost interest, now she'd ceased to fight him. He'd collapsed on the bed beside her. Amid the churned-up bloodied bedclothes he would sleep.

It was like slipping beneath the surface of water: Rebecca kept losing consciousness, then waking. A very long time seemed to pass before she had the strength to wake fully, and get to her feet. She moved so slowly, so awkwardly, she expected Tignor to wake, and grab her arm. Almost, she could hear his grunted words. *Cunt! Where're you going!* But Tignor did not wake, Rebecca was safe. She went to the child, where he lay on the floor. Her face was bleeding, her left eye swollen shut. She could barely see him yet knew: he was all right. He would be all right, he too was safe, there could be nothing seriously wrong with him. It could not be. His father loved him, his father would not have wished to hurt him.

She whispered to Niley. He was safe, Mommy had him. But not to cry any more.

Niley was breathing, in shallow erratic gasps. His head fell forward at a sharp angle. *His neck is broken* Rebecca thought even as she knew it could not be so, and it was not. She had no strength and yet she lifted Niley, staggered beneath his weight carrying him out of the bedroom. He was breathing, he was not seriously hurt. She was certain.

In her dazed state Rebecca would not have supposed herself capable of walking from the bedroom to the kitchen and yet she managed to carry Niley into the kitchen, and did not drop him. In the brighter light of the kitchen she saw that the child's small face was bleeding, and swollen; there was an ugly scratch at his hairline, leaking blood; his skin wasn't flushed as usual but waxy-pale, with a bluish cast. His eyelids were not fully closed, crescents of white showed faintly. For here was the mechanism of vision, and yet there was no vision. Like a doll's glassy eyes if you pushed the lid up with a thumb.

"Niley. Mommy has you."

He was alive, he was breathing and alive and beginning to stir, whimpering, in Rebecca's arms.

"You're all right, honey. Can you open your eyes?"

His thin arms, legs: they did not appear to be broken.

Femur, clavicle, pelvis: not broken.

Cranium . . . Not broken.

Oh, she wanted to think so! Groping with her fingers, running her fingertips over him, the weakly stirring arms and legs, the head pitched forward against her chest. If his skull was fractured, how could she know? She could not know.

She washed Niley's face, and her own. The child was groggy, but waking. He had not the strength to cry loudly, for which Rebecca was grateful. Rebecca washed her hands, her arms, her chest that was smeared in blood. Pausing to listen, if Tignor was waking and would come after them.

But the fury had spent itself, for now.

She had known for weeks that she would leave him and yet: she had not acted. Now she was desperate, and must act. She could not think where to go that would not be a mistake, a net to capture her and Niley and return them to Tignor.

Not the Meltzers'. Not the Chautauqua Falls police.

Never the police! She shared her father's distrust and dislike of the police. She seemed to know that these men, men so very like Niles Tignor, would sympathize with Tignor, the husband and father. They would not protect her and Niley from him.

Niley was lying now on the kitchen floor, she'd placed a towel beneath his head. He was all right now, he was breathing almost normally. His face was not so white, some color had returned to his cheeks.

She would carry him out to the car, she would not take time to change his clothes. She would not even force a jacket on him, only just wrap him in a blanket.

It seemed to Rebecca then that she had done this: wrapped Niley in a blanket. She had carried him out to the car in the driveway, and placed him gently in the backseat. And there he would sleep.

She returned to the bedroom where Tignor lay on the bed as she'd left him, snoring. She would not have thought herself courageous enough or reckless enough or desperate enough to return to this room of such devastation, that smelled still of her terror, and yet she had no choice. The way out was through Tignor, she had no choice but to reach into his trouser pocket, to extract his car keys.

He did not stir, he had no awareness of her. His mouth was like an infant's mouth, opening wetly as he sucked in air. His eyes were like Niley's, partially shut, a crescent of sickly white exposed.

Such snoring! A sound of rude animal health Rebecca had always thought it, smiling as she'd lain beside Tignor in their countless beds. For more than five years, she had lain beside this man. She had listened to him snore, she had listened to his quieter breathing. How attentive she had been to every nuance of his body's mood, that fascinated her as if his body were another facet of Tignor's soul, of which she might be aware in ways that he himself was not.

Now the fury in the man was spent, Rebecca felt it reviving in her.

She had the car keys. Now they were hers.

Tignor lay in the rumpled bedclothes with a look of profound astonishment as if he'd fallen from a great height only to land on this bed, unhurt. He would sleep like this for ten, twelve hours. Without Rebecca to wake him he would be incapable of dragging himself from the bed to urinate, urine would leak from him in his sleep, soiling the bed. In the morning he would be shamed, disgusted. Yet in his stupor he could not prevent it from happening.

By which time, Rebecca and Niley would be gone.

She smiled to think so! There was a kind of peace in the room, now.

Deftly Rebecca was packing. She would not take time to change her soiled clothes. A few things of hers, and Niley's, folded and tossed into the suitcase Tignor had bought for her years before. And then she picked up all the bills she could find in the room. She was methodical, determined. So much money! Tignor had won big at cards, he'd wanted her to know. She would not touch Tignor's wallet, however, that lay on the floor where he'd dropped it.

From the top closet shelf she took the money she'd hidden away since March. Now it was fifty-one dollars. And the ratty sweater in which she'd wrapped the seven-inch piece of scrap steel.

Now Rebecca knew, why she'd kept this makeshift knife. Why she'd hidden it away in this room.

She tested the tip of the steel with her thumb. It was sharp as any ice pick. If she struck Tignor swiftly and accurately and with all her strength, against the thick artery pulsing in his neck, she believed she could kill him. He would not die immediately but he would bleed to death. The carotid artery, this was. She knew from her biology textbook. Deep inside Tignor's massive chest was his heart, that would have to be pierced in a single powerful blow. She did not think she was capable of such a blow. If the steel struck bone, it would be deflected. If she missed by a fraction of an inch, the man might revive, in a paroxysm of anguish he might take the steel from her and turn it upon her, he might kill her with his bare hands. Her neck was bruised even now, from his half-strangling her. The carotid artery, so vulnerable, was more practical. And yet, even so Rebecca might miss. She was aroused, trembling in anticipation and yet: she might miss.

And did she want to kill this man, she was hesitant, uncertain. Did she want to kill any human being. Any living creature. To punish Tignor, to hurt him badly. To allow him to know how he had hurt her, and their child, and must be punished.

The child was waiting for her. She had no choice, she must hurry.

Rebecca lay the piece of scrap steel on the bed beside the sleeping man.

"He will know, maybe. That I have spared him. And he will know why."

45

❀ ❀ ❀

Three days later on October 29, 1959, the Pontiac registered in the name of Niles Tignor would be discovered, gas tank near-empty, keys on the floorboards beneath the front seat, in a parking lot close by the Greyhound bus station in Rome, New York. This was approximately two hundred miles north and east of Chautauqua Falls. Left behind in the car was no note, only just several wadded bloodstained tissues on the floor of the backseat of which one contained a woman's ring: a small milky-pale synthetic stone resembling an opal in a slightly tarnished silver setting; and, in the glove compartment a flashlight with a cracked glass, a pair of soiled men's leather gloves, and a much-creased road map of New York State to be identified by the car's owner as his.

II

IN THE WORLD

I

❀ ❀ ❀

Even as a small child he was shrewd enough to know *It's like she and I have died. And now nothing can hurt us.*

2

❀ ❀ ❀

At first it was play. He believed it must be play. Like singing, humming.
Under your breath. In secret. A way of being happy, the two of them needing no one else.

Speaking to strangers in her quiet proud voice *His name is Zacharias. A
name from the Bible. He was born with a musical gift. His father is dead, we never
speak of it.*

He believed it had to do with *keeping-going.* She spoke of what their lives
were as *keeping-going,* for now. The names of towns, mountains, rivers, counties ever changing. Never in one place for more than a few days. One day
Beardstown, the next Tintern Falls. One day Barneveld, the next day Granite Springs. The Chautauqua River became the Mohawk River, the Mohawk
River became the Susquehanna. He saw the signs beside the highway. He
was eager to pronounce the names for he loved the sounds of new names
strange in his mouth and he was eager too to learn their spellings but the
names so frequently changed he could not remember and she seemed to
have no wish that he remember as she had no wish that he remember his
old name now that he was *Zack, Zack-Zack* she hugged and adored telling
him solemnly *Now you are Zack. My son Zacharias. Blessed of God for your father*—her eyes vague, bemused—*has returned to Hell where they've been waiting
for him.* Laughing, and lifting his hands inside hers in the patty-cake game
she'd begun when he was a baby clapping the soft palms of his hands together inside hers so that he was made to laugh and their laughter mingled
breathless, joyous.

As he could not recall when memory began. When first he'd opened his eyes. When first he'd drawn breath. When first he'd heard music, that startled him, quickened his pulse. When first she'd sung and hummed with him. When first she'd danced with him. Though recalling how in one of the cafés there had been a piano, a jukebox and a piano and the jukebox an old Wurlitzer, wide, squat, stained-glass colors darkened by a patina of grime through which a glaring light shone throbbing with the beat of simple loud percussive popular songs, when in the late evening the jukebox lapsed into silence Mommy led him (so sleepy! his head so heavy!) to the old upright yellow-keyed Knabe back beside the bar, Christmas tinsel and strings of red lights, a powerful smell of beer, tobacco smoke, men's bodies, Mommy was saying in her excited voice clear as a bell for others to hear *Try it, Zack! See if you can play piano* gripping him in her strong warm arms so he would not slip from her lap, her sturdy knees, at such times he was a clumsy child, a stricken-shy-mute little rat of a child, the badly scruffed piano stool too low for him he could have barely reached the keyboard, there were men looking on, always there were men in these cafés, taverns, bars to which Mommy brought him, the men were uttering words of hearty encouragement *Come on, kid! Let's hear it* and her breath was hot and beery against the back of his neck, trembling with excitement she seized his small pliant hands and placed them on the keyboard, never mind the ivory keys were stained and warped and their sharp edges hurt his fingers, never mind the black keys had a tendency to stick, the piano was stained and warped and out of tune, Mommy knew to place her son's hands at the center of the keyboard, Mommy knew to place his right thumb at middle C, each of his fingers sought its key by instinct, there was comfort to it *He was born with the gift, God has designated him special. He don't always talk so well.* At such times she spoke strangely, forcefully, with such certainty and her eyes unwavering and her mouth shaped in a smile of such raw hope, though he was hurt at her words, he felt the falsity of her words even as he supposed he understood their logic *Feel sympathy for us! Help us* he was frightened for her, not for himself that he had no gift, he had been born with no gift and no god had designated him special, it was for her sake he was frightened that the men who'd seemed captivated by her a few minutes before should suddenly laugh at her, but when he began to strike the keys at once he would cease to hear the men's jokes and laughter, he would cease to hear his father's low mocking outraged voice in the voices of these strangers, he would cease to be aware of the tension in his mother's body and the heat radiating from her, depressing the keys, those that weren't sticking, in a rapid run, the scale of C major executed with childish enthusiasm though he had no idea it was the scale of C major he played, almost harmoniously both hands together though the left trailed the right by a fraction of a second, now he was striking chords, trying to depress the sluggish keys, striking black keys, sharps, flats, no idea what he was doing but it was play, piano was play, play-for-Zack, what he did felt right, felt natural, out of the piano's unfathomable interior (he imagined it densely wired and with a glowing tube, like a radio) these wonderful sounds emerged with an air of surprise, as if the old upright Knabe shoved into an alcove of a roadside café in Apalachin, New York, had been silent for so long, unused except for purposes of drunken keyboard banging for so long, the very instrument had been startled into wakefulness, unprepared.

What his mother meant by *designated by God*. Not his hands which were fumbling blind-boy hands, but the piano-sounds that were like no sounds he had ever heard so intimately. Out of the radio he'd heard music since infancy and some of this had been piano music but it was nothing like the strange vivid sound that sprang into life from his fingertips. He was dry-mouthed in wonder, awe. He was smiling, this was such happiness. Discovering the way individual notes fused with others as if his fingers moved of their own volition. Not a child to be at ease in the presence of strangers and the roadside places to which his mother brought him were populated exclusively by strangers and most of these were men perceiving him with the glazed-eyed indifference of the male for any offspring not his own. Except he had their attention now. For he was discovering in the maze of stained, warped, sticking and dead keys enough live keys to allow him to play a pattern of related notes he could not guess would be instantly familiar to these strangers' ears, Bill Monroe's "Footprints in the Snow" he'd been hearing repeated on the jukebox in that dreamy state between sleep and wakefulness his head lowered onto his mother's folded coat in one of the café booths, he had no idea that the succession of notes constituted a song composed and performed by individuals unknown to him and that those who heard it would be drawn to marvel at it—"Jesus, how's he do it? Kid so little, he don't take lessons does he?"

He wasn't listening to their voices. Eyes shut tight in concentration. The fingers of his right hand picked out the predominant pattern as if already it was familiar to him, the fingers of his weaker left hand provided chords, a filling-in of gaps in the sound. Play. Playing. This was happiness! The old piano's notes running through him—fingers, hands, arms, torso—like an electric current.

"Ask can he play 'Cumberland Breakdown.' "

Mommy told them he could not. He could only play songs he'd heard on the jukebox.

" 'Rocky Road Blues'? That was on the jukebox."

He was discovering that he could play a cluster of notes and then replay it as an echo, in a different key: raised by a half-note, or lowered. He could change the pattern of the cluster by playing the notes faster or slower or with emphasis upon certain notes and not on others, yet the pattern remained recognizable.

He could not reach a full octave of course, his hands were far too small. He could not reach the pedals of course. Had no idea what the pedals were. Nor would his mother know. The piano-sounds were choppy, broken up. This was not the smooth music you heard on the radio.

The men who'd been drawn by the child's piano playing began to lose interest. Began to drift away. Soon their loud voices resumed, their braying laughter. One man remained, and came closer. He placed his foot on the right-hand pedal and depressed it. At once the choppy sounds melted into one another.

"You need the pedal. You pump it."

This man, a stranger. But not like the others. He was smiling, he'd been drinking but he knew something the others didn't know. And he cared, he appeared to be genuinely interested in the child fumbling to play an instrument he'd never touched before, astonishing how raw and instinctive the child's playing was. And there was the child's young mother holding him in her arms, smiling, so proud, a glisten of madness in her face.

Afterward asking who they were, where they were from. And the young woman said evasively, though she was still smiling, "Oh, up farther north. Nowhere you would know." And the man persisted, "Try me, honey: where?" and the young mother laughed fixing the man with her calm dark seemingly imperturbable eyes shadowed with tiredness and yet beautiful to him, saying, as if she'd rehearsed these words many times, "Nowhere is where we are from, mister. But somewhere is where we are going."

A roadside café in Apalachin, New York. Just south of the Susquehanna River and a few miles north of the Pennsylvania border. It was late winter 1960, they had been in flight from Niles Tignor for nearly five months.

It was the first time he'd played any piano. The first time she'd led him to any piano. Possibly she'd been drinking, she had seen the piano shoved into an alcove of the café and the idea came to her as so many ideas came to her now: "The breath of God."

Not that she believed in any god. Hell, no.

Still there were these wayward breezes, sometimes. Sudden gust of wind. Whipping-wind of the kind she'd grown up with, rushing at the old stone cottage from the vastness of Lake Ontario. A cruel suffocating wind, you could not breathe. Laundry was torn from the line, sometimes the very posts collapsed. But there were gentler winds, there were breezes gentle as breaths. These she was learning to recognize. These she awaited eagerly. These she would guide her life by.

Beyond this night there would be other cafés, taverns and restaurants, hotels. There would be other pianos. If circumstances were right, she would lead her gifted child Zacharias to play. If circumstances were not so right, sometimes she would lead her gifted child Zacharias to play anyway. For he must be heard! His musical gift must be heard!

Each time Zack played there was applause.

You don't look closely into the motive for applause.

And each time there would be a man who lingered afterward. A man who marveled, admired. A man who had money if only a few dollars to spend on the strange young mother and her spindly-limbed little boy with his pale, intense face and haunted eyes.

Tell me your name, honey. You know mine.

You know my son's name. That's enough for now.

No. I need to know your name, too.

My name is Hazel Jones.

"Hazel Jones." That's a pretty name.

Is it? I was named for someone. My parents kept the secret but now they are gone. But one day I will know, I think.

3

❊ ❊ ❊

"If we haven't been killed by now, no reason to think we ever will be."

She laughed, such delicious wisdom.

Fleeing with the child she had not looked back. This would be her strategy for weeks, months, eventually years. *Keeping-going* she called it. Each day was its own surprise, and reward: *keeping-going* was enough. From the house on the Poor Farm Road she'd taken money thrown at her body in contempt of her very body and in repudiation of her love as a naive young wife defrauded in marriage. She had this money, these crumpled bills of varying denominations, she might tell herself she'd earned it. She would supplement it by working when necessary: waitress, cleaning woman, chambermaid. Ticket seller, movie theater "usherette." Salesclerk, shopgirl. On her knees gracefully slipping shoes onto men's stockinged feet, Hazel Jones with her dazzling American-girl smile: "Now, sir, how does that feel?"

Frequently men offered to buy her meals, drinks. Her and her little boy. Frequently they offered to give her money. Sometimes she refused, sometimes she accepted but she provided no sexual favors for money: her puritanical soul was revulsed at such a thought.

"I'd rather kill us. Zack and me. And that will never happen."

She felt no remorse for leaving the child's father as she'd done. She felt no regret, and no guilt. She did feel fear. In that vague fading way in which we contemplate the fact of our own deaths, not imminent but impending. *So long as we keep going, he will never find us.*

It did not occur to Rebecca that the man who had beaten her and the child had committed criminal acts. No more would she have thought to flee to Chautauqua Falls police than Anna Schwart would have fled to Milburn police in terror of Jacob Schwart.

You made your bed, now lie in it.

It was the wisdom of peasants. It was a gritty wisdom of the soil. It was not to be questioned.

Her wounds would heal, her bruises would fade. There remained a faint high ringing in her right ear at times, when she was tired. But no more distracting than the springtime trill of peepers or the midsummer hum of insects. There were angry reddened scabs on her forehead she fingered absently, almost in awe, a curious gratified pleasure. But these she could hide, beneath strands of hair. She worried more for the child than for herself, that the child's father would be maddened with the need to reclaim him.

Hey you two: love ya.

There was Leora Greb shaking her head, saying you don't step between a man and his kids, if you want to stay alive.

This was Rebecca's plan: to abandon Tignor's car in a public place, that it would be found by authorities immediately and its ownership traced and Tignor would come into possession of it and have less reason to pursue her. She knew, the man would be infuriated by the theft of his car.

She laughed, thinking of the man's rage.

"He would kill me now, would he? But I'm out of his reach."

She smiled. She touched the scabs at her hairline, that were nearly painless now. She would not speak of Tignor to the child nor would she ever again tolerate the child whimpering and whining after *Dad-dy*.

"There is Mommy now. Mommy will be all to you, now."

"But Dad-dy—"

"No. There is no Dad-dy. No more. Only just Mommy."

She laughed, she kissed the anxious child. She would kiss away his fears. Seeing that she laughed, he would laugh, in childish imitation. Wishing to please Mommy and to be kissed by Mommy, he would quickly learn.

Never again would she utter aloud the name of the man who had masqueraded as her husband! He had tricked her into believing that they were married, in Niagara Falls. It had been her stupidity that tricked her, she would think no more of it. The man was dead now, his name erased from memory.

The child's name, that was the father's. A diminutive of the father's. A curious name, that made others smile quizzically. She would never call him by that name again. She must re-name the child, that the break with the father would be complete.

Leaving Chautauqua Falls she'd driven the stolen Pontiac on back roads north and east through the foothills of the Chautauqua Mountains and into and past the rolling farmland of the Finger Lakes region and at last into the Mohawk Valley where the river moved swift and sullen and steel-colored beneath shifting columns of mist. She had not dared to stop anywhere she and the child might be recognized and so she pushed on, pain-wracked and exhausted. In a shallow rocky stream beside one of the roads she washed the child and herself, tried to clean their wounds. She kissed the child repeatedly, overcome with gratitude that he hadn't been seriously injured; at least, she didn't believe he had been seriously injured. His small supple bones appeared to be intact, his skull that had seemed so delicate to his anxious mother, the eggshell-skull of infancy, was in fact tough and resilient and had not been cracked by the raging man.

Grateful too that the child couldn't see his own swollen and blackened eyes, his distended scabby upper lip, his blood-edged nostrils. And that the child was so impressionable, he would take his emotional cues from her: "We got away! We got away! Nobody will ever find us, we got away!"

Strange how happy Rebecca was becoming, as the Poor Farm Road swiftly receded into the past.

Strange how jubilant she felt, despite her swollen face and aches in all her bones.

Leaning over to kiss and hug the child. Blow in his ear and whisper nonsense to make him laugh.

In cornfields they hid from the road and relieved themselves like animals. Afterward running and hiding from each other, shrieking with laughter.

"Mom-my! Mom-my where are you!"

Rebecca came up behind him, closed her arms about him in a swoon of happiness, possessiveness. She had saved her son, and she had saved herself. She would see that her life, though mauled and shaken as if in the jaws of a great beast, was blessed.

The child's true name came to her then: " 'Zacharias.' A name from the Bible."

She was so very happy. She was inspired. She would abandon the stolen car in Rome, an aging city beyond Oneida Lake of about half the size of Chautauqua Falls. This was a city that meant nothing to her except the man who'd masqueraded as her husband had business dealings there, he'd spoken of Rome often. She would leave the car there to confound him, as a riddle.

Parked the car, gas tank near-empty, near the Greyhound bus station. *He will reason that we are traveling east. He will never find us.*

She reversed the course of their flight. At the Greyhound station she bought two adult tickets to Port Oriskany, 250 miles back west.

Adult tickets in case the ticket seller was queried about a fleeing mother and her child.

Neither she nor the child had ever ridden on a bus before. The Greyhound was massive! The experience was exhilarating, an adventure. Nothing to do on a bus but stare out the window at the landscape: rapidly passing in the foreground beside the highway, slowly passing at the horizon. Though she was very tired and her bones ached yet she found herself smiling. The child lay sleeping beside her, snug and warm. She stroked his silky hair, she pressed her cool fingers against his swollen face.

Will you take my card at least.

If you should wish to contact me.

Accept from me your legacy. Hazel Jones.

" 'Dr. Hendricks' is the name. 'Byron Hendricks, M.D.' "

The uniformed man, very dark skinned, with a narrow mustache and heavy-lidded eyes, regarded her with surprise.

"Fourth floor, ma'am. Except I don't b'lieve he is there."

Rebecca had not thought of this possibility. It had seemed to her since that evening on the canal towpath that the man in the panama hat had so sought her, of course he was awaiting her.

Rebecca stared at the wall directory. Wigner Professional Building. There was HENDRICKS, B.K. SUITE 414.

The child Zacharias was prowling about the ornate, high-ceilinged foyer of the Wigner Building, inquisitive and restless. Newly named, in this new city Port Oriskany beside an enormous slate-blue lake, he seemed subtly altered, no longer shy but frankly curious, staring rudely at well-dressed strangers as they pushed through the revolving doors entering from busy Owego Avenue. Until now he'd been a country boy, the only adults he'd seen had dressed and behaved very differently than these adults.

When he wasn't staring at strangers rushing past him he was stooping to examine the polished ebony marble beneath his feet, so unlike any floor he'd ever walked on.

A dark mirror! Inside which, beneath his feet, the ghostly reflection of a boy whose face he could not see moved jerkily.

"Zack, come here with Mommy. We're going up in an *elevator*."

He laughed, the name *Zack* was so strange to him, like an unexpected pinch you didn't know was meant to be playful or hurtful.

Zacharias meant blessed, his mother had told him. Already he was going for his first elevator ride. Though he still limped from what the drunken man had done to him, and his small pale face looked as if it had been used as a punching bag, he knew he was entering a world of unpredictable surprises, adventures.

The uniformed man had entered the elevator and taken his position at the controls. He said, "Ma'am, I can take you to Dr. Hendricks's office. But like I say, I don't b'lieve he is there. I ain't seen any of 'em for some time."

It was as if Rebecca hadn't heard this. In the elevator she gripped the child's small-boned hand. A hot dry hand. She hoped that he wasn't feverish, she had no time for such foolishness now. In Port Oriskany, about to see Byron Hendricks! He'd expressed surprise that Hazel Jones was married, what would he think that Hazel Jones had a child? Rebecca was feeling uncertain, confused. Maybe this was a mistake.

Her lips moved. She might have been talking to herself.

"Dr. Hendricks has to be there. He gave me his card only a few days ago. He's expecting me, I think."

"Ma'am, you want I should wait for you? Case you comin' right back down?"

The uniformed man loomed over her. She had to wonder if he was teasing her, that she might become shaken, tearful; and he might comfort her. Yet he appeared to be sincere. He was wearing white gloves to operate the elevator. She smelled his hair pomade. She had never been in such proximity to a Negro man before, and she had never been in a position of needing help from a Negro man before. At the General Washington Hotel the "Negro help" had mostly kept to themselves.

"No. That isn't necessary. Thank you."

The uniformed man stopped the elevator at the fourth floor and opened the door with a flourish. Quickly Rebecca stepped out into the corridor, pulling the child with her.

He is thinking I want Dr. Hendricks to examine my son. That's what he is thinking.

"He down there, that dir'ection. You want for me to wait, ma'am?"

"No! I told you."

Annoyed, Rebecca walked away without glancing back. The elevator doors clattered shut behind her.

Zack was fretting he didn't want any old doctor, he *did not*.

Suite 414 was at the farther end of the medicinal-smelling corridor. On a door whose upper half was set with a sheet of frosted glass had been hand-lettered BYRON K. HENDRICKS, M.D. PLEASE ENTER. But the interior appeared to be darkened, the door was locked. There was a begrimed and derelict air to this end of the corridor.

Desperate, Rebecca knocked on the frosted glass.

She could not think what to do. In her fevered but vague fantasies of seeking out Byron Hendricks, anticipating that moment when the man's

eyes perceived her, when he smiled in delight in recognition of Hazel
Jones, she had not anticipated him not being where he had promised he
would be.

Zack was fretting he didn't like the smell in this place, he *did not*.

Well, Rebecca had money. She had several hundred dollars in bills of
varying denominations. She would not have to find work for a while, if she
was careful with the money. She would find an inexpensive hotel in Port
Oriskany, she and Zack would stay the night. They were badly in need of
rest. They would bathe, they would sleep in a bed with clean, crisp sheets.
They would lock themselves in a room in a hotel populated by strangers,
they would be utterly safe. For three nights in succession they had slept in
the Pontiac, parked beside a country road, shivering with cold. The bus trip
from Rome had been five long hours.

"In the morning. I can telephone him. Make an appointment."

Zack saw his mother was becoming anxious. Coming to nudge himself
against her thighs murmuring Mom-*my*? in his plaintive child's voice.

She was thinking it had been unwise to come directly to Dr. Hendricks's office from the bus station. She should have telephoned to see
if the doctor was in. She could look up his telephone number in a directory. It was what people did, normal people. She must learn from normal
people.

Another time, Rebecca turned the knob of the locked door. Why wasn't
Hendricks here!

When he saw her, he would know her. She believed this. Whatever
would happen next would happen without her volition. He had summoned
her to him, he'd begged her. No one had ever begged her in such a way. No
one had ever looked into her heart in such a way.

The man in the panama hat. He'd followed her from town, he had
known her. He had altered the course of her life. She'd been a deluded
young woman living with a man not her husband. A violent man, a criminal. She would not have had the courage to leave this man if she had not
met Hendricks on the canal towpath.

Very possibly, she would not have aroused the jealousy of the man
who'd masqueraded as her husband, if Hendricks had not approached her
on the canal towpath.

"You see, you have changed my life! Now I'm here in Port Oriskany, and this is my son Zacharias . . ."

She would not lie to him. She would not claim to be Hazel Jones.

Though she could not absolutely deny it, either. For there was the possibility that she'd been adopted. Hadn't Herschel suggested this, they'd found her, an infant, newly born on a ship in New York Harbor . . . "My parents are gone, Dr. Hendricks. I will never be able to ask them. But I never felt that I was theirs." In her exhausted and deranged state this seemed to her more than theoretically possible.

The child frowned up at her. Why was Mommy talking to herself? And smiling, biting at her scabby lip.

"Mommy? C'n we go now? It smells bad here."

She turned, numbly. She groped for the child's hand. She was thinking hard and yet no thoughts came to her. In the wan reflective surfaces of frosted-glass doors they were passing her face was obscured and only her thick straggling hair was sharply defined. She looked like a drowned person.

One of the frosted-glass doors opened. The sickly medicinal smell was intensified. An individual was leaving suite 420, occupied by Hiram Tanner, D.D.S. On an impulse Rebecca entered the waiting room. Did D.D.S. mean dentist? A woman receptionist frowned at her from behind a desk. "Yes? Can I help you, miss?"

"I'm looking for Dr. Hendricks in suite four-fourteen. But the office seems to be closed."

The receptionist's crayon-eyebrows lifted in exaggerated surprise.

"Why, haven't you heard? Dr. Hendricks died last summer."

"Died! But . . ."

"All his patients were notified, I thought. Were you one of his patients?"

"No. I mean . . . yes, I was."

"His office hasn't been vacated yet, there's some problem. It was left in pretty bad shape and has to be cleaned."

The receptionist, middle-aged, tidily dressed, was looking from Rebecca to the child nudging against her thigh. She was staring at their battered faces.

"There's other doctors you could see in the building. Down on floor two there's—"

"No! I need to see Dr. Hendricks. It's the son I mean, not the father."

The receptionist said, "There hasn't been anybody around that office since last summer, that I've seen. People say somebody comes in after hours. There's things get moved around, there's debris in boxes for the janitor to take away. I used to see the son, but not recently. It was a stroke that killed Dr. Hendricks, they said. He had a lot of patients but they were getting old, too. I never heard the son was a doctor."

Rebecca protested, "But he is! 'Byron Hendricks, M.D.' I've seen his card. I was supposed to make an appointment . . ."

"A man about forty, is he? Nervous, like? With a kind of strange way about him, and eyes? Always dressed kind of different, wearing a hat? In cold weather it was a fedora, other times it was a straw hat. He wa'n't never any M.D. that I ever heard of but I could be wrong. He might've gone to medical school but wasn't practicing, there's some like that."

Rebecca stared at the woman, as Zack nudged and twisted impatiently against her legs. Seeing Rebecca's shock, the woman laid her hand on her bosom: "See, miss, I don't feel comfortable passing on rumors. Dr. Tanner was one to say hello to the old man, and they'd chat for a few minutes, but Dr. Tanner didn't know them, either of them, real well."

Rebecca said, confused, "Can you be a doctor and not 'practice'? But . . ." Seeing in the woman's eyes a measure of pity, yet of satisfaction. She thought she had better get accustomed to it.

She thanked the receptionist, pulled Zack with her out of the office and shut the door behind her.

Out in the corridor Zack wrenched out of her grasp and ran limping ahead of her, flailing his arms foolishly and making a whistling-gagging noise as if he couldn't breathe the stale air. He was becoming unruly, obstinate. He had never behaved this way in any public place in the past.

Rebecca half sobbed, "Zack! Damn you get back here."

He was about to punch the elevator button *down*. Rebecca was surprised he knew to do such a thing, at his age. She slapped his hand away. She didn't want to summon the elevator operator, the uniformed Negro with the neat narrow mustache and playful-brooding eyes, knowing how he would look at her with pity, too.

"We'll take the stairs, honey. Stairs are safer."

A windowless stairway three steep flights down, to a heavy door marked EXIT on a back street.

The ringing in her ear was louder, distracting. Almost, she thought there were nocturnal insects somewhere near.

Thinking *Hendricks wanted you to believe him, trust him. On the towpath. At that time. He had no thought that you would ever try to find him here.*

"Just the two of us. One night. My son and me."

They would spend the night in a walk-up hotel in a brownstone, a few blocks from Owego Avenue. Rebecca checked several rooms before taking one: examined sheets and pillowcases, lifted a corner of the mattress from the box springs to check for bedbugs, lice. The desk clerk was amused by her, eyeing her long straggly hair and bruised face. "You want the Statler, honey, you're in the wrong place."

The double bed took up most of the space in the room between stained-wallpaper walls and a melancholy window looking out into an air shaft. There was no bath, the toilet was in the hall.

Rebecca laughed, wiping at her eyes.

"Five-fifty a night. This is the right place."

When they were alone in the room, Zack poked about in imitation of his mother. Pretended to be a dog sniffing in corners. Stooped to peer beneath the bed.

"Mommy, what if Dad-dy—"

Rebecca raised a warning finger. "No."

"But Mommy! If Da—"

"There is Mommy now, I told you. From now on only Mommy."

She would not scold the child. She would never frighten him. Instead she embraced, tickled him.

Eventually, he would forget. She was determined.

She took him for a meal before bedtime at an automat on Owego Avenue. The bright-lit, noisy atmosphere and the way in which food was acquired, pushed along on shiny plastic trays, fascinated the child. After their meal she debated taking him across the wide, windy square to the Port Oriskany Statler which was the city's most distinguished hotel. Wanting to show him the spacious, ornate lobby crowded with well-dressed men and women. Marble floor, leather sofas, potted ferns and small trees. An open atrium to the mezzanine floor. Uniformed doormen, bellboys.

The Port Oriskany Statler sparkled with lights. At least twenty-five floors. On the far side of the sandstone building was a waterfront park, and Lake Erie stretching to the horizon. Rebecca had a vague memory of a view from high windows. He'd brought her to stay at the hotel years ago, the man who'd masqueraded as her husband. She had been so deluded, believing she'd been happy at the time! Her role too had been a masquerade.

"I was his whore. Even if I didn't know it."

Zack glanced up at her quizzically. As if she'd been talking to herself, laughing. He was of an age to know that adults didn't do such things in public.

She was trying to recall if it had been here in Port Oriskany, or in another city, she'd been followed from the hotel by a man in a navy jacket and navy cap. He'd turned out to be (she surmised, she had never been certain) someone sent to test her loyalty, faithfulness. She wondered for the first time what would have happened to her if she had smiled and laughed with the man, allowed herself to be picked up.

She wasn't sure if that had been Port Oriskany, though. But she did recall that the man who'd masqueraded as her husband had taken her to an obstetrician in this city, who had examined her and run a test on her urine and told her the good news that she was going to have a baby in eight months' time.

The man who'd masqueraded as her husband had said in his blunt bemused voice *You're pregnant are you, girl.* He had not said *You're going to have a baby.*

Years later, with her surviving child, she contemplated these words. The distinction between each statement.

"Mommy are you sad? Mommy are you *crying*?"

She wasn't, though. She'd swear she was laughing.

Next morning was brightly cold, invigorating. In the night she'd decided not to try to telephone Byron Hendricks, M.D. She would make her own way, she had no need of him. Nor did she take time to scan the telephone directory for *Jones*.

She was in a very good mood. She had slept the sleep of the dead, and so had the child. More than nine hours! He'd wakened only just once, needing to be taken out into the hall to the toilet.

Shivering with cold. Sleep-dazed. She'd led him by the hand and helped him open his pajamas, afterward guiding his hand to flush the toilet. Kissing him tenderly on the nape of the neck where there was a pear-sized ugly bruise. "Such a big boy! Such a good boy."

In hotels like this brownstone walk-up above a shuttered restaurant, as at the glamorous Port Oriskany Statler, it happened that individuals sometimes checked in with or without luggage, safety-locked their doors and pulled their blinds and in some way—clumsy, inspired, calculated, desperate—managed to kill themselves, usually by climbing into the bathtub clothed or naked and slashing their wrists with a razor blade. At the General Washington Hotel such incidents had been spoken of in whispers, though Rebecca had never been a witness to any bloody scene nor had she been asked to help clean up afterward.

Suicide in hotel rooms was not uncommon, but murder was very rare. Rebecca had never heard of anyone killing a child in any hotel.

Why do they do it, why check into a hotel, Rebecca had asked someone, possibly Hrube himself at a time when they must've been on reasonably good terms, and Hrube had shrugged saying, "To fuck the rest of us up, why else d'you think?" Rebecca had laughed, this was so inspired a reply.

Couldn't remember why she was thinking of him now: Hrube? Hadn't thought of that flat-faced bastard in years.

Back in the room she'd safety-locked the door, pulled the frayed blind farther down, hoisted the groggy child back into bed and climbed in beside him hugging him.

Sleep of the dead! Nothing sweeter.

In the morning using the tiny sink in the cubbyhole-toilet she managed to wash the child, including his hair. He resisted, but not vehemently. Thank God there was soap! She washed his fair fine thin hair and combed out of it the last remaining small snarls of dried blood.

Her own hair was too thick, too long and matted and snarled with dried blood to be shampooed in any sink. She hated it, suddenly. Heavy greasy rank-smelling dragging at her soul. Like her brother Herschel she was, you'd think was an Iroquois Indian.

She left the child at the automat instructing him not to move an inch, to wait for her. Hungrily he was eating a second bowl of hot oatmeal lavishly topped with milk and crystalline brown sugar of a kind he'd never before tasted. Rebecca went to have her hair shampooed and cut in Glamore Beauty Salon around the corner from the automat. She'd noticed the beauty salon on their walk the previous night, she'd studied the prices listed in the window.

How sick she was of Rebecca Schwart's hair! Her former husband had loved her hair long, heavy, sexy twining in his fingers, burying his face in her hair as he made love to her, moaning and pumping his life into her, between the legs he'd greedily kissed and nuzzled her, the coarse wiry pelt of hair she could hardly bear to touch, herself. But that time was past. The time of her love-delusion was past. She'd come to hate her thick shapeless hair that was always snarled beneath, couldn't force a comb through it, oily if it wasn't shampooed every other day and of course it was not shampooed every other day, not any longer. And now the hopeless bits of dried blood snarled in it. She would have it cut off, all but a few inches covering her ears.

In the Glamore Salon she paged through *Hair Styles* until she found what she was looking for: Hazel Jones's breezy short cut, with bangs scissor-cut just above the eyebrows.

There he sat in the automat, where she'd left him. Very still as if his thoughts had collapsed in upon themselves. His expression was intense, absorbed. He was gripping himself oddly, arms folded across his chest in a tight embrace. She thought *He is playing piano, his fingers are making music for him.*

He trusted her utterly. He had no doubt that she would return to him. Seeing her now he glanced upward, blinking.

"Mommy you're *pret-ty*. Mommy you look *nice*."

It was so. She was pretty, she looked nice. When her bruises and swellings faded, she would look more than nice.

The new feathery haircut drew eyes to her. Something in her walk, her manner. Purchasing two adult tickets at the Greyhound Bus counter, impulsively choosing a destination ("Jamestown" somewhere to the south of Port Oriskany) because the bus was leaving in twenty minutes and she was wary of lingering in this busy public place where she and the child might be observed. (Zack was wearing a cloth cap on his head. He was sitting where she'd positioned him, on the farther side of the crowded waiting room, his back to the room and to her. They would be seen together only outside at the curb as the bus loaded, and then briefly. And on the bus they would sit together as if by chance, at the very rear.) Rebecca was smiling at the ticket seller, rousing the man from his late-morning torpor. "A beautiful day, so *sunny*." The ticket seller, male, youngish, rounded shoulders and morose eyes brightening in turn, seeing a pretty-breezy American girl with shiny dark bangs across her forehead, feathery strands of shiny dark hair lifting about her ears, smiled at her blinking and staring, "Yeah! Man it sure is."

The remainder of her life. Maybe it would be easy.

The Greyhound to Jamestown was loading. She signaled the child to follow her. Made him a gift of two discarded comic books she'd found in the waiting room. Kissing and cuddling in their seat on the bus. "They didn't find us, sweetie! We're safe." It was a game, only Mommy knew the rules and the logic behind the rules. By the time the bus was lumbering into the hilly countryside south of Port Oriskany the child had become absorbed in one of the comic books.

Cartoon animals! Walking upright, talking and even thinking (in balloons floating over their heads) in the way of human beings. They did not seem to the child any more bizarre or even illogical than the actions of those human beings he'd witnessed.

Waking later, alone in his seat. Mommy was in the back playing gin rummy with a couple sitting in the rear seat that ran the width of the bus.

The Fisks, they were. Ed and Bonnie. Ed was a flush-cheeked fattish bald man with sideburns and a genial laugh, Bonnie was big-busted, glamorously made up with flashing fingernails. Across Ed's spread knees was a cardboard suitcase upon which Ed was dealing cards for himself and the women seated on either side of him.

It wasn't like Mommy to behave like this. On the bus trip from Rome she'd kept to herself not meeting anyone's eye.

" 'Gypsy-gin-rummy.' It's a variation of the other but there are more options. With gypsy, you have 'wild cards' and 'free draw' if you earn it. I can show you, if you're interested."

The Fisks were interested. Bonnie said she'd heard of gypsy-gin-rummy but had never played.

Zack watched the game for a while. He liked it that his mother was smiling, laughing in the new way. He liked her pretty new haircut. From time to time she glanced up at him leaning over the back of his seat, and winked. He drifted off to sleep hearing the slap-slap-slap of cards, exclamations and laughter from the players. He took comfort from the immediate fact *They didn't find us, we're safe*. It was all he wished to know at this time.

Later, at another time, there would be other facts to know. He would wait.

Already Port Oriskany, that had been so exciting to arrive in, was receding into the past. The brownstone hotel with the creaky double bed. The automat! The surprise of Mommy returning to him, her hair so short and shiny, bangs across her forehead to hide the bruises and worry lines. The child was beginning to know the satisfaction of departure. You arrive in a city in order that you might leave that city at a later time. There is a thrill in arrival but there is a greater thrill in departure.

It was Mommy's turn to deal. She laughed and joked with her new friends she would never see again after the bus deposited them at a farm just outside Jamestown. It was intoxicating to think that the world was crammed with individuals like the Fisks, good-natured, quick to laugh, ready for a good time. She said, "The world is a card game, see? You can lose but you can win, too." She was Hazel Jones laughing in the new way, shuffling and dealing cards.

4

❀ ❀ ❀

In Horseheads, New York, in late winter/early spring 1962 befriended Willie James Judd, state-licensed notary public and head clerk, Department of Records, Chemung County Courthouse. At that time waitressing at the Blue Moon Café on Depot Street, Horseheads. A young widow, just her and the little boy. A popular presence at the Blue Moon where most of the customers were men but the men quickly learned to respect the young widow. *See, Hazel is like your own sister. You don't come on to your own damn sister do you?*

Willie James Judd was near to retirement from his longtime county employment. Ate most of his meals at the Blue Moon where he became acquainted with the new waitress Hazel Jones who was also known to him through his younger sister Ethel Sweet who'd married the owner of the ramshackle Horseheads Inn where the young widow and her child rented a room by the week. Ethel Sweet liked publicly to marvel how uncomplaining Hazel Jones was. Not like other boarders. Quiet, kept to herself. Never any visitors. Never wasted towels, linens, hot water, soap. Never went out without switching off all the lights in her room. Nor did she allow the child to run on the stairs, to play noisily even outdoors behind the Inn. Nor did she allow the child to sneak downstairs and watch TV in the parlor with other boarders.

Almost, Ethel said approvingly, you would not know a child was *there*.

And Hazel's life had not been easy: gradually it was revealed to Ethel Sweet how the young widow had lost both her parents as a child, her father in a house fire when she was four years old, her mother to cancer-of-the-breast when she was nine. Taken in then by relatives up in Port Oriskany who were begrudging to her, never found room for her in their hearts made her quit school at age sixteen to work as a chambermaid till at last at age eighteen she ran away with a man twice her age, married him and realized her mistake afterward learning he'd been married twice before, had children he was not supporting, he was a heavy drinker, beat her and their child and threatened to kill them both so at last unable to bear it she'd run away one night taking the terrified child with her this had been three years now and she had not stopped running out of fear of the man finding her.

No they had not been divorced. He would never give her a divorce. He would wish to see her dead first. And their son, too.

Ethel Sweet reported how, telling this, Hazel began to tremble. It was so real to her!

But now, in Horseheads, she wished to remain. In Horseheads she'd made friends, she was happy. She was content. She wished to enroll Zacharias in the elementary school next fall. He would be almost six years old in September.

Saying to Ethel maybe she'd noticed, Zacharias is not like other boys? Doesn't play with other children, he's shy and fearful of being hurt, his father had beat him so often, only just needed to raise his fist and the child would become terrified so she had to shelter him from the roughness of men and boys, boys' games and loud shouting, also Zacharias had a musical gift, he would be a *concert pianist* someday and so he must not injure his hands.

Ethel Sweet was so touched! That Hazel who had a reputation in Horseheads for keeping to herself and avoiding personal remarks and questions at the Blue Moon by simply smiling and saying not a word should suddenly open her heart to Ethel, whose own daughters were grown and gone and didn't give a damn for their mother they'd always taken for granted.

Except Ethel saw that the young woman was nervous and worried-like. Asked what was wrong and Hazel says she don't have the right papers to enroll Zacharias in school.

Like what kind of papers, Ethel asked. Birth certificate?

Hazel said yes. Birth certificate for her son but also one for her, too.

What had happened was: Hazel's birth certificate had burned in the house fire when she was four years old. There was no record of her birth anywhere! The fire had been in some town upstate, Hazel did not even know for certain, for her mother had taken her away to live elsewhere in one town after another in the Chautauqua Valley. And her mother had died when Hazel was nine. And her relatives she lived with had no care for her. She had been told she'd been born on a boat from Europe, in New York harbor, her parents had been immigrants from Poland or maybe Hungary but she had not been told which boat, she wasn't sure when it had crossed, she had seen no record of her birth. It was like they wished to erase me soon as I was born, Hazel told Ethel. But not complaining-like, only just stating a fact.

And Zacharias's birth certificate was in the possession of his father unless it too had been lost or willfully destroyed.

Hearing this Ethel said hotly it was ridiculous, a person is alive in front of you she or him was certainly *born*. Why you'd need a document to prove this fact made no God-damn sense.

Saying hotly, What it is is just damn-fool lawyers. The law. Willie over at the Courthouse thirty-eight years could tell you tales to make you laugh like hell, or throw up you'd be so disgusted. And that goes for the judges, too.

Saying yet more hotly, What it is, Hazel, is *men*. Shooting off their mouths, and charging for it like you wouldn't believe—seventy-five dollars an hour some of 'em charge! If it was up to women, you would not need legal documents for any damn thing from buying or selling a henhouse to making out your own will.

Hazel thanked her for being so understanding. Hazel said she had gone a long time not confiding in another person. It was a thorn in her heart, she had no proof that either Zacharias or her had ever been born. It wasn't like the old days now, you needed legal documents to make your way. There was no avoiding it. At the Blue Moon she was paid off the books and of course tips are off the books but if she kept on this way she would be retired someday and an old woman with no Social Security payments, not a penny.

Ethel said without thinking, "Oh honey you got to get *married*. That's what you got to do, get *married*."

And Hazel said biting her lower lip, looking like she wanted to cry and Ethel could've bit her own tongue speaking as she'd done, "I can't. I am already married, I can never be married again."

Right away then Ethel called her brother Willie. She knew Willie had a generous heart. In Horseheads he had a reputation for being a prickly old bastard liked to boss folks around but that was only toward individuals who rubbed him the wrong way. He was a decent man. Felt sorry for the girl Hazel Jones. And the little boy quiet like a deaf-mute. At the County Hall of Records Willie Judd was the man to see for any kind of document you required. Had access to any kind of document you could name. Birth certificate, wedding certificate, death certificate. Two hundred years of yellowing old wills in faded ink, real estate documents dating back to the 1700s, deeds executed with the Six Nations of the Iroquois. Legal forms of any damn kind you wished. And Willie was a notary public owning his own New York State notary seal.

In this way in spring 1962 Willie Judd took pity on Hazel Jones. Willie was not a man given to ease with others and very rarely to pity, sympathy. It would have to be secret. Invited the young woman to his office in the basement of the courthouse just at 5 P.M. closing time of a weekday to explain her situation to him which she did, carefully writing down for Willie certain facts. As she wrote these, she paused to wipe at her eyes. Her birth name was "Hazel Jones" but her married name of course was a different last name she did not care to say; Zacharias's last name was not "Jones" of course but the name of her husband she was in terror would find the boy, if his legal name was revealed. That was why, Hazel said, they had always to keep going, to live in different places where they would not be known. But now in Horseheads they hoped for a permanent residence.

Willie brushed aside these details as he'd brush aside a swarm of gnats. Head clerk at the Hall of Records for thirty-eight years plus he was a notary public. Had the power of any damn judge in the U.S. almost. Could draw up any document he damn well wished and to anybody's eye it would be legal.

So! A few swigs of good malt whiskey and Willie Judd was God-damn *inspired*.

Drew up surrogate birth certificates for Hazel Jones and her son. Willie's imagination in full gear. There was a form, Chemung County Courthouse letterhead, allowed for such documents to replicate documents that had existed but had been lost or destroyed. Only in recent decades did you need "certificate of birth" anyway. Old-timers, nobody gave a damn. Like adoption. You'd take in a kid, any-age kid, he was yours, no formal adoption papers, none of that bullshit. Now it would be a matter of public record, she'd have the documents to prove it: *Hazel Esther Jones born May 11, 1936 New York harbor, New York parentage unknown*.

For Zacharias, he'd had to type in a name for the father. Could not see a way around it. Any suggestions? he asked Hazel and she said all smiling and without thinking—Willie? I mean, William.

William—what?

We could say Judd.

Christ he was pleased by this. Flattered to hell.

But that might make for complications, Willie observed. Maybe it would be wiser to reverse these. Hazel Judd, William Jones. And so, Hazel Jones when married.

Hazel laughed, a wild stricken cry. Her son's birth certificate would read *Zacharias August Jones born November 29, 1956 Port Oriskany New York mother Hazel Jones father William Jones*.

Now her own name—*her* name—would be, not Hazel Jones, but Hazel Judd. Yet only on this stiff sheet of paper with the Chemung County Courthouse letterhead.

Thanking the old man, Hazel burst into tears. No one had been so kind to her in a long long time.

(Nobody was to know. Not Ethel, even. The woman had a mouth on her, she'd blab. She'd be proud of her brother interceding like he'd done on behalf of Hazel Jones, she'd blab and get them into trouble. This way, Hazel has the documents, nobody will challenge them, why'd anybody challenge them?

Each year he lived, Willie Judd came to see there was no clear logic to why things happened as they did. Could've just as easy happened some other way.

You typed out a form. You typed out another form. You signed your name. Administered the seal of the State of New York, Notary Public. That's it.)

At the Blue Moon Café next evening Willie Judd came in earlier than usual for supper and stayed later. Ordered the chicken pot pie which was a Blue Moon special. Sat in Hazel Jones's row of booths as always elbows on the table gazing smiling at the waitress with his tea-colored eyes. It was raining outside like hell, Willie'd worn his black oilcloth slicker people kidded him made him look like a sea lion. This enormous shiny garment he'd hung at the coatrack dripping wet onto the floor. He would ask Hazel Jones to marry him. He had not married, the only one in the family who had not and why exactly he'd never known. Shy, maybe. Beneath his Willie mask. He'd been damn proud of himself rising to head clerk. Only one of the family till then to graduate from high school. So it was a curse, maybe! Willie was the special son, hadn't found a girl to marry him like the others had done with lower expectations. Time's a whirlpool, Christ he was sixty-four. Would retire next birthday. Pensioned off by the county, that was a good thing but melancholy, too. Enough to sober you. He had seen in Hazel's eyes a certain warmth. A certain promise. *She'd made him the father of her son.* Hazel was always so sweet and transparent smiling at everybody like who's it Doris Day but there was a touch-me-not air about the girl, everybody remarked upon. A man had to respect. Bringing Willie a draft ale foaming to the top of the heavy stein and over. Bringing Willie one of the least fly-specked menus with BLUE MOON SPECIALS stapled to the front like Willie who'd been coming to the Blue Moon half his lifetime needed to be reminded what to order. And bringing Willie extra butter to smear on his Parker House rolls, and the rolls piping-hot.

Somehow it happened. Willie must've had too much ale. Not like Willie who'd used to be a drunk but had reformed, to a degree. Could not burn off the alcohol like he'd done. Your liver starts to weaken. Once you turn fifty. Telling Hazel when she brought him his chocolate cream custard pie and coffee about the old days in Horseheads, when him and Ethel had been kids. And Hazel nodding and smiling politely though she had other customers to serve, and tables to clear. And Willie hears this loud old-man's voice asking, "D'you know why Horseheads is named like it is, Hazel?" and the young woman smiles saying no she guesses she don't, Willie is all but touching her elbow to keep her from running off saying, "There was actual horseheads here! I mean actual horse-heads. A long time ago, see. We're talking like—1780s. Before the settlers came. Some of 'em were Judds, see. My people. Me and Ethel's people. Great-great-great-great somethin', if you figured it. A long time ago. There was this General Sullivan fighting the Iroquois. Had to come up from Pennsylvania. There was three hundred horses for the soldiers and to carry things. They fought the damn Indians, and had to retreat. And the horses collapsed. There was three hundred of 'em. It was said the soldiers had to shoot 'em. But didn't bury 'em. You can see you wouldn't, huh? You would not bury three hundred horses if you were near to collapsing yourself, huh? Fighting the Iroquois that'd as soon tear out your liver and guzzle it as look at you. They did that to their own kind, other Indians. Tried to wipe 'em out. The Iroquois was the worst, like the Comanches out west. Sayin' then it was the white man brought evil to this continent, bullshit! The evil was in this continent in this actual soil when the white man showed up. My people came from somewhere in north England. Landed in New York right where you was born, Hazel, ain't that a coincidence? 'New York harbor.' There ain't many folks born in 'New York harbor.' I b'lieve in coincidences. The settlers pushed all the way out here. Damn if I know why. Must've been a wilderness then it ain't exactly Fifth Avenue, New York, now, huh? Anyway, the settlers come out here, a year or so later, first damn thing they see is these horse skeletons all over. Along the riverbank and in the fields. Three hundred horse skulls and skeletons. They couldn't figure what the hell it was, there was not much knowledge of history in those days. You'd hear things by rumor I suppose. You could not turn on the radio, TV. Three hundred horse skulls all bleached in the sun so they called it 'Horseheads.' " Willie was panting by this time. Willie had reached out to grasp the waitress's elbow by this time. In the Blue Moon everybody had ceased talking and even the jukebox had gone abruptly silent where Rosemary Clooney had been singing just a minute ago. Could hear a pin drop it would be reported. Ethel Sweet would be stricken to the heart next day. Hearing how her big brother Willie had gotten drunk and lovesick over Hazel he'd done a favor for and would have reason to think she would do some favor for him not wishing to consider would a woman that young and pretty wish to marry a man his age, and girth.

So Willie starts to stammer. Flush-faced, knowing he's made a spectacle of himself. But not knowing how to back out of it saying, guffawing, "Anyway, Hazel. That's how 'Horseheads' came to be. What you got to wonder, is why'd they stay here? Why the hell'd anybody stay here? Poke through the grass there's not one or two or a dozen horse heads there's *three hundred*. And you decide to stay, settle down and stake out a claim, build a house, plow the land and have your kids and the rest is history. That's the twenty-four-dollar question, Hazel, God damn ain't it?"

Hazel was startled by Willie's vehemence. Loud-laughing and red in the face as she'd never seen him. Murmuring some muffled words not overheard by anyone except Willie, the waitress slipped away from his grasp and hurried through the swinging doors into the kitchen.

Willie'd seen the repugnance in her face. All that talk of horse skeletons, skulls, "Horseheads"—he'd ruined any beauty the moment might have had.

Next morning, Hazel Jones and the child were gone forever from Horseheads.

It was an early, 7:20 A.M. Greyhound bus they'd caught out on route 13 with all their suitcases, cardboard boxes, and shopping bags. The Greyhound was southbound from Syracuse and Ithaca to Elmira, Binghamton and beyond. Hazel would leave their room spic-and-span Ethel Sweet would report. Her bed and the child's cot stripped of all linens including the mattress covers and these neatly folded for the wash. The bathroom Hazel and the child had shared with two other boarders, Hazel left equally clean, the bathtub scrubbed after she'd used it very early that morning, her towels folded for the wash. The single closet in the room was empty, all the wire hangers remaining. Every drawer of the bureau was empty. Not a pin, not a button remained. The wicker wastebasket in the room had been emptied into one of the trash cans at the rear of the Inn. On the bureau top was an envelope addressed to MRS. ETHEL SWEET. Inside were several bills constituting full payment for the room through the entire month of April (though it was only April 17) and a brief note, heartbreaking to Ethel Sweet who was losing not just her most reliable boarder but a kind of daughter as she was coming to think of Hazel Jones. The neatly handwritten note would be shown to numerous individuals, read and reread and pondered in Horseheads for a long time.

Dear Ethel—

Zacharias and I are called away suddenly, we are sorry to leave such a ~~warm~~ good place. I hope this will suffise for April rent.

Maybe we will all meet again sometime, my thanks to you and to Willie from the bottom of my heart.

Your friend "Hazel"

5

❀ ❀ ❀

It was an old river city on the St. Lawrence at the northeast edge of Lake Ontario. It looked to be about the size of the city of his earliest memory on the barge canal. On the far side of the river which was the widest river he'd ever seen was a foreign country: Canada. To the east were the Adirondack Mountains. *Canada*, *Adirondack* were new words to him, exotic and musical.

Observers would have assumed she'd traveled south with the child. Instead she'd changed buses at Binghamton, traveled impulsively north to Syracuse, and to Watertown, and now beyond to the northernmost boundary of the state.

"To throw them off. Just in case."

That shrewdness that had become instinctive in her. In no immediate or discernible relationship with available logic or even probability. It was *keeping-going*, the child knew. He'd become addicted to *keeping-going*, too.

"Come on come *on*! God damn it *hurry*."

Gripping his hand. Pulling him along. If he'd run ahead on the cracked and potholed pavement impatient after the long bus ride she'd have scolded him for she always worried he might fall, hurt himself. He felt the injustice of her whims.

She walked swiftly, her long legs like scythes. At such times she seemed to know exactly where she was going, to what purpose. There was a two-hour layover at the Greyhound station. In several lockers she'd stored their bulky possessions. The keys were safe in her pocket wrapped in tissue. She'd zipped up his jacket in haste. She'd tied a scarf around her head. They'd left the Greyhound station by a rear exit opening onto a back street.

He was out of breath. Damn he couldn't keep up with her!

He'd forgotten the name of this place. Maybe she hadn't told him. He'd lost the map on the bus. Much-folded, much-wrinkled map of New York state.

Keeping-going was the map. Staying in one place for so long as they'd done back there (already he was forgetting the name Horseheads, in another few days he would have forgotten it entirely) was the aberration.

"See, there's been a sign. There might be more."

He had no idea what she meant. The excited glitter of her eyes, the set of her jaws. She walked so quickly and so without hesitation people glanced at her in passing, curious.

Mostly men. There were mostly men here, at the river's edge.

He was thinking again he'd never seen such a wide river. She'd told him there were a thousand islands in that river. He shielded his eyes against splotches of sunshine like fiery explosions on the choppy water.

Drowsing on the bus his head knocking against the smeared window and he'd seen through half-shut eyes long featureless stretches of countryside. At last farmland, human habitations. A cluster of mobile homes, tar paper shanties, auto graveyard, railway crossing and granary, Jefferson Co. Farm Bureau, banners wind-whipping at a Sunoco gas station, a railway crossing. Wherever they were traveling was less green than wherever they'd been hundreds of miles to the south.

Backward in time? There was a wintry glare to the sun here.

The countryside ended abruptly. The road descended between three-storey brick buildings steep-gabled and gaunt looking like elderly men. There was a jarring ascension to a hump-backed old iron bridge above a railroad yard. Quickly he told himself *We are safe, it won't fall in.* He knew this was so because his mother showed no alarm, not the slightest interest or even much awareness of the old nightmare bridge across which the massive Greyhound was moving at less than ten miles an hour.

"See! Over there."

She was leaning eagerly across him to look out the window. Always when they entered any town, any city, whether they were going to disembark or remain on the bus, his mother became alert, excited. In such close quarters she gave off a damp sweetish odor comforting to him as the odor of his own body in slept-in clothes, underwear. And there was the harsher smell of her hair in those days just after she'd had to dye it, not wanting Hazel Jones's hair to be black but dark brown with "russet-red highlights."

She was pointing at something outside the window. Below was a vast lot of freight cars BALTIMORE & OHIO, BUFFALO, CHAUTAUQUA & NEW YORK CENTRAL, ERIE & ORISKANY, SANTA FE. Words he'd long ago learned to recognize having seen so often though he could not have said what they meant. Exotic and musical such names seemed to him, the province of adult logic.

His mother was saying, "Almost I'd think we have been here before except I know we have not."

She didn't seem to mean the freight cars. She was pointing at a billboard erected above a giant oil drum. SEALTEST ICE CREAM. A curly-haired little girl lifted a spoon heaped with chocolate ice cream to her smiling mouth. A flash came to him Ike's FOOD STORE glimmering like a surfacing fish for the briefest of moments before sinking away again into oblivion.

She was saying people had been good to them. All through her life when she'd needed them, people had been good to her. She was grateful. She would not forget. She wished that she could believe in God, she would pray to God to reward these people.

"Not in heaven but here on earth. That's where we need it."

He had no idea what she meant but he liked it that she was happy. Entering a town or a city she was always edgy but the little curly-haired girl in the Sealtest billboard had made her smile.

"We're actual people now, Zack. We can prove who we are like everybody else."

She meant the birth certificates. On the long journey from Binghamton she'd shown him these official-looking documents several times as if unable to believe that they existed.

Zacharias August Jones born 1956. Hazel Esther Judd born 1936. He liked it that both birthdates ended in *6*. He had not known that his middle name was *August,* that seemed strange to him, the name of a month like June, July. He had not known that his mother's last name was *Judd* and wondered if this was so. And his father—*William Jones?*

Drawing his thumb slowly over the stamp of the State of New York that was slightly raised, whorled like a thumbprint the size of a silver dollar.

"That's who we are?" He sounded so doubtful, Mommy had to laugh at him.

She'd begun to complain he was getting so damned independent-minded, and not yet six years old! And not yet in first grade! Her little billy goat he was. Sprouting horns she'd have to saw off, that was what you did with billy goat horns growing out of a naughty boy's forehead.

Where was that, he'd asked. And Mommy had poked his forehead with two blunt fingers.

Though she'd relented, seeing his face. She'd relented and kissed him for Hazel Jones never scolded her child or scared him without a ticklish wet kiss or two to make everything well again.

"Yes. That's who we are."

By the time they filed off the bus, she had replaced the birth certificates carefully inside the zippered compartment of her suitcase, between pieces of stiff cardboard to keep them from tearing.

On the wharf was a weatherworn sign creaking in the wind.

Malin Head Bay

He supposed that was the name of this town. He shaped the words silently MALIN HEAD BAY noting the rhythmic stresses.

"What is a 'bay,' Mommy?"

She was distracted, not listening. He would look up *bay* in the dictionary, later.

She was walking more slowly now. She'd released his hand. She seemed to be sniffing the air, alert and apprehensive. On the massive river were fishing boats, barges. The water was very choppy. The barges were much larger than he'd ever seen on the canal. In the water fiery sun-splotches came and went like detonations. In the wind it was chilly but if you stood sheltered in the sun it was warm.

In front of a tavern men stood drinking. There were men fishing from a pier. There were run-down hotels ROOMS DAY WEEK MONTH and on the crumbling steps of these hotels sickly-looking men sprawled in the sun. He saw his mother hesitate, staring at a man on crutches fumbling to light a cigarette. He saw her staring at several men of whom one was shirtless, basking in sunshine drinking from brown bottles. They walked on. She reached for his hand again, but he eluded her. He kept pace with her, however. Wanting to return to the bus station but knowing that they would not, could not until she wished it. For her will was all: vast as a net encompassing the very sky.

Ma lin Head Bay. His fingers played the keys, the chords.

All that he could make music of was a consolation to him. And there was nothing however ugly he could not make music of.

His mother stopped suddenly. He nearly collided with her. He saw that she was staring at a grotesquely obese old man who sat sprawled in the sunshine, only a few feet away. He'd lowered his bulk onto an overturned wooden crate. His skin was white as flour, strangely whorled and striated, like reptile skin. His shirt was missing several buttons, you could see the scaly folds and creases of his flesh, warm-looking in the sun. In his fatty face his eyes were deep set and appeared to be without focus and when Hazel Jones passed before the man at a distance of no more than ten feet he gave no sign of seeing her only just lifted his bottle to his sucking hole of a mouth, and drank.

"He's blind. He can't see us."

The child understood this to mean *He can't hurt us.*

Which was how Zack knew they would stay in Malin Head Bay, for a while at least.

6

❀ ❀ ❀

"You don't look like you're from around here."

A slight emphasis on *you*. And he was smiling.

She didn't seem to have heard, exactly. Poised yet childlike in her manner. The slightest flicker of attention directed upward at him as her red-lacquered nails took his ticket from him yet there came her blinding flash of a smile: "Sir, thank you!" As if he'd won a prize. As if for the late-afternoon half-price $2.50 he'd been granted entrance to a holy shrine and not the mildewy-smelling interior of the Bay Palace Theater where a rerun of *West Side Story* was showing.

Deftly she tore the green ticket in two and handed him back the stub already looking past his shoulder with that luminous smile at whoever was pushing close behind him: "Sir, thank *you*!"

New usherette at the Bay Palace Theater. Dove-gray trousers with flared legs, snug-fitting little bolero jacket with crimson piping. And, on the just-perceptibly padded shoulders, gold braid epaulettes. Prominent shiny bangs across her forehead, skimming her eyebrows. Dark brown, dark-red-brown hair. And the long-handled flashlight she took up with girlish zest, leading older patrons, or moms with young children, into the shadowy interior of the movie house where on the frayed carpet you might unknowingly kick a discarded box of popcorn or a part-eaten candy bar tangled in its wrapper: "*This* way, please!"

She might have been any age between nineteen and twenty-nine. He wasn't a keen judge of ages as he wasn't a keen judge of character: wishing to see the best in others as a way of wishing that others might see only the best, the crispy rind of surface charm and American decency, in him.

He couldn't recall having taken notice of any usher/usherette at the local movie house before. It was rare for anyone to make an impression upon him. Nor was he a frequent patron of movies, in fact. American pop culture bored him to hell. The only twentieth-century music that engaged him was jazz. His was a jazz sensibility meaning *at the margins*. In a white man's skin by accident of birth.

Here in Malin Head Bay at the northern edge of New York State in the off-season everyone was local. Few summer residents lingered beyond Labor Day. The usherette had to be local, but new to the area. Gallagher was himself a new local: one of those summer residents who'd lingered.

His family had had a summer place on Grindstone Island, a "camp" as such places were called, for decades. Grindstone Island was one of the larger of the Thousand Islands, a few miles west of Malin Head Bay in the St. Lawrence River. Gallagher had been coming to the island in the summer, for much of his life; since his divorce in 1959 he'd taken to spending more and more of the year in Malin Head Bay, alone. He'd bought a small house by the river. He played jazz piano at the Malin Head Inn two or three nights a week. He still owned property near Albany, in the suburban village of Ardmoor Park, where the Gallaghers lived; he remained a co-owner of the house in which his former wife lived, with her new husband and family. He did not think of himself *in exile* nor as *estranged from the Gallaghers* for that made his situation appear more romantic, more isolated and significant than it was.

What ever became of Chet Gallagher?
Moved away from Albany. Living up by the St. Lawrence.
Divorced? Estranged from the family?
Something like that.

He'd been seeing the new usherette in Malin Head Bay, he realized. Not gone looking for her but, yes he'd seen her. Maybe at the Lucky 13 over the summer. Maybe at the Malin Head Inn. Maybe on Main Street, Beach

Street. In the IGA pushing a wobbly wire cart in the early evening when there were few customers for most residents of Malin Head Bay ate supper at 6 P.M. if not earlier. He seemed to recall that the girl had had a young child with her.

Hoped not.

They ever have children, Chet and his wife?

She does, now. But not his.

The usherette had smiled at him as if her life depended upon it but had tactfully ignored his inane remark. He was thinking now he might have alarmed her. He was thinking now he'd made her uneasy and he'd meant only to be friendly as an ordinary guy in Malin Head Bay might be friendly, maybe he should go back and apologize, yes but he wasn't going to, he knew better. *Leave this one alone* was the wisest strategy as he groped for a seat in the darkened near-deserted smokers' loge at the rear of the theater.

And a second time, a few weeks later at the Bay Palace Theater he saw her, he'd forgotten her in the interim and seeing her again felt a stab of excitement, recognition. A man might make the mistake in such a situation thinking the woman will know him, too.

This evening the usherette was selling tickets. In her pert little military-style costume, in the ticket booth in the brightly lighted lobby. He was struck as before by the young woman's manner: her ardent smile. She was one whose face is transformed by smiling as by a sudden implosion of light.

Her hair was different: pulled back into a ponytail swinging between her shoulder blades, partway down her back. You could see that she liked feeling it there, took a childlike sensuous pleasure in shaking, shifting her head.

The mood came over Gallagher at once. Weak-jointed, swallowing hard as if he'd been drinking whiskey and was dehydrated. *You ain't been blue. No no no.*

Yet, oddly he'd forgotten this young woman until now. Since the evening of *West Side Story* weeks ago. Now it was October, a new season. Though Gallagher was emotionally estranged from his father Thaddeus and had not been close to the family for much of his adult life, yet he was involved in some of the Gallagher Media Group properties: radio-TV stations in Malin Head Bay, Alexandria Bay, Watertown. He remained a consultant and sometime-columnist for the *Watertown Standard* and its half-dozen rural affiliates in the Adirondack region: the only liberal Democrat associated with Gallagher Media, tolerated as a renegade. And he had his jazz gigs which paid little except in pleasure and were coming to be the center of his unraveled life.

When he wasn't actively drinking he had AA meetings in Watertown, forty miles south of Malin Head Bay. There, Chet Gallagher was something of a spiritual leader.

Which is why, Gallagher thought, waiting in the brief line to buy his ticket for *The Miracle Worker*, a man yearns to meet an attractive young woman who doesn't know him. A woman is hope, a woman's smile is hope. No more can you live without hope than you can live without oxygen.

"Hello! That's two-fifty, sir."

Gallagher pushed a crisp new five-dollar bill beneath the wicket. He'd vowed he would not make a fool of himself this time, yet heard his voice innocently inquire, "Do you recommend this movie? It's supposed to be"—pausing not knowing what to say, not wanting to offend the dazzling smile—"pretty arduous."

Regretting *arduous*. Really he'd meant *tough going*.

The smiling young woman took Gallagher's money, deftly punched cash register keys with a flash of her red-lacquered nails, pushed change and green ticket toward him with a flourish. She was looking even more attractive than she'd looked back in September, her eyes were warmly dark-brown, alert. Her carefully applied red lipstick matched her nails and Gallagher saw, couldn't prevent the rapid search of his gaze, she wore no rings on any of her fingers.

"Oh no, sir! It isn't arduous it's hopeful. It kind of breaks your heart, but then it makes you"—in her breathy downstate voice, almost vehement, as if Gallagher had challenged the deepest beliefs of her soul—"rejoice, you are *alive*."

Gallagher laughed. Those intense dark-brown eyes, how could he resist. His heart, a wizened raisin, stirred with feeling.

"Thanks! I will certainly try to 'rejoice.' "

Without glancing back Gallagher walked away with his ticket. Already the young woman was smiling up into the face of the next customer, just as she'd smiled at him.

Beautiful but not very bright. Transparent (breakable?) as glass.

Her soul. Can see into. Shallow, vulnerable.

In the smokers' loge in a rear seat. Ten minutes into the movie he became restless, distracted. He very much disliked the music score: obtrusive, heavy-handed. The stalwart melodrama of *The Miracle Worker* failed to engage him, who had come to see that failure is the human condition, not victory over odds; for each Helen Keller who triumphs, there are tens of millions who fail, mute and deaf and insensate as vegetables tossed upon a vast garbage pile to rot. In such moods the shimmering film-images, mere lights projected onto a tacky screen, could not work their magic.

Yet we yearn for the miracle worker, to redeem us.

Gallagher's bladder ached. He'd had a few beers that day. He rose from his seat, went to use the men's lavatory. This tacky tawdry smelly place. In fact he knew the owner, and he knew the manager. The Bay Palace Theater had been built before the war in a long-ago era. Art deco ornamentation, a slickly Egyptian motif popular in the 1920s. His father's boyhood, adolescence. When the world had been glamorous.

Wanting to look for the ponytailed young woman. But he would not. He was too old: forty-one. She was possibly half his age. And so naive, trusting.

The way she'd lifted her beautiful eyes to his. As if no one had ever rebuffed her, hurt her.

She had to be very young. To be so naive.

He hadn't wanted to stare at her left breast where a name had been stitched in crimson thread. He wasn't that kind of man, to stare at a girl's breasts. But he could call the manager, whom he knew from the Malin Head bar, and inquire.

That new girl? Selling tickets last night?

Too young for you, Gallagher.

He wanted to protest, he felt young. In his soul he felt young. Even his face still looked boyish, despite the lines in his forehead, and his receding hair. When he smiled, his pointed devil's-teeth flashed.

In some quarters of Malin Head Bay he was known and respected as a Gallagher: a rich man's son. Deliberately he wore old clothes, took little care with his appearance. Hair straggling past his collar and often didn't shave for days. He ate in taverns and diners. He was one to leave inappropriately large tips. He had an absentminded air like one who has been drinking even when he has not been drinking only just thinking and taxing his brain. Finding his way back to his seat without drifting out into the lobby looking for the usherette. He felt a stab of shame for the way he'd spoken to her, as a pretext for provoking her into reacting; he hadn't been sincere but she had answered him sincerely, from the heart.

When *The Miracle Worker* ended in a swirl of triumphant movie-music at 10:58 P.M., and the small audience filed out, Gallagher saw that the ticket seller's booth was darkened, the young ponytailed woman in the usherette's costume was gone.

7

⚜ ⚜ ⚜

"Hide most things you know. Like you would hide any weakness. Because it is a weakness to know too much among others who know too little."

He was Zacharias Jones, six years old and enrolled in first grade at Bay Street Elementary. He lived with his mother for his father was *no longer living*.

"That's all you need to tell anyone. If they ask more, tell them to ask your mother."

He was a sly fox-faced child with dark luminous shifting eyes and a mouth that worked silently when other children spoke as if he wished to hurry their silly speech. And he had a habit, disconcerting to his teacher, of drumming his fingers—all his fingers—on a desk or tabletop as if to hurry time.

"If they ask where we're from say 'downstate.' That's all they need to know."

He didn't have to ask who *they* were, it was *they*, *them* who surrounded. By instinct, he knew Mommy was right.

They lived in two furnished rooms upstairs over Hutt Pharmacy. The outdoors stairs ascended the churchy dark-shingled building at the rear. A sharp medicinal smell lifted through the plank floorboards of the apartment, Mommy said was a good healthy smell—"No germs." There were three windows in the apartment and all three overlooked an alley bordered by the rears of garages, trash cans and scattered debris. Always a smudged look through the windowpanes which Mommy could wash only from inside. A mile and a half away was the St. Lawrence River, visible as a dull-blue glow at dusk that seemed to shimmer above the intervening rooftops. There were other tenants living above Hutt Pharmacy but no children. "Your little boy will be lonely here, no one for him to play with," the woman next door said with an insincere twist of her mouth, but Hazel Jones protested in her liquidy movie-voice, "Oh no, Mrs. Ogden! Zack is fine. Zack is never lonely, he has his music."

His music was a strange way of speaking. For never did he feel that any music was *his*.

Friday afternoons at 4:30 P.M. he had his piano lesson. Stayed at Bay Street Elementary (with his teacher's permission, in the makeshift library where by November first he'd read half the books on the shelves including those for fifth and sixth graders) until it was time then hurried over tense with anticipation to the adjoining Bay Street Junior High where, in a corner of the school auditorium backstage, Mr. Sarrantini gave piano lessons in half-hour sessions of sharply varying degrees of concentration, enthusiasm. Mr. Sarrantini was music director for all public schools in the township, also organist at Holy Redeemer Roman Catholic Church. He was a wheezing big-bellied man with a flushed face and wavering eyes, of no age a six-year-old might guess except *old*. Listening to his pupils' lessons, Mr. Sarrantini allowed his eyes to shut. Close up, he smelled of something very sweet like red wine and something very harsh and acrid like tobacco. By late afternoon of a Friday when Zacharias Jones arrived for his lesson, Mr. Sarrantini was likely to be very tired, and irascible. Sometimes when Zack began his scales Mr. Sarrantini interrupted, "Enough! No need to beat a dead horse." At other times, Mr. Sarrantini seemed displeased with Zack. He discerned in his youngest pupil a deficient "piano attitude." He'd told Hazel Jones that her son was gifted, to a degree; he could play "by ear" and would one day be able to "sight read" any piece of music. But the steps to playing piano well were arduous, and specific, "piano discipline" was crucial, Zacharias must learn his scales and study pieces in the exact order prescribed for beginning students before plunging on to more complicated compositions. When Zack played beyond his assignment in *My First Year at the Piano*, Mr. Sarrantini frowned and told him to stop. Once, Mr. Sarrantini slapped at his hands. Another time, he brought the keyboard lid halfway down over Zack's fingers as if to smash them. Zack yanked his hands away just in time.

"One thing all piano teachers despise is a so-called 'prodigy' getting ahead of himself."

Or, with a wet-wheezing laugh, "Here's little Wolfgang. Eh!"

Hazel Jones had offended Mr. Sarrantini, Zack knew, by telling him that her son was *meant to be a pianist*. He'd cringed, hearing such a flamboyant statement put to the music director of the township.

" 'Meant to be,' Mrs. *Jones*? By whom?"

Another parent, addressed with such sarcasm by Mr. Sarrantini, would have said nothing further; but there was Hazel Jones speaking in her earnest, liquidy voice, "By what we all have inside us, Mr. Sarrantini, we can't know until we bring it out."

Zack saw with his shrewd child's eye that Mr. Sarrantini was impressed by Hazel Jones. At least in Hazel Jones's presence, he would behave in a more kindly manner with his pupil.

Scales, scales! Zack tried to be patient with the tedium of "fingering." Except there was no end to scales. You learned the major keys, then came the minor keys. Didn't your fingers know what to do, if you didn't interfere? And why was *timing* so important? The formula was so prescribed Zack could hear every note before his finger depressed it. Even worse were the study pieces ("Ding Dong Bell," "Jack and Jill Go Up the Hill," "Three Blind Mice") which provoked his fingers to swerve out of control in derision and mockery. Recalling the boogie-woogie piano pieces that made you smile and laugh and want to get up and jump around they were so playful, making-fun-of other kinds of music, he'd been so captivated by long ago hearing on the radio in the old farmhouse on the Poor Farm Road he wasn't to think of for that would make Mommy unhappy, if Mommy knew.

If Mommy knew. But Mommy could not always know his thoughts.

Here in Malin Head Bay, in their apartment above Hutt Pharmacy, there was a plastic portable radio Mommy kept on the kitchen table. Restlessly turning the dial seeking "classical music" but encountering mostly loud jokey talk and news broadcasts, jingly advertisements, pop songs where the women were breathy-voiced and the men were bawling, and static.

He would play pieces by Beethoven and Mozart one day, Mommy said. He would be a real pianist, on a stage. People would listen to him, people would applaud. Even if he didn't become famous he would be respected. Music is beautiful, music is important. In Watertown, there was a "youth concert" every Easter. Maybe not next Easter—that would be too soon, she supposed—but the following Easter maybe he might play at this concert if he followed Mr. Sarrantini's instructions, if he learned his assignments and was a good boy.

He would! He would try.

For nothing mattered more than making Mommy happy.

Arriving twenty minutes early for his lesson with Mr. Sarrantini so that he could listen to the pupil who preceded him, a ninth grader whose spirited playing Mr. Sarrantini sometimes praised. She was one who executed her scales dutifully, doggedly; kept to the metronome's pitiless beat almost perfectly. A husky girl with bristly braids and damp fleshy lips whose book was the blue-covered *My Third Year at the Piano*; she sounded as if she were playing piano with more than ten fingers, and sometimes with her elbows: "Donkey Serenade," "Bugle Boy March," "Anvil Chorus."

At home Zack had no piano upon which to practice. This shameful fact Hazel Jones didn't want anyone to know.

"We can make our own keyboard. Why not!"

They made the practice-keyboard together, out of white and black construction paper. They laughed together, this was a game. Between the keys they drew lines in black ink to suggest cracks. Zack's hands were still too small to reach octaves but they prepared the keyboard to scale. "You're practicing not just for Mr. Sarrantini, but for all of your life."

Now, making supper, Hazel glanced over to watch Zack's hands moving over the paper keyboard. He was a demon, executing scales!

"Sweetie. Too bad those damn keys don't make any sound."

Without pausing in his playing Zack said, "But they do, Mommy. I can hear them."

8

❀ ❀ ❀

Now they were no longer *keeping-going* there was danger. Even in Malin Head Bay at the northern edge of the state by the Canadian border hundreds of miles from their old home in the Chautauqua Valley there was danger. Now that Zacharias Jones was enrolled in elementary school and Hazel Jones was working six days a week at the Bay Palace Theater where anyone could walk up and buy a ticket there was danger.

He, him was the danger. His name unspoken he had become strangely powerful with the passage of time.

It was like a fair, cloudless sky. Here at the edge of the lake you glanced up to see that the sky has become suddenly mottled with cloud, thunderheads blown across Lake Ontario within minutes.

His mother's games! Out of nowhere they came.

He would struggle to comprehend the nature of the game even as he was playing it. For always there were rules. Games have rules. As music has rules. Where such rules come from, he had no idea.

The Game-of-the-(Disappearing)-Pebbles.

Fifteen pebbles of varying size and shapes Hazel placed on the windowsill of the largest of the windows overlooking the alley behind Hutt Pharmacy. One by one, these disappeared. By early winter only three remained.

It was a rule of the game that Zack could note the absence of a pebble but not question who'd taken it, or why. For obviously his mother had taken it. (Why?)

In later years Zack would understand that these were childish games of necessity, not of choice.

They'd gathered the pebbles on the stony beach by the bridge to St. Mary Island. One of their favorite walking places, at the edge of the St. Lawrence River. The pebbles were prized as "precious stones"—"good luck stones." Several were strikingly beautiful, for common stones: smooth and striated with colors like a kind of marble. Zack never tired of staring at them, touching them. Other pebbles were not beautiful but dense and ugly, clenched like fists. Yet they exuded a special power. These Zack never touched but took a strange comfort in seeing on the windowsill each morning.

In no discernible order, over a period of months the pebbles began to disappear. It seemed not to matter if a pebble was beautiful or ugly, one of the larger pebbles, or smaller. There was a randomness to the game that kept Zack in a state of perpetual uneasiness.

Obviously, his mother was taking the pebbles away. Yet she would not admit to it, and Zack could not accuse her. It seemed to be an unspoken rule of the game that the pebbles disappeared during the night by a kind of magic.

It was an unspoken rule, too, that Zack could not remove any of the pebbles. He'd taken one of the beautiful pebbles away to hide under the mattress of his bed but Mommy must have found it there for it, too, vanished.

"If he doesn't find us by the time all the pebbles are gone, it's a sign he never will."

He, him. This was Daddy-must-not-be-named.

Now that Hazel Jones was an usherette at the movie theater, she had a way of speaking in mimicry of certain Hollywood actresses. As Hazel Jones she could allude to things that Zack's mother would not wish to allude to. There was Mommy who'd had another name in that time living in the big old farmhouse on the Poor Farm Road close by the canal where he'd played and there was Daddy who'd had a name not to be recalled for Mommy now would be very upset, he lived in dread of upsetting Mommy.

There is Mommy now. Mommy will be all to you now.

And so whatever Hazel Jones said in her airy insouciant way was somehow not "real" yet it could be used as a vehicle for "real" speech. As one might speak through the mouth of a mask hidden by the mask.

The other game was the fearful game. For he could never be certain that it was a game.

Sometimes on the street. Sometimes in a store. In any public place. He would sense his mother's sudden apprehension, the way she froze in mid-speech, or squeezed his hand so that it hurt, staring at someone whom he, Zack, had not yet seen. And might not see. His mother might decide no, there was no danger, or his mother might suddenly panic and push him into a doorway, pull him into a store and hurry with him to the rear exit, paying no heed to others staring at them, the white-faced young mother and her child half-running as if in fear of their lives.

Always it happened so quickly. Zack could not resist. He would not have wished to resist. There was such strength in Mommy's desperation.

Once, she'd pushed him down behind a parked car. Tried clumsily to shield him with her body.

"Niley! I love you."

His old name, baby-name. Mommy had uttered it without realizing in her panic. Later he would realize that Mommy had expected to be killed, this was her farewell to him.

Or, she'd expected him to be killed.

Only a few times did Zack actually see the man his mother saw. He was tall, broad-backed. In profile, or turned away from them entirely. His face wasn't clear. His hair was close-cropped, glinting gray. Once he was coming out of the Malin Head Inn, pausing beneath the marquee to light a cigarette. He wore a sport coat, a necktie. Another time he was just outside the IGA as Mommy and Zack were leaving with their shopping cart so that Mommy had to reverse her direction, panicked, colliding with another customer just behind them.

(The cart containing their meager groceries, they'd had to abandon in their haste to escape by a rear exit. Fortunately by this time Hazel Jones was known to the IGA manager and her groceries would be set aside for her to retrieve the next morning.)

Zack was left shaken, frightened by these encounters. For he knew that any one of them might be *he*, *him*. And that he and Mommy would be punished for whatever it was they'd done, *he* would never forgive.

Back in the apartment, Mommy would pull down all the window blinds. At dusk she would switch on only a single lamp. Zack would help her drag their heaviest chair in front of the door that was locked, and double-locked. Neither would have much appetite for supper that evening and afterward practicing piano at the make-believe keyboard, Zack would be distracted hearing behind the sharp clear notes and chords of the imagined piano a man's upraised voice incredulous and furious and not-to-be-placated by even a child's abject terror.

"It wasn't him, Zack. I don't think so. Not this time."

Hunched over the make-believe keyboard. His fingers striking the paper keys. The piano sound would drive out the other sound, if his fingers did not weaken.

In the morning, the pebbles on the windowsill.

If it was a clear day, sunshine flooded through the glass making the pebbles hot to the touch. Zack would realize the pebble-game was not a game merely. It was real as Daddy was real, though invisible.

Mommy would not allude to what had happened the day before, or had almost happened. That was a rule of the game. Hugging him and giving him a smacking wet kiss saying in her brisk Hazel Jones voice to make him smile, "Got through the night! I knew we would."

A curious variant on the Game of *He/Him* gradually evolved. This was Zack's game entirely, with Zack's rules.

By chance, Zack would sight the man, not Mommy. A man who closely enough resembled the man of whom they could not speak, yet somehow it happened that Mommy did not see him. Zack would wait, with mounting tension Zack would wait for Mommy to see this man, and to react; and if Mommy did not, or, seeing the man, took no special notice of him, Zack would feel something snap in his brain, he would lose control suddenly, pushing into his mother, nudging her.

"Zack? What's wrong?"

Zack seemed furious suddenly. Pushing her, striking with his fists.

"But—what is it? Honey—"

By this time the danger might have passed. The man, the stranger, had turned a corner, disappeared. Possibly there'd been no man: Zack had imagined him. Yet, in childish fury, Zack drew back his lip, baring his teeth. It was a facial mannerism of his father's, to see it in the child was a terrifying sight.

"You missed him! You never saw him! *I* saw him! He could walk right up to you and blam! blam! blam! shoot you in the face and blam! he'd shoot me and you couldn't stop him! I hate you."

In astonishment Hazel Jones stared at her raging son. She could not speak.

9

❀ ❀ ❀

Stunned. Struck to the heart. Somehow her son had known, his father had owned a gun.

Somehow, the son had memorized certain of the father's expressions. That look of disgust. That look of righteous fury, you dared not approach even to touch in helpless love.

❀   ❀   ❀

10

Fallin' in love with love.

Savin' all my love. For you.

It was in the early winter of 1962 that he began to see the young woman in the smoky piano bar of the Malin Head Inn. Where he was CHET GALLAGHER JAZZ PIANO advertised in a blown-up glossy photo on display in the hotel lobby.

At first half-disbelieving his eyes, it could be her. The usherette from the Bay Palace Theater.

The one whose name Gallagher had learned from his friend who managed the theater. (Though he had not made use of this information, and vowed he would not.)

She arrived early at the piano bar, about 8 P.M. Sat alone at one of the small round zinc-topped tables beside the wall. Left before the lounge became really crowded, shortly after 10 P.M. Always she was alone. Conspicuously alone. Declining offers of drinks from other, male patrons. Declining offers of company from other, male patrons. She smiled, to soften her refusal. You could see that she was resolved to listen to the jazz pianist, not to be drawn into conversation with a stranger.

Each time, she ordered two drinks. She did not smoke. She sat watching Gallagher, attentively. Her applause was quicker and more enthusiastic than the applause of most of the other patrons as if she wasn't accustomed to applauding in a public place.

"Hazel Jones."

He mouthed the name to himself. He smiled, it was so innocent and naive a name. Purely American.

The first time Gallagher saw her had been one of his brooding evenings. Picking his way through Thelonious Monk's "Round About Midnight." Minimalist, meditative. Like making your way through the dream of another person and it's easy to lose your way. Gallagher loved Monk. There was a side of him that *was Monk*. Unyielding, maybe a little cranky. Eccentric. Beautiful music Gallagher believed it, this very cool black jazz. He wanted so badly for others to hear it as he did. To care about it as he did.

That's the problem. To be supremely cool, you don't care. But Gallagher cared.

It's her. Is it her?

A woman by herself in the Piano Bar. You expect a man to join her, but no one does. This striking young woman in what appeared to be a cocktail dress of some cheaply glamorous dark red material threaded with silver. Her hair was feathery and floating at the nape of her neck. She smiled vaguely about her not seeing the frank stares of men and as the waiter approached she looked up at him, appealing. As if to ask *Is it all right, that I am here? I hope I am welcome.*

Gallagher fumbled a few notes. Finished the meandering Monk piece to scattered applause and his agile fingers leapt to something more animated, rhythmic, sexy-urgent "I Can't Give You Anything But Love, Baby." Which Gallagher hadn't played in a very long time.

Hadn't realized he'd been thinking of her. "Hazel Jones." In a way, he resented thinking of any woman. He'd have thought that he was beyond that, the tight hot sensation in his chest and groin. Since *The Miracle Worker* that summer he'd returned to the Bay Palace Theater only once; and that evening he hadn't allowed himself to seek out the pretty usherette, to inveigle her into speaking with him. No, no! Afterward he'd been proud of himself for avoiding her.

The compulsion to be happy only complicates life. Gallagher had had enough of complications.

That night, Gallagher took his break without glancing out at the young woman. He walked quickly away. When he returned, her table was occupied by someone else.

Too bad. But just as well.

Had to ask the waiter what the young woman had been drinking and was told Coke on ice. She'd left a thirty-five-cent tip, dimes and nickels.

This curious phase of Chet Gallagher's life: woke up one morning to find himself an affable small-town eccentric who played jazz piano at the Malin Head Inn, Wednesday/Thursday/Friday evenings. (Saturday was a country-and-western dance combo.) He lived in a small wood-frame house near the riverfront, sometimes drove out to the family camp on Grindstone Island for a few days in seclusion. It was off-season in the Thousand Islands, there were few tourists. Locals who lived year-round on the islands were not exactly sociable. Not long ago Gallagher might have brought a woman friend to stay with him on the island. In an earlier phase, the woman would have been his wife. But no longer.

Too damned much trouble to be shaving every morning. Too much trouble to be warmly humorous, "upbeat."

The compulsion to be upbeat only exhausts. He knew!

Gallagher's family lived on the farther side of the state, in Albany and vicinity. In their own intense world of exclusivity, family "destiny." He hadn't spoken to any of them in months and not to his father since the previous Fourth of July, at the Grindstone camp.

And so he'd become an entertainer in the sometime hire of the Malin Head Inn, whose owner was a friend of Gallagher's, a longtime acquaintance of his father Thaddeus Gallagher. The Malin Head was the largest resort hotel in the area, but in the off-season only about a fifth of its rooms were occupied even on weekends. Gallagher played piano Hoagy Carmichael style, loose-jointed frame hunched over the keyboard, long agile fingers ranging up and down the keys like making love, cigarette drooping from his lips. Didn't sing like Carmichael but frequently hummed, laughed to himself. In jazz there are many private jokes. Gallagher was an impassioned interpreter of the music of Duke Ellington, Fats Waller, Monk. In the Piano Bar, he received requests for "Begin the Beguine," "Happy Birthday to You," "Battle Hymn of the Republic," "Cry." Smiled his fleeting polite smile and continued playing the music he liked, with strains of cruder music woven in. He was versatile, playful. Good-natured. Not mocking and not malicious. A man of youthful middle age whom most other men liked, and to whom some women were powerfully attracted. And not often drunk.

Some nights, Gallagher drank only tonic water on ice, spiked with lime gratings. Tall glass beading with moisture on the piano top, ashtray beside it.

Gallagher had local admirers. Some drove up from Watertown. Not many, but a few. They came to hear CHET GALLAGHER JAZZ PIANO, they were mostly men, like himself unmarried, formerly married, separated. Men losing their hair, gone flaccid at the waist, stark-eyed, needing to laugh. Needing sympathy. Men for whom "Stormy Weather," "Mood Indigo," "St. James Infirmary," "Night Train" made perfect sense. There were a few local women who liked jazz, but only a few. (For how could you dance to "Brilliant Corners"? You could not.) The hotel guests were a mixed bag, especially during the tourist season. Sometimes there were true jazz enthusiasts. Most often, not. Customers came into the lounge to drink, smoke. Listened a while, became restless and departed for the less restrained atmosphere of the tap room where there was a jukebox. Or they stayed. They drank, and they stayed. Sometimes they talked loudly, laughed. They were not intentionally rude, they were supremely indifferent. You couldn't help but know, if you were Chet Gallagher, that they were disrespectful of the musical culture that meant so much to him, Gallagher wasn't so damned affable he didn't feel the sting of insult not to himself but to the music. *Privileged white sonsofbitches* he thought them, having eased into the dark subversive skin of jazz.

It was one of the things his father detested in him. An old story between them. Gallagher's politics, his "pinko"—"Commie"—tendencies. Soft-hearted about Negroes, voted for Kennedy not Nixon, Stevenson not Eisenhower, Truman not Dewey back in '48.

That had been the supreme insult: Truman not Dewey. Thaddeus Gallagher was an old friend of Dewey's, he'd given plenty of money to Dewey's campaign.

Lucky for Gallagher he didn't drink much any longer. When his thoughts swerved in certain directions, he could feel his temperature rise. *Privileged white sonsofbitches* he'd been surrounded by most of his life. *Fuck what do you care. You don't care. The music doesn't depend on you. A privileged white sonofabitch yourself, face it, Gallagher. What you do at the piano is not serious. Nothing you do is serious. A man without a family, not serious. Playing piano at the Malin Head isn't a real job only something you do with your time. As your life isn't a real life any longer only something you do with your time.*

"Blue Moon" he was playing. Slow, melancholy. Maudlin raised to its highest pitch. It was mid-December, a snow-flurried evening. Languid flakes blown out of the black sky above the St. Lawrence River. Gallagher never allowed himself to expect Hazel Jones to turn up in the Piano Bar as he never allowed himself to expect anyone to turn up. She'd come several times, and departed early. Always alone. He had to wonder if she worked alternate Friday evenings at the Bay Palace or maybe she'd quit altogether. He'd made inquiries and knew that ushering paid pitifully little. Maybe he could help her find better employment.

His friend who managed the Bay Palace had told him that Hazel was from somewhere downstate. She knew no one in the area. She was somewhat secretive but an excellent worker, very reliable. Always friendly, or friendly-seeming. Very good selling tickets. "Personality plus." That smile! Good with troublesome (male) patrons. You hired a good-looking girl to fill out the usherette uniform but you didn't want trouble. Unlike the other female ushers Hazel Jones didn't become upset when (male) patrons behaved aggressively with her. She spoke calmly to them, smiled and eased away to call the manager. Never raised her voice. The way a man might do, not letting on what he's feeling. *Like Hazel is older than she looks. She's been through more. Anything now is chicken shit to her.*

Gallagher glanced out into the smoky lounge, saw a young woman just coming in, heading for an empty table near the wall. *Her!*

He smiled to himself. He made no eye contact with her. He felt good! Improvising, liking how his lean fingers flashed. He eased from "Blue Moon" to "Honeysuckle Rose" playing vintage Ellington for one who he guessed knew little of jazz, still less of Ellington. Badly wanting her to hear, to know. The yearning he felt. Thinking *She came to me. To me!* In a showy run of notes to the top of the keyboard Chet Gallagher fell in love with the woman known to him as Hazel Jones.

At his break, Gallagher went directly to her table.

Looming over the surprised young woman who'd clapped with such childlike enthusiasm.

He thanked her, said he'd been noticing her. Introduced himself, as if she wouldn't have known his name. And stooped to hear the name she told him: " 'Hazel'—what? I didn't quite hear."

"Hazel Jones."

Gallagher laughed with the pleasure of a thief fitting a key into a lock.

"Mind if I join you for a few minutes, Hazel Jones?"

He could see that she was flattered he'd approached her. Other patrons had been waiting to speak with the pianist but he'd brushed past them heedless. Yet Gallagher would recall afterward to his chagrin that Hazel Jones had hesitated, staring at him. Smiling, but her eyes had gone slightly flat. Maybe she was alarmed by him, looming over her so suddenly. He was six foot three, whippet-lean and loose-jointed and his high balding dome of a head glowed warm with the effort of his stint at the piano; his eyes were shadowy, kindly but intense. Hazel Jones had no choice but to move her chair to make room for him. The zinc-topped table was small, their knees bumped beneath.

Close up, Gallagher saw that the young woman's face was carefully made up, her mouth very red. Hers was a poster-face at the Bay Palace. And she was wearing the cocktail dress made of some dark red glittery fabric that fitted her breasts and shoulders tightly. The upper sleeves were puffed, the wrists tight. In the smoky twilight of the cocktail lounge she exuded an air both sexual and apprehensive. Politely she declined Gallagher's offer to buy her something stronger than Coke: "Thank you, Mr. Gallagher. But I have to leave soon."

He laughed, hurt. Protested, "Please call me Chet, Hazel. 'Mr. Gallagher' is my sixty-seven-year-old father way off in Albany."

Their conversation was wayward, clumsy. Like climbing into a canoe with a stranger, and no oars. Exhilarating and also treacherous. Yet Gallagher heard himself laughing. And Hazel Jones laughed, so he must have been amusing.

How flattered a man is, that a woman should laugh at his jokes!

How childlike in his soul, wishing to trust a woman. Because she is attractive, and young. Because she is alone.

Gallagher had to concede, he was excited by Hazel Jones. In the Bay Palace in her ridiculous uniform, now in the Piano Bar in her glittery-red cocktail dress. Her eyebrows were less heavy than he recalled, she must have plucked and shaped them. Her hair was cut in feathery, floating layers, like a loose cap on her head. Brunette, streaked with russet-red highlights. And her skin very pale. It was like leaning toward an open flame, leaning toward Hazel Jones. The sensation Gallagher felt was tinged with dread for he was not a young man, hadn't been a young man for a long time, and these feelings were those he'd had as a young man and they were associated with hurt, disappointment.

Yet, here was Hazel Jones smiling at him. She, too, was edgy, nervous. Unlike other women of Gallagher's wide acquaintance, Hazel seemed to speak without subterfuge. There was something missing in her, Gallagher decided: the mask-like veneer, the scrim of will that came between him and so many women, his former wife, certain of his lovers, his sisters from whom he was estranged. With girlish aplomb Hazel was telling him that she admired his "piano playing"—though jazz was "hard to follow, to see where it's going." Surprising him by saying that she'd used to listen to jazz music on a late-night program on a Buffalo radio station, years ago.

Immediately Gallagher identified the program: "Zack Zacharias" on WBEN.

Hazel seemed surprised, Gallagher knew the program. Gallagher had to resist telling her that late-night jazz programming on a number of stations through the state was his, Chet Gallagher's idea. WBEN was an affiliate of Gallagher Media, one of the stronger urban stations.

"Do you know him? 'Zack Zacharias'? I always wondered if he was— you know, Negro."

Delicately Hazel enunciated the word: *Ne-gro*. As if to be *Ne-gro* was a kind of invalidism.

Gallagher laughed. "His name isn't 'Zack Zacharias' and he's no more Negro than I am. But he knows good jazz, the program is in its ninth year."

Hazel smiled, as if confused. He didn't want to seem to be laughing at her.

"You're from Buffalo, are you?"

"No."

"But western New York, right? I can hear the accent."

Hazel smiled again, uncertainly. Accent? She had never heard the flat nasal vowels, herself.

Gallagher didn't want to make her self-conscious. She was so vulnerable, trusting.

"Why've you come so far north? Malin Head Bay? Must've come here in the summer, yes?"

"Yes."

"D'you know people here? Relatives?"

This blunt question Hazel seemed not to hear. Surprising Gallagher with a remark he'd have had to take as flirtatious, from another woman: "You haven't been back to the movies for a long time, Mr. Gallagher. At least, I haven't seen you."

Gallagher was flattered, Hazel remembered him. And was willing to allow him to know that she remembered him.

Telling her again, poking at her arm, please call him Chet.

Now Gallagher leaned over Hazel feeling the blood course warm and exhilarated in his veins. How pretty she was! How desperately grateful he was, she'd come back! A man plays jazz piano hoping to attract a woman like this one. Telling her that really he didn't like movies, much. He wasn't very American, very normal in that regard. His family background was "media"—not films, but newspapers, radio, TV. Trading in images, dreams. Always the film industry had been primed to sell tickets, that was its aim. If you knew this, you were not so likely to be seduced. What Gallagher most disliked about Hollywood films was the music. The "score." Usually it grated against his nerves. The sentimental employment of music to evoke emotions, to "set scenes" offended him. A holdover from silent films when an organist played in each theater. All was exaggerated, perverse. Sometimes he shut his ears against the music. Sometimes he shut his eyes against the images.

Hazel laughed. Gallagher was himself exaggerating, to be amusing. He loved seeing her laugh. He guessed that, in other circumstances, Hazel didn't laugh much. A warm flush rose into her face. One of her mannerisms was to brush unconsciously at her hair, lifting and letting fall the neatly scissor-cut bangs that lay across her forehead. It was a childlike gesture that called attention to her serene face, her shining hair, ringless fingers and red-painted nails. Also, she shifted her shoulders in the tight dress, leaning forward, and back. Her body seemed awkward to her, as if she'd grown up too soon. The red-glittery dress was a costume like the usherette's costume; Gallagher knew without needing to check that Hazel would be wearing very high-heeled shoes.

Gallagher wanted to protect this young woman from the hurt that such naiveté would surely bring her. He wanted to make her trust him. He wanted to make her adore him. Wanted to caress her cheek, her slender throat. That squirmy, partly bared shoulder. Wanting to cup her breast in his hand. He felt a swoon of desire, imagining Hazel naked inside her clothes. The shock of it, seeing a woman naked for the first time, such *trust*.

Gallagher was talking rapidly. This was all coming fast, careening at him. And he hadn't had anything stronger than beer all evening. Just he was a little drunk with Hazel Jones.

That old familiar shiver of dread. Yet a perverse comfort in it. Never had Gallagher made love to a woman without that anticipatory sensation of dread. Except in his marriage, he'd become numbed to extremes of emotion. As soon as sex becomes companionable, habitual, it ceases to be sex and becomes something else.

This one, you won't marry.

Wishing to comfort himself.

Gallagher heard himself ask Hazel how she liked movies?—having to see them continuously as she did.

He cared nothing for her reply. Her voice engaged him, not her words. Yet she surprised him, saying she saw only fragments of movies at the Bay Palace, never anything whole. And before working as an usherette she had not seen many movies—"My parents didn't approve of movies." So now she saw just broken parts of movies and these many times repeated. She saw the ends of scenes hours before she saw the beginnings. She saw the beginnings of movies soon after having seen their dramatic endings. Stories looped back upon themselves. No one got anywhere. She knew beforehand what actors would say, even as the camera opened upon a "new" scene. She knew when an audience would laugh, though each audience was new and their laughter was spontaneous. She knew what music cues signaled even when she wasn't watching the screen. It gave you a confused sense of what to expect in life. For in life there is no music, you have no cues. Most things happen in silence. You live your life forward and remember only backward. Nothing is relived, only just remembered and that incompletely. And life isn't simple like a movie story, there is too much to remember.

"And all that you forget, it's gone as if it has never been. Instead of crying you might as well *laugh*."

And Hazel laughed, a thin anxious girl's laugh that ceased as abruptly as it began.

Gallagher was astonished by the young woman's outburst. He had no idea what she was talking about. And her curious emphasis upon the word *laugh* as if English were a foreign, acquired language to her. He didn't want to think he'd underestimated her intelligence yet he couldn't quite grant to a young woman who looked like Hazel Jones any subtlety of analysis, reasoning; it had been Gallagher's experience that most women spoke out of their emotions. He laughed again, as if she'd meant to be amusing. Took her hand in his, in a gesture that could be interpreted as gallant, playful. Her fingers, chilled from her cold glass, were unexpectedly strong, not small-boned or delicate; her skin was slightly roughened. Gallagher's pretext to touch her was a handshake of reluctant farewell for he must return to the piano, his break was over.

It was nearly 9:30 P.M. More customers were entering the Piano Bar. Nearly all the tables were taken. Gallagher was feeling good, he'd have a sizable audience and Hazel would be further impressed.

"Any requests, Hazel? I'm at your command."

Hazel appeared to be pondering the question. A small frown appeared between her eyebrows.

A young woman to take all questions seriously, Gallagher saw.

"Play the song that makes you happiest, Mr. Gallagher."

" 'Chet,' honey! My name is 'Chet.' "

"Play what makes you happiest, Chet. That's what I would like to hear."

11

It was the New Year. Zack was made to understand by certain veiled
and enigmatic remarks of his mother's that there would be a surprise for
him, soon.

"Better than Christmas. Much better!"

Much had been made of Christmas at school. Now in the New Year
much was made of 1963. All first-graders had to learn to spell *JANUARY*
not forgetting the *U*. Stony-faced Zacharias Jones drummed his fingers on
his desk top lost in a trance of invisible notes, chords. Or, if his teacher
scolded him, he folded his arms tight across his chest and depressed his
fingers secretly, compulsively. Scales, formula patterns, contrary motions,
arpeggio root positions and inversions. He didn't know the names for these
exercises, he simply played them. So vividly did he hear the notes in his
head, he always heard a misstrike. When he made a mistake, he was obliged
to return to the very beginning of the exercise and start over. Mr. Sarrantini
was an invisible presence in the first-grade classroom. Out of Miss Humphrey's sallow-skinned face emerged the fattish flushed face of the piano
teacher. Neither Miss Humphrey nor Mr. Sarrantini was more than grudging in their praise of Zacharias Jones. Clearly, Mr. Sarrantini disliked his
youngest pupil. No matter how fluently Zack executed his weekly lesson,
always there was something less-than-perfect. This new scale, F minor with
four flats. After only a day of intensive practicing Zack could play it as fluently as he played the scale of C major with no sharps or flats. Yet he knew

beforehand that Mr. Sarrantini would make the wet chiding sound with his lips.

Smirking *Here's little Wolfgang. Eh!*

Miss Humphrey was nicer than Mr. Sarrantini. Mostly she was nicer. Though sometimes she became exasperated and snapped her fingers under Zack's nose to wake him causing the other children to giggle. She had not liked it when the entire class was instructed to make construction-paper Santa Claus figures and paste silky white fluff on them as "hair" and Zack had been clumsy—purposefully, Miss Humphrey believed—with scissors, paper, glue. She had told the child's anxious mother that Zack read at the sixth grade level and his math skills were even better but *Your son has problems of deportment, attitude. Social skills. Either he's restless and can't sit still or he goes into a trance and doesn't seem to hear me.*

He was six years old. Already the knowledge lodged in him sharp as a sliver in flesh that if people don't like you it doesn't matter how smart, how talented you are. *Doesn't seem to hear me* was the charge.

Mrs. Jones apologized for her son. Promised he would "try harder" in the New Year.

In the New Year it was bitter cold. Minus-twenty degrees Fahrenheit "warming" to a high of minus-five if the sun appeared through layers of sullen cloud. At such times Hazel was practical-minded, uncomplaining. Laughed at the radio forecaster's dour tone. It was comical, how the local radio station played the brightest, most cheerful music—"Sunny Side of the Street," "Blue Skies," "How Much Is That Doggie in the Window?"—on the darkest winter mornings.

Heavy mugs of steaming hot chocolate Mommy prepared for Zack and herself. It was the principle of the thermos bottle, Mommy said: hot liquid in your tummy, you'll be kept warm until you get to where you're going.

On blizzard days, no one was expected to go anywhere. What happiness! Zack was allowed to stay home from school luxuriating in snowy quiet and Hazel could stay home from the Bay Palace Theater. No need to make up her face like a movie poster or brush-brush-brush her hair till it gleamed like fire. Singing slyly under her breath *Savin' all my love for you!* glancing sidelong at her son so fiercely absorbed in piano practice at the kitchen table. On those blindingly sunny mornings that often followed blizzards, Mommy would bundle Zack up in long woollen itchy underwear, shirt and two sweaters, zip him into his stiff new sheepskin jacket from Sears, pull his woollen cap down low on his head and wrap a woollen muffler 'round and 'round his neck covering his mouth as well so that if Zack breathed through his mouth outdoors, and not his nose, which he couldn't help doing, the wool dampened, and smelled bad. Two pairs of winter socks inside his rubber boots, also newly purchased at Sears. And two pairs of mittens forced on his hands, the outer pair made of fake leather lined with fake fur. "Your precious fingers, Zack! Your little toes can freeze and fall off, honey, but not your fingers. These fingers will be worth a fortune someday."

Laughing at what she called Zack's pickle-puss, and kissing him wetly on the nose.

❊ ❊ ❊

12

"You have a new friend, Zack! Come meet him."

He had not seen his mother so breathless, excited. She was taking him into the brightly lighted hotel on the river, the Malin Head Inn, he'd seen only from the exterior when, in warm weather, it seemed long ago they'd gathered the special stones along the beach.

They were awkward together, stumbling into a single compartment of the revolving door. A blast of warm air struck their faces when they spilled out into the hotel lobby. So many people! Zack stood blinking. Mommy gripped his mittened hand tight and led him across the crowded floor. On all sides there was activity, movement. Too much to see. A rowdy party of skiers had only just arrived, moving to register at the front desk. They wore brightly colored canvas jackets and carried expensive skiing gear. Several of the young men observed Hazel Jones as she made her way through the lobby. Her cheeks smarted from the cold and she appeared distraught as if she'd been running. In a lounge area, she paused to unzip Zack's sheepskin jacket and to remove her own shapeless coat which was made of a gray fuzzy material, with a hood. Beneath the coat, Hazel Jones was wearing one of her two "party" dresses as she called them. This one, Zack's favorite, was dark purple jersey with tiny pearls across the bosom and a satin sash. Hazel had bought both dresses for nine dollars at a fire sale downtown. You'd have had to look close to see where the fabric of each dress was damaged.

"He's waiting, sweetie. This way!"

Hazel grabbed Zack's hand, now bare, and pulled him along. Zack liked it that there were no other children in the lobby. He was made to feel special for it was late for a child to be up: past 8:30 P.M. Zack rarely became sleepy until past ten o'clock, sometimes later if he was listening to music on the radio. He was hearing music now, and it excited him.

"It's a wedding. But I don't see the bride."

Hazel had stopped outside an enormous ivory-and-gold ballroom where, on a raised platform against the farther wall, a five-piece band was playing dance music. This was music to make you smile, and want to dance: "swing." Strange that most of the dressily attired men and women in the ballroom were not dancing but standing in tight clusters, holding drinks, talking and laughing loudly.

Zack wondered if this—the wedding?—was the surprise.

The surprise could not be Daddy, he knew. Now that the pebbles were gone.

But Daddy himself is gone. He had to remember that.

Zack nudged Mommy in the leg. Such a young-looking mother like one of the female faces in the posters at the Bay Palace Theater, and in her purple jersey party dress it scared him she wasn't any mother at all.

"Why do people get married, Mommy? Is it the only way?"

"The only way *what*?"

Zack had no idea. Hoping that Mommy would finish his thought for him, as often she did.

They were walking then swiftly along a corridor of brightly lighted shop displays. Jewelry, handbags. Hand-knit Shetland sweaters. At the end of the corridor was a dimly-lit room, shadowy as a cave: PIANO BAR. Zack heard a piano being played. Here was his surprise! Hazel pulled him inside shivery and excited. Across the room a man was sitting at a beautiful gleaming piano, not a small upright like the piano in the Junior High auditorium but a "grand" piano, the kind with an opened lid. The man was playing music Zack knew from the radio, long ago on the Poor Farm Road: "jazz."

A number of people were sitting at small tables scattered across the smoky room. At a bar, more customers sat on stools. Some were talking and laughing among themselves but most were listening to the pianist play his quick bright startling music. Zack felt the glamor of the Piano Bar, his heart beat hard with happiness.

There was a small round zinc-topped table reserved for Hazel Jones, near the piano! Hazel positioned Zack where he could watch the pianist's hands. He had never seen such long, supple fingers. He had never heard such music, close up. It was astonishing to him, overwhelming. Zack guessed that the man at the piano could reach twelve keys—fifteen!—with his long agile fingers. He watched, he listened enthralled. It would be one of the great memories of his life, hearing Chet Gallagher play jazz piano that night in January 1963 at the Malin Head Inn.

"If It Isn't Love"—"A-Tisket, A-Tasket"—"I Ain't Got Nobody" Fats Waller style: pieces Gallagher played that night, that Zack would come to know in time.

At the break, Gallagher came to sit at Hazel Jones's table. Zack saw that they were known to each other: Gallagher was the "friend." In that instant he understood the logic of the new sheepskin jacket and boots from Sears, the newly installed telephone in their small apartment, Hazel's air of secrecy and well-being. He would not wonder at this for he'd long ago understood that it was futile to wonder at the logic of adult behavior. It was not astonishing that Chet Gallagher should know Hazel Jones, but that Chet Gallagher, the man who'd only now been playing the piano, should wish to know him, shaking his hand, smiling and winking—"H'lo, Zack! Your mother has been telling me, you play piano, too?" Zack was too stricken to speak, Hazel nudged him and said in an undertone to Gallagher, "Zack is shy with adult men," and Gallagher laughed, in a way that allowed you to see how fond he was of Hazel Jones. "What makes you think I'm an 'adult man'?"

Gallagher had an oversized, oblong head like something carved out of wood. His dark, crinkled hair framed a bald front and his nose was long and narrow with amazing dark holes for nostrils. His mouth was always smiling. His head was aimed forward. At the piano, his spine had looked like a willow, easily bent. Gallagher wore the strangest clothes Zack had ever seen on a man: a black silk shirt with no collar, that fitted his sinewy, narrow torso snug as a glove; suspenders made of a showy iridescent-blue fabric, you would associate with a party dress like Hazel Jones's. Zack had never seen any man with a face like Gallagher's, he supposed was an ugly face and yet the more you stared at this face, the more attractive it became. Nor had Zack ever seen such kind eyes on any man.

Gallagher rose. Time to return to the piano. He'd brought his drink to the table with him, a clear-looking liquid in a tall glass. As he turned away, his hand drifted against Hazel's shoulder lightly, in passing. Zack would fall asleep listening to Gallagher's fingers moving up and down the keyboard in a wild antic rhythm that made his own fingers twitch in emulation: "boogie-woogie."

> *I knew then that a man could love.*
> *A man can love.*
> *With his music, with his fingers a man can love.*
> *A man can be good, a man does not have to hurt you.*

Zack was wakened, later. The Piano Bar had closed. The bartender was cleaning up. Chet Gallagher had ordered roast beef sandwiches for them: four sandwiches for three people of whom one was a six-year-old child dazed with sleep. Of course, Chet Gallagher was famished. He would eat two and a half sandwiches, himself. He was thirsty, too. After his stint at the piano he was in a mood to celebrate. Hazel was laughing protesting it was late, after 2 A.M., wasn't he tired, Gallagher shook his head vehemently— "Hell, no."

Zack went eagerly to the piano. Had to stand, for the piano stool was too low. At first he just touched the keys, depressed them cautiously, hearing the sudden sharp, clear tones, the notes out of the piano's mysterious interior that always excited him, the wonder that any such sound might exist in the world and that it might be summoned out of silence by an effort of his own.

That was the wonder: that sound might be summoned out of silence, emptiness. That he might be an instrument of that sound.

Gallagher's voice came teasing and fondly familiar, as if they'd known each other for a long time: "Go on, kid. Piano's yours. Play."

Zack played the scale of F minor, right hand alone, left hand alone and both hands together. His fingers fitted the keys as if he'd played this beautiful piano before! The tone was very different from the piano he played for Mr. Sarrantini, though. It was far clearer, the notes more distinctive. Here, his fingers began to take on the movements and syncopation of Gallagher's fingers, jazz rhythms, boogie-woogie. He heard himself playing, trying to play, one of the catchy melodies Gallagher had played earlier in the evening: the one that sounded like a child's song—"A-Tisket, A-Tasket." Out of this, too, he fashioned a clumsy boogie-woogie. Gallagher came laughing to the piano to lean over him. There was a smell of Gallagher's breath that was sweetish-stale, smoky. "Jesus, kid. You play by ear, eh? Terrific." Gallagher's enormous hands descended beside Zack's small hands on the keyboard; his long black-sleeved arms enclosed Zack, without touching him. His fingers that were so long and supple moved with authority up into the treble keys, down deep into the bass keys, lower and lower until the notes were almost too deep to hear. Gallagher was snorting with laughter, it was so funny that Zack's child-fingers tried to follow his, slipping and faltering, striking the wrong notes, yet not giving up, like a clumsy puppy running after a long-legged dog. Zack's face was warm, he was becoming excited. Gallagher struck the keys hard, his hands leapt. Zack struck the keys hard, too. His fingers stung. He was becoming overly excited, feverish.

"Kid, you're a firecracker. Where the hell'd you come from!"

Gallagher rested his chin on top of Zack's head. Very lightly, as Hazel sometimes did when he was practicing piano at the kitchen table and she was in a playful mood. "Just a touch, kid. No need to pound. You draw the music out, you don't beat it out. All you need is a touch. Then move quick, see?—the left hand is mostly chords. One-two-three-four. One-two-three-four. Keep the beat. Keep the beat. With the beat you can play any damn thing. 'St. James Infirmary.' "

Gallagher's big hands struck the keys with dirge-like authority. To Zack's astonishment Gallagher began to sing in a sliding, bawling, nasal voice, you didn't know if you were meant to cry or laugh:

> *"Let 'er go, let 'er go, God bless her—*
> *Wherever she may be—*

She can look this wide world over—
She'll never find a sweet man like me."

Gallagher returned to the table, to Hazel who laughed and applauded with childlike enthusiasm.

Zack remained at the piano, determined to play like Gallagher. Left-hand chords, right-hand melody. The melodies were rather simple when you knew them. Over and over, the identical notes. Zack began to feel a strange dizzying sensation, he was coming close to possessing the secret of the piano through these notes that Gallagher had played with such assurance, one day he would be able to play any music he heard for it would exist (somehow) in his fingers as it seemed to exist in this man's superior fingers.

Hearing and not-hearing his mother confide in Chet Gallagher that she wasn't happy with Zack's piano teacher, Mr. Sarrantini was an older man who seemed to dislike teaching children and who was very critical of her son, often hurting his feelings. "And Zack tries so hard. It will be the purpose of his life, music."

He didn't have a piano at home, though. He had little opportunity to practice.

Quickly Gallagher said, "Hell, come by my place. I have a piano, he can use mine. All he wants." Hazel said hesitantly, "You would do that for Zack?" and Gallagher said, in his warm easy way, "But why not? The boy is talented."

There was a pause. Zack was playing piano, echoing Gallagher: "St. James Infirmary." But his fingers were faltering, less certain now. With a part of his mind he heard his mother's low anxious voice, "But—it could leave him, couldn't it? 'Talent.' It's like a flame, isn't it? Not anything real."

Zack heard this, and did not hear. He could not believe that his mother was saying such things about him, betraying him to a stranger. Hadn't she boasted of him, for years? Urging him to play piano in the presence of strangers, hoping for their applause? She had insisted upon the lessons with Mr. Sarrantini. She had told Zack more than once that his fingers would be worth a fortune someday. Why was she speaking so doubtfully now? And to Chet Gallagher of all people! Zack was angry, striking high treble notes and chords to accompany them. He'd lost the beat. God damn the beat. His fingers struck almost at random. He could hear his mother and her new friend speaking earnestly in lowered voices as if not wanting him to hear nor did he want to hear yet there was Hazel saying, protesting, "I—I don't think I could do that, Mr. Gallagher. I mean—Chet. It wouldn't be right," and Gallagher saying, "Not right? In who the hell's eyes?" and when Hazel didn't reply he said, more sympathetically, "Are you married, Hazel? Is that it?"

Now Zack tried not to hear. His mother's voice was almost inaudible, abashed.

"No."

"Divorced?"

Zack's fingers groped at the keys, fumbling a melody. He was searching for the melody. Strange how once you lose a melody it's gone totally, though when you have it, nothing seems so easy and so natural. His eyelids were heavy. So tired! Hearing his mother in her glamorous purple jersey party dress confess to Gallagher that she was not married, and not divorced, she had never been married—"Not ever married to any man."

This was a shameful thing, Zack knew. For a woman with a child, not to be married. Why this was, he had no idea. Just the words *Having a baby* pronounced in a certain insinuating tone provoked sniggering laughter. At school, older children teased him asking if he had a father, where was his father, and he'd told them his father had died, as Mommy had instructed him, and he'd backed off from them, their cruel jeering faces, he turned in desperation to run away. Mommy had told him never run away, like dogs they will pursue you, and yet he could not help it, he was frightened of them shouting after him gleeful and aroused, tossing chunks of ice at him. Why did they hate him, why did they shout *Jo-nes* as if the name was something ugly?

Mommy said they were jealous. Mommy said he was special, and she loved him, and nobody loved them the way she loved him that was why they were jealous, and because Zacharias really was special in the eyes of the world and all the world would know, one day.

Gallagher was saying, "Hazel, that doesn't matter. For Christ's sake."

"It matters. In people's eyes."

"Not in mine."

Zack was not watching the adults. Yet he saw the man lay his big hand over Hazel's hand, on the zinc-topped table. And the man leaned forward awkwardly, brushing his lips against Hazel Jones's forehead. Zack was striking keys with his left hand, low, and lower. High in the treble like a bird's nervous chattering. Every damn melody he'd thought he knew, he'd lost. And the beat, he'd lost. His fingers began to strike the keyboard harder. He held his thumbs and fingers like claws, striking ten keys at once, as an ordinary ill-tempered child might do, banging at the keyboard he could no longer play, up and down the keyboard like thunder.

"Zack! Honey, stop."

Hazel came to him, seizing his hands.

It was time to leave. Lights in the Piano Bar were being switched off. The bartender had departed. Chet Gallagher stood, taller than Zack had imagined him, stretching luxuriantly like a big cat, yawning.

"C'mon. I'll drive you Joneses home."

He was being helped into the rear of a car. Such a big car, wide as a boat! The backseat was cushioned like a sofa. His eyes kept closing, he was so sleepy. Seeing by the green-luminous clock in the dashboard that it was 2:48 A.M. Mommy was sitting in the front seat of the car beside Mr. Gallagher. Last thing Zack heard, Gallagher was saying extravagantly, "Hazel Jones, this has been the happiest night of my misspent life. So far."

13

✳   ✳   ✳

In the late winter of 1963 they would move from Malin Head Bay to Watertown, New York. This was *keeping-going* in a new way. Not by Greyhound bus and not poor and desperate but driven in Chet Gallagher's comfortable 1959 Cadillac wide and floating as a boat.

"We have a new life, now. A decent life. No one will follow us, here!"

Over a flurried weekend it was arranged: Hazel would be employed as a salesclerk at Zimmerman Brothers Pianos & Music Supplies in Watertown. And Zack would be taking piano lessons with the older Zimmerman brother who gave lessons to serious pupils only.

From Malin Head Bay they would move forty miles south to the much larger city of Watertown, where they knew no one. From the cramped and ill-smelling apartment above Hutt Pharmacy they would move to a two-bedroom apartment with freshly painted white walls on the second floor of a brownstone on Washington Street, a five-minute walk from Zimmerman's.

Hazel Jones would be paying her own rent for this apartment. Mr. Gallagher would not be paying her rent. Her salary at Zimmerman's was almost three times as much as her usherette's salary had been at the Bay Palace Theater.

"When you sell music, you are selling beauty. From now on, I will be selling beauty."

From now on, Zack would be taking serious piano lessons. Zack would have his own piano. Zack was a child-not-a-child.

From Bay Street Elementary, Zack would be transferred to a new school, North Watertown Elementary. Here, he was enrolled in second grade. There was the possibility, too, that he might be advanced another grade if he continued to excel in school.

One day, Mr. Gallagher had driven Zack and his mother to the Watertown school, where Zack spent several hours taking tests: reading, writing, arithmetic, matching up geometrical figures. The tests were not difficult, Zack completed them quickly. Afterward was an interview with the principal of North Watertown Elementary, and this too seemed to go very well.

It must have been, Chet Gallagher had made these arrangements, too. Mommy hinted this was so. Mommy assured Zack he would be very happy in the new school, happier than he'd been at the old.

"Mrs. Jones, do you have your son's birth certificate?"

"Yes. I do."

Such a document was required in the Watertown public school district for all children seeking enrollment. Zack's birth certificate declared that *Zacharias August Jones* had been born November 29, 1956, in Port Oriskany, New York. His parents were *Hazel Jones* and *William Jones* (now deceased).

The birth certificate, new-looking, was a fascimile, Hazel explained to the principal. For the original had been lost years ago in a house fire.

Goodbye to Malin Head Bay! Except he'd been tormented by older children, and never much encouraged by Mr. Sarrantini, Zack had liked living in the old river town.

Walking along the pebbly beach with Mommy, just the two of them. And snowbound days at home, just the two of them. And that night in the Malin Head Inn, that had changed their lives.

Chet Gallagher was Mommy's friend, and Zack's friend, too. No sooner had Mommy and Zack moved into the new apartment in Watertown than there was the possibility that they might move again: to a house that Mr. Gallagher was negotiating to buy, or had already bought.

Too excited to sleep Zack lay very still in his bed listening to the adults speaking together in another room of the new apartment.

Through the wall he heard them. His fingers twitched striking notes on an invisible keyboard.

For speech is a kind of music. Even when words are blurred, their tone, their rhythm prevails.

. . . but wouldn't you want to, Hazel?

Yes, but . . .

What?

It wouldn't be right. If . . .

Bullshit. That's no reason.

People would talk.

So who gives a damn, if people talk? What people? Who even knows you here?

At Zimmerman's, they know me. And they know you.

So what?

And there's Zack.

Let's ask him, then.

No! Please don't wake him, it would only make him upset. You know how he admires you.

Well, I admire him. He's a terrific kid.

He's had so much upset in his life, he's only six years old . . .

You want to get married, Hazel? That's it?

I . . . I don't know. I don't think . . .

Marry me, then. What the hell.

They were not quarreling exactly. Hazel Jones was not one to quarrel. Her manner was soft, earnest. Her voice was liquidy and pleading like a song. Hearing Hazel Jones was like listening to a radio song. Gallagher, the man, was the one to lose his temper, unexpectedly. Especially when he'd been drinking. And often when he came to visit Hazel he'd been drinking. Zack would be drifting off to sleep, awakened suddenly by Gallagher's raised voice, the sound of a fist striking something, a chair being pushed away from a table, Gallagher on his feet swearing and headed for the door and Hazel Jones's voice pleading *Chet, please. Chet!* But away Gallagher would go like a waterfall of notes cascading along a keyboard, once the momentum begins it can't be stopped, heavy footsteps on the stairs, a man's pride wounded, wouldn't return for days, holed up back in Malin Head Bay and would not even telephone allowing Hazel Jones to know God damn he could walk out of her life as he'd walked into it he could walk out of any woman's life as he'd walked into it and then what?

"Because I'm not a whore. I am not."

It was a small upright, the piano Gallagher bought for Zack. Insisting it was "secondhand"—"a bargain." Not a new piano, Gallagher had bought it at Zimmerman's at a discount. A gift for the boy, Gallagher said Hazel need feel no indebtedness.

"It isn't a Steinway, it's a Baldwin. Really, Hazel. It didn't cost much."

The keys were not ivory but plastic, glaring white. The wood was veneer, though very smooth, teak-colored. The piano was the size of the battered piano in the Bay Street Junior High School but had a far clearer tone. Zack was stunned by the gift. Zack had seemed almost to recoil from it, at first, overcome. Hazel had seen in the child's face the stricken look of an adult woman. Like no normal child in such a circumstance, Zack had begun to cry.

Hazel thought uneasily *He feels the burden of the gift. He won't be equal to it.*

The deliverymen had brought the piano to ZACHARIAS JONES. On a card prominently attached to the piano was Gallagher's scrawl—

Play your heart out, Zack!
("No strings attached")
Your friend C.G.

Gallagher spoke, in his teasing way, of the house he was buying in Watertown: "The feature that will attract you most, Hazel, is its two separate entrances: we can come and go without seeing each other for weeks."

She hated it, the child was eavesdropping on her. No business of a child's, Mommy's private life. Nudging her with his elbow hard enough to hurt. "But why, Mommy? Don't you like Mr. Gallagher?" and Hazel said evasively, "Yes. I like Mr. Gallagher." And the child said, in that pleading-bullying way of a willful child, "He's real nice, isn't he? Mom*my*?" and Hazel said, "A man can seem nice, Zack. Before you come to live with him."

Between mother and child there passed the shadow of *that man*. In their shared speech *that man* was never given a name and Hazel had to wonder if Zack remembered his father's name.

It was not a name to be uttered aloud. Yet, still it haunted her in weak moments.

Niles Tignor.

Wondering if Zack recalled his own, early name. So many times uttered in Mommy's voice, in love.

Niley.

As if somehow Niley had been her firstborn. And this older, more difficult and willful Zacharias was another child whom she could not love quite so much.

Zacharias was growing from her, she knew. His allegiance was shifting from Mommy to the adult man in their lives, Gallagher. She supposed it was inevitable, it was altogether normal. Yet she must protect her son, as she must protect herself.

Saying, as she stroked his warm forehead, "I don't think that we are ready to live with a man, Zack. I don't think that we can trust a man. Not yet." Speaking so frankly was not Hazel's favored mode of speech with her child, she worried she would regret it.

"But when, Mommy?"

"Someday, maybe. I can't promise."

"Next month? Next week?"

"Certainly not next week. I said—"

"Mr. Gallagher told me—"

"Never mind what Mr. Gallagher told you, he has no right to talk to you behind my back."

"Wasn't behind your back! He told me!"

Suddenly Zack was angry. It was like snapping your fingers, how quickly the child became angry. Demanding to know why couldn't they live with Mr. Gallagher if he wanted them! Nobody else wanted them did they! Nobody else wanted to marry them! If Mr. Gallagher was buying a house for *them*! Hazel was stunned to see the rage in her son's hot little face, a contorted little fist of a face, and the threat of violence in his flailing fists. *He wants a father. He thinks I am keeping his father from him.*

She tried to speak calmly. It was not Hazel Jones's style to become emotional in response to others' emotions.

"Honey, it's none of your business. What passes between Mr. Gallagher and me is none of your business, you're just a child."

Now Zack was truly furious. Shouted outrageously he was not a child, he was not a damn stupid child *he was not.*

He pushed out of her arms and ran from her, trembling. He did not strike her with his fists but pushed from her as if he hated her, slammed into his room and shut the door against her as she stared after him dazed and shaken.

The tantrum passed. Zack emerged from his room and went at once to the piano. Already that day he'd practiced for two hours. Now he would play and replay his lesson for Mr. Zimmerman, then reward himself (Hazel supposed this was the logic, a bargain) with random playing, more advanced compositions in his *John Thomson's Modern Course for the Piano* book or jazz/boogie-woogie Chet Gallagher style.

Hazel teased him: "Play 'Savin' All My Love For You.' "

Maybe. Maybe he would.

Hazel took comfort, hearing her son at the piano. Preparing dinner for the two of them. Even when Zack played loudly or carelessly or repeated sequences of notes compulsively as if to punish both himself and her she thought *We are in the right place in all the world, Hazel Jones has brought us here.*

14

❀ ❀ ❀

"When you sell music, you are selling beauty."

Never had Hazel Jones been so proud of any work of hers. Never so smiling, exalted. Light flashed from her young face like a shard of sunlight reflected in a mirror. Her eyes blinked rapidly overcome by the moisture of gratitude, disbelief.

Zimmerman Brothers Piano & Music Supply was an old Watertown establishment, housed in a shabbily elegant brownstone on South Main Street in a part-residential, part-commercial neighborhood of distinguished old apartment buildings and small shops. The first thing you saw, approaching Zimmerman's, was the graceful bay window in which a Steinway grand piano was on permanent display. At dusk, and on dreary winter days, the bay window was lighted. The piano shone.

Hazel stopped to stare. The piano was so beautiful, she was left feeling weak, shaken. The thought came to her *Not a one of them can follow you here.*

From Milburn, she meant. That life. Soon she would be twenty-seven years old, the gravedigger's daughter who had been meant to die at thirteen.

What a joke, her life! That good, decent, kindly man Gallagher believed he loved her, who had not the slightest knowledge of her.

She felt a pang of guilt, for deceiving him. But how much more powerfully, a strange giddy pleasure.

In the early morning especially, when she walked to the music store hearing her high heels strike the sidewalk in brisk Hazel Jones staccato, she found herself thinking of the stone house in the cemetery. Her brothers Herschel, August. How old would they be now, if they were living: Herschel in his mid-thirties, August nearly as old. She wondered if she would know them. If they would now recognize her in Hazel Jones.

They would be proud of her, she believed. Both her brothers had liked her. They would wish her well—wouldn't they? Herschel would shake his head, disbelieving. But he would be happy for Hazel Jones, she knew.

And there were the adult Schwarts.

Jacob Schwart would be damned impressed with Zimmerman's. The very look of the brownstone, the store. And it was a large store, with parquet floors in the piano display room, and piped-in classical music. Though Jacob Schwart despised Germans. As he despised the well-to-do. Never could Jacob Schwart resist mocking, belittling any accomplishment of his daughter.

You are ignorant now. You know nothing of this hellhole the world.

Hazel Jones did know. But no one in Watertown would guess Hazel Jones's knowledge.

Anna Schwart would be proud of her! Working in a store that sold pianos!

Though Hazel Jones, like the other female salesclerks, was not entrusted with piano sales: that was the province of Edgar Zimmerman.

Hazel sold music instruction books, sheet music, classical records. Such musical instruments as guitars, ukeleles. Zimmerman Brothers was a major outlet for ticket sales for local concerts, recitals, musical performances of all kinds and these tickets Hazel proudly sold as well. Sometimes, she was given two free tickets to these events, and she and Zack went together.

"A new life, Zack. We have begun our new life."

In honor of this new life Hazel often wore white gloves arriving at Zimmerman's. In emulation of President Kennedy's glamorous socialite wife she sometimes wore a black pillbox hat with a gossamer veil. Gloves and hat she removed when she arrived at the store. Of course she wore high-heeled shoes and nylon stockings without a run and always she was perfectly groomed as a young woman in an advertisement. Her hair was now a deep chestnut color, so clean and fiercely brushed it crackled with static electricity, worn shoulder-length with bangs across her forehead.

There were fine white scars at her hairline, hidden beneath the bangs. No one but her son had ever seen. And very likely, her son had forgotten.

At Zimmerman's, there were two other female employees: middle-aged, busty Madge and Evelyn. Madge was a receptionist for Edgar Zimmerman who ran the store, and something of an accountant. Evelyn was a sales-clerk specializing in lesson books and sheet music, known to every public school music teacher in the county. Both Madge and Evelyn wore shape-less dark dresses, often with cardigan sweaters draped over their shoulders. They were rather short women, hardly more than five feet tall. By contrast, Hazel Jones was a tall, striking young woman who wore only clothes that fitted her figure to advantage. She had not many clothes but understood shrewdly how to vary her "outfits": a long pleated black wool skirt with a matching bolero top, embroidered in red rosebuds; a long gray flannel skirt with a kick pleat in back, waist cinched in by a black elastic belt; fussily feminine "translucent" blouses; crocheted sweaters with tiny jewels or pearls; tight-fitting dresses made of shiny fabrics. Behind her glass-topped counter Hazel sometimes resembled a Christmas ornament, all glittering innocence. Her employer Edgar Zimmerman was bemused to note how when a customer entered the store, if that customer was male, he would glance quickly at Evelyn, at Madge if she was out on the floor, and at Ha-zel, and make his way without hesitation to Hazel who stood pert and smil-ing in expectation.

"Hello, sir! May I be of assistance?"

Sometimes, Hazel was observed behind her counter in a posture of sudden unease. As if she'd heard someone calling her name at a distance or had glimpsed, through the store window, a passing figure that alarmed her. "Hazel? Is something wrong?" Edgar Zimmerman might ask, if he didn't feel he was being intrusive at that moment; but Hazel Jones would imme-diately wake from her trance to assure him, smilingly, "Oh no! Nothing at all, Mr. Zimmerman. 'A goose walked over my grave'—I guess."

The remark was so silly, so senseless, Edgar Zimmerman exploded into laughter.

So funny! Hazel Jones had that rare gift, to make an aging melancholy-at-heart gentleman laugh like an adolescent boy.

Only Edgar Zimmerman sold pianos. Edgar Zimmerman's life was pianos. (His more distinguished brother Hans was not involved in sales. Hans disdained "finances." He appeared in the store only to give piano instructions to selected students.) Yet Hazel Jones was often in the piano showroom, eager to dust, polish, buff the beautiful gleaming pianos. She came to love the distinctive smell of the special brand of lemon polish favored by the Zimmermans, an expensive German import sold in the store. She came to love the smell of real ivory. Zimmerman Brothers had even acquired an antique harpsichord, a small exquisite instrument made of cherrywood inlaid with gilt and mother-of-pearl, which Hazel particularly admired. It may have been that Edgar Zimmerman, widower, a short dapper man with gray bushy hair in sporadic clumps and a spiky goatee which his fingers compulsively stroked, was flattered by his youngest employee's enthusiasm for her work for often he was seen talking animatedly with her in the showroom; often, he would seek out Hazel Jones, and neither Madge nor Evelyn, to assist him in making a sale.

"Your smile, Hazel Jones! That cinches the deal."

It was a little joke between them, rather daring on Edgar Zimmerman's part. His fingers caressed the spiky goatee, with unconscious ardor.

Edgar Zimmerman, too, was a pianist: not so gifted as his brother Hans but very capable, demonstrating pianos for customers by playing favorite passages from Schubert, Chopin, the thunderous opening of Rachmaninoff's "Prelude in C-sharp Minor" and the romantic-liquidy opening of Beethoven's so-called "Moonlight Sonata." Edgar spoke of having heard Rachmaninoff play the Prelude, long ago at Carnegie Hall, Manhattan. An unforgettable evening!

Hazel said, smiling her ingenuous smile, "You didn't ever hear Beethoven, I guess?—in Germany? That was too long ago, I guess?"

Edgar laughed. "Hazel, of course! Beethoven died in 1827."

"And when did your family come to this country, Mr. Zimmerman? A long time ago, I guess?"

"Yes. A long time ago."

"Before the war?"

"Before both wars."

"You must have had relatives. Back in Germany. It is Germany the Zimmermans came from, isn't it?"

"Yes. Stuttgart. A beautiful city, or was."

" 'Was'?"

"Stuttgart was destroyed in the war."

"Which war?"

Edgar Zimmerman saw Hazel smiling at him, though less certainly. She was an awkward schoolgirl, twining a strand of hair around her forefinger. Her red-lacquered nails flashed.

He said, "Someday, Hazel, maybe you will see Germany. There are some landmarks that remain."

"Oh, I would like that very much, Mr. Zimmerman! On my honeymoon, maybe."

They laughed together. Edgar Zimmerman was feeling giddy, as if the floor had begun to tilt beneath him.

"Hazel, much said about Germany—about Germans—has been luridly exaggerated. The Americans make a fetish of exaggeration, like in Hollywood, you see?—for a profit. Always for a profit, to sell tickets! We Germans have all been tarred with the same brush."

"What brush is that, Mr. Zimmerman?"

Edgar edged closer to Hazel, stroking his chin nervously. They were alone together in the lavish piano showroom.

"The Juden brush. What else!"

Edgar spoke with a bitter laugh. He was feeling reckless suddenly, this naive attractive girl staring at him with widened eyes.

" 'Juden'?"

"Jewish."

Hazel was looking so perplexed, Edgar regretted he'd brought the damned subject up. It was never a subject that quite justified the expenditure of emotion it seemed to require.

He said, in his lowered voice, "What they have claimed. How they—

424 ⊛ JOYCE CAROL OATES

Jews—have wished to poison the world against us. Their propaganda about 'death camps.' "

Still Hazel was looking perplexed. "Who is 'us,' Mr. Zimmerman? Do you mean Nazis?"

"Not Nazis, Hazel! Really. *Germans*."

He was very excited now. His heart beat in his chest like a deranged metronome. But there was Madge in the doorway, summoning Edgar to the telephone.

The subject would never again be brought up between them.

"Hazel Jones, you keep us all young. Thank God for people like you!"

It was Hazel's idea to bring flowers in vases, to display on the most beautiful of the pianos in the showroom. It was Hazel Jones's idea to organize a raffle for tickets to Hans Zimmerman's annual student recital, held each May; and to offer "complimentary" tickets to customers who spent a certain sum of money at the store each month. Why not television advertisements, instead of just radio? And why not sponsor a competition for young pianists, it would be such wonderful publicity for Zimmerman Brothers . . .

Hazel grew breathless, expressing such ideas. Her older companions in the store smiled in dismay.

It was then Madge Dorsey made the remark about Hazel Jones keeping them all young. And thank God for people like her.

" 'People like me'? Who?"

Hazel seemed to be teasing, you never knew quite what she was getting at. Her girlish laughter was infectious.

Madge Dorsey made up her mind then not to hate Hazel any longer. These several weeks since the new salesclerk—lacking not only experience in sales, but totally ignorant of music—had been hired by Edgar Zimmerman, Madge had felt hatred blossoming inside her, in the region of her bosom, like a fast-growing cancer. But, to hate Hazel Jones was to hate the much-awaited spring thaw of upstate New York! To hate Hazel Jones was to hate the warm blinding flood of sunshine itself! And there was the futility, Madge conceded: Edgar Zimmerman had hired the girl, and Edgar Zimmerman was clearly taken with her.

Evelyn Steadman, salesclerk at Zimmerman Brothers for twenty-two years, was slower to be won over by Hazel Jones's "personality." At fifty-four, Evelyn was yet unmarried, with a waning and ever-waxing hope that Edgar Zimmerman, widower now for twelve years, in his early sixties, might take a sudden romantic interest in her.

Still, Hazel Jones prevailed. Thinking *I will make you love me! So you will never wish to hurt me.*

"How's my girl Hazel doin' here, Edgar? Any complaints?"

A few weeks after Hazel began working at Zimmerman Brothers, Chet Gallagher began dropping by in the late afternoon, in the wintry dusk when the store was about to close. Out of nowhere Gallagher appeared. He was known to the Zimmermans, and he appeared to be known to Madge and Evelyn, who brightened at his appearance. Hazel was always taken by surprise. Hazel had no idea that Gallagher was in town, and planning to surprise her with a dinner invitation that evening; often, Gallagher had failed to call her for several days, in the aftermath of a temper tantrum.

At such times, entering the store, Gallagher was smiling and exuberant and very much in control. He wore an expensive, rumpled camel's hair coat, his high forehead gleamed and his hair straggled over his shirt collar. Often he hadn't shaved for a day or two, his jaws glinted like metal filings. Hazel felt the glamor of her friend's sudden presence, the flurry of drama that accompanied his every gesture. In the tastefully decorated interior of Zimmerman Brothers Pianos & Music Supplies, on the polished parquet floor, Gallagher seemed somehow larger than life, like a figure that has stepped down off a movie screen. He made much of Edgar Zimmerman, zestfully shaking the man's small hand. He seemed even to enjoy the attention of Madge Dorsey and Evelyn Steadman who fluttered about him, calling him "Mr. Gallagher" and imploring him to play the piano.

"Just for a few minutes, Mr. Gallagher. Please!"

It was a lively scene. If business at Zimmermans had been slow, Chet

Gallagher's appearance would end the day on a bright note. For it seemed that the jazz pianist was something of a local figure, and well liked.

Glancing at Hazel with a sardonic smile *You see? Chet Gallagher is a big deal in some quarters.*

Hazel removed herself to the side, not entirely comfortable. When Gallagher made one of his appearances she was obliged to show pleasure as well as surprise. Her face must *light up*. She must hurry to him in her high-heeled shoes, allow him to squeeze her hand. She could not hold back. She could not wound him. This was the man who had paid for her move to Watertown, who'd loaned her money for numerous items including the deposit on her apartment. ("Loaned" at no interest. And no need to repay him for a long time.) Gallagher insisted there were "no strings attached" to his friendship with them yet Hazel felt the awkwardness of her situation. Gallagher was becoming ever more unpredictable: driving from Malin Head Bay to Watertown on an impulse, to see her, and driving back to Malin Head Bay that night; capable of not turning up in Watertown when he'd made arrangements to see her, with no explanation. Though he expected explanations from Hazel, he refused to explain himself to her.

In the music store, Hazel saw Gallagher staring at her with an expression of confused tenderness and sexual arrogance and she was filled with anxiety, resentment. *He wants them to think I'm his mistress. He owns Hazel Jones!*

It was a masquerade. Yet she could not abandon it.

"Come play for us, Chester! You must."

"Must I? Nah."

Gallagher had been a pupil of Hans Zimmerman's as a boy. There was an air of the renegade boy about him, amid these admiring elders. Implored to sit at a Steinway grand, Gallagher eventually gave in. Stretched and flexed his long fingers, lunged forward suddenly and began to play piano music of unexpected subtlety, beauty. Hazel had been expecting jazz and was surprised to hear music of an entirely different sort.

The adoring women identified Liszt: "Liebesraum."

Gallagher was playing from memory. His playing was uneven, in sudden rushes and runs of showy dexterity, then again elegantly understated, dreamy. And then again showy, so that you were watching the man's hands, arms, the sway of his shoulders and head, as well as listening to the sounds the piano produced. Yet Hazel was impressed, enthralled. If she and Zack lived with Chet Gallagher, he would play piano for them in this way . . .

You must love this man. You have no choice.

She felt the subtle coercion. If Anna Schwart could stand beside her now!

But Gallagher was striking wrong notes, too. Some of these he managed to disguise but others were blatant. Amid a virtuoso run of treble notes he broke off with "Damn!" He was embarrassed, making so many mistakes. Though the others praised him and urged him to continue, Gallagher turned obstinately on the piano stool like a schoolboy, his back to the keyboard, and fumbled to light a cigarette. His face was flushed, his prominent, pointed ears were flushed red. Hazel could see that Gallagher was furious with himself, and impatient with Edgar Zimmerman explaining fussily to the three women, "You see, it is the style of Liszt himself, how Chester plays the 'Liebesraum.' How his arms roll with the notes, the strength in his arms, flowing from his back and shoulders. It is the revolutionary manly style Liszt made so famous, that the pianist could be equal to the composer's art."

To Gallagher, Zimmerman said with paternal reproach, "You should never have abandoned your serious music, Chester. You would have made your father so proud."

"Would I."

Gallagher spoke flatly. He was lighting a cigarette carelessly, Hazel dreaded sparks falling onto the piano.

Now Gallagher lapsed into teasing Edgar Zimmerman, as he teased Hazel asking how "my girl was doin'" and so Hazel eased away with an embarrassed laugh. She knew, it was through Gallagher's connection with Hans Zimmerman that she owed her job here, she must be grateful to Gallagher as to the Zimmermans and such gratitude was best expressed by not standing about idly like everyone else. Hazel had been shutting up the cash register when Gallagher had appeared and she returned to the task now. She would spend minutes deftly stacking nickels and dimes into rolls for the bank.

Such a tedious, exacting ritual! Neither Madge nor Evelyn could bear it but Hazel executed it flawlessly and without complaint.

"Hazel, my dear. Time to call it a day."

There was Gallagher in his rumpled coat, advancing upon Hazel with her own coat opened to her, like a net.

Sorry for barging in on you like that, Hazel. You weren't expecting me tonight I guess.

No.

But why's it matter? You haven't anything you're hiding from me have you?

Not likely that he would follow them into this new life.

For this was *keeping-going* in their new way. She smiled to think how astonished he would be, if he could know!

Zimmerman Brothers Pianos & Music Supplies. In a row of brownstones on South Main Street, Watertown. The bay window, visible up and down the street, and the Steinway grand piano illuminated in the bay window. And a vase of tall white lilies on the piano waxy in perfection.

And the brownstone at 1722 Washington Street where H. Jones and her son lived in #26. Where in the vestibule beside the aluminum mailbox for #26 the name H. JONES was neatly handprinted on a small white card as a concession to the U.S. Postal Service.

(Hazel protested to the mailman: "But I don't get any mail except bills—gas, electric, telephone! Can't bills be delivered just to 'occupant, #26'? *Is it a law?*" It was.)

She did remember: the Watertown Plaza Hotel.

Where as *Mrs. Niles Tignor* she had signed her name in the registration book. As *Mrs. Niles Tignor* she had been known. Only vaguely did she remember the rooms in which she and Niles Tignor had stayed and she could not remember at all his face, his manner or his words to her for a mist obscured her vision as, when she was tired, the faint high-pitched ringing was discernible in her (right) ear. Mostly Hazel avoided the regal old Watertown Plaza Hotel. Except, Gallagher liked the Plaza Steak House. Naturally, Gallagher liked the Plaza Steak House where he was known, his hand warmly shaken. Gallagher was a steak man: plank steak, onion rings, very dry martinis. When he visited Watertown he insisted upon taking Hazel and Zack to the Steak House. Hazel was conscious of the danger. Though instructing herself *Don't be ridiculous, Tignor isn't a brewery agent any longer. All that is finished. He has forgotten you. He never knew Hazel Jones.* For those evenings at the Steak House, Hazel dressed somewhat conspicuously. Gallagher was in the habit of surprising her with attractive "outfits" for such occasions. Ever vigilant of the roaming eyes of other men, Gallagher yet took a perverse pride in Hazel's appearance at his side. In the lobby of the Watertown Plaza, holding Zack's hand and walking close beside Chet Gallagher, Hazel felt the sickish sliding *glissando* of male eyes moving upon her yet surely there was no one here who knew her, who knew Niles Tignor and would report her to him.

She was certain.

A woman opens her body to a man, a man will possess it as his own.
   Once a man loves you in that way, he will come to hate you. In time.
   Never will a man forgive you for his weakness in loving you.

15

❀ ❀ ❀

"Repeat, child."

A Czerny study that was twenty-seven bars of allegretto sixteenth-notes in four flats. Zack had played it once, slightly rushed, in small anxious surges as his piano teacher beat out the time with a pencil exact as the antiquated metronome on the piano. Zack had not missed or struck any wrong notes at least. Now at Hans Zimmerman's request, he played the study again.

"And another time, child."

Again, Zack played the Czerny study. Half-shutting his eyes as his fingers flew rapidly up, up into the treble, up, up into the treble in repetitive gliding motions. It was a time, it would be months, years of such studies: Czerny, Bertini, Heller, Kabalevsky. Acquiring and refining piano technique. When Zack finished, he did not remove his slightly trembling hands from the keyboard.

"You have memorized it, yes?"

Mr. Zimmerman closed the exercise book.

"Again, child."

Zack, half-shutting his eyes as before, replayed the study, twenty-seven bars of allegretto sixteenth-notes in four flats. The four/four time of the composition never varied. No compositions in the *Royal Conservatory of Music Pianoforte Studies* ever varied. When he finished, the elderly Hans Zimmerman murmured in approval. He'd removed his smudged eyeglasses, he was smiling at his youngest pupil.

"Very good, child. You have played it four times, it can be no mistake you have hit only right notes."

In Watertown, New York, where Mr. Gallagher had brought them. Where days-of-the-week were crucial as they had not been crucial in Malin Head Bay. Where Saturday was so crucial that Friday, which was the day-before-Saturday, soon became for Zack a day of almost unbearable excitement and apprehension: he was distracted in school, at home feverishly practiced piano for hours not wanting to take time to eat supper and refusing to go to bed until late: midnight. For Saturday morning at 10 A.M. was his weekly lesson with Hans Zimmerman.

Saturday was Zack's favorite day! All of the week built up to Saturday morning when his mother brought him with her to Zimmerman Brothers arriving at 8:45 A.M. and they would not leave until the store closed early Saturday afternoon at 3:30 P.M.

How old is he, Hazel?

Six and a half.

Only six and a half! His eyes . . .

There was the excitement of Zack's lesson with the elder Mr. Zimmerman which sometimes ran over ten, fifteen minutes while the next pupil waited patiently in a corner of the music instruction room at the rear of the brownstone. But there was the excitement, too, of being allowed to remain behind to observe certain of Mr. Zimmerman's advanced students at the keyboard for this, too, was a way of acquiring technique.

"So long as you promise to sit very still in the corner, child. Still as a little *Maus.*"

Zack thought *A mouse is not still but nervous.*

Zack found the other pupils' lessons of great interest. For he understood that these more advanced lessons would be his one day. He did not doubt that this was so, Mr. Gallagher had set into motion a sequence of actions and his trust in Mr. Gallagher was absolute.

He's allowing Zack to observe other pupils, Chet. Isn't that wonderful!

If it isn't too much for the kid.

Too much, how can it be too much?

Children turn against music if they're pushed too hard.

Strange he felt no envy of the other piano pupils except envy of their larger hands, their greater strength. But these too would be his one day.

What relief, Hans Zimmerman never made personal or hurtful remarks to his students, as Sarrantini had done! He cared only for the execution of music. He seemed to make little distinction between older and younger pupils. He was a kindly teacher who praised when praise was due but did not wish to deceive, for always there was more work: "Schnabel took it as his ideal, he wished to play only those piano works that cannot be fully mastered. Only those pieces 'greater than they can be played.' For what can be played, is not the transcendental. What can be played easily and well, is *Schund*."

The disdainful expression on Hans Zimmerman's face allowed his pupils to know what the German word must mean.

Zimmerman had himself studied with the great Artur Schnabel, Gallagher informed them. In Vienna, in the early 1930s. He was now retired from the Portman Academy of Music in Syracuse where he'd taught for decades. He was long retired from the concert stage. Gallagher surprised Hazel and Zack bringing several records Zimmerman had made in the late 1940s with a small prestigious classical record label in New York City.

The records were piano pieces by Beethoven, Brahms, Schumann, and Schubert. Hazel would have spoken to Hans Zimmerman about them except Gallagher cautioned her: "I don't think Zimmerman wants to be reminded."

"But why not?"

"Some of us feel that way about our pasts."

At Zimmerman Brothers, Hans Zimmerman kept to the rear quarters of the brownstone while Edgar Zimmerman ran the business. The two were co-partners, it was believed, yet Hans had virtually nothing to do with the selling of merchandise, employees, finances; Edgar ran everything. Hans was known to be only four or five years older than his brother, but he appeared of another generation entirely: courtly in manner, rather detached and deliberate in his speech, with smudged bifocals that were often drooping out of his vest pocket, untrimmed steely whiskers, a habit of breathing noisily through his teeth when he was concentrating on a pupil's playing. Hans who was tall, gaunt, noble in his bearing wore mismatched coats, sweaters, unpressed trousers. His favored footware was a pair of very old penny loafers. You could see that he'd been a handsome man once, now his face was in ruins. He was reticent, elliptical in criticism as in praise. From out of his corner Zack witnessed entire lessons when Mr. Zimmerman murmured no words except "Good. Move on" or "Repeat, please." Several times Zack had heard the terrible words: "Repeat the lesson for next week. Thank you."

It was common for Mr. Zimmerman to have Zack repeat pieces, but he had never yet asked Zack to repeat an entire lesson. He called him "child"— he didn't seem to remember his name. For why should he remember a name? Why a face? His interest in his pupils was in their hands; not their hands exactly but their fingers; not their fingers exactly but their "fingering." You could assess a young pianist by his or her "fingering" but you could make nothing of significance out of a name or a face.

The whole of the magnificent *Hammerklavier* Hans Zimmerman had memorized more than fifty years before remained in his memory intact, each note, each pause, each tonal variant yet Hans could not be troubled to remember the names of people he saw frequently.

And here was the gifted child, a rarity in Hans Zimmerman's life now: out of nowhere he'd seemed to have come with his eager, somehow old-European eyes, not at all an American boy, to Zimmerman's way of thinking. He would ask no personal questions of the boy's mother, he did not want to know about the boy's background, he did not want to feel anything for the boy. All that was extinguished in him now. And yet in weak moments the piano teacher found himself staring at the boy as he played his exercise pieces, one of the tricky little Czernys perhaps. Presto in six/eight time, three sharps. Left and right hands mirroring each other rapidly ascending, descending. In the concluding bars, left and right hands were nearly a keyboard apart, the little boy stretched his arms as in an antic crucifixion.

Hans Zimmerman surprised himself, laughing aloud.

"Bravo, child. If you play Czerny like Mozart, how will you play Mozart?"

16

❀ ❀ ❀

Makes me happy. What makes me happy. O Christ what!

No idea in hell what to play. No one had ever made such a request of the jazz pianist before. His fingers fumbled at the keyboard. So much of his adult life had become mechanical, his will suspended and indifferent. The emptiness of his soul opened before him like a deep well, he dared not peer into it.

His fingers would not fail him, though. Chet Gallagher at the keyboard. That old classic "Savin' All My Love For You."

And that turned out to be so.

17

A love ballad, a bluesy number.

Driving this snowswept landscape.

Gallagher drifting in a dream, at the wheel of his car. All his life he has been hearing music in his head. Sometimes the music of others, and sometimes his own.

> *Driving to Grindstone Island*
> *in the St. Lawrence River floating*
> *in reflected sky*
> *Lovesick Gallagher redeemed*
> *on Grindstone Island*
> *in the St. Lawrence River floating*
> *in reflected sky*

"Anybody want to turn back? *I* don't."

They were driving to Grindstone Island. They were planning to spend Easter weekend at the Gallagher lodge. The three of them: Gallagher's little family. For he loved them, out of desperation that the woman did not love him. The child he loved, who seemed at times to love him. But in the rearview mirror since they'd left Watertown, the child's face was averted, Gallagher could not catch the child's eye to smile and wink in complicity repeating his brash challenge, "Anybody want to turn back? *I* sure as hell don't."

What could the Joneses say. Captive in Gallagher's car being driven at less than forty miles an hour on icy-slick Route 180.

Then Hazel murmured what sounded like *No* in her maddening way that managed to be both enthusiastic and vague, doubtful.

It was the way in which Hazel allowed Gallagher to make love to her. To the degree to which Hazel allowed Gallagher to make love to her.

In the backseat of Gallagher's car the child Zack had disappeared from the rearview mirror entirely. He'd brought along his *Royal Conservatory Pianoforte Studies* and was lost in frowning concentration, oblivious of the snowy highway and occasional abandoned vehicles at the roadside.

Gallagher had assured him there was a piano at the lodge. He could practice at the lodge. Gallagher had banged on that piano plenty of times. He'd entertained his relatives. He'd played for himself. Summers on Grindstone Island, Gallagher's happiest memories. Wanting to convey to the child as to the child's mother how happiness is a possibility, maybe even a place you might get to.

Impulsively he'd bought the house in Watertown. But Hazel wasn't ready for that yet.

Easter weekend on Grindstone Island. It had been a very good plan except on Thursday morning a freezing rain began and within a few hours the rain had become sleet and the sleet became a wet wind-driven snow howling across Lake Ontario. Nine to twelve inches by Friday morning, and drifting.

Still, the region was accustomed to freak storms. Snow in April, sometimes in May. Quick blizzards, and a quick thaw. Snowplows had been operating through the night. Roads into the Adirondacks would be impassable but Route 180 north to Malin Head Bay and the bridge to Grindstone Island was more or less open: traffic moved slowly, but was moving. By Friday afternoon the wind had blown itself out. Sky clear and brittle as glass.

God damn: Gallagher wasn't going to change his plans.

The snow would melt by Sunday. Certainly it would melt. Gallagher was insisting. He'd been on the phone that morning with the caretaker who'd assured him that the driveway would be plowed by the time Gallagher and his guests arrived. The lodge would be open, ready for occupancy. The power would be on. (McAlster was sure there'd be power out at the camp, there was power elsewhere on the island.) In the lodge there was a kitchen, stocked with canned and bottled goods. Refrigerator and stove. All in working order. McAlster would have aired out the rooms. McAlster was a man you could rely upon. Gallagher had not wanted to change his plans and McAlster agreed, a little snow wouldn't interfere with anyone. The island was so beautiful covered in snow. A shame such a beautiful place was deserted most of the year.

A shame it belongs to people like you.

McAlster, now in his sixties, had been entrusted with overseeing summer residents' properties for decades. Since Gallagher had been a small child. Not once had McAlster spoken with the slightest air of reproach, in Gallagher's hearing. It was Gallagher who felt shame, guilt. His family owned ninety acres of Grindstone Island of which less than five or six were actually used: the rest was woodland, pines and birches. There was a mile of river frontage, of surpassing beauty. Thaddeus Gallagher's father had acquired the property and built the original hunting lodge in the early 1900s, long before the Thousand Islands region was developed for summer tourism. It had been a wilderness, at a remote northern edge of New York State. The small native population of Grindstone Island lived mostly in the area of Grindstone Harbor, in asphalt-sided houses, tar paper shanties, trailers. They owned bait-and-tackle shops, gas stations and roadside restaurants. They were trappers, guides, commercial fishermen and caretakers like McAlster, hiring themselves out to absentee residents like the Gallaghers.

Don't you feel guilty, owning so much property you rarely see Gallagher had asked his father Thaddeus as a young man provoked to ideological quarrels and Thaddeus's reply had been hotly uttered, unhesitating *Those people depend upon us! We hire them. We pay property taxes to pay for their roads, schools, public services. There's a hospital in Grindstone Harbor now, didn't used to be! How'd that happen? Half the population in the Thousand Islands is on welfare in the off-season, who the hell d'you think pays for that?*

Gallagher's anger with his father so choked him, he had trouble breathing in the old man's presence. It was like an asthma attack.

"My father . . ."

Beside him in the passenger's seat of his car Hazel gave Gallagher a shrewd sidelong look. Unconsciously he'd been sucking in his breath. Drumming his fingers on the steering wheel.

"Yes?"

". . . says he wants to meet you, Hazel. But that won't happen."

He'd told her very little about his father. Very little about his family. He supposed she'd heard, from others.

In fact, Thaddeus had telephoned Gallagher the previous week to inquire *This new woman of yours, a cocktail waitress is she, a stripper, call girl with a bastard retarded son? Correct me if I'm wrong.*

Gallagher had hung up the phone without speaking.

Prior to this call, Gallagher had not heard from his father since Christmas 1962 and then it had been Thaddeus's private secretary calling, with the message that his father was on the line to speak with him and Gallagher had said politely *But I'm not on this line. Sorry.*

"Well. If you don't want me to meet your father, I won't."

"You and Zack. Either of you."

Hazel smiled uncertainly. Gallagher knew he made her uneasy, she couldn't read his moods: playful, ironic, sincere. As she couldn't interpret the tone of the more tortuous and meandering of his jazz piano pieces.

"You're too good to meet the man, Hazel. In your soul."

"Am I."

"Hazel, it's true! You're too good, too beautiful and pure-minded to meet a man like Thaddeus Gallagher. You'd be despoiled by his eyes on you. By breathing the same air he breathes."

Why Gallagher was so angry suddenly, he didn't know. Possibly it had something to do with McAlster.

Hazel Jones, William McAlster. Individuals of the servant class. Thaddeus Gallagher would identify Hazel Jones at once.

Behind a slow-moving truck spreading salt on the highway, they were approaching Malin Head Bay. It was nearly 6 P.M. yet the sky was still light. There was an icy glaze over many trees, flashing sunlight like fire. Traffic moved sluggishly along Main Street where only a single wide lane had been plowed.

Gallagher didn't want to think what Grindstone Island would be like.

McAlster had promised him, though. McAlster would never go back on his word.

McAlster would never disappoint Thaddeus Gallagher's son.

Relenting, Gallagher said they could always stay at the Malin Head Inn, if the island didn't work out.

"You aren't worried, Hazel? Are you?"

Hazel laughed. "Worried? Not with you."

She touched his arm to reassure him. A strand of her hair fell against Gallagher's cheek. He felt a choking sensation in his chest.

She'd told him a man had hurt her. He supposed the man had been Zack's father, who had left her, hadn't married her. This would have been almost seven years ago. She'd kissed him and drew away from him telling him she had no wish to be hurt by a man again.

"I'll make it up to you, Hazel. Whatever it was."

Gallagher groped for Hazel's hand and brought it to his lips. He kissed her fingers greedily. Not an erotic kiss unless you knew the desperate ways of Eros. Gallagher had not kissed Hazel that day. They had not been alone together for five minutes. He was weak with desire, and outrage mixed with desire. He would marry Hazel Jones, next time he crossed St. Mary Bridge to Grindstone Island she would be his wife.

McAlster was right, the island was beautiful in snow.

"Our property begins about here. That stone wall."

Hazel was staring through the windshield. The child in the backseat was at last alert, watchful.

"All that is Gallagher property, too. Miles uphill. And along the river."

The River Road had been plowed, if haphazardly. Gallagher drove very slowly. His car was equipped with chains, he was accustomed to driving on icy graveled surfaces. On the island, there were more trees covered in ice, tilted at sharp angles like drunken figures. Some of the birches had shattered and collapsed. Evergreens were tougher, not so extensively damaged. In the road there were fallen tree limbs, Gallagher drove carefully around them.

"You can tell it isn't winter, can't you. By the sun. Yet so much snow. Jesus!"

The river was choppy, wind-churned. Vast, and very beautiful. Before the sudden freeze, the river had thawed; now at the water's edge amid enormous boulders there were jagged ice-spikes, jutting up vertically like stalagmites. Gallagher was conscious of the woman and her child seeing this for the first time.

"That's the lodge, at the top of that hill. Through those evergreens. Over there are guest cabins. It looks as if McAlster has plowed us out, we're in luck for tonight."

The Adirondack-style lodge was the size of a small hotel, made of logs, fieldstone and stucco. Its roof was steep and shingled and it had two massive stone chimneys. Adrift in snow at the crest of a hill was a tennis court. There was a gabled three-car garage, a former stable. High overhead a hawk drifted, lazily dipped and turned on widespread wings. The sky looked like glass about to shatter. Gallagher was seeing Hazel Jones at last beginning to see *He is rich. His family is rich.*

That hadn't been Gallagher's reason for bringing them here. He didn't think so.

18

❋ ❋ ❋

A rough wild game! Driving her like a panicked animal along the rows of cornstalks. Drunk-looking cornstalks broken and dessicated in the heat of early autumn and the browned tassels slapping and cutting at her face. Herschel clapped his hands laughing his high-pitched heehaw laugh *Git along little dawgie git along little weenie* long-limbed and loose-jointed and he was breathing through his mouth as he ran, as she ran, a flame-like sensation in her belly, she too was laughing, clumsy and stumbling on her small legs so she fell to one knee, she fell more than once, scrambled to her feet before the scraped welt filled in with gritty blood, if she could make her way to the end of the row of cornstalks to the edge of the farmer's field and to the road and to the cemetery beyond—

How the cornfield game ended, Rebecca could never recall.

19

※ ※ ※

"Mom*ma*? Are we?"

It was morning. The morning of Holy Saturday. Bright, and gusty with wind. Hazel Jones was brushing her hair in swift punishing strokes ignoring the fretting child pulling at her.

In the bureau mirror a face floated wan and indistinct as if underwater. Not her face but Hazel Jones's young face smiling defiantly.

You! What right, to be here!

She'd gotten through the first night on Grindstone Island and she believed she would get through the second night on Grindstone Island and by that time it would be decided.

"Momma? *Mom*ma!"

The child had slept fitfully the night before. She'd heard him, in the room adjoining her own, whimpering in his sleep. Lately, he'd begun grinding his teeth, too. The wind!—the damned wind had kept him awake, unnerved him. Not a single wind but many winds blowing off the St. Lawrence River and across Lake Ontario to the west confused with human voices, muffled shouts and laughter.

You! you! such laughter seems to accuse.

Hazel had wakened early in the unfamiliar bed not knowing where she was at first and which time in her life this was and her heart pounded hotly in her chest as the voices grew bolder, jeering *You! Jew-girl you have no right to be here.*

She had not heard such voices in years. She had not had such a thought in years. She rose from bed shaken, frightened.

But it was Gallagher who'd brought her here. Gallagher, her friend.

Through the front windows of the room you could see another island floating in the glittery river. Beyond that the dense Canadian shore at Gananoque.

Gallagher's family lodge was even larger than it appeared from the foot of the driveway. It had been built into a hill, three floors and a more recently constructed wing connected to the main house by a flagstone terrace, now drifted in snow.

Hazel Jones, seeing the lodge, had laughed. A private residence, of such dimensions!

For the briefest of moments seeing the Gallagher property as Jacob Schwart might see it. The man's mocking laughter mingling with Hazel Jones's laughter.

Embarrassed, Gallagher had said yes the place was large, but it was really very private. And most of the lodge was shut off for the winter, they'd be using only a few rooms.

Hazel understood that Gallagher was both ashamed of his family's wealth, and vain of it. He could not help himself. He had no clear knowledge of himself. His hatred of his father was a sacred hatred, Hazel knew not to interfere. Nor would she believe in this hatred utterly.

Gallagher had brought her to this room that was more a suite than a room, with a child's room adjoining, for Zack. His own room, he told her, was close by, down the hall. His manner was outwardly contained, exuberant. This was the first time the three of them had gone away together, he was their host and responsible for their well-being. Setting Hazel's lightweight suitcase onto her bed—old, brass, four-poster, with a quilt coverlet in pale blues and lavenders—he stood staring at it for a long moment his breath quickened from the stairs and his face flushed and uncertain and Hazel could see him summoning the precise words he wished to speak, to impress upon her.

"Hazel. I hope you will comfortable here."

It was a remark that carried with it a deeper meaning. At that moment Gallagher could not bring himself to look at Hazel.

If Zack had not been with them, investigating his room (a boys' room, with bunk beds, Zack would sleep in the upper bunk), Hazel knew that Gallagher would have touched her. He would have kissed her. He would have framed her face in his large hands, and kissed her. And Hazel would have kissed him in return, not stiffening in his embrace as sometimes she did involuntarily but standing very still.

Pleading *Don't love me! Please.*

As Gallagher would relent with his hurt, hopeful smile *All right Hazel! I can wait.*

Zack nudged against Hazel's thigh: "Momma! Are we going to marry Mr. Gallagher?"

Rudely she was wakened from her trance. She'd been brushing her hair in long swift strokes in front of the crook-backed mirror.

Overnight Zack had begun to call her "Momma"—no longer "Mommy." Sometimes the word was a grudging syllable: "Mom" pronounced "M'm."

By instinct the child knew that speech is music, to the ear. And speech can be a music to hurt the ear.

He'd been awake and out of bed for more than forty minutes, and was restless. Maybe he was feeling uncomfortable in this new place. Pushing against Hazel's thigh, nudging her hard enough to bruise if she didn't prevent him. With the back of the hairbrush she swiped playfully at him but he persisted, "I said *are we*, Momma? Are we going to marry Mr. Gallagher?"

"Zack, not so loud."

"Momma I *said*—"

"No."

Hazel gripped his shoulders, not to shake him but to hold him still. His small body quivered in indignation. His eyes that were dark, moist and glittering, were fixed on hers in a defiant look that roused her to anger, except Hazel was never angry. She was not a mother who raised her hand to her child, nor even her voice. If Gallagher should overhear this exchange! She would be mortified, she could not bear it.

Her face wasn't yet Hazel Jones's face, but darker-skinned, a rich oily-olive skin she would disguise with lighter makeup, liquid and then powder. This makeup she would take care to extend onto her throat, gradually tapering off, always subtly, meticulously. And she would take care to disguise the fine pale scars at her hairline, that Gallagher had never seen. But her hair had been brushed vigorously and bristled now with static electricity, it was a warm chestnut hue streaked with dark red, it was a hue that seemed altogether natural to her, as Hazel Jones. She wore neatly pressed gray woollen slacks and a rose-colored woollen sweater with a detachable lace collar. For this weekend visit to Grindstone Island Hazel had brought two pairs of neatly pressed woollen slacks and a beige cable-knit sweater and the sweater with the lace collar and two cotton blouses. Hazel Jones was a young woman of the utmost propriety in her dress as in her manner. Gallagher laughed at her Hazel Jones ways, she was so proper. Yet Hazel understood that Gallagher adored her for those Hazel Jones ways and would not wish her otherwise. (Gallagher continued to see other women. Meaning, Gallagher slept with other women. When he could, when it was convenient. Hazel knew, and was not jealous. Never would she have inquired after Gallagher's private, sexual life apart from her.) As, at Zimmerman Brothers Pianos & Music Supplies, the salesclerk Hazel Jones had established for herself a personality distinct as a comic strip character: Olive Oyl, Jiggs-and-Maggie, Dick Tracy, Brenda Starr Girl Reporter. The deepest truth of the American soul is that it is shallow as a comic strip is shallow and behind her shiny glass-topped counter in Zimmermans' there was Hazel Jones prettily composed, smiling in expectation. Like Gallagher, Edgar Zimmerman adored Hazel Jones. Could not stop touching her with his fluttery little-man's hands that were dry and hot with yearning. *Bastard. Nazi.* Hazel Jones's smile wavered only when Edgar too emphatically touched her arm as he spoke with her in a lull between customers, otherwise her hands rested slender and serene on the shiny glass-topped counter. And Zimmerman's customers had grown to know Hazel, and stood by patiently, ignoring the other salesclerks until Hazel was free to wait on them.

"Momma *are we*! Are we going to marry Mr. *Gallag*her!"

"Zack, I've told you—"

"No no no no *no*. No *Mom*ma."

Hazel resented it, Zack pretending to be a child. Childish. She knew, in his heart he was an adult like Hazel Jones.

"Zack, what is this 'we'? There is no 'we.' Only a man and a woman get married, nobody else. Don't be silly."

"I'm not silly. *You're* silly."

Zack was becoming wild, uncontrollable. Back home he would never have dared ask such questions. He was forbidden to speak familiarly about "Mr. Gallagher" who had come into their lives to change their lives as he was forbidden to speak familiarly about "Hazel Jones."

As, in Malin Head Bay, a very long time ago now it seemed, he had been forbidden to ask about the pebbles vanishing one by one from the windowsill.

This snowy-glaring island called Grindstone in the choppy St. Lawrence River seemed to have unleashed, in Zack, a mutinous spirit. Already this morning he'd left their rooms and had been running on the stairs and skidding on carpets in the hallway and when Hazel had called him back he'd come reluctant as a bad-behaving dog. Now, restless, he was prowling about her room: poking in a step-in cedar closet, bouncing on the brass four-poster bed which Hazel had neatly made up as soon as she'd slipped from between the bedclothes. (No unmade or rumpled beds in any household in which Hazel Jones lived! It was the one thing that roused Hazel to something like moral indignation.) On the bureau was a carved antique clock with a glass face that opened: Zack was moving the black metallic hands around, and Hazel worried he might break them.

"You're hungry, honey. I'll make breakfast."

She snatched his hands in hers. For a moment it seemed he might fight her, then he relented.

Unfamiliar surroundings made Zack nervous, antic. He'd badly wanted to come to Grindstone Island for the weekend, yet he was anxious about changes in the routine of his life. Hans Zimmerman had told Hazel that for the young pianist as gifted as her son, his life must revolve around the piano. Always Zack woke at the same time each morning, early. Always he practiced a half-hour at the piano before leaving for school. After school, he practiced no less than two hours and sometimes more, depending upon the difficulty of the lesson. If he struck a wrong note he made himself start a piece from the beginning: there could be no deviating from this ritual. Hazel could not interfere. If she tried to make him stop, to go to bed, he might lapse into a temper tantrum; his nerves were strung tight. Hazel had seen him seated at the piano with his small shoulders raised as if he were about to plunge into battle. She was proud of him, and anxious for him. She took comfort in hearing him practice piano for at such times she understood that both Hazel Jones and her son Zacharias were in the right place, they had been spared death on the Poor Farm Road for this.

"And you can play piano, honey. All you want."

As Gallagher had promised, there was a piano downstairs in the lodge. The previous evening, Gallagher had played before supper, boisterous American popular songs and show tunes, and Zack had sat beside him on the piano bench. At first Zack had been shy, but Gallagher had drawn him into playing with him, jazzy companionable four-hand renditions of popular songs. And they'd played one of Zack's Kabalevsky studies from the *Pianoforte* lesson book, boogie-woogie style that made Zack laugh wildly.

The piano was a matte-black baby grand, not in prime condition. It had not been tuned for years, and some of the keys stuck.

Gallagher said, "Music can be fun, kid. Not always serious. In the end, a piano is only a piano."

Zack had looked mystified by the remark.

In the kitchen, Gallagher had helped Hazel prepare supper. They'd bought groceries together in Watertown, for the weekend. Hazel had asked him, "*Is* a piano only a piano?" and Gallagher had said, snorting, "Only a piano, darling! Sure as hell not a coffin." Hazel had not liked this remark which was typical of Gallagher when he'd had a drink or two and was in his swaggering boisterous mood out of which his eyes, plaintive and accusing, adoring and resentful, swung onto her too emphatically. At such time Hazel stiffened and looked away, as if she had not seen.

I don't know what your words mean. I am shocked by you, I will not hear you. Don't touch me!

She could guess what it had been like, living with Gallagher as his former wife had done for eight years. He was the kindest of men and yet even his kindness could be engulfing, overbearing.

With some comical mishaps, and a good deal of eye-watering smoke, Gallagher started a birch-log fire in an immense cobblestone fireplace in the living room, and they ate on a small plank table in front of the fire;

Zack had been very hungry, and had eaten too quickly, and nearly made himself sick. In the kitchen, he'd been upset by the tile floor: a black-and-white diamond pattern that made him dizzy, it seemed to be moving, writhing. In the living room, he'd been concerned that sparks from the fire would fly out onto the hook rug, and he'd been fascinated and appalled by the several mounted animal heads—black bear, lynx, buck with twelve-point antlers—on the lodge walls. Gallagher had told Zack to ignore the "trophies," they were disgusting, but Zack had stared, silent. Especially, the buck's head and antlers had drawn his attention for it was positioned over the fireplace and its marble eyes seemed unnaturally large, glassily ironic. The animal's fur was a burnished brown, but appeared slightly matted, marred. A frail cobweb hung from the highest point of the antlers.

Hazel had taken the boy upstairs to bed shortly after nine o'clock though she doubted he would sleep, he was over-stimulated and hot-skinned, and had never before slept in a bunk bed.

Still, he'd insisted upon climbing the little ladder, to sleep in the top bunk. The thought of sleeping in the lower bunk seemed to frighten him.

Hazel had allowed him to keep a lamp burning beside the bed, and she'd promised not to shut the door between their rooms. If he woke agitated in the night, he would need to know where he was.

"Please be good, Zack! It's a beautiful morning, and this is a beautiful place. We've never been in such a beautiful place, have we? It's an island. It's special. If you want to 'marry' Mr. Gallagher you would have to live with him in a house, wouldn't you? This is like living with him, this weekend. This is his house, one of his family's houses. He will be hurt if you aren't good."

She spoke as if to a very young child. There was the pretense between them, that Zack was a child.

Hazel rebuttoned his flannel shirt, he'd buttoned crookedly. She pulled a sweater over his head, and combed his hair. She kissed his warm forehead. So excited! Feeling the child's pulses beat quick as her own.

Neither of them belonged here. But they had been invited, and they were here.

Hazel led Zack out of the room. The air in the hallway was rather drafty, with an acrid smoke-smell from the previous night.

Except for the wind, and a sound of ice melting, dripping from the eaves, and the harsh, intermittent cries of crows, the house was very still. The sky was scribbled in fine, faint clouds through which the sun shone powerfully. It would be one of those balmy-wintry days. Hazel gripped Zack's hand to keep him from running along the corridor and a wild thought came to her that she and the child might enter Gallagher's bedroom, which was close by: tease the sleep-dazed man awake, laugh at him. Gallagher was a man who loved to be teased and laughed at, to a degree. She and Zack could climb onto the bed in which Gallagher slept . . .

Instead they paused outside the door of his bedroom, to hear him snoring inside: a wet, gurgling sound labored as if the man were struggling uphill with an awkwardly shaped weight. It was somehow very funny that the snoring-snorting noises were not at all rhythmic, but uneven; there were pauses of several seconds, pure silence. Zack began laughing, and Hazel pressed her fingers over his mouth to muffle the sound. Then Hazel too began laughing, they had to hurry away.

The flame of madness leapt between them. Hazel feared that the child would catch it from her, he would be uncontrollable for hours. Zack slipped from Hazel's grasp, to prowl about the downstairs of the lodge. There was so much to see, with Gallagher not present. Hazel was most interested in a wall of framed photographs of which Gallagher had spoken slightingly, the day before. Clearly, the Gallagher family thought highly of themselves. Hazel supposed it was a sign of wealth: naturally you would think highly of yourself, and wish to display that thought to others.

Amid the faces of strangers she sought Gallagher's familiar face. Suddenly, she was eager to see him as a Gallagher, a younger son. There: a photograph of Chet Gallagher with his family, taken when Gallagher was in his mid-twenties, with a startlingly full head of dark hair, a squinting, somewhat abashed smile. There was Gallagher a skinny boy of about twelve, in white T-shirt and swim trunks, squatting awkwardly on the deck of a sailboat; there was Gallagher a few years older, muscled in shoulders and upper arms, gripping a tennis racquet. And Gallagher in his mid-twenties in a light-colored sport coat, surprised in the midst of laughter, both arms flung around the bare shoulders of two young women in summer dresses and high-heeled sandals. This photograph had been taken on the lawn outside the lodge, in summer.

Beautiful women! Far more beautiful than Hazel Jones could ever make herself.

Hazel wondered: was one of the women Gallagher's former wife? Veronica, her name was. Gallagher rarely spoke of his former wife except to remark it was damned good luck they hadn't had children.

Hazel knew, Gallagher had to believe this. He was a man who told himself things to believe, in the presence of witnesses.

In many of the Gallagher photographs there was a broad-chested man with a large, solid head, a blunt handsome face like something hacked out of stone. This man was stocky, self-confident. Always in the photographs he was seated at the center, hands on his knees. In photographs taken when he appeared older, he was gripping a cane in a rakish gesture. His face resembled Gallagher's only around the eyes, that were heavy-lidded, jovial and malicious. He was of moderate height with legs that appeared foreshortened. There was something stubby about him as if a part of his body were missing but you could not see what.

This had to be the father, Thaddeus.

In a cluster of photographs, Thaddeus was seated with a mannequin figure that looked familiar to Hazel: ex-Governor Dewey? A short man with sleekly black hair, prim little mustache like something pasted on his upper lip, shiny protuberant black eyes. In those photographs in which others appeared, Thaddeus Gallagher and Dewey were seated together at the very center, glancing toward the camera as if interrupted in conversation.

These were summer photos of years ago, judging from the men's attire. Thomas E. Dewey a dapper little mannequin in sports clothes, very stiff in his posture, purposeful.

Those others. Who surround us. Our enemies.

The flat of his hand striking the newspaper's front page, on the oilcloth covering of the kitchen table. His rage spilled out suddenly, you could not predict.

Except she'd come to know: all politicians, public figures were objects of his hatred. All figures of wealth. Enemies.

"It's another time now, Pa. History has changed, now."

Strange, Hazel had spoken aloud. She was not one to speak aloud even when safely alone.

Seeing then another photo of Gallagher as a boy: looking about sixteen, long-faced, somber, with a mildly blemished skin, posed in a suit and tie in front of a small grand piano, on what appeared to be a stage. Beside him stood an older man in formal clothes, regarding the camera sternly: Hans Zimmerman.

"Zack! Come look."

Hazel smiled, Gallagher was so young. Yet unmistakably himself as Zimmerman, though much younger, in his early forties perhaps, was unmistakably himself. You could see that the piano instructor took a certain pride in his pupil. Hazel felt a curious sensation, almost of pain, dismay.

"I don't love him. Do I?"

It came over her then, she would never fully know him. The previous night in bed in these unfamiliar surroundings she had thought of Gallagher close by, she'd known he was thinking of her, hoping that she would come to him; she had felt a stab of panic, in her dread of knowing him. Since Tignor, she had not wanted to make love with any man. She did not trust any man, not to enter her body in that way.

Yet now it seemed obvious, she could not know Chet Gallagher even if she became his lover. Even if she lived with him. Even if he became a father to Zack, as he wished. So much of the man's soul had been squandered, lost.

"Zack? Honey? Come see what I found."

But Zack was preoccupied, elsewhere. Hazel went to find him, hoping he wasn't being destructive.

There he was standing on one of the leather sofas, peering at the "trophy" mounted over the fireplace mantel. The air here smelled of woodsmoke. How like her son, drawn to morbid things!

"Oh, honey. Come down from there."

In daylight the buck was more visible, exposed. A large, handsome head. And the antlers remarkable. You knew this was merely an object, lifeless, stuffed and mounted, eyes shining with ironic knowledge but in fact mere glass. The heraldic antlers were foolish, comical. The deer's silvery brown hair was matted and marred and Hazel saw numerous wisps of cobwebs on them. Yet the trophy was strangely imposing, unnerving. Somehow, you believed it might still be alive. Hazel understood why her son was drawn to stare at it in fascination and revulsion.

Hazel came up quietly behind him, to nudge him in the ribs.

Saying, in her playful Hazel Jones voice, "Somebody 'married' him."

By the time Gallagher came downstairs, in the late morning, Hazel and Zack had had breakfast. Hazel had cleaned the kitchen: the stove top, and oven; the counters, that were mysteriously sticky; the cupboards that required fresh paper liners, and which Hazel neatly arranged, turning the labels of cans to face out. She'd opened windows to air out the woodsmoke and musty odors. She'd straightened stacks of back issues of *Life, Collier's, Time, Fortune, Reader's Digest*. Dragging a chair to stand on, she'd dusted each of the "trophies," taking most care with the buck's antlers. When Gallagher saw her Hazel was sitting in a patch of sunshine leafing through *My Thousand Islands: From the Time of Revolution to Now*. Close by, Zack was practicing one of his Kabalevsky studies.

"My little family! Good morning."

Gallagher meant to be jokey, jocular, waking so much later than his guests, but his quivering red-rimmed eyes swam with tears, Hazel glanced up involuntarily to see.

20

❀ ❀ ❀

He was saying, reasoning, "Why should it matter so much, Hazel? If people are married, or not? McAlster is only a caretaker. He doesn't know you, or anyone who knows you."

But Hazel Jones did not want to meet the caretaker.

"But why not, Hazel? You are here, and he knows I have guests. It's perfectly natural. He opened the house for us, he'll want to know if there is anything he can do for you or Zack."

But Hazel did not want to meet the caretaker.

Running away upstairs when McAlster's pickup approached the house.

Gallagher was amused. Gallagher was trying not to be annoyed.

He loved Hazel Jones! He did respect her. Except her quick bright laughter grated against his nerves, sometimes. When her eyes were frightened, and her mouth persisted in smiling. Her way of speaking airily and lightly and yet evasively like an actress reciting lines in which she can't believe.

Gallagher understood: she'd been wounded in some way. Whoever was the father of the child had wounded her, surely. She was uneasy in situations that threatened to expose her. It was a wonder she hadn't worn white gloves, pillbox hat, high-heeled shoes to Grindstone Island. Gallagher vowed to win her trust, that he might set about correcting her: for Hazel Jones's imagination was primitive.

His Albany relatives would see through her awkward poise, at once. Gallagher dreaded the prospect.

His father! But Gallagher would not think of his father, in terms of Hazel Jones. He was determined that they would never meet.

Yet it was ironic, that he should fall in love with a woman who, in her soul, was more a Gallagher than he was. More conventional in her beliefs, her "morality." What is good, what is bad. What is proper, what is not-proper. Hazel hid from the caretaker because she could not bear it, that a stranger might suppose she was Gallagher's mistress, spending Easter weekend with him.

Other women whom Gallagher had brought to stay with him on Grindstone Island hadn't been so self-conscious. These were women of a certain degree of education, experience. An employee like McAlster had no existence for them. Nor would they have cared what he thought of them, not for a moment.

Not that McAlster wasn't the most tactful of men. All Gallagher employees, on Grindstone Island or on the mainland, were tactful. They were hardly likely to ask their employers awkward questions, or in fact any questions at all. McAlster had known Chet Gallagher's wife Veronica for six or seven years always politely calling her "Mrs. Gallagher" and several summers ago when there apparently ceased to be a "Mrs. Chet Gallagher," McAlster had certainly known not to inquire after her.

When McAlster drove away in his pickup truck, Gallagher called teasingly up the stairs:

"Haz-el! Hazel Jones! Coast's clear."

They went outside. They hiked down to the river, to the Gallaghers' dock.

In the bright sunshine the river was starkly beautiful, a deep cobalt-blue, not so rough as usual. The wind had dropped, the temperature was 43° F. Everywhere snow was melting, there was a frenzy of melting, dripping. Gallagher wore dark glasses to shield his eyes against the sun clattering like castanets inside his skull.

Am I hungover? I am not.

A manic little tune, of castanets. Fortunately, Hazel could not hear it.

How striking the view of the St. Lawrence, from the Gallaghers' thirty-foot dock! Gallagher, who had not been out on the dock since the previous summer, and certainly would not be there now except for his guest, pointed out the lighthouse at Malin Head Bay, several miles to the east; in the other direction, a smaller lighthouse at Gananoque, in Ontario.

Hearing himself say, who had not sailed in twelve years, "In the summer, maybe we can sail here. You and I and Zack. Would you like that, Hazel?"

Hazel said yes she would like that.

It was like Hazel to revert to her usual mood. As soon as she'd come downstairs, the issue of the caretaker was forgotten. There could be no protracted hardness or opposition in Hazel, always her moods were melting, quicksilver. Gallagher had never met so intensely feminine a woman, she was fascinating to him. Yet she would not make love with him, she held herself at a little distance from him, uneasy.

He couldn't resist teasing her. She was shielding her eyes against the sun-glare, looking out. "He did ask after my guests. The caretaker. Asking if your rooms were all right and I told him yes, I thought so."

Quickly Hazel said yes their rooms were fine. She was not to be baited by Gallagher. She asked if Mr. McEnnis would be coming back the next day.

Gallagher corrected her: " 'McAlster.' His name is 'McAlster.' His people emigrated from Glasgow when he was two years old, he's lived on Grindstone Island for more than sixty years. No, he won't be coming back tomorrow."

They were hiking along the river's edge. Hazel would have descended a treacherous rocky path to the beach, where broken slabs of ice glittered in the sun like enormous teeth, and where storm debris lay in tangled heaps amid sand hardened like concrete, but Gallagher restrained her, alarmed. "Hazel, no. You'll turn an ankle."

They'd hiked more than a half-mile along the river and had some distance to retrace, uphill. From this perspective the Gallagher property appeared immense.

Zack had preferred to remain indoors practicing piano. Because of Easter weekend his Saturday lesson had been postponed until Tuesday after school. Hazel had told Gallagher that Zack had been outdoors for a while, earlier that morning; she spoke apologetically, as if the child's lack of interest in the outdoors would annoy Gallagher.

Not at all! Gallagher was on the boy's side. He intended always to be on the boy's side. His own father had not much interest in his youngest son except to be "disappointed" at crucial times, and Gallagher did not intend to model himself after that father. *I will make both of you need me and then you will love me.*

Gallagher was surprised, Hazel Jones turned out to be so much more robust than he'd expected. She was hiking uphill with less effort than he, scarcely short of breath. She was sure-footed, eager. She exuded an air of happiness, well-being. The mid-April thaw was exhilarating to her, the great flaring sun did not overwhelm her but seemed to draw her forward.

Gallagher had wanted to talk with her. He must talk with her, alone. But she eased away from him, as if impatient. Slipping and sliding in the melting snow, that didn't vex her but made her laugh. Nor did she seem to mind that evergreen boughs were dripping onto her head. She was sure-footed and exuberant as a young animal that has been penned up. Gallagher sweated inside his clothes, began to fall behind. Damned if he would call out to the woman, to wait for him. His heart beat hard in his chest.

You love me. You must love me.

Why don't you love me!

Hazel was charmingly dressed for their hike. She wore a windbreaker and a girl's rubber boots and on her head was a fawn-colored fedora she'd found in a closet at the lodge. Gallagher was forced to recall how when he touched Hazel, in their tender, intimate moments, when he kissed her, she went very still; like a captive animal that does not resist, yet remains slightly stiff, vigilant. You would not guess that the woman's body was so young, supple and tremulous with life. Behind her clothes the female body, hot-skinned.

Overhead, hawks were circling. Always there were wide-winged sparrow hawks on Grindstone Island, along the river's edge. They swooped to their prey in open areas, it was rare for a hawk to penetrate the pine woods. Now their swift shadows passed over the snow-stubbled grass and over Hazel's figure, several hawks cruising so low that Gallagher could see the sharp outlines of their beaks.

Hazel, too, noticed the hawks, glancing up uneasily. She began to walk faster as if to elude them.

Damn! Gallagher saw that she was ascending a trail, the rutty remains of a trail, leading farther uphill; Gallagher had intended that they take another fork and return to the lodge, he'd had enough of hiking for one day. But Hazel hiked on, oblivious of her companion. The hill they were climbing was a small mountain, densely wooded, with a jagged, uneven surface, sharp diagonal outcroppings of shale ridged with ice; for sunshine came only in sporadic patches here, the interior of the pine woods was shaded, chill. The summit of the hill was impassable, Gallagher recalled. He had not hiked this damned trail in twenty-five years.

"Hazel! Let's turn back."

But Hazel plunged ahead, unheeding. Gallagher had no choice but to follow.

He'd bought a house for her and the child in Watertown. A handsome red-brick colonial with two separate entrances, overlooking a Watertown park. But Hazel would not step inside.

In her soul, a shopgirl. An usherette. Shrinking in shame from the judgment of a hired caretaker.

A mistake, loving Hazel Jones. It would be a terrible mistake to marry her.

Gallagher wasn't accustomed to such physical stamina in any female. On Grindstone Island, it was rare for females to hike this mountain. His former wife would have laughed at him if he'd suggested such a hike in the melting snow. Gallagher had come to associate females with smoky bars, cocktail lounges, dimly lighted expensive restaurants. At least, females he found sexually desirable. And there was Hazel in her windbreaker and man's hat, hiking a steep hill without a backward glance. Other female guests at Grindstone Island, strolling with Gallagher on his family property, had stayed close beside him, attentive to his conversation.

Another peculiar thing: Hazel was the only visitor to the lodge in Gallagher's memory, female or male, who had not commented on the display of photographs. Guests were always exclaiming at the "known" faces amid the Gallaghers and their friends, looking so thoroughly at home. Some of the individuals pictured with the Gallaghers were wealthy, influential men whose faces Hazel would not have recognized, but there were numerous public figures: Wendell Wilkie, Thomas E. Dewey, Robert Taft, Harold Stassen, John Bricker and Earl Warren, Dewey's vice-presidential running mates in

1944 and 1948. And there were Republican state congressmen, senators. It was Gallagher's habit to speak disdainfully of his father's political friends, but Hazel had not given him the opportunity for she'd said nothing.

She was ignorant of politics, Gallagher supposed. She had not been educated, hadn't graduated from high school. She knew little of the world of men, action, history. Though she read the occasional newspaper columns Gallagher wrote, she did not offer any criticism or commentary. *She knows so little. She will protect me.*

At last, Hazel had stopped hiking. She was waiting for Gallagher where the trail ended in a snarl of underbrush, in the pine woods. When he joined her, out of breath, sweating, she pointed at a scattering of feathers on the ground, amid pine needles and glistening ice-rivulets. The feathers were no more than two or three inches long, powdery-gray, very soft and fine. There were small bones, particles of flesh still attached. Gallagher identified the remains of an owl's prey. "There are owls everywhere in these woods. We heard them last night. Screech owls."

"And owls kill other birds? Smaller birds?" The question was naive, wondering. Hazel spoke with a pained expression, almost a grimace.

"Well, owls are predators, darling. They must kill something."

"Predators have no choice, have they?"

"Not unless they want to starve. And eventually, as they age, they do starve, and other predators eat them."

Gallagher spoke lightly, to deflect Hazel's somber tone. Like most women she wished to exaggerate the significance of small deaths.

Hazel's cheeks were flushed from the climb, her eyes were widened and alert, glistening with moisture. She appeared feverish, still excited. There was something heated and sexual about her. Almost, Gallagher shrank from her.

He was taller than Hazel Jones by several inches. He might have gripped her shoulders, and kissed her, hard. Yet he shrank from her, his eyes behind the dark glasses tremulous.

Damn: he was sweating, yet shivering. At this height the air was cold enough, thin gusts of wind from the river struck his exposed face like knife blades. Gallagher felt a stab of childish resentment, here was a woman failing to protect a man from getting sick.

He pulled at her arm, and led her back down the trail. She came at once, docile.

" 'The owl of Minerva soars only at dusk.' "

Hazel spoke in her strange, vague, wondering voice as if another spoke through her. Gallagher glanced at her, surprised.

"Why do you say that, Hazel? Those words?"

But Hazel seemed not to know, why.

Gallagher said, "It's a melancholy observation. It's the German philosopher Hegel's remark and it seems to mean that wisdom comes to us only too late."

" 'The owl of Minerva.' But who is Minerva?"

"The Roman goddess of wisdom."

"Some long-ago time, we're talking of?"

"A very long time ago, Hazel."

Afterward Gallagher would recall this curious exchange. He would have liked to ask Hazel whom she was echoing, who'd made this remark in her hearing, except he knew that she would become evasive and manage not to answer his question. Her manner was naive and girlish and somehow he did not trust it, not completely.

"Why is it, do you think, 'the owl of Minerva soars only at dusk'? Must it always be so?"

"Hazel, I have no idea. It's really just a remark."

She was so damned literal-minded! Gallagher would have to be careful what he told Hazel, especially if she became his wife. She would believe him without question.

They left the densely wooded area and were descending the hill in the direction of the lodge. Here in the open sunshine Gallagher would have been blinded without his dark glasses. A smell of skunk lifted teasingly to their nostrils, faint at first and then stronger. It might have been emanating from a stand of birch trees, or from one of the guest cabins. At a distance the smell of skunk can be half-pleasurable but it is not so pleasurable at close range. That inky-cobwebby odor that can turn nauseating if you blunder too close.

Families of skunks sometimes hibernated beneath the outbuildings. The warm weather would have roused them.

"Skunks have to live somewhere. Just like us."

Hazel spoke playfully. Gallagher laughed. He was liking Hazel Jones again now that she wasn't leading him up the damned mountain to a heart attack.

Gallagher tried the doors of several cabins until he found one that wasn't locked. Inside, the air was cold and very still. Like an indrawn breath it seemed to Gallagher who was feeling unaccountably excited.

The cabin was made of weatherized logs, built above a small glittering stream. Nearby were birch trees whose trunks were blindingly white in the sunshine. The interior of the cabin was partly shaded and partly blinding. There was a faint but pungent odor here of skunk. There were twin beds, new-looking mattresses loosely covered with sheets, and pillows without pillowcases. On the floor was a hook rug. Standing inside the cabin, with Hazel Jones, Gallagher felt a rush of emotion so powerful it left him weak. He had an urgent impulse to talk to her, to explain himself. He had not talked very seriously with her since coming to the island and their time together was rapidly running out. Tomorrow he would have to drive his little family back to Watertown, their individual lives would resume. He had bought a beautiful house for Hazel and the child but they had not yet come to live with him.

No child. He had no child. *If you have lost your way it is best to have no child.*

It was then that Gallagher began to speak haphazardly. He heard himself tell Hazel Jones how as a boy he'd camped in the woods on summer nights, alone. Not with his brothers but alone. He had a "pup" tent with mosquito netting. The guest cabins hadn't been built yet. Noises in the woods had frightened him, he'd hardly slept at all, but the experiences had been profound, somehow. He wondered if all profound experiences occur when you're alone, and frightened.

It was like wartime in a way, sleeping outdoors, in tents. Except in wartime you are so exhausted you have no trouble sleeping.

He told Hazel that his father had built most of the cabins after the war. Thaddeus had expanded the lodge, bought more land along the river. In fact, the Gallaghers owned property elsewhere in the Thousand Islands which was being developed, very profitably. Thaddeus Gallagher had made money during wartime and he'd made a lot more money, after: tax laws highly favorable to the Gallagher Media Group had been passed by the Republican-dominated New York State Legislature in the early 1950s.

(Why was Gallagher telling this to Hazel Jones? Did he want to impress her? Did he want her to know that he was a rich man's son, yet innocent of acquiring riches, himself? Hazel could have no way of knowing if Gallagher shared in any of his family money or if—just maybe!—he'd been disinherited.)

Hazel had never asked Gallagher about his family, no more than she would have asked him about his former marriage. Hazel Jones was not one to ask personal questions. Yet now she asked him, with a startling bluntness, if he'd been in the war?

"The war? Oh, Hazel."

Gallagher's wartime experience was not a subject he spoke of easily. His brash swaggering jocular manner could not accommodate it. His eyes snatched at Hazel Jones's eyes, that were so glistening, intense. Just inside the cabin door they stood close together yet not touching. They were very aware of each other. In this small space their intimacy was unnerving to Gallagher.

"Did you see the death camps?"

"No."

"You didn't see the death camps?"

"I was in northern Italy. I was hospitalized there."

"There were no death camps in Italy?"

It seemed to be a question. Gallagher was uncertain how to answer. While he'd been overseas, at first in France and then in the Italian countryside north of Brescia, he had known nothing about the infamous Nazi death camps. He had not really known much about his own experience. Twenty-three days after landing in Europe he'd been struck by shrapnel in his back, knees. Around his neck he'd worn a collar thick as a horse collar and he'd gotten very sick with infections, and later with morphine. He understood that he'd witnessed ugly things but he had no access to them, directly. It was as if a scrim had grown across his vision, like a membrane.

Now Hazel Jones was regarding him with a curious avid hunger. Gallagher could smell the fever-heat of the woman's body, that was new to him, very arousing.

"Why did the Nazis want to kill so many people? What does it mean, some people are 'unclean'—'impure'—'life unworthy life'?"

"Hazel, the Nazis were madmen. It doesn't matter what they meant."

"The Nazis were madmen?"

Again it seemed to be a question. Hazel spoke with a peculiar vehemence, as if Gallagher had said something meant to be funny.

"Certainly. They were madmen, and murderers."

"But when Jews came to the United States, the ships carrying them were turned away. The Americans didn't want them, no more than the Nazis wanted them."

"Hazel, no. I don't think so."

"You don't think so?"

"No. I don't."

Gallagher had removed his dark glasses. He fumbled to slip them into his jacket pocket, but they slipped from his fingers to the floor. He was startled and somewhat repelled by Hazel's intensity, her voice that was strident, uncanny. This was not Hazel Jones's melodic female voice but another's, Gallagher had never heard before.

"No, Hazel. I'm sure that wasn't the case, what you're saying."

"It wasn't?"

"It was a diplomatic issue. If we're talking about the same thing."

Gallagher spoke uncertainly. He wasn't sure of his information, the subject was vague to him, distasteful. He was trying to remember but could not. His breathing was coming quickly as if he were still hiking uphill.

"The ships docked in New York harbor but immigration officials wouldn't let the refugees in. There were children, babies. There were hundreds of people. They were sent back to Europe, to die."

"But why did they return to Europe?" Gallagher asked. He had a flash of insight: he could debate this. "Why, if they might have gone elsewhere? Anywhere?"

"They couldn't go anywhere else. They had to return to Europe, to die."

"There were refugees who went to Haiti, I think. South America. Some refugees went as far away as Singapore."

Gallagher spoke uncertainly. He really didn't know. Vaguely he recalled the editorials in the Gallagher newspapers, as in many American newspapers, in the years before Pearl Harbor, arguing against American intervention in Europe. The Gallagher newspapers were very much opposed to F.D.R., in editorials F.D.R. was charged with being susceptible to Jewish influences, bribery. In the columns of certain commentators F.D.R. was identified as a Jew, like his Secretary of the Treasury Henry Morgenthau, Jr. For a confused moment the scrim shifted in Gallagher's memory and he saw with a child's curious eyes, a sign in the lobby of a dazzling Miami Beach hotel JEWISH PERSONS ARE ASKED NOT TO FREQUENT THESE PREMISES. When had that been, in the early 1930s? Before the Gallaghers acquired their private Palm Beach residence on the ocean.

Gallagher said, faltering, "Much of this has been exaggerated, Hazel. And it wasn't only Jews who died, it was all sorts of people including Germans. Many millions. And more millions would die under Stalin. Children, yes. Babies. Upheavals of madness like volcanos spewing lava . . . You understood, if you were a soldier, how impersonal it is. 'History.' "

" 'You're defending them, then. 'Much has been exaggerated.' ' "

Gallagher stared at Hazel, perplexed. He felt an undercurrent of revulsion for the woman, almost a fear of her, she seemed so different to him, suddenly. He touched her shoulders. "Hazel? What is it?"

" 'Much has been exaggerated.' You said."

Hazel laughed. She was blinking rapidly, not looking at him.

"Hazel, I'm so sorry. I've been saying stupid things. You lost someone in the war?"

"No. I lost no one in the war."

Hazel spoke harshly, half-jeering. Gallagher made a move to embrace her. For a moment she held herself rigid against him, then seemed to melt, to press herself against him, with a shudder. A wave of sexual desire struck Gallagher like a fist.

"Hazel! Dear, darling Hazel . . ."

Gallagher framed the woman's face in his hands and kissed her, and she startled him with the vehemence of her response. They stood in a patch of blinding sunshine. Beyond the cabin, air shimmered with sunshine, there was a glare like fire. Hazel Jones's mouth was cold, yet seemed to suck at

Gallagher's mouth. Awkwardly, like one unaccustomed to intimacy, with a kind of desperation she pressed against him, her arms around him tightening. There was something fierce and terrible in the woman's sudden need. Gallagher murmured, "Hazel, dear Hazel. My dear one," in a rapt, crooning voice, a voice distinct from his own. He drew her into the cabin, stumbling with her, their breaths steamed, nervously they laughed together, kissing, trying to kiss, fumbling to embrace in their heavy outdoor clothing. Gallagher drew Hazel to one of the twin beds. Beneath the loose, discolored sheet the mattress was bare. A smell of skunk, bestial, intimate, lifted through the floorboards. It was a strangely attractive odor, not so very strong. Fumbling, laughing, yet without mirth, for she seemed very frightened, Hazel was pulling at Gallagher's jacket, and at the belt of his trousers. Her fingers were clumsy, deliberate. Gallagher thought *As she has undressed the child, the mother undressing the child*. He was astonished by her. He was utterly captivated by her. So long had Hazel Jones resisted him, and now! In a swath of blinding sunshine they lay on the mattress, kissing, straining to kiss, continuing to fumble with their clothing. Gallagher had long advised himself *She is not a virgin, Hazel Jones is not a virgin, I will not be forcing myself upon a virgin, Hazel Jones has a child and has been with a man* but now, this Hazel Jones was astonishing to him, gripping him tightly, drawing him to her, deeply into her. In a frenzy the woman's mouth sucked at his, he was losing consciousness of himself, in a delirium of animal urgency and submission. In the woman's arms he would be obliterated, this was not natural to Gallagher, had not been his experience, not for many years. Not since late adolescence, when Gallagher's sexual life had begun. Now, he was not the stronger of the two. His will was not stronger than Hazel Jones's will. He would succumb to the woman, not once but many times for this was the first of many times, Gallagher understood.

Her hair that was damp with perspiration stuck to his face, his mouth. Her breasts were much larger, heavier than he'd imagined, milky-pale, with nipples large as berries. He was not prepared for the lavish dark hair of her body, spiky-black at her groin, lifting into her navel. He was not prepared for the muscular strength of her legs, her knees gripping him. *I love love love you* choked in his throat as helpless he pumped his life into her.

By quick degrees the sun expanded to fill the sky.

❀ ❀ ❀

21

"The breath of God."

A wayward breeze that would drive her in a sudden, unexpected direction that was yet determined, purposeful. She, and the child who was her own purpose.

22

❀ ❀ ❀

A man wants to know. A lover wants to know. Wants to suck the very marrow of your bones wants to *know*.

A man has a right. A lover has a right. Once your body is entered in that way, he will have the right.

Telling him of what can't be told. A lover wants to know what can't be told. For some secret must be offered. It was time, and more than time. She knew, though she was not his wife and would not be. *This girl at my high school in Milburn, d'you know where Milburn is,* and he said *No I don't think so* and she said *When we were thirteen her father killed her mother, her older brother and her, and then himself, with a double-barreled shotgun in a back bedroom of their house they lived in a funny old stone house like a storybook cottage except it was old, it was sinking into the earth.* And he said *Jesus! what a terrible thing* shifting uneasily *was she a close friend of yours* and quickly Hazel said *No* then *Yes but not a close friend then, when we were in grade school she'd been* and Gallagher asked *Why did the father do such a terrible thing, was he insane? desperate? poor?* with surprising naiveté for one who'd been in the war and had been wounded in the war Gallagher asked and Hazel smiled in the darkness, not Hazel Jones's bright yearning smile but a smile of rage *Are those reasons for killing your family and yourself, are those the recognized reasons* but Gallagher mistook Hazel's trembling for emotion holding her tightly in his arms to protect her as always he would protect her *Poor darling Hazel! It must have been horrible for you, and for everyone who knew them* and Hazel smiled *Was it?* for the thought had never occurred to her. Saying

He was the town gravedigger. As if that was the explanation. Gallagher would accept this explanation.

Hazel knew it was not true of course. No one in Milburn would have thought it was horrible. It was the gravedigger murdering his family, and himself.

Because he'd murdered them all. No one remained to grieve.

23

❀ ❀ ❀

Why? Because it was time.

Hazel Jones would come to live with Gallagher in the red-brick house he'd bought for her in Watertown and of course she would bring her son. *For the child's sake she had consented, they would remain as long as seemed expedient as long as the man believed he loved her for the gravedigger's daughter had not the right to bypass such an opportunity* and when two years later the child was offered a piano scholarship at the Portman Academy of Music Gallagher would buy a house in Syracuse and they would move there.

My little family they were to him. Never in his adult life had Chet Gallagher been so happy.

It was meant to be. It was the breath of God. That my son would be a pianist, he would play before large audiences and they would applaud him.

"But why do you care so much, Hazel?"

Gallagher put the question to her gently. He was smiling, and stroking her hand. Always he was touching her, caressing her. He adored her! But the stubbornness in her, the curious adamant unyielding will, concerned him. Her primitive soul he thought it, then was ashamed of himself for such a thought. For he did adore her, he believed he would die for her. And the child he loved too, though not as he loved the mother.

"Because"—Hazel paused, wetting her lips, confused or seeming-so as at such times she seemed shy, uncertain, her eyes avoiding his so that Gallagher could not confound her with his equanimity—"music is beautiful. Music is—" It was here that Hazel's voice dipped in that way Gallagher found both charming and maddening, you had to lean your head close to hers, to hear. And if you didn't hear, and asked Hazel to repeat what she'd said, she would shrink away in shyness, self-conscious as a young girl: "Oh, nothing! It's too silly."

Afterward hearing the solemn muttered words he had not quite heard at the time *Music is the one thing.*

" 'Why do fools fall in love' . . ."

Why the hell not? He was forty-two years old and not getting any younger, smarter, or better-looking.

Laughed at himself in the bathroom mirror, shaving. This was the face he'd used to shield his eyes against—literally!—seeing at any hour and especially in the clinical unsparing light of a bathroom mirror. No thanks! But now, Hazel Jones downstairs in the kitchen preparing breakfast for him and Zack, a woman who *actually liked to prepare breakfast and wore a floral-print apron while preparing it,* Gallagher was in a mood to confront his own face without that old urge to slam a fist into the mirror, or puke up his guts into the sink.

And he loved, the boy, too.

My boy. Occasionally even *My son* he would hear himself say, in casual conversation.

My little family he kept to himself and Hazel. *My new life* he kept strictly to himself.

"Music isn't 'the one thing,' darling. There are plenty of other 'one things.' "

Was it so? Gallagher, a former child piano-prodigy, burnt out and for a time suicidal at the age of seventeen, certainly thought so.

He wouldn't tell Hazel this, however. Of the many things Gallagher rehearsed to tell Hazel, this was one he would not tell her out of a fear of upsetting her, wounding her.

Out of a fear of telling the truth.

No longer was Chet Gallagher playing jazz piano at the Malin Head Inn, he'd moved one hundred miles south to Syracuse to a house within three blocks of the music school where Zack now took intensive lessons with a pianist who'd been one of Hans Zimmerman's favored protégés. Zimmerman had arranged for the scholarship, there would be other costs and some of them considerable if Zack was to embark upon a serious professional career. Gallagher had not needed to tell Hazel that he would pay for this embarkment, happily he would pay what was required. No longer did Gallagher play much jazz piano, wanting to avoid smoky bars, occasions for drinking too much, occasions for meeting lonely seductive women, oh Christ he so much preferred staying at home evenings with his little family he adored.

Out of a fear of telling the truth.

Yet Hazel was reluctant to marry Gallagher! It was the great mystery of his life.

A mystery, and a deep hurt.

"But Hazel, why not? Don't you love me?"

As always Hazel's reasons were vague, evasive. She spoke hesitantly. You would almost think that words were thistles, or pebbles, scraping her throat. The Gallaghers would not approve of her, an unwed mother. They would despise her, they would never forgive her.

"Hazel! For Christ' sake."

He held her in his arms, she was so distressed. Gallagher didn't want to upset her further. Now that they were living together he was more able to gauge her moods. Like an upright flame Hazel Jones appeared, the eye was drawn to her, dazzled by her, yet a flame is after all a delicate thing, a flame can be suddenly threatened, extinguished.

Unwed mother, despise. Forgive! Gallagher winced at such clichés. What the hell did he care, if the Gallaghers disapproved of his liaison with Hazel Jones? They knew nothing of her, really. The most absurd, malicious things were said of her, in Albany. And now that Gallagher was openly living with her . . . They would never meet Hazel, if he could avoid it. By now, Gallagher was very likely disinherited. Thaddeus would have written him out of his will years ago.

"Is it money you're worried about? I don't need their money, Hazel. I can make my own way."

It wasn't exactly true: Gallagher received money from a trust established by his maternal grandparents. But he'd returned to newspaper work, he was producing radio programs. If Hazel was anxious about money, he would make more money!

He would protect Hazel Jones, that was a principle of his character. He wanted to think this was so: he was a man of principle. Even his father, supremely indifferent to the sufferings of masses of human beings like most "conservatives," was nonetheless loyal, at times fiercely and irrationally loyal, to individuals close to him.

Thaddeus, too, had women; or had had women when he'd been younger, fitter. A primitive and seemingly insatiable sexual itch the man had satisfied with whoever was available. Yet, Thaddeus had remained a "faithful" husband in society's eyes. He had not betrayed his wife publicly and perhaps in her naiveté (Gallagher wanted to think) his mother had never known that Thaddeus had betrayed her at all.

Gallagher heard himself ask, plaintively, "But don't you love me, Hazel? I certainly love you."

His voice broke. He was making a fool of himself. He seemed to be accusing her.

Hazel moved into Gallagher's arms, as if too stricken to speak. This was proof that she loved him: wasn't it? Pressing herself against him as, in their bed, she pressed against him, never resisting now, warmly affectionate, her arms around his neck, her mouth opened to his. He felt her heartbeat, now. He felt the quickened heat of her body. It came to him *She is remembering another man, the man who hurt her.* Gallagher felt an impulse to break her in his arms, as the other had done. To break her very bones, gripping her tight, burying his hot furious face in her neck, in a coil of her red-glinting hair.

He hid his contorted face, he wept. Tears no one need acknowledge.

Not in Watertown, and not in Syracuse had she had a glimpse of any man who resembled the man who'd masqueraded as her husband yet it came to her in a swoon of bitter certitude *If I marry this man, if I love this man the other will hunt us down and kill us.*

He could make money for his little family, certainly Chet Gallagher could. "Hazel Jones, you have the gift of happiness! You have brought such happiness into my life." It was so: Gallagher was a young man again. An ardent lover, a fool for love! A man who'd once joked that his heart had shrunken to the size of a raisin, and was of the wizened texture of a raisin, now Gallagher's heart was the good healthy size of a man's fist, suffused with hope as with blood. His face appeared younger. Always he was smiling, whistling. (Zack had to ask Gallagher please not to whistle so loud, the tunes Gallagher whistled got into Zack's head and interfered with the music Zack was playing in his head.) He drank red wine at dinner, that was all. He ate less compulsively, he'd lost twenty pounds in his gut and torso. His hair was still falling out but what the hell, Hazel stroked his bumpy bald head, twirled her fingers in the wiry fringe that remained, and pronounced him the most handsome man she'd ever met.

His ex-wife had wounded Gallagher sexually, other women had disappointed him. But Hazel Jones obliterated such memories.

Virtually overnight, Gallagher had gone from being a man who went to bed at 4 A.M. and staggered awake next day at noon, to being a man who went to bed at 11 P.M. most weekday nights and woke at 7 A.M. He produced a series of radio programs ("Jazz America," "American Classics") that originated in Syracuse, at a local station, and was broadcast eventually through New York State, Ohio, Pennsylvania. He'd been befriended by the editor in chief of the *Syracuse Post-Dispatch*, a Gallagher-owned paper, yet one of the more independent of the chain, and had begun writing newspaper columns for the editorial page on ethical/political issues. Civil rights, school desegregation, Martin Luther King, Junior. Racial discrimination in labor unions. The need for "radical reform" in New York State divorce law. The "morally suspect" war in Vietnam. These were impassioned columns, leavened with humor, that soon drew notice. *Chet Gallagher* was the sole liberal voice published in the Gallagher newspapers, a controversial presence. When the editors endorsed, as invariably they did, Republican candidates for office, Gallagher flamboyantly criticized, dissected, exposed. That he could be as critical of Democratic candidates was a measure of his integrity. Angry letters were published condemning his views. The more controversy, the more papers sold. Gallagher loved the attention! (His columns were never censored in the Syracuse paper, but other papers in the Gallagher chain sometimes declined to print them. These decisions had nothing to do with Thaddeus Gallagher, who rarely interfered with the operations of any of his papers if they were making profits. Very likely, Thaddeus read every column of Gallagher's, for he was a man who kept a close scrutiny on all aspects of Gallagher Media, but he never made any comment on his youngest son's columns, so far as Gallagher knew, and he'd never exercised his power to censor a column. It had long been a principle of the old man to detach himself from his youngest son's career as a way of establishing his own moral superiority to him.)

And so, Gallagher was happy. To a degree.

Is she married? Is that it? And not divorced? She has lied to me, is that it?

Unbidden the thought came to him, even when they were making love. Even when they were sitting side by side, clasping hands, listening to the child Zacharias play piano. (His first public recital, at the Portman Academy. Aged nine, Zack was the youngest performer of the evening and drew the most enthusiastic applause.) Sometimes he was stricken by jealousy, a misery like tight-coiled snakes in his gut.

Hazel had told him she had never been married. She spoke with such pained sincerity, Gallagher could not doubt her word.

More and more, Gallagher wanted to adopt the child. Before it was too late. But to adopt the child, he must be the mother's husband.

In his soul, Gallagher loathed the very idea of marriage. He loathed the intrusion of the state into the private lives of individuals. He quite agreed with Marx, he'd used to quote Marx to inflame Thaddeus, for Marx had got it right, mostly: the masses of humankind sell themselves for wages, capitalists are sons of bitches who'd slit your throat and collect your blood in vials and sell it to the highest bidder, religion is the opium of the masses and the churches are capitalist ventures organized to make money, secure power, influence. Of course, laws favor the rich and powerful, power wishes only to engender more power as capital wishes only to engender more capital. Of course the industrial world is pitched to madness, World War I, World War II, always the specter of World War, the ceaseless strife of nations. Marx had got most of it right and Freud had got the rest of it right: civilization was the price you paid for not getting your throat slashed, but it was too damned high a price to pay.

Getting a divorce in New York State in the mid-1950s! Gallagher was one of the walking wounded, almost a decade later.

"Asshole. Whose fault but my own!"

The irony was, he'd married to placate others. His mother had been very ill at the time, she would die shortly after the wedding. The tyranny of the dying mother's role in civilization cannot be overestimated! Gallagher had returned from overseas wishing not to succumb to despair, depression, alcoholism like other veterans of his acquaintance, for an entire generation the only salvation had been marriage.

Gallagher had been young: twenty-seven. Grateful not to have been killed and not (visibly) crippled. As a way of showing his gratitude for being alive he had hoped to placate others, above all his parents. A mistake he would not make again.

Living in Albany, capital of New York state, Gallagher had been aware of the intrusion of the state into individuals' lives, even as a boy. Impossible not to be aware of politics if you live in Albany! Not the politics of idealism but grub-politics, the politics of "deals." There was no goal higher than "deals" and no motive higher than "self-interest." Gallagher's disgust reached its peak in 1948 with the sordid politicking that accompanied the Taft-Hartley law which the Republican-dominated U.S. Congress passed over Truman's veto. And Dewey's sneering campaign against Truman, to which Thaddeus contributed a good deal of money, not all of it a matter of public record.

He'd quarreled with Thaddeus, and moved away from Ardmoor Park. He would never be on comfortable terms with the old man again.

That Hazel Jones should consider herself unworthy of the Gallaghers, and of him! Preposterous.

To his shame he heard himself begging.

"Hazel, I could adopt Zack as my son, if we were married. Don't you think that's a good idea?"

Quickly Hazel kissed Gallagher saying yes, she supposed so.

Someday.

"Someday? Zack is growing up, the time is now. Not when he's an adolescent who won't give a damn about any father."

Wanting to say *won't give a shit about any father*. The anger in him was mounting, to desperation.

In the music room at the rear of the house Zack was playing piano. Must have struck a wrong note, the music broke off abruptly and after a brief pause began again.

Seeing that he was upset, Hazel took Gallagher's hand that was so much larger and heavier than her own, lifted and pressed it against her cheek in one of Hazel Jones's impulsive gestures that pierced her lover's heart.

"Someday."

For the Young Pianists' Competition in Rochester, in May 1967, the boy was preparing Schubert's "Impromptu No. 3." At ten and a half, he would be the youngest performer on the program, which included pianists to the age of eighteen.

The next-youngest was a Chinese-American boy of twelve who was being trained at the Royal Conservatory of Music in Toronto, and who had recently placed second in an international competition for young pianists in that city.

Day following day and often into the late evening the child practiced. Such precise, cleanly struck notes, such rapidity of execution, you would not have thought the pianist was so young a child and if, like Gallagher, you were drawn to the doorway of the music room, the child's intense unblinking eyes would remain fixed upon the keyboard (the piano was no longer the Baldwin upright but a Steinway baby grand Gallagher had bought from Zimmerman Brothers) and his small fingers striking the keys as if of their own volition for the piece must be memorized, not a note, not a pause, not a depression of the pedal left to chance.

Gallagher listened, entranced. No doubt about it, the boy played more beautifully than Gallagher had done at his age, and older. Gallagher would boast *He's inherited all I had to give him. Quite a talent, isn't he!*

By degrees Gallagher was becoming the child's father. Strange that he did not much wonder who the child's true father was.

In the doorway of the music room Gallagher lingered, uncertain. Waiting for the boy to break off practice at which point Gallagher would clap enthusiastically—"Bravo, Zack! Sounds terrific"—and the boy would blush with pleasure. But the practice continued, and continued, for if Zack made the smallest error he must return to the beginning and start again, until Gallagher at last lost patience and slipped away, unseen.

Didn't I promise you, Ma? You would be proud.

"Zack" is his name. A name out of the Bible. For he is blessed of God, Ma. None of us would have guessed!

My son. Your grandson. His face will be known to you, when you see him. It's a face you will recognize, Ma. The father is not in him, much.

His eyes, Ma! His eyes are beautiful, like yours.

Maybe they are Pa's eyes, too. A little.

At the piano, I hear him and I know where he is. In all the world he is here, Ma. With us.

He is safe in this house.

I should not have left you, Ma. I stayed away so long.

Sometimes I think my soul was lost in those fields. Along the canal. I stayed away from you so long, Ma.

I am paying for that, Ma.
If you hear him, Ma, you will know. Why I had to live.
I love you, Ma.
This is for you, Ma.
It is called "Impromptu No. Three" by Schubert.

24

❋ ❋ ❋

So quickly it happened, he would replay it many times in his memory. Always he was invisible, helpless to intervene. If something had happened to his mother, helpless.

Thinking *I didn't warn her. It was like I wasn't there, no one saw me.*

Out of nowhere the man appeared.

Out of nowhere staring at Hazel Jones as if he knew her.

Though in fact Zack had been seeing the man for perhaps ten, twenty seconds. Zack who never took notice of anyone had been seeing this man watching his mother from a distance of about thirty feet, as Hazel walked on the graveled path through the park, oblivious.

There was a repair truck parked in the roadway nearby. The man must have been a repairman of some sort, in soiled work clothes, work shoes. In cities (they lived always in cities now, and traveled only to cities) you learn not to see such individuals who are not likely to be individuals whom you know, or who know you.

Except this man was watching Hazel Jones, very intently.

This day! "Free time" for Zack. The day following a piano recital. For perhaps seventy-two hours his senses would be alert, aroused. He continued to hear music in his head yet the intensity of the music abated, and the need of his fingers to create it. His eyes felt new to him at such times, raw, exposed to hurt. They filled with moisture easily. His ears craved to hear, with a strange hunger: not music but ordinary sounds. Voices! Noises!

He felt like a creature that has pushed its way out of a smothering cocoon, unaware of the cocoon until now.

The man in work clothes was no age Zack could judge, maybe Gallagher's age, or younger. He looked like one whom life has chewed up. He was perhaps six feet tall, yet there was a broken, caved-in look to his chest. His lower jaw jutted, his skin was coarse and mottled and flamey as if with burst boils. His head appeared subtly deformed like partly melted wax and strands of colorless hair lay like seaweed across his scalp. A ravaged-angry face like something scraped along pavement yet out of this face eyes shone strangely with yearning, wonderment.

It's him.

Is it—him?

An afternoon in September 1968. They were spending the weekend in Buffalo, New York. They were guests of the Delaware Conservatory of Music. A party of six or seven persons, all adults with the exception of Zack, were walking in the direction of the Park Lane Hotel where the Joneses and Gallagher were staying. They had had lunch together at the Conservatory where, the previous evening, the young pianist had performed; he would not be twelve until November, but had been accepted as a scholarship student at the prestigious music school, and would play with the Conservatory Chamber Orchestra the following spring.

Hazel and Zack were walking more slowly than the others. By instinct wanting to be alone together. Ahead, Gallagher was talking animatedly with his new acquaintances. He had established himself as Zacharias Jones's protector, manager. Vaguely it was implied that Gallagher was the boy's stepfather and when Hazel Jones was called "Mrs. Gallagher" the misassumption was accepted in silence.

The remarkable young pianist Zacharias Jones was the subject of the adults' conversation as he had been the subject of the luncheon but the young pianist himself was not much engaged. *He, him, the boy* he overheard, at a distance. Long he'd been adept at detaching himself from the attentions of others. In the roadside cafés where his hands had first discovered the piano keyboard he had begun knowing that it made little difference what others said, what others thought, there was only the music, finally. From Hazel Jones he'd learned to be both *here* and *not-here* simultaneously; how to smile even as your mind has retreated elsewhere. Zack behaved rudely and impatiently, at times. He would be forgiven, for he was a gifted young pianist: you had to assume he was playing music in his head. Hazel too played a continuous music in her head, but no one could guess what that music was.

During the lunch in the Conservatory dining room Zack had glanced up at Hazel Jones, to see her watching him. She'd smiled, and winked so that no one else could see, and Zack had blushed, looking quickly away.

They had no need to speak. What was between them could not be uttered in words.

Make his debut. Zacharias Jones would *make his debut* in February 1969 with the Delaware Chamber Orchestra among whom there were few musicians younger than eighteen.

February 1969! At the luncheon, Hazel had laughed uneasily saying it seemed so far off, what if something happened to . . .

Others looked at Hazel so quizzically, Zack knew that his mother had misspoken.

Gallagher intervened. Showing his devil's-point teeth in a smile remarking that February 1969 would be here quickly enough.

Zack would play a concerto, yet to be chosen. The orchestra conductor would be working closely with him of course.

Feeling at that moment a sensation of alarm, the cold taste of panic. *If he failed* . . .

Afterward, Hazel Jones had touched his arm, lightly. They would allow the others to walk ahead through the park. It was a wan warm sepia-tinted autumn afternoon. Hazel paused to admire swans, both dazzling white and black, with red bills, paddling in the lagoon in surges of languid energy.

How the company of *those others* oppressed them! Almost, they could not breathe.

After the previous evening's recital, Gallagher had hugged Zack and kissed the top of his head playfully saying he should be damned proud of himself. Zack had been pleased, but embarrassed. He was deeply in love with Gallagher yet shy and self-conscious in the man's presence.

Pride puzzled Zack Jones! He had never understood what pride was.

Nor did Hazel seem to know. When she'd been a Christian girl she'd been taught that pride is a sin, pride goeth before a fall. Pride is dangerous, isn't it?

"Pride is for other people, Zack. Not us."

Zack was thinking of this when he saw the man in work clothes, at the edge of the roadway. The park was not very populated, traffic moved on the road slowly, intermittently. No one in view was dressed in work clothes except this individual who was staring at Hazel as if trying to decide if he knew her.

It was not unusual for strangers to stare at Hazel Jones in public but there was something different about this individual, Zack felt the danger.

Yet he said nothing to his mother.

Now the man had decided to approach Hazel, and was walking toward her with surprising swiftness. Suddenly you could see that he was a man who acts with his body. Though he looked unhealthy with his caved-in chest and boiled face yet he was not weak, and he was not indecisive. Like a wolf coming up swiftly and noiselessly behind a deer, that has not yet sensed its presence. The man made his way slantwise across a patch of grass in which PLEASE! DO NOT WALK ON THE GRASS was prominently displayed, and along the graveled path. Massive plane trees bordered the path and sun fell in coin-sized splotches on pedestrians as they passed beneath.

There was something of the deer to Hazel Jones in her high-heeled shoes and stylish straw hat, and there was something of the wolf, coarse-haired, ungainly, to the man in work clothes. Fascinating to Zack to see his mother through this stranger's eyes: the scintillant chestnut-red hair, lacquered flash of red nails and red mouth. The perfect posture, high-held head. For luncheon in the elegant Conservatory dining room Hazel had worn a very pale beige linen suit with several strands of pearls and a wide-brimmed straw hat with a green velvet ribbon. Zack had noticed people looking at her, in admiration; but no one had stared rudely. After the Rochester Young Pianists' Competition when Zack, the youngest performer, had received a special citation from the judges, photographs of the honored pianists and their parents were taken and one of the photographers had told Hazel, "You're so beautiful with your hair and skin tone, you should certainly wear black." And Hazel had laughed, disdainfully, "Black! Black is for mourning, and I'm not in mourning."

Now the man in work clothes had caught up to Hazel and was speaking with her. Zack saw his mother turn to stare at him, startled.

"Ma'am? Excuse me?"

Blindly Hazel groped for Zack, who stood out of reach.

He saw the panic in her face. He saw her frightened eyes inside the Hazel Jones mask.

"Just I'm wondering if—if you know me? Like do I look like anybody you know, ma'am? My name is Gus Schwart."

Quickly Hazel shook her head *no*. She would regain her composure, smiling her polite, wary smile.

Ahead, Gallagher and the others had not noticed. They continued on, in the direction of the hotel.

"Ma'am, I'm real sorry to bother you. But you look familiar to me. Used to live in Milburn? It's a small town maybe a few hundred miles east of here, on the Erie Canal? I went to school there . . ."

Hazel stared at him so blankly, the man began to falter. His scabby face flushed red. He tried to smile, as an animal might smile showing yellowed, raggedy teeth.

Zack stood close by to protect his mother but the man took not the slightest interest in him.

Hazel was saying apologetically no she didn't know him, she didn't know Milburn.

"I been sick, ma'am. I ain't been well. But now I'm over it, and I . . ."

Hazel was tugging at Zack's arm, they would make their escape. The man in work clothes swiped at his mouth, embarrassed. Yet he could not let them go, he followed them for a few yards, clumsy, stammering, "Just you look kind of—familiar, ma'am? Like somebody I used to know? My brother Herschel and me, and my sister Rebecca, we used to live in Milburn . . . I left in 1949."

Tersely Hazel said over her shoulder, "Mister, I don't think so. No."

Mister was not a word Hazel Jones ordinarily used, not in this tone.

There was something crude and dismissive in her speech, that was unlike Hazel Jones.

"Zack! Come on."

Zack allowed himself to be pulled with Hazel, like a small child. He was stunned, unable to comprehend the encounter.

Not my father. Not that man.

His heart beat heavily, in disappointment.

Hazel pulled at Zack's arm and he jerked it from her. She had no right to treat him as if he was five years old!

"Who was that man, Mom? He knew you."

"No. He didn't."

"And you knew him. I saw that."

"No."

"You used to live in Milburn, Mom. You said so."

Hazel spoke tight-lipped, not looking at him. "No. Chautauqua Falls. You were born in Chautauqua Falls." She paused, panting. She seemed about to say more, but could not speak.

Zack would taunt his mother now. In the aftermath of the encounter in the park he felt strangely aroused, unsettled.

In the aftermath of the recital he was free to say, to do anything he wished.

He was furious at Hazel in her linen suit, pearls and wide-brimmed straw hat.

"You did know that man. Damn liar you *did*."

He nudged Hazel. He wanted to hurt her. Why did she never raise her voice, why did she never shout at him? Why did she never cry?

"He was looking at you so *hard*. I saw that."

Hazel maintained her dignity, gripping the rim of her straw hat as she crossed a roadway, hurriedly. Zack wanted to rush after her and pound her with his fists. He wanted to use his fists to hit, hit! Halfway he wanted to break his hands, that were so precious to the adults.

Gallagher and the others were waiting for Hazel and Zack, beneath the hotel portico. Gallagher stood with crossed arms, smiling. The visit to Buffalo had gone as well as he'd hoped. Gallagher would look for a new house, in the Delaware Park area which was the most exclusive residential area in the city; in Syracuse, he would put their present house on the market. If he hadn't quite enough money for a spacious old house in Delaware Park, possibly he'd borrow from a Gallagher relative.

The look in Gallagher's face when Hazel came to him: like a light switched on.

Zack was trailing behind Hazel hot-faced, sullen. He must say goodbye to the adults, shake their hands and behave sensibly. The attention of strangers was blinding, like stage lights. Except onstage you have no need to stare into the lights, you turn your attention onto the beautiful white-and-black keyboard stretching in front of you.

Zack would be returning to Buffalo, in less than a month. He would take piano instructions with the most revered member of the Delaware Conservatory, who had studied with the great German pianist Egon Petri when Petri had taught in California.

If he failed . . .

He had not failed, the previous evening. He'd played the Schubert "Impromptu" which Hazel so loved, and a newer piece with which he'd been less satisfied, a Chopin nocturne. The tempo of the nocturne seemed to him maddeningly slow, the pianist had felt exposed as if naked. Not music to hide inside!

Still, the audience had seemed to like him. The Conservatory faculty, including his new teacher, had seemed to like him. Waves of applause, a waterfall drowning out the hot beat of blood in his ears. *Why! why! why! why!* He was dazed at such times, scarcely knowing where he was. Like a swimmer who has nearly drowned, struggling desperately to save himself and in this way drawing the attention of admiring strangers who applaud. Gallagher had told him to be proud of himself, and Hazel who was less demonstrative than Gallagher in public had squeezed his hand, allowing him to know that she was very happy, he'd played so well.

"You see? I told you!"

And so, Zack had not been defeated. He had not failed, yet. And he would practice harder, ever harder. Predictions had been made of him, lavish predictions he must live out. He felt the bitter weight of such responsibility, he resented it. Overhearing Hans Zimmerman remarking to his brother Edgar *My youngest pupil has the oldest eyes.* Yet he was giddy with relief, he had been spared. This time.

He would go upstairs to their suite in the Park Lane Hotel and fall onto his bed and sink into a deep dreamless sleep.

Mother and son went upstairs to the ninth floor, Gallagher remained behind to have a drink in the hotel lounge, with the conductor of the chamber orchestra. How tireless Gallagher was, plotting the future! His life was his little family, he adored without question. Upstairs Hazel removed her stylish straw hat and tossed it in the direction of the bed. Before she could see where it might land, she'd already turned away. Neither she nor Zack had spoken since Zack had shouted at her. In the elevator ascending to the ninth floor they had not looked at each other, nor touched. Zack was very tired now, fatigue was overtaking him like an eclipse of the sun. He saw his mother standing quietly at one of the tall windows, gazing down toward the park. He went to use the bathroom, making as much noise as he could, and when he returned Hazel was still standing there, leaning her forehead against the windowpane. Always when they checked into hotels Hazel would examine their rooms for cleanliness and she would not neglect the windows, frowning to see if they were polished clean or if they had been sullied by a stranger's forehead. Zack observed her in silence. He was thinking of the man in work clothes, who had not been his father. Who the man was, Zack would not know. If he went to Hazel, to peer at her face, he would see that it was a vacant face, no longer young and not very beautiful. The eyes would be without luster, the light drained from them. The shoulders were beginning to slump, the breasts were becoming heavy, graceless. He was furious with her. He was frightened of her. He would not speak to her, however. Certainly Hazel was aware of him, her son's hot accusing eyes, but she would not speak. Alone together, mother and son often did not speak. What was between them, knotted together like a tangle of guts, they had no need to utter.

Zack turned away. Went into his room adjoining the adults' suite, shut the door but did not lock it. Fell onto the bed not removing any of his clothing nor even kicking off his shoes that were dusty from the park.

Woke with a start later that afternoon to discover that the room was partially darkened, for Hazel had drawn the venetian blinds, and there was Hazel Jones lying beside Zack on top of the bed, fully clothed as well but with her high-heeled shoes kicked off, sunk into a sleep deep and exhausted as his own had been.

25

❀ ❀ ❀

Dragging the stunned boy by his arm. As if wanting to tear his arm out of its socket. Yelling at him, punching and kicking. On the ground the boy tries to escape, crawling on hands and knees and then dragging himself as his father catches him, brings his booted foot down on the boy's hands: first the right, then the left. Hearing the small bones crack. Hearing the boy screaming Daddy don't hurt me! Daddy don't kill me! and where is the mother, why isn't the mother intervening, for the assault isn't over, will not be over until the boy lies unconscious and bleeding and still the wrathful father will cry You're my son! My fucking son! My son. Mine.

26

❁ ❁ ❁

Yet it took her weeks to make the call. In fact it had taken her years.

And then, dialing the number that was suddenly familiar again to her, steeling herself hearing the phone ring at the other end of the line, she was struck by a sudden vision of the Meltzers' house she had neither contemplated nor envisioned in years and in that instant from the side door of the Meltzers' house she was seeing the farmhouse next door which was the house in which she'd lived and nursed her baby in a delirium of unspeakable happiness she knew now to be the only purely happy time of her life, and she began to tremble, and could not speak with the ease and clarity Hazel Jones had wished.

"Mrs.—Mrs. Meltzer? You won't remember me—I lived next door to you eight years ago. In that old farmhouse. I lived with a man named Niles Tignor. You took care of my little boy when I worked in town, in a factory. You—"

Hazel's voice broke. She could hear, at the other end of the line, an intake of breath.

"Is this Rebecca? Rebecca Tignor?"

The voice was Mrs. Meltzer's, unmistakable. Yet it was an altered voice, older and oddly frail.

"Hello? Hello? Is this Rebecca?"

Hazel tried to speak. She managed to speak, in choked monosyllables. Her heart was beating dangerously hard in her chest. The damned ringing in her ear, to which she'd grown so accustomed she rarely heard it during the day, was confused now with the pulsing of her blood.

"Rebecca? My God, I thought you were dead! You and Niley both. We thought he'd killed you, all those years ago."

Mrs. Meltzer sounded as if she was about to cry. Hazel silently begged her *no*.

Edna Meltzer had not been her mother. It was ridiculous to confuse the two women. It was ridiculous to be trembling like this gripping the phone receiver so her hand shook.

At least, she was making the call in an empty house. Both Gallagher and Zack were out.

"Where is he, Mrs. Meltzer?"

"*He's* dead, Rebecca."

"Dead . . ."

"Tignor died in Attica, Rebecca, two-three years ago. That's what Howie heard. He was sent away on assault, 'extortion'—I'm not sure what 'extortion' is, some kind of blackmail I guess. None of it had anything to do with Four Corners or with what he'd done to you, Rebecca. We never saw him after that time he came to our house crazy-like wanting to know where you were, and we said we did not know! He was set to kill you, or anybody stood in his way, we could see. Saying you stole his son, and you stole his car. Saying no woman had ever insulted him like that and you would pay for it. He was like a wild man, saying he would murder you with his bare hands for betraying him, and he'd murder us if he found out we were hiding you. Howie has a shotgun, Howie ain't one to back down, I told Howie just let it be, don't rile the man up any worse than he is. Well, Tignor went off! Left the house like it was, mostly." Mrs. Meltzer paused to catch her breath. Hazel saw the older woman warming to her subject, thrilled, smiling. Her voice had gained strength. It was no longer the voice of an old woman. "Such a time it was, then! But now it's real quiet here. People moved in next-door, nice family and kids and they fixed up the house some. Oh, there never was anyone like Tignor in Four Corners before or since, I have to say."

Hazel was sitting down. In an acid-bright patch of sunlight Hazel Jones was sitting down.

Mrs. Meltzer was asking how Niley was, such a sweet little boy, and Hazel managed to say that Niley was fine, healthy, he was eleven years old and played piano, and Mrs. Meltzer said this sounded wonderful she was so happy to hear this, her and Howie and other neighbors in Four Corners had the bad thought for years that Tignor had murdered them both and hid their bodies in the canal maybe where nobody would ever find them, and now Tignor himself was dead, probably killed by somebody like himself, they was killing one another all the time in Attica and the guards were almost bad as the prisoners, thank God the prison wasn't any closer than it was, but how was Rebecca? where was Rebecca living now? was she married again, did she have a family?

"Rebecca? *Rebecca?*"

She had to lie down. She was dazed, dizzy as if he'd slapped the side of her head only just a few minutes ago, the ringing in her ear was high-pitched as a deranged cicada.

She would call Mrs. Meltzer back, another time. Only just not now.

❀ ❀ ❀

27

" 'Hazel Jones.' A mysterious name out of the past."

The elderly invalid leaned forward in his wheelchair to grip both Hazel's hands in his, rather hard. She had no idea what he meant: mysterious? The man's large glassy veined eyes of the hue of pewter gazed up at Hazel with such intensity, she was unnerved not knowing if Thaddeus Gallagher meant to be naively adoring, or was mocking such adoration of a young woman visitor. His hands gripping hers were doughy, warmly moist, seemingly boneless. Yet the man was strong. You understood that Thaddeus Gallagher was strong in his heavy upper body if not in his lower body and that he exulted in this strength, all the while continuing to smile at his startled visitor with the smiling air of a benevolent host. Hazel felt a shiver of dread that he would not release her, Gallagher would have to intervene and there would be an unpleasant scene.

Don't let my father manipulate you, Hazel! Immediately we step into his presence, he will exert his will upon us like a fat spider at the center of its web.

The shock of meeting Gallagher's father! Not only was the old man confined to a wheelchair but his body appeared deformed, a shapeless mass of mollusc-flesh inside weirdly jaunty tartan plaid bathing trunks and a white cotton T-shirt strained to bursting. Massive thighs and buttocks were squeezed against the unyielding sides of the wheelchair. Thaddeus's arms were muscled while his legs hung useless, pale and atrophied. Yet his feet were large and wedge-like, resting bare against the wheelchair's padded footrest. The big bare toes twitched in obscene delight.

An invalid! Thaddeus Gallagher! Hazel cast her companion Gallagher a look of dismay. How like Gallagher to complain of his father to her for years while neglecting to mention that the man was an invalid in a wheelchair.

Thaddeus winked at Hazel as if they shared an intimate joke, too subtle for Gallagher to grasp. "You seem surprised, dear? I apologize for greeting you so casually dressed but I swim, or try to swim, every day at this time. I confess that I also feel less constrained by decorum and fashion in my seventies than I did at your young age. My son 'Chet Gallagher,' the prize-winning journalist and public seer, might have warned you what to expect." Thaddeus laughed, sucking at his fleshy lips. He was reluctant to release Hazel's hands that were damp and numbed from his grasp.

All the while, Gallagher stood awkwardly beside Hazel, staring at his father in vague unease. He had said very little. He seemed as confused as Hazel. The sight of his father whom he had not seen in several years must have alarmed him. That the elderly man was in a wheelchair and they were on their feet seemed to put the couple at a disadvantage.

Thaddeus said fussily, "Please do sit, both of you! Pull those chairs a little closer. We'll have drinks now. After, I hope you will both join me for a swim in the pool. It's a very warm day, and both of you are overdressed, and are looking uncomfortable."

Thaddeus had been awaiting his visitors outside, by the pool. An Olympic-sized pool it was, exquisitely tiled in a deep rich aqua intended to suggest, as Gallagher had explained to Hazel, the Mediterranean. Yet the water exuded a warm sulphurous odor as of stale bathwater. Hazel's nostrils pinched. She could not imagine herself in that water, she felt a wave of faintness at the prospect.

Gallagher was saying, quickly, "I don't think so, Father. We don't have time for that. We—"

"You've said. You must get back to the 'music festival' in Vermont. Of course." Thaddeus spoke with dignity, though looking rebuffed. He pressed a button on the arm of the wheelchair and the motorized chair moved forward. Sunlight illuminated oily beads of perspiration on his wide sallow face. "But sit with me a while, at least. As if," smiling up at Gallagher, "we had something in common beyond a name."

———

It was late August 1970. At last, Gallagher had brought Hazel to Ardmoor Park to visit his aging father. In the past year Thaddeus had several times invited them, with a hint that his health was "worsening"; he had learned that Hazel's son Zacharias Jones was one of the young musicians in residence at the Vermont Music Festival in Manchester, Vermont, less than an hour's drive from Ardmoor Park. Reluctantly, Gallagher had given in. "Maybe my father is really ill. Maybe he's repentant. Maybe I'm crazy." Gallagher joked in his usual mordant way but Hazel understood that he was genuinely fearful of the visit.

Through the 1960s, the Gallagher newspapers had remained staunchly in favor of the Vietnam War. Yet, most of the papers continued to run Chet Gallagher's column, that had won national awards and appeared now in more than fifty newspapers. Gallagher also published opinion pieces in popular magazines and occasionally appeared on television panels discussing politics, ethics, American culture. Hazel had become his assistant; she liked best doing research for him at the University of Buffalo library. It was becoming more difficult for Gallagher to maintain his distance from Gallagher Media, and from Thaddeus. Through intermediaries he heard that his father was "proud" of him—"damned proud"—though he would never agree with his youngest son's "rabid radical politics." Gallagher had been told, too, that Thaddeus was eager to meet his "second family."

Gallagher would introduce Hazel to Thaddeus as his friend and companion, he would not even call her his fiancée. He would not be bringing Zack to Ardmoor Park at all.

He had warned Hazel not to be drawn into personal conversation with his father, still less into answering questions she didn't want to answer. "I know he's curious about you. He will interrogate you. He's an old newspaper man, that's what he knows. Poking and prodding and stabbing until the blade finds a soft spot, then he shoves it *in*."

Hazel laughed nervously. Gallagher had to be exaggerating!

"No. It's impossible to exaggerate Thaddeus Gallagher."

Gallagher's newspaper column was accompanied by a line-drawing caricature: a comically quizzical horsey face with a high forehead, deep-pouched eyes, lopsided smile, jutting chin and prominent ears. Around the near-bald dome of a head a fringe of kinky curls like a wreath. "Caricature is the art of exaggeration," Gallagher told Hazel, "yet it can tell the truth. In times like ours, caricature may be the only truth."

Yet on the drive from Manchester to Ardmoor Park, Gallagher's composure leaked from him like air from a deflating balloon. He was chain-smoking, distracted. He avoided the subject of Thaddeus Gallagher and spoke only of Zack whom they'd heard perform the previous evening at the music festival. Zack was now thirteen, no longer a child. He was becoming lanky, loose-jointed. His skin had an olive-dark pallor. His nose, eyebrows, eyes were striking, prominent. In the company of adults he was withdrawn, rather reserved, yet his piano performances were praised as "warm"—"reflective"—"startlingly mature." Where many child prodigies perform with mechanical precision and a deficiency of feeling, Zacharias Jones brought to his playing an air of emotional subtlety that was beautifully reflected in such pieces as the Grieg sonata he'd played at the festival. Gallagher could not stop marveling over the performance.

"He isn't a child, Hazel, in his music. It's uncanny."

Hazel thought *Of course he isn't a child! There wasn't time.*

"But we're not going to discuss Zack with my father, Hazel. He will want to know about your 'talented' son, he will hint that Gallagher Media could 'put him on the map.' He will interrogate you, he will stick and stab if you let him. Don't fall into the trap of answering Thaddeus's questions. The one thing he wants to know—to put it bluntly—is whether Zack might be his grandson. Because of all the things he has, he doesn't have grandchildren. And so—"

Hazel saw that her lover's face was creased, contorted. He looked both angry and aggrieved, like a gargoyle. He was driving too fast for the narrow road curving through hilly countryside.

Hazel said, "But you and I didn't even meet, until Zack was in school, in Malin Head Bay. How can your father—"

"He can. He can imagine anything. And it's a fact he can't know, even if he has hired private investigators to look into our relationship, when we first met. That, he can't know. So I will field his questions, Hazel. We will stay for an hour, maybe an hour and a half. All this I've explained, but he will try to dissuade us of course. He will try to dissuade you."

They were passing large estates set back from the road like storybook houses. Vast green lawns in which fugitive rainbows leapt and gleamed among sprinklers. Enormous elms, oaks. Juniper pine. There were ponds, lagoons. Picturesque brooks. The estates were bordered by primitive stone walls.

Gallagher said, "And please don't exclaim that the house is 'beautiful,' Hazel. You aren't obliged. Sure, it's beautiful. Every damn property in Ardmoor Park is beautiful. You bet, anything can be beautiful if you spend millions of bucks on it."

By the time they arrived at his father's house, the house of his boyhood, Gallagher was visibly nervous. It was a French Normandy mansion originally built in the 1880s but restored, refurbished and modernized in the 1920s. Hazel did not tell Gallagher that it was beautiful. Its enormous dull-gleaming slate roofs and hand-hewn stone facade reminded her of the elaborate mausoleums in Buffalo's vast Forest Lawn Cemetery.

Gallagher parked beyond the curve of the horseshoe drive, like an adolescent preparing for a quick departure. He tossed his cigarette onto the gravel. With the bravado of an afflicted man mimicking his own discomfort, he thumped his midriff with his fist: he'd been having gastric attacks lately, dismissed as "nerves."

"Remember, Hazel: we are not staying for dinner. We have 'other plans' back in Vermont."

Thaddeus Gallagher turned out not to be eagerly awaiting his visitors inside the massive house, but at the rear, by the pool. A female servant unknown to Gallagher answered the door, and insisted upon leading them to the pool area though Gallagher certainly knew the way. "I used to live here, ma'am. I'm your employer's *son*."

Along a flagstone path, beneath a wisteria archway, through a garden whose roses were mostly spent, fallen. Hazel glanced into tall windows bordered by leaded-glass panes. She saw only her own faint and insubstantial reflection.

And there, in his motorized wheelchair, in white T-shirt and tartan plaid trunks: Thaddeus Gallagher.

An invalid! Elderly, and obese! Yet the man's eyes snatched at Hazel Jones, hungrily.

Close beside the pool they sat. A festive gathering! A male servant in a white jacket brought drinks. Thaddeus talked, talked. Thaddeus had much to say. Hazel knew, from Gallagher, that Thaddeus continued to oversee Gallagher Media, though he'd officially retired. Thaddeus woke at dawn, was on the phone much of the day. Yet he talked now with the air of one who has not spoken to another human being in a long time.

For this visit to Ardmoor Park, Hazel was wearing a summer dress of pale yellow organdy with a sash that tied at the back, a favorite of Gallagher's. On her head, a wide-brimmed straw hat of an earlier era. On her slender feet, high-heeled straw sandals, with open toes. In a playful mood to celebrate Zack's three-week residence at the Vermont Music Festival, she had painted both her fingernails and toenails coral pink to match her lipstick.

On the wheelchair footrest Thaddeus Gallagher's toes twitched and writhed. The abnormally thick nails were discolored as old ivory. Like embryonic hooves they seemed to Hazel who could not help staring, revulsed.

This old man, Thaddeus Gallagher! A multi-millionaire. A much-revered philanthropist. Hazel recalled the wall of photographs in the lodge at Grindstone Island: a younger, less monstrous Thaddeus with his politician friends.

The shadow of death is upon him Hazel thought. She saw it, the fleeting shadow. Like the hawk-shadows passing over her and Gallagher as they'd climbed the steep hill on Grindstone Island.

Yet the older man confronted and confounded the younger. By quick degrees Gallagher lapsed into muttered monosyllables even as Thaddeus talked with zestful animation. Gallagher shifted uneasily in his chair, he seemed unable to catch his breath. Ordinarily, Gallagher did not drink alcohol at this hour of the day but he was drinking it now, very likely to show his father that he could. Hazel saw how he was refusing to glance at her. He was refusing to acknowledge her. Nor did he look Thaddeus Gallagher fully in the face. Gallagher looked like a man whose vision had gone blank: his eyes were open but he did not seem to be seeing. Hazel understood that she, the female, was meant to observe father and son: son and father: the elder Gallagher and the younger: meant to appreciate how the elder was the stronger of the two, in this matter of masculine will. This scene, Thaddeus had arranged.

At first, Hazel felt sympathy for Gallagher. As she'd felt a maternal protectiveness for Zack when he'd been a younger boy, at the mercy of older boys. But also impatience: why didn't Gallagher confront his bully-father, why didn't he speak with his usual authority? Where was Chet Gallagher's corrosive sense of humor, irony? Gallagher had a superbly modulated "radio" voice he could turn on and off at will, playfully. He made his little family laugh, he could be devastatingly funny. Yet now at his father's house the man who never stopped talking from morning to night was speaking vaguely, hesitantly, like a child trying not to stammer. This was the first Gallagher had returned to his childhood home since his mother's death years before. It was the first Gallagher had seen his father in such intimate quarters since that time. *He is remembering what hurt him. He is helpless as a child, remembering.* Hazel felt a wave of contempt for her lover, unmanned by this overbearing invalid.

Hazel would have wished not to be a witness to Gallagher's humiliation. But she knew herself, by Thaddeus's design, the crucial witness.

Beyond the flagstone terrace and the swimming pool with its rich aqua tiles was a stretch of gently sloping lawn. Not all of the lawn was mowed, there were patches of taller grasses, rushes and cattails. On a hill above a glittering pond, a stand of birch trees looking in the sun like vertical stripes of very white paint. Hazel remembered how in the drought of late summer, birches are the most brittle and vulnerable of trees. As in a waking dream she saw the trees broken, fallen. Once beauty is smashed it can't ever be made whole.

Seeing where Hazel was looking, Thaddeus spoke with childlike vanity of having designed the landscaping himself. He'd worked with a famous architect, and he'd had to fire the architect, finally. In the end, you are left with your own "genius"—such as it is.

Adding, in a pettish tone, "Not that anyone much gives a damn, among the Gallaghers. My family: they've all but abandoned me. Nobody comes to visit me, hardly."

"Really! I'm sorry to hear that, Mr. Gallagher."

Hazel doubted it was true. There were many Gallagher relatives and in-laws in the Albany area, and she had not heard that Thaddeus's other adult children, a brother and a sister, were estranged from him as Gallagher was.

"You have no family, Hazel Jones?"

There was a subtle emphasis on *you*. Hazel felt the danger, Thaddeus would try to interrogate her now.

"I have my son. And I have . . ."

Hazel's voice trailed off. She was stricken by a sudden shyness, reluctant to speak Chet Gallagher's name in his father's presence.

"But you and Chester are not married, eh?"

The question came blunt and guileless. Hazel felt her face heat with discomfort. Beside her, withdrawn and seemingly indifferent, Gallagher lifted his glass to his mouth and drank.

Hazel said, "No, Mr. Gallagher. We are not married."

"Though you've been together for six years? Seven? Such free-thinking young people! It's admirable, I suppose. 'Bohemian.' Now in the 1970s, when 'anything goes.' " Thaddeus paused, shifting his bulk eagerly in the wheelchair. His groin appeared swollen as a goiter in the snug-fitting plaid trunks. His flushed scalp was damp beneath thin floating wisps of silvery hair. "Though my son is not so young, is he? Not any longer."

Gallagher let this remark pass, as if unhearing. Hazel could think of no reply that was not fatuous even for Hazel Jones.

Thaddeus persisted, gaily: "It is admirable. Throwing off the shackles of the past. Only we, the elderly, wish to retain the past out of a terror of being thrust into the future where we will perish. One generation must make way for another, of course! I seem to have offended my own children, somehow." He paused, preparing to say something witty. "There's a distinction naturally between children and heirs. I no longer have 'children,' I have exclusively 'heirs.'"

Thaddeus laughed. Gallagher made no response. Hazel smiled, as one might smile at a sick child.

The old man must have his melancholy jokes. They were this afternoon's audience for his jokes. Gallagher had estimated, Thaddeus would leave an estate valued somewhere beyond $100 million. He had a right to expect to be courted, visited. The fat dimpled spider at the center of his quivering web. He wished now to persecute his youngest son whom he loved, who did not love him. He would poke, prod, stab at his son, he would demoralize his son, try to rouse him to fury. He hoped to make Gallagher squirm with guilt as with the most severe of gastric pains. Long he'd planned this passionate love-encounter, that was also revenge.

Winking at Hazel *You and I understand each other, eh? My fool son hasn't a clue.*

The suggestion of complicity between them left Hazel shaken, uncertain. Her face was very warm. Here was an old man long assured of his appeal to women. He was suffused with a thrumming life that seemed to have drained from his son.

"Of course, none of us are. Is. Any longer. Young."

Now Thaddeus began to complain more generally of the United States federal government, saboteurs in the Republican party and outright traitors among the Democrats, America's cowardly failure to "pull out all stops" in Vietnam. And what of the "media manipulation" of leftist intellectuals in the country, that Senator Joe McCarthy had been onto but got sidetracked, and his enemies bludgeoned the poor bastard to death. Why, Thaddeus wondered, were Jews invariably the ones most opposed to the war in Vietnam? Why were most Jews, when you came down to it, Communists, or Commie-sympathizers! Even Jew-capitalists, in their hearts they're Communists! Why the hell was this, when Stalin had loathed Jews, the Russian people loathed Jews, there had been more pogroms in Russia than in Germany, Poland, Hungary combined? "Yet in New York City and Los Angeles, that's all you will find. In broadcast journalism, newspapers.

The 'paper of record'—the *Jew York Times*. Who was it founded the NAACP—not the 'colored people,' you can bet, but the 'chosen people.' And why? I ask you, Hazel Jones, *why*?"

Hazel heard these sputtered and increasingly incoherent words through a steadily mounting ringing in her ears. Mixed with the mad cries of cicadas.

He knows. Knows who I am.

But—how can he?

At last Gallagher roused himself from his stupor.

"Is that so, Thaddeus? *All* Jews? They don't disagree with one another, about anything? Ever?"

"To their enemies, Jews present a unified front. The 'chosen people'—"

"Enemies? Who are the enemies of Jews? Nazis? Anti-Semites? *You*?"

With a look of indignation Thaddeus drew back in his wheelchair. The subtlety of his argument was being misunderstood! His disinterested philosophical position was being crudely personalized!

"I meant to say, non-Jews. They call us *goyim*, son. Not enemies per se except as Jews perceive us. You know perfectly well what I mean, son, it's a matter of historic *fact*."

Thaddeus was speaking solemnly now. As if his earlier baiting had been a pose.

But Gallagher rose abruptly to his feet. Mumbling he had to go inside for a few minutes.

Gallagher stumbled away. Hazel worried he was having one of his gastric attacks, that sometimes led to spasms of vomiting. His face had gone sickly white. Gallagher had begun to experience these attacks when he'd first been heckled at anti-war rallies several years ago, in Buffalo. Sometimes he suffered milder attacks before one of Zack's public performances.

Damn him: Hazel couldn't help resenting it, being left behind with Gallagher's father. This grotesque old man in his wheelchair glaring at her.

Saying, in Hazel Jones's way that was both breathless and apologetic, and her widened eyes fixed upon the glaring eyes in a look of utter distress, "Chet doesn't mean to be rude, Mr. Gallagher. This is an emotional—"

"Oh yes, is it, for 'Chet'? And for me, too."

"He hasn't been in this house, he said, since—"

"I know exactly how long, Miss Jones. You needn't inform me of facts regarding my own God-damned family."

Hazel, shocked, knew herself rebuffed. As if Thaddeus had leaned over and spat on her yellow organdy dress.

God damn your soul to hell, you bastard.

Sick dying old bastard I will have your heart.

The gravedigger's daughter, Hazel Jones was. There was never a time when Hazel Jones was not. Saying, in an embarrassed murmur to placate the enemy, "Mr. Gallagher, I'm sorry. Oh."

The white-jacketed servant hovered at the edge of the terrace, perhaps overhearing. Thaddeus noisily finished his drink, a vile-looking scarlet concoction laced with vodka. He too might have been embarrassed, speaking so sharply to a guest. And to so clearly innocent and guileless a guest. His glassy eyes brooded upon the swimming pool, its lurid artificial aqua. In the ripply surface, filaments of cloud were reflected like strands of gut. Thaddeus panted, grunted, scratched viciously at his crotch. He then rubbed his hefty bosom up inside the T-shirt, with a sensuous abandon. Hazel lowered her eyes, the gesture was so intimate.

The photographs she'd seen of Thaddeus Gallagher in the lodge at Grindstone Island were of a stout man, heavy but not obese, with a large head and a self-possessed manner. Now his body appeared swollen, bloated. His jaws had the look of jaws accustomed to ferocious grinding. Hazel wondered what cruel whimsy had inspired him to dress that day in such clothes, exposing and parodying his bulk.

"Bullshit he's 'emotional.' He's a cold-hearted s.o.b. You will learn, Hazel Jones. Chester Gallagher is not a man to be trusted. I am the one to apologize, Miss Jones, for *him*. His idiotic 'politics'! His Ne-gro jazz! Failed at serious piano, so he takes up Ne-gro jazz! Mongrel music. Failed at his marriage so he takes up women he can feel sorry for. He's shameless. He's a mythomaniac. He told me, bratty kid of fifteen, 'Capitalism is doomed.' The little pisspot! These newspaper columns of his, he invents, he distorts, he exaggerates in the name of 'moral truth.' As if there could be a 'moral truth' that refutes historical truth. When he was a drunk—and Chester was a drunk, Miss Jones, for many more years than you've known him—he inhabited a kind of bathosphere of mythomania. He has invented such tales of me, my 'business ethics,' I've given up hoping to set them straight. I'm an old newspaper man, I believe in facts. Facts, and more facts! There's never been an editorial in any Gallagher newspaper not based upon facts! Not liberal crap, sentimental bullshit about 'world peace'—the 'United Nations'—'global disarmament'—but facts. The bedrock of journalism. Chester Gallagher never respected facts sufficiently. Trying to make himself out some kind of white Ne-gro, playing their music and taking up their causes."

Hazel was gripping a sweating glass in her hand. She spoke evenly, just slightly coquettishly. "Your son is a mythomaniac, Mr. Gallagher, and you are not?"

Thaddeus squinted at her. His chins jiggled. As if Hazel had reached over to touch his knee, he brightened.

"You must call me 'Thaddeus,' Hazel Jones. Better yet, 'Thad.' 'Mr. Gallagher' is for servants and other hirelings."

When Hazel made no reply, Thaddeus leaned toward her, suggestively. "Will you call me 'Thad'? It's very like 'Chet'—eh? Almost no one calls me 'Thad' any longer, my old friends are falling away—every season, like dying leaves."

Hazel's lips moved numbly. " 'Thad.' "

"Very good! I certainly intend to call you 'Hazel.' Now and forever."

Thaddeus moved the wheelchair closer to Hazel. She smelled his old-man odor, the airless interior of the old stone cottage. Yet there was something sweetly sharp beneath, Thaddeus Gallagher's cologne. A monster-man, crammed into a wheelchair, yet he'd shaved carefully that morning, he'd dabbed on cologne.

Unnerving how, close up, you could see the younger Thaddeus inside the elder's face, exultant.

" 'Hazel Jones.' A lovely name with something nostalgic about it. Who gave you that name, my dear?"

"I—don't know."

"Don't know? How is that possible, Hazel?"

"I never knew my parents. They died when I was a little girl."

"Did they! And where was this, Hazel?"

Gallagher had warned, his father would interrogate her. Yet Hazel could not seem to prevent it.

"I don't know, Mr. Gallagher. It happened so long ago . . ."

"Not that long ago, surely? You're a young woman."

Hazel shook her head slowly. Young?

" 'Hazel Jones' The name is known to me, but not why. Can you explain why, my dear?"

Hazel said lightly, "There are probably 'Hazel Joneses'—Mr. Gallagher. More than one."

"Well! Don't let me upset you, my dear. I'm feeling guilty, I suppose. I seem to have upset my overly sensitive radical son, who has run off and left us."

Briskly then Thaddeus pressed one of the buttons on the wheelchair. Hazel heard no sound but within seconds a male attendant appeared, in T-shirt, swim trunks, carrying terry cloth robes and towels. This young man called Thaddeus "Mr. G." and was called by the older man what sounded like "Peppy." He was about twenty-five, darkly tanned, with a blandly affable boy's face; he had a swimmer's physique, long-waisted, with broad wing-like shoulders. Hazel saw his eyes slide onto her, swiftly assessing yet vacant. He was one who knew his place: a wealthy invalid's physical therapist.

"Will you join me, Hazel? They say I must swim every day, to keep my condition from 'progressing.' Of course, my condition 'progresses' in any case. Such is life!"

Hazel declined the invitation. She came to assist Peppy as he helped Thaddeus into the pool, at the shallow end: this was a Hazel Jones gesture, spontaneous and friendly.

"My dear, thank you! I hate the water, until I get into it."

Peppy fastened red plastic water wings onto the obese man, over his fatty shoulders and across his immense drooping bosom. Slowly then he helped Thaddeus into the water with the frowning attentiveness of a mother helping her clumsy, somewhat fearful child into the water, that shimmered and quaked about him. Hazel offered her hand. And how grateful Thaddeus was, gripping her hand. As his weight slipped into the water like a bag of concrete Thaddeus squeezed Hazel's slender fingers in a sudden helpless panic. Then, as if miraculously, Thaddeus was in the pool, wheezing, paddling with childlike abandon. Peppy walked and then swam beside him slowly. Thaddeus was laughing, winking up at Hazel who followed his slow progress through the now choppy water, walking at the edge of the pool.

"Hazel! You must join us. The water is perfect, isn't it, Peppy?"

"Sure is, Mr. G."

Hazel laughed. Her pretty dress had been splashed, and would stink of chlorine.

"Really, Hazel," Thaddeus said, holding his head erect out of the water, with an absurd dignity, "you must join us. You've come so far." The motions of his hefty arms were energetic, those of his atrophied legs feeble.

"I don't have a bathing suit, Mr. Gallagher."

" 'Thad'! You promised."

" 'Thad.' "

Thaddeus was enlivened again, with a frantic gaiety.

"There are women's bathing suits in the changing rooms, over there. Please, go look."

Hazel stood irresolute. Almost, to spite her lover she was tempted.

As if reading her thoughts Thaddeus said slyly, "You must, dear! To show up my cowardly son. He fled, he's afraid of his old crippled father who has prostate cancer, and a touch of colon cancer to boot. But do you see Thaddeus slinking away in cowardly defeat? *You do not.*"

Hazel knew not to react to this disclosure. Never must she make any reference to Thaddeus Gallagher's health. She would pretend she had not heard. Carefully she removed her high-heeled sandals, to walk barefoot at the edge of the pool. Her legs were long, supple with muscle. Her legs were smooth, shaven. It was a fetish with Hazel Jones to shave her legs, thighs and armpits and other areas of her body that might betray her by sprouting dark, rather curly coarse hairs. As Hazel Jones ate sparingly, to remain Hazel Jones who was slender, very feminine and very pretty. In the smelly aqua water, Thaddeus Gallagher strained to watch her.

He could not speak very clearly, paddling and splashing with his absurd water wings. Yet he kept calling to Hazel as one might call to a perverse child. "Surely you can swim, dear? Nothing would happen to you, with Peppy and me at hand."

Hazel laughed. "I don't think so, Thad. Thank you."

"And if I gave you a gift, dear? A thousand dollars."

Thaddeus meant to speak in such a way that Hazel could interpret the remark as a joke, and not be offended. But the words came out awkwardly, his glassy blinking eyes stared and strained at her.

Hazel shook her head, no.

"Five thousand!" Thaddeus cried gaily.

An old man's harmless teasing. He was falling in love with Hazel Jones. Cavorting in the water, making even Peppy laugh. Paddling and splashing and kicking and wheezing like a baby elephant. His behavior was so ludicrous, so strangely touching, Hazel had to laugh.

"My dear, don't abandon me! Please."

He'd thought that Hazel was walking away. She'd gone only to examine a lattice of crimson climber roses, against a cream-colored stucco wall.

After a few more minutes, Thaddeus abruptly ordered Peppy to haul him out of the pool. Again, Hazel Jones came to help: took the old man's big fleshy hand, that gripped hers tightly. Hazel also brought towels, terry cloth robes for both men. Thaddeus wrapped the enormous towels about his body, rubbing himself briskly. His thinning hair that lay now flat against the big dome of his head, he dried as energetically as he might have done in his youth when his hair was thick. It was exactly Gallagher's practice. Hazel saw this, and felt some tenderness for Thaddeus.

In his wheelchair, wrapped in towels large as blankets, Thaddeus puffed and panted and smiled, exhilarated. The white-jacketed servant had brought him another scarlet drink as well as a silver bowl of mixed nuts which he ate noisily.

"Hazel Jones! I must confess I'd heard certain things about you. Now I see, none of them were true."

Thaddeus spoke in a lowered voice. He kept glancing back at the house, concerned that his son would reappear.

He reached out to take Hazel's hand. She shivered but did not pull away.

"My son is a man of integrity, I know. I have quarrels with him but in his own way, yes of course he is 'moral.' I wish that I knew how to love him, Hazel! He has never forgiven me, you see, for things that happened long ago. He has told you, I suppose?" Thaddeus squinted wistfully at Hazel.

"No. He has not."

"He has *not*?"

"Never."

"He complains about my politics, surely? My convictions that are so very different from his?"

"Chet only speaks of you with respect. He loves you, Mr. Gallagher. But he's afraid of you."

"Afraid of me! Why?"

There was something furtive and sick in Thaddeus's face. Yet a glimmering of hope.

"You should ask Chet, Mr. Gallagher. I can't speak for him."

"Yes, yes: you can speak for him. Far better you can speak for him, Hazel Jones, than he can speak for himself." The old man's pose of drollery had quite fallen away, now he was fully earnest. Almost, he was pleading with Hazel. "He loves me? He respects me?"

"He thinks that your political beliefs are mistaken. That's all."

"He has never said anything about—his mother?"

"Only that he loved her. And misses her."

"Does he! I do, too."

Thaddeus and Hazel were alone on the terrace. Both Peppy and the servant in the white jacket had departed. Thaddeus sat swathed in white terry cloth, sighing. Still he continued to glance back at the house nervously. "You have no family, Hazel? No one living?"

"No one."

"Only just your son?"

"Only just my son."

"Are you and Chet secretly married, dear?"

"No."

"But why? Why aren't you married?"

Hazel smiled evasively. No, no! She would not say.

Wistfully Thaddeus asked, "Don't you love my son? Why would you live with him, if you don't love him?"

"He loves me. He loves our son."

The words escaped from Hazel Jones as in a dream. For all her shrewdness she had not known she would utter them until that moment.

She saw in the old man's face an expression of shock, triumph.

"I knew! I knew that was it!"

Worriedly Hazel said, with the air of one who has confided too much, "He can't know that I've told you, Mr. Gallagher. He can't bear the thought of being talked about."

Thaddeus said, panting, "I knew. Somehow, seeing you. I did know. Hazel Jones: this will be our secret."

A blind, dazed expression came over the old man's face. For some seconds he sat silent, breathing hard. Hazel felt the terrible pounding of his heart in that massive body. Thaddeus was deeply gratified yet suddenly very tired. Cavorting in the pool had exhausted him. This long scene had exhausted him. Hazel would summon one of the servants to help him but Thaddeus continued to grip her hand, hard. Pleading, "You won't stay for dinner, Hazel? You don't think that Chet could be talked into changing his mind?"

Gently Hazel said no. She didn't think so.

"I will miss you, then. I will think of you, Hazel. And of—'Zacharias Jones.' I will hear the boy play piano, when I can. I will not push myself upon you, I understand that that would be a tactical error. My son is a sensitive man, Hazel. He's also a jealous man. If—if Chester ever disappoints you, dear, you must come to *me*. Will you promise, Hazel?"

Gently Hazel said yes. She promised.

In a sudden clumsy gesture Thaddeus lifted her hand to his lips, to kiss. Long Hazel would feel the imprint of that kiss on her skin, the fleshy, unexpectedly chill sensation.

The fat dimpled spider, the gravedigger's daughter. Who might have predicted!

28

❋ ❋ ❋

The wound was such, Gallagher would not speak of it initially.

In silence they drove back to Vermont. Gallagher's face was still unnaturally pale, drawn. Hazel surmised he'd been sick to his stomach vomiting in one of the bathrooms of his father's house and he was deeply ashamed.

She did love him, she supposed. In the man's very weakness that filled her with a wild flailing contempt like a maddened winged creature trapped against a screen she loved him.

The remainder of the day passed in a kind of dream. They were uneasily aware of each other without speaking, nor even touching. They had dinner with Zack and some others. By quick degrees, Gallagher recovered from the visit at Ardmoor Park. He was very much his usual self at dinner, and at a reception following that evening's symphony concert. Only when he and Hazel were alone together in their hotel room did Gallagher say at last, in a genial tone to allow Hazel to know he was bemused and not angry: "You and my father got along very well, didn't you! I heard you laughing together. From the window of my old room I saw him wheezing and splashing in the pool like a deranged elephant. Something of a couple: Beauty and the Beast."

Gallagher was brushing his teeth in the bathroom, the door ajar. Spitting into the sink, harshly. Hazel knew without seeing that he was grimacing into the mirror.

She said, "He seems sad, Chet. A lonely old man fearful of dying."

"Is he!" Gallagher spoke flatly, yet wanting to be appeased.

"He seems hurt by life."

"By me, you mean."

"Are you all of 'life' to your father, Chet?"

It was an unexpected response. When Hazel Jones said such things, Gallagher seemed often not to hear.

Later she slipped her arms around his chest. She held him tight, gravely she intoned, " 'My son is a man of integrity, I wish that he would let me love him.' "

Gallagher's laughter was startled, uneasy.

"Don't try to tell me my father said that, Hazel."

"He did."

"Bullshit, Hazel. Don't tell me."

"He has prostate cancer, Chet. He has colon cancer."

"Since when?"

"He doesn't want you to know, I think. He made a joke of it."

"I wouldn't believe anything he says, Hazel. He's quite the joker." Clumsily Gallagher moved about the room, not-seeing. The staring vacant look had come into his face. "That crap about the '*Jew York Times*'—he's got a feud going, the *Times* wins Pulitzer Prizes every year and the Gallagher chain wins a Pulitzer every five years if they get lucky. That's what's behind *that*." Gallagher was incensed, close to tears.

"He loves you, though. Somehow, he feels ashamed before you."

"Bullshit, Hazel."

"It may be bullshit, but it happens to be true."

In bed, in Gallagher's ropey-muscled arms, Hazel felt at last that she might tease him. She felt the heat of her lover's skin, she lay very still against him. He would forgive her now. He adored Hazel Jones, always he was looking for plausible ways to forgive her.

Hazel whispered in his ear how shocked she'd been, to discover that Thaddeus Gallagher was an invalid in a wheelchair!

"He is? An invalid?" Gallagher squirmed and twitched beneath the bedclothes, staring toward the ceiling. "Christ. I guess he is."

29

❀ ❀ ❀

Hazel Jones: this will be our secret.

For the remainder of his life he would send her small gifts. Flowers. Every four or five weeks, and often following a public performance of Zack's. Somehow he knew, he made it his business to know, when Gallagher would be gone from the house, and timed deliveries for those mornings.

The first came soon after Hazel returned to Delaware Park, Buffalo, to the house Gallagher had bought for them near the music school. Numerous red climber roses, small-petalled roses, in a thorny cluster that was awkward to fit into even a tall vase. The accompanying note was handwritten, as if in haste.

August 22, 1970

Dearest Hazel Jones,

I have not stopped thinking of you for a single momment since last week. I had a (secret!!!) tape made of Zachiaras playing at the music festival, truly your son is a suberb musician! So hard to believe he is only 13. I have photographs of him, he is so young. Of course in his heart he is no child is he! As I at 13 was no longer a child. For my heart was hardened young, I knew the "way of the world" from boyhood on & had no illusions of the "natural good" of mankind etcetera. Dear Hazel, I hope I am not offending you! Your husband must not know. We will keep our secret will we! Tho' I think always of you, your beautiful dark kind eyes that forgive & do not judge. If you would be so kind Hazel you might call me sometime, my number is below. This is my privvate line Hazel, no one will pick up. <u>But if not</u> dear, I will not be hurt. You have brought into the world the re-markable boy. That he is my grandson is our secret (!!!) & I will meet him sometime but in secret. Do not fear me. You have given me so much I did not expect or hope. I will not be hurt. I will think of you always. Chester is a good man I know, but he is weak & Jealous as his father at that age. Utnil another time, dear

Your Loving "InLaw" Thad

Hazel read this letter in astonishment, distracted by the numerous spell-ing errors. "He's crazy! He's in love with her." She had not expected such a response. She felt a pang of guilt, if Gallagher should know.

She threw the letter away, she would not reply to it. Never would Hazel Jones reply to Thaddeus Gallagher's impassioned letters, which became more incoherent with time, nor would she thank him for the numerous gifts. Hazel Jones was a woman of dignity, integrity. Hazel Jones would not encourage the old man, yet she would not discourage him. She supposed that he would be true to his word, he would not confront her or Zack. He would admire them from a discreet distance. Gallagher seemed never to notice the gifts in the household: vases of flowers, a heart-shaped crystal paperweight, a brass frame for a photograph, a silk scarf printed with rose-buds. The old man was discreet enough to send Hazel only small, relatively inexpensive and inconspicuous gifts. And never money.

In March 1971 there came by special delivery a packet for Hazel Jones that was not a gift, but a manila envelope with the return address GALLAGHER MEDIA INC. Inside the envelope were photocopies of newspaper articles and one of Thaddeus Gallagher's hastily scrawled letters.

At last my assistant gathered these matrials, Hazel. Why it has takken so long I frankly DO NOT KNOW. Thought you would be intriguing,

Hazel Jones. "Only a Conincidence" I know. [THANK GOD THANK
GOD this poor Hazel Jones was not <u>you</u>.]

There were several pages more, but Hazel tossed them away without
reading them.

In an upstairs room of the Delaware Park house where no one was likely
to disturb her, Hazel removed the photocopied material from the manila
envelope and spread it out on a table. Her movements were deliberate and
unhurried and yet her hands shook slightly, she seemed to know beforehand that the revelation Thaddeus Gallagher had sent her would not be a
happy one.

The newspaper articles had already been arranged in chronological order. Hazel tried to keep from glancing ahead to learn the outcome.

Yet, there it was:

GRISLY DISCOVERY IN NEW FALLS

FOLLOWS DOCTOR DEATH

Female Skeletons Unearthed

And,

DECEASED NEW FALLS M.D.

SUSPECT IN UNSOLVED 1950S ABDUCTIONS

Property Searched by Police, Skeletons Found

Both clippings included an accompanying photograph, the same likeness of a genially smiling man of middle age: Byron Hendricks, M. D.

"Him! The man in the panama hat."

Both articles, from the *Port Oriskany Journal*, were dated September
1964. New Falls was a small, relatively affluent suburb north of Port Oriskany, on Lake Erie. Hazel told herself sternly *It is over now. Whatever it was, is
over now. It has nothing to do with me now.*

It was so. It had to be so. She had not given a thought to Byron Hendricks, M.D., for eleven years. Virtually all memory of the man had faded from her consciousness.

Hazel turned to the first of the articles, also from the *Journal*, and dated June 1956.

NEW FALLS GIRL REPORTED MISSING

POLICE, VOLUNTEERS EXPAND SEARCH

Hazel Jones, 18, "Vanished"

This Hazel Jones had attended New Falls High School but had dropped out at the age of sixteen. She had lived with her family in the country outside New Falls and had supported herself by "babysitting, waitressing, housecleaning" locally. At the time of her disappearance, she had just begun summer work at a Dairy Queen. Numerous parties had seen Hazel Jones at the Dairy Queen on the day of her disappearance; at dusk she had left to ride her bicycle home, a distance of three miles; but she had never arrived home. Her bicycle was subsequently found in a drainage ditch beside a highway, about two miles from her home.

Apparently it was not a kidnapping, there was no ransom demanded. There were no witnesses to any abduction. No one could think of any person who might have wanted to harm Hazel Jones nor did Hazel Jones have a boyfriend who might have threatened her. For days, weeks, eventually years Hazel Jones was the object of a search but she, or the body she had become, was never found.

Hazel stared at the girl in the photograph. For here was a familiar face.

Aged seventeen at the time of the photograph, Hazel Jones had thick wavy dark hair that fell to her shoulders and across her forehead. Her eyebrows were rather heavy, she had a long nose rather broad at the tip. She was not pretty but "striking"—almost, you might say "exotic." Her mouth was fleshy, sensuous. Yet there was something prim and even sullen about her. Her eyes were large, very dark, untrusting. For the camera she tried to smile, not very convincingly.

How like Rebecca Schwart at that age, this Hazel Jones! It was unnerving. It was painful to see.

Former New Falls classmates said of Hazel Jones that she was "quiet"—"kept to herself"—"hard to get to know."

Hazel Jones's parents said she would "never have gotten into any car with anybody she didn't know, Hazel wasn't that kind of girl."

A subsequent article depicted Mr. and Mrs. Jones posed in front of their "modest bungalow-style" home on the outskirts of New Falls. They were a middle-aged couple, heavy-browed and dark-complected like their daughter, staring grimly at the camera like gamblers willing to take a risk though expecting to lose.

The fake-brick siding on the Joneses' house was water stained. In the Joneses' grassless front yard, debris had been raked into a mound.

The next several articles were dated 1957, from upstate newspapers in Port Oriskany, Buffalo, Rochester and Albany. (The Rochester and Albany papers belonged to the Gallagher chain, coincidentally.) In June 1957 another girl was reported missing, this time from Gowanda, a small city thirty miles south and east of Port Oriskany; in October, yet another girl was reported missing from Cableport, a village on the Erie Barge Canal near Albany, hundreds of miles east. The girl from Gowanda was Dorianne Klinski, aged twenty; the girl from Cableport was Gloria Loving, aged nineteen. Dorianne was married, Gloria engaged. Dorianne had "vanished into thin air" walking home from her salesclerk job in Gowanda. Gloria had similarly vanished walking home from Cableport on the Erie Canal towpath, a distance of no more than a mile.

How like Hazel Jones of New Falls these girls looked! Dark-haired, not-pretty.

In the several articles about Dorianne and Gloria there were no references to Hazel Jones of New Falls. But in articles about Gloria Loving, there were references to Dorianne Klinski. Only in later articles, about girls missing in 1959, 1962, and 1963, were there references to the "original" missing girl Hazel Jones. It had taken law enforcement officers, spread across numerous rural counties and townships through New York State, a long time to connect the abductions.

Hazel was reading with mounting difficulty. Her eyes flooded with tears of hurt, rage.

"The bastard! So that's what he wanted with me: to murder me."

It was a supreme joke. It was the most fantastical revelation of her life. "Hazel Jones": all along, from the first, a dead girl. A murdered girl. A naive trusting girl who, when Byron Hendricks had approached Rebecca Schwart on the towpath outside Chautauqua Falls, had been dead for three years. Dead, decomposed! One of the female skeletons to be one day unearthed on Byron Hendricks's property.

Hazel forced herself to continue reading. She must know the full story even if she would not wish to recall it. The final articles focused on Byron Hendricks, for now in September 1964 the man had been exposed. The most lavish article was a full-page feature from the *Port Oriskany Journal* in which "Dr. Hendricks's" benignly smiling face was positioned in an oval surrounded by oval likenesses of his six "known" victims.

At least, Hendricks was dead. The bastard wasn't locked away somewhere in a mental hospital. There was that satisfaction, at least.

Hendricks had been fifty-two at the time of his death. He had lived alone for years in a "spacious" brick home in New Falls. His medical degree was from the University of Buffalo Medical School but he had never practiced medicine, as his deceased father had done for nearly fifty years; he identified himself as a "medical researcher." New Falls neighbors spoke of Hendricks as "friendly-seeming but kept to himself"—"always a kind word, cheerful"—"a gentleman"—"always well dressed."

Hendricks's only previous contact with any of his victims, so far as police could determine, had been with eighteen-year-old Hazel Jones who'd done "occasional housecleaning" for him.

Hendricks had been found dead in an upstairs room of his home, his body badly decomposed after ten or more days. Initially it was believed that he'd died of natural causes, but an autopsy had turned up evidence of a morphine overdose. Police discovered scrapbooks of news clippings pertaining to the missing girls as well as "incriminating memorabilia." A search of the house and overgrown two-acre lot led to the eventual discovery of an "estimated" six female skeletons.

Six. He'd led away six Hazel Joneses.

How eagerly, with what naive hope had they gone with him, you could only imagine.

Hazel had not been seated at the table, which was a long, narrow worktable to which she often retreated (here, on the airy third floor of the house Gallagher had bought for her, Hazel felt most comfortable: she was taking night school courses at nearby Canisius College, and spread out her work on the table), but leaning over it, resting her weight on the palms of her hands. By degrees she'd become dizzy, light-headed. Pulses beat in her brain close to bursting. She would not faint! She would not succumb to fear, panic. Instead, she heard herself laughing. It was not Hazel Jones's delicate feminine laughter but a harsh mirthless hacking laughter.

"A joke! 'Hazel Jones' is a joke."

There came a rebuking wave of nausea. A taste of something black and cold at the back of her mouth. Then the worktable's nearest corner flew up at her. Struck her forehead against something sharp as the edge of an ax blade, abruptly she was on the floor and when she managed to rouse herself from her faint some minutes later, might've been five minutes, might've been twenty, there she was dripping blood not knowing where the hell she was or what had happened, she was still laughing at the joke she couldn't exactly remember, or trying to laugh.

That night, beside Gallagher. Thinking *I will wake him. I will tell him who I am. I will tell him my life has been a lie, a bad joke. There is no Hazel Jones. Where I am, there is no one.* But Gallagher slept as always Gallagher did, a man oblivious in sleep, hot-skinned, prone to snoring, twitching and kicking at bedclothes and if he woke partially he would moan like a forlorn child and reach out for Hazel Jones in the night to touch, to nudge, to caress, to hold, he adored Hazel Jones and so finally she did not wake him and eventually, toward dawn, Hazel Jones slept, too.

III

BEYOND

I

❀ ❀ ❀

Through the summer and fall of 1974 the house rang with Beethoven's "Appassionata." That music!

As in a dream she who was the mother of the young pianist moved open-eyed and unseeing. Lovesick she found herself standing outside the closed door of the music room, entranced.

"He will. He will play it. This is his time."

She who lacked an ear for the subtleties of piano interpretation could not have said if the sonata she heard bore a profound or a merely superficial relationship to the recording by Artur Schnabel she'd heard twenty-five years before in the parlor of the old stone cottage in the cemetery.

Inside the music room her exacting son was forever starting, and stopping. Starting, and stopping. Now the left hand alone, now the right. Now both hands together and back to the beginning and ceasing abruptly and returning again to the beginning in the way of a small anxious child beginning to walk upright, stumbling and flailing for balance. If he had wished, Zack could play the sonata unimpeded: he could play it straight through, striking every note. He had that ability, the mechanical facility of the piano prodigy. But a deeper resonance was required. A deeper desperation.

The desperation beneath, Hazel supposed to be inside the music itself. It was that of the composer, Beethoven. It was the man's soul into which the young pianist must descend. She listened, wondering if the choice of the sonata had been a mistake. Her son was so young: this was not music for youth. She became excited, almost feverish in listening. Stumbling away exhausted not wanting Zack to know she'd been listening outside the door of the music room for it would annoy and exasperate him, who knew his mother so intimately.

Bad enough I'm trying not to go crazy myself, Mother I don't intend to be responsible for you going crazy too.

He was restless! At the age of fifteen he'd placed second in the 1972 Montreal Young Pianists Competition, and at the age of sixteen he'd placed first in the 1973 Philadelphia Young Pianists Competition, and now nearing his eighteenth birthday he was preparing for the 1974 San Francisco International Piano Competition.

Hours. Each day at the piano. At the Conservatory, and at home. And into the night hours and through the night in the throes of music rushing through his sleep-locked brain with the terrible power of cascading water over a falls. And this music was not his and must not be impeded, choked-back. A vast tide to the very horizon! It was a tide that encompassed time as well as space: the long-dead as well as the living. To choke back such a force would be to suffocate. At the piano sometimes leaning into the keyboard suddenly desperate for air, oxygen. That piano smell of old ivory, fine wood and wood polish, this was poison. Yet at other times away from the piano knowing he must take a break from the piano for sanity's sake at such times in even the outdoor air of Delaware Park and in the presence of another (Zack was in love, maybe) a sensation of helplessness came over him, the panic that he would suffocate if he could not complete a passage of music struggling to make its way through him except: his fingers were inadequate without the keyboard and so he must return to the keyboard or he would suffocate.

Trying not to go crazy Mother. Help me!

In fact he blamed her.

Rarely allowed her to touch him, now.

For Zack was in love (maybe). The girl was two years older than he was, in his German language class and a serious musician: a cellist.

Except not so good a cellist as you are a pianist, Zack. Thank God!

It was this girl's way to speak bluntly. Her way to laugh at the expression on his face. They were not yet intimate, they had not yet touched. She could not console him with a kiss, for the shock she'd caused him. For he was one to whom music is sacred, no more to be laughed at than death is to be laughed at.

You could laugh at death though. From the farther side recalling the grassy canal bank they'd walked along, how on the farther side was the towpath but the nearer side where no one walked except Mommy and him (so little, Mommy had to grip his hand to keep him from stumbling!) was grassy and overgrown.

Laugh at death if you could cross over why the hell not!

She knew. A mother knows.

Beginning to be wary, anxious. Her son was growing apart from her.

It wasn't the piano, the demands of practice. Hazel was never jealous of the piano!

Thinking when she heard him playing *He is in the right place now of all the world. Where he was born to be.* Taking comfort knowing he was hers. Rather, it was a reaction against the piano she feared.

Against his own talent, "success." His own hands she saw him studying sometimes, examining with a clinical and faintly bemused detachment. *Mine?*

If he injured his hands. If somehow.

He was interested in European history: World War II. He'd taken a course at the university. He was interested in philosophy, religion. There was a feverish tone to his voice, an uneasy tremor. As if the world's secrets might yield to him, if only he had the key. To Hazel's dismay Zack began talking of the most preposterous things! One day it was the ancient Indian Upanishads, one day it was the nineteenth-century German philosopher

Schopenhauer, one day it was the Hebrew Bible. He began to be argumentative, aggressive. Saying suddenly at the dinner table, as if this were a crucial issue they'd been avoiding: "Of all the religions, wouldn't the oldest be closest to God? And who is 'God'? What is 'God'? Are we to know this God, or only just one another? Is our place with God or with one another, on earth?" His expression was quizzical, earnest. He was leaning his elbows on the table, hunched forward.

Gallagher tried to talk with his stepson, more or less seriously. "Well, Zack! Glad you asked. My personal feeling is, religion is mankind trying to get a handle on what's outside 'man.' Each religion has a different set of answers prescribed by a self-appointed priestly caste and each religion, you can be sure, teaches it's the 'only' religion, sanctified by God."

"But that doesn't mean that one of the religions isn't *true*. Like if there are twelve answers to an algebra problem eleven might be wrong and one *right*."

"But 'God' isn't a provable math problem, Zack. 'God' is just a catchall term we give to our ignorance."

"Or even, maybe," Zack said excitedly, "the different ways of human speech are crude and clumsy and are actually pointing toward the same thing, but different languages make them confused. Like, 'God' is behind the religions, like the sun you can't look at directly, you'd go blind, except if there was no sun, see, then you would really be blind, because you couldn't see a damned *thing*. Maybe it's like that?"

To Hazel's knowledge, Zack had never spoken so passionately about anything before, except music. He was leaning his elbows onto the table clumsily so that the lighted candles wavered, screwing up his face in a way that reminded Hazel horribly of Jacob Schwart.

Her son! In hurt and chagrin Hazel stared at him.

Gallagher said, trying to joke, "Zack, I had no idea! What a budding theologian we have in our midst."

Zack said, stung, "Don't condescend to me, 'Dad,' O.K.? I'm not somebody on your TV show."

Now Zack was Gallagher's legally adopted son sometimes he called Gallagher "Dad." Usually it was playful, affectionate. But sometimes with a twist of adolescent sarcasm, like now.

Gallagher said quickly, "I don't mean to condescend, Zack. It's just that discussions like this make people upset without enlightening them. There is a similarity between religions, isn't there, a kind of skeleton in common, and like human beings, with human skeletons—" Gallagher broke off, seeing Zack's look of impatience. He said, annoyed, "Believe me, kid, I know. I've been there."

Zack said sullenly, "I'm not a kid. In the sense of being an idiot I'm not a fucking *kid*."

Gallagher, smiling hard, determined to charm his stepson into submission, said, "Intelligent people have been quarreling over these questions for thousands of years. When they agree, it's out of an emotional need to agree, not because there is anything genuine to 'agree' about. People crave to believe something, so they believe anything. It's like starving: you'd eat practically anything, right? It's been my experience—"

"Look, 'Dad,' you aren't *me*. Neither one of you is *me*. Got it?"

Zack had never spoken so rudely in the past. His eyes glittered with angry tears. He'd had a strained session with his piano teacher that day, perhaps. His life was complicated now in ways Hazel could not know, for he kept much to himself, she dared not approach him.

Gallagher tried again to reason with Zack, in Gallagher's affably bantering way that was so effective on television (Gallagher now had a weekly interview show on WBEN-TV Buffalo, a Gallagher Media production) but not so effective with the boy who squirmed with impatience and all but rolled his eyes as Gallagher spoke. Hazel sat forlorn, lost. She understood that Zack was defying her, not Gallagher. He was defying her who had taught him since childhood that religion was for *those others*, not for them.

Poor Gallagher! He was red-faced and breathless as a middle-aged athlete grown complacent in his skills who has just been outmaneuvered by a young athlete whom he has failed to take seriously.

Zack was saying, "Music isn't enough! It's only a part of the brain. I have a whole brain, for Christ's sake. I want to know about things other people know." He swallowed hard. He shaved now, the lower half of his face appeared darker than the rest, his short upper lip covered in a fine dark down. Within seconds he was capable of childish petulance, good-natured equanimity, chilling hauteur. He had not once glanced at Hazel during the exchange with Gallagher nor did he look at her now, saying, in a sudden rush of words, "I want to know about Judaism, where it comes from and what it *is*."

Judaism: this was a word never before spoken between Hazel and Zack. Nor even the less formal words *Jews, Jewish*.

Gallagher was saying, "Of course, I can understand that. You want to know all that you can know, within reason. Beginning with the old religions. I was the same way myself . . ." Gallagher was fumbling now, uncertain. He was vaguely conscious of the strain between Hazel and Zack. As a man of the world with a certain degree of renown he was accustomed to being taken seriously, certainly he was accustomed to being deferred to, yet in his own household he was often at sea. Doggedly he said, "But the piano, Zack! That must come first."

Zack said hotly, "It comes first. But it doesn't come second, too. Or third, or fucking *last*."

Zack tossed his crumpled napkin down onto his plate. He'd only partly eaten the meal his mother had prepared, as she prepared all household meals, with such care. She felt the sting of that gesture as she felt the sting of the purposefully chosen expletive *fucking*, she knew it was aimed at her heart. With quavering adolescent dignity Zack pushed his chair back from the table and stalked out of the room. The adults stared after him in astonishment.

Gallagher groped for Hazel's limp hand, to comfort her.

"Somebody's been talking to him, d'you think? Somebody at the university."

Hazel sat still and unmoving in her state of shock as if she'd been slapped.

"It's the pressure he's under, with that sonata. It's too mature for him, possibly. He's just a kid, and he's growing. I remember that miserable age, Christ! Sex-sex-sex. I couldn't keep my mind on the keyboard, let me tell you. It's nothing personal, darling."

To spite me. To abandon me. Because he hates me. Why?

She fled from both the son and the stepfather. She could not bear it, such exposure. As if the very vertebrae of her backbone were exposed!

She was not crying when Gallagher came to comfort her. It was rare for Hazel Jones to cry, she detested such weakness.

Gallagher talked to her, tenderly and persuasively. In their bed she lay very still in his arms. He would protect her, he adored his Hazel Jones. He would protect her against her rude adolescent son. Though saying of course Zack didn't mean it, Zack loved her and would not wish to hurt her, she must know this.

"Yes. I know it."

"And I love you, Hazel. I would die for you."

He talked for a long time: it was Gallagher's way of loving a woman, with both his words and his body. He was not a man like the other, who had little need of words. Between her and that man, the boy's father, had been a deeper connection. But that was finished now, extinct. No more could she love a man in that way: her sexual, intensely erotic life was over.

She was deeply grateful to this man, who prized her as the other had not. Yet, in his very estimation of her, she understood his weakness.

She did not want to be comforted, really! Almost, she preferred to feel the insult aimed at her heart.

Thinking scornfully *In animal life the weakest are quickly disposed of. That's religion: the only religion.*

Yet she'd returned in secret several times to the park where the man in soiled work clothes had approached her and spoken to her.

My name is Gus Schwart.

Do I look like anybody you know?

Of course, she had not seen him again. Her eyes filled with tears of dismay and indignation, that she might have hoped to see him again, who had sprung at her out of nowhere.

How it had pierced her heart, that man's voice! He had spoken her name, she had not heard in a very long time.

My sister Rebecca, we used to live in Milburn . . .

She'd looked up *Schwart* in the local telephone directory and called each of the several listings but without success.

In Montreal, and in Toronto, where they'd traveled in recent years, Hazel had also looked up *Schwart* and made a few futile calls for she had the vague idea that Herschel was somewhere in Canada, hadn't Herschel spoken of crossing the border into Canada and escaping his pursuers . . .

"If he's alive. If any 'Schwarts' are alive."

She began to be anxious as she had not been anxious before the earlier competitions reasoning *He is young, he has time* for now her son was nearly eighteen, rapidly maturing. A taut tense sexual being he was. Impulsive, irritable. Nerves caused his skin to break out, in disfiguring blemishes on his forehead. He would not confide in his parents, that he suffered indigestion, constipation. Yet Hazel knew.

She could not bear it, that her gifted son might yet fail. It would be death to her, if he failed after having come so far.

"The breath of God."

That roadside café in Apalachin, New York! The hot-skinned child on her lap snug in Mommy's arms reaching up eagerly to play the broken keyboard of a battered old upright piano. Smoke haze, the pungent smell of beer, drunken shouts and laughter of strangers.

Jesus how's he do it, kid so little?

She smiled, they'd been happy then.

He was an affably drunken older man acquainted with Chet Gallagher eager to meet Gallagher's little family.

Introduced himself as "Zack Zacharias." He'd heard that Gallagher's stepson was a pianist named "Zacharias," too.

This was at the Grand Island Yacht Club to which Gallagher took his little family to celebrate, when Zack was informed he'd been selected as one of thirteen finalists in the San Francisco competition.

Gallagher's philosophy was: "Celebrate when you can, you might never have another chance."

Weaving in the direction of their riverside table was the affably drunken man with stained white hair in a crew cut, lumpy potato face and merry eyes reddened as if he'd been rubbing them with his knuckles.

He'd come to shake Gallagher's hand, meet the missus but mostly to address the young Zacharias.

"Coincidence, eh? I like to think coincidences mean something even when likely they don't. But you're the real thing, son: a musician. Read about you in the paper. Me, I'm a broke-down ol' d.j. Twenty-six friggin' yeas on WBEN Radio Wonderful broadcasting the best in jazz through the wee night hours"—his voice pitched low into a beautifully modulated if slightly mocking Negro radio voice—"and the lousy sonsabitches are dropping me from the station. No offense, Chet: I know you ain't to blame, you ain't your old man friggin' Thaddeus. My actual name, son"—stooping over the table now to shake the hand of the cringing boy—"is Alvin Block, Jr. Ain't got that swing, eh?"

Shaking his hips, wheezing with laughter as the white-jacketed maître d' hurried in his direction to lead him away.

(The Grand Island Yacht Club! Gallagher was apologetic, also a bit defensive, on the subject.

As a local celebrity Chet Gallagher had been given an honorary membership to the Grand Island Yacht Club. The damned club had a history—invariably, Gallagher called it a "spotty history"—of discrimination against Jews, Negroes, "ethnic minorities," and of course women, an all-male all-Caucasian Protestant private club on the Niagara River. Certainly Gallagher scorned such organizations as undemocratic and un-American yet in this case there were good friends of his who belonged, the Yacht Club was an "old venerable tradition" in the Buffalo area dating back to the 1870s, why not accept their hospitality that was so graciously offered, so long as Chet Gallagher wasn't a *dues-paying member*.

"And the view of the Niagara River is terrific, especially at sunset. You'll love it, Hazel."

Hazel asked if she would be allowed into the Yacht Club dining room.

Gallagher said, "Hazel, of course! You and Zack both, as my guests."

"Even if I'm a woman? Wouldn't the members object?"

"Certainly women are welcome at the Yacht Club. Wives, relatives, guests of members. It's the same as at the Buffalo Athletic Club, you've been there."

"Why?"

"Why what?"

"Why'd women be 'welcome,' if they aren't? And Jews, and Ne-groes?" Hazel gave *Ne-groes* a special inflection.

Gallagher saw she was teasing now, and looked uncomfortable.

"Look, I'm not a dues-paying member. I've been there only a few times. I thought it might be a nice place to go for dinner on Sunday, to celebrate Zack's good news." Gallagher paused, rubbing his nose vigorously. "We can go somewhere else, Hazel. If you prefer."

Hazel laughed, Gallagher was looking so abashed.

"Chet, no. I'm not one to 'prefer' anything.")

Sometimes I'm so lonely. Oh Christ so lonely for the life you saved me from but he would have stared at her astonished and disbelieving.

Not you, Hazel! Never.

In Buffalo they lived at 83 Roscommon Circle, within a mile's radius of the Delaware Conservatory of Music, the Buffalo Historic Society, the Albright-Knox Art Gallery. They were invited out often, their names were on privileged mailing lists. Gallagher scorned the bourgeois life yet was bemused by it, he acknowledged. Overnight Hazel Jones had become *Mrs. Chet Gallagher, Hazel Gallagher.*

As, young, she'd been an able and uncomplaining chambermaid in an "historic" hotel, now in youthful middle age she was the caretaker of a partly restored Victorian house of five bedrooms, three storeys, steeply pitched slate roofs. Originally built in 1887, the house was made of shingle-board, eggshell with deep purple trim. Maintaining the house became crucial to Hazel, a kind of fetish. As her son would be a concert pianist, so Hazel would be the most exacting of housewives. Gallagher, away much of the day, seemed not to notice how Hazel was becoming overly scrupulous about the house for anything Hazel did was a delight to him; and of course Gallagher was hopeless about anything perceived as practical, domestic. By degrees, Hazel also took over the maintenance of their financial records for it was much easier than waiting for Gallagher to assume responsibility. He was yet more hopeless with money, indifferent as only the son of a wealthy man might be indifferent to money.

With the instinct of a pack rat, Hazel kept receipts for the smallest purchases and services. Hazel kept flawless records. Hazel sent by registered mail photocopied materials to Gallagher's Buffalo accountant on a quarterly basis, for tax purposes. Gallagher whistled in admiration of his wife. "Hazel, you're terrific. How'd you get so smart?"

"Runs in the family."

"How so?"

"My father was a high school math teacher."

Gallagher stared at her, quizzically. "Your father was a high school math teacher?"

Hazel laughed. "No. Just joking."

"Do you know who your father was, Hazel? You've always said you didn't."

"I didn't, and I don't." Hazel wiped at her eyes, couldn't seem to stop laughing. For there was Gallagher, well into his fifties, staring at her gravely in that way of a man so beguiled by love he will believe anything told him by the beloved. Hazel felt she could reach into Gallagher's rib cage and touch his living heart. "Just teasing, Chet."

On tiptoes to kiss him. Oh, Gallagher was a tall man even with shoulders slouched. She saw that his new bifocals were smudged, removed them from his face and deftly polished them on her skirt.

Mrs. Chester Gallagher.

Each time she signed her new name it seemed to her that her handwriting was subtly altered.

They traveled a good deal. They saw many people. Some were associated with music, and some were associated with the media. Hazel was introduced to very friendly strangers as *Hazel Gallagher*: a name faintly comical to her, preposterous.

Yet no one laughed! Not within her hearing.

Gallagher, the most sentimental of men as he was the most scornful of men, would have liked a more formal wedding but saw the logic of a brief civil ceremony in one of the smaller courtrooms of the Erie County Courthouse. "Last thing we want is cameras, right? Attention. If my father found out . . ." The ten-minute ceremony was performed by a justice of the peace on a rainy Saturday morning in November 1972: the exact tenth anniversary of Gallagher and Hazel meeting in the Piano Bar of the Malin Head Inn. Zack was the sole witness, the bride's teenaged son in a suit, necktie. Zack looking both embarrassed and pleased.

Gallagher would believe he'd been the one to talk Hazel Jones into marrying him, at last. Joking that Hazel had made an honest man of him.

Ten years!

"Someday, darling, you'll have to tell me why."

"Why what?"

"Why you refused to marry me for ten long years."

"Ten very short years, they were."

"Long for me! Every morning I expected you to have disappeared. Cleared out. Taken Zack, and left me heartbroken."

Hazel was startled, at such a remark. Gallagher was only joking of course.

"Maybe I didn't marry you because I didn't believe that I was a good enough person to marry you. Maybe that was it."

Her light enigmatic Hazel Jones laugh. She'd tuned to perfection, like one of Zack's effortlessly executed cadenzas.

"Good enough to marry *me*! Hazel, really."

As Gallagher had arranged to marry Hazel in the Erie County Courthouse, so Gallagher arranged to adopt Zack in the Erie County Courthouse. So proud! So happy! It was the consummation of Gallagher's adult life.

The adoption was speedily arranged. A meeting with Gallagher's attorney, and an appointment with a county judge. Legal documents to be drawn up and signed and Zack's creased and waterstained birth certificate issued as a facsimile in Chemung County, New York, to be photocopied and filed in the Erie County Hall of Records.

Legally, Zack was now *Zack Gallagher*. But he would retain *Zacharias Jones* as his professional name.

Zack joked he was the oldest kid adopted in the history of Erie County: fifteen. But, at the signing, he'd turned abruptly away from Gallagher and Hazel not wanting them to see his face.

"Hey, kid. Jesus."

Gallagher hugged Zack, hard. Kissed the boy wetly on the edge of his mouth. Gallagher, most sentimental of men, didn't mind anyone seeing him cry.

Like guilty conspirators, mother and son. When they were alone together they burst into laughter, a wild nervous flaming-up laughter that would have shocked Gallagher.

So funny! Whatever it was, that sparked such laughter between them.

Zack had been fascinated by his birth certificate. He didn't seem to recall ever having seen it before. Hidden away with Hazel Jones's secret things, a small compact bundle she'd carried with her since the Poor Farm Road.

Zack asked if the birth certificate was legitimate, and Hazel said sharply Yes! It was.

"My name is 'Zacharias August Jones' and my father's name is 'William Jones'? Who the hell's 'William Jones'?"

" 'Was.' "

" 'Was' what?"

" 'Was,' not 'is.' Mr. Jones is dead now."

———

Secrets! In the tight little bundle inside her rib cage in the place where her heart had been. So many secrets, sometimes she couldn't get her breath.

Thaddeus Gallagher, for instance. His gifts and impassioned love letters to *Dearest Hazel Jones!*

In fall 1970, soon after Hazel received the first of these, an individual wishing to be designated as an *anonymous benefactor* gave a sizable sum of money to the Delaware Conservatory of Music earmarked as a scholarship and travel fund for the young pianist Zacharias Jones. Money was required for the numerous international piano competitions in which young pianists performed in hope of winning prizes, public attention, concert bookings and recording deals, and the donation from the *anonymous benefactor* would allow Zacharias to travel anywhere he wished. Gallagher who intended to manage Zack's career was keenly aware of these possibilities: "André Watts was seventeen when Leonard Bernstein conducted him in the Liszt E-flat concerto, on national television. A bombshell." And of course there was the legendary 1958 Tchaikovsky Competition in which twenty-four-year-old Van Cliburn took away the first prize and returned from Soviet Russia an international celebrity. Gallagher knew! But he was damned suspicious of the *anonymous benefactor*. When administrators at the Conservatory refused to tell him the benefactor's identity, Gallagher became suspicious and resentful. To Hazel he complained, "What if it's *him*. God damn!"

Naively Hazel asked, "Who is *him*?"

"My God-damned father, who else! It's three hundred thousand dollars the 'anonymous benefactor' has given the Conservatory, it has to be him. He must have heard Zack play in Vermont." Gallagher was looking fierce yet helpless, a man cut off at the knees. His voice pitched to a sudden pleading softness. "Hazel, I can't tolerate Thaddeus interfering in my life any more than he has."

Hazel listened sympathetically. She did not point out to Gallagher *It isn't your life, it's Zack's life.*

———

It was a mother's predatory instinct. Seeing how her son's skin glowed with sexual heat. His eyes that guiltily eluded her gaze, hot and yearning.

Restless! Too many hours at the piano. Trapped inside a cage of shimmering notes.

He went away from the house, and returned late. Midnight, and later. One night he didn't return until 4 A.M. (Hazel lay awake, and waiting. Very still not wanting to disturb Gallagher.) Yet another night in September, with only three weeks before the San Francisco Competition, he stayed away until dawn returning at that time stumbling and disheveled, defiant, smelling of beer.

"Zack! Good morning."

Hazel would not rebuke the boy. She would speak only lightly, without reproach. She knew, if she even touched him he would recoil from her. In sudden fury he might slap at her, strike her with his fists as he'd done as a little boy. *Hate you Momma! God damn I hate hate hate you.* She must not stare too hungrily at his young unshaven face. Must not accuse him of wishing to ruin their lives any more than she would plead with him or beg or weep for that was never Hazel Jones's way smiling as she opened the back door for him to enter, allowing him to brush roughly past her beneath the still-burning light breathing harshly through his mouth as if he'd been running and his eyes that were beautiful to her now bloodshot and heavy-lidded and opaque to her gaze and that smell of sweat, a sex-smell, pungent beneath the acrid smell of beer, yet she allowed him to know *I love you and my love is stronger than your hatred.*

He would sleep through much of the day. Hazel would not disturb him. By late afternoon he would return to the piano renewed, and practice until late evening. And Gallagher, listening in the hallway would shake his head in wonder.

She knew!

(He had to wonder what she'd meant in her playful teasing way *Mr. Jones is dead now.* If she meant that his father was dead? His long-ago father who had shouted into his face and shaken him like a rag doll and beat him and threw him against the wall yet who had hugged him too, and kissed him wetly on the edge of his mouth leaving a spittle-taste of tobacco behind. *Hey: love ya!* As his fingers executed the rapidly and vividly descending treble notes in the final ecstatic bars of the Beethoven sonata he had to wonder.)

Strange: that Chet Gallagher was losing interest in his career. Had lost interest in his career. Following the abrupt and shameful ending of the Vietnam War the most protracted and shameful war in American history strange, ironic how bored he'd become almost overnight with public life, politics. Even as his career as *Chet Gallagher* soared. (The newspaper column, 350 words Gallagher boasted he could type out in his sleep with his left hand, was nationally reprinted and admired. The TV interview program he'd been asked to host in 1973 was steadily gaining an audience. Also in 1973 a collection of prose pieces he'd cobbled together whimsically titled *Some Pieces of (My) Mind* became an unexpected bestseller in paperback.)

Losing interest in *Chet Gallagher* in proportion as he was becoming obsessed with *Zacharias Jones*. For here was a gifted young pianist, a truly gifted young pianist Gallagher had personally discovered up in Malin Head Bay one memorable winter night . . .

"It happens, he's my adopted son. My *son*."

Gallagher had to concede this was a phenomenon his own father had been denied. For he'd let his father down. *He* had failed as a classical pianist. Maybe to spite his father he'd failed but in any case *he had failed*, all that was finished. He played jazz piano only occasionally now, local gigs, fund-raisers and benefits and sometimes on TV, but not serious jazz any longer, Gallagher had become so Caucasian bourgeois, damned boring middle-aged husband and father, and *happy*. There's no edge to *happy*. There's no jazz-cool to *happy*. So devoted to his little family he'd even given up smoking.

How strange life was! He would manage the boy's career for the responsibility lay with Chet Gallagher.

Not to push the boy of course. From the first he'd cautioned the boy's mother.

"We'll take it slow. One thing at a time. Must be realistic. Even André Watts, after his early fantastic success, burned out. And so did Van Cliburn. Temporarily." Gallagher was not seriously expecting Zack to win a top prize at the San Francisco Competition: for one so young and relatively inexperienced, it was a remarkable honor simply to have qualified. The judges were of various ethnic backgrounds and would not favor a young Caucasian-American male. (Or would they? Zack was playing the "Appassionata.") Zack would be competing with prize-winning pianists from Russia, China, Japan, Germany who had trained with pianists more distinguished than his teacher at the Delaware Conservatory. To be realistic, Gallagher was planning, plotting: the Tokyo International Piano Competition in May 1975.

Her name was Frieda Bruegger.

She was a student at the Conservatory, a cellist. Beautiful blunt-featured girl with almond-shaped eyes, thick dark bristling hair exploding about her head, a young animated very shapely body. Her voice was a penetrating soprano: "Mrs. Gallagher! Hel*lo*."

Hazel was smiling and fully in control but staring rather vacantly at the girl Zack had brought home, whom he had introduced to her as a friend he was preparing a sonata with, for an upcoming recital at the Conservatory. Hazel was admiring the beautiful gleaming cello in the girl's hands, she would ask questions about the instrument, but something was wrong, why were the young people looking at her so oddly? She realized she hadn't replied. Numbly her lips moved, "Hello, Frieda."

Frieda! The name was so strangely resonant to her, she felt almost faint.

Realizing that she'd seen this girl before, at the music school. She had even seen the girl with Zack though the two had not been alone together. Following a recital, among a group of young musicians.

It's her. She's the one. He is sleeping with her. Is he?

So without warning Zack had brought the girl home with him, Hazel wasn't prepared. She'd expected him to be secretive, circumspect. Yet here the girl stood before Hazel calling her "Mrs. Gallagher." Really she was a young woman, twenty years old. Beside her Zack was still a boy, though taller than she was by several inches. And awkward in his body, uncertain. In personal relations Zack had not the zestful agility and grace he had at the piano. He was swiping at his nose now, nervously. He would not look at Hazel, not fully. He was excited, defiant. Gallagher had told Hazel it was the most natural thing in the world for a boy Zack's age to have a girlfriend, in fact girlfriends, you had to assume that kids were sexually active today as they generally had not been in Hazel's generation, hell it was fine as long as they took precautions and he'd had a talk (how awkward, Hazel could only imagine) with Zack so there was nothing to worry about.

And so Zack had brought home this bluntly beautiful girl with almond-shaped eyes and rather heavy dark unplucked eyebrows and the most astonishing explosive hair: Frieda Bruegger.

Informing Hazel that they would be performing a Fauré sonata for cello and piano at a Conservatory recital in mid-December. This was the first Hazel had heard of it and did not know how to respond. (What about the "Appassionata"? What about San Francisco, in eight days?) But Hazel's opinion was not being sought. The matter had been decided.

"It will be my first recital in that series, Mrs. Gallagher. I'm very nervous!"

Wanting Hazel to share in her excitement, the drama of her young life. And Hazel held back from her, resisting.

Yet Hazel remained in the music room longer than she might have expected. Busying herself with small housewifely tasks: straightening the small pillows on the window seat, opening the venetian blinds wide. The young people talked together earnestly about the sonata, looking through their photocopied sheets of music. Hazel saw that the girl stood rather close to Zack. She smiled frequently, her teeth were large and perfectly white, a small charming gap between the two front teeth. Her skin was beautifully smooth, with a faint burnished cast beneath. Her upper lip was covered in the faintest down. She was so animated! Zack held back from her, just perceptibly. Yet he was amused by her. Zack had several times brought other young musicians home to practice with him, he was a favored piano accompanist at the Conservatory. Possibly the girl was only a friend of his, a classmate. Except less experienced musically than Zack and so she would depend upon his judgment, she would defer to him musically. She brandished her beautiful cello as if it were a simulacrum of herself: her beautiful female body.

Hazel was forgetting the girl's name. She felt a vague fluttery panic, this was happening too quickly.

For a student at the Conservatory, the girl was provocatively dressed: lime green sweater that fitted her ample breasts tightly, metal-studded jeans that fitted her ample buttocks tightly. She had a nervous mannerism of wetting her lips, breathing through her mouth. Yet she did not seem truly ill-at-ease, rather more self-dramatizing, self-displaying. A rich girl, was she? Something in her manner suggested such a background. She was assured of being cherished. Assured of being admired. On her right wrist she wore an expensive-looking watch. Her hands were not extraordinary for a cellist, rather small, stubby. Not so slender as Zack's hands. Her nails were plain, filed short. Hazel glanced at her own impeccably polished nails, that matched her coral lipstick . . . Yet the girl was so young, and suffused with life! Hazel stared and stared lost in wonder.

She heard herself ask if the young people would like something to drink? Cola, coffee . . .

Politely they declined, no.

The terrible thought came to Hazel *They are waiting for me to leave them alone.*

Yet she heard herself ask, "This sonata, what is it like? Is it—familiar? Something I've heard?"

Frieda was the one to answer, bright and enthusiastic as a schoolgirl: "It's a beautiful sonata, Mrs. Gallagher. But you probably haven't heard it, Fauré's sonatas aren't very well known. He was old and sick when he wrote it, in 1921, it's one of his last compositions but you would never guess! Fauré was a true poet, a pure musician. In this sonata there's a surprise, the way the mood shifts, the 'funeral theme' becomes something you wouldn't expect, almost ethereal, joyous. Like, if you were an old man, and sick, and soon to die, still you could lift yourself out of your body that is failing you . . ." The girl spoke with such sudden intensity, Hazel felt uneasy.

Why is she talking to me like this, does she believe that I am old? Sick?

As it had been Hazel's custom to place flowers on the Steinway grand piano in the display window at Zimmerman Brothers, so it was Hazel's practice to place flowers on the piano in the music room. Zack took no notice of course. In the Gallagher household Zack seemed to take notice of very little, only music fully absorbed him. But his friend would notice the flowers. Already she had noticed. She had noticed the polished hardwood floor, the scattered carpets, the brightly colored pillows arranged on the window seat, the tall windows overlooking the vividly green back lawn where in wet weather (it was raining now, a fine porous mist) the air glowed as if undersea. Brought into the house and led through the downstairs by Zack she would certainly have noticed how beautifully furnished the Gallaghers' house was. She would go away marveling *Zack's mother is so . . .*

Hazel stood forlorn, uncertain. She knew she should leave the young musicians to their practice but another time she heard herself ask if they needed anything from the kitchen and another time they politely declined *no*.

As Hazel left, Frieda called after her, "Mrs. Gallagher, thanks! It was so nice to meet you."

But you will meet me again won't you? You will.

Yet Hazel lingered outside the door of the music room, waiting for the practice to begin. The cellist tuned her instrument: Zack would be seated at the piano. Hazel felt a pang of envy, hearing the young musicians begin. The cello was so rich, so vivid: Hazel's favorite instrument, after the piano. She much preferred the cello to the violin. After a few bars, the music ceased. They would return to the beginning. Zack played, the girl listened. Zack spoke. Another time they began the sonata, and another time ceased. And another time began . . . Hazel listened, fascinated. For here was beauty she could comprehend: not the thunderous cascading of piano notes that left the listener breathless, not the strongly hammered repetitions, the isolation of the great Beethoven sonata but the more subtle, delicately entwined sounds of two instruments. The cello was predominant, the piano rather muted. Or so Zack chose to play it. Twined together, cello and piano. Hazel listened for some time, deeply moved.

She went away. She had work to do. Elsewhere in the house, her own work. But she could not concentrate, away from the music room. She returned, lingering in the hall. Inside, the young musicians were talking together. A girl's quick robust laughter. A boy's low-pitched voice. Was the practice over for the day? It was nearing 6 P.M. And when would they practice again? On the other side of the door, the youthful voices were animated, melodic. Zack's voice was so warmly entwined with the girl's, they were so at ease together, as if they spoke together often, laughed together. How strange: Zack had become wary with Hazel, guarded and reticent. She was losing him. She had lost him. It was very recent in her memory, when Zack's voice had changed: his voice that had been a child's thin high-pitched voice for so long. Even now sometimes it wavered, cracked. He was not yet a man though no longer a boy. Of course, a boy of seventeen is sexually mature. A girl of Frieda's type, full-bodied, sensual, would have matured sexually at a much younger age. Hazel had not seen her son naked in a very long time nor did she wish to see him naked but she had occasional glimpses of coarse dark hair sprouting in his armpits, she saw that his forearms and legs were covered in dark hairs. The girl would be less of a stranger to Hazel than Zack: for the girl's body would be known to her, familiar as her own lost girl's body.

Frieda must have been answering a question of Zack's, she was speaking now of her family. Her father was an eye surgeon in Buffalo, he'd been born in that city. Her mother had been born in a small German village near the Czechoslovakian border. As a girl she'd been transported to Dachau with all of her family, relatives, neighbors but later she was reassigned to a labor camp in Czechoslovakia, she'd managed to escape with three other Jewish girls, she'd been a "displaced person" after the liberation and she'd emigrated to Palestine and in 1953 she'd emigrated to the United States, aged twenty-five. The Nazis had exterminated all of her family: there was no one remaining. But she had this belief: "There should be some reason why she survived. She really believes it!" Frieda laughed to show that she understood that her mother's belief was naive, she wished to dissociate herself from it. Zack said, "But there was, Frieda. So that you can play Fauré's second sonata, and I can accompany you."

Hazel went away from the music room feeling as if her soul had been annihilated, extinguished.

———

So lonely!

She could not cry, there was only futility in crying. With no one to witness, a waste of tears.

Made your bed now lie in it.

Made your bed your bed. Now lie in it, you!

The coarse, crude voices of her childhood. The old voices of wisdom.

On the third floor of the house in the sparely furnished attic space that had become Hazel's private space she hid away like a wounded animal. At this distance she could not hear if the young couple resumed their practice. She could not hear when the girl left. She could not hear if Zack left with her. If he'd called out to her on his way out of the house, she had not heard. If the girl called out to her in that warm penetrating voice *Goodbye Mrs. Gallagher!* she had not heard.

Never what you've told yourself. Never escaped from him. Pa was too smart, and too quick. Pa was too damned strong. Aimed the shotgun at your scrawny girl-chest and pulled the trigger. *And that was it. And afterward turning from what lay bleeding and mangled on the bedroom floor like a hunk of butchered meat triumphant his enemies would not subdue and humiliate him another time he reloaded the shotgun that like the console model Motorola radio was one of the astonishing purchases of his American experience awkwardly he turned both barrels on himself and fired and in the aftermath of that terrible blast there was only silence for no witness remained.*

Laugh at death. Why not and yet he could not bring himself to laugh.

The earth's soil was steeped in blood. He knew, before he'd met Frieda Bruegger. He knew of the Nazi death camps, the Final Solution. Seemed already to know what he might spend years learning. *Laugh at death* was not possible this side of death.

How airy, how ephemeral and trivial music seemed, of all human efforts! Fading into silence even as it's performed. And you had to work so very hard to perform it, and very likely you would fail in any case.

Revolted by his own vanity. His ridiculous ambition. He would be exposed, on a brightly lighted stage. Like a trained monkey he would perform. Before a panel of "international judges." He would desecrate music, in the display of his own vanity. As if pianists were racehorses to be pitted against one another, that others might wager on them. There would be a "cash prize" of course.

Six days before they were scheduled to fly to San Francisco he informed the adults who surrounded Zacharias Jones: he wasn't going.

What a commotion! Through the day the telephone rang, Gallagher was the one to answer.

The young pianist refused to listen to his piano teacher. Refused to listen to other musicians at the Conservatory. Refused to listen even to his stepfather whom he adored who pleaded with him, begged and cajoled and bartered: "This can be your last competition, Zack. If you feel so strongly."

The young pianist's mother did not plead with him, however. She knew to keep her distance. Perhaps she was too upset, she avoided speaking with anyone. Oh, the boy knew how to wound his mother! If Hazel had tried to plead with him as Gallagher did, he'd have laughed in her face.

Fuck you. Go play yourself. Think I'm your fucking trained monkey, well I am not.

In this way three days passed. Zack hid away, he was beginning to be ashamed. His decision was coming to seem to him like mere cowardice. The moral revulsion in his soul was coming to seem like mere nerves, stage fright. His face was inflamed. His bowels now spat liquid shit in a scalding cascade. He could not bear his exhausted reflection in any mirror. He could not even speak with Frieda, who had begun by being sympathetic with him but was now not so certain. He had not meant to draw attention to himself. He had meant to remove himself from attention. He had been reading the Hebrew Bible: *All is vanity*. He had been reading Schopenhauer: *Death is a sleep in which individuality is forgotten*. He had meant to withdraw himself from the possibility of acclaim and "success" as much as from the possibility of public failure. Now, he was beginning to reconsider his decision. He had tossed something very precious into the dirt, now he must pick it up and wash it off. Maybe it would be better to kill himself after all . . .

Or he might run away, disappear across the border into Canada.

The Conservatory had not yet notified the organizers of the competition, that Zacharias Jones had decided to drop out. And now he was reconsidering his decision. And there was Gallagher to speak reasonably saying that nobody expected him to win, the honor was in qualifying. "Look, you've been playing the Beethoven sonata here for months, so play it out there. What's the difference, essentially? There is no difference. Except Beethoven composed his music to be heard, right? He kept the 'Appassionata' from being published prematurely because he didn't believe that the world was ready for it yet, but we're ready for it, kid. So play your heart out. And for Christ's sake stop moping."

Taken by surprise, Zack laughed. As usual, Dad was right.

2

❀ ❀ ❀

In San Francisco the streets shone wetly. So steep, as in an ancient cataclysm. The air was harshly pure, blown inland from the fog-obscured ocean.

And the fog! Outside the windows of their twentieth-floor suite in the San Francisco Pacific Hotel the world had collapsed to a few feet.

The world had collapsed to a gleaming piano keyboard.

"The breath of God."

It was so. There could be no other explanation. That he'd become at the age of seventeen a young pianist named *Zacharias Jones*, his thumbnail-sized photograph in the glossy program of the 1974 San Francisco International Piano Competition. And she'd become *Hazel Gallagher*.

In their hotel suite, a dozen red roses awaited. A cellophane-wrapped wicker basket stuffed with gourmet foods, bottles of white and red wine. They would have laughed wildly together like conspirators except they'd grown wary of each other in recent months. The son had aimed at the mother's heart, he'd struck a deep stunning blow.

Unknowing, Gallagher had become the mediator between them. He had not the slightest awareness of the tension between mother and son. Nudging Hazel, when they heard Zack whistling in his adjoining hotel room, "Listen! That's a good sign."

Hazel did not know if it was a good sign. She, too, had become strangely happy in San Francisco, in the fog. It was a city of wetly gleaming near-vertical streets and quaintly clamorous "trams." It was a city utterly new to her and Zack. It had a posthumous feel to it, a sense of calm. The breath of God had blown them here, as whimsically as elsewhere.

Downstairs in the hotel gift shop, Hazel bought a deck of cards.

Alone in the suite she tore the cellophane from the deck and rapidly shuffled the cards and slapped them out onto a glass-topped table facing a window, for a game of solitaire.

So happy, to be alone! Gallagher had badly wanted her to come with him and Zack, to the luncheon honoring the pianists. But Hazel remained behind. On the plane, she'd seen two teenaged girls, sisters, playing double solitaire.

So happy. Not to be Hazel Jones.

"Hazel? Why the hell are you wearing black?"

It was a new dress of softly clinging jersey, graceful folds of cloth at the bodice. Long-sleeved, long-waisted. The skirt fell to mid-calf. She would wear black satin pumps with it. The October night was cool, she would wrap herself in an elegant black wool shawl.

"Shouldn't I? I thought . . ."

"No, Hazel. It's a gorgeous dress but too damned funereal for the occasion. You know how Zack interprets things. Especially coming from you. A little more color, Hazel. Please!"

Gallagher seemed so serious, Hazel gave in. She would wear a cream-colored suit in light wool, with a crimson silk scarf, one of Thaddeus Gallagher's more practical gifts, tied around her neck. It was all a masquerade.

Outside the tall windows, the fog had cleared. San Francisco emerged at dusk, a city of stalagmites glittering with lights to the horizon. So beautiful! Hazel wondered if she might be forgiven, remaining in the room. Her heart clenched in terror at the prospect of what lay ahead.

"Hey Dad? Come help."

Zack was having trouble with his black tie. He'd been in and out of his own room, lingering in their bedroom. He had not been very comfortable that day, Gallagher had said. At the luncheon, and afterward. The other pianists were older, more experienced. Several exuded "personality." Zack had a tendency to withdraw, to appear sullen. He had showered now for the second time that day and he had combed his hair with compulsive neatness. His blemished forehead was mostly hidden by wings of fawn-colored hair. His angular young face shone with a kind of panicked merriment.

The men were required to wear black tie. Starched white cotton dress shirts with studs, elaborate French cuffs. Gallagher helped Zack with both the necktie and the French cuffs.

"Chin up, kid. A tux is a ridiculous invention but we do look good. Dames fall for us." Gallagher snorted with laughter at his feeble joke.

Through a mirror Hazel observed. She could not help but feel that the little family was headed for an execution and yet: which one of them was to be executed?

Gallagher fussed with Zack's tie, undoing it entirely and trying again. Almost, you would see that the two were related: middle-aged father with a high bald dome of head, adolescent son nearly his height, frowning as the damned tie was being adjusted for him. Hazel guessed that Gallagher had to restrain himself from wetly kissing the tip of Zack's nose in a clown's blessing.

The more edgy Gallagher was, the more jocular, antic. At least he wasn't doubling up with gastric pains, vomiting into a toilet as he'd done at his father's house. In semi-secrecy (Hazel knew, without having seen) he'd unlocked the minibar in the parlor and taken a swig or two of Johnnie Walker Black Label Whiskey.

It was believed to be contrary to nature, that a man might love another man's son as if he were his own son. Yet Gallagher loved Zack in this way, Gallagher had triumphed.

Of five pianists scheduled to perform that evening in the concert hall of the San Francisco Arts Center, Zacharias Jones was the third. Next day the remaining eight pianists would perform. The announcement of the first, second, third prize winners would be made after the last pianist played that evening. The Gallaghers were relieved that Zack would play so soon, the ordeal for him would be more quickly over. But Gallagher worried that the judges would be more inclined to favor pianists who played last.

"Still, it doesn't matter," Gallagher told Hazel, stroking his chin distractedly, "how Zack does. We've said this."

Their seats were in the third row, on the aisle. They had a clear, unimpeded view of the keyboard and the pianists' flying hands. As they listened to the first two pianists perform, Gallagher gripped Hazel's hand tightly, leaning heavily against her. He was breathing quickly and shallowly and his breath smelled of a lurid mixture of whiskey and Listerine mouthwash.

After each of the performances, Gallagher applauded with enthusiasm. He'd been a performer himself. Hazel's arms were leaden, her mouth dry. She'd heard hardly a note of music, she had not wanted to realize how talented her son's rivals were.

Abruptly then Zack's name was announced. He moved onto the stage with surprising readiness, even managing to smile toward the audience. He could see nothing but blinding lights and these lights made him appear even younger than he was, contrasting with the preceding pianist who'd been in his early thirties. At the piano, Zack seated himself and leaned forward and began playing the familiar opening notes of the Beethoven sonata without preamble. Though Hazel had seen Zack perform in numerous recitals it was always something of a shock to her, how abruptly these performances began. And, once begun, they must be executed in their entirety.

There were only three subtly contrasting movements to the intricate sonata, that would pass with unnerving swiftness. Ever more swiftly Zack seemed to be playing it, than at home. So many months in preparation, less than a half-hour in performance! It was madness.

Gallagher was leaning so heavily against Hazel, she worried he would crush her. But she dared not push him away.

She was in a state of suspended panic. She could not breathe, her heart had begun to pound so rapidly. She had told herself repeatedly, Zack could not possibly win in this competition, the honor was in simply qualifying. Yet she feared he would make a mistake, he would blunder in some way, he would humiliate himself, he would fail. She knew that he would not, she

had absolute faith in him, yet she was in dread of a catastrophe. Vivid crystalline notes exploded in the air with hurtful volume yet seemed almost
immediately to fade, then to swell, and to fade again out of her hearing. She
was becoming faint, she'd been holding her breath unconsciously. Gallagher's hand was so very heavy on her knee, his fingers so tight squeezing
hers she felt he would break the bones. The music that had been familiar to
her for months had become suddenly unfamiliar, unnerving. She could not
recall what it was, where it was headed. There was something deranged,
demonic about the sonata. The swiftness with which the pianist's fingers
leapt about the keyboard . . . Hazel's eyes filled with moisture, she could
not force herself to watch. Could not imagine why such a tortuous spectacle was meant to be pleasurable, "entertaining." It was sheerly hell, she
hated it. Only during the slower passages, which were passages of exquisite
beauty, could Hazel relax and breathe normally. Only during the slower
passages when the demonic intensity had ceased. Truly this was beautiful,
and heartrending. In recent weeks Zack's interpretation of the "Appassionata" had begun to shift. There was less immediate warmth to his playing
now, more precision, percussion, a kind of restrained fury. The rapid,
harshly struck notes tore at her nerves. Zack's piano teacher had not liked
the newer direction in which Zack had been moving, nor had Gallagher.
Hazel could hear it now, the fury. Almost, there was a disdain for the fact
of the sonata itself. There was disdain for the showy act of "performance."
Hazel saw that Zack's jaws were tight-clenched, his lower face was contorted. A patch of oily moisture gleamed on his forehead. Hazel looked
away, flinching. She saw that others in the audience were staring at the pianist, fascinated. Rows of rapt listeners. The hall had five hundred seats in
the orchestra and balcony, and appeared to be full. It was a musical audience, familiar with the pieces the pianists would perform. Many were
pianists themselves, piano teachers. There was a contingent of supporters
from the Conservatory, Frieda Bruegger among them: Hazel sought out
the girl's face but could not find it. Here and there in the elegantly appointed concert hall with its plush seats and mosaic wall tiles were faces
you would not expect to see in such a setting. Very likely they were relatives
of the performers, ill-at-ease among the other, more knowledgeable listeners. A crack of memory opened, sharp as a sliver of glass. Herschel telling

her that their parents had once sung arias to each other, long ago in Europe. In Munich, it would have been. In what Anna Schwart had called the Old Country.

Blurred with distance as with time, their faces hovered at the rear of the concert hall. The Schwarts!

They were stunned, disbelieving. They were immensely proud.

We always had faith in you Rebecca.

No. You didn't.

We always loved you Rebecca.

No. I don't think so.

It was hard for us to speak. I did not trust this new language. And your father, you know what Pa was like . . .

Do I!

Pa loved you Rebecca. Used to say he loved you most, you were most like him.

Hazel's face was a brittle doll-face, covered in cracks. She was desperate to hide it, that no one would see. Tears gushing from her eyes. She managed to cover part of her face, with one hand. Seeing the neglected and overgrown cemetery. Always the cemetery was close behind her eyelids, she had only to shut her eyes to see it. There, grave markers were toppled over in the grass, cracked and broken. Some of the graves had been vandalized. The names of the dead had been worn away. No matter how carefully engraved into the stone the names of the dead had vanished. Hazel smiled to see it: the earth was a place of anonymous graves, every grave was unknown.

She opened her eyes that were flooded with tears. On the stage, the pianist was completing the final, turbulent movement of the Beethoven sonata. All of his young life was being channeled into this moment. He was playing his heart out, that was clear. Hazel's face must have shone with happiness, that had been strained and hard for so long. There came the final chord, and the pedal holding. And the pedal released. At once, the audience erupted into applause.

With childlike eagerness the pianist bounded from his seat to bow to the audience. His young, vulnerable face gleamed with perspiration. There was something glaring and fanatic in his eyes. Yet he was smiling, a somewhat dazed smile, he bowed as if stricken with humility like sudden pain.

By this time Gallagher was on his feet, lifting his hands to applaud with the rest.

"Hazel, he did it! Our son."

There should be some reason why she survived.

She knew. She knew this fact. Yet she did not know what the reason was, even now.

So restless!

It was 2:46 A.M. Though exhausted she could not sleep. Though spent with emotion she could not sleep. Her eyes burned as if she'd rubbed them in sand.

Beside her Gallagher slept, heavily. In sleep he was childlike, strangely docile. Leaning his hot, humid body against her, nudging her like a blind creature ravenous for affection. Yet his breathing was so loud, labored. Sounds in his throat like wet gravel being shoveled, scraped. In such breathing she foresaw his death: then, she would know how deeply she loved this man, she who could not articulate that love now.

She was one whose childhood language has been taken from her, no other language can speak the heart.

Must get out! Slipped from the bed, left the darkened bedroom and the sleeping man. Insomnia drove her like red ants swarming over her naked body.

In fact, she wasn't naked: she was wearing a nightgown. Sexy-silky champagne-colored nightgown with a lace bodice, a gift from Gallagher.

In the parlor she switched on a lamp. Now it was 2:48 A.M. By such slow degrees a life might be lived. It was five hours since Zack had played the "Appassionata." At the reception afterward the girl with the blunt beautiful face had embraced Hazel as if they were old friends, or kin. Hazel had held herself stiff not daring to embrace the girl back.

Zack had gone away with her. Her, and others. He'd asked Gallagher and his mother please not to wait up for him, they'd promised they would not.

Rain was pelting against the windows. In the morning again there would be fog. The nighttime city was beautiful to Hazel but not very real. At this height of twenty floors, nothing seemed very real. In the near distance there was a tall narrow building that might have been a tower. A red light blurred by rain rotated at its pinnacle.

"The eye of God."

It was a curious thing to say. The words seemed to have spoken themselves.

She wouldn't take time to dress, she was in too great a hurry. Her trench coat would do. It was a stylish olive-green coat with a flared skirt and a sash-belt to be tied at the waist. The coat was still damp from that evening's rain. Yet she would wear it like a robe over the nightgown. And shoes: she could not leave the room barefoot.

Looking for her flat-heeled shoes she found a single shiny black dress shoe of Gallagher's lying on the carpet where he'd kicked it. She picked it up and placed it in a closet beside its mate.

They had returned to the hotel suite to celebrate, together. Gallagher had called room service to order champagne. On the marble-topped coffee table was a silver tray and on the tray a spillage of wrappers, bottles, glasses. Remains of Brie cheese, rye crackers, kiwi fruit and luscious black Concord grape seeds. And almonds, Brazil nuts. After the emotional strain of that evening's program Gallagher had been famished but too excited to sit still, he'd paced about the parlor as he ate, and talked.

He had not expected Zack to play so well, perhaps. He, too, had expected some sort of catastrophe.

In May, the elder Gallaghers had had a medical scare. Gallagher's gastric pains continued, something cloudy had showed up on an X-ray but was not malignant. An ulcerous condition, treatable. They'd decided not to tell Zack, this would be their secret.

Zack had gone off with friends from the Conservatory and other young musicians they'd met in San Francisco. After his controversial performance Zack would be something of a hero, among pianists of his own generation at least.

Hazel would not approach the door to Zack's adjoining room. She would not turn the knob, gently: she knew it would be locked.

Yet surely the girl would not be in that room with Zack. In that bed. In such proximity to the Gallaghers. She had a room elsewhere in the hotel and she'd come alone to San Francisco and if she and Zack were alone together in any bed, exhausted now in the aftermath of lovemaking, they would be in her room. Probably.

She would not think of it. She was no one's daughter now, and she would be no one's mother. All that was over.

She would say, You can live your own life now. Your life is your own, to live.

She'd brought with her, to San Francisco, the most recent of Thaddeus's letters. Love letters they were, of increasing passion, or dementia. Opening the stiff, much-folded sheet of stationery, to read by lamplight as her husband slept oblivious in the adjoining room. The letter was clumsily typed as if in lunges, in the dark; or by one whose eyesight is dimming.

Dearest Hazel Jones,

You wld tickel an old mans vanity if youd replied to my appeals but I see now, you are Hazel Jones and <u>a good wife</u> and you are a <u>worthy Mother</u> to your son. So you wld not reply, I rever you for it. I think that I will not write to you agin this side the grave. You & the boy will recieve a consumat Reward for your fathfulness & goodness. Your shallow husband the Mouth of Liberal Consience does not have a clue! He is a fool unworthy of you & the boy, that is our secret Hazel Jones isnt it. In my will you will all see. The scales will fall from the eyes of some. God bless you Hazel Jones & the boy whose music of beauttu is to outlive us all.

Hazel smiled, and folded up the letter again, and put it away in her handbag. A voice echoed faintly as if in rain beating against the window-panes *You—you are born here. They will not hurt you.*

Pushed her arms into the sleeves of the still damp trench coat, and tied the belt tight around her waist. No need to glance at herself in the mirror: she knew her hair was disheveled, the pupils of her eyes dilated. Her skin smarted with a kind of erotic heat. She was excited, jubilant. She would take money with her, several twenties from her purse. She would take several items from the mini bar: miniature bottles of whiskey, gin, vodka. She would take the playing cards, dropping them loose in a pocket of her coat. And she must not forget the key to room 2006.

She stepped into the empty corridor. Shut the door behind her waiting for the lock to click into place.

The corridor leading to the elevators was longer than she recalled. Underfoot were thick crimson carpets and on the walls beige silk wallpaper in an Oriental design. At the elevators she punched DOWN. Swiftly she would descend from 20 to G. Smiling to recall how in the past elevators had moved much more slowly. You had plenty of time to think, descending in one of those.

At this hour the hotel appeared deserted. Floor G was very quiet. The piped-in Muzak of daytime, a chirping of manic sparrows Gallagher called it, had been silenced. Though she had never been in this hotel before Hazel moved unerringly past windowless doors marked EMPLOYEES ONLY and PRIVATE: NO ADMITTANCE. At the end of a long corridor smelling of food was KITCHEN: EMPLOYEES ONLY. And ROOM SERVICE: EMPLOYEES ONLY. Twenty-four-hour room service was a feature of the San Francisco Pacific Hotel. Hazel heard voices on the other side of the door, a sound of dishes being stacked. Radio music with a Latino beat. She pushed open the door, and stepped inside.

How the eyes snatched at her, in astonishment! Yet she was smiling.

There were kitchen workers in soiled white uniforms, and a man in a dark, neatly pressed uniform who had just returned to the kitchen pushing a cart loaded to capacity with trays of dirtied plates, glasses and bottles. The kitchen lights were very bright, the air much warmer than the corridor had been. Amid the strong kitchen odors of grease and cleanser was a sharp garbagey odor. And a beery odor as well, for some of the kitchen workers were drinking beer. Even as the alarmed-looking man in the dark uniform began to speak, "Ma'am, excuse me but—" Hazel was saying quickly, "Excuse me, I'm hungry. I can pay you. I have my own drinks but I don't want to drink alone. I didn't want to order room service, it takes too long." She laughed, they would see that she was in a festive mood and would not send her away.

Hazel would not afterward recall the sequence of events. She would not recall how many men there were for at least two continued working, at sinks; another came in later by a rear door, yawning and stretching. Several befriended her, cleared a place for her at their table setting aside tabloid papers, a crossword puzzle book, emptied Coke, 7-Up, beer cans. They were grateful for the miniature bottles she'd brought from the room. They would not accept her offer of $20 bills. They were: César, a youngish Hispanic with pitted skin and liquidy eyes; Marvell, a black man with skin the color of eggplant and a fleshy, tender face; Drake, a Caucasian of about forty, with an oddly flat face like a species of fish and glinting wire-rimmed glasses that gave him the look of an accountant, you would not take for a nighttime cook. And there was McIntyre, suspicious of Hazel initially but by quick degrees her friend, in his fifties, the man in the hotel uniform who made room service deliveries on call through the night. They were so curious of Hazel! She would tell them only her first name which was a name strange to them: "Haz-el" pronounced as if it were an exotic foreign word. They asked where she was from and she told them. They asked was she married, was her husband sleeping up in their room, what if he woke and saw that she was gone?

"He won't wake. When he wakes, I will be there. It's just I can't seem to sleep now. This time of night . . . They say that people check into hotels who are planning to commit suicide. Why is that? Is it easier, somehow? I used to work in a hotel. When I was a girl. I was a chambermaid. This was back east, in upstate New York. It was not so large and luxurious a hotel as this. I was happy then. I liked the other hotel workers, I liked the kitchen staff. Except . . ."

The men listened avidly. Their eyes were fixed upon her. The Latino music continued. Hazel saw that the kitchen was vast, larger than any kitchen she had ever seen. The farther walls were obscured in shadow. Numerous stoves and all the stoves were mammoth: a dozen gas burners on each. There were large refrigerators built into a wall. Freezers, dishwashers.

The space was divided into work areas of which only one was currently lighted and populated. The linoleum floor shone wetly, recently mopped. Plates were removed from carts and garbage scraped into plastic bags, the bags were tightly tied and placed inside large aluminum cans. The mood of the kitchen workers was heightened, jocular. Hazel might wonder if her presence had something to do with it. She'd taken the playing cards out of her pocket and stacked and shuffled them. Did they know gin rummy? Would they like to play gin rummy? Yes, yes! Very good. Gin rummy. Hazel shuffled the cards. Her fingers were slender and deft and the nails had been lacquered deep crimson. Skillfully Hazel dealt the cards to the men and to herself. The men laughed, their mood was exuberant. Now they knew Hazel was one of them, they could relax. They played gin rummy laughing together like old friends. They were drinking chilled Coors beer, and they were drinking from the miniature bottles Hazel had brought them. They were eating potato chips, salted nuts. Brazil nuts like those Gallagher had devoured up in the room. A phone rang, a hotel guest calling room service. McIntyre would have to put on his jacket, and make the delivery. He went away, and within a few minutes returned. Hazel saw that he was relieved she hadn't left yet.

Cards were tossed onto the table, the set was over. Who had won? Had Hazel won? The men didn't want her to leave, it was only 3:35 A.M. and they were on room-service duty until 6 A.M. Hazel stacked the cards together and shuffled and cut and shuffled again and began to deal. The front of her trench coat had loosened, the men could see the tops of her breasts pale and loose in the silky champagne-colored nightgown. She knew that her hair was disheveled, her mouth was a cloudy smear of old lipstick. Even one of her fingernails was chipped. Her body exuded an odor of old, stale panic. Yet she supposed she was an attractive woman, her new friends would not judge her harshly. "D'you know 'gypsy gin rummy'? If I can remember, I'll teach you."

Epilogue

1998—1999

Lake Worth, Florida
September 14, 1998

Dear Professor Morgenstern,

How badly I wish that I could address you as "Freyda"! But I don't have
the right to such familiarity. I have just read your memoir. I have reason
to believe that we are cousins. My maiden name is "Schwart" (not my
father's actual name, I think it was changed at Ellis Island in 1936) but
my mother's maiden name was "Morgenstern" and all her family was
from Kaufbeuren as yours were. We were to meet in 1941 when we
were small children, you and your parents and sister and brother were
coming to live with my parents, my two brothers and me in Milburn,
New York. But the boat that was carrying you and other refugees, the
Marea, was turned back by U.S. Immigration at New York Harbor.

(In your memoir you speak so briefly of this. You seem to recall a name
other than *Marea*. But I am sure that *Marea* was the name for it seemed
so beautiful to me like music. You were so young of course. So much
would happen afterward, you would not remember this. By my calculation you were 6, and I was 5.)

All these years I had not known that you were living! I had not
known that there were survivors in your family. It was told to us by my
father that there were not. I am so happy for you and your success. To

think that you were living in the U.S. since 1956 is a shock to me. That you were a college student in New York City while I was living (my first marriage, not a happy one) in upstate New York! Forgive me, I did not know of your previous books, though I would be intrigued by "biological anthropology," I think! (I have nothing of your academic education, I'm so ashamed. Not only not college but I did not graduate from high school.)

Well, I am writing in the hope that we might meet. Oh very soon, Freyda! Before it's too late.

I am no longer your 5-year-old cousin dreaming of a new "sister" (as my mother promised) who would sleep with me in my bed and be with me always.

Your "lost" cousin

Rebecca

Lake Worth, Florida
September 15, 1998

Dear Professor Morgenstern,

I wrote to you just the other day, now I see to my embarrassment that I may have sent the letter to a wrong address. If you are "on sabbatical leave" from the University of Chicago as it says on the dust jacket of your memoir. I will try again with this, care of your publisher.

I will enclose the same letter. Though I feel it is not adequate, to express what is in my heart.

Your "lost" cousin

Rebecca

P.S. Of course I will come to you, wherever & whenever you wish, Freyda!

Lake Worth, Florida
October 2, 1998

Dear Professor Morgenstern,

I wrote to you last month but I'm afraid that my letters were mis-addressed. I will enclose these letters here, now that I know you are at the "Institute for Advanced Research" at Stanford University, Palo Alto, California.

Its possible that you have read my letters and were offended by them. I know, I am not a very good writer. I should not have said what I did about the Atlantic crossing in 1941, as if you would not know these facts for yourself. I did not mean to correct you, Professor Morgenstern, regarding the name of the very boat you and your family were on in that nightmare time!

In an interview with you reprinted in the Miami newspaper I was embarrassed to read that you have received so much mail from "relatives" since the memoir. I smiled to read where you said, "Where were all these relatives in America when they were needed?"

Truly we were here, Freyda! In Milburn, New York, on the Erie Canal.

Your cousin

Rebecca

Palo Alto CA
1 November 1998

Dear Rebecca Schward,

Thank you for your letter and for your response to my memoir. I have been deeply moved by the numerous letters I've received since the publication of *Back From the Dead*: *A Girlhood* both in the United States and abroad and truly wish that I had time to reply to each of these individually and at length.

Sincerely,

[signature]

Freyda Morgenstern

Julius K. Tracey '48 Distinguished Professor of Anthropology, University of Chicago

Lake Worth, Florida
November 5, 1998

Dear Professor Morgenstern,

I'm very relieved now, I have the correct address! I hope that you will read this letter. I think you must have a secretary who opens your mail and sends back replies. I know, you are amused (annoyed?) by so many now claiming to be relatives of "Freyda Morgenstern." Especially since your television interviews. But I feel very strongly, I am your true cousin. For I was the (only) daughter of Anna Morgenstern. I believe that Anna Morgenstern was the (only) sister of your mother Dora a younger sister. For many weeks my mother spoke of her sister Dora coming to live with us, your father and your Elzbieta who was older than you by 3 or 4 years and your brother Joel who was also older than you, not by so much. We had photographs of you, I remember so clearly how your hair was so neatly plaited and how pretty you were, a "frowning girl" my mother said of you, like me. We did look alike then, Freyda, though you were much prettier of course. Elzbieta was blond with a plump face. Joel was looking happy in the photograph, a sweet-seeming boy of maybe 8. To read that your sister and brother died in such a terrible way in "Theresienstadt" was so sad. My mother never recovered from the shock of that time, I think. She was so hoping to see her sister again. When the *Marea* was turned back in the harbor, she gave up hope. My father did not allow her to speak German, only English, but she could not speak English well, if anyone came to the house she would hide. She did not speak much afterward to any of us and was often sick. She died in May 1949.

Reading this letter I see that I am giving a wrong emphasis, really! I never think of these long-ago things.

It was seeing your picture in the newspaper, Freyda! My husband was reading the *New York Times* & called me to him saying wasn't it strange, here was a woman looking enough like his wife to be a sister, though in fact you & I do not look so much alike, in my opinion, not any longer, but it was a shock to see your face which is very like my mother's face as I remember it.

And then your name *Freyda Morgenstern*.

At once I went out & purchased *Back From the Dead: A Girlhood*. I have not read any Holocaust memoirs out of a dread of what I would learn. Your memoir I read sitting in the car in the parking lot of the bookstore not knowing the time, how late it was until my eyes could not see the pages. I thought "It's Freyda! It's her! My sister I was promised." Now I am sixty-two years old, and so lonely in this place of retired wealthy people who look at me & think that I am one of them.

I am not one to cry. But I wept on many pages of your memoir though I know (from your interviews) you wish not to hear such reports from readers & have only contempt for "cheap American pity." I know, I would feel the same way. You are right to feel that way. In Milburn I resented the people who felt sorry for me as the "gravedigger's daughter" (my father's employment) more than the others who did not give a damn if the Schwarts lived or died.

I am enclosing my picture taken when I was a girl of sixteen. It is all I have of those years. (I look very different now, I'm afraid!) How badly I wish I could send you a picture of my mother Anna Morgenstern but all were destroyed in 1949.

Your cousin,

Rebecca

Palo Alto CA
16 November 1998

Dear Rebecca Schwart,

Sorry not to have replied earlier. I think yes it is quite possible that we
are "cousins" but at such a remove it's really an abstraction, isn't it?

I am not traveling much this year trying to complete a new book before my sabbatical ends. I am giving fewer "talks" and my book tour
is over, thank God. (The venture into memoir was my first and will be
my last effort at non-academic writing. It was far too easy, like opening
a vein.) So I don't quite see how it would be feasible for us to meet at
the present time.

Thank you for sending your photograph. I am returning it.

Sincerely,

JM

Lake Worth, Florida
November 20, 1998

Dear Freyda,

Yes, I am sure we are "cousins"! Though like you I don't know what
"cousins" can mean.

I have no living relatives, I believe. My parents have been dead since 1949
& I know nothing of my brothers I have not glimpsed in many years.

I think you despise me as your "American cousin." I wish you could
forgive me for that. I am not sure how "American" I am though I was
not born in Kaufbeuren as you were but in New York harbor in May
1936. (The exact day is lost. There was no birth certificate or it was
lost.) I mean, I was born on the refugee boat! In a place of terrible filth
I was told.

It was a different time then, 1936. The war had not begun & people of our kind were allowed to "emigrate" if they had money.

My brothers Herschel & Augustus were born in Kaufbeuren & of course both our parents. My father called himself "Jacob Schwart" in this country. (This is a name I have never spoken to anyone who knows me now. Not to my husband of course.) I knew little of my father except he had been a printer in the old world (as he called it with scorn) and at one time a math teacher in a boys' school. Until the Nazis forbade such people to teach. My mother Anna Morgenstern was married very young. She played piano, as a girl. We would listen to music on the radio sometime if Pa was not home. (The radio was Pa's.)

Forgive me, I know you are not interested in any of this. In your memoir you spoke of your mother as a record-keeper for the Nazis, one of those Jewish "administrators" helping in the transport of Jews. You are not sentimental about family. There is something so craven to it isn't there. I respect the wishes of one who wrote *Back From the Dead* which is so critical of your relatives & Jews & Jewish history & beliefs as of post-war "amnesia." I would not wish to dissuard you of such a true feeling, Freyda!

I have no true feelings myself, I mean that others can know.

Pa said you were all gone. Like cattle sent back to Hitler, Pa said. I remember his voice lifting NINE HUNDRED REFUGEES, I am sick still hearing that voice.

Pa said for me to stop thinking about my cousins! They were not coming. They were *gone*.

Many pages of your memoir I have memorized, Freyda. And your letters to me. In your words, I can hear your voice. I love this voice so like my own. My secret voice I mean, that no one knows.

I will fly to California, Freyda. Will you give me permission? "Only say the word & my soul shall be healed."

Your cousin,

Rebecca

Lake Worth, Florida
November 21, 1998

Dear Freyda,

I am so ashamed, I mailed you a letter yesterday with a word misspelled: "dissuade." And I spoke of no living relatives, I meant no one remaining from the Schwart family. (I have a son from my first marriage, he is married with two children.)

I have bought other books of yours. *Biology: A History. Race and Racism: A History.* How impressed Jacob Schwart would be, the little girl in the photographs was never *gone* but has so very far surpassed him!

Will you let me come to see you in Palo Alto, Freyda? I could arrive for one day, we might have a meal together & I would depart the next morning. This is a promise.

Your (lonely) cousin

Rebecca

Lake Worth, Florida
November 24, 1998

Dear Freyda,

An evening of your time is too much to ask, I think. An hour? An hour would not be too much, would it? Maybe you could talk to me of your work, anything in your voice would be precious to me. I would not wish to drag you into the cesspool of the past as you speak of it so strongly. A woman like yourself capable of such intellectual work & so highly regarded in your field has no time for maudlin sentiment, I agree.

I have been reading your books. Underlining, & looking up words in the dictionary. (I love the dictionary, its my friend.) So exciting to consider *How does science demonstrate the genetic basis of behavior?*

I have enclosed a card here for your reply. Forgive me I did not think of this earlier.

Your cousin

Rebecca

Palo Alto CA
24 November 1998

Dear Rebecca Schwart,

Your letters of Nov. 20 & 21 are interesting. But the name "Jacob Schwart" means nothing to me, I'm afraid. There are numerous "Morgensterns" surviving. Perhaps some of these are your cousins, too. You might seek them out if you are lonely.

As I believe I have explained, this is a very busy time for me. I work much of the day and am not feeling very sociable in the evening. "Loneliness" is a problem engendered primarily by the too-close proximity of others. One excellent remedy is work.

Sincerely,

FM

P.S. I believe you have left phone messages for me at the Institute. As my assistant has explained to you, I have no time to answer such calls.

Lake Worth, Florida
November 27, 1998

Dear Freyda,

Our letters crossed! We both wrote on Nov. 24, maybe it's a sign.

It was on impulse I telephoned. "If I could hear her voice"—the thought came to me.

You have hardened your heart against your "American cousin." It was courageous in the memoir to state so clearly how you had to harden your heart against so much, to survive. Americans believe that suffering makes saints of us, which is a joke. Still I realize you have no time for me in your life now. There is no "purpose" to me.

Even if you won't meet me at this time, will you allow me to write to you? I will accept it if you do not reply. I would only wish that you might read what I write, it would make me so happy (yes, less lonely!) for then I could speak to you in my thoughts as I did when we were girls.

Your cousin

Rebecca

P.S. In your academic writing you refer so often to "adaptation of species to environment." If you saw me, your cousin, in Lake Worth, Florida, on the ocean just south of Palm Beach, so very far from Milburn, N.Y., and from the "old world," you would laugh.

Palo Alto CA
1 December 1998

Dear Rebecca Schwart,

My tenacious American cousin! I'm afraid it is no sign of anything, not even "coincidence," that our letters were written on the same day and that they "crossed."

This card. I admit I am curious at the choice. It happens this is a card on my study wall. (Did I speak of this in the memoir, I don't think so.) How you happen to come into possession of this reproduction of Caspar David Friedrich's *Sturzacker*—you have not been to the museum in Hamburg, have you? It's rare that any American even knows the name of this artist much esteemed in Germany.

Sincerely,

JM

Lake Worth, Florida
4 December 1998

Dear Freyda,

The postcard of Caspar David Friedrich was given to me, with other cards from the Hamburg museum, by someone who traveled there. (In fact my son who is a pianist. His name would be known to you, it's nothing like my own.)

I chose a card to reflect your soul. As I perceive it in your words. Maybe it reflects mine also. I wonder what you will think of this new card which is German also but uglier.

Your cousin

Rebecca

Palo Alto CA
10 December 1998

Dear Rebecca,

Yes I like this ugly Nolde. Smoke black as pitch and the Elbe like molten lava. You see into my soul, don't you! Not that I have wished to disguise myself.

So I return *Towboat on the Elbe* to my tenacious American cousin. THANK YOU but please do not write again. And do not call. I have had enough of you.

FM

Palo Alto CA
11 December 1998/2 A.M.

Dear "Cousin"!

Your sixteen-yr-old photo I made a copy of. I like that coarse mane of hair and the jaws so solid. Maybe the eyes were scared, but we know how to hide that, don't we cousin.

In the camp I learned to stand tall. I learned to be big. As animals make themselves bigger, it can be a trick to the eye that comes true. I guess you were a "big" girl, too.

I have always told the truth. I see no reason for subterfuge. I despise fantasizing. I have made enemies "among my kind" you can be sure. When you are "back from the dead" you do not give a damn for others' opinions & believe me, that has cost me in this so-called "profession" where advancement depends upon ass-kissing and its sexual variants not unlike the activities of our kindred primates.

Bad enough my failure to behave as a suppliant female through my career. In the memoir I take a laughing tone speaking of graduate studies at Columbia in the late 1950s. I did not laugh much then. Meeting my old enemies, who had wished to crush an impious female at the start of her career, not only female but a Jew & a refugee Jew from one of the camps, I looked them in the eye, I never flinched but they flinched, the bastards. I took my revenge where & when I could. Now those generations are dying out, I am not pious about their memories. At conferences organized to revere them, Freyda Morgenstern is the "savagely witty" truth-teller.

In Germany, where history was so long denied, *Back From the Dead* has been a bestseller for five months. Already it has been nominated for two major awards. Here is a joke, and a good one, yes?

In this country, no such reception. Maybe you saw the "good" reviews. Maybe you saw the one full-page ad my cheapskate publisher finally ran in the *New York Review of Books*. There have been plenty of attacks. Worse even than the stupid attacks to which I have become accustomed in my "profession."

In the Jewish publications, & in Jewish-slanted publications, such shock/dismay/disgust. A Jewish woman who writes so without sentiment of mother & other relatives who "perished" in Theresienstadt. A Jewish woman who speaks so coldly & "scientifically" of her "heritage." As if the so-called Holocaust is a "heritage." As if I have not earned my right to speak the truth as I see it and will continue to speak the truth for I have no plans to retire from research, writing, teaching & directing doctoral students for a long time. (I will take early retirement at Chicago, these very nice benefits, & set up shop elsewhere.)

This piety of the Holocaust! I laughed, you used that word so reverentially in one of your letters. I never use this word that slides off American tongues now like grease. One of the hatchet-reviewers called Morgenstern a traitor giving solace to the enemy (which enemy? there are many) by simply stating & re-stating as I will each time I am asked, that the "holocaust" was an accident in history as all events in history are accidents. There is no purpose to history as to evolution, there is no goal or progress. Evolution is the term given to what *is*. The pious fantasizers wish to claim that the Nazis' genocidal campaign was a singular event in history, that it has elevated us above history. This is bullshit, I have said so & will continue to say so. There are many genocides, so long as there has been mankind. History is an invention of books. In biological anthropology we note that the wish to perceive "meaning" is one trait of our species among many. But that does not posit "meaning" in the world. If history did exist it is a great river/cesspool into which countless small streams & tributaries flow. In one direction. Unlike sewage it cannot back up. It cannot be "tested" —"demonstrated." It simply *is*. If the individual streams dry up, the river disappears. There is no "river-destiny." There are merely accidents in time. The scientist notes that without sentiment or regret.

Maybe I will send you these ravings, my tenacious American cousin. I'm drunk enough, in a festive mood!

Your (traitor) cousin,

JM

Lake Worth, Florida
15 December 1998

Dear Freyda,

How I loved your letter, that made my hands shake. I have not laughed in so long. I mean, in our special way.

It's the way of hatred. I love it. Though it eats you from the inside out. (I guess.)

Its a cold night here, a wind off the Atlantic. Florida is often wet-cold. Lake Worth/Palm Beach are very beautiful & very boring. I wish you might come here & visit, you could spend the rest of the winter for its often sunny of course.

I take your precious letters with me in the early morning walking on the beach. Though I have memorized your words. Until a year ago I would run, run, run for miles! At the rain-whipped edge of a hurricane I ran. To see me, my hard-muscled legs & straight backbone, you would never guess I was not a young woman.

So strange that we are in our sixties, Freyda! Our baby-girl dolls have not aged a day.

(Do you hate it, growing old? Your photographs show such a vigorous woman. You, tell yourself "Every day I live was not meant to be" & there's happiness in this.)

Freyda, in our house of mostly glass facing the ocean you would have your own "wing." We have several cars, you would have your own car. No questions asked where you went. You would not have to meet my husband, you would be my precious secret.

Tell me you will come, Freyda! After the New Year would be a good time. When you finish your work each day we will go walking on the beach together. I promise we would not have to speak.

Your loving cousin

Rebecca

Lake Worth, Florida
17 December 1998

Dear Freyda,

Forgive my letter of the other day, so pushy & familiar. Of course you would not wish to visit a stranger.

I must make myself remember: though we are cousins, we are strangers.

I was reading again *Back From the Dead*. The last section, in America. Your three marriages—"ill-advised experiments in intimacy/lunacy." You are very harsh & very funny, Freyda! Unsparing to others as to yourself.

My first marriage too was blind in love & I suppose "lunacy." Yet without it, I would not have my son.

In the memoir you have no regret for your "misbegotten fetuses" though for the "pain and humiliation" of the abortions illegal at the time. Poor Freyda! In 1957 in a filthy room in Manhattan you nearly bled to death, at that time I was a young mother so in love with my life. Yet I would have come to you, if I had known. Though I know that you will not come here, yet I hold out hope that, suddenly yes you might! To visit, to stay as long as you wish. Your privacy would be protected.

I remain the tenacious cousin,

Rebecca

Lake Worth, Florida
New Year's Day 1999

Dear Freyda,

I don't hear from you, I wonder if you have gone away? But maybe you will see this. "If Freyda sees this even to toss away . . ."

I am feeling happy & hopeful. You are a scientist & of course you are right to scorn such feelings as "magical" & "primitive" but I think there can be a newness in the New Year. I am hoping this is so.

My father Jacob Schwart believed that in animal life the weak are quickly disposed of, we must hide our weakness always. You & I knew that as children. But there is so much more to us than just the animal, we know that, too.

Your loving cousin,

Rebecca

Palo Alto CA
19 January 1999

Rebecca:

Yes I have been away. And I am going away again. What business is it of yours?

I was coming to think you must be an invention of mine. My worst weakness. But here on my windowsill propped up to stare at me is "Rebecca, 1952." The horse-mane hair & hungry eyes.

Cousin, you are so faithful! It makes me tired. I know I should be flattered, few others would wish to pursue "difficult" Professor Morgenstern now I'm an old woman. I toss your letters into a drawer, then in my weakness I open them. Once, rummaging through Dumpster trash I retrieved a letter of yours. Then in my weakness I opened it. You know how I hate weakness!

Cousin, no more.

FM

Lake Worth, Florida
23 January 1999

Dear Freyda,

I know! I am sorry.

I shouldn't be so greedy. I have no right. When I first discovered that you were living, last September, my thought was only "My cousin Freyda Morgenstern, my lost sister, she is alive! She doesn't need to love me or even know me or give a thought of me. It's enough to know that she did not perish and has lived her life."

Your loving cousin,

Rebecca

Palo Alto CA
30 January 1999

Dear Rebecca,

We make ourselves ridiculous with emotions at our age, like showing our breasts. Spare us, please!

No more would I wish to meet you than I would wish to meet myself. Why would you imagine I might want a "cousin"—"sister"—at my age? I like it that I have no living relatives any longer for there is no obligation to think *Is he/she still living?*

Anyway, I'm going away. I will be traveling all spring. I hate it here. California suburban boring & without a soul. My "colleagues/friends" are shallow opportunists to whom I appear to be an opportunity.

I hate such words as "perish." Does a fly "perish," do rotting things "perish," does your "enemy" perish? Such exalted speech makes me tired.

Nobody "perished" in the camps. Many "died"—"were killed." That's all.

I wish I could forbid you to revere me. For your own good, dear cousin. I see that I am your weakness, too. Maybe I want to spare you.

If you were a graduate student of mine, though! I would set you right with a swift kick in the rear.

Suddenly there are awards & honors for Freyda Morgenstern. Not only the memoirist but the "distinguished anthropologist" too. So I will travel to receive them. All this comes too late of course. Yet like you I am a greedy person, Rebecca. Sometimes I think my soul is in my gut! I am one who stuffs herself without pleasure, to take food from others.

Spare yourself. No more emotion. No more letters!

Chicago IL
29 March 1999

Dear Rebecca Schwart,

Have been thinking of you lately. It has been a while since I've heard from you. Unpacking things here & came across your letters & photograph. How stark-eyed we all looked in black-and-white! Like X-rays of the soul. My hair was never so thick & splendid as yours, my American cousin.

I think I must have discouraged you. Now, to be frank, I miss you. It has been two months nearly since you wrote. These honors & awards are not so precious if no one cares. If no one hugs you in congratulations. Modesty is beside the point & I have too much pride to boast to strangers.

Of course, I should be pleased with myself: I sent you away. I know, I am a "difficult" woman. I would not like myself for a moment. I would not tolerate myself. I seem to have lost one or two of your letters, I'm not sure how many, vaguely I remember you saying you & your family lived in upstate New York, my parents had arranged to come stay with you? This was in 1941? You provided facts not in my memoir. But I do remember my mother speaking with such love of her younger sister Anna. Your father changed his name to "Schwart" from—what? He was a math teacher in Kaufbeuren? My father was an esteemed doctor. He had many non-Jewish patients who revered him. As a young man he had served in the German army in the first war, he'd been awarded a Gold Medal for Bravery & it was promised that such a distinction would protect him while other Jews were being transported. My father disappeared so abruptly from our lives, immediately we were transported to that place, for years I believed he must have escaped & was alive somewhere & would contact us. I thought my mother had information she kept from me. She was not quite the Amazon-mother of *Back From the Dead*... Well, enough of this! Though evolutionary anthropology must scour the past relentlessly, human beings are not obliged to do so.

It's a blinding-bright day here in Chicago, from my aerie on the fifty-second floor of my grand new apartment building I look out upon the vast inland sea Lake Michigan. Royalties from the memoir have helped pay for this, a less "controversial" book would not have earned. Nothing more is needed, yes?

Your cousin,

Freyda

Lake Worth, Florida
April 13, 1999

Dear Freyda,

Your letter meant much to me. I'm so sorry not to answer sooner. I make no excuses. Seeing this card I thought "For Freyda!"

Next time I will write more. Soon I promise.

Your cousin

Rebecca

Chicago IL
22 April 1999

Dear Rebecca,

Rec'd your card. Am not sure what I think of it. Americans are ga-ga for Joseph Cornell as they are for Edward Hopper. What is *Lanner Waltzes*? Two little-girl doll figures riding the crest of a wave & in the background an old-fashioned sailing ship with sails billowing? *Collage?* I hate riddle-art. Art is to *see*, not to *think*.

Is something wrong, Rebecca? The tone of your writing is altered, I think. I hope you are not playing coy, to take revenge for my chiding letter of January. I have a doctoral student, a bright young woman not quite so bright as she fancies herself, who plays such games with me at the present time, at her own risk! I hate games, too.

(Unless they are my own.)

Your cousin,

Freyda

Chicago IL
6 May 1999

Dear Cousin: Yes I think you must be angry with me! Or you are
not well.

I prefer to think that you are angry. That I did insult you even in your
American soft heart. If so, I am sorry. I have no copies of my letters
to you & don't recall what I said. Maybe I was wrong. When I am
coldly sober, I am likely to be wrong. When drunk I am likely to be
less wrong.

Enclosed here is a stamped addressed card. You need only check one
of the boxes: angry not well.

Your cousin,

Freyda

P.S. This Joseph Cornell *Pond* reminded me of you, Rebecca. A doll-
like girl playing her fiddle beside a murky inlet.

Lake Worth, Florida
September 19, 1999

Dear Freyda,

How strong & beautiful you were, at the awards ceremony in Washington! I was there, in the audience at the Folger Library. I made the trip
just for you.

All of the writers honored spoke very well. But none so witty & unexpected as "Freyda Morgenstern" who caused quite a stir.

I'm ashamed to say, I could not bring myself to speak to you. I waited
in line with so many others for you to sign *Back From the Dead* & when

my turn came you were beginning to tire. You hardly glanced at me, you were vexed at the girl assistant fumbling the book. I did no more than mumble "Thank you" & hurried away.

I stayed just one night in Washington, then flew home. I tire easily now, it was a mad thing to do. My husband would have prevented me if he'd known where I was headed.

During the speeches you were restless onstage, I saw your eyes wandering. I saw your eyes on me. I was sitting in the third row of the theater. Such an old, beautiful little theater in the Folger Library. I think there must be so much beauty in the world we haven't seen. Now it is almost too late we yearn for it.

I was the gaunt-skull woman with the buzz cut. The heavy dark glasses covering half my face. Others in my condition wear gaudy turbans or gleaming wigs. Their faces are bravely made up.

In Lake Worth/Palm Beach there are many of us. I don't mind my baldie head in warm weather & among strangers for their eyes look through me as if I am invisible. You stared at me at first & then looked quickly away & afterward I could not bring myself to address you. It wasn't the right time, I had not prepared you for the sight of me. I shrink from pity & even sympathy is a burden to some. I had not known that I would make the reckless trip until that morning for so much depends upon how I feel each morning, it's not predictable.

I had a present to give to you, I changed my mind & took away again feeling like a fool. Yet the trip was wonderful for me, I saw my cousin so close! Of course I regret my cowardice now, its too late.

You asked about my father. I will tell you no more than that I do not know my father's true name. "Jacob Schwart" was what he called himself & so I was "Rebecca Schwart" but that name was lost long ago. I have another more fitting American name, & I have also my husband's last name, only to you, my cousin, am I identified as "Rebecca Schwart."

Well, I will tell you one more thing: in May 1949 my father who was the gravedigger murdered your aunt Anna and wished to murder me but failed, he turned the shotgun onto himself & killed himself when I was thirteen struggling with him for the gun & my strongest memory of that time was his face in the last seconds & what remained of his face, his skull & brains & the warmth of his blood splattered onto me.

I have never told anyone this, Freyda. Please do not speak of it to me, if you write again.

Your cousin

Rebecca

(I did not intend to write such an ugly thing, when I began this letter.)

Chicago IL
23 September 1999

Dear Rebecca,

I'm stunned. That you were so close to me—and didn't speak.

And what you tell me of—What happened to you at age thirteen.

I don't know what to say. Except yes I am stunned. I am angry, & hurt. Not at you, I don't think I am angry at you but at myself.

I've tried to call you. There is no "Rebecca Schwart" in the Lake Worth phone directory. Of course, you've told me there is no "Rebecca Schwart." Why in hell have you never told me your married name? Why are you so coy? I hate games, I don't have time for games.

Yes I am angry with you. I am upset & angry you are not well. (You never returned my card. I waited & waited & you did not.)

Can I believe you about "Jacob Schwart"! We conclude that the ugliest things are likely to be true.

In my memoir that isn't so. When I wrote it, forty-five yrs later it was a text I composed of words chosen for "effect." Yes there are true facts in *Back From the Dead*. But facts are not "true" unless explained. My memoir had to compete with other memoirs of its type & so had to be "original." I am accustomed to controversy, I know how to tweak noses. The memoir makes light of the narrator's pain & humiliation. It's true, I did not feel that I would be one of those to die; I was too young, & ignorant, & compared to others I was healthy. My big blond sister Elzbieta the relatives so admired, looking like a German girl-doll, soon lost all that hair & her bowels turned to bloody suet. Joel died trampled to death, I would learn afterward. What I say of my mother Dora Morgenstern is truthful only at the start. She was not a kapo but one hoping to cooperate with the Nazis to help her family (of course) & other Jews. She was a good organizer & much trusted but never so strong as the memoir has her. She did not say those cruel things, I have no memory of anything anyone said to me except orders shouted by authorities. All the quiet spoken words, the very breath of our lives together, was lost. But a memoir must have spoken words, & a memoir must breathe life.

I am so famous now—infamous! In France this month I am a new bestseller. In the U.K. (where they are outspoken anti-Semites which is refreshing!) my word is naturally doubted yet still the book sells.

Rebecca, I must speak with you. I will enclose my number here. I will wait for a call. Past 10 P.M. of any night is best, I am not so cold-sober & nasty.

Your cousin,

Freyda

P.S. Are you taking chemotherapy now? What is the status of your condition? *Please answer.*

Lake Worth, Florida
October 8

Dear Freyda,

Don't be angry with me, I have wanted to call you. There are reasons I could not but maybe I will be stronger soon & I promise, I will call.

It was important for me to see you, and hear you. I am so proud of you. It hurts me when you say harsh things about yourself, I wish you would not. "Spare us"—yes?

Half the time I am dreaming & very happy. Just now I was smelling snakeroot. Maybe you don't know what snakeroot is, you have lived always in cities. Behind the gravedigger's stone cottage in Milburn there was a marshy place where this tall plant grew. The wildflowers were as tall as five feet. They had many small white flowers that look like frost. Very powdery, with a strange strong smell. The flowers were alive with bees humming so loudly it seemed like a living thing. I was remembering how waiting for you to come from over the ocean I had two dolls Maggie who was the prettiest doll, for you, and my doll Minnie who was plain & battered but I loved her very much. (My brother Herschel found the dolls at the Milburn dump. We found many useful things at the dump!) For hours I played with Maggie & Minnie & you, Freyda. All of us chattering away. My brothers laughed at me. Last night I dreamt of the dolls that were so vivid to me I had not glimpsed in fifty-seven yrs. But it was strange Freyda, you were not in the dream. I was not, either.

I will write some other time. I love you.

Your cousin,

Rebecca

Chicago IL
12 October

Dear Rebecca,

Now I am angry! You have not called me & you have not given me your telephone number & how can I reach you? I have your street address but only the name "Rebecca Schwart." I am so busy, this is a terrible time. I feel as if my head is being broken by a mallet. Oh I am very angry at you, cousin!

Yet I think I should come to Lake Worth, to see you.

Should I?

About the author

About the book

Read on

Ideas,
interviews
& features . . .

Profile of Joyce Carol Oates

by Eithne Farry

ON THE WALL above Joyce Carol Oates's desk is a 1957 quote from the film director Alfred Hitchcock. It says: 'It's only a movie, let's not go too deeply into these things.' These simple words of advice were given to Kim Novak when she was feeling agitated and despondent on the set of *Vertigo*. 'I thought it was good advice,' says Joyce Carol Oates. 'Writers can get too intense and too emotionally involved with their work. Sometimes I tend to get a little anxious and nervous about my writing, and I can make myself unhappy, so I look up at that quote and think, it's only a book, don't worry, it's not your life.'

But writing is an intrinsic part of Joyce Carol Oates's life, the biographical details overshadowed by her literary output. To date, Oates has thirty-nine novels, nineteen collections of short stories, and numerous plays and non-fiction works (including monographs on boxing and the American artist George Bellows) to her name – as well as those of her pseudonyms Rosamond Smith and Lauren Kelly. By the time this interview appears that number, in all likelihood, will have increased. 'I like writing, and I'm always working on something; if it's not a novel, then it'll be a short story, or an essay, or a book review.'

From an early age Oates was fascinated by words; she began writing when she was very young. 'Even before I could write I was

emulating adult handwriting. So I began writing, in a sense, before I was able to write.' Her first stories were about cats and horses. 'I love animals. I'm very close to animals.' Born on Bloomsday – 16 June 1938 – she grew up on a small farm in Lockport, New York, and studied at the same one-room school her mother attended. Her grandparents had a hard life: Joyce's father and his mother moved frequently 'from one low-priced rental to another'; Joyce's mother was handed over to the care of an aunt when her father died suddenly and left the family impoverished. 'Is die too circumspect a term?' asks Joyce. 'In fact, my maternal grandfather was killed in a tavern brawl.'

Oates is the eldest of three and her childhood territory was mapped out in books. She was a voracious reader; by the time she was in her teens she was devouring Henry David Thoreau, Hemingway, Emily Brontë, Faulkner – and she can track the influence of these major writers in her own work. She explains: 'I think we are most influenced when we are adolescents. Whoever you read when you're fifteen, sixteen, seventeen, eighteen are probably the strongest influences of your whole life.' She adds, 'I think it's true for all artists: as an adolescent you don't have much background, you don't know much. I can imagine a young artist who's, say, thirteen years old and seeing Cézanne for the first ▶

Profile of Joyce Carol Oates *(continued)*

◀ time being very, very overwhelmed. But it's not going to have the same impact when you're forty.'

Oates majored in English at Syracuse University (to which she won a scholarship) and won the *Mademoiselle* 'college short story' competition in 1959, when she was just nineteen (Sylvia Plath received this coveted award in 1951). She gained her master's degree from the University of Wisconsin in just a year, and had already embarked on her prolific writing career at this point, at times publishing two or three books in the space of twelve months. In 1962 she and her husband Raymond Smith moved to Detroit and stayed there until 1968, witnessing at first hand the civil unrest that overtook many American cities. She was 'shaken' by the experience, and 'brooded upon it'. She is now a professor at Princeton, but the violence and unease of the Detroit years still make their unnerving way into her fiction almost forty years later.

The sheer amount of Oates's output can be bewildering. Her biographer Greg Johnson recalls his first visit to the Oates archive at Syracuse University, when he was beginning research for *Invisible Writer*, his book on Oates. 'My overwhelming impression was of the sheer amount of labor represented by these manuscripts . . . the novel manuscripts in particular were astonishing in their complexity.' Oates explains, 'I like writing. I'm not a person who thinks in terms of her career. I think in terms of the work I'm doing.' She adds, 'I don't think I'm incredibly disciplined. I write in the mornings, I sometimes write through the afternoon, even the evening, but not every day. It's not a schedule that's rigid.'

Her earlier fiction was written in 'one headlong plunge', a rush of words across the page. Then she would 'systematically rewrite the entire manuscript, first word to last . . . and this was the triumph of Art . . . control imposed upon passion'. Oates still writes every manuscript in longhand first, and then continues her work on a typewriter, editing each book as many as five times before she is happy. 'I don't have a computer. And I won't let things go until I'm happy.' She doesn't have hobbies, but likes to run, hike and cycle in the summer, before heading back to the study to get back to her writing. 'I'm just trying to do the best work I can. Most writers are trying to do the best they can. You hope someone responds to the work, but then you move on to a new project.' It's a pragmatic attitude to a prolific career. 'People can get depressed and suicidal and upset with their work, but I look at that Hitchcock quote on my wall and remind myself it's only a book, don't worry, it's not your life. It's a good cautionary tale.' ■

Joyce Carol Oates' Favourite Passionate Works of Fiction

Wuthering Heights
Emily Brontë

Light in August
William Faulkner

The Rainbow
D.H. Lawrence

Moby Dick
Herman Melville

The Song of the Lark
Willa Cather

The Wings of the Dove
Henry James

Crime and Punishment
Fyodor Dostoyevsky

Ulysses
James Joyce

Middlemarch
George Eliot

Sister Carrie
Theodore Dreiser

In Our Time
Ernest Hemingway

Edmund White Interviews Joyce Carol Oates

EDMUND WHITE: *The Gravedigger's Daughter* has some connections to your own life, I've been told, or at least to your grandmother's. Could you tell me what those links are?

JOYCE CAROL OATES: The novel is an imagined journey through the life of my 'Jewish' grandmother who had hidden her Jewishness, like most of her family background, from everyone including her husband and son. Because my grandmother Blanche Morgenstern – the name was changed to 'Morningstar' – seemed to have no history, she came to seem to others admirably selfless; only decades later did I come to realise that she must have been terribly lonely, bereft of a family background and any ancestral history if even a despairing one. My grandmother was the person who bought me my first typewriter when I was fourteen, and always gave me books as presents; she has come to seem to me, across the decades, as across an abyss whose depths are obscured by picturesque mists, an utterly mysterious woman: the 'muse' of much of my writing, which has always been for me an exploration of mystery, though not invariably an explanation of it.

EW: This novel seems to me to be about the Holocaust, though it takes place entirely in America and mostly in the period after ▶

Edmund White Interviews
Joyce Carol Oates *(continued)*

◄ World War II. Would you ever consider writing a direct, head-on account of the Holocaust – or do you feel more at home with this indirect approach?

JCO: No, I would never wish to attempt writing about the Holocaust since there is no point of entry for me. Such an obsessive quest would belong to the descendants of Holocaust sufferers or survivors who would likely be haunted by their relatives' memories.

EW: Tignor is a vibrant male who gradually falls apart and becomes dangerously jealous and violent. Another character, glimpsed fleetingly, is a serial killer. What I find remarkable is how well-rounded your representations of these characters are. Do you find it difficult to humanise these monsters?

JCO: I don't consider these men 'monsters' really; they are not so very different from us, but the trajectories of their life-stories take them in ways radically different from our own. Writers are fantasists, not unlike serial killers who are utterly enthralled by the contents of the unconscious which they cannot expel or comprehend but which seems to guide them in their acts. Only when obeying the dictates of the unconscious is the serial killer 'really alive'—so too for many artists, only when immersed in art are they 'really alive'.

EW: Just when it seems you have exploited all the possibilities of your tale you shift into a new, unexpected epistolary mode at the end of the book which provides a shocking and deeply moving coda. You have always struck me as a writer fully in command of her craft, but if anything to me it seems that in *Blonde* and the novels that have followed you have reached new technical heights. Not that you are showing off your skills for their own sake; rather, you seem now to be able to go anywhere at any time with a resourcefulness that is always surprising.

JCO: I had always intended the cousins Rebecca and Freida to meet after many years. In fact, it isn't clear if they will meet. The letters at the end of the novel – though written by me – yet have the power to bring tears to my eyes, after repeated readings. Isn't this strange! I think it must be because I feel that I am a kind of Freida, though more benign than this Freida, writing to my grandmother who has been dead for decades...

EW: Do you see any direct relationship between your teaching of fiction at Princeton and your own finesse as a writer? Between your work as a critic and as a novelist?

JCO: I don't think that there is much connection between my teaching and my writing. The one is so very social and ▶

Edmund White Interviews
Joyce Carol Oates *(continued)*

◄ outgoing, the other very solitary and often exhausting.

EW: Though your main female character changes her name several times in the course of the novel, this variability only serves to underline her rock-solid toughness, her amazing ability to endure. Are you an optimist about human nature – or are her survival skills merely idiosyncratic?

JCO: I don't think that I am particularly optimistic or pessimistic: so much of life is sheer contingency, sheer luck, good or bad, one's perspective is inevitably an expression of one's luck, good or bad. The optimist is someone to whom the bad things have not yet happened … (this sounds like an Oscar Wilde aphorism, though Oscar would have been more perversely witty in expressing it).

EW: What are your favourite parts of the book?

JCO: My favourite parts of *The Gravedigger's Daughter* are the scenes in the gravedigger's miserable little house and in the graveyard; the exchanges between the father, the brothers, and Rebecca. The strange haunting rawness of a certain kind of utterly uncivilisable being like Rebecca's older brother and the furious befuddlement of the father who'd once been a maths teacher and must now dig graves in a Christian cemetery; next, the scenes with Tignor. I think that this is a powerful 'nostalgia for the depths' (is that the expression?) that evokes distant memories from my childhood, not to be replicated in any way in my present life, and not desirable in any case. I grew up amid men not unlike these, and while the warm and loving women of my childhood are not at all absent from my present life, these men are utterly absent and seem to belong almost to a pre-history. ■

Have You Read?

Other books by Joyce Carol Oates

My Sister, My Love
Published in 2008
My Sister, My Love: The Intimate Story of Skyler Rampike recounts the saga of a murder through the eyes of the nineteen-year-old 'survivor' of a family torn apart by intense media scrutiny. In this ingeniously constructed novel – part mystery, part elegy for the narrator's six-year-old sister, and part exposé of the pretensions of upper-middle-class suburbia – Joyce Carol Oates explores with sympathy and subtlety the intimate lives of those who dwell in Tabloid Hell.

Black Girl, White Girl
Fifteen years after the mysterious death of Minette Swift – a 19-year-old black girl enrolled as a scholarship student in an exclusive liberal arts college – her former roommate Genna begins an official enquiry into the traumatic event. In reconstructing the girls' tumultuous freshman year at the college, Genna is led also to reconstruct her life as the daughter of a famous radical lawyer of the 1960s, among whose clients were anti-Vietnam War protestors wanted by the FBI.

'Oates digs her pen into the sensitive heart of the race question with all the intelligence and humanity we have come to expect from this brilliant writer'   *The Times*

On Boxing

'No other subject is, for the writer, so intensely personal as boxing. To write about boxing is to write about oneself – however elliptically, and unintentionally. And to write about boxing is to be forced to contemplate not only boxing, but the perimeters of civilization – what it is, or should be, to be "human".

'The sport seems in crisis, its best practitioners no less than its most dubious contaminated by association with fixed fights, manipulated judges, questionable referees. Demands for its abolition are made, indignation is aroused, well-argued editorials are printed, deals continue to be made, boxers continue to be "managed". Occasionally there is a boxing match that, in its demonstration of skill, courage, intelligence, hope, seems to redeem the sport – or almost. Perhaps boxing has always been in crisis, a sport of crisis. Without doubt, it is our most dramatically "masculine" sport, and our most dramatically "self-destructive" sport. In this, for some for us, its abiding interest lies.'

JOYCE CAROL OATES, from the Foreword

'Oates concedes boxing's brutality and often seamy side but finds positive merits as tragic theater. Good fare for fans and haters alike'
Library Journal ▶

Have You Read? *(continued)*

◄ *Mother, Missing*

Nikki Eaton, single, thirty-one, sexually liberated, and economically self-supporting, has never particularly thought of herself as a daughter. Yet, following the unexpected loss of her mother, she undergoes a remarkable transformation during a tumultuous year that brings stunning horror, sorrow, illumination, wisdom, and even – from an unexpected source – a nurturing love.

'A brilliant, unmissable novel'   *The Times*

The Falls

A man climbs over the railings and plunges into Niagara Falls. A newlywed, he has left behind his wife, Ariah Erskine, in the honeymoon suite the morning after their wedding. 'The Widow Bride of The Falls', as Ariah comes to be known, begins a relentless, seven-day vigil in the mist, waiting for his body to be found. At her side throughout, confirmed bachelor and pillar of the community Dirk Burnaby is unexpectedly transfixed by the otherworldly gaze of this plain, strange woman, falling in love with her though they barely exchange a word. What follows is their passionate love affair, marriage and children – a seemingly perfect existence.

But the tragedy by which their life together began shadows them, damaging their idyll with distrust, greed and even murder. What unfurls is a drama of parents and their children; of secrets and sins; of lawsuits, murder and, eventually, redemption. As Ariah's children learn that their past is enmeshed with a hushed-up scandal involving radioactive waste, they must confront not only their personal history but America's murky past: the despoiling of the landscape, and the corruption and greed of the massive industrial expansion of the 1950s and 1960s. 'If you read one new novel this autumn, make it this . . . you'll be hooked within pages'   *Mail on Sunday*

The Tattooed Girl

Joshua Seigl, a celebrated but reclusive author, reluctantly hires a young assistant named Alma to ease the stress of his complicated professional and personal affairs. As the tattooed assistant is allowed deeper and deeper into his life, Seigl remains unaware that he has brought into his home an enemy: an anti-Semite who despises him virulently and unquestioningly. Soon, however, their closeness forces Seigl and Alma to make discoveries that cut to the core of their identities.

'The storytelling is extraordinary . . . a completely gripping tale'   *Guardian*

I'll Take You There

Anellia is a student at Syracuse University, and away from home for the first time in her life. Headstrong, vibrant and occasionally obsessive, she embraces new experiences with a headlong enthusiasm for life and love. In her quest to belong, Anellia discovers the ▶

Have You Read? *(continued)*

◀ risks and rewards of confronting the world so passionately.

'Oates knows few contemporary rivals for her expertise at conjuring up the frenetic compulsion of forbidden desires'
New York Times Book Review

Middle Age: A Romance
When Adam Berendt collapses suddenly, his death sends shock waves through his home town, the affluent hamlet of Salt-on-Hudson. Its inhabitants are beautiful, rich and middle-aged, and, following the demise of Berendt, suddenly forced to confront their own mortality and morality in this richly comic study of middle-class mores.

'A stylish and wise chronicle of transformation and regeneration'
Sunday Telegraph

Faithless: Tales of Transgression
In this collection of twenty-one stories Joyce Carol Oates explores the darkest territory of the human psyche – these stories are shot through with sexual and emotional violence. The characters consider suicide, plot and murder, are the victims and perpetrators of sexual assault and stalking. *Faithless* is a startling look into the heart of contemporary America.

'Mesmerizing . . . illuminating . . . astonishing. Not only does it cut close to the

bone, it cuts close to the headlines. The
writing is so vivid it's breathless'
Boston Globe

....

Blonde

Blonde is the deeply moving exploration of
the inner life of the woman who became
Marilyn Monroe and a portrait of American
culture hypnotized by its own myths.
Poetically sensual and compulsively readable,
it traces the destruction of a cultural icon,
but never loses sight of the real woman
behind the invention.

'*Blonde* is an epic achievement, a
masterpiece, a piece of art so shatteringly
well-conceived and lavishly wrought that at
times it does not seem like a mere book'
Independent on Sunday ∎